PRAISE FOR
# CAVITATION

The word 'book' is too dead for what happens on these pages. I experience an emergency transformation of self toward something more alive and relational.
- Jim Rough, author of *Society's Breakthrough*, originator of *Wisdom Council*

Every time I engage with or read something from Clinton Callahan, I feel changed... not just mentally or emotionally, but on a cellular level. Then my world starts to work more interestingly.
- Betsy Chasse, writer, director, producer of *What The Bleep Do We Know?!*

"The treasure is endless, if you let it flow through you," explains one of the characters in *Cavitation*. And what a flow! I was swept up by the wide and deep stories forming this novel, each a tributary to larger wholeness. I encourage you to let this visionary work inspire you to practice another way of being.
- Laura Grace Weldon, Ohio Poet of the Year, author of *Free Range Learning*

*Cavitation* creates bubbles of liquid state all over inside of me. I feel as if I have changed into a glass of sparkling water!
- Ana Norambuena, Co-Founder of On-Tree Archiarchy Invention Center

*Cavitation* is a book of doorways to seemingly impossible worlds, but if you go through a doorway, the new world is no longer impossible because the book gives you the tools to bring it to life yourself.
- Sophia Wegele, Possibility Management Trainer in Training

As I cradle *Cavitation* in my arms, my eyes brim over with tears. I've been aching to read this book my whole life.
- Nicole Hartley Bradford, Possibilitator

While reading *Cavitation*, I began feeling strange, effervescent sensations throughout my body, a pleasant, energizing flow coursing directly from the book through my cells, drawing me into its thrilling evolutionary current. It's fun and thrums the chords of my soul.
- Marc Tognotti, founder of Infinity Point CDFI

Each time I put Cavitation down, I long to hold it in my hands again. I don't want the book to be over too soon, but I can't resist reading further to find out what becomes of me as I continue on this journey.
- Michaela Kaiser, co-founder of *Feelings Practitioners*

These stories, filled with resilience and resourcefulness, point humanity towards a viable way forward. Cavitation is so well researched and told. We are reminded that it is the question that leads us to the answers we seek. This is a journey of self-exploration and contemplation, leaving us to choose what we shall embody, or not.
-   Rick Pursell, Oracle of Consciousness

Clinton Callahan has put together an intriguing and beautifully written saga that pulled me right in through the writing, the ideas, and the depth of the book.
-   Meredith Little, co-author of *Vision Quest*, co-founder *School of Lost Borders*

By reading *Cavitation*, it is quite possible that you will begin to orbit in its constellation, mysteriously including aspects of its clarity and inventiveness in your daily life.
Clinton Callahan and his teams are entirely unique in the scale, focus, persistence, and passion of their life-changing work. After forty years of exploration, I have found no other body of work that is so well equipped to support and empower sincere practitioners as we reach out to create truly new possibilities, new ways of thinking, being, relating and reconnecting with life. Thank you, Clinton, for the realness and gravitas you include in *Cavitation*. The scale and power of your creations never cease to amaze me.
-   Dean Walker, author of *The Impossible Conversation,* originator of *Safe Circles*

Why hasn't this already happened? Maybe because no one thought of it before. From the distinctions in these stories, so many projects could be created, so many films could be made. The awareness expansions are so real and inspiring. Cavitation reveals the secrets for starting over.
-   Anne-Chloé Destremau, co-originator of *Women of Earth*

Some Evolutionaries leave trails of breadcrumbs in their books. Clinton shows up at your door, enthusiastically ringing the bell with a crate full of tasty and deliciously diverse loafs, baguettes, doughnuts... and cakes... with frosting on top. He does not want anything in return. Neither does he expect that you will accept the gift. He simply enjoys the possibility that you can finally nurture your Self. But if you let him in, it turns out he also brought a bag of seeds, should you want to grow the grains yourself, a design for a water powered mill and rocket oven, recommended contacts for people who are enthusiastic about baking, plus a list of websites with the best recipes and a short guide of how you could make a living baking bread should you chose to do so. You blink in disbelief. A few months later you find yourself ecstatically baking bread, with a joyous bunch of new friends, in a city you never heard of before, for a consciousness-expanding, archetypally-creative co-laboratory event that you yourself have initiated. Here is how your life could start over. You have been warned...
-   Jan Mizkajski

# CAVITATION

# TITLES BY CLINTON CALLAHAN

Building Love That Lasts
(new edition, previously published as *Radiant Joy Brilliant Love*)

Conscious Feelings
(new edition, previously published as *Directing The Power of Conscious Feelings*)

Goodnight Feelings (children's book)

No Reason

White Witch of Tenerife

# CAVITATION

## THE EMERGENCE OF ARCHIARCHY

CLINTON CALLAHAN

Thoughtware Press
Boulder, Colorado

Editing, cover, and layout by Anne-Chloé Destremau: annechloedestremau.org
Thanks to Luís Trindade for impeccable writer kick-ass services: luis-trindade.com
Thanks to Qinu Stempka for awesome standing rage hold sketches: qinu.art
Thanks to Mark Tognotti for hawk-eye typo and verb tense error finding. infinitypointcdfi.org

Many of the ideas woven throughout these pages emerged during the past twenty-five years of intense research sessions in five-day trainings from Possibility Management. The author is grateful for the opportunity to participate in so many transformational vulnerabilities and personal revelations: possibilitymanagement.org

Message to the author: *You don't already know this story. The story is only known through writing it. Just write the damn story. Keep answering the question, "What happens next?"*

ISBN: 979-8-9854058-7-3

Version 2, printing 1, 25 December 2024.

The purpose of this book is to provide transformational entertainment that inspires edgeworkers to intentionally affiliate for practicing skills needed for taking care of each other and life on Earth better than ever before. May this book serve as a doorway to jewels for growing up and shifting to regenerative, initiation-centered radically responsible human culture – Archiarchy.

DISCLAIMER: Any personal names or institutions mentioned in these pages are used for story telling purposes only. This publication is designed to provide accurate and authoritative information regarding the subject matter covered. It is sold with the understanding that the publisher is not engaged in rendering relationship, emotional, or psychological counseling, medical treatment, or other professional services. If professional advice or expert assistance is required, readers are advised to seek the services of a competent professional from your preferred context.

Thoughtware Press
1724 Broadway, STE 1
Boulder, Colorado 80302
www.thoughtwarepress.org

To Amethyst and Aurora, daughters who, during our homeschooling years together, insisted that I write my stories down someplace other than on empty toilet paper tubes.

"...It is as though you are being born. Do you understand?"
"No."
"You were incomplete when they brought you here. You are somewhat less incomplete now, but your recovery is necessarily a complexly organic process. If you are very fortunate, it will continue for the rest of your life. 'Recovery' is perhaps a deceptive word for this. You are recovering some aspects of yourself, certainly, but the more important things are things you've never previously possessed. Primary aspects of development. You have been stunted in certain ways. Now you are being given an opportunity to grow."
"But that's good, isn't it?"
"Good, yes. Comfortable? Not always."

– William Gibson in *Zero History*

## WARNING TO THE READER

It is true that this book is a work of fiction. At the same time, it is also true that woven into nearly every page are powerful distinctions which may have an effect on your worldview. In your everyday life, you use many distinctions for example, avocados are not ripe until they are a little soft to the touch, or, the red light means stop until it changes color, but at a stop sign you can stop and go again, or, some dogs are friendly but not all of the time. The distinctions in this book may rewire or replace distinctions that you have already been using for a long time. For this reason, I strongly recommend not reading this book too fast. Please pace yourself. If you start to feel nauseous, dizzy, shivery, shaky, headachy, confused, angry, frightened, weak, sad, or ecstatically joyful for no apparent reason, it could be that you are in a thoughtware-upgrade liquid state. If you pause in your reading, or read slower, or re-read what you just read, or have a conversation with others about the ideas you are exploring, or document in your *Beep! Book* which new distinctions are arriving in your world, your symptoms will soon go away. However, your new thoughtware won't. We recommend that you drink lots of water as you read. The extra water helps you diminish the natural stresses of 'Box expansion'. If you wish for more clarity about certain words used in this book, we offer you a free, online 'Distinctionary' at the website distinctionary.mystrikingly.com.

# CONTENTS

# Gaia

Due to recent actions and inactions of humankind, Gaia, the living spirit of planet Earth, has come to fear for her life.

Her wish to continue playing the infinite game of evolution is the same wish as humankind – although many individual humans have forgotten.

Gaia is a gentle and kind Being, playing against unimaginable forces of darkness. There is not much hope of success for her experiment of creating an organic form with a nervous system sophisticated enough to experience self-awareness.

She gives her naked monkeys free will. What is the first thing they do? Organize into hierarchies which are immediately hijacked by psychopathic personalities who banish the formidable adulthood initiatory processes required to liberate radical responsibility of authentic adulthood. Humans remain uninitiated.

Intelligent life on the watery planet appears to be doomed.

After painful deliberation, Gaia decides for intervention.

Using insight rather than force, Gaia delicately unbalances chaos in such a way that her allies can more easily unfurl their true inner potentials.

After that... she can only wait and see what happens.

# Phoenix, South Africa 1

Grandmother's hard-learned dying words circle in Mandisa's head like hungry vultures, waiting to peck her eyes out because she ignored the wisdom. "You have a gift to give, Mandisa. The gift appears through creation. Creation is different from procreation. The village needs your creative gifts, not more children."

Heat waves shimmer beyond the wall of the dirt-floored compound. Cicadas shift to a higher pitch, intensifying their shriek, rudely interrupting her thoughts.

Mandisa's gaze drops to her arms where her baby, only a few days old, stops breathing, shudders once, and dies. The flies are already eating his face.

She doesn't move. She does not cry out. There is nothing anyone can do to help, and no one there to do it, besides. Her son's death goes unnoticed in the world.

She waits a few moments to establish contact with his soul and then speaks the death prayer to guide his passage. "To the one who did not yet have a name..."

An hour passes. The scene is unchanged but for shadows of wooden kraal slats drifting silently across ancient dust. No one has come. No one has gone. Every clue indicates this is yet another deserted South African village.

*We are asaXhosa – the fierce people!* Mandisa wills the familiar words to return things to the old normal again. Nothing changes. She is forced to suffer alone at the summit of agony, cornered on this peak of pain. Finally she cries out the question that has been tearing silently at her heart for so long. "If we are asaXhosa, then where is the 'we'?"

The money stopped coming in when the gold mines closed. Families battered each other with vicious bickering – utterly unheard of until recent years. Unsolved murders occurred. Men and animals wandered off. Fields were untended. Young people sought money in Cape Town, or Johannesburg. Old people had no way to leave and, anyway, no place else to go. One after another, they died.

*And what about me? Mandisa? Sweetness. My one-night stand for cash gave us a few days umngqusho to eat, plus this mockery of life, this insult to human dignity, a baby that dies of starvation in its own mother's arms.*

Her ego does not have enough calories to function. It drifts into a stupor. An ancient and natural channel dilates.

*If my purpose is to bring my original story to life in the world, then I have something other to do than having babies. But what is it? What is my original story?*

The insight comes without words. It is an image of caring for geniuses. She does not understand.

Another insight comes. This one has words: *Questions are the key. What does that mean?*

Confusion crashes against the starkness of death. *The longer a question remains unanswered, the further the soul changes, because questions are fuel for evolution, a completely regenerative fuel.*

Mandisa's soul refuses clear-seeing like a dry rag rejects water. Her energy body is stiff and brittle. But clarity abides in patience. Clarity persists, unoffended. Long seconds continue ticking by.

*What is my original story?* The question lingers, like a honey bon-bon calling moisture into a dry mouth. She sighs in the sweetness. Without leaving any residue, an ancient misunderstanding that had prevented her from perceiving the bigger picture loses its power to blind. The impediment dissolves. The question redefines itself. *What did my future look like just before I was born?*

The question caresses a part of her she cannot remember was ever caressed before. *It was never so safe as it is right now.*

*Safe?* She sniggers out loud at her own irony. *With my cold dead baby in my arms? With me starving, the village broken and gone? This is safe?*

*It is never so safe as after losing everything you ever loved.*

A few minutes pass. The idea further clarifies itself.

*Death is safe. It is living that is dangerous.*

A fragile smile creeps unbelievably across Mandisa's dry lips, but she doesn't notice. A warmth glowing around her heart pulls her deeper within. *What is my original story?* Having the safe space in which to consider this question injects a nectar into her veins that oozes through her cells, like resting in a warm bath. Her soul unfolds and becomes inexplicably alive.

*At last. At last. Can this happen? But what is it? I thought my heart needed love to unfold like this? But no one here is loving me! My baby is dead. My village is gone.*

An answer comes. *Your soul is being fed with soul food. Now keep going.*

A single tear trickles down her left cheek, a flash flood streaking through the dust. A passer-by would think she grieves the death of her child, but it's the opposite. She has gratitude, immense wonder for life itself.

*Of course my village is gone! Being fierce people, we forced other people away. Fierce people! That strategy did not ultimately work, did it?*

Time passes. She keeps breathing. The questions persist. *So, what new story do I bring? Who am I really?*

Unrelenting introspection redirects her attention to an ancient seed potential. The seed sprouts. Tendrils unfurl, seeking something to wrap around. Tiny roots and shoots weave a network of exchange with other roots and shoots inside of her, densifying into a protective bird's nest incubating something precious. These critical inner connections mold a catch-basin for a pearlescent cloud so that it cannot blow away.

Suddenly, Gaia has a new home inside of her.

*Other souls long to unfold in the nectar produced by your inner weaving. We unfold together if there is a woven thing to hold us. The weaving is the village: a woven nest for unfolding together. The old village has died. Who will weave the next village?*

Grandmother used to say, "When you see a job to do, it is your job."

*Well, I see a job to do. I am a village weaver.*

Mandisa's new understanding relaxes every cell in her body, but then her familiar self-image erupts in outrage. *You are no village weaver! You are a slut, a failed mother, a crazy starving woman. Your village is dead, and soon you. You're already insane. Don't embarrass your insanity by also being ridiculous.*

Fortunately, truth requires no defense. It maintains itself while story-fortified denial bashes its clever brains out on truth's simplicity. In a contest between clarity and denial, denial has no chance.

Mandisa's destiny stands revealed in extended radiance without regard for her present circumstances: *village weaver.*

Awareness walks a one-way road.

Try not to think of a green monkey? Too late.

*I am here to weave new people together. All my time before now has been preparation. At last life begins. Death is a strange way to begin life, but come to think of it, it's the only way.*

The next defensive wave arrives. Long forgotten emotional patterns grip Mandisa's heart and awaken her inner little girl's whining litany: *I don't know how to be a village weaver. Nobody ever showed me how. I might make mistakes. I might embarrass the village. I can't. I can't. I might fail. I don't want to try. People will ridicule me, hate me, kill me.*

As her inner ranting loses momentum, a new and devastating revelation surfaces: *Be known or be unknown. Either way you die. It doesn't matter to death which way you choose.*

She remembers. *The child Mandi died long ago when I embraced my rite of passage into adult asaXhosa woman. Then I knew who I was because I was knotted into my village culture.*

*But if the asaXhosa culture dies... what is then my source?*

Grandmother seems to whisper into her ear. "Old stories die to make room for new stories. When a source outside of you dies, you become the source. Like a phoenix bird, you weave a new culture out of the ashes of the old. All around the world it is time for phoenix cultures to arise."

Mandisa opens her eyes and looks around for someone to tell. *This is it! I found it! My original story!*

A sudden breeze spins a miniature dust devil between the huts. The switch has been turned on, and it will never turn off again. No amount of arguing can dissuade Mandisa of her direct experience.

Clarity ignites unquenchable inspiration.

*I weave phoenix-culture villages. This is what I came here to do. I will weave a new asaXhosa culture. But this time the 'we' is bigger. The 'we' is everyone, every Being of the Earth.*

When no one is there to remember the old stories, they must fall off and disintegrate. New stories emerge from new longings.

*What if it's no longer 'us and them'?* thinks Mandisa. *What if it is 'us and us'? 'Us' the woven, and 'us' the not-yet-woven. I am a village weaver. This is my new name. I awaken other village weavers.*

The great golden sun ball passes over the top of its arch and starts its long journey down toward the opposite horizon. *The sun may die, but clarity has eternal life.*

Her mission comes into focus. *I shall let my heart remain broken so I can bathe in undefended contact with others.*

*I shall let my soul forever ache so it can speak freely.*

*I shall stay hungry for service.*

*I shall weave villages for life.*

*And I shall keep moving so all can experience the new opportunities.*

It amazes Mandisa that sitting here in full ruin, in the lowest most hopeless hell of the underworld, a prostitute's burden dead in her arms, nowhere to turn, no strand of dignity or faith remaining, she hits bottom, and discovers that, strangely enough, she now has something solid to stand on.

*If I simply endure at the bottom, appropriate next actions will reveal themselves.*

A few seconds tick by while Mandisa waits attentively alive at the bottom of her underworld. Then it comes, *I must bury my baby.*

She moves.

# Aleppo, Syria 1

Zenobia Darwish's Diary – 29 February 2012

I know now that by experientially mixing emotional fear with emotional sadness in the center of my own heart, I create horrific sensations of despair. If I do not want to experience despair, then I unmix these two emotions and the despair vanishes instantly. In its place I feel pure sadness, and I also feel pure fear.

If I was not skilled at making practical use of my sadness and my fear, I might think I would be better off feeling despair.

But me? I hate despair. And I have learned how to put my sadness and my fear to very good uses.

Also my anger.

But I did not know these things at first. At first, I only knew that I had to try to survive, along with twenty-two million other Syrians.

My name is Zenobia Darwish. I was born in 1998 on my grandfather's farm near Palmyra, Syria, four years after my father's mother died... four years after the Afqa Spring dried up.

That miraculous Afqa Spring, located in the middle of the vast Syrian desert, had nurtured human settlements for ten thousand years, ever since the Stone Age when Syria was covered in forests. Now the Afqa Spring is gone. So are the forests. Something big is amiss, bigger than most people realize.

On the farm we speak Levantine Arabic. When friends or neighbors visit, many other languages are spoken. Grandfather grows olives, barley, and apricots to sell, and sheep for wool. I milk the sheep and learn to make delicious cheeses for our family. Sometimes there is enough cheese to give to our relatives, or even to sell at the market.

When I first learned that this area of Earth was named the 'Fertile Crescent', I asked Papa to explain to me what 'fertile' and 'crescent' mean. It is not long before I begin wondering where all the fertility went.

Ancient ruins prove that roof beams and second floors in large buildings were constructed using huge timbers carved from abundant local trees. Where did all the trees go? Where did the rich soils go?

When I could articulate my question, I asked Papa to explain. But he could not. This became our first (of many) 'Co-Research Projects'.

Our obsessions sometimes drove Mama crazy. She was taught that 'respectable little girls' do not ask about such things. At other times I had the impression that Mama was secretly proud of me, but she never directly told me. I had to guess from sentiments hidden behind frowns on her face, and from the things she did not say.

Eventually, Papa and I discovered that for 3000 years, Syria was home to the remarkable Natufian culture, from 12,500 BC to about 9500 BC. Back then, the lands were forested with oak, pine, cedar, olive, pistachio, almond, wild fruits and berries, and abundant natural cereals. The Natufians settled in villages year-round, thriving on a rich diet gathered from their immediate surroundings. They hunted gazelles, aurochs, deer, wild asses, and wild boar with bows and arrows, gathered sea turtles, shellfish, and hunted seafood and freshwater carp with bone hooks and harpoons, while also collecting and storing wild fruits, roots, nuts, and seeds from the local grasses. They made sickles with flint blades set into straight bone handles for harvesting wild grains. But they did not farm. These humans made villages without making civilization!

Natufians carved mortars in large boulders and made pestles to grind seeds and nuts into flour. These mortars were not to carry around with them as in a nomadic hunter-gatherer lifestyle. They were fixtures of their permanent villages. By grinding various seeds along with dried roots from a cousin of papyrus, they made a pita-like flatbread. They even used the local grains they harvested for fermenting beer.

They sharpened stone tools on rotating grinders, made stone-drilling and string-spinning devices for pendants and beaded jewelry, and carved figures in stone and bone. Natufians are the first known humans to depart from the hunter gatherer lifestyle, yet their villages thrived for two millennia before humans in other locations domesticated farm animals and practiced agriculture.

Some Natufians lived in caves. Most built permanent multi-family villages of circular stone houses near fresh water sources, decorating their dead with bone and shell ornaments and burying them in little cemeteries or under their own houses. After a person's body decomposed, the villagers dug up the bones and rearranged them, adding carvings and coloring, then reburied them, often with new bodies in the same grave. One elderly lady was even buried with her hand resting on the skeleton of a small dog! Was this the first pet?

I was excited to learn that the Natufian culture was discovered and named in 1929 by a woman, Dorothy Annie Elizabeth Garrod, a British archeologist, the first woman to hold an archeology professorship at the University of Cambridge. Her hand-picked digging teams that excavated the Natufian ruins were almost all women!

Two millennia after the Natufians vanished, civilization emerged. It was the pottery cultures and then the bronze cultures who cut down forests for firewood, construction, shipbuilding, and the expanding desire for agricultural lands, which they irrigated decade after decade until the soil became salty and lifeless. The last of the Fertile Crescent was squandered when Romans, Mongols, and Muslims ransacked Syria, destroying aqueducts and canals, burning cities, chopping down orchards, destroying the precious infrastructure that took thousands of years to build by hand. When local people are dead, no one rebuilds. Forests are never replanted. Tree stumps turn to dust. Soil blows away. The desert takes over.

Now each year the weather grows dryer and hotter. Everyone is affected. An intensifying drought kills our food. Barley, apricot trees, sheep, drying to death before our eyes. It is unimaginably horrible.

The government does nothing. Neighbors become frantic. We meet in the evenings, frightened, in small groups, gathering at different neighbors' houses hoping someone has answers. We try to organize. Nothing seems to work. We are helpless, and, over time, we become hopeless.

On 15 March 2011, men come into our meeting with jubilant words. They call themselves 'Rebels of the Free Syrian Army' and promise to take back control from President Bashar al-Assad and his family. They say they will stop government corruption, free other Rebels from prisons, and bring us a new Syria.

People cheer and give them food and money.

They already have guns.

How did it come to this?

I remember Papa ranting one night after spending hours researching foreign news reports about the Syrian 'situation'. "Newscasters say the fighting is created by terrorists! How naïve! Yet how deceptively clever! Blaming 'the terrorists' is such a reasonable story to cover-up darker political agendas. The fighting in Syria is not created by terrorists. This so-called 'Syrian Civil War' is created by global warming. The drought has changed us into crazed animals. The government is too corrupt to provide any aid, so we fight each other to distract ourselves from the madness of slowly starving to death like our sheep. Fanatical terrorism is only a side effect!"

I remember feeling scared about Papa's fury while Grandfather only shakes his head in shame, and Mama says nothing.

In January 2012 my parents decide to leave what remains of the farm and move the three of us to the slums of eastern Aleppo, near the center of rebel activities, in the part of town they call 'Free Aleppo'. My parents figure that in the chaos of civil war, they can find work and survive better in the city than they can in the desert where there is only dust.

I still remember how cold it is the day we depart, and the blank stare on Grandfather's face as we roll away by donkey-cart leaving him stubbornly alone with the farm. He knows that his son and his life are leaving him, but he rejects our invitations to come along. I never see Grandfather again.

Many others give up on Syria altogether. They become refugees on boats headed for Europe, or they go on foot across the border into Türkiye. My parents refuse to run away.

We don't have enough money to rent an apartment, so we find a deserted lot full of rubble west of Karm al-Deadea by the Queiq Riverbed. I help my father hammer corrugated tin roofing onto a shack we build from scrap boards. Between us and the street are unoccupied bombed-out buildings. It is so cold, but the shack keeps out most of the wind.

Mama finds work as a nurse's aide in the hospitals. Papa provides re-construction clean-up, collecting bits and pieces here and there to improve our 'house'. Both of them work during the night and get paid in cash.

Papa loves history and listening to the news. He would rather find out what is really going on in Syria than eat dinner. He doesn't stop explaining to me about who is doing what to whom, where, how, and why.

Eventually his information urgency infects me. Together we use our minimized budget to obtain a used unlocked quad-band GSM cell phone on the black market and keep it running on a local SIM card. We rig a portable solar panel to charge the phone when the electricity is down.

We search the global internet using a free international VPN. It shocks us how the various news agencies report such dissimilar – sometimes even contradictory – reports. It also shocks us how little the people in other countries know about what is really occurring over here in Syria... and how little they actually care. It is as if we live on a different planet from the western world, as if there are secrets at work that those in the west do not wish exposed. I figure someone derives benefits from us living in a secret hell world.

Papa proposes that he and I draw up a war map to keep track of where the numerous factions are located. "Let's use coins to represent Assad's Army strongholds backed by Russia and Iran, bottlecaps for ISIS encampments, stones for the Rebels and Syrian Democratic Forces backed by USA and NATO, and bent paperclips to indicate how many forces and which armaments are deployed. We can try to outguess their next moves."

I enthusiastically agree. Sometimes I think our strategies are better than theirs. Too bad nobody asks us for consultation services.

By 29 February 2012 I am fourteen years old. It is a 'leap year'. Luckily, my parents are too distracted by our circumstances and too dis-connected from local society to try to force me to get married. My job is to guard our shack from being taken over during the nights, and to keep up with the latest news. This leaves me plenty of time to read books that I find in the rubble of destroyed buildings, and watch Hollywood movies on our phone.

This evening my parents wake up, eat mixed porridge, and ride their bikes off to work. I am proud of those two bikes. I pulled them out of the wreckage of ruined buildings. Papa and I hammer their handlebars and frames back to a usable shape. I patch two of the tires, mount generator lights on the front, and get them working again so my parents can dodge debris in the streets and travel to and from work faster than walking.

After I wash up our dishes, I sit at our rickety wooden table outside the shack. By the light of my kerosene lantern I read a hard-back edition of *The Kin of Ata Are Waiting for You* written by the American author Dorothy Bryant.

It is after sunset but before total blackness. My father often says, "Nighttime is when mischief creeps out of the corners," so my alertness is tuned high. Therefore, it is no surprise when I hear gravel scrape against something leathery twenty meters away at my two o'clock. I slowly raise my head and look over – so as not to scare whoever, or whatever, is approaching into taking aggressive action.

Two young girls walk towards me from the blocked-off street. To get this close they had to climb over rubble from collapsed buildings.

They approach carefully. I watch for clues about how to treat them, arriving unannounced out of the dusk. I see that they also search for clues about whether they should come closer to me or run away. I say nothing and I do not move.

Both of them are wiry, dirty, and looking hungry. Their long dark hair is tied back behind their heads under simple scarves. The older one wears boy's blue pants and a dark-green hoodie. The younger one wears a knee-length pink and white dress, torn at the hem, with a gray sweater over her chest. Perhaps the sweater was white at one time. They hold hands and seem scared, which makes total sense. Their city is dying around them, and their parents are gone.

Possibly gone...

Appearances can be deceiving.

Deceptions can be fatal.

This could be a trap.

I avoid making assumptions, don't move, refuse to say anything, and persist in noticing details. My right arm hangs loosely at my side with my fingers caressing the rusty surface of the iron wrecking-bar leaning behind my chair.

They stop about five meters away. The older girl speaks to me in Arabic.

I stare warily into her eyes without giving any hint of interest or understanding. She pauses, then looks down at the book I hold closed with my left hand, my fingers marking my page. I learned from watching Denzel Washington in *Equalizer 2* that I can also use my book as a weapon.

"Oh," she says. "You speaking English! Me too! Us too!"

I still do not speak.

"Sorry," says the older girl. "I am Jamila. She is Aziza, my sister. I am twelve years. She ten. We lost. Not know what doing, where going. We walking across Aleppo for days."

Still I wait.

"Our building attacked from boys with guns. They kill parents and take food and money. They not find us in closet. But then..." She looks down and starts crying softly. Her chest quivers from her efforts to hold back sobs. Her little sister cries with her but keeps a fierce glare at me.

I say, "Wait here, please," while I release the wrecking bar, stand up very slowly, and slide a fragment of red ribbon between the pages of my book as a bookmark. I turn my back and step inside the shack. Soon I return with two glasses filled with water. "I boiled this yesterday," I say. "It is okay to drink."

They each hold their glass in two hands and drink carefully to the last drop.

"Please sit down here. We can talk." I indicate the simple bench on their side of the wooden table. They glance at each other and wordlessly agree to approach me. As they sit down, I take their glasses back inside and refill them.

Before stepping outside again, I pause at the doorway, taking in the shadowy scene. The crumbled buildings have become mere silhouettes. A few stars dot the darkening sky. My lantern creates a circle of light around the table. There is no wind.

I scan the street from where they came. No movement. Good.

I scan the two girls. It feels comforting to have someone closer to my age sit down across the table from me. We might understand each other.

If they were boys, this would be impossible. I would not trust a single word out of their mouths. I would probably have to kill them.

But these are girls.

We have a common understanding of the world.

We have a common enemy.

There are no social rules to help protect us here, but also no rules against how we can protect ourselves. I am sure neither Jamila nor Aziza saw my wrecking bar, or the straight and very sharp kitchen knife slid into its leather sheath just inside my pants.

Probably they have protections too, or they would not have made it walking alone through this darkened city.

That is why we can talk.

That is why we could possibly become friends.

I quietly lower a portion of my defendedness and say, "My name is Zenobia. I am..."

They stare at each other with such wide eyes that I stop speaking. Their mouths hang open yet move speechlessly. Their heads shake in wonder and disbelief.

Aziza stares at me and says, "We hear from you! We dream you. You are real!"

"What did you hear?"

"We hear you come from desert," says Jamila wide eyed..

I nod, vaguely.

Aziza continues. "We hear you beautiful. And strong... And you someday lead us to new future, to a better place."

"Who told you this?", I demand incredulously, leaning forwards, both hands on the table ready to jump somewhere... anywhere...

"The lady..." says Jamila. "The lady who make string bags and read fortunes at Wednesday market. She sits in corner near dried fish and..."

"I know where she sits. My parents took me to that market once when we first came here. She is still alive?"

"She was okay before attack," says Jamila sadly shaking her head. "Now, I don't know."

Aziza closes her eyes with relaxed intention. We wait a moment, watching her sigh deeply. "Yes," says Aziza quietly. "She still alive. I feel her thread." Then Aziza opens her eyes and looks at me with squinted eyes. "She send you good greetings." Pause. "And she say, 'Good luck!'"

This does not make me feel any better at all.

I decide to shift the conversation to practical matters. "You can sleep here tonight. I live with my parents in the shack, but they work at night, so you can sleep in their bed. I sleep in the little bed across. I will give you some bread to eat. The toilet is behind that wall there. Be careful. It is just a hole and some boards. We don't have much water."

I turn the lantern down low and place it inside the shack on the floor so Aziza and Jamila can find their way around. They crawl into the bed, but I remain outside for a long time, crouched in the shadows around the corner of the shack. I want to assure myself that the two of them were not followed.

Squatted down, leaning against the rough boards, I sigh, thinking, *These are not easy times. This is not a fine place to live. We do not experience dignity and respect here. Little joy. Only survival. Is this my future? More of the same? How could I get us out of here? What is needed to properly prepare?*

I drift into thinking about my namesake, the *real* Zenobia, born in Palmyra in the year 240, a couple hundred years after Christ dies.

I remember reading that the first Zenobia received an extensive education, learning to speak not only Aramaic, but also Egyptian, Greek, and Latin. Her favorite activity was hunting.

Zenobia was soon noticed by a Roman senator in Palmyra, named Septimus Odaenathus. Around 254, when she was 14 years old, he took her as his second wife. His first wife already gave him a son, named Hairan, but Zenobia gave him a second son, named Vaballathus.

This is a time when the Persians launch a series of devastating attacks against the Roman province of Syria. The Roman emperors prove incapable of protecting the area. Septimus Odaenathus gathers his Palmyran followers and takes the lead in its defense.

Odaenathus had not inherited his royal title from his bloodline, so his legitimacy comes from personal loyalty from others. That means, if Odaenathus were to die, there is a good chance his son would not be welcomed to leadership with open arms. Odaenathus tries to bypass this problem by, after a great victory in the defense of Rome, crowning himself and his son 'Co-Kings' of Syria. This way, his son can start building up loyalty before his father dies.

By now, Zenobia accompanies Odaenathus and Hairan on many

of their Roman military campaigns. Her presence raises the morale of the troops, and gives her political presence plus military leadership experience.

Odaenathus and Hairan inflict several defeats on the Persians, and by 260, when Zenobia is twenty, have twice pursued the Persians as far as the walls of their capital city, Ctesiphon, with the militia of Palmyra and Roman troops. Ctesiphon was an ancient Iranian city, located on the eastern bank of the Tigris, about 35 kilometers southeast of present-day Baghdad.

When Rome's Emperor, Gallienus, hears about this victory, he is so happy that in 262, he confers upon Odaenathus the title 'independent Lieutenant of the Emperor for the Eastern Roman Empire'.

Through further successful battles, Odaenathus and Hairan restore the rule of Rome in the East, and by 264, Odaenathus celebrates his victories by crowning both himself and his son Hairan 'King of Kings', a very special title.

Since Gallienus is not technically a 'king', and certainly is not called 'King of Kings' in Rome, Odaenathus using the Persian title does not challenge Gallienus' position as Emperor of the Roman Empire.

Odaenathus' battle campaigns continue to unite the east under Rome's banner until on the way back to Palmyra in 267, at a dinner party – possibly as drunken revenge for a short confinement imposed on him by Odaenathus for being disrespectful – Odaenathus' nephew, Maeonius – technically next in line to the throne – poisons both Odaenathus and Hairan, announcing that now he himself is 'King of Kings'.

Zenobia is twenty-seven years old when this happens. What a mess.

Rome would be unable to protect Zenobia, or her beloved Palmyra. What is she to do? Slink away? Leave her fate to political chaos? No!

Odaenathus' troops love Zenobia, not Maeonius. Zenobia rallies her Generals to dispose of Maeonius, declares herself Regent for her own young son, Vaballathus, thereby making herself the de facto Queen of Palmyra.

She asserts that her teenage boy is the new 'King of Kings', also inheriting Odaenathus' Roman titles, all the while assuring Palmyra's continued loyalty to Rome. Things settle down for the future of Palmyra.

But Zenobia does not settle down. She makes audacious proposals and negotiates agreements with her Generals. Using wealth from Silk Road caravans that carry treasures from Persia, India and China through Palmyra to the Roman Empire, Zenobia raises her new Queendom to a thriving hub of trade, culture, and learning. She leads her armies to unite most of the middle east, including Egypt!

Soon after that, Zenobia declares freedom from Rome and establishes Palmyra as a thriving multicultural beacon of creativity. She promotes religious tolerance and intellectual growth, encouraging a blend of Hellenistic, Semitic, and Egyptian traditions.

This story has been repeated to me so many times...
Yet... hmmm... I wonder...
It always seemed like a child's fantasy to me... It always seemed to be an ancient, long-dead history...
Until tonight. Until the girls' shared their legendary vision.
Now I begin to wonder...
Perhaps... Zenobia of Palmyra was not the 'real' Zenobia.
Perhaps she was just the *first* Zenobia.

# Fontainebleau, France

Remington Smith's *Beep! Book* – 13 March 2023

I loved being homeschooled in Fontainebleau. My grandmother gave me the freedom and encouragement to learn whatever I wanted so I could live my life exploring the world.

She demonstrated how to trust my anger, and how to use it for making my way. My anger took me straight to *Fight Club, V for Vendetta, the Matrix, World War Z,* David Attenborough, Ken Robinson, and *everything* from Derrick Jensen, Guy MacPherson, and Paul Chefurka.

I recommend that you try the following experiment: Radically trust your anger.

The experiment is more effective if you detect whether your anger is mixed or unmixed, whether it is a feeling or an emotion, and what percentage intense it is. When you can distinguish these things in yourself, you start being able to distinguish these things in the anger of others. But I get ahead of myself...

Whenever I am frustrated (an emotion I make by mixing anger with sadness...) from watching *Mission Impossible, The Man From U.N.C.L.E., Indiana Jones, Pirates of the Caribbean, Star Wars, Star Trek,* and *Tarzan*, my anger tells me that I want to learn how to live alone in the forest, sword fight, ride a horse, throw knives, work with leather, command a sailboat, shoot bow and arrow, pick locks, make bombs, tell bold-faced lies without flinching, improvise, go nonlinear, do hand-to-hand fighting Jason Bourne-style with weapons made out of anything, and go where no woman has gone before.

Since I am homeschooled, I have been learning these skills to whatever degree of expertise I desire, either under my own recognizance or under the careful eye of any tutor with whom I can arrange to do experiments.

I am experimenting right now, telling you that I don't really care what you think and feel about what I will tell you. The words will stay in black and white right here in what Michelle my grandmother calls my *Beep! Book*, even if you don't like them. I am alchemically transforming these words from concepts into solid physical objects on paper. These words won't go anywhere even if you ignore them, or refuse to understand them. They will last longer than you. Even if you delete the file or burn the book, you cannot make these words disappear because I have already arranged that there are copies, and copies of copies.

I first wrote these particular words by hand into my *Beep! Book #13*. Now I am compiling my *Beep! Books* into a treasure map. Why? Because I love treasure maps! I have followed other people's treasure maps since I first learned to read. Now it is my turn to make a map that others can use to go hunting for transformational treasures.

I know this is a treasure map because I have been exploring it for years and I keep finding more treasures, the kind of treasures that grow by giving them away. I will be trying to give you as many of these transformational treasures as possible.

Let's start here: There are hints about a path that leads you sideways out of the bleak future bearing down upon us even in this moment, from overpopulation, aquifer depletion, climate change, biodiversity loss, ocean dead zones, nuclear wastes, and multiple failed bureaucracies.

Somewhere, somehow, I think the right people will read these lines. If that is you, then you are already a friend of mine. Please say hello when you can...

My name is Remington Smith, a joke from my dad, I think. Some people try to call me 'Remi'. I rarely answer. Anyone who gets to know me calls me by my real name.

I am twenty-two years old. Earth years. I carry a French driver's license for cars, tractors, trucks, and motorcycles. I earned a sea captain's license, and a single engine aircraft pilot's license. I am certified in First Aid, CPR and SCUBA diving. I can grow squash, build with wood, weld metal, hitch a horse to a wagon, and cook a feast for 70 people. I can dismantle, clean, reassemble, load, and accurately fire an M-16.

None of these skills are counterfeit. They are not video-game fantasy-skills. I worked hard to gain these skills for real. Try it yourself. I guarantee you will discover what I did: Reality is hard and persistent, and will kick you in the ass every time.

I have the bruises to prove how hard I practiced, but I had to trust myself each day, each moment, to keep practicing, because learning a new skill only happens at the edge of what you already can accomplish.

Not trusting yourself comes from fear, *unconscious* fear, which means this fear is running your life from beneath your awareness. You are afraid, but you don't know what you are afraid of. You don't even know you are controlled by your unconscious fears!

The result is that you cannot hold yourself accountable to yourself.

Is that any way to live?

Trust is a decision, not a feeling.

I can feel afraid and still trust myself.

In fact, my fears empower my trust. I trust my fears to alert me to what needs to be taken care of. Et voila! I take care of it before it even appears as a problem for me.

I carry my French passport in case I ever need to cross international borders, but it is not my real passport. I think of my French passport like a ticket to Disneyland. It lets me get into Disneyland, but I don't live in Disneyland. I visit there as a guest, as a tourist. Where I really live is in my own country, a nanonation, currently a nomadic nanonation, contexted in authentic adulthood initiatory processes and radical responsibility.

You may not know what all this means right now, but for my whole life I have been an unschooling experimenter. By now I am living proof that anyone can figure these things out if they want to. There are certain platforms online where people who have been implementing these possibilities in their own lives make their practices available for free, describing thousands of precise experiments to try that truly change what you are able to create for yourself, in your relationships, and in your teams. You can then verify what is proposed by trying it yourself.

People sometimes ask me, "If you live in your own country, how do you make friends?" I have friends from my Rage Club, horse riding classes, the Krav Maga dojo, and my own Possibility Team. Good, strong, intense friends.

But I think the question is bigger than this. I think it has to do with being terrified of the radical consequences of taking responsibility for choosing what you value.

For example, if you take responsibility for choosing what you value, you might bear the weight of feeling unsatisfied with your life, hopeless, unfulfilled, rejected, and lonely from not fitting in. You might conclude that no matter what you try, life does not work out for you. You stored up plenty of evidence to validate your conclusion, and your conclusion makes you feel enough depression or despair that you sometimes think of killing yourself. Yes?

What if the evidence you use to prove your conclusion comes from applying a false value system?

What? (you exclaim!) There is a false value system?

Are you claiming there is a true value system?

If there were a true value system, is it the values of the Muslim Church? The values of Walmart? The values of the President of the United States? Or of China?

If there is no true value system, then you can choose any value system you wish.

If you can choose to value any value you wish to value, then why are you using a value system that supports you being unfulfilled and rejected?

If you use a value system that swampifies you, what is your purpose?

Your purpose is to drown in self-hatred, confusion, and resentment.

Q.E.D.

For example, are you deceiving yourself into adopting the value that earning a lot of money through stable employment in a corporate career is success? Or that earning another certificate, or another degree, is success? Or that going viral on Instagram is success? Or that not getting divorced is success? If so, then you may have plenty of evidence to prove you are a failure.

But are those values true?

Or are they purely subjective?

Who chose those values for you to use as your measure? You did.

Why did you choose to choose those particular values?

A more relevant question is, why have you chosen those values as your criteria if they are going to dump you into self-hatred if you are not successful?

Answer: Because part of you wants to be drowning in self-hatred. Hmmm...

You might be asking yourself which values truly define success?

Why value success?

I will tell you about my current experiment.

If I am in an experience, and I notice myself comparing my immediate experience to any previous standard of experience, and I conclude that my current experience would be more satisfying if it were like my previous experience, or like an imagined experience, to the degree that I judge how my current experience *should* be or *could* be, then I am not in my current experience. I am in 'it', meaning, I am in my modeled-up experience. I am in my mind, comparing and contrasting my current experience, instead of being in my here-and-now free-of-comparisons immediate and awesome experience.

When I am relating to my experience as 'it', over there, and I judge it, I actually have no connection to what is really happening in my 5 bodies because I am cycloning around in my intellectual fantasy world, complaining about what is or is not happening in the real world when I compare it with a false value system.

The shocking thing I discovered is that I may be doing this to myself on purpose.

What purpose?

The purpose of using up so much of my genius energy and awareness making the judgments and comparison that I can only end up sinking in depression and self-hatred.

Why would I want to put myself into depression and self-hatred?

The answer to this question is also shocking: I do it to survive.

Putting myself into self-hatred is a childhood survival strategy.

I figured out how to devour my wild creation force with self-hatred so that I do not have enough energy to kill myself due to being rejected, not being seen, not fitting in, not being supported, not being collaborated with.

By interviewing others, I see that more people than I ever thought are natural-born geniuses and inventors. Think about it. If awareness is a bell curve, then there should be as many geniuses as idiots. There are obviously a lot of idiots. Where are all the geniuses?

I watched my neighborhood friends get sent off to school. Their magical worlds died immediately. Their love of trees and animals, water and rocks was hidden away. They hid their talents and knacks. They changed from being question marks in action to plastic coated Barbies and Kens, or the opposite, to bad boys on the block. It was horrifying to me that there were no police or authorities to report these criminal actions to. The way school and teachers annihilated life joy was abusive and ugly. I wanted to scream at their parents. "You sent my friends to school and it killed them." One of my six-year-old friends did kill himself that first summer. Rather than returning to school, he 'slipped and fell' off a rock.

Kids who went to school were being dumbed down enough to work as a slave employee in a corporation, or a soldier in an army, either way fighting to protect the wealth of the rich.

Ordinary people do not try to *not* see geniuses. They simply don't detect that geniuses exist. You exceed their perception limits, as if you reflect frequencies of light that the rods and cones in their retinas cannot perceive.

Is being an invisible genius good or bad? Useful or destructive?

Who decides?

What value system do you use to evaluate your condition?

If you invent your life according to a value system different from the mainstream-marketed value system for the half-dead, almost no one will support you.

So what?

You are already so far beyond a zombie's perception horizon that they cannot even make fun of you, or attack you.

But if you feel depressed, hopeless, unfulfilled, worthless... that is when zombies can help you! They are delighted to sell you more alcohol, plastic surgeries, a new car, antidepressant brain drugs, electroshock therapy, or a frontal lobotomy.

What if, instead, you consider changing your value system?

Hmmm?

What values could you try that would generate new conclusions about the world, or about yourself? (This is not a rhetorical question... But I will not make suggestions about what values you could choose to value. I encourage you to create a list right now of values that make sense to you to value.) (Yes, I am sharing a second experiment to try!)

What if you decide to assess your life and your creations against values that indicate that you are succeeding?

Suddenly you would no longer need to use 80% of your own creation force to punish yourself for failing to fulfill other people's values!

What could you do with 80% more personal energy?

What could your new self-image story be?

It requires an entirely new identity to value your new values.

Shifting to an identity with upgraded values can be a rough

process! Watch *Edge of Tomorrow*, *Batman Begins*, *The Mask of Zorro*, *Ender's Game*, the first *Matrix* film, *Groundhog Day*, the 2002 *Spiderman*, *Captain America: the first avenger*, *Willow*, *Pleasantville*, *Cast Away*, *Source Code*, *Hook*, *John Carter*, *Doctor Strange*, *Rock the Kasbah*, *Sorcerer's Apprentice*, *King Arthur: Legend of the Sword*, *Earthsea*, *Peaceful Warrior*, *Postman*, *The Game*, *Harold and Maude*, *Little Big Man*, *Lord of the Rings*, the first *Men In Black*, *Galaxy Quest*...

Yeah, I know. All men... Okay, there is also *Spy* with Melissa McCarthy, *Resurrection* with Ellen Burstyn, *True Lies* with Jamie Lee Curtis, uh..., *French Kiss* with Meg Ryan...

So? Don't complain to me! Go make the female versions yourself! We need them.

If you stop your self-torture, you suddenly have five times more rocket-star-fire-energy available than you did before. Are you prepared to manage that much life, and love, and awareness? Are you willing to do whatever it takes to shed your childhood survival chrysalis and learn to fly?

If so, prove it.

No one can do it for you.

On the other hand, no one can stop you from doing it.

When I was 13, Michelle, my grandmother, took me to the Oceania section of the Museum Five Continents in Munich, when we visited Germany. In one corner she showed me the beautifully carved teakwood board which the Polynesian villagers reserved for carrying the bodies of their dead children back to the village to honor them for trying to get initiated.

I didn't understand.

Michelle explained that traditional cultures put their youth through formidable adulthood initiatory processes – 'formidable' because they are real, not theoretical. On average a village would lose 10% of their adolescents. She told me that the psychopaths were in the 10% who died. Anyone not initiated was never permitted to hold a position of power in the village.

At the time, I could suddenly sense how ready I was for my initiations to begin.

But I had a question. "Now that this board is in a museum, what has happened to the initiations? And what has happened to the initiators?"

I went researching. Six thousand years ago, as the hierarchies of modern civilization started forming, the men most adept at doing whatever it takes to climb the power ladder to the top in a hierarchy – the psychopaths – protected themselves by eliminating authentic initiatory processes from their modern culture.

The answer to my question is that the Polynesians have been modernized. The initiations have been banished, and the initiators are in hiding, perhaps even from themselves.

This tells me that if I want to shift out of Patriarchy, it starts with getting initiated. And if I want to get initiated, it starts with escaping Patriarchy.

Which opens a new question. "How does anyone get initiated these days? And, what kind of culture – political, economic, technical, ecological, educational – emerges if no one is initiated into adulthood anymore?"

I was born in 1996 in Paris, France. I speak French, but also English with an American accent I picked up from loving to watch Hollywood films without subtitles.

My father, Alexander Smith, is Scottish, or was Scottish. I don't know if he still lives. He came to France as a student of French history at la Sorbonne, where he met my mother, Valerie du Pont, who was studying Law.

My grandmother told me that I was with my mother when she was carrying groceries across a street in Paris and was killed by a drunk driver. I was 4 years old.

I don't remember.

Apparently, my father broke down completely after that. He left everything behind, including me, and returned to Scotland. I haven't seen or heard from him since.

No one knew what to do with me, so they left me in Fontainebleau with my mother's mother, my grandmother, Michelle Piment du Pont.

Michelle was born 1929 in Fontainebleau. When she was 17 years old, she began studying the teachings and practices of George Ivanovich Gurdjieff, who was born in 1866 in Georgia – the country in Eastern Europe, not the American state Georgia, home of peach pie and Coca-Cola.

In case you don't already know, Gurdjieff was a philosopher, Sufi mystic, composer, dance teacher, consciousness researcher, mage, and originator of *The Fourth Way*. He lived nearby Michelle, but died in 1949, three years after she met him. But by then, Michelle can already navigate transformational research spaces. Without authorization she ran her own weekly Study Group for 67 years, from 1950 until she died, in 2017, at 88 years of age. That was nearly six years ago.

Once I asked her, "Michelle..." – she always wanted me to call her by her name instead of *Bonne-Maman*, or *Granny* – "...what happened to my grandfather?"

She says, "My husband's name was Jean-Luc du Pont. We met at a dance bar in Paris, and loved each other at first sight. But he was so rebellious of his aristocratic family that, soon after we were married and I was pregnant with your mother, Valerie, he joined the French Foreign Legion. He was immediately killed in a skirmish in Tunisia, leaving me with this house, a wild child, and enough pension for us to live."

I held Michelle's hand as she died peacefully at 3 minutes after midnight on Christmas eve, leaving me with the old 2-story stone house and the pension.

Michelle's last words to me were, "Write it down, Remington.

That makes it real. You have a good life ahead of you. Make it real."

When she dies, I am lost.

I spend a couple years either camping alone in the French wilderness areas, or sequestered in libraries where I allow my immediate questions to navigate me through the internet. I am driven to know what is going on in the world, and what I am going to do about it.

Getting frustrated with staring at screens, I lock up the house and journey a few more years through the South Pacific, Southeast Asia, and Asia, partly following in Gurdjieff's footsteps.

Then my aim changes. I start searching for a project I can join that is making a practical contribution towards rectifying the horrors currently being wreaked upon the Earth by humanity. A month ago, I found one.

Suddenly I recognize that I am not properly skilled to assist in their efforts. I need someone to train me. I apply for an intern program with the Nature Conservancy in Eugene, Oregon, U.S.A.

After a telephone interview, they accept me. I book my tickets to depart 3 days later – which is today – and I pack my bag.

But... just last night... I had a dream.

In the dream I am cuddled up in Michelle's lap. We sit in the circle of chairs in our attic where she holds her weekly meetings. I must have been 4 or 5 years old to fit in her lap like this, which makes it just after my mother died.

There are mostly women in the circle, a few men, about 18 people altogether. They speak respectfully, yet ecstatically. The attic is only dimly lit, but filled with bright loving energy. I feel delighted reverie emanating from the human beings in this space.

As I look around, I notice how the magic has always been here, waiting for us to leave behind enough psychoemotional baggage that we can find this chamber.

I feel deeply connected to nature in the dream, and completely accepted by the others in the group, even welcomed. I am at home here.

Then Michelle leans down and gently whispers something into my ear. What she says shocks me, and I wake up.

I do not understand her message.

I am not scared. It is more like what she tells me does not make sense to me in that moment.

I open my eyes and look out the window near my bed. It is already getting light outside, so I decide to ascend to the attic. I haven't been here for over five years, ever since Michelle got sick and the Study Group moved to the next woman spaceholder's house.

The wooden stairs creak, just as I remember.

I turn the handle and push open the door to the left. It bumps into a low table with a dusty, cut-crystal vase standing on it, still filled with long dead flowers. I can't see much else in the room except what is revealed by the light beaming through the small window behind the table.

When I flick on a light switch, the magical world returns. I step forward into what I remember as my favorite room in the world. The writing desk by the wall, the workbench with the large, mounted magnifying lens and the small hand tools. The meeting chairs, still undisturbed in the familiar circle. Why haven't I come back here in all this time?

I duck under a wooden beam and run my fingers along the dusty bookshelves filled with titles from René Daumal, Robert de Ropp, George Ivanovich Gurdjieff, Peter D. Ouspensky, Claudio Naranjo, John C. Lilly, Lee Lozowick, Alan Watts, Robert A. Heinlein, Marilyn Ferguson, A. S. Neill, Clinton Callahan, Paramahansa Yogananda, Irina Tweedie, Buckminster Fuller, Valerie Lankford, James P. Carse, Lewis Carroll, Dorothy Bryant, Eric Berne, Lyall Watson, Aleister Crowley, Carlos Castaneda, C. S. Lewis, Kurt Vonnegut Jr., Oscar Ichazo, Robert Silverberg, Arnaud Desjardins, William Gibson, Joseph Chilton Pearce, Frank Herbert, John Holt, E. J. Gold, Alejandro Jodorowsky, Malidoma Patrice Somé, Carl Rogers, Robert Wolff, Thomas Gordon, John Welwood, Neil Postman and Charles Weingartner, H. P. Blavatsky, Pema Chödrön, J. R. R. Tolkien, Thich Nhat Hanh, Isaac Asimov, Philip K. Dick, Arthur C. Clark, J. G. Bennett, Eckhart Tolle, Orson Scott Card, Aldous Huxley, Daniel Quinn, John Fowles, Olaf Stapledon, Terry Pratchett, Chogyam Trungpa, Harper Lee, Robert Graves, Suzuki Roshi, Ursula K. Le Guinn, José Silva, Werner Erhard, Neal Stephenson, Abraham Maslow... on and on, the wizards.

I am overwhelmed with an urge to stay in this room for a year, only reading what I have not yet read. But my plane leaves for Oregon in a few hours!

I gaze over at the circle, then slowly approach Michelle's chair, the one in which she cuddles me in the dream. I brush the dust off, sit down, pull up my legs and hug my knees, crying softly for a long while.

My heart and soul ache. I am crying because things change, because things that I love have the power to disappear.

*Did I make the most of the time I had with Michelle? Did I ask my real questions? Did I make myself available to all the initiations she could have given me?*

Something else niggles at me. From the dream? Is it what Michelle whispers in my ear that I cannot understand?

Then I remember. She says, "The treasure is endless if you let it flow through you."

And... something more! Something about this chair... something...

My right hand reaches down under the front of the seat. I feel a small cold metal panel. I leap out of the chair and tilt it backwards to peer underneath. The panel slides easily to the left. Out drops a brass key.

A key!

Michelle! Who were you! What were you really doing?

I hold the key out before myself, using it like a dowsing rod, turning slowly from side to side, letting the key scan for its home. Perhaps the locked object is no longer even in this room. It could be a cabinet downstairs, perhaps in the basement. It could be buried outside. I don't have time for this!

Something drags me vaguely towards the table in the far corner under the window, half blocked behind the door through which I entered the attic.

The table is covered with a white tablecloth trimmed in red and blue embroidery, well sprinkled with dry mouse turds. I lift the front flap of the tablecloth and bend over to peer underneath. There sits a wooden storage trunk!

I pull it forward and insert the key nervously into the lock. It turns easily!

*Click!*

I get such a chill down my spine that I want to scream.

No one else is around, so I cut loose. My shrieking shivery squeals of fear and excitement are far louder than I expected. Just for the hell of it, I jump around shrieking even more. It is fun! I laugh at myself.

Then I grab the trunk by both sides, and pull it fully out from under the table. It slides easily. The lid opens without a squeak.

The first thing I see inside the trunk is a saber lying diagonally across the rest of the contents, ready to be grabbed by a right-hander.

Was Michelle right-handed? I think so .

I check for boobie traps, just in case... knowing Michelle... Then I carefully lift out the sword and stand with it *en garde*. Nice balance! I suppose if I were in the *Fellowship of the Ring,* or a crew member on the *Black Pearl* in *Pirates of the Caribbean*, this weapon would be useful. As I am in the modern world, I place the sword on the table and search beneath where it had lain.

Assorted artifacts and implements of bronze, bone, wood, clay, horn, and crystal, some for ritual, some with obvious practical uses, lie scattered on top of paper folders and old notepads.

I begin thinking practically to myself.

(Wasn't it Robert Heinlein who said, "Women are the practical ones."?)

*In a few hours I am going nomadic for I don't know how long. Which of these things am I willing to lose if this house burns down?*

This question makes it utterly simple to divide the contents into two piles.

The pile I am NOT willing to abandon consists of nearly 15 kilograms of paperwork, notepads, folders, and documents including a leather-bound manuscript titled *Handbook*. Most of the papers are written in Michelle's own handwriting. Glancing at a few, I see distinctions, experiments, diagrams, group exercises, and processes.

What an unbelievable treasure!

*Are these ideas handed down from the past?* I don't think so. If they came from previous efforts, human beings around the world would already have adopted them from artwork, hieroglyphs, traditions, or literature from ancient cultures. From what I have seen, humanity knows nothing of these things. Therefore, Michelle must have newly invented the instructions for how to build and run her healing and transformational village society.

Out of the blue it comes to me. This! This needs to be transcribed! If these notes are lost, they would be gone forever. But if I can digitize these notes into a workbook or manual, they could spread around the world and serve as an alchemical doorway to a new future!

I run down the stairs to my bedroom, grab my packed-for-Eugene roller bag, dump the entire contents onto the floor of a closet, retrieve my toiletries and three panties and toss them back in the suitcase, shut the closet door, then carry the bag upstairs and fill it to the brim with papers and notebooks. It is weighty, but manageable.

Just like my life...

Now that I am the guardian of something with real substance, I understand what Michelle meant when she said, "Write it down. Make it real."

I am an ambassador of the culture that could come next, a bridge to something beyond what currently exists on Earth.

Thirteen hours ago, an ambassador of the next culture departed from the Charles de Gaulle airport in Paris, France, and will shortly land in Portland, Oregon. I wonder what awaits me there.

# San Francisco, California

Edith Goldman's third day as a legal intern in the offices of Bach, Becker, and Benowitz on Market Street, starts at Mazarine Coffee, 'the place with exquisite muffins'. After earning a double degree in Economics and Law from Columbia University in New York, and la Sorbonne University in Paris by her twenty-third year, the future looks bright for Edith. She has her own desk, her own telephone, her own little office, and her own view on the city. Her father will be proud.

At ten-twenty, the secretary knocks gently on her door, sticks her head in, and says, "Mr. Benowitz would like to see you in his office in ten minutes."

"Sure! No problem," says Edith. The head disappears and the door closes. Edith worries about not knowing proper protocol for head-popping-through-the-door conversations in a top legal office in San Francisco.

But that was not a conversation. This secretary is as emotionless as a blow-up doll. She subserviently delivers a message from her boss, and coldheartedly refuses to give the new girl – Edith – any clues about what is up. That woman is nothing more than a message girl, a decoration, a slave.

As Edith steps quietly down the hall, she runs into Kyoko, the other new intern, headed in the same direction. They say nothing to each other, equally unsure of what is about to occur.

Edith takes the risk of knocking on the dark wooden door. A lot is revealed about a person by the way they knock. A lot is revealed about a person if they stand back and let the other person take the risk of knocking.

A male voice from behind the door says, "Come in."

Edith looks at Kyoko standing there and thinks, *Ahh... The 'doing nothing is safer' strategy. Fuck this shit!* Edith reaches over and twists the polished brass doorknob, steps forward into a classic lawyer's office.

Kyoko follows.

The shelves behind Mr. Benowitz' chair are packed neatly with law books. Edith wonders if they are real books or simply decoration put there to add fake legitimacy to video conferences. It could be both. A curved bronze lamp with a green blown-glass lampshade rests at the corner of his desk.

"Well, well, young ladies! Welcome to Bach, Becker, and Benowitz!" says the round-faced man with wire rimmed glasses and almost nonexistent gray hair. He remains seated in his leather-covered swivel chair, looking each of them thoroughly up and down. He proudly says, more to himself than to them, "It is certainly a pleasure to work with beautiful young women in my office!"

There is so much creepiness in this man's leer that Edith becomes speechless. She feels like she just opened a cupboard door and stands nose to nose with a gigantic cockroach eyeing her up for lunch. The cockroach continues to speak. "I simply wanted to look you over and say hello. Let me know if either of you needs... anything." Then he nods his head towards the door, and looks down at his papers, signaling that they can go now.

Outside in the hallway, Edith looks at Kyoko, searching for any kind of recognition that what just happened was a short stroll on a naked catwalk. Kyoko betrays nothing.

*Of course she doesn't react!* thinks Edith furiously. *She's from Tokyo, where women are supposed to be obedient little dolls.*

They silently part ways. Edith steps pensively back into her office and slowly shuts the wooden door behind her. Her true urge is to lock the door from the inside, but there is no key.

She remains standing.

She glances at the leather swivel chair behind the desk that she was only minutes before so proud of.

*I cannot sit there anymore*, she says to herself. *It has been ruined.*

Five minutes go by. Nine minutes... she stands motionless, staring out the window at the hard, cold, lifeless buildings smashed together as far as she can see.

Horns honk meanly at each other. Engines roar on the streets below. A police siren wails bleakly in the distance. Her mind races a thousand miles an hour, telling her nothing.

It is her heart that speaks first.

*I'm not doing this*, it says.

*The truth has been revealed*, it says.

*I refuse to degrade myself like this.*

*Never again!*

*There is nothing here for me but empty days doing meaningless neurotic busy-work for fucked-up jerks until I get so bored, I am willing to have sex with that bastard.*

*I worked my ass off for five years to earn these degrees, to be accepted in this intern position. What is the result?*

*Having to act like a slave without a voice for the next twenty years?*

*Having to obey pointless orders from sleazy men and play dead like the secretaries?*

*My life is not available to be consumed by others.*

*If I choose to stay here, I would be abusing myself.*

*I won't do that.*

*After three days, I see the truth.*

*Staying here will ruin the rest of my life.*

*I do not care about the consequences.*

*I have no idea where to go next, but I am damn sure that I'm leaving this behind.*

*I refuse to participate in this disgusting, debasing, drooling, debauchery of a profession.*

*I am out of here.*

It takes three months to complete the terms of her contract without getting sued... but Edith Goldman is true to her word.

# Phoenix, South Africa 2

Burying her baby takes longer than Mandisa imagines. Even digging a baby-sized hole in the parched clay with a worn-down shovel demands every effort her starving body can muster. *The grave must be deep so hyenas cannot eat the dead.*

She wraps her tattered scarf around the tiny lifeless body, lays it carefully into the pit, and gently pushes dirt in.

*The hyenas will fight over the flesh, and then shit the gnashed bones ungraciously over the fields.* To prevent this Mandisa uses the shovel handle to pry a large stone off another grave nearby and roll it onto the dirt over her baby. She stands unsteady, breathing hard, stunned, bewildered.

Near the burial grounds grow big yellow guavas. Without thinking she eats two and puts a dozen more into her shoulder bag. She collects a bundle of dry guava twigs and drags a dead branch back to the kraal.

Although exhausted, sleep is not what she wants. She wants company. If no one is to join her then a small fire will provide easy access to the company of the ancestors.

Mandisa pulls a yellow BIC lighter out of her bag. She has cherished this talisman for years as a symbol of modern culture's wealth and power. Caressing its smooth sides and chromed metal parts, Mandisa remembers how it promised such glorious expectations for her clan, for all the people in the world. If such a simple device can flick a fire to life, heaven on earth could be accessible to everyone.

*So naïve we have been...*

She scornfully stares at this plastic device in the fading light, alone in the kraal on the day her baby dies.

A veil falls away.

If a grain of sand reveals the design of the universe, a disposable plastic lighter reveals the design of modern culture.

Mandisa's illusion of a bright future is shattered, like peeling a candy wrapper and finding a scorpion.

Modern culture's promise hides a toxic betrayal, a plastic carrot, dangled before the gullible by uninitiated adolescents who love power and money more than life, twisted boys who do not care the slightest bit about her.

The lighter is a trap, camouflaged as comfort. Long ago she and her village were fooled.

With the village destroyed, and the heart of the clan stolen by other people's illusions, the lighter's false promises no longer jail her intelligence. The spell is broken. *I am no longer a prize for modern culture. I have become empty. Empty of illusion, deception, and dreams that were not mine.*

*What can arise in a space that is full? Nothing.*

*What can arise in a space that is empty? Everything.*

The lighter is a decoy for catching consumers. Mandisa's soul is no longer deceived. Her longing for the illusion permanently died with her son's last breath. Without smoke and mirrors, modern culture's economic plan reveals its insane and horrifying goal: empire... the soul-sick greedy few devouring the life of the many.

But inside Mandisa, clarity blazes. Her soul discerns actuality from fiction. The greedy few have a big surprise coming... as modern civilization collapses in its consumerism frenzy, those who can live well without technology will do so. And the rest?

*When my lighter is empty, what do they intend for me to do with it?*

*Throw it away and buy another one?*

*Where do they plan to obtain the plastic and gas and metal for infinite replacements?*

*And for whom must I become a prostitute to get the money to buy it?*

*And what do they imagine when they say, 'Throw it away?' Do they still think the world is flat. Do they think they can walk to the edge of the Earth and drop off their empty plastic lighters?*

*The world is not flat! The world is round. On a round world there is no place called 'away' where lighters can be dropped off. We all live together inside this delicate bubble of life.*

*If my wastes do not nurture my food, I poison and starve my own children.*

*If everybody wants new lighters, the plastic and metal and gas will run out, forever. Then what? Isn't anybody thinking about this? The system which is fiercely advertised to old and young, is headed for suicide, and it will take all life with it.*

*If I use money, then I am owned by the ones who print the money. When I believe I must work to get money to live, then I am not living. I am only struggling for survival, being a slave to someone else's delusion.*

The final dismay puts a shudder in her breath. *This is what happened to the asaXhosa. We were captured by a fantasy world, tricked like monkeys to abandon our freedom by refusing to let go of the juicy apple in the jar. We left behind our living village to join the hungry ghosts in the cities. The asaXhosa are dead.*

An eternity of silent grieving passes.

Eventually thought returns.

*I want fire. How can I get it? Long ago father showed me that fire comes from rubbing sticks together, concentrating sunlight, or a tree ignited by lightning. I have no sunlight. I have no lightning. But I do have sticks.*

She crawls under the flap door into her dusty hut, then stands up and gropes in the rafters for the ancient firesticks and dry tinder. They are still wrapped in stiff goat skin.

Back outside her fingers remember father showing her how to shape a tiny tinder nest. She gets to her knees, arranges the sticks over the tinder and begins the rhythmic movements, making a sound not heard in the kraal since before the plastic lighters arrived.

The strange noise is what draws Tandra out of her hut. Mandisa's cousin, the daughter of her mother's sister, stands skin and bones unsteadily in the dusk. She is the only other remaining resident of the village, too stubborn to leave, too angry to adapt, too tough to die.

Tandra stands in the doorway of her hut, staring warily at Mandisa. "What are you doing? Are you crazy?" She pauses a moment, then says, "Do you want to use my lighter?"

Mandisa's eyes blaze wildly into the dusk. *"Nyo kanyoko!"* she screams. ['Your mother's cunt!' in Xhosa.] "Come over here!"

A puff of smoke drifts from the whizzing fire-drill. It is working. Mandisa cradles the tiny glowing ember in her nest of shredded bark and raises it to her lips, but her breath is too feeble to bring the ember to flames. She looks dizzily to Tandra for help. Tandra kneels down.

The two women blow alternate breaths into Mandisa's hands. Smoke billows. They cough with stinging eyes. Mandisa adjusts the tinder nest around the fragile ember and they blow again.

Suddenly, magically, victoriously, a little flame leaps to life.

Mandisa slides the flickering ball of fire under a small teepee made of broken guava twigs. A fire quicky grows.

After a few minutes, Mandisa tosses her yellow plastic BIC lighter into the flames. It whooshes abruptly into hydrocarbon smoke.

Mandisa turns to Tandra. "Give me your lighter. Now, cousin! This game is over."

# Aleppo, Syria 2

Zenobia Darwish's Diary – 1 March 2012

My parents return home shortly after dawn. I hear their bicycle tires crunch across the gravel. First my mother, then five minutes later my father. Jamila, Aziza and I are already awake and have prepared food for them. They seem to accept Jamila and Aziza's presence in stride, even seeming to relax a bit, perhaps feeling glad that now I might have some company. They go to bed.

Strangely enough, that afternoon, a scraggly but bright blond-haired little girl walks towards our shack smiling and holding up an improvised cloth sack hanging on a bindle stick. She shouts at me in Arabic, *"Uhdir lak altaeam."* ['I bring you food!']

I can't help but smile, thinking, *If that is actually food in her bag, it is a small peace offering. She must eat like a sparrow…*

"What is your name?" I shout at her in English, the one language people in Aleppo have in common.

"Mitzi," she shouts back, not slowing her approach at all.

"Mitzi what?" I demand.

This question stops her cold in her tracks. The girl's eyes grow wide. From this distance I cannot tell if she is shocked or angry.

"Why is it a problem for you to tell me your last name?" I shout at her.

"Nobody ever asked for my last name before…" she yells back. "I… I don't have a last name. I don't remember if I have a last name or not. Do I have to have a last name to come visit you?"

"Good question," I shout at her. "Come closer so we can speak with each other in a more civil tone." She lowers her satchel and approaches cautiously.

When she stops three meters distance, I say, "How old are you?"

"Five," she says rather belligerently.

"I never thought about your question before, Mitzi. Let us think about it together. This is Aziza Hamdi Ahmed. Over there is Jamila Ali Ahmed. They are sisters and just arrived here yesterday. My parents also live here, but they are trying to sleep now in the shack. They work in the city at night. We came here from near Palmyra two months ago. We have not yet established our traditions, except to not shout so much in the daytime that my parents cannot sleep. Meanwhile, what food did you bring us?"

The smile comes back to her face, not so bright as before, but more authentic. "Barley!" she says, handing me the bag. I estimate three kilos. I sigh. I wonder, *What is happening that suddenly more people are arriving?*

"Çima tu ewqas baş bi îngilîzî diaxivî?" I ask her in Kurmanji Kurdish. ['Why do you speak English so well?']

"Vorovhetev yes goyatevum yem shrjapati mardkants' het lav shp'velov," she immediately answers in Armenian. ['Because I survive by talking with the people around me.']

I switch back to English. "Aziza, would you please quietly bring Mitzi a glass of water to drink?" Aziza nods and moves towards the shack. "Mitzi with no last name, would you like some porridge? It is left over from our breakfast?"

"Yes, please," she says, giving us a little curtsy. *Where did she learn that gesture?* I wonder apprehensively. *It seems overly coquettish. Well... I suppose we will have time for such stories later. Right now there are other matters to attend to, such as, where are we all going to sleep? Where will we get more food and water?*

I indicate for Mitzi to sit quietly at our flimsy table.

Eventually Mama and Papa wake up. It is evening. They happily eat their breakfast, which is our dinner, and head out on their bikes to work. Soon after that, we four go to sleep.

When Mama and Papa arrive home the next morning, I tell them our plan to find more food and water. They agree. After they go to bed, we walk into parts of Aleppo I never visited before. I feel a new sense of confidence due to the strength of our numbers. But in reality, we are only four, and I hear Papa's voice in my mind, "Bravado is not far from stupidity."

We walk in a diamond shape, with a point person, two flanks and a rear guard. Our objective is to find food, water, and extra blankets in places that have already been scoured clean of usable resources. We don't know where to go without entering territory claimed by the rebels, Assad's Army, ISIS, or impromptu citizen militias roaming the streets desperately but hopelessly trying to protect their neighborhood from marauders. By now we are far away from my known territory.

"You shouldn't go down that street." It is a directionless female voice, stern and cynical. It scares us witless. We reflexively move closer and grab each other's hand. The voice echoes off weird angles of collapsed stone walls at this intersection. We frantically look around trying to locate the speaker. Should we run or drop to the dirt?

"You ladies are pitiful," the voice continues, this time laced with enhanced scorn.

"So then, help us," I demand, shouting with rage in no particular direction.

"That's more like it," says the voice. "Somebody is home in there..."

"Where is *your* home?" I shout back, accusingly. "You think you can make it alone out here as a single fighter?"

We wait. No response.

"What's the matter? Cat got your tongue?" I taunt.

"What does that mean?" she asks. A tall figure dressed in green army fatigues steps half-way out from a shadowy crevice carrying an AK-47 pointed in our direction but slightly towards the ground.

"It's an old English idiom," I explain loudly. "Harvey Keitel says it to Brad Pitt in *Thelma and Louise*."

She makes no response. I have the impulse to build further connection, so I continue answering her question. "In the 1700's, the English Royal Navy invented a short whip with nine knotted leather thongs. They used it on their own men for corporal punishment. They called it a 'Cat o' nine tails'. If a sailor was told a secret by a higher officer, the sailor would be threatened with 'the cat' if they ever told the secret. The question, 'Has the cat got your tongue?' came to mean, 'Are you afraid to tell?' I thought you would be educated about things like this." I try to sound as scornful as she.

The business end of the AK-47 rises slightly.

I shout at her. "We are weaponless, you idiot! You feel angry? Your anger will not be solved by pointing your Kalashnikov at us. Anger is solved by talking. Even if you shoot us, you will still be angry. Don't you get it? If you want to talk with us, great. We have questions for you. What do you say?" I tremble in my shoes saying such things, but, well, this is what I say.

The assault rifle sinks towards the ground again. "You jerks are *albatat albalisa* out there in the middle of the street." ['Sitting ducks' in Arabic.]

Silence.

I look to Jamila, then Aziza, then Mitzi. We agree. We are hungry, hot, tired, and thirsty. On top of that, now we are scared. What a fine day!

I shout, "Okay then. We come over to you."

The gun toter takes a cautious step forward into the light of day, scanning the intersection in all directions, also glancing up towards possible sniper positions. To me it seems overdramatic. But what do I know? This woman has survived. It cannot be too wrong what she is doing. She has her hair tucked up into a keffiyeh men's head wrap, dark gray with red patterns. I approach her earnestly with my empty hand out-stretched in a western man's greeting. "Hello. My name is Zenobia Darwish. This is Jamila and Aziza Ahmed. Mitzi has no last name. What is your name?"

She reflexively goes for the handshake, playing out her masculine character, catching herself only after it is too late to back down. "I am Israa Nabih, at your service." This she follows with a slight formal bow, never losing eye contact in case I might try something.

I long to tell this 'Israa Nabih' person our entire story and ask about hers, but caution takes the lead. I say, "We are looking for water."

"No, you're not!" Israa says derisively. "Water is heavy. If you were truly looking for water, you would have brought transportation to carry a heavy load back to wherever it is you are staying. You have no wheelbarrow, no wagon, no jugs, not even good backpacks. Your teamwork looks sloppy and crude. I bet this is the first time you ever went out on patrol together. Am I right?"

I don't even look at the others to answer this one. "You are right." I am not embarrassed. It is the simple truth. "What is your story, Israa? How have you survived so far?"

We silently wait. No answer comes.

Israa nervously scans the street again, then looks me in the eyes and says the most unexpected thing. "Can I invite you in for tea?"

Aziza blurts out, "Yes! We accept invitation. Do you have place to pee?"

We all laugh. Israa does an 'about face' and we follow her back through a maze of passageways under the collapsed structures. The buildings must have been five stories tall before being shelled and battered.

"Toilet is there," Israa indicates a broken wooden door on her left without slowing down. "Meet us back through here," leading the rest of us into a dark hallway then opening a door on the left into a cramped apartment. I guess it is a refurbished storeroom.

Our eyes adjust to the dim light as Israa starts up a single-burner gas stove and puts a teapot full of water on the fire. There are no chairs. We sit on the wool carpeted floor. Aziza finds us, comes inside, sits down.

"I never had guests before, so I improvise my teacups." Israa hands me a soup bowl. Jamila gets a chipped coffee cup. Aziza and Mitzi get Turkish style tea glasses. For herself, Israa keeps a clear glass beer stein bearing a circular logo with the word 'Paulaner' and the profile of a bearded monk. Then she steps outside, turns left, disappears.

We glance quizzically at each other, but Israa returns a moment later, her beer stein stuffed with a handful of freshly picked mint. She carefully breaks off sprigs and places them into our teacups. We look silently at each other until Mitzi says, "This could be the first of many times that we have tea together. Next time I will make scones."

"What are scones?" Aziza and Jamila ask in unison.

We laugh, but Israa cuts us off sternly. "Here you sit in the middle of a war zone. There are factions on every corner not caring who they shoot, as long as they shoot first. The city is being destroyed by fanatical terrorists of every variety, and you want to talk about scones?"

"It depends on what one regards as important," I suggest. "People can go crazy and shoot at each other because they have different ideas about what is important. I am not interested in joining their party. I want to start a different kind of party. More like a tea party. More like what we are doing here."

"But the brigades could break in here right now and rape and kill each one of us. What about that?" demands Israa. "How would you protect yourselves?"

"Yes, this is true," I say. "I think there are various ways to approach this problem. For example, if we do not join their party, then we are forced to make ourselves into an army with more fighters and weapons and bullets than they have, keeping watch day and night for when they might attack us. Or we could attack them first until they are all dead and gone. The game is: either they kill us, or we kill them. The outcome is that the evilest team wins. This means we all lose because we are all trying to become more evil and treacherous than the others. I do not want to play that game. I want to find another way, play a different game."

"What different game?" demands Israa. "Where is the different game to play?"

"I have been looking around the world," I say. "For example, there is a place called Bali, an island in Indonesia. The intention of the Balinese people is to praise the local spirits. That is their game. Anything else going on in their lives is regarded as less important than praising the spirits. The other details of their lives fall where they may around the central purpose of praising the spirits. It turns out that if you praise the spirits, the spirits praise you in return. As a result, the island of Bali has become abundant in blessings. Everybody wins. This is more like a game I want to play."

"So! You are going to Bali, then?" demands Israa furiously.

"No. Not necessarily. It is only one example, one possibility. I want to think with you about how we could create other overall interaction strategies here in Aleppo."

The tea kettle shrieks its whistle and quickly fills the space with steam.

Israa jumps up, turns off the flame, uses a dish towel to lift the kettle, then not-so-carefully splashes bubbling hot water over our tea lives. The fragrance of fresh steamy mint fills our nostrils.

"What are you children really up to?" demands Israa, slamming the kettle back on the stove and plopping herself on the carpet again.

"Right now, we need to bring some more food back to camp. I have a sense that more people might be coming, and we need to feed ourselves," answers Jamila. "How are you growing mint here in these ruins, by the way?"

"The usual way. 'I water it. I pull the weeds. Carrots grow from carrot seeds.'"

"You can grow carrots?" asks Mitzi. "I did not eat a carrot for such a long time!"

I interrupt. "Back to the important question Israa asked us. What are we up to? We were talking about that this morning, Israa. Here are the answers we came up with so far. We want to learn how to not only survive, but also to thrive in an environment like Aleppo. I want to improve our English so that we can have better access to online global resources. I am learning to grow, store, and cook chickpeas, fava beans, eggplant, and tomatoes. We will need to build single-story wooden shelters. And to practice self-defense skills."

"What style of self-defense?" demands Israa.

I am beginning to get the impression that Israa is a very demanding person.

"What do you propose? We are not skilled in this area..."

"I suggest you learn stick fighting. And Krav Maga."

"What is Krav Maga?" asks Aziza.

"Better you should ask me what is stick fighting. It is easier to explain."

"What is Krav Maga?" repeats Aziza, unphased.

"It is an uncontrollable form of hand-to-hand fighting developed in the 1930's by European Jews. It is simultaneously offensive and defensive."

"Can you teach us?" asks Mitzi.

Israa refuses to answer.

I change the subject. "Are you willing to help us find some food? We would also like to show you where our place is. It's a few kilometers west from here, over near the Queiq riverbed."

Israa lets out a long sigh.

*Where did that sigh come from?* I wonder. *Is she regretfully saying goodbye to her isolated way of surviving, while timidly saying hello to being part of a solid little team? Or something else?* I can't figure it out.

"Finish your tea, and then let's go," Israa says abruptly. We are unanimously surprised. "Jamila, please dig into that shelf behind you and grab an armful of canvas bags. I am not giving them to you. I am loaning them to you for this mission. I want them back afterwards."

"Deal," says Jamila.

"Thanks for the drink, Israa," says Aziza, smiling. "Can we take some of your mint plants to put in our gardens?"

Israa regards us for a moment, then leans over and reaches behind Aziza's back pulling two plastic yogurt containers out of a drawer. "I have a little shovel outside. Come with me and hold these so I can give you some mint, and some rosemary."

We excitedly jump to our feet and exit the tiny room.

After digging up the herbs, Israa shoves a spare 30-round magazine into her belt, slips the AK-47's strap over her right shoulder, and takes us through a crazy back-alley maze of tiny streets and passages. Aziza cradles our new mint and rosemary plants. Jamila carries the empty bags.

We hike up several flights of half-shattered stairs, then climb out through a broken window onto an improvised scaffolding over to a crushed warehouse. We enter through a gaping hole in the roof and clamber after Israa down into the basement which is packed with bags of wheat and canned food. It does not take long to load up as much as we can carry. Food is heavy.

"Do we have to go back the same way we got here?" asks Mitzi.

She kept up with us bravely on the way here, but she is clearly afraid of heights.

"No," says Israa. "I know a different way out to the main street, but from there one of you needs to take over navigating."

"No problem," I affirm, at the same time noticing being drenched with sweat. I am feeling thirsty to the point of dehydration.

While scurrying along one alley, we pass the ruins of a western-style café, crushed beneath a collapsed apartment building. Digital nomad foreigners must have come here to drink cafe lattes, write messages on their iPhones, read books, and socialize. I can make out a smashed cooler in the gloom, door twisted open, plastic bottles of fresh water scattered on the floor. If only I could grab a few.

"I want to take some water from back in there."

"Stop!" whispers Israa fiercely. "It could be booby-trapped."

We all freeze and stay silent. Israa digs an LED flashlight out of her belt-pouch and clips it to the front of her rifle. She turns it on. All her senses follow the beam of light as she scours the chaotic interior for wires, strings, or mines. Israa takes a few cautious steps, then turns and signals for me to go ahead of her towards the cooler.

I slide past her in the rubble, but on my next step I slip on something buried in the debris. I grab onto a splintered bookshelf on the wall for balance, then bend down to find a fat book sprawled open and face down in the dust.

I pick up the book and shake grit out of the pages. "This is no place for a book to die," I mumble to no one in particular. Israa says nothing.

I wipe dust off its leather cover with my sleeve and read the title: *Handbook*.

I flip through a few pages and see photos and drawings with words in English. I vaguely say, "It is no accident that we find this book. It could prove useful."

Israa wordlessly nods.

*Where are these ideas coming from?* I tuck the book under my arm and approach the crumpled cooler, collect five dusty one-liter bottles of water from the floor, and drop a few coins on the floor to avoid having a debt.

We scrabble with our load of scavenged contraband over tons of crumbled gray cinderblock, squeezing past bent iron bars through a narrow dark alleyway and out into bright afternoon sunlight of the main road.

I easily remember the way back to camp. Israa wordlessly takes up a rear position with her weapon. We arrive before my parents wake up, me hugging the *Handbook* to my chest as if I had been searching for this book my whole life. It feels very weird, but it also feels true, even if I know nothing more about it.

I turn to Israa and say, "Israa, we invite you to stay with us for supper. Would you do us the honor of accepting our invitation?" As I speak, the others gather around, hoping to hear Israa's affirmative answer.

In that moment, my father sticks his head out the door of the shack, sees us all standing there in a circle, then speaks back over his shoulder, "Mama, I think you should come see. Our little flock seems to be growing!"

Both my parents stroll over. We five step backwards a little to widen the circle and let them join. I feel a peaceful joy grow in our hearts. Suddenly tears come to Israa's eyes. She slowly turns and carefully sets her assault rifle down behind her on a concrete block, then uses one arm to hug me on her left side, and the other to hug Aziza on her right side.

Wordless smiles grow on all our faces while we glance around, eye to eye. I can sense lonely hearts bonding and wounds of betrayal healing. If there would be nothing else for dinner, this is already a feast.

But an additional surprise comes during our meal together around our outdoor table. In a pause during our chatter, Israa clears her throat and says, "I know of a man..."

I think to myself, *Now, this is a particularly effective segway phrase to remember!*

We anxiously look at her, waiting to learn if there is more to her sharing. A tense minute ticks by in silence. *Is this all she will ever say to us about herself? We know so little about Israa Nabih. She could in reality be some kind of psychological nut case.* There are already bits of evidence that could be twisted around to support this diagnosis. I would prefer that it not be true. I sigh and keep waiting, trying to be patient.

Finally Israa's eyes come back into focus and she speaks. "When I first went to school in 2001, I was five years old. I sat behind a boy in class named Montassar Bilal Khaled. 'Montassar' means victorious genius protector. 'Bilal' is the name of one of the ten companions of Muhammed. 'Khaled' means immortal. To me, he really had these qualities. I liked him, but then he stopped coming to school. I asked about what happened, but no one would tell me. I was devastated. One day I went to the market and was attracted to approach an old lady sitting near the dried fish, reading cards, telling people about their future."

"That's crazy!" shouts Aziza.

"What?" demands Israa, at first scared, then irritated about being interrupted while remembering her painful past.

"Sorry for my sister yelling out in the middle of your sensitive story," interrupts Jamila. "What she means to tell you is that we know this *Sahira*. ['witch' or 'wise woman' in Arabic]. She helped us to come here and find Zenobia. We tell you later about that. Please tell us more about Montassar."

Israa looks around for agreement. We are all nodding. I clamp my hand over Aziza's mouth to emphasize that we are on Israa's side. Israa smiles briefly at my theatrics, and decides to continue.

"I remember it so clearly even though it was so long ago. I am maybe nine years old at the open-air market. I sit down on a wooden crate and tell the old lady about how my heart broke when Montassar did not come to school anymore. She saves my life back then because she took me seriously. She pretends to read her cards, but I could see her eyes are glazed over and she scans somewhere else. Then she starts to talk. She tells me not to worry. She carefully explains to me that there was a scandal between Montassar's father and a woman in the government. The father had to move his family away to protect them from social ridicule. She tells me that one day, Montassar will come back into my life, that he will help me do something big. Well, I did not know what to make of that, but I could feel my soul settling down. The thought that I would meet Montassar again helped me stay tough and survive when my family splits up. It happened like this for so many... One day my brothers come home and proudly announce that they had become rebels. My parents explode in rage because they are committed to defending Assad's regime. Suddenly everyone in my family hates everyone else and wants to call in the officials to arrest the others as enemies. I cannot stand this tormenting insanity. One night I run away. Since then I have been alone." She pauses for a moment, looking down at her hands, breathing heavily. "Sometimes I think they must all be dead by now. I don't know. I had to cross the city so I could hide out in those ruins."

We remain in silence. It is such a moving story, but I do not get the point of it. I glance at my parents, wondering about how late it is getting, thinking I should end this conversation, afraid about them not making it to work on time. They silently shake their heads for me to not worry. I never saw them be like this before.

Then Israa continues. "Two weeks ago, I saw Montassar crossing through my part of town, on foot. He was with two other men on some kind of patrol. The one at the rear carried a gun. Montassar was studying a map. The third man carried a backpack. I followed them for a while, but then it got too dangerous for me. I was afraid of being seen. Since then I have scouted the area and tracked their movements a few times. I think I know their routine. In truth, I do not know who Montassar is anymore. But my heart tells me he did not change his basic nature. I think he is surviving, like the rest of us, pretending to be whoever he needs to be to get through this. I had the idea that... well... if he would come here, it could be good for him. I know it is a wild thing to say..."

"No, no! My dear child!" Mama blurts. "Don't worry! Thank you for telling us. I remember what happened and how people changed it into a scandal. It was long ago." She glances at Papa, who nods, and then she continues. "I think you are right about Montassar. In any case, it is time for Papa and I to go to work. Will you stay with us tonight? I think you can all fit into our beds. Later on, we can work out a plan for how to meet with Montassar Bilal Khaled. What do you say?"

Israa is quick to answer. "What I say is that my belief in miracles is quickly being restored. I say, yes. I say, thank you for your kindness, your generosity, and your compassion."

We send my parents off into the night on their bikes, clean up the dishes, and crawl into the shack.

I watch Israa professionally check the magazine of her AK-47 to make sure the first bullet is correctly positioned in the chamber, and that the safety is off. Then she slides the gun gently under the big bed where she is to sleep with Aziza and Jamila, making sure the barrel points towards the door, then arranging herself to lie on the edge of the mattress.

For some reason, I sleep better that night than I have in a long time.

# Eugene, Oregon 1

Remington Smith's *Beep! Book* – 20 March 2023

What a strange place America is. City after city constructed out of ticky-tacky, all labeled with franchised corporate brand names. Such big roads. So many cars. Shopping center parking lots large enough to contain an entire French village.

And what strange people, at once so familiar from the cinema screen, and yet so disconnected from real life.

After a week I feel aligned with the challenges that the Nature Conservancy has taken on. People seem to like me okay here, but I do not understand my peers. They worry about boyfriends, and how they look in the mirror.

Yesterday my boss, Evelyn Starfield, says, "Nature Conservancy has given us Fridays off if we participate in the *Fridays For Future* rally. Are you coming?"

I hesitate... but rather than staying alone at work, I say, "Yes. What shall I wear?" The other girls laugh.

Their sense of reality seems dangerously attenuated. I wish to be better prepared, so I search the Extinction Rebellion website to learn more. They suggest wearing pants, boots, long-sleeve shirt, and sunhat, all black or dark colored, personal ID, water bottle, high-protein snacks, painter's breathing mask with an activated carbon filter, goggles, notepad and pen, flashlight.

As I walk towards the center of town, I feel afraid... 54% afraid. Yet I trust myself to take care of myself regardless of what happens.

I carry no placard.

I am on a private expedition to research the effectiveness of *sheeple* gathering in the streets to 'petition the lord with prayer'.

Those words are from Jim Morrison's song: *Soft Parade*. He sings, "*You cannot petition the lord with prayer.*" It means, Town Hall will not bend to your wishes, even if you propose to create a better future for Earthlings.

This is because 'creating a bright future for humanity' is not on a psychopath's agenda. The only thing on a psychopath's agenda is power over others to protect the psychopath's security, which is self-defined as their wealth.

I tell you these things because so many people live in denial about how the dominant culture's design is sending humanity and other living Beings over the cliff to extinction. Many people live in denial and ignorance about psychopathology. Since you are reading my *Beep! Book*, you cannot say I didn't warn you!

A psychopath's life-plan originates in their unconscious fear of being found out. It is huge fear, in fact, it is terror, mostly unconscious terror, frequently masked by blathering idiotic arrogance. Regardless of their bluff, psychopaths live in terror. You can see it behind their eyes if you pay attention.

This is why the word 'terrorist' has replaced the word 'witch' as the worst name you can call someone.

Psychopathy is in the core of a terrorist.

Psychopaths are deeply terrified that others will notice the disconnect between their mind and their heart which causes them to have no conscience. They are afraid of being discovered as 'damaged goods', and then singled out for destruction.

A psychopath's survival ploy is to pretend to serve humanity by hunting down those evil 'terrorists' out there – making a 'Global War on Terror', imprisoning 'terrorists' outside of America in Guantanamo Prison – when in fact, *psychopaths are terrorists*.

This explains a lot about America, doesn't it?

How do I know all this? Because I myself have a mild form of dyslexia. I too noticed that I was different from the other kids. I too did not want to be found out and isolated. I learned to hide my dyslexia by being a 'nice girl'.

I am still alive, so my 'nice girl' survival strategy worked. But every survival strategy has a price. Right now, the 'nice girl' part of me wants to go back home and not hike towards a potential police confrontation zone.

I tell myself, *I wear the mask. The mask does not wear me*. I keep walking.

Approaching our meeting point, I sense butterflies in my stomach, as if there are deep tectonic rumbles in the local energetic field from social rules breaking down, liberating something that feels exuberant about being less conscious.

Hmmm... now... I wonder... What gets exuberant about being less conscious? It smells like gremlin to me. I feel like I just slipped into Steven Spielberg's *Gremlin* movie and am entering a gigantic gremlin feeding frenzy in the middle of town. Holy crap...

The crowd sounds angry and belligerent, yet giddy, like victims who find a chance to take revenge.

Paris must have felt like this when its citizens attacked the Bastille, later that afternoon in 1789. (Watch the film *Start The Revolution Without Me* to get the joke... It's with Gene Wilder and Donald Sutherland.)

Over in a parking lot I see about 20 people standing in two concentric circles, facing each other. They are not marching to storm the castle of the rich. They seem to be practicing yelling at each other, "No!"

"Yes!" "Hah!" while throwing their hands into the air. Not one is smiling. Not one is aggressive. I instinctively change course to discover more about what they are up to.

I become so entranced that I fail to notice a roar from behind me. A woman screams in the distance. A siren wails. Someone shouts, "Police! They have teargas!" A pulse jets through the crowds faster than I can think. People panic. Someone shatters a plate-glass shopwindow across the street. I freeze. People start running. It is coming apart.

I turn around and see a mob from my right swarming to confront the police approaching from my left. I am about to be crushed in the middle. I drop to the ground and roll sideways under a parked SUV while reaching into my backpack and strapping on my mask and goggles.

Time stops. I see police riot boots running past, smoking teargas canisters. I hear bullhorn commands and screams from marchers being beaten with sticks, handcuffed, and dragged away. Then a damp gray cloud of gas blocks my view.

The thought passes through my mind, *This is when I die...*

After a lifetime, the sounds fade. The gas slowly dissipates. A puddle of blood oozes slowly towards my hiding place. I drag myself out from under the car and peek around. *I have never been dirtier in my life.* I feel completely contaminated by human insanity.

I see no one from the Nature Conservancy, but I notice two young women who look familiar. From where? Ah, yes! The circle who practiced yelling at each other. How did they avoid having a confrontation with the police?

Without knowing why and with no plan, I move towards their friendly faces. I hear one of them comment, "Getting their head bashed and their eyes pepper-sprayed does not create a new future. Too bad they are using such outdated thoughtware..."

I blurt out, "I have to know what you are talking about."

They scan me up and down, then say, "Come with us."

It is early evening. We walk quite a distance together, mostly in silence. The women are named Francis Atkins and Carol Washington. I feel glad for the walk... time to digest some of what just happened. The sun is setting when we trudge up the front steps of the *Horsehead Bar*, looking like a nondescript hangout for alcoholics, a place that I would ordinarily avoid.

I crash into Francis and Carol when they unexpectedly stop in the entryway. Carol slides open a black velvet curtain on the left to reveal a narrow door which she pushes open. We all step through onto a small platform where a bare bulb lights wooden stairs leading down into a dimly lit, cement floored basement. I close the cellar door behind me and follow them down and to the right into a room with about twelve people sitting in chairs around a collapsable table.

A skinny man with gold, wire-rimmed bifocal eyeglasses and a short white beard in his middle-sixties bangs a small gavel on the table several times and then says, "Welcome everyone to *Shadow Knights of the Mysterium*. My name is Robert Maxwell, chairman. I hereby call this meeting to order!"

Weirdly enough, Robert Maxwell seems to be using protocol from *Robert's Rules of Order*, an 1876 American manual of guidelines for 'parliamentary procedure' which I read when I was 12.

He starts with an agenda, discusses issues, and tries to make decisions. The interactions are dry, masculine, hierarchical, under rigid control, and not producing very creative outcomes.

Michelle, my grandmother, allowed me to participate in her Study Group whenever I wanted... which was always. She introduced us to *Torus Technology*, meeting protocols, and processes for making the most of non-hierarchical group intelligence.

I sit here with a few people in a basement in the town of Eugene, Oregon, a town in which there was just a police action against a peaceful rally, painfully watching the people at this meeting ignore precious doorways and waste potentials until I cannot stand the loss anymore.

I raise my hand.

Robert eventually allows me to speak.

"Hello everyone. My name is Remington Smith. I know I am new here, but, well, I would like to share something important that I learned from my grandmother in France. She said, 'You can only experiment at the edge.' So far today, we are not at the edge. We look at the edge, we talk about the edge, but we are not *at* the edge. For example, this team's intelligence is being partly blocked by keeping this table between all of us. If we get rid of the table, we can meet in an open circle with nothing in the middle. Then we are free to connect with every other person here while each of us becomes creative due to being exposed at our personal edges. Would you like to try the experiment of meeting without this table?"

Robert says, "Ms. Remington Smith has made the motion that we remove the table from our meeting space. Any further discussion about that?" 5 seconds tick by. "No? Then let us vote. All those in favor say, 'Aye.'"

Everyone says, "Aye!"

All those opposed say, "Nay!"

No one says, "Nay."

"Let it be recorded that the 'Ayes' have it unanimously."

One of the women writes the motion and the vote on her yellow minutes notepad.

Robert says, "I move that we recess so as to put this table back out in the basement. Is there a second?"

"I second the motion," says Carol Atkins.

Robert continues. "Let us reconvene in five minutes."

Everyone helps.

The little meeting room feels much larger with the table removed. Sitting with open space before them, most people are visibly relieved, already chatting freely with whoever sits next to them. Yet some nervously fidget in fear of being so physically exposed in the circle.

The most nervous is Robert Maxwell.

Without the table in front of him, he has nothing on which he can bang his hammer to get people to quiet down and play dead again. It reminds me of what being in school must be like. I am so glad I was unschooled. It gives me liberty to speak when speaking needs to happen rather than having to wait for permission. Like now...

"A circle establishes a different kind of teamwork. It is radically different from a hierarchy. In order to fly, the circle needs a pilot, a spaceholder. The spaceholder is not a 'leader'. She is more like an optimizer. 'Plus, the spaceholder's job is temporary. The role can be passed to the next spaceholder even after only a few minutes, if desired. I suggest, Robert, that someone else besides you or me starts as the first spaceholder of this circle. Okay?"

"Sure thing, Remington! We are experimenters! Who would like to be the first spaceholder?"

"I would!" It is Carol Atkins. "How does it go, Remington?"

"You simply get centered in yourself, stay grounded deep into the Earth, surround yourself with your own personal bubble of radically responsible space, and then say and do whatever needs to be said and done to fly this spacecraft!"

"Uh, okay! Does anyone have anything?"

Across the circle from Carol, a woman says, "Yes! Thank you, Remington! My name is Patricia Wells. Nice to meet you! We now have the physical space in here to try an exercise I once read about on a website that I always wanted to try with you. It is a way to transform your frustrations into useful actions. It will take about 45 minutes. Is this okay for everyone?"

"Excuse me for interrupting," I say, "but since we are using *Torus Technology*, you may as well try *Resistance Decision Making*. It goes like this. Patricia just made a proposal to do a 45-minute exercise. As a circle we need to decide if we do the exercise or not. Instead of checking all those in favor and all those opposed, counting who wins and who loses, we use a two-handed symbol for consulting resistance. Resistance has group-intelligence because if you feel resistance, you may have information, or perhaps knowledge from past experiences, that the rest of us do not have. The group needs the value of your wisdom. The hand symbol is easy. Patricia says, 'Please show your resistance to doing this exercise. One, two, three!' If you hold up two closed fists showing no extended fingers, that means you have 'zero resistance', which means we could not stop you from doing the exercise. If you hold up ten fingers, that means you have 'ten resistance', meaning we could never force you to do the exercise. Holding up any other number of fingers shows your degree of resistance from zero to ten. Then we consult with those people who have the highest levels of resistance to see what they know that we don't know. New proposals can be made at any time to incorporate new information. Ready Patricia?"

"Yes! Please show your resistance to doing this exercise. One, two, three!"

I see zero resistance everywhere, so I hold up four fingers just to show how to collect wisdom from resistance.

Patricia says, "I see we have level 4 resistance from Remington. What is your resistance?"

"My resistance is that I don't know what you mean by the word 'frustration.' I know about feelings and emotions that are either anger, sadness, fear, or joy. What are 'frustrations'?"

"Frustrations would be anger. This exercise changes your anger into productive actions."

"What I am asking is, do you mean the *feeling* of anger that comes up right now in the moment, gets used, and then completely vanishes as an experience? Or do you mean the *emotion* of anger that has been hanging around for a long while, never quite going away no matter what you do?"

"Ah! I see! You are offering us a further distinction that I didn't think about before. Thank you, Remington! This exercise is about changing your longtime emotional anger into real time immediately productive actions. Is that clearer?"

"Yes, perfect!" I say.

"What is everyone's resistance now?" says Patricia. "One, two, three!"

Only fists are shown around the room. No fingers up.

"Okay. I see zero resistance. Here we go. We begin by stacking all these chairs in the corner, and choosing a partner. It works better if everyone takes off their shoes and socks, and if you each choose a partner who is more-or-less your same physical size. Then we all circle up, facing your partner. Good! Now put both your hands on your partner's shoulders and lean towards them. Yes! Like that! This is not a power struggle. This is working together to create a safe enough space to express your anger consciously.

"See how we are standing in two concentric circles? The inner circle will speak first. Outer Circle, your job is to encourage your partner to let their frustrations speak loudly while you listen carefully to help them remember. After you both have a chance to find the specifics behind your personal emotional anger, you will help each other remember what your anger said and write it down."

"In our *Beep! Books?*" I ask.

"What's a '*Beep! Book*'?" asks Carol.

"A *Beep! Book* is one of these..." I say, pulling my own *Beep! Book* and pen out of my belt pouch, "a small notepad you carry around for instantly documenting new distinctions, new ideas, or feedback and coaching from others, before your Box and gremlin cause you to forget."

"What do you mean 'box and gremlin'?" asks Francis.

"Your 'Box' has many other names: your psychological defense strategy, your memetic construct, your comfort zone... it is the worldview you live inside of that gives your life its look and feel. Your 'gremlin' is the active part of your Box that does whatever it takes to keep things the same in your life, because if anything changes or evolves in your survival strategy, it might no longer work to assure your survival."

The space stays silent a moment as people consider what I said.

"Are we good to go?" asks Patricia.

Robert says, "How do I find my frustrations?"

"You are doing it right now, Robert!" says Patricia. "You are speaking your frustration about not knowing how to find your frustrations. Do you get this? It is simple and natural. Just keep going like that. Start speaking about small frustrations that are close to you right now, and work up to bigger frustrations about things around you that have bothered you for a longer time. Any other questions?"

I shout out, "Yes! Can I say, 'I feel angry', instead of 'I feel frustrated?'"

"Yes, you can say that! It might even be more accurate to say, 'I feel angry!' Any other questions? No? Okay. Inner circle, you push and speak first. Outer circle, you push back, give encouragement, and remember what your partner says. I will tell you when to switch roles. You only have about 3 minutes, so jump right into the important stuff. One, two, three, go!"

We go.

I stand in the inner circle, pushing on Anton Pirelli's shoulders shouting, "I feel angry that no one ever showed me this exercise before. So many people have so much good wisdom and energy for changing things for the better! And we do nothing! And say nothing! Instead we try to be acceptable as nice people! I hate this! It wastes so much potential! I feel angry that I have adopted values from my mother as a way to have a souvenir of my mother in my life who died when I was 4 years old! I am frustrated that I am forced to use words one after another instead of being able to communicate everything I want to say all at once. The stuff that makes me angry is so big! And my anger is so massive! It is not okay with me that human beings let war crimes happen instead of making war itself a crime. I feel angry that I never knew about *Shadow Knights of the Mysterium* before! I have been looking for you my whole life! Why are you so hidden? I have finally found my tribe, way over here in Eugene, Oregon! Why were you hiding from me? I don't even know you and I want to be with you the rest of my life! We have a future together! There is so much to change! So far to grow! So much potential to bring to life! The schools have to be dismantled! People need to prepare for their initiations instead of going to classes and sitting in rows trying to remember facts they can find on the internet! There is no time to waste! So many unconscious things are happening that lead us into a cul-de-sac! A dead end! A very dead end! I hate it! Where is human intelligence? Why do we have to pretend to be normal and then hide underground like this to research what is important to us? Is the Inquisition still going on? I want things to change. I want a wake-up revolution! I want to know you Anton, and Carol, and Robert, and Patricia, and Francis, and everyone! Who are you? And what do you want? I don't want people to be afraid of trying new things to create a future on Earth that does not depend on burning fossil fuels and using up rare minerals so fast that future generations will have none to use! We are behaving like selfish short-sighted children, like mindless bacteria! I do not want that for my future! I don't want that to be the culmination of human presence on Earth, overpopulating until we die in our own shit! No! Not that! I feel angry that the good people I know are still giving away their authority to psychopaths at the top of insane hierarchies! This is insane! I want to be initiated into a new kind of adulthood! I want to initiate others so they can be centered and grounded and take their authority back to relate with each other so that more love happens! Not just money! Not just survival! I want what really matters to happen, like love and transformation and integrity and high-level fun, like we are having now! This does not depend on making more cars or phones or buying more plastic shit from China! I want to walk through towns that are not designed around cars but instead around radical relating and joyful intimacy! I want..."

I could have kept going, but Patricia shouts to interrupt us. "Okay! Okay! Thank you! Please come to a pause! So much fabulous frustration and anger! Thank you for your courage to speak it out. Listener, be sure to take a kind of inner photograph of everything you just heard your partner say so you can help them write it all down in a few minutes. Now we change roles. Outer Circle, it is your turn to speak. Please stay in the same position. Keep your hands on your partner's shoulders. Make sure you are grounded, centered, and bubbled. Take a deep breath. One! Two! Three! Go!"

Anton starts yelling. His whole body shakes, but he stumbles with finding the right words. I shout, "Change to Italian!"

That is the doorway.

He shouts, "I am not Italian! I am Sicilian! "Io sugnu sicilianu! Io nun sugnu italianu! Mi sta mali ca la genti è accussì ignoranti di quantu culturi diffirenti ci sunnu supra la Terra! Ci su' miliuna di culturi, ognuna cù' a so preferenza è puntu di vista e cuntribuzioni preziosi da fà! Mi fa mali ca tanti preziosi cuncetti e risorsi sunnu pisati di la mediocrità! Ognunu cerca di essiri accittatu, ma cancella la so' squisita individualità! Vogghiu tutta la ansalata di frutta! Non di na lattina! Frescu tagghiatu e succusu, culuritu, deliziosu! Vogghiu livari li pirsuni di la rete e libbirarili ntô largu oceanu accussì putissiru amari la vita di novu ppi tuttu! Vogghiu ca l'umani ritrovanu la nostra libertà caòtica picchì chistu è comu è la vita!"

Pure Latin rage! I can hardly hold him back. He's spitting fire like a dragon! It is marvelous to feel and see him come so alive in his mother tongue. I wish I could speak Sicilian to better understand him.

Patricia brings the second shouters to a halt, then invites us to sit and help each other write down what we said. Because of my French, I picked up enough key words to help Anton document the fierce desires roaring behind his forced politeness and civility. He does the same for me.

Then Patricia says, "Please find new partners and sit in groups of 3."

I end up with Francis Atkins and Sophia Bentley.

Patricia continues, "You now have 3 minutes per person to translate the clarity each person just captured from their inner frustration dynamo, into a clearly defined project. What did your rage scream at you to change? What project would transform your anger into ecstasy? Write clear mission statements for several projects for each person, based on what they are angry about. Please begin."

The 3-minute time limitation forces us to access invention resources that are unhampered by our linear minds. We create huge value for each other simultaneously, using every person's wealth of intelligence in parallel. This is full-out, parallel play. I love it!

The mission statements we created for me are:

- Provide transformational spaces like *Shadow Knights of the Mysterium*.
- Establish a United Nations Network of regenerative communities.
- Train people how to dismantle obsolete institutions, such as schools, franchises, religions, armies, and corporations.
- Depave downtown Eugene and create a Human Intimacy Zone.
- Write a Handbook of Transformational Exercises.

We read our projects out loud to detect potential synergies. The joy this visibly brings to each person is boundless.

I am shocked by how clear and accurate our mission statements are.

My shock is amplified in the next part of the exercise. Patricia says, "Please sit across from a new partner. Give your partner your *Beep! Book*. For each of your missions, they ask you, 'Why are you afraid to do this part of your destiny?' You answer in radical honesty. They write down your fears."

My fears are:

- I am only one person, too small to make a difference. I am afraid of failing.
- I am afraid that obsolete institutions will defend themselves by hiring Security Forces to kill me.
- I am afraid about not knowing how to fully dismantle obsolete institutions.
- I am afraid that police will arrest me if I am caught depaving the streets of Eugene.
- I feel afraid of losing my anonymity. If I write a book and become recognizable, I am afraid that people will project things on me, or expect things from me. If I become famous, I may become a target of abuse, like what happened to Charles Lindburg after he flew alone across the Atlantic.

Patricia says, "The last step in this exercise, which altogether is called *Push Shoulders*, is to shift into a new group of 3 people, then help each person design two or three experiments which use the intelligence of their fears to build a path to their destiny instead of a block.

The experiments I receive are:

- Call teams together for each of my projects so I am no longer small and alone. If someone is interested in my team, they already like me.
- Change "I don't know how to..." into, "I love inventing new ways to..." For example, "I love inventing new ways to write the book, dismantle institutions, depave downtown," etc.
- Live in a shortened timeline so that I can do the step that is immediately at hand, rather than trying to handle all eventualities at once. For example, the police have not arrived in a paddy wagon to arrest me for depaving Eugene even though I have already begun doing it here at this meeting.

These experiments are so exciting that I want to start doing them immediately. I raise my hand while looking hard at Carol Atkins. Carol says, "Go ahead, Remington."

I stand up and say, "I am doing one of my experiments right now. I lived with my grandmother in Fontainebleau, France, since I was 4 years old. Her name was Michelle Piment du Pont. She was some kind of alchemist of human potential, a student of George Gurdjieff, a spaceholder for healing and evolutionary circle-meetings like this one, for 67 years. She died a year after passing on the spaceholding for her circle. Just before coming here, in a dream, Michelle gave me access to a secret trunk full of handwritten papers filled with distinctions, instructions, discoveries, and diagrams... Those papers are all that I brought with me from France."

People around the circle gasp in amazement. I start crying, probably from amazement too. People offer me tissues and consolation, but I refuse to sit down.

"I have mostly been a loner. I did not fit in anywhere. Now I find you all, and I am suddenly home. Part of my experiment is to keep talking even if I am crying..." People chuckle, but making them laugh is not the point. I am not finished.

"The actual experiment is to invite two of you to create a team with me to transcribe the useful parts of my grandmother's notes into a kind of handbook so others can have access to this treasure. I have never done this before... make a team... or write a book. Are there two of you who would like to join me in this project?"

There are four: Patricia Wells, Francis Atkins, Carol Washington, and Sophia Bentley. Sophia says, "We can start tomorrow evening at 6 over at my house. I have a large table in my study where we would have plenty of room to work together. My internet connection is strong."

I simply shake my head in disbelief, stand there crying.

Patricia says, "What is it, Remington? Talk to us!"

"I have a team now for a project that is truly dear to me. How did that suddenly happen? I can't believe it. This is ecstatic... I probably don't look ecstatic... But, I am ecstatic... I feel really, really happy. I never dared to imagine this would be possible."

Sophia says, "Well, if you bring your suitcase full of secret papers over to my place tomorrow, you will have to believe it."

What a day.

"Would everyone please take a deep breath?" says Carol, the spaceholder. "It is rather late. I feel sad to say it, but we are about to exit this extraordinary chamber and step back out there, into the ordinary world. Shifting from this context to that context may be quite a stark transition. Please drive carefully. You may be in an altered state of consciousness, but your car is not. Please drink lots of water. Does anyone need a ride?"

I definitely do not need a ride. I already feel like I am on a rollercoaster!

# Death Valley, California

No food. No shelter. No one else for company. No phone. No electricity. No heating. No air conditioning. No lighting. No internet connection. No walls. No roof over my head. No windows. No doors. No flat smooth floors. No square corners. No curtains or blinds. No water faucet. No sink. No mirror. No trash can. No bed. No carpeting. No toilet. No refrigerator. No closets. No bookshelves. No basement. No attic. No neighbors above or below. No shops. No sidewalks. No roads. No electric wires strung between telephone poles. No buses. No car. No bicycle. No garage. No ice. No fruit. No salad. No coffee. No dogs. No cats. No packages from Amazon. No music. No pizza or Thai food deliveries. No other shoes. No police. No laws. No fences. No protection from wild animals, rattlesnakes, scorpions, hawks, mountain lions. Wild pigs. Coyotes. Cockroaches. Mice. Bats. Wind. Dust. Rain. Sandstorms. Thunderstorms. Crazy people... with guns... or knives...

"This is my space," whispers Edith Goldman, to no one there.

Leaning back against the boulder, she glances furtively left and right over both shoulders.

She sees rocks, creosote bushes, sky, and the hill behind her. A wide valley spreading out below. Mountains rising in the distance beyond that. Gravel and sand under her butt. A faint breeze. Mostly silence. Sitting alone in the desert, there is, of course, no one, and nothing glaring at her to be quiet.

*Why did I look around?* She asks herself. *To see if I disturbed someone by speaking? That's insane. There is no one here but me.*

*The desert is not annoyed by my voice.*

*Shit!*

She shakes her head, disgusted that adaptive childhood survival habits still operate automatically out of context.

She sighs deeply.

With greater resolve she tries again, louder this time.

"This is my circle in the sand! My straw hat, my jug of water, my wool blanket, and my journal to write in. This is my bottle of ink! I mixed it together. And my feather pen! I carved it. This is my space! I start over here and now, with just this."

Memories flick across her mind's eye. Exiting the Bach, Becker, and Benowitz offices for the last time. No one even said good-bye.

Wandering aimlessly through San Francisco streets, uninspired. Nursing cafe lattes for hours while searching online for hints about what should be next for her, how to grow up, how to face life as an adult woman.

That was an initiation in itself! Sifting through philosophical hogwash and confidence-building pep talks, bypassing Instagram divas and gurus, skipping indigenous rituals, circumventing psychedelic mushrooms and ayahuasca ceremonies, avoiding rites of passage into secret societies or religions, finally googling 'authentic adulthood initiatory processes' and discovering a video showing a list of initiations flowing up the screen 'star wars' style for seven full minutes.

She remembers watching the video three times, then closing her eyes and choosing one. What he finger pointed at was: Vision Quest.

*What the hell is Vision Quest?*

*Only one way to find out...* and here she is, in the middle of day six of a twelve-day Vision Quest initiation with *School of Lost Borders*. Four days of sitting in a circle and camping out with the other candidates, preparing. Four days and nights alone in the desert, without food, now. Four days of debriefing, later.

Vision Quest is only one of the hundreds of authentic adulthood initiatory processes mentioned in the film from initiations.mystrikingly .com, where they claim that humans need a wide variety of 'matrix-building' experiences to activate functional adult responsibility in regenerative culture.

Hunger has faded. Plans and appointments are nonexistent. No tech or distractions. Time expands. Spaciousness opens up.

Edith reviews her current condition. She still shakes inside from arbitrarily abandoning a solid legal career. Still afraid of what her father might say... Not attracted by any known profession. She looks at her future, thinking, *I am a lost baby chicken, sticking only one foot out of my eggshell. I have a long way to go...*

Then she notices that her chicken story contains a previously uninspected assumption: that there is 'some place' other than here and now to get to...

Without that assumption, there is nothing to compare herself to, no justification for beating herself up.

*If there is nowhere else than here and now, then... this is it. This is all there really is.*

She slowly rolls over onto her side and curls up in the partial shade of a sage bush and a boulder on the western slopes of Death Valley in California, an environment that has killed many unprepared white people.

Edith naps.

Eventually she wakes up with a 1967 *Who* song whispering in her head. She opens her eyes and sits up, only to find that the song is true. She sings the words out loud: "I can see for miles and miles and miles and miles and miles..."

The song takes over her heart. She stands up, stretches her arms out wide, and can't help but sing and dance full out into a vastness that extends to a distant horizon where a dust storm meets a rainstorm. Nature's aliveness feeds her soul.

She sits down and writes, 'This desert view is so clear that it seems to be without air. Only space.'

She feels giddily free, yet afraid, doubting her arrogance to claim so much certainty.

Sitting alone in the dust, Edith considers her self-image. It has been days since there was anyone around to judge who she is anymore. With no one pressuring her to behave consistently with how she behaved just a moment before, there is no need to edit herself.

She chuckles at her own personal pun: The unedited Edith is alive and well in Death Valley!

This little bubble of space is free of other people's worlds.

She writes, 'I sit in my newly declared empty space in the middle of the desert. I leave behind me all the reference frames given to me by other people, by modern technology, religion, society, culture, worldview... they are all somewhere else. Not here. Not in my space. No parents. No university curriculum. No fellow students. No teachers. No city. No American flag. No debts. No beliefs. No plans. Only a still and silent present, with an unknown future.'

She speaks out, "I want to start over again. I want a new beginning... I want a drink of water." She drinks.

She has no device for telling the time. Approximately two hours pass.

The Earth turns. Flies buzz.

A lone raven perched on the branch of a dead tree in the nearby ravine has been keeping silent watch over Edith. *In case I die, probably. Then Mrs. Raven would squawk to call in her friends to feast.*

Edith decides the raven is female. Why not?

Edith writes, 'Silence has a presence of its own. It waits with eons of patience. This space is not empty. Something beyond comprehension occupies it. This structure was always here, and it can never go away. I can sense it.'

'But me? I am temporary, an animal, a creature with all my thoughts, needs, confusions... all my dissatisfactions. Yet I sit in a new culture of my own making, starting over, not yet knowing what this culture is, or how it goes.'

'Every culture is made each moment by the people operating it. They must agree on how things go to live together. But since I am the only one in my culture, no agreement is necessary. I am free to expand and explore in places that would ordinarily scare or offend me.'

'This is why I see the bare bones of the Universe exposed here right now, uncolored by familiar meaning, without instructions for how to interpret the scenery. It has always been this way. It will always be this way. I just never saw it before.'

'Even the Earth itself can be left behind from this perspective. Without the inherited human inner infrastructures, something reveals itself from behind a curtain. Something steps forward from the other side. An energetic truth appears, a framework that existed before the Earth was born. The word 'archetypal' comes to mind.'

'If I represent simple adulthood, then this space serves me as a doorway to the archetypal domains. The prerequisite for going through is being centered, present, and thriving in a stable, uncontaminated adultness.'

'Whole new realms await anyone who can meet the requirements and find this doorway. Imagine stepping through together with another... Imagine the intimate exploratory research journeys.'

'It seems so obvious now, that I... that humans... are designed to engage with this framework, the neutral bones of the Archetypal Universe. Otherwise I would not now be able to directly sense this preexisting structure. The clarity is beautiful. Simple. Clean. Free of beliefs or philosophies.'

'Clever men built hierarchies and positioned themselves as priests, the 'chosen ones' at the top, intermediaries licensed to talk to God. Common people would have to pay tithing and bow down for the priests to arrange intercessions. But that game is over. Anyone can talk with God. It is so simple. Each of us is designed to talk directly with God.'

'Archetypal considerations are impersonal, yet fully comprehensive. There is so much to learn here!'

'Collaboration with the Archetypal involves new forms and new gestures.'

'What are appropriate actions?'

'I can build and care for an altar to pure consciousness that anchors the doorway in my daily life.'

'I can perceive and relate in the language of nothingness, and everythingness.'

'I can wait without expectation.'

'I can notice without collapsing experience into vocabulary.'

'I can choose and move.'

'Including archetypal dimensions of the Universe opens archetypal culture.'

'I have the potential to live with archetypal agency in an archetypal culture.'

'I am archetypal woman.'

'Where are the archetypal men?'

'I remember the last 'man' I was with, a lawyer, during the summer before my legal internship. Our power struggles were not as subtle as I imagined back then. He thought he owned me as his possession, a sex object to please him whenever he wanted. He would not escape the Patriarchy to be with me, and I was unwilling to remain in the Patriarchy. But there I was...'

'Then I participated in my first *Rage Club*. I learned to say, *"No!"*

*"Stop that!" "This is not okay with me!" "That is not what we agreed to."* Suddenly I could make boundaries and proposals. I started saying what I want and don't want. I got my voice back.'

'I made new kinds of proposals to this 'man'. He suddenly lost interest in me. He claimed to be confused about what I wanted, as if his awareness hit an internal barrier, as if I had already evolved beyond what he could experience this lifetime.'

'I remember packing my bag and walking out the door. He does not object. In my last glance, I see fear swirling behind his 'handsome holy tribal man' mask. It is a sad parting of ways, yet somehow also glorious.'

'Since I had a few weeks of time before the internship started, I could read what I wanted from my booklist in the back of my journal. I chose the thin unfinished manuscript: *Mount Analogue* by René Daumal. It is the notes in the appendix that give the book its impact, added by René's wife, Vera Milanova, after he died of tuberculosis in 1944.'

Edith looks over to the raven and shouts, "Thanks be to the Women!"

Mrs. Raven ruffles her feathers in response.

Edith keeps shouting. "I am going to recite to you René Daumal's last letter to Vera Milanova. I love this letter so much that I memorized it! Listen carefully!"

The raven cleans both sides of her beak on the branch upon which she stands, then waits attentively.

Edith writes each word into her journal as she slowly shouts them to Mrs. Raven, and whoever else is listening:

*I am dead because I lack desire.*
*I lack desire because I think I possess.*
*I think I possess because I do not try to give.*
*In trying to give, I see that I have nothing.*
*Seeing that I have nothing, I try to give of myself.*
*Trying to give of myself, I see that I am nothing.*
*Seeing that I am nothing, I desire to become.*
*In my desire to become, I begin to live.*

Edith continues writing, not knowing what words will tumble out next.

'Earth is so old, but humans are new. I can sit here with nearly nothing from civilization for a few days, but then I would die. Yet all humans are faced with the same question: How do I live in a place like this?'

'Archeologists say that the first humanoids evolved in jungles and lush green forests. Our closest relative is the chimpanzee. Roving tribes of early humans regarded Earth as an all-you-can-eat salad bar open 24/7/365 provided by Gaia. This is how we start, children in the Matriarchal Garden of Eden.'

'Then we feel the jealous fears of scarcity. We start claiming ownership, compete for territory, make walls and fences, organize into hierarchies with leaders at the top, build armies of soldiers to protect our village's food from marauders. Uninitiated men take over, assuming they are the boss because they can make stone-tipped weapons, then bronze weapons, then iron weapons, then flying weapons, then nuclear weapons, then cyber weapons. Whoever can coerce the others, wins. It is a world of uninitiated adolescent boys, the patriarchal empire, corrupted with capitalist delusions, led by psychopaths, empowered by AI.'

'I am done with excusing corruption. My space here is from another culture. It is not Matriarchy, and not Patriarchy. But what else is there? What else could there be besides Matriarchy or Patriarchy?'

The Earth turns.

Darkness reveals a sparkling indigo dome. A stellar map fills the whole sky. Billions of stars smear the arch of the Milky Way across the heavens.

Edith comes awake with a start, sobbing in raw joy, both hands pressing against her heart. It is barely dawn. She blinks her eyes, teetering in the space in between being awake and being asleep.

This was a special dream, lucid and important. She wants to stay in the dream space, yet must write it down lest she forget. She grabs her journal and pen.

'A man stands on my right, looking forward, not at me. He holds his sword at the ready in his right hand, and holds my right hand solidly in his left. I carry an energetic device in my left hand, an untruth sensor. Together we emanate a bright field of clarity and possibility. We stand in a circle with others who are fit and ready like us. Not all are partnered, but all celebrate being in the same field under the arch of bright stars. We stand together in a new culture.'

'There is a flash. The man and I are alone, walking rapidly through a forest, on a mission to find something, still holding hands. The path leads us to a cliff overhanging a valley. On the other side rises gigantic, snow-covered peaks, far into the sky. Buddhist style prayer flags are strung from tree to tree.'

'Suddenly the man is gone. A large black raven stares at me from a tree branch near my right shoulder. His yellow eyes demand my complete attention. "Find Archiarchy," he says, then touches my chest with his wingtip. A warm fire starts in my heart. I wake up with both of my hands pressed over my heart, feeling glad about the instructions, scared of what comes next, and sad that the man is gone.'

After writing all this down, Edith shakes her head in some degree of disbelief.

*Find Archiarchy? Were those the Himalayas? Was that Nepal? Do I need to go to Nepal?*

*What is Archiarchy?*

She remembers the question she fell asleep pondering. *What else could there be besides Matriarchy and Patriarchy?*

She turns to the next blank page in her journal, dips the tip of her feather pen into the uncorked bottle of ink, and writes:

'It is 13 April 2024. The name of the culture I live in is 'Archiarchy'.

I don't know where it is. But now I know what it is. Archiarchy is initiated adult women creatively collaborating with initiated adult men in a regenerative radically responsible nonmaterial Gaian centered culture. Neither the 'matri' nor the 'patri' prevails. After matri-archy and patri-archy comes 'archi'-archy. Archiarchy! The culture that naturally emerges from the archetypal nature of the Universe!'

She looks out at the desert, breathing fresh creosote and sage scented air, then spots the raven perched on her branch.

"I am finally home!" Edith shouts to Mrs. Raven. "Thank you for helping me!"

The raven squawks back, the cry echoing off the rocks.

Then Edith shouts, "Where are my friends?"

Mrs. Raven flaps her great wings, lifts into the air, and flies away, presumably to go be with her friends.

Making friends in a newly invented cultural context is Edith's challenge, not the raven's.

Edith throws off her blanket, stands fully upright, scans the far horizon, then shouts to the entire planet Earth, including Mrs. Raven, "Alrighty then! I am ready for this challenge! I will start by writing an article and making a website!"

# Aleppo, Syria 3

Zenobia Darwish's Diary – 17 March 2012

We already transported Israa's things out of her closet in the rubble and into our camp. She prefers to sleep alone in a broken-down car by the side of the next building over. Meanwhile she offers so many practical ideas to help us collect our wits in this chaotic environment. This morning will be our second attempt at finding Montassar Bilal. My parents sacrifice another day of sleep to participate in our plan.

Over a period of twenty minutes, we arrive randomly one-by-one at an intersection located between shattered lifeless buildings which Israa specified. Each of us stands or sits in our assigned positions. Random people and vehicles roll by now and then, but no one has business here. How can you have business in a cemetery unless you are a gravedigger?

This time, he comes. It is as Israa said, a team of three young men, Montassar with the map. He must be 16 years old. He wears a military pistol at his waist, and writes notes onto the map on his clipboard. They seem particularly interested in finding access to the basement under a collapsed mosque. Perhaps they are assigned to enter one of the ancient tunnel systems under Aleppo. But who are they fighting for? Which side are they on? This is the important question.

Mama wears her finest shopping dress and headscarf but walks out into the sun carrying nothing. She moves on a diagonal intercept towards the three men, limping weirdly on her right leg. She smiles, but the men do not smile back. The gunman turns in her direction warily. She stops. "I am looking for my future relative," says Mama.

Since the idea is incomprehensible, the men hesitate, confused.

"The reason is not the cause," Mama declares, spreading out her empty hands as if explaining something obvious to a child.

The men still do not understand, of course, but they are not meant to. I have heard Mama use this sentence on patients to disconnect their reasoning mind, thereby decreasing their imagined fears so she can heal them more effectively.

"I am searching for Bilal the unbreakable," Mama explains helplessly, looking down like a destitute victim, acting innocent and lost. She has quoted a popular nonsense saying, Bilal being one of the ten companions of Muhammed.

Montassar is quick to respond. He says, "Better to search for Allah than to search for Muhammed." It is a religious idea suggesting that humans are fallible, but God is not, so it is wiser to avoid trying to follow a mere man.

"I search for the searcher," Mama says. "You look like searchers to me."

"I am Bilal," says Montassar sternly, ending the verbal game. "What do you want? How do you know me?"

"You are Montassar," says Mama, matter of factly, looking straight into his eyes, daring him to deny it.

The interaction suddenly becomes treacherous. Nobody wants to move next. This could be interpreted as the silence of confusion, or the silence of surprise. But it is not. This is the silence of men about to commence in lethal battle.

Whatever strategy Montassar has been using to explain his life to these others – and perhaps also to himself – has just now disintegrated. Everyone waits to see what will happen next.

"You told us your name is Bilal!" accuses the gun-toting man with a threatening tone in his voice.

"My name is Montassar Bilal Khaled. I am not lying," states Montassar, staring unwaveringly into the gunman's eyes while trying to keep his voice from shuddering with the violent beats of his heart. "Long ago there was a family scandal. It was not my fault. It ruined my life. I needed to disconnect from the disgrace, to get far away from it, that's all. From then on, I used my middle name, Bilal." He switches from defensive to offensive. "How can I be sure that your name is 'Rafiq Abadi'? Or that yours is 'Farhan Kader'?" he asks the second man. "I simply trust you as my friends. I do not really care what your names are!"

Neither man offers a rebuttal. Their love for each other clearly weaves too deeply to be undermined by trifling squabbles. A connection built around years of life-threatening adventures cannot be broken by a well-intentioned misnomer.

Mama takes a breath to brace herself, then says, "Montassar, I personally know the woman your father fell in love with."

Montassar's hands jerk desperately towards her to stop her from talking, but Mama moves even closer and scolds him, "Shhhhhush! Do not interrupt me! This is important for you. This woman's parents married her off young to a pigheaded businessman, much older than her. I met her at the market. She was my neighbor. She escaped that man's abuses by getting a job pushing paper in Assad's bureaucracy in Aleppo. She was a wonderful woman, and a wonderful friend to me, so I could see how life was being drained out of her. She became severely depressed. No one could pull her out of it. She confided in me that she was addicted to brain drugs and was thinking of suicide. I was frantic, but I knew of no way to help her other than to pray. Soon after that I saw a sparkle return to her eyes. I asked what was going on. One afternoon she met me for lunch, and told me she had a conversation with a man who came into her office for documents. She was radiant. I was so glad. I could not stop smiling. Your father, Montassar, saved my friend's life. After meeting with him she gained a new kind of self-worth. He confirmed in her the kind of self-respect a woman like her deserves. She regained enough aliveness to escape from her husband. Your father was married so she ran away by herself. I don't know where she went or where she is now, but she lived because of your father's courage. Her husband was outraged and tried to destroy your father for the insult. Your father is a true hero in my eyes, Montassar. He gave life to a wonderful woman. And to you, I see. A fine young man."

Montassar cannot take his wet eyes away from Mama's face.

Mama continues. "I come to you now because there is a new need for your true qualities, Montassar, an opportunity that does not require so much deception. So many dimensions are at play, yet love can prevail. Are you willing to lower your weapon and have tea with us?"

"Who is us?" demands Rafiq, the gunman.

Mama raises her left hand slowly into the air. This is the signal for us to step out of the shadows and make ourselves visible, but not to approach. Papa remains hidden. Our idea is that if we are only women, the alpha-male threat response won't trigger fears in these men.

It seems to work. We women reveal ourselves and the men say nothing, even if they are outnumbered. Mama lowers her hand to tell us we can approach.

These three wary soldiers check for dangers in the new arrivals, Aziza, Mitzi, Jamila, me, and Israa. I have my eyes on Israa. Her breathing is shallow and fast. Israa had left her Kalashnikov in Papa's care, so she appears to be unarmed. I know that she is not, but at this point, it is appearances that matter.

Montassar's eyes meet Israa's. His heart visibly skips a beat. "Who are you?" he demands with quiet intensity.

She does not answer.

I am outraged!

Here we have made all this effort just for her to meet Montassar again, and she stands there saying nothing! Is she petrified? Too afraid to speak? Or what?

Then she speaks one word, in Arabic. "مبتذل" (It sounds like: "*Rady-on.*")

This is an informal word, difficult to translate accurately. The closest meaning I can find in English is 'pipsqueak'.

She continues softly, "That is what you used to call me."

Seconds tick by.

"I... I can see I was wrong about that," says Montassar, looking to the ground in front of Israa's feet, then raising his eyes to meet hers again, this time with a combination of disbelief and honor-filled respect. "You have no idea how sad I was when they dragged me away from you. And how angry! I fought against them to let me return to school, even for one more day, but they were too big and too strong for me to win! It broke me."

She says nothing. Tears roll down her dusty cheeks.

He speaks again. "You gave me joy, Israa. Yes, I still remember your name. You brought life to my life, but for far too short a time. I hated them for taking me away and not letting me contact you. I still hate them for that now."

Israa nods her agreement. She cannot speak because she is feeling too much.

Israa slowly lifts her hand, reaches her fingers towards him, first to see if he is real, then to see if he is still in there, to see if he will reach half-way back towards her, now, rather than staying stuck in all those pain-filled memories from the past.

He increases the offer in return. Without breaking eye contact from Israa, Montassar hands his clipboard and pencil over towards Farhan Kader who takes it carefully. Then Montassar holds both his hands out towards Israa's shoulders.

She gradually moves towards him until she is close enough that he wraps her up in his arms.

Both are sobbing.

Everyone is sobbing.

This goes on for the longest time.

I am so glad that it goes on and on.

"I always wanted to do this," mumbles Montassar quietly without letting her go. "I always wanted to smell your hair. But it was not time."

Israa only nods her head, burying her face further into his chest.

Unexpectedly I realize that I must say something. "We don't know what you have been doing, Montassar, which side you are on, who you work for, or what your plans are. Nevertheless, we make a provisional offer to the three of you to join our little Learning Village. What do you say?"

Montassar gently releases Israa, takes half-a-step backwards, and looks to his buddies.

Mama speaks into that pause with a demanding voice. "Montassar, which faction do you fight for?"

All three men jump as if avoiding a bear trap. This is the exact dangerous question they most try to avoid. It crawls just under their skin, keeping them on the edge. Quick glances between them, then an impish grin appears on the lips of the one they call Farhan. "We fight for no faction," he says, looking into Mama's eyes to see if she believes him. "Our craft is in being invisibly crafty. We hide in plain sight, looking serious while we collect intel for staying away from hot zones. We call ourselves 'the neutrinos' because we carry no charge, express no political bias."

Montassar adds, "We help others whenever it is clear that intelligent coincidence has placed them into our path."

"What is the 'Learning Village'," asks Rafiq Abadi.

Israa says, "It is where we are building a new future."

"Who has the plans?" asks Farhan Kader. I soon learn that in

Farhan's mind, if he can get his hands on the plans, he can build or repair anything.

"We were given a *Handbook*," I explain.

"By whom?" insists Farhan.

I hesitate to tell Farhan what I regard as the most probable truth of the matter. But then I think, *No time like the Present. He will be exposed to this sooner or later. Why not sooner?*

"The *Handbook* was given to us by the Earth Coincidence Control Office. We call it E.C.C.O. for short. Where did we learn about E.C.C.O., you might ask? Well, we learned about E.C.C.O. from the *Handbook*. The gang out there at E.C.C.O. seems to be on our side. They want us to go ahead."

I examine Farhan. He does not ridicule me, so I continue. "I come to this conclusion because it is beyond all calculations of probability that Jamila Ali Ahmed, and her sister Aziza Hamdi Ahmed, and Mitzi with no last name, stroll into our camp bearing gifts of unknown things. And that Israa with her AK-47 stops us dead on her street and does not shoot us, but instead invites us in for tea. And that Israa spots Montassar three weeks ago passing through this ruined neighborhood. And that my own mother personally knew the woman who Montassar's father scandalously brought back to life. And that Rafiq Abadi and Farhan Kader are such trustworthy men. And that we stand here talking about all these impossible things with such radical honesty. How else do you explain all this?"

No one answers. I continue. "The thing that comes to me next is to tell my Papa, who has been over there quietly hiding in the shadows, that we are all fine so he can come out now and give Israa back her AK-47..." I wave that Papa should join us... "and I should tell you now that we invite you all over to dinner at our place to figure out what happens next. What do you say?"

The newly assembled characters in our live-action playbook glance around at each other, uncertainly at first. They gradually smile their agreement.

I nod towards Jamila to lead the way home.

Now and then I glance over my shoulder and notice that Israa walks at the rear with the AK-47 hanging over her right shoulder, her right-hand fingers caressing the trigger, and her left hand gripping Montassar's right hand. She squeezes his hand extra hard from time-to-time just to make sure all this is not a dream.

*And Zenobia?* I ask myself. *How is Zenobia doing at this moment? What does Zenobia need?*

Hmmm... I experience these as amazing circumstances, not very likely to have occurred without some kind of paranormal intervention. I decide to trust the forces at work behind the curtain, just as Dorothy Gale eventually comes to trust the Wonderful Wizard of Oz.

Something astonishing could come from all this. I don't see what, yet. But I don't think it matters if I see it or not.

What I think I truly need is what I have been reading about in the *Handbook*. I need to jack-in to my archetypal resources so that I have the extraordinary intelligence and energy needed to collaborate with a rapidly approaching yet unplannable future. And I need as many other courageous persons as possible to do this with me.

At this moment I detect a strategic difference between me and the first Zenobia who ruled Palmyra one thousand six hundred and forty years ago. Her only role model demonstrated how to be a king. She adopted this to being in a female body, and became head warrioress of her armies, the top of the hierarchy, conquering lands around her until the Caesar in Rome had to march over and take her down.

We are trying something different here. My model is to – as efficiently as possible – replace myself in whatever my current roles are, and to empower others everywhere in our project to do likewise. Then an outcome might be possible with more resilience than what 'Zenobia the First' was able to create, vastly more interconnected, highly skill redundant. I think of it as a worthy experiment to try.

I quicken my pace to catch up with my parents and insert myself between the two of them, grabbing ahold of both of their hands. We walk in silence.

I never felt so happy before in my life.

"Something big is cooking up," I say. "And I did not have to fight my parents to make it happen. In fact, they are here with me now, in the thick of things."

They glance at each other saying nothing, trying to suppress smiles so I understand that they take me seriously.

I think to myself, *The 'it', whatever 'it' is, is nowhere near the center of the culture that is actively generating catastrophe for Syria, for its tribes, its soils, its plants and animals. What is being born around us feels like a new spirit, and its name is no longer 'Syria'.*

"Mama, Papa..." I say. "Thank you so much for being a part of my new life. Today was a victory of immense proportions. I could not have created it without you."

Mama and Papa remain silent, but they stop hiding their smiles.

# San Pedro, California 1

The liquid-crystal wall-clock noiselessly changes its display from 12:59 to 13:00. It hangs anachronistically on a stone wall above ancient wooden shelves overstuffed with books and parchment scrolls in a small workspace.

There is a light knock on the heavy steel door.

With the clock at his back, Balthazar Blake sits facing the door across his great oakwood workbench. He wears a black buttoned shirt, black slacks held to his waist by a black belt, black all-leather shoes, and a high-collared black cotton overcoat. He studies a cryptic diagram in an ancient, oversized book lying open before him. In his left hand he holds what looks to be a copper and bronze steam-punk blaster with an ash-wood handle. His right hand uses a screwdriver to hold his shoulder-length silver-black hair away from his eyes. He avoids attending to the knocking.

The door handle slowly rotates, and the door opens silently inwards. Dave Stutler cautiously peaks his head inside.

Without looking up Balthazar says, "I could hear your All Stars squeaking up the stairs."

"But I had these made with leather soles!"

Balthazar does not look up. "Then maybe I was hearing your guilty conscience. I haven't seen you for too long. How's your witch?"

"We're... We're good."

Balthazar still focuses on the diagram.

"Can I come in?" asks Dave.

"Take a seat.... Just don't..."

Dave enthusiastically bursts through the door and slams himself into the chair opposite Balthazar, accidentally bumping the table, the jiggling of which triggers a loud blue energy-blast from the device in Balthazar's hands.

The blast shoots over Balthazar's left shoulder and annihilates a section of ancient books that explode into bits of burning parchment skins and black smoke. Since Newton's Third Law also applies to blasters, the device jerks out of Balthazar's grip and flies across the table into Dave's hands with its business end pointed directly at Balthazar while it audibly winds down from its energy charge.

"...bump the table!" shouts Balthazar gesticulating furiously, pushing the barrel of the blaster away from his face. He cannot believe that he is still astonished at Dave's unconscious competence for calling forth Chaos.

Flaming paper shards and smoke drift away to reveal a watermelon-sized hole burnt clean through the books.

"Didn't you hear me?" demands Balthazar.

"You want me to hear what you say before you say it?" asks Dave, examining the device in his hands.

"Yes!" shouts Balthazar glaring at Dave, "Of course I want that! You are a sorcerer!"

Dave looks into Balthazar's eyes. "This is exactly what I came to speak with you about... sir..." says Dave, shifting the dangerous direction in which this conversation seems to be heading.

Balthazar sighs in frustrated amazement. "What is it?"

A moment passes. Dave says, "Things are going badly, aren't they? I scan for Bright Forces, but everywhere I search, all I see are dark forces. Me and the witch deliver our transformational trainings. The Work works! I mean, people actually heal from their childhood wounds, redesign their memetic constructs, change old decisions, cancel out past life vows, remove energetic blocks, bypass mind machines, sew up brain splits, jack-into their infinite resources, upgrade their thoughtware, take steps in their initiations... but in the over-all circumstances of the world, things just keep getting worse. I no longer see a chance for humans and animals to keep living on Earth. Species are going extinct each and every hour of the day, right now as we speak. They die out forever, do you get this? Never to return!" Despair creeps into Dave's voice, echoing in the cracks of his breaking heart. "What the hell can I do to stop all this? It is insane for humans to destroy ecological habitats on the only planet that sustains life! How can a sorcerer work if there is no life?"

Balthazar leans compassionately towards Dave and welcomes eye countenance. Silence prevails. The sorcerer-to-sorcerer connection is happening. Dave gets it that he has been heard. He can now risk asking about a deeper level of concerns.

"Killing bad guys is no answer! I've tracked the strategic causes, and there are no individual bad guys behind the scenes pulling strings. It is the design of the systems, implemented by ordinary scared greedy people doing what they think is best for themselves. We are facing planetwide human systems failure.

"I think people cower within suicidal systems because they are terrified of stepping outside their comfort-zone. They are not initiated into making use of conscious fear – like you did with me – so when the fear of discovering the edge of the system shivers up their spines, they just leap back into the middle of the old system. They do this ten times a day and don't even know it. Fuck!

"How can I permanently take down suicidal gameworld systems? That is my question. This is what I need to know from you. How to demolish dinosaur gameworlds. I am ready for my next level of training. I need it. I need you to help me, Balthazar Blake."

The space is charged with silent salient connection. By Balthazar saying nothing, he affirms that the Master Wizard agrees with the Apprentice Wizard's assessment.

Dave goes on. "I do not want to spend the rest of my life rearranging deck chairs on the sinking Titanic! I did not come all this way for that! It is not a mistake that you found me. What am I not seeing? What can I do to change the course of the river?"

Balthazar nods and says, "I feel glad you did not ask: 'What can *you* do about it?', meaning me. I see that my time spent chasing you down was a wise investment. Are you telling me that you take the stand to be radically responsible for causing new results on a global scale even though you do not know how?"

"Yes, exactly!" shouts Dave desperately. "I truly thank you for understanding me instead of calling me a wacko."

Balthazar sits more upright in his chair and takes a pensive breath to allow Dave's desperation to drift into the past so they can start afresh in a new space.

"I will tell you two things." A few seconds drift by. "One. From time to time, a 'torus' assembles. The torus is a small group of prominent people who do not view themselves as prominent. This means they are neither politicians nor priests nor businesspeople. The torus functions as a catalyst. A catalyst is an agent that causes radical change without itself being..."

"I know what a catalyst is," interrupts Dave impatiently.

Balthazar stops dead, squints pointedly at Dave, and says very sincerely, "You owe me one hundred dollars, cash."

"Shit!" mumbles Dave, throwing up his hands helplessly and looking away. "You are right. That was our Pirate Agreement. I just shot an 'I Know Torpedo' at you. I killed what you said to me before what you said could land in my Being and deliver its transformative communication."

"Yes. That is precisely what you did, David Stutler," says Balthazar, narrowing his eyes. "But knowing what you did does not change the fact that you owe me one hundred dollars cash, in my hand. Right now!" Balthazar holds out his left hand, palm up.

*But what is he doing with his right hand?* wonders Dave. *Balthazar is right-handed...*

Balthazar continues. "People don't change unless it hurts too much to keep doing things the old way. One hundred. Cash in my hand. Actual paper..."

Dave carefully puts down the blaster and reaches to his back pocket. He opens his wallet, digs out most of its contents, and soberly hands the bills over to Balthazar.

"I ask for a do-over, sir," says Dave, without complaint, returning his wallet to his pocket.

"Do-over granted," pronounces Balthazar without the slightest tone of recrimination. Sliding the bills into his coat pocket, Balthazar starts over exactly where he left off when he was so rudely interrupted. "The torus functions as a catalyst. A catalyst causes radical change without itself being changed." He momentarily pauses to assure himself that Dave is able to resist having to give him another hundred dollars.

Dave intently clenches his jaw and keeps his lips pinched shut.

"When the torus gathers, the chosen ones in the circle may think they are serving their conceived purpose, but their raw dedication to their conceived purpose is enough to cause the torus to authenticate itself at the Archetypal level, which simultaneously upgrades human thoughtware in the morphogenetic field of Earth."

Dave clasps his hands into a tight ball in front of him on the table to keep them from moving or bumping into something. Then he bites his knuckles to keep himself from speaking. He sits like a cat ready to pounce on prey without any visible prey before him, staring fiercely into Balthazar's eyes. He trusts Balthazar to eventually deliver the punchline, but Dave wants it yesterday.

Patience is not Dave's strongpoint.

Balthazar enjoys Dave's efforts, knowing that every moment of authentic practice builds matrix that holds more consciousness.

Finally, Balthazar nods, satisfied at the young sorcerer's discipline, and proceeds perfunctorily. "Human thoughtware upgrades in the moment when humans learn an uncanny new skill. The particular skill that catalyzes the assembly of the torus must be a skill that humans never thought of before, but which has been staring them in the face for centuries, perhaps even millennia. It is something they can already do as soon as they become able to think of the possibility of doing it."

"What skill is that?" Dave demands leaping half out of his seat in an outburst of frustrated curiosity, hands gesticulating wildly, unable to restrain himself even a nanosecond longer.

The look on Balthazar's face becomes inscrutable. "I... don't know," Balthazar says, looking down at his own helpless hands.

Dave is so stupefied he cannot speak.

"I do not contain this answer. I am sorry. It is not available to me. The next catalytic talent can never be predicted. Therefore, it cannot be found in a book already written. I've been searching for it anyway," gesturing helplessly over his shoulder at the exploded bookshelves.

Balthazar continues. "Catalytic talents have been documented from previous torus assemblies. But knowing past talents only interferes with discovering the talent needed now. Each new catalytic talent unfolds new memetic pathways in the brain, so that new kinds of attention can flow. There is no connection between existing catalytic talents and the next talent needed. There is no pattern to recognize. The catalytic talent needed now serves the purpose that has arisen now. The catalytic talent and current necessity fit together like a spark and gunpowder." Balthazar pauses a moment, then says, "Clearly what is called for is masses of people each taking back their individual authority and stepping out beyond the hypnotic grip of what you called 'suicidal gameworld systems'."

"Yes!" exclaims Dave, coming to tears of relief from being so well met by his friend the sorcerer. "But how do those masses of people take back their authority? I mean, they *could* do it! Of course they could. Instantly. Any of them. All of them. Of course it could be done. In reality, nothing stops them. And yet, something stops them! They are not doing it. Why not?"

"Probably because they never thought of doing it."

"But thinking of it is easy! It is so obvious!"

"Could you stay centered before you thought of trying it?" demands Balthazar. "Before you knew how to do it?"

Dave seriously remembers the personal learning breakthroughs that learning to be centered entailed for him. He admits it. "Before I knew how to be centered, I only did it once. And that was the first time I kept my center. After that I could do it again because by then, I already knew how to do it. But that fist time... that first time being centered was scary as hell. I was terrified of being so different from how I normally was. It was a leap over a bottomless void. I had to stay centered to avoid being adaptive, to keep paying attention and not get hooked into a story world full of false assumptions and useless conclusions. I would go so far as to say that staying centered has even saved my life from time to time. It is true that real necessity was present. The urgent circumstances kicked my ass enough to keep my center and not give it away, even if I was scared shitless and did not know how.

"But what I don't understand is why people don't feel the necessity of the ecosystems dying? I feel it! My witch feels it. I can see that you feel it. Every day and every night the pain creates such a huge necessity driving me that I want to take immediate drastic actions. I want to tear down government offices and rip corporate headquarters out of the ground and throw them into the sun! Are people so numb?"

"Were *you* numb?" asks Balthazar. "When I found you, didn't you fight me tooth and nail, trying to survive by fitting in, pretending to look like an ordinary person, not a sorcerer?"

"Yes, but... people thought I was crazy if I did anything cool! They tried to lock me up in a psych ward! They wanted to give me brain drugs!"

"Then let's take it one step at a time, shall we?" offers Balthazar.

"Uh... Well... Okay... I mean... I will temporarily accept your proposal," says Dave with a sigh. Then he squints his eyes and asks, "What is the second of the two things, the thing after the torus generates the catalytic talent?"

Balthazar's eyes acquire a certain inscrutable sparkle which the wizard obviously enjoys for a moment before saying, "Go have a ginger ale with Sandra Bullock."

Dave knows better than to challenge the vagueness of such an assignment placed upon him by Balthazar. He breathes a few breaths, realizing sadly that probably this precious conversation with his colleague and friend is coming to an end. Cautiously he pushes his chair back, slowly stands, gently cradles the steam-punk blaster with two hands and offers it butt first across the table to Balthazar, and then asks, "How is it with you and your witch?"

"Eh... Right. Well... This chance you gave us to reunite after such an extended time of longing was tremendously healing for both of us. Yet... after some months... we both came to recognize that we were fulfilling wishes that were no longer current. Even during our tortured stasis conditions, we had each evolved. By you making it possible for us to be together again, we could complete what we so long ago started. Then we could start over, but not *ensemble*." Dave winces compassionately but stays silent. Balthazar continues, "Since quite some time she has been co-teaching in several esoteric monasteries in Asia. I don't even know where she is now."

Balthazar sighs and looks down at his hands. "And me... Well... it is not easy to make a wizard happy. I keep trying to evolve my shape to be of useful service to E.C.C.O. When the next relational experiment becomes possible, I sincerely hope to be ready to engage. Believe it or not, I have been trying to learn from you how to not be such a jerk..."

"I appreciate your gratitude... But I must say, my world just shattered, learning that you two are not together anymore. It was so legendary. I don't know what to say..."

"Your silence is enough reward for me..."

Balthazar smiles weakly.

Dave grimaces, then looks straight into Balthazar's eyes. "I am sorry about your books."

"No problem," says Balthazar. "Now they are holy."

The sorcerer does not smile at his own joke. He watches his apprentice turn and depart, knowing neither when nor if he will ever set eyes on the sorcerer's apprentice again. The Earth Coincidence Control Office cannot be manipulated by a mere mage.

# Phoenix, South Africa 3

"Here. Eat." Mandisa puts three yellow guavas into Tandra's bony fingers. "We have work to do."

The fire supplies whatever body heat they haven't enough calories to generate.

"Work to do," mumbles Tandra, guava juice dribbling out the side of her mouth. "Who's paying?"

"There is no money anymore," says Mandisa.

"I know! That's why I'm eating guavas instead of goat stew."

"No Tandra. That is *not* why you are eating guavas instead of goat stew. You are eating guavas because you choose to eat guavas. You have other options to choose from."

"Oh, yes? Where's the menu?"

"Tandra, the change is bigger than 'Who's paying'? You were tricked. You were fooled. We all were. We were seduced into making insane choices. You are still making insane choices. There are options to choose from that are not offered on the menu of modern culture. That culture has gone mad. And our two-thousand-year-old Xhosa culture is dead."

Mandisa pauses. It takes effort for her to stay focused and speak. "But you and I? We are still here. We are still here because we have a job to do, a job that no one else can do."

"What is that job, Mandi? Sweep the kraal one last time before we burn the place down?"

"Tandra!" Mandisa scolds. "The ancestors hear every word you say! They see who you are! They feel what you feel. It is not by accident that you and I are still alive. It is not by accident that all our people have gone and my baby starved to death. These things have a bigger purpose. If you cannot see what has happened or feel its purpose, then it is time for the encrusted cynical old Tandra to die so you get a new heart and eyes."

After catching her breath, Mandisa continues. "Has it been so good in your life being Tandra the small-hearted righteous one? What did it give you all these years? Being alone? Spitting rage? What if you put that poor old Tandra's life into the fire with mine? Let her die right now so you can help me build the next asaXhosa culture."

"No! What craziness are you speaking about, child?" scolds Tandra, offended. "You don't get to judge me! This is who I am! There is no other Tandra! Don't call me ugly names! I survived this far being like I am! It's my life! My life... My life is gone... Everyone is gone... Except you. Why are you still here? Why do you still care about me? It has been lonely trying to fight everyone all the time... I thought I was protecting something important, but I was only blaming others to avoid facing reality..."

The two black-skinned women sit in the dirt hugging each other, crying softly. The sun has set. The fire crackles.

"Mandisa the child does not speak anymore, Tandra. She has died. I don't know the one speaking to you now. This could be the first time Mandisa the woman speaks. It feels more dignified, more powerful, more true. Put your acid memories into the fire, Tandra. Let them burn to dust. Return your memories to the past where memories belong. We cannot change what happened to us, Tandra. Let us abandon all hope of that. But we can change our *relationship* to what happened to us. Let us get real here. Let memories of past suffering burn away. The old must die before the new can be born. Like a phoenix bird."

"No, no, no, no, no, no, no...." Tandra hugs her knees, crying and rocking back and forth. Mandisa cradles her in her arms.

"Let go of it all, Tandra. Just let it go, or else I have no one to work with me. I need a new Tandra... a grown woman Tandra. I need you. Let little Tandicha's memories burn to ashes and smoke. Let us be together here now, as freshly born women. We have this chance to start over."

"I can't. I can't. I can't. It hurts too much to let it go, Mandisa! Ohhhhhhhh."

"Yes, it hurts. The pain is the burning. Let it burn. You can do this, Tandra! You are even stronger in your heart than I am. You can do this!"

"But you are stronger in your soul..."

"Yes. This makes us a good team, doesn't it?" They both manage a slight grin as they look in each other's eyes.

Mandisa continues, "I need you, Tandra. I cannot do this alone. Remember old Ozawa the initiator? Remember how she took us out into the woods all those days and nights so long ago?"

"Yes," says Tandra between shuddering breaths. "She dragged us out there even during festival time."

"Remember that invocation she made at sunrise? How the desert opened up and cool water poured out. The sea goddesses came to bless us! After it was all over Ozawa said she could not do such things without us being there. Remember that? She said it takes at least two with a shared purpose to open a new future. Remember?"

"Yes. But she also said we should practice this over and over... I never practiced."

"I never practiced either," admits Mandisa. "But I am practicing now, here, with you... We are the two with a shared purpose. We are opening the new future... You seem to breathe easier now Tandra. Look at you... do you have more space inside now?"

Tandra's eyes drift towards one of the huts. "I see how each and every day I lived with my vow to kill father for beating me at the village gathering. I am soaked in outrage that he never respected my ideas. I have acid vengeance towards mother for not protecting me when Keakala raped me. She blamed me for my weakness instead of making it not happen... It was the worst thing, how she sacrificed me instead of being a problem in the village. And then there is Benji..." holding her sides as she howls out the fear, the grief, the rage, shaking her head from side to side.

"I remember..." Mandisa has tears too. "Chief Tintalo gave my laughing little brother Benji to the priest with the other children so they could be schooled in the sickness of the white man. I hated Chief Tintalo for his weakness and confusion. By the time I saw Benji again, he had stopped smiling. His spirit was so thoroughly broken at the seminary. The moment I saw his empty heart I vowed revenge against God for permitting the priest to speak in God's name, promising lies, twisting Chief Tintalo's mind and heart so he gave our children to the church... If God was truly God, He would have struck the church dead!"

Tandra sighs heavily. "You are right Mandisa. So much hatred I have been carrying... I wake up each morning with visions of revenge... And it is all from the past. But where is everyone now? Gone. Who cares about all this now? Only me. I care because I vowed I would carry this vengeance forever... These vows have crippled my life for so long... so long... long enough! I put the vows into the fire... Arrrrrrnnnghaaa! It hurts! Nnnggghhhhhaaa! I announce to the world that my vows are finished now! They have no purpose anymore here. I am the one who made the vows. I have the power to disassemble them. I burn the vows now. I put them in the flames. The vows release me. They turn to ashes and blow away in the winds of healing... Aaaahhhhhhh.... I breathe in a new way. Hmmmmmhhhaaaaa. I become fluid. Arrrrrrrhhhhhaaaaaa."

Tandra lays back in the dirt, holding her ribs, sobbing and laughing freely. Mandisa's hand rests on Tandra's leg, so Tandra knows she is not alone.

After a while, still with her eyes closed, Tandra asks, "Is this crazy? Have I gone crazy? Or is this a bit of joy I feel? I haven't felt this good for so long! Is it freedom? Space? Expansion? Whatever it is, it feels just fine to let go of such painful self-torture."

"You look so beautiful!" says Mandisa. "Don't ever think about anything else."

# Salt Lake City, Utah 1

JET's *Beep! Book* – 27 March 2023

I keep searching for the enemy against whom the revolution must be fought.

At first, I assume the enemy is the government, the lumbering mindless hierarchical system of money-hungry egocentric sociopathic politicians and their minions trying to obey their psychopathic overlords.

After some research, it becomes clear who are the puppets and who are the puppeteers. Behind so-called 'political decisions' made 'for the public good' are international banking interests, providing endless deceptions that profit the few.

"Here, we will generously loan you money to install G5 telephone and glass fiber internet after the war so we can better sell you our online products and services. The same contractors who supported our invasion will be happy to help you rebuild your infrastructure."

"Here, we will generously loan you money to construct a modern harbor out of which you can easily sell us your trees, your coal, your oil and minerals, and the food from the land we already purchased and manage so we can feed our people at home, and then we will loan you more money to build the train tracks and bridges over which we can offload our shipping containers full of cheap child-labor clothes and plastic disposables from the harbor so as to shut down your local shops and export your local economy. And, by the way, if you default on any of these high-interest loans, the fine print of the contract says we take ownership of all the new infrastructure we built and charge you steep tariffs for its use."

Even the United States Supreme Court is obviously bought.

Which means that the law-making function of the U.S.A. serves the Dark Side.

Which means that the Rule of Law of Western Civilization is invalid. It has lost its legitimacy. Western Law is killing off life on Earth. This does not herald a happy destiny for humanity.

Which means that anyone following the Rule of Law of Western Civilization is criminally insane. (By following the Rule of Law, you exterminate life on Earth! That is criminally insane!)

And anyone who enforces the Rule of Law of Western Civilization has already forfeited their life. (They are fighting *against* life. They are *already dead*. They have made themselves into zombies.)

Upon closer examination I notice how terrified the businessmen are of being truly present and living their moment-to-moment lives. You can see it on their faces, in their eyes, the minimal way they interact with people, the evil side-comments they make 'off camera'. These guys are numb and number. How could authentic intimacy possibly happen in a family where money trumps love?

Then I start thinking that the enemy is money itself.

I remember saying, "Jeffrey..."

Oh, yeah. Jeffrey Stump. He's not my father. He is my mom's current boyfriend, been around enough years that I can sometimes talk with him, if I'm desperate enough...

"Jeffrey, I hate it that the government is spending our tax money to send soldiers over to kill people in other countries. How do I make them stop?"

He says, "Well, John. This is a democracy. That means next time there is an election, you can vote for a president who won't do that."

I say, "But *this* president already promised he wouldn't do that, and he is doing it just as badly *or worse* than the president before him! I need more immediate changes."

He says, "Well, John, in a democracy you have freedom of speech. That means you can write letters to your Senator and your state Representatives. You can write opinion articles for the alternative online press, or the newspapers. You can write a blog, or make a vlog for your Instagram page. You could even go downtown to the courthouse and stand on a soap box and say what you want to say."

"What difference would that make?" I ask.

"Well, you could bring more people to your cause, and build a coalition for a political campaign to influence the next elections. If you get enough people on your side, you could start an independent political party and offer candidates for office."

I say, "I don't want a campaign. I want a revolution. I want real change. I want a new life experience."

He says, "Well, I suggest you start with the soap box. See what happens."

Soap comes in boxes?

It's Friday afternoon. The park in front of the courthouse is busy with shoppers and students. I balance precariously on a stack of cardboard boxes holding a hand-painted placard, "NO MORE OIL WAR!" I try to speak with anyone who comes near me. People seem nervous, irritated, and embarrassed. Only one couple stops. They try to convert me to Christianity.

I shout, "Don't you realize your tax money for building a regenerative future is being wasted?" Some people yell back. "Stop making noise!" "Go get a job!"

More people gather to watch. It isn't long before a police officer saunters through the crowd. "Come down off there, sonny. You're disturbing the peace."

"But that's exactly why I am standing up here, 'occifer'. *There is no peace.* There is war. This is a democracy! I have freedom of speech! I can say whatever I want..." stomping my feet.

"May I see your permit?"

"I don't have a permit!" I stomp once more, and the boxes collapse under me. I tumble through them to the ground. People laugh at me and walk away. The police officer extends a hand to me as I try to untangle myself from the boxes.

I say, "Thanks," regaining a bit of my composure, but not losing my passion.

I drop my placard and say, "Look, officer, I want to ask you a serious question. Why should I stop talking? Don't you care that the U.S. is stupidly blowing up foreign cultures, spending billions, killing millions, and getting our own soldiers killed?"

"Sure, it bothers me, son. But that's not the point."

"What is the point, then, sir?"

"The point is that you are being a public nuisance. People come here to shop. The store owners don't want them scared away by political weirdos like you."

"So let me get this straight. You are a police officer in this town. You are hired by the local government and paid by town citizens to serve the Rule of Law. But in fact, you serve businessmen who are afraid their customers will be scared away. Is that it? You protect the rich, but not the citizens?"

"Are you resisting arrest?"

"No sir, just packing up my soap boxes."

# Eugene, Oregon 2

Davis Hatcher arrives at the hospice in one hour and seventeen minutes without getting flashed. *He taught me where the cops set speed traps*, he thinks. It is thirteen minutes earlier than the hour-and-a-half he had promised his sister Barb.

Davis strides into the secluded hospice still wearing his red ski parka and black stretch pants. To come here he sacrificed the last good skiing day this year in a skiing season rapidly shrinking due to the onset of global warming. He unzips his coat while pecking Barbara's cheek. "Thanks, Sis."

She exits the room to give the two men privacy.

Family life with Police Captain Henry Hatcher had been far from fun-filled. *That is all water under the bridge now*, thinks Davis.

When their mother was devoured by cancer two years before, a secret was revealed. Dad loved Mom more than he ever let on. When she faded away, he did also.

Wearing pajamas instead of a uniform, the police officer lies in a hospital bed with an oxygen tube in both nostrils, gray colored lifeless skin, barely breathing, both hands clutching a letter-sized gold-rimmed picture frame face-down on his chest. Davis sits in the bedside chair Barbara just vacated, afraid he might have come too late. He leans over and places his right hand gently on top of both his father's, wondering what is in the frame.

Henry's eyes flutter, then half-open, sees his son sitting by his side. Unbelievably a crooked smile creeps visibly over his lips. "Davis..." in a croaky voice, then a spasm of weak coughing. He shuts his eyes again.

"Easy Dad. Take it easy!" Davis notices his own left-hand reach over to stroke his father's forehead. His crew-cut hair is so thin now. Davis expresses a level of care he never imagined himself having. He presses his own lips together to hold back tears as he takes in the weakened condition of a once proud and stern representative of law and order in the City of Eugene, Oregon.

Henry opens his eyes again, turns his head to the right, and locates Davis's face. He faintly utters three words, "You did it."

Davis reacts. *What did I do this time? Is it reproach? Blame? How have I failed him now? Is there something I forgot to do? Crap! Not this again...*

Henry makes an effort to lift up the picture frame, trying to gaze at it one more time. His lips quiver, smiling, unfamiliar with being used to express joy. Henry's eyes focus on the frame for a moment, then work their way back over to Davis's face. After more hard breathing, Henry forces important words out of his heart, "You gave my life meaning... by following in my footsteps."

Henry's head falls back. He struggles to breathe, swallowing hard several times, fighting against his unfamiliar physical frailty. "I am so proud of you." His eyes slam closed and he fades into a distant world.

These are the last words Davis will ever hear from his father.

Davis grabs at the picture frame to keep it from flopping onto his father's placid face.

In the frame, Davis sees his own image on the certificate given to him the day he was officially accepted into the Eugene City Police Force, one month ago.

# Aleppo, Syria 4



Everyone seems to have found shelter for the night. Fighting continues everywhere in Aleppo, but we use the chaotic background energy as a springboard for inventing what we need for our Learning Village.

Papa and I continue to document the horrors and insanities we discover in a separate notebook. I will copy them here later. Right now, you simply need to know that all around us, human beings are mad from despair. Yet what our tiny group puts at the center of our lives is the transformational context of the *Handbook*, not anybody's political propaganda or religious dogma.

The *Handbook* is a treasure that has been given to us. We make ourselves into an energetic citadel to protect it. We use the treasure to its maximum potentials, which turns out to be bigger than we ever imagined.

In the afternoon after Farhan, Rafiq, and Montassar came to camp, Montassar asks to borrow the *Handbook*. He spontaneously starts reading the book out loud from page one to anyone who wants to listen. He sits on a makeshift cushion in the shade shelter we built from a large canvas tarpaulin on the north side of a broken-down cinder-block wall. Through his resonant voice and his commitment to clarity, a new kind of food begins pouring into our little tribe.

Previous to now, we focused on having physical food for our physical bodies. But with daily input from the *Handbook*, practicing the new skills, trying the experiments, we receive a storm of intellectual food for our minds, and energetic food for our souls. The sudden abundance of new kinds of food reveals that – unbeknownst to us – we were starving.

While we dedicate our afternoons to village projects, building more sleeping quarters, spreading compost and mulch in our vegetable and herb gardens, digging a deeper well for water, and helping local people in our neighborhood, our mornings are dedicated to upgrading our thoughtware.

Before now, we did not even know we were using 'thoughtware'. Now thoughtware is a central topic even during mealtime conversations.

Montassar's reading voice is deep and steady. He pronounces the words from the *Handbook* with such simplicity and clarity that the ideas seem easy to understand, at first. However, as each idea sinks further in, it begins to disassemble or replace the ideas that we each secretly hold onto and defend at the core of our identities.

A private battleground forms inside each one of us where a memetic war is being fought. Fortunately for us, the new memes from the *Handbook* are winning.

On the first day, Montassar invents the tradition that during reading, whenever someone feels lost, tired, or confused, or does not understand a word, they immediately put up their hand. Montassar stops reading and together they go back and find which word it is that was not understood.

The first time this happens is with the word 'memetics'. Israa interrupts Montassar's reading by shouting, "Stop, Montassar! Stop reading! What good is it to read words we do not understand? What is 'memetics'? How are we supposed to know what 'memetics' is?"

Then Thomas Taha – a young Iranian-looking teen who wandered into camp two weeks ago but never speaks – suddenly says, "Just a minute! I will look it up!" He finds the word in his Dictionary App on his beat-up old phone and tells us the definition of 'memetics' in English: "Memetics is the study of the evolution and transfer of 'memes'. A 'meme' is the smallest instruction for the design of your intellectual body – your mind – in the same way that a 'gene' is the smallest instruction for the design of your physical body. Memetic evolution is analogous to Darwinian genetic evolution. The word 'meme' was invented by Clinton Richard Dawkins in his 1976 book, *The Selfish Gene.*"

Then Thomas spontaneously translates the definition into Arabic for anyone whose English is not so strong. "Memetics hi dirasat tatawur wanaql 'almimati'. 'Almim' hu 'asghar taelim litasmim jasadik alfikrii – eaqluk – binafs altariqat alati yakun biha 'aljin' 'asghar taelim litasmim jasadik almadiyu. Altatawur almimiu mushabih liltatawur aljinii aldaarwyni. Kalima 'mim' aikhtaraeaha klintun ritshard dukinz fi kitabih 'Aljin Al'Anani' eam 1976."

After the definition and examples are given, Montassar goes back and re-reads the offending sentence in the *Handbook*.

In this case, he reads:

*'Memetics' is the study of memes and memetic interactions, just like 'Mechanics' is the study of machines and mechanical interactions. Memes are what you use to think with, in other words, your 'thought-ware'. Each bit of your thoughtware is assembled out of memes.*

*Certain memes have the particular quality of being a 'distinction'. A distinction is a meme combination that weaves together with your existing memes to augment your ability to experientially differentiate between one thing and another thing. An example of a distinction meme is: There are three Worlds: the Middleworld, the Upperworld, and the Underworld. Contrary to some religious beliefs, the Underworld is located between the Middleworld and the Upperworld. (More will be said about this later...)*

*Integrating a new distinction changes the inner structure of your Being by 'building matrix'.*

*'Matrix' is the network of distinctions your Being uses to catch its current level of consciousness.*

*There is consciousness everywhere. What makes a difference in your personal awareness is adding to your internal network of distinctions by building matrix. When your matrix changes shape it changes the shape of your Being.*

*When your Being changes shape, it forces the Universe to interact with you differently, the same way that digging a new harbor forces the ocean to interact with the shore differently.*

*Through 'building matrix', you detect finer distinctions, which increases your 'pain of awareness'. This increased sensitivity makes you more responsible due to changing your behavior to avoid painful consequences. That is why we can say, 'responsibility is applied consciousness.'*

This is heavy-duty thoughtware, right? But with this avalanche of dense clarifications, the *Handbook* gives us fabulously interesting new ways to talk about things between us.

When Montassar arrives at a confusing word, he tries to repeat its meaning in Arabic, which is hilarious, because Montassar's first language is Armenian. His pronunciation of Arabic is horribly funny, but he boldly tries over and over with dignity.

During this process, whoever sits closest to Mitzi helps her write the English word and its Arabic meaning into a blank book in alphabetical order – with 5 pages reserved for each letter in the English alphabet – for future reference, thus creating an *English Arabic Dictionary* of the new language. The *Handbook* tells us the new language is called 'Archan'. Therefore, Mitzi is writing an *English Arabic Archan Dictionary*. But the definitions are full of new distinctions, so Mitzi's is actually writing an *English Arabic Archan Distinctionary*.

What is 'Archan'? It is the language spoken in Archiarchy.

What is 'Archiarchy'?

Ah, now, the story becomes interesting. Below here I copy or paraphrase some pages from the *Handbook*.

It is only a smattering, so if you like this stuff, I suggest you get yourself a copy...

*Each of us is born into a culture.*

*But no culture until now teaches us truthfully about itself. The culture does not teach you that the culture itself is bullshit. All cultures are fictitious stories, fabricated by human beings out of nothing, including religions, economics, politics, values, laws, and worldviews.*

*The culture may be Armenian, Iraqi, Palestinian, Greek, Assyrian, Circassian, Mandean, Eritrean, Turkish, Kurdish, Babylonian, Celtic, Saxon, Germanic, Greek, French, Mongolian, Xhosan, Inca, Phoenician, Aztec, Mayan, Iroquois, Blackfoot, Siamese, Lao, Minoan, Chinese, Egyptian, Eskimo, Māori, on and on and on, it does not matter, because all cultures created in the last ten-thousand years are patriarchal*

*– even if a woman is at the top of the hierarchy – and use the same basic tenets:*

- *Men are more important than women.*
- *Men can own women and slaves such as employees.*
- *Men can own land.*
- *Whoever has the most 'toys' when they die, wins ('toys' such as land, slaves, money, cars, houses, technology, weapons, defenses).*
- *Society is hierarchical.*
- *The top of the hierarchy is the King, and the King is appointed by God.*

*Even communists are capitalists, and atheists are theists, because whether you follow a rule or go against the rule, you are still defined by the rule.*

*Regardless of whether a male or female is at the top of a patriarchal hierarchy, it is a 'me'-centered, competitive, material-scarcity, adolescent-level-responsibility culture.*

*Before Patriarchy emerged, humans roamed the 'Great Mother' Earth in tribes, hunting and gathering their way through a giant salad bar in baby-level-responsibility Matriarchal cultures.*

*Now that the baby-level-responsibility Matriarchal cultures and the adolescent-level-responsibility patriarchal cultures have run their course, a more adult-level-responsibility culture is emerging where neither the Great Mother nor the Patriarchs are regarded as the ideal. Instead, authentically-initiated radically-responsible adult feminine or masculine archetypes are the ideal. Thus emerges Archiarchal cultures.*

*Archans create, hold, and navigate space in circular power structures rather than hierarchical power structures. If the central value of Archiarchy is not money, power, and possessions, then what is at the center of an Archan circle? Nothing. Initiated Archan adults use Nothingness as an infinite resource.*

*Humanity has entered an epochal culture shift, leaving behind Matriarchy and Patriarchy, and inventing Archiarchy.*

*Archiarchy never existed on Earth before now.*

*Since Patriarchy has selfishly dug up, pumped out, and burned the easy-to-reach minerals while contaminating the air, land, and water, there is almost no time to make the culture shift to the regenerative human culture of Archiarchy. Rather than having thousands of years, as was the case in the shift from Matriarchy to Patriarchy, now we have perhaps one hundred years, and half of those years have already ticked by.*

*By the time you hear and understand these words, you have barely enough time to 'upgrade your thoughtware' and reboot yourself into Archiarchy.*

*What is 'thoughtware'?*

*We thought you would never ask.*

*Thoughtware is what you use to think with. If you go to school, they teach you what to think about. Before you went to school, you already knew how to think, or they would not have let you into school.*

*Where did you get your thoughtware? From your parents.*

*Where did your parents get their thoughtware? Right. From their parents.*

*This means you are probably using very outdated thoughtware, passed on from generation-to-generation for thousands of years.*

*The culture you were born in gave you its Standard Human Intelligence Thoughtware (S.H.I.T.).*

*Upgraded thoughtware is available.*

*How often do you upgrade the application programs in your phone?*

*How often have you upgraded the thoughtware in your head?*

*What stops you from upgrading your personal thoughtware?*

*Fear.*

*What stops you from inventing upgraded thoughtware?*

*Fear.*

*Your fear stops you because you are using antiquated thoughtware about fear. This ancient thoughtware blocks you from consciously feeling and making use of the intelligence and energy of your fear. This means you lack the inner resources to navigate the frightening groundless liquid state that is naturally experienced in the gaps between letting go of your existing thoughtware and gaining agency with the upgraded thoughtware.*

*S.H.I.T. thoughtware stops you from upgrading your thoughtware.*

*After discovering the epochal culture shift from Matriarchy to Patriarchy to Archiarchy, the next recommended thoughtware upgrade to make is that you have Five Bodies, not simply a mind and a body as modern culture teaches.*

*You have physical, intellectual, emotional, energetic, and Archetypal bodies. Part of your Archan education is to learn to become centered, grounded, and bubbled in each of your five bodies.*

*Your emotional body can consciously distinguish and make use of four feelings: anger, sadness, fear, and joy.*

*Inner navigating your four feelings can be simple and clear! Communicating your four feelings with other people can be intimate and rewarding!*

*Your four feelings are either feelings or emotions. This is a world-changing distinction.*

*Feelings are radically different from emotions, and your emotions may be mixed.*

*Mixed emotions can be unmixed.*

*How can you detect the difference between feelings and emotions? It is so straightforward. Feelings last less than three minutes in your experience.*

*With feelings, you consciously feel anger, sadness, fear, or joy, then you use the energy and information of your feeling to handle things. After the energy and information are used up, the experience of the feeling vanishes from your body in less than 3 minutes. That was a feeling!*

*But have you ever felt angry for an hour? A day? A week? This is not the feeling of anger. This is the emotion of anger. Did you ever feel fear hang around you for an hour? Or sadness? Or joy? Yes, even joy can be emotional. Much of what people think of as 'being happy' is actually emotional joy, a fantasy world.*

*Emotions at first feel exactly like anger, sadness, fear, or joy, but they last longer than three minutes. Why? Because emotions do not come from you in the present moment. Emotions are incomplete feelings from your past, staying around you as a memory, or they come from other people – they may not even be yours, or they come from a religious or political belief system, or from a corporation or politician or priest trying to manipulate your opinions and beliefs to keep your loyalty.*

*Each emotion that you have is a doorway for healing something.*

*Unhealed emotions do not go away, even if you keep your numbness bar raised high. Suppressing your emotions can result in psychological illnesses and physical diseases.*

*The old thoughtmap of feelings says that there are three 'bad' or 'negative' feelings (anger, sadness, and fear), and only one 'good' or 'positive' feeling (joy).*

*The new thoughtmap of feelings says that feelings and emotions are neutral energy and information resources, not negative or positive, not good or bad.*

*Lowering your numbness bar empowers you to use your feelings and your emotions as valuable resources in your daily life and relating.*

*Feelings are for handling things.*

*Emotions are for healing things.*

*Imagine not being able to experientially distinguish between feelings and emotions, then trying to relate with other human beings... You have just discovered the cause of war.*

*People using S.H.I.T. thoughtware would rather kill other human beings than heal their own emotions. This is because we have not been initiated into radical responsibility, and have not learned how to provide Emotional Healing Processes for each other...*

Whoa... I can't write anymore right now. My previous world wobbles, crystallizes, falls over, shatters from its own weight, drops into a pile of dust at my feet, and blows gently away in the winds of evolution...

I think to myself, *We have been idiots. I have been an idiot. We have been S.H.I.T. heads, using Standard Human Intelligence Thoughtware on each other – and also on ourselves – competing to be right with each other in senseless psycho-emotional battles, attacking each other and beating ourselves up our whole lives.*

I see that these paragraphs include huge thoughtware upgrades that won't happen simply from reading the *Handbook*.

What will we do with all of this? What will I do with it?

It feels like I am being given the chance to walk through a thoughtware bazaar from a culture I never knew existed. There are so many new possibilities to choose from, and I don't know how to apply any of them. It is like strolling through a hardware store full of shiny new tools, trying to assemble an effective toolbox, without knowing how any of the tools work. How can I figure out what to start with?

Obviously I need to develop my ability to discern the varieties of thoughtware!

Reading time is often interrupted due to the *Handbook* telling us to go do a particular experiment right now, immediately! Through experimenting we gain new skills to match our new understandings. Otherwise our understandings are useless.

After a few mornings of study, I realize that we are becoming researchers!

The *Handbook* demands that every reader carry a blank book with them at all times – called a *Beep! Book* – in order to document what we learn, what we think, what we feel, and to be absolutely certain about whether what we feel is a feeling or an emotion. This also means having a watch with a minute hand for measuring how long three minutes is. Our scavenger team has been supplying us with wrist watches, blank books, pens, and fanny packs.

We write feelings in the front part of our *Beep! Book* (anger, sadness, fear, or joy) along with what actions they tell us to take or avoid taking. But the *Handbook* is fiercely clear about this: my feelings DO NOT DECIDE to take my actions. I decide. It is me who decides. Not my feelings.

Just because my psycho-emotional defense strategy – what the *Handbook* calls my 'Box' – is having a feeling about something, does not mean I must do or not do anything. My Box can be over there in my hand freaking out about something, but I can decide to do or not do something entirely different from whatever makes my Box freak out. I have a Box. But I am NOT my Box.

We write emotions into the BACK of our *Beep! Book* (anger, sadness, fear, or joy, or the mixed emotions, like shame, jealousy, aggression, sentimentality, revenge, guilt, despair, envy, etc.) plus what triggered the emotion, in a short sentence. Each emotion is the doorway to an Emotional Healing Process (EHP) to do as soon as possible.

By practicing what the *Handbook* suggests, I discover that I feel emotional fear far more often than I ever realized.

It is called a '*Beep! Book*' because to learn, we must try new things.

The *Handbook* says: *If you try new things, you will make mistakes. Mistakes are valuable coaching from reality. Mistakes inform you about how to better design your next experiment.*

Our books of *Beeps!* are our books of treasures.

Our objective becomes to make, document, and share the learnings from as many new mistakes as possible. This quickly makes our culture wiser, much faster than a culture that values putting on the show of 'looking good' or 'being perfect'.

This is how we figure out how to collaborate in our new circumstances. We furiously write ideas and observations in our *Beep! Books* and share them with each other in circle. Our little village erupts in a new level of aliveness.

The *Handbook* explains: *School is about learning what is already known. What is already known got us to where we are now. Duplicating what is already known only reproduces what does not work. The age of school is over. This is now the age of Research Circles.*

*Wherever you are, whatever is going on, call together your Research Circle. A Research Circle is between three and thirty people. Sit in chairs so that your back is straight and your stomach is not bent over upon itself. If your stomach is bent over, this makes it more difficult for you to feel your feelings and your intuitive impulses. You need feelings and emotions and intuition as resources in your Research Circle.*

We don't have chairs, or a classroom. Instead we sit in the shadows of crumbled buildings on plastic crates, buckets, cinder blocks, or stacks of broken wood. We use old clothing or burlap sacks for padding. Thus we begin developing our improvising skills more consciously.

The *Handbook* goes on: *In a circle there is no leader. Instead, you take turns serving as spaceholders. Having a leader forces you to have followers. By having a leader and followers you establish a hierarchy with power positions located further up the ladder. That is how to create a patriarchal hierarchy.*

*Power is scarce in a hierarchy. People struggle against each other because there are fewer and fewer power positions the further up the hierarchy you go.*

*The people who are most effective at doing whatever it takes to climb the hierarchical ladder and take the power positions are the psychopaths. Psychopaths are damaged human beings who lack a connection between their heart and their mind. This prevents them from having a conscience. Psychopaths use situational morals, justifying doing whatever it takes to protect their power.*

*The most effective way to detect psychopaths is authentic adulthood initiatory processes. Psychopaths fail initiations.*

*Be wary of allowing psychopaths into your circle. Their survival strategy won't work, but they could waste your energy and time. You may not have as much time as you may think.*

Reading these words scares us, but the words ring true, so we continue.

*In a circle, the spaceholders rotate positions and coach each other to become better spaceholders. Coaching provides distinctions for your matrix to grow. The more matrix you grow, the more responsible you become. Distinctions create clarity. Clarity creates agency.*

*An authentic initiation is any process after which you are able to be more responsible. Responsibility is consciousness in action.*

*Agency and awareness are side-effects of responsibility.*

*The capacity to take responsibility is power.*

*In a circle, power is not scarce because a circle offers unlimited available space for taking responsibility. In a circle, people are empowered.*

*The opposite of scarcity is not abundance. The opposite of scarcity is creation.*

*Whatever creates matrix builds better spaceholders.*

*Building spaceholders creates true wealth.*

*The purpose of a circle is to grow spaceholders who train others to replace themselves to create more nonmaterial wealth on Earth.*

I am amazed to discover that our job as navigators, as spaceholders in our Research Circle, is to keep inventing new ways for each individual person to build matrix, and to train others to replace ourselves. This is far more interesting to me than fighting against others to merely survive.

I have a new purpose! I am a Matrix Engineer! I design and deliver distinctions and experiences which can build matrix in people's Beings!

NOTE TO MY BEEP BOOK: I just figured out that in English, the word 'nowhere' can be split into two words: 'now here'.

Now / Here is a very small place in time and space, almost infinitely small, as small as one can inhabit.

As Albert Einstein explains, time is relative. A moment with your hand touching a hot wood-burning stove is far longer than a moment holding a handsome boy's hand.

This means that if it is actually measured with a stopwatch, now can have widely varying dimensions. For example, the size of a now chewing a stalk of lemongrass while lying in the shade of an olive tree in the summer would be significantly longer in real-time than the size of a now kicking along the ball on the soccer field near your goal in the last seconds of the game.

This means that 'now / here' can be so small that it instantly vanishes into the past, whereas 'nowhere' can be so vast and empty that it feels like it can remain forever. The same letters have diametrically opposite meanings, both extremely useful and interesting.

When I flip ahead through the *Handbook,* I see hints that 'now here' and 'nowhere' are both Infinite Resources which we can learn to jack into and use. This is so exciting I want to run in circles, jumping up and down, screaming and shouting!

# Possibilica, Florianópolis 1

A fit-looking short-haired young man in his thirties pedals his cross-country bike past the wooden 'Welcome To Possibilica' sign upon which ravens chat brazenly to each other. The man slows to a squeaky stop on the dirt road in front of a south-facing building and dismounts. A hand-carved wooden sign hangs from the eaves that says *Possibilica Bakery & Intimacy Café*.

Even before he enters, the roasty sweet odors of baking bread start his mouth watering. He waits his turn at the counter.

Eventually, the middle-aged baker wearing a white chef's hat, a white sleeveless T-shirt, a flour-encrusted blue-denim apron, and nearly nothing else, says, "Hello there, young man. What's your name?"

"Gareth," he says. "I'd like a loaf of bread."

"Don't you want to know what my name is?"

"Um... I would call you Baker."

"Well, then. I would call you Monkey."

Gareth stands stunned. "Um... then, Mr. Baker..."

"Yes, Mr. Monkey?"

A couple of the other customers pause with wide grins on their faces, interested to see the outcome of an interaction they seem to have witnessed before.

"I'm sorry..." says the bike rider.

"Hello Sorry. My name is Alfred. Welcome to the Possibilica Bakery and Intimacy Café. What can I do for you?"

"No, no!. My name is Gareth. And I feel sorry. I did not mean to offend you."

"No offense taken. What country do you think you are standing in?"

"Um... Brazil."

"I have evidence to believe that you think you are standing in *Zombieland*. You keep using that zombie invocation mantra, 'Um'. Why are you saying that word so often? I don't even think you know that you are saying it. In my opinion, there are already enough zombies in the world. I am certain that I do not want zombies coming into this Café. We are dedicated to bringing people to life here, not lulling them off to sleep. Why do you keep saying 'Um'?"

"Um..."

People in the Café erupt in good-humored laughter, disbelieving the demonstrated depth of Human Awareness Disfunction.

"I am serious!" demands Alfred, seriously.

"Hello Sirius", says Gareth. "You seem to be confused about your name."

The laughter explodes three-fold. Even Alfred cannot keep a straight face. "Ahh, there *is* someone home in there! Welcome to my Bakery, Gareth! Would you like whole wheat, rye, or sourdough?"

"Whole wheat, please."

Alfred chooses a fine loaf of freshly baked whole wheat bread and places it on the counter.

Gareth pulls twenty-five Brazilian Reals out of his wallet and slides them over the counter towards Alfred.

Alfred stands back warily, staring at the bills as if looking at a rattlesnake ready to strike. He makes no move to take the money. "I will give you the benefit of the doubt, Gareth. Perhaps you do not know what that is."

"This?" says Gareth, eyebrows up, eyes wide. "This is money to pay for your bread!"

Alfred says, "That stuff you just put on my counter is a false paradigm."

"A what?"

"Money has misbehaved."

"What do you mean, misbehaved?"

"What I mean is that people foolishly give value to that paper or to numbers on their bank's website. It's an enormous deception."

"But this is worth at least five U.S. dollars! It's a medium of exchange!"

"That is exactly my point, Gareth. People have come to value the medium rather than the value it is supposed to transport in an exchange. Then they spend their lives trying to collect more and more of the medium, thinking they are rich. But the menu is not the meal. You believe that piece of paper has value. I don't. There is no exchange-rate between that paper and the currency I use."

"How do I pay you for the bread, then? What's your currency?"

"My currency is creative collaboration."

"What?"

"I don't bake bread for money. I bake bread because it turns me on to work alongside this amazing team of bread bakers making bread for people in our community who are creating clarity and possibilities for our village and others around the world. If I exchanged my bread for your money, then I would contaminate our local culture with an artifact from a culture that is rapidly destroying itself and taking down most of life on Earth with it. I won't do that. My culture is too precious to contaminate it with your money."

"Should I pay you in Euros? I have some Euros with me..." he digs further through his wallet.

"No. Euros are the equivalent contamination as Dollars or Reals."

"What? Why? I don't get it!"

"It's like this. I creatively collaborated with my bakery team to produce this loaf of bread out of grain that was given to me by a local farmer. He grew and harvested his grain the same way, by creatively collaborating with his team. My team baked this bread using wood we were given from the woodsman's team through creative collaboration. The foresters love the bread I make and want me to keep making it, because the people who eat our bread – including them – are creatively engaged in projects which they know and love and want to support. The farmer and the woodsman and I are partners in this Creative Collaboration Bakery. What we actually bake here are Creative Collaborations."

"Alright. That makes sense."

"This bakery is not a business. It is a growness. We do not work together for the purpose of making a profit. We work together for the purpose of evolving consciousness through our dedication to making excellent bread as a team. These are entirely different purposes."

"So?"

"So, this loaf of bread could feed you and your family for a day or two. What will you be working on during that time?"

"What?"

"If you eat our bread, then you have food while you work on your project, and then you and I are creatively collaborating to succeed in your project. I am asking you what your work is so that I can decide whether or not I find value in that. As your potential partner, I want to know if what you are creating turns me on. I want to know my Ecstasy Return On Investment for my bread. My E.R.O.I."

"Well, I work at a grocery shipping company, managing food imports."

A middle-aged woman who just enters the bakery immediately asks, "But does that turn you on, really?"

Gareth turns to look the woman directly in her eyes. "No..." he says slowly. "It does not turn me on. Not really. I do it to earn money to pay for food and rent."

Alfred, wordlessly, but with a smile and a nod, hands a big loaf of sourdough to the woman who spoke. She slides the loaf into her canvas shopping bag, turns, and heads out the door having given the baker no money.

Then Alfred reaches back for his bread knife, lining it up to slice off one-third of the whole wheat loaf. "This is my point. You are using one-third of your time and energy to merely survive. That does not turn me on either. What else are you creating besides survival?"

"What do you mean? Everybody needs money for food and rent!"

"It is no fun for me to listen to your badly outdated thoughtware... Look, what is your archetypal lineage? What nonmaterial service do you provide to support something greater than yourself? What part of your original agreement for being born are you delivering on? Please let the sense behind your life speak to me."

"I have a wife and a seven-year-old daughter."

"Did you already send her to prison in kindergarten and school?"

"No. We did not! We organize with other families to unschool our kids together."

"Well, now! This turns me on! Could you cut down your hours at the shipping company and increase your time for unschooling?"

"Well... yes, I could decrease my hours. But how do I make money for food and rent?"

"Are you listening? Do you have something on which you can write this down? I don't give possibility to someone if they don't write it down. Their Box would have them forget what I said before they even stepped out the door!"

Gareth digs into his backpack, finds a pen and pad, gets ready to write, looks expectantly at the Baker.

Alfred says, "You create the resources you need by building a local team that supports and organizes other people to unschool their own children while they learn to grow their own food in the new gardens that you build together. In the meantime, I will help with food. Twice a week I will give each family involved in your project two loaves of bread. When you have sweet potatoes and squash from your gardens, bring some to me. I have an old soup recipe I want to try out, and I want to bake sweet potato bread this winter to feed my other collaborators."

Alfred places the knife down on the counter and reaches back to grab a second loaf of bread to place by the first loaf on the counter Then he puts his hand out to shake. "Do we have a deal?"

"Interesting bakery you have here," says Gareth, looking Alfred straight in the eyes and firmly shaking his hand. "Yes, we have a deal."

On his way out the door with two loaves of whole wheat Creative Collaboration Bakery bread sticking out of his backpack, Gareth sees Alfred hand over a loaf to a new customer and ask, "How are our composting toilets coming along?"

# Salt Lake City, Utah 2

JET's *Beep! Book* – 7 to 20 April 2023

I hate lies.

I think that is what finally pushes me to look for the Revolution. Too many lies too often from too many people who should know better.

Deep in my soul I long to serve a good king. The government promises us a good king for president. Until now, I never allowed myself to feel the depths of the government's betrayal. With the president's true colors flying, my illusion is shattered. Simultaneously, my longing to serve a good king is intensified due to the obvious contrast between what I want and what currently exists. My desire to experience what I want is now keener than ever.

I think the government's plan backfired. My longing to serve a good king drives me to make the distinction: the president is not a good king. He is a puppet, a phantom, a ghoul.

Realizing that the commonly-accepted and often-used concept: 'the President of the United States' is such a blatant lie, initiates me to take a real stand for what I now know is possible.

Everyone gets the king he serves.

If you remain a sheeple, the king you get fleeces you down to your skin once each spring, at tax time.

How can I assure that I serve a good king?

By being one.

Where is the good king in me? I am longing to live in a real kingdom. Is the true king outside or inside?

What I can tell you for sure is that I am no longer willing to be the victim of a stupid president.

I can develop the inner qualities of being a good king. I can learn to serve in my world as if it is a kingdom, or even a queendom. My people are the people in my circle. Our life is about experimenting in new territories, discovery, healing, transformation, creation. Can I be a good king, serving something greater than myself? Or is a good king the slave of his people?

I can sense a good king as a possibility, as a potential, alive within me in each moment of my life.

What would a good king tell me about being a good king? He

would say, "Get to work, JET. Quit complaining about your circum-stances. Your circumstances do not determine who you are or what you do.

You do.

Fulfill the mission you came here to serve. Bring your people together. Feed them with clarity, possibility, and adventure. Empower them distinction-by-distinction to take their steps of becoming more aware and capable. And ask them to help you do the same for others."

Holy shit! This is Holy Shit!

Long live the evolution!

It's not the liars that bother me. Just the lies. Liars are slugs in their own slime. Thanks to our responsible Universe, words and actions / silence and hesitation automatically deliver unavoidable consequences. As the hippies figured out, "What goes around, comes around."

I do not understand how a person – even a president – could sell their integrity so cheaply, except that they must be scared for their own survival. Terrified enough to believe their own bullshit.

Through lack of integrity, the empire crumbles by itself. This is why we must stay alert to the lies. These days, that's just about all we are given.

I need a tool, something to keep me alert. I hereby install a functional crap detector as a red-light and buzzer gizmo on the left shoulder of my energetic body. It instantly flashes and signals, "Beep! Beep! Beep!" to warn me whenever bullshit is in the air.

TWO DAYS LATER

Man, was I surprised when my bullshit detector leapt into action. I was instantly and eternally forced to recognize the truth in what Neil Postman and Charles Weingartner wrote in *Teaching As A Subversive Activity*: "The greatest source of bullshit with which you must contend is *yourself.*"

I innocently stand at the bus stop, or in the school cafeteria, doing nothing, minding my own business, and my bullshit detector blinks red screeches in my left ear. At first, I think it is beeping at the others, all their blah-blah, a waste of good oxygen. But then I look closer at the readouts and see that what triggers the beeps is my internal cynicism and hubris, my ongoing disgust machine generating revolting stories about each and every person around me. This critical commentary is my own mind sucking down most of my creative energy to keep me from connecting with people and making transformational proposals. No wonder all I can see is brown.

A few days ago I wrote, "I hate lies."

What if that statement is a lie?

What if I actually love lies?

What if I think that lies are inescapable, that everybody all around me is lying all the time?

Yes. It makes sense that I would think that. Nobody sees me.

Nobody listens to me. Nobody answers my real questions. This would explain a lot about the way I understand the world and the other people in it. They lie all the time.

If I concluded through direct observation that everybody lies all the time, it would make sense that I would need to figure out some kind of survival strategy in such an insane environment. Maybe I decided: *If you can't beat 'em, join 'em!*

Is this what I have done?

How come they don't know that they are lying?

How come their lies don't fuck up their world more than they do, enough that they might start to notice they are lying.

How can they have friends if they are so fake and their 'friends' are fake? Maybe they don't have friends, only the self-deceiving delusion of friends.

How can they be intimate with another human being? Maybe they are not intimate with anyone. Maybe it is all superficial, pretend intimacy. "Let's pretend to be intimate."

How can anyone trust anyone all, except to trust that they are lying all the time?

Where is the real world?

Is there anyone out there who has integrity?

Or accountability?

Is there anyone who is their word?

What would it take for me to source integrity, even if it cuts me off from everyone else around me? My fear is that I would be like Paul Simon, *the only living boy in Salt Lake City*. But I guess being like Paul Simon is not so bad...

THREE DAYS LATER

I did an experiment.

I stood or sat as close as I could to other people in numerous places, the cafeteria line, the lawn in front of the library, the convenience store, and I listened to what other people were saying to each other.

They were all lying.

Not vicious, spiteful or deceitful lies. Mostly just innocent lies, childish lies.

I also watched films where the main characters lied to each other, causing horrendous outcomes. "Are you okay?" "Yes..." It's a lie. Nobody is truly okay, ever.

The answer to the question, "How are you?" is 45 minutes long. If you are not ready to spend 45 minutes listening, do not ask the question.

I started making a list of the types of lies I was hearing, adding in my own ways of lying as well. I came up with:

1. Deny the truth with blatantly false claims of innocence.
2. Claim to be ignorant of what is real or true. Ignorance of the law.
3. Omit crucial facts to make one thing seem like something else.
4. Make up fake facts and act as if you believe them to be the truth.

5.　Distort the truth to minimize your responsibility in causing it to occur.
6.　Dramatically amplify or exaggerate the story so as to twist reality.
7.　Pretend to be someone you are not.
8.　Create a cover story with really good excuses woven in.
9.　Pretend to hate anyone who does exactly what you are doing.
10.　Confuse the questioner by burying the facts in an avalanche of hogwash.
11.　Threaten to freak out emotionally if someone forces you to find the truth.
12.　Tell only half-truths to make it not sound so bad, and later claim to not have really been lying.
13.　Divert your focus to irrelevant issues hoping they will follow your lead.
14.　Attack the questioner with scorn about their overreaction to what you did.
15.　Withhold incriminating information to defuse possible reactions.
16.　Claim to have forgotten what you really know about.
17.　Say the opposite of what you know to be the truth.
18.　Devalue the importance or relevance of observations.
19.　Make an assumption, conclusion, expectation, justification or projection.
20.　Make a promise and do not keep it, or only fulfill the easy part of it.
21.　Make a decision based on a reason, because then it is the reason's fault if the decision goes bad.
22.　Blame, complain, resent, or plot revenge to try to avoid responsibility.

My central discovery? Words are lies. All words. A wordsound in any language is an agreed upon sonic symbol to mean approximately something. Since a word is a symbol of a meaning, it is not true. If it is not true, it is a lie.

Things are not looking brighter in my world.


FIVE DAYS LATER

This afternoon I sit at my desk and seriously ask, 'Who is it talking in there?'

The voice sounds like my second-grade teacher's constant criticisms, plus my mom's sister endlessly commenting on my eating habits, my posture and my speech patterns, plus the stupid advertising jingles on radio and TV, plus sex messages in the media. Always some external authority figure speaking in my head.

Okay. But the voices have been chattering in there for years. Why haven't I noticed before? Has my self-generated bullshit become too normal to distinguish? Too loud to hear myself think?

That's not the real question. The real question is why would I keep it going? Just because my bullshit is normal? Yee-gads! It's like there's a giant unconscious troll in there, crapping all over my life.

I mean, what if I stop it?

What if I distrust *every* voice in my head?

What if I blast them away?

I shape my hand into the form of a pistol...

I could do this.

I am going to do it!

'They are idiots!' *Blam!* The sharp sound echoes back from the walls of my room.

I do not stop.

'I am special!' *Blam!*

'Nobody understands me!' *Blam!*

Poof!.... Silence.

Then the next voice creeps in.

'I am not good enough!' *Blam!*

'I will never be successful!' *Blam!*

Silence again. Longer this time.

Another voice comes!

'I am an idiot for listening to these voices for so long!' *Blam! Blam! Blam! Blam!* just for the hell of it!

'You are doing so good, JET!'

What? I hesitate a moment... Yes, this is definitely a voice. But it is praising me... telling me how wonderful I am. A part of me just loves hearing sweet positive praises. It means my mother loves me. It means... It means that I am being fucking adaptive to someone else!

*Blam! Blam! Blam! Blam! Blam!*

Holy crap! What a nightmare!

No voice is trustworthy.

Staying alert now. Blaster in hand. Waiting for any vampire voice to show its ugly or angelic little face.

Just waiting.

Waiting...

I may have turned the tide.

Instead of the vampire voices feeding on me, I have become a vampire hunter, using my... Voice Blaster!

Jeeeez. It is actually quiet in here.

THREE DAYS LATER

I train myself to dedicate part of my awareness to the possibility that a voice might return at any moment, and hold my Voice Blaster at the ready with a hair trigger.

At first this is exhausting.

After some days... it becomes more and more my way of life.

I am alert to voices like I am alert to dogshit on the sidewalk.

My attention narrows to shorter than my breathing. I can feel and hear myself breathe. When was the last time I was present to that?

What if.... Naw, can't be...

What if all those opinions I've been spouting for all these years are not really my own? What if the positions I've held onto so strongly, the beliefs, the judgments, the criticisms... what if all my hard-held conclusions – even about myself, or the way the world treats me – are not mine?

'I am so gullible...'

*Blam! Blam!* Gotcha!

What if the vampire voices have been sucking away my ability to be simply present?

What if keeping me away from being present keeps me away from being powerful.

Why would I want to avoid being powerful?

That one is easy to answer: So I don't have to be abused or killed by my mother's boyfriends, or by the school system.

And what if, now that I have survived and am away from existential threats, I can stop the chatter machine?

It did its job perfectly, and... I don't need it anymore.

I paid the price of disempowering myself in order to survive my childhood and adolescence. I made it through. I succeeded. I survived. Now I can stop hiding out.

'Congratulations, JET! Good job!

*Blam! Blam!* Shot from the hip.

'Whoa! That's cool!'

*Blam! Blam! Blam! Blam! Blam! Blam! Blam! Blam! Blam! Blam! Blam!*

Breathing hard... then a question comes. Does this mean that all my life before now was a lie?

Yes.

Does this mean that the 'me' that other people currently know is a false image?

Yes.

Listening to voices made my life into a Grade C movie, the life of a pathological liar. If I believe my own lies, I am just as much a liar as when making the lies. It means I am a double liar, a meta liar, lying to myself about lying to myself, and then believing my second level lies. That's how I made my lies believable to others. I believed them myself. Or did I?

What have others seen about me that I did not see? My voices always told me I was right – always right, in fact, superior – so I never listened to other people much. Even when I punished myself for being wrong, I still held that I was right about being wrong.

This way I never had to listen to anyone else's feedback to me. Ever.

Who am I then? Just a hubristic, pathological liar pretending to be a survival hero so I can feel betrayed by having to do what I didn't really want to do, which gives me license to take revenge by suffocating everyone around me in a black cloud of resentment and self-pity...

Jeeez. This feels like hitting bottom.

Can it get worse than this?

Maybe I don't really want to know the answer to that question...

Scratch it from the record!

I could try to get away from this wasteland of devastated nothingness, but then... what would I be? What would I stand on?

*Blam! Blam!* (I am sure some kind of voice was creeping back from some corner...)

I don't have a plan.

I don't know what to do next.

At least there aren't any vampires right now.

How do I know?

Breathing is happening.

My bullshit detector is actuated, and, for the moment, silent.

Things certainly look different without my usual bullshit worldview filters in place, warping and twisting everything I perceive and everything I can express to fit that worldview's preexisting requirements.

My analytical mind informs me: *If it fits the permissible assumptions, then it can be classified as 'true' and 'real'.*

This drives my bullshit detector to the maximum limits, bending the needle as it tries desperately to go past 100% bullshit.

I feel intensely bad, actually... the horror of the situation... the fear of what might be coming next... and yet... conceivably... I am seeing reality for the first time in a long time... perhaps the first time ever...

Could it be that hitting bottom is the first step of growing up?

Could hitting bottom be starting over?

# Phoenix, South Africa 4

The sky glows orange and pink. Dawn comes. Mandisa lies on her side facing Tandra. "I've been having a clarity storm, Tandra. Here is how we make a new asaXhosa culture. Are you ready for this?"

"As ready as a newly hatched crocodile."

"We start with a new name. *Asa* means *fierce*. *Fierce* because we were afraid of all the others and had to frighten them away. That is a child's view. This is childhood's end. We aren't against anyone. We don't have to be against anyone when you get it that all people are the same. No more 'us and them'. We are the Earth come awake to think out loud, to learn and share what we learn. We are the Earth's conscious eyes, ears, hands, mind, heart and soul. I am the Earth talking to you, the Earth. There is only us, the Earth. Let us henceforward be called the *connected* ones, the fiercely connecting ones, the *AsamangaXhosa*."

Tandra nods assent.

"Modern culture separates us from others and wants us to compete, to work against each other. Then we barely survive. Competing between tribes... it used to seem so natural, so important. Now it seems so silly. Competition makes one winner and many, many losers. Our village was a loser. Our culture died and the people lost their story and went away because we were fiercely disconnected. We fought against everyone else in the world. Anyone not of our tribe was not even a human being. They were the enemy..."

"Yes!" says Tandra. "They are the edible ones!"

"*Were* the edible ones!" corrects Mandisa. "It seems you are still hungry..."

"Got anything besides guavas?"

"You listen better when you're hungry. So listen well... our culture failed, but modern culture is even worse. It is a virus taking over people's souls, spread by plastic products that make life seem easier. But the secret is found out. Modern culture is suicidal. It thinks the world provides it with unlimited slaves and resources for the masters' indulgent lifestyle. While modern culture devours the world, it dies in its own psychopathological shit.

"Culture is a story. My heart aches wishing to have a new story. Here we are, Tandra, you and I, with no culture. You and I get to weave the new story. The new story is that we are a phoenix culture."

"Who are you Mandisa? Who is talking to me now? How did you suddenly become wise?"

"It's from behind me, Tandra, through my nerves. It is not some ancestor or spirit. This is me. My roots have grown down into the Earth now. And behind me is a force of clarity. Your roots have grown too. I can see them. The clarity of Earthmother naturally comes through when the way has been cleared. It is time for us to decide."

"Decide what?" demands Tandra.

"We can wish. We can imagine. We can worry. We try to figure things out. But nothing changes until we decide. An uninhibited decision changes the shape of the universe. Put a rock in the stream and the stream changes course to flow around the rock. Are you ready to be a rock, Tandra?"

"Yes."

"How do we say it?"

"I represent the next culture," says Tandra.

"I am next culture." The words roll over Mandisa like warm rain. She continues, "We do not have to fight the old culture to live in next culture. It is a matter of discernment, not force. Our next culture already exists because we are it. We cause it to happen here between us, around us like a cloud, like a resilient bubble, clear, flexible, and tough as a warthog's hide. Then we behave only in accordance with our new culture. That's it."

"Then the decision has been made," says Tandra.

"And if we can do it, so can anyone else. Any person in the world can make this same decision."

"Yes. Who decides which culture I live in? I do."

Tandra's brow furrows with a new picture. "Mandisa, we two make a seed. You are the outer part. I am the inner part. We are a seed of a new culture. You know how seeds are. They wait until conditions are right, until the soil is warm and moist. Lord, we have waited long enough! We have waited our whole lives and so many bad things have happened. But if even one of those bad things had not happened, this good thing could not be happening now because we would not be ready."

"Who is calling things good or bad?" asks Mandisa.

"The one who is tired of waiting. But you are right, my friend. Think of the seed we are, waiting, begging, hoping. Sometimes seeds don't sprout until a fire clears away the brush. That's us, Mandisa! With everyone gone we have space now, but our little culture is so fragile. We must protect it. We must keep it to ourselves so no one comes to stomp on it."

"I don't think stomping can stop us anymore, Tandra. This is a phoenix culture. We started by being thoroughly stomped on. Each stomp gets us reborn, only smarter."

"Smarter? Do you already know how to do all that we have to do?"

"No. Deciding comes before we know how."

"You call this smart?" asks Tandra.

"Well, think about it. Would the universe go out of its way, bend coincidences, provide resources, and show us how to do all we need to do if we are not already committed?"

"Not if I was the universe. It would be too risky," says Tandra.

"So, we commit first, *before* we know how. Our commitment creates the necessity to call the universe into new actions."

"Alrighty then! I commit to being next culture with you," says Tandra.

"Me too," says Mandisa.

"Yesterday I thought life was hell," says Tandra. "Today I can't wait to jump up and make things happen. How did you do that?"

"By committing to do what I don't know how to do alongside of you," says Mandisa. "This I would call high level fun!"

The fire crackles and a shower of orange sparks shoots high up into the air in some kind of agreement.

And the sun dawns a new day.

# Eugene, Oregon 3

Remington Smith's *Beep! Book* – 1 May 2023

Sophia Bentley greets me with a happy squeal and a hug, plus a kiss on each cheek in the French tradition. Then she invites me into her foyer even though I am 15 minutes early. I automatically remove my shoes. Sophia takes my coat. I won't let her touch my roller bag. That has been my policy since the moment I zipped it shut on my bed in Michelle Piment du Pont's old house in Fontainebleau.

Sophia leads me silently through a maze of overstuffed furniture on wall-to-wall carpeting, then three steps down into a multipurpose bonus room which Americans refer to as 'the den', variously used for gaming, movie watching, playing music, reading, or a home office. In this case we will turn it into a *pièce où on écrit* to assemble an alchemist's manuscript. To my surprise, Patricia Wells, Francis Atkins, and Carol Washington are already sitting around the dark oak table!

I should have noticed the extra cars.

Sophia asks us for our drink wishes. I accept her offer of fresh cold lemonade.

Without further ado, I lift my bag, place it carefully in the center of the table, and slowly unzip it. Then wait until Sophia returns to the den carrying a tray of refreshments. She wordlessly places the tray onto a folding side table, and slips into our work chamber.

I look around at my four new women friends, then slowly lift the lid.

"Can you smell that?" I ask, inhaling pure inspiration. "This is the smell of my grandmother's attic! I've known this smell my whole life. This is the smell of magic happening."

The excitement continues to soar in our workspace. But these women are skilled navigators. There is no idle chatter, nor gossip, only bright attentiveness.

"I grabbed these papers out of an old trunk in the attic which, for all the years of my life, I never knew existed. In my dream, Michelle hinted to me where the key was, tucked behind a metal panel screwed to the bottom of the chair she always sat in in our circle meetings. I only had time to empty my roller bag of non-essentials and stuff these papers inside before leaving for the airport. I have not looked through anything.

The papers I found at the bottom of the trunk are the papers at the top of my roller bag, so they are presumably the oldest. I propose that we simply start pulling the top papers out first and try to classify them into themes or possible chapters as we go. What do you think?"

Sophia says, "I will bring out the flip-chart board from the closet. We could begin drafting a table of contents there, and make piles of papers to match over on the sideboard. I have reserved this workspace for the duration of our project. No one will disturb our work between meetings."

"Thank you for arranging this, Sophia," I say. "I feel nervous. Do any of you speak French? Although Gurdjieff spoke primarily Armenian and Russian in his meetings, Michelle could see that English would replace French as the *lingua franca* of the world, and she ran her meetings in English. Most of her notes seem to be in English, but I saw a few French paragraphs fly by."

"I understand some French," says Francis.

"Let's you and I be the French department, then." Francis nods and silently changes chairs to sit near me.

I am still standing. I reach into the suitcase and carefully lift out the top three pages. I read the first sentences out loud. "Attention is your only resource. Everything else flows from where you place your attention. Are you placing your attention consciously and being alive? Or are you placing your attention unconsciously, reactively, mechanically, and being dead? This will be an exercise in consciously placing and guarding your attention. The purpose is to build your attention-placing, attention-holding, and attention-splitting muscles." I pause for a moment, looking from woman to woman with tears in my eyes. I can't speak anymore.

"You are biting your lips," says Patricia. "If you put your attention on your lips and slowly release the biting, what emotions come?"

I dare to follow her invitation, unclamping my teeth from the insides of my lips. Suddenly I break down and begin weeping for some reason I don't understand.

"Let it get bigger," says Patricia. "We are holding space for you. Which feeling is this?"

"Sadness," I blubber.

"Sadness has words," says Patricia. "Let your sadness speak. We are listening."

"Michelle is dead!" I cry. "She died. My Mama who I never knew died, and then Michelle, my unschooling grandma died. Michelle lived an amazing life, and then she died. I was holding her hand when she passed over, but I never got to say goodbye to her. Not really."

I keep sobbing and sobbing, and letting the sobs speak. The others keep listening. "The truth is, I never wanted to say goodbye to her. She died too early for me. I feel sad that she died at all. She should never have died. She created so many treasures for so many people. So many healings. How can I ever live up to that? She was so special, and only a few people knew of her specialness. She should be remembered more than

Kings or Queens, more than rock stars or stupid politicians, but she is mostly forgotten. Oh! Michelle... I won't forget you!"

I sob away. The women have me sit as they tightly gather around me and with me.

This establishes our team protocol for organizing Michelle's notes.

We read sentences or paragraphs out loud to each other and maybe do the exercise together, or do the Emotional Healing Process for one or more of us who are thrown into a liquid state from Michelle's notes. More than once all 5 of us drop into a liquid state together. We do not get much collating done that night. But it is so worth it.

Thursday nights are *Mysterium* meetings.

Friday nights are Notes meetings. Often we also have Notes meetings on Sunday and Tuesday nights.

Six or eight weeks pass before we realize it.

"Hey, everyone," I say. "There is something I just remembered today that I forgot to tell you."

We have such stimulating discovery conversations while parsing through Michelle's papers that me saying this is nothing special

"When I first opened the trunk in Michelle's attic, the first thing on top of the papers was a short, curved sword with no scabbard. It looked like an authentic pirate's cutlass from the 1700s, but most things in France look like they are from the 1700s, so I thought nothing of it. Besides, I wanted to bring my bag as carry-on, and no way would they let a girl with a cutlass through airport security, even if she was a real pirate!"

I was glad they laughed. They might not laugh at the next thing I was about to say.

"Just under the cutlass was a leather-bound book embossed with the title *Handbook*. I did not open the book. I only threw it into the bottom of my bag and then piled all papers and spiral bound pads on top of it. What I am saying is that, down there, under all those papers, is this *Handbook*, probably just sitting there waiting for us to find it. For some reason, I remembered the *Handbook* this morning on my way to work. What I am thinking now is that it might be a good idea for us to dig down in there and take a look at it. Otherwise, it will be another six months before we excavate to that level in this dig. What do you say?"

"Oui! Pourquoi pas?" says Francis.

"I am excited already," says Patricia, "which is an emotion created by mixing fear with joy."

"What is the fear about?" asks Sophia.

"I have read too many... or not enough... secret treasure map books. Usually somebody gets cursed or kidnapped, or falls into a pit of vipers..."

"Stop! Too much information!" cries Carol. "Just do it already, Remington!"

"But be careful!" warns Francis. "Some of the papers are already brittle and tear easily."

"Okay," I say, sliding my hands down the inside panel of my roller bag while moving the page aside. "I feel it! It's still there!"

I detect the old book still resting where I put it, dead center under all the other papers. I pull it gently sideways as the others hold the papers back to keep me from dragging them out onto the table and making even more of a mess of our mess.

There it is. In my hands. Heavy, both physically and energetically.

"I propose we all move up to the couches in your living room, okay? I think we might need the extra space to properly digest what we are about to do."

There are no objections.

We take a pee and water break, then gather around Sophia's coffee table where I had placed the book.

I take a deep breath. "Does somebody want to do the honors?"

"It's you, Remington," says Carol. "You can't get out of this honor. We are lucky to be here with you, but it's your job to take us to the next level."

I sigh again, reach over, and cradle the book in my hands.

It feels like an encyclopedia, like a bible, like *Merlin's Book of Magic*. I slip the middle finger of my right hand under the top right corner of the leather cover and slowly open the tome. Nothing cracks. Nothing leaps out at me. I breathe easier.

It says, "Handbook." I turn the book around to show the calligraphic font to the others. Or perhaps it is actual calligraphy, hand drawn? I turn the book back around and squint at the title sideways to the light, but I can't tell. I turn to the next page and show it to the others. It says, 'Contents,' and then lists 13 chapter titles with their page numbers.

"No author. No date. No publishing house. No copyright information. No dedication..."

"But the text is printed on a printing press, right?" asks Sophia. "It's not handwritten by some monk by candlelight in some basement somewhere, right?"

"Right. Printing press," I confirm.

I turn to the pages inside of the back cover. "The last words of the *Handbook* are, 'The way lives as you develop agency for loving life and not the shell of one.'"

I look up at the others, then pass the book to Francis on my right. "Take your time, honey," I say. "I would like to hear what each of you makes of this."

We go far past our ordinary end time. Sophia calls for pizza delivery. Her husband comes home, witnesses the hubbub of women, gives Sophia a peck on the lips and disappears upstairs.

We are caught in a tidal wave of doubts, fraught with worry, guffawing in disbelief, yet feeling victorious at each new hint we uncover. We keep wrestling with the question, 'What is really going on with this book and these notes?' We can't piece it together yet.

Sophia finds it. "Listen to this." She reads out loud. "Attention is your only resource. Everything else flows from where you place your attention. Are you placing your attention consciously and being alive? Or are you placing your attention unconsciously, reactively, mechanically, and being dead? This will be an exercise..." She looks up, mouth open, eyes wide... "What... does this m-m-mean?" she stutters.

"The notes are already in the *Handbook*?" I ask, incredulously.

"Or else the notes are in fact the *Handbook* in shredded form..." says Francis.

"The notes come from the *Handbook*?" asks Carol. "But that is ridiculous! Why would Michelle copy out the notes from the *Handbook* if she already has the *Handbook*?"

"Exactly!" I say. "But if the notes are already made into the *Handbook*, why did she keep the notes? And why don't I remember the *Handbook* from her study circle? And why didn't she ever tell me about the *Handbook*?"

"But, she did tell you!" exclaims Sophia. "In the dream! Maybe she had to wait until you were ready to listen."

"Did she print any more *Handbooks* than this one?" asks Francis. "And if so, where are they? Who has them now? And what are they doing with them?"

"And what do we do now?" demands Patricia.

"I suspect," continues Francis, "that our gameplan has just been changed. I would estimate that the quantity of notes in the suitcase would approximately fill up the *Handbook*. *C'est un gros livre*, as one would say in French. A 'fat book' in every sense of the word. If we are fanatical, which a few of us are... we would want to make sure that all of the valuable contents of the notes have been included in the *Handbook*. But doing this by hand – no pun intended – would be considered by some to be excessively tedious. However, if the contents of the *Handbook* were digitized, then we could search the document file for the contents of the notes, and our cross-check would go rather quickly."

"We could even scan the pages of the *Handbook*, and then use an Optical Character Recognition app to convert the scanned PDF file into a Word DOC file."

"But then our transformational party is over..." complains Sophia, clearly forlorn about this idea.

I can only commiserate.

It is late.

We agree to sleep on it and decide next Friday evening.

All week, I feel like I am in some kind of altered state of consciousness. My life-focusing mission suddenly vaporizes due to it having already been accomplished, perhaps before I was even born. Now what do I do with myself?

On Friday we decide to assure ourselves that the best of the notes are indeed in the *Handbook* and then print out a new copy for ourselves to use as a resource during *Shadow Knights of the Mysterium* meetings.

I am shocked by how sad and depressed I secretly feel about this radical turn of events.

# Kathmandu, Nepal

Three months after quitting her lawyer internship in San Francisco, Edith Goldman walks thoughtfully along the dusty uneven streets of Kathmandu with a pack on her back and a walking stick in her hand. She feels insignificantly small compared with the gray monster Himalayan mountains that have on this clear morning taken over the horizon. She steps gingerly towards a month-long *November Course* at Kopan Buddhist Monastery: *the Foundation for the Preservation of the Mahayana Tradition*, with no idea what their slogan means. She intends to sit on her butt for a month and wait for instructions from the great unknown about what to do next.

After a couple weeks of meditation in the great hall, Edith is given the opportunity to meet alone with a senior practitioner and ask questions. The first words out of Edith's mouth are, "If a Nun is egoless, how does she make choices in her life?"

The senior nun says, "She chooses whatever brings the greatest good, whatever serves the most."

"But I am asking about daily choices, like what to eat for lunch, noodles or rice? Which of my two pairs of socks should I wear? Where should I buy underwear?"

"Every circumstance fits into the overall flow of benedictions in a perfect way. The nun relies on the great field of benediction to take care of her personal needs."

Edith bows her head to show gratitude, yet senses she has been lied to. Not intentionally, of course, but dogmatically. Her true question is brushed aside by the senior practitioner, who either does not want to look stupid by admitting she cannot offer an answer, or is brainwashed to the extent that she does not understand the validity and importance of Edith's question.

This is not a fun thing for Edith, a lawyer-economist in search of greater clarity about how the world works. She thinks, I *am rejected from abstaining from my life at the monastery due to the obstinacy of the teacher*.

After thirty days, Edith finds herself again walking the dusty crowded streets of Kathmandu. The difference from last time is that, this time, she has no plan.

A window full of fine-looking pies grabs her attention. She steps through the open door into the Snowman Café on Old Freak Street. A woman sits against the wall reading a book titled *Conscious Feelings*. A large chai latte and a half-eaten slice of crumb-top apple pie sit on the table before her. Edith impulsively steps to her table and says, "Excuse me. Can I ask you a question?"

The woman looks up over the top of her book. Edith takes this for a 'yes' and says, "I am sorry if I am being rude, but I need to speak with someone real. You look real enough to me. My question is, what cool stuff do you know about? What experiments are you doing? I am fresh out of the monastery and don't know what to do next."

The book gets placed face down on the table. A large forkful of pie goes into the woman's mouth. She lifts her cup of chai latte, leans back in her chair slowly chewing, and then tilts her head, indicating that Edith could sit down next to her at the end of the table if she wants.

Edith sits and continues speaking. "Every culture has its beliefs, its traditions, its unspoken rules. Everyone knows how to build a proper house. What clothes the man wears. What jobs the woman does. How to die. What to eat for breakfast. And none of these traditions from any culture are true, right? It is all simply a matter of preference, right?"

The woman nods her head solemnly in Edith's general direction, keeping steady yet slightly uncertain eye contact with Edith. The uncertain contact is to communicate to Edith that she is not being believed, only acknowledged. Not being rescued, only listened to.

"So when I go about figuring out who I am, none of those things help me, do they? The real me is somehow deeper than all this."

The woman nods again while squinting her eyes ever so slightly.

"In the monastery I made a list of what I would do with a one-hundred-million dollars. In that process, I figured out that one army tank costs as much as one ecovillage. Since governments in the world invest in tanks and not in ecovillages, I realized that no government has any interest in creating a regenerative future for humans on Earth."

"That's not entirely true," says the woman at the table, speaking for the first time. "The government of Senegal has an ecovillage development department focused on shifting fourteen-thousand traditional Senegalese villages to ecovillages. You can find their organization by searching on REDES ECOVILLAGES. I visited there last year and saw a village of five-hundred families with many youths. They received us with local music and dance. I saw how they derive electricity from solar power and biogas. They cook with rocket stoves, compost their organic wastes, and grow a wide variety of food crops using permaculture methods. They forbid plastic disposables. I saw how immensely their standards of living have improved using ecovillage techniques. Every family has enough to live. The stresses on the surrounding trees and soils have decreased, and they have become more abundant with life. The community seems to be unified in their support of one another."

"Why aren't you living there, then?"

"Because they use only outer permaculture. Inner permaculture is missing. Being regenerative depends on using whole permaculture which combines the inner with the outer. Some people call it *Archan permaculture*. There's another place I just heard of, an experiment of living in what they call 'phoenix culture' with the asamangaXhosa people, in eastern South Africa."

"Could you please write the name here in my notebook? How did you become such a global citizen? Where are you from?"

"I am from here, and now. How did I leave my birth culture behind? That was easy. It was bullshit from the get-go. When I was four years old, they sent me to public school. Suddenly all my little toys became lifeless. The sparkling fairyland in the trees behind my house turned colorless and dead. I knew something was very, very wrong indeed. I abandoned the whole system. I pretended to agree with them until I felt old enough to leave home. I was thirteen. They put me in a boarding school and I focused on sports instead of academics. At eighteen I could legally abandon the whole parents and school thing. That was twenty years ago."

"What about having a house and a husband? What about children?"

"I was married for a while. Luckily, I did not get pregnant. It seems nearly impossible for a man to escape the Patriarchy. I don't know how it has been for you, but I notice you are traveling alone. I'm not into women as partners. Children? Well... perhaps you should read about John B. Calhoun's 'Mouse Utopia' experiments. The Earth these days is suffocating under an invisible pressure from human overpopulation, which also causes confusion and perversions just like it does in overpopulated mice. People are not talking about it yet. Having a kid these days subjects them to social and psychic forces difficult to protect them from. It is not pretty."

"Well... shit." Edith looks down at her hands. "That explains a lot. Why are you reading that *Conscious Feelings* book?"

"I saw Dr. Ousmane Aly Pame reading it at the Global Ecovillage Network last summer. He sources the REDES projects in Senegal. I figured if it is good for him, it would be good for me. Actually, it's bizarre. This is the second time I'm reading it. I read it once while traveling in South India. I wrote my name in the inside cover and left it in a café in Kanyakumari for someone else to find. Then I come here and my exact same book is sitting over there on that giveaway bookshelf! I figured it is E.C.C.O. talking to me. The book is part of the Possibilitator Library..." She flips to the inside cover and shows the website link. "See... this is my signature here. Three other people read it since me. The book came back to me here, so I guess it is my turn again. I think I read it too quickly the first time. I did not actually do the experiments."

"What do you mean, 'echo talking to you'?"

"It's an acronym, E. C. C. O. It stands for Earth Coincidence Control Office. It is the agents out there arranging all the coincidences, like you walking into the Snowman Café just now so we can have this conversation.

Making myself useful to E.C.C.O. adds excellence to being a nomad."

"How do you make money?"

"I deliver online Emotional Healing Processes and Rage Clubs. My turn."

"What?" asks Edith.

"My turn to ask questions. Where did you get your genes?"

Edith looks at her pants, "They're not jeans, they're... oh... uh, my other genes? My mother got fed up with Russia as a teenager and escaped to Rio de Janeiro where she met my dad, an American investment banker at Carnival."

"Ah! That explains your amazing Ashkenazi green eyes. So then?"

"So then... my older brother, Adler, commits suicide, and my father has a heart attack." Edith looks down at her hands gripping each other in her lap

"Holy... shit."

Joni Mitchell sings softly in the background at the Snowman Café. *Don't it always seem to go, that you don't know what you got 'til it's gone. Pave Paradise, put up a parking lot...* which amplifies a wistful silence between these two women.

Men have never been the solution for them, but when the men suddenly vanish from their life, it creates a particular anti-satisfaction shock. They both want men transformed, not dead.

Edith speaks. "Adler was in the U.S. Air Force in Iraq. He told me he betrayed his men and couldn't live with it. Said he would die soon anyway, from being exposed to toxins. I never had a chance to say goodbye to him."

"My name is Prescott. Claire Prescott."

"You introduce yourself like James Bond..."

"What specific toxins?" Claire keeps her center.

"In 1991 they called it *Gulf War Syndrome* and claimed ignorance of its origins. In the Iraq Afghanistan war, and later in the Balkan War, they didn't call it anything, but it still happened. Of the 700,000 soldiers deployed in 1991, 250,000 came home and got sick a few weeks later. After Adler drove himself off the road and died, I began researching. In Operation *Desert Storm*, the U.S. government littered the Iraqi countryside with over 350 metric tons of Depleted Uranium shot from A10 Warthog jets built around the GAU-8 Avenger Gatling Gun. The 30-millimeter bullets from the jet's rotary cannon cut through armor plating on tanks like a hot knife through butter, exploding into a fireball releasing nanoparticles of radioactive dust. They won the war and left radioactive dust everywhere. Then, in Iraq again, in 2003, the U.S. disposed of over 1000 metric tons of Depleted Uranium, same way. It is an insanely irresponsible technique for dumping your nuclear waste in other countries. Maybe that is why the U.S. has to start so many wars... to dispose of Depleted Uranium."

"Holy Kali – loosed upon the world!" murmurs Claire.

Edith feels remorse about the shock and awe of human stupidity for a few moments, then asks Claire, "What did you do before? I ask this because I spent five years earning Master's degrees in economics and law. Then on my third day on the job in San Francisco I met the boss lawyer and quit as soon as my contract would let me get out the door. After a Vision Quest in Death Valley, I found my way to Kathmandu."

"You are lucky! As soon as I got out of high school, I decided to make enough money to be secure for the rest of my life. I got a job in technical sales at Microsoft. It took me ten years to realize that the word 'business' actually means 'busy-ness'. They knew how to keep me so busy I did not have enough attention left to wonder why I was always so busy. Years flew by. I was as dead as a zombie. Sure, I had plenty of money. But the false intensity of the work sucked me dry. I had zero time for myself. I took early retirement and moved into a Bridge-House."

"How old were you?"

"Twenty-nine."

"What's a Bridge-House?"

"There is an amazing website about that: bridge-house.mystrikingly.com. I was sick of ordinary society, and too afraid of trying to start something on my own. I went googling and ended up locating a Bridge-House in Brazil that was open for participants. Simply put, a Bridge-House is a small team of people coming together in an agreed upon context to help each other heal their wounds and remove their blocks so they can access enough radical freedom to responsibly grow up. All I can tell you is that Bridge-Houses are the most powerful human transformational environments I ever found on Earth."

"Better than a monastery?"

"You already answered that question for yourself."

"What are you doing alone up here in Kathmandu, then?"

"You make an assumption."

"Which is?"

"That I'm alone. I'm not. Our entire Bridge-House went nomadic, starting three months ago. We are currently on expedition here in Nepal, searching for artifacts and ancient secret teachings, plus connecting with other projects and people we find while exploring evolutionary hotspots."

"Hotspots like Kathmandu!"

"Exactly!"

"People like me!"

"Now you are getting the picture!"

"You mean, I am the fly, and you are the Venus Flytrap?"

"Something like that."

"What are you planning to do with me now that I am caught?"

"Are you caught?"

"Not really. It was a theoretical question. What would you do with me if I had said yes?"

"I would have said goodbye."

"Why?"

"Because I am not interested in people who are catchable."

"What are you up to, really?"

Claire takes a sip of her chai latte. "Like I said, collecting artifacts."

"So, I'm an artifact?"

"Think about it. You have been carving your Being into something unusual, wouldn't you say? Sure, you had some help. It sounds like your parents welcomed your genius. I would bet your mother challenged your thinking skills even more than school. You go to top universities to study the legal memetics of the most dangerous and out-of-control gremlin gameworld on Earth, the United States of America. Then that gameworld's government kills your brother for no good reason. Then you enter the valley of death for solace. The desert with one of the lowest places on Earth sends you to a monastery in the highest mountains of the world, but within a few months you fire your guru. And here you are, sitting in the best pie shop in Asia having a nonlinear possibility conversation with a stranger. And you are trying to tell me you are not an artifact? Do you write anything?"

"What?"

"Have you uploaded any articles? Do you have a website to document your discoveries?"

"Uh..."

"Here, give me your diary. I'll write down a few links for you to check out. This conversation is not about us. It is not just for entertainment."

Claire looks up from writing and says, "I'll tell you a story. One night, a few years ago, never mind how many exactly, I was standing alone at midnight in the Basel train station after having delivered a wildly successful transformational training and then eaten five one-hundred-gram Ritter Sport chocolate bars to calm down. A doorway opens up to communicating directly with my bright principles. During that exchange I make a deal with the principles of clarity and possibility. I say, 'If you will give me everything you've got, I will pass it on to ten thousand people.' They accept the offer. Since then, I am jacked-in to these infinite archetypal resources, and my life has been about trying to give it all away as fast as I can. I shot past the ten-thousand people marker after a couple of years with my first books. They are not best sellers, but they will also never fade away. People pass them around to their friends for years. The books are filled with distinctions and experiments to try. This conversation would be irresponsible unless I tell you that I think this time has come for you too. I think you are standing at a start over moment."

"What are you saying?"

"I am saying that I think your lawyer's future is gone. Your attraction to the kind of 'success' that is marketed by modern culture is burned away. Since your dad just had a heart attack, he is probably also ready to start over with you."

"You might be right about that. He recently messaged me an invitation to meet him in San Diego this spring at a wedding of the daughter of his friend."

"Since you are dropping off the baggage of your comforts and your beliefs, fate can step in and provide you with new opportunities. Here at this café table, you and I sit together at the cutting edge of human consciousness. We may each be collaborating with other edgeworker alchemists, but we have our unique part to play. Others are counting on us to do our part, just like we count on them to do theirs. We may meet with them at some point. Meanwhile, let's paint the vision here, in this space, for the people we already know. This conversation is the speaking of the vision of what is possible. No organization that has been captured can speak for me, or you. We must speak for ourselves. And what I say is: *Something completely different from this is possible right now.* Therefore, I beg a favor of you. I am going to ask you a question and write down what you say. Will you please simply tell me the first answer that comes to you when you hear my question?"

"Yes."

"Which memetic virus will cut the unbreakable link between a shrinking food supply and a growing population?"

"*I already have everything that I need.*"

"Whaa!" says Claire, eyes wide. Seconds tick by in this gravity-free limbo as Claire writes down her own question and Edith's answer. "Bingo! Yes! I get it. Thank you so much! That is perfectly true! The only problem being that, standing in a world where I already have everything that I need is the orientation of an initiated adult. No one could see what you saw, or authentically say what you said, without first decontaminating their adult egostate from their child egostate or parent egostate, or gremlin egostate. So we are still at the same problem."

"Which is?"

"Which is, how to provide authentic adulthood initiatory processes to eight billion children so they have a chance to grow up?"

"Ask me that one."

"Okay. Which memetic virus will cut the unbreakable link between a childhood survival strategy that worked, and the comforts of staying a slave zombie in modern culture's candy-coated economic machine?"

"*Death, or death,*" says Edith.

"Uh... can you say more about that, please?"

"Staying stuck in the chrysalis kills the butterfly. Right?"

Claire nods her head while listening with full intention.

"And being a zombie is being the walking dead. A 'zombie' is any person serving a gameworld without knowing the true values of that gameworld. This transformational meme, *Death or Death*, wakes you up to seeing that the choice you are being offered is either death by staying in your uninitiated juvenile survival strategy as an employee, or death by pretending to be an adult by having a dead managerial job in a corporation or government. Without thinking, people choose death either way. It is hilarious, isn't it? The human biological machine is so amazingly designed that it can be used as a transformational apparatus.

But we choose death instead of transformation. We live inside this incredibly delicate system – the human body – and twenty-four hours a day it offers us aliveness. Instead, we choose death. We prefer death over fear."

"Say more about that," says Claire, writing furiously in Edith's notebook.

"The chrysalis – our survival strategy – is known, familiar, comfortable territory for us, even if what we are familiar with is to beat ourselves up, judge ourselves, criticize ourselves, strangle ourselves, violently hate ourselves, diminish ourselves to enough worthlessness that we live as a zombie and call it 'modern life'. If that is how we survived our family and school, then that is what feels safe and familiar to us. So we keep doing it, because – now get this – we keep doing it because, by doing even the slightest little thing differently, we might not survive! We are afraid of not surviving, so we kill ourselves. We are afraid of changing, so we become petrified. We are afraid of living... so we make sure we stay dead." Tears pour down Edith's cheeks.

"Tell me what the tears are about."

"I am sad and shocked by how many years I spent dead inside of my own little habitual neurotic shut-in chrysalis. I am so sad and angry about how many friends have faded out of my life recently because they are choosing to stay in the groove that is marketed to them by modern culture media. If I grow up, I leave them behind. We were taught to consume! Copy! Obey! Stay numb with alcohol or dope or shopping ourselves into debt, or having children as a single mom with no community around, which drives a woman into neurotically insane overwhelm." Edith's fingers jitter and tap loudly on the wooden tabletop.

"What's with your fingers, Edith?"

"Anger. Rage. I want to scream. I hate the deadness. I hate the fear of fear."

"Hold on one second, Edith."

Claire stands up. There are two other customers in the café, one flipping through Instagram, one wearing earbuds, plus there are three staff behind the counter. Claire speaks in a loud adult voice, "Excuse me everyone! Hello there! My friend here has been sitting on a mountain of rage for her whole life, and she is going to make a loud noise now for a few seconds. Don't worry, okay? Everything will be fine. It will just be really loud for a short time, that is all. I am holding space for her to scream for a few seconds as loud as she can, then we will be quiet again. Everybody ready? Hold your ears if you want. Here we go! Edith! One. Two. Three!"

Edith stands up abruptly, knocking her chair over backwards. She balls her hands into fists, opens her mouth full wide and yells a roar of rage suitable for a dragon to crack open its eggshell.

Claire shouts back just as loudly, "Words Edith! Take another breath and use words! Give your rage words!"

One of the staff ladies and the guy flipping Instagram shout out enthusiastically together, "Go! Louder! Go all the way!"

Edith's next shout breathes fire on her world. "I hate it that people are dead! I hate it that I was dead for so long and nobody! Fucking nobody ever told me I could live out loud! I hate school, and the military! I hate fucking insane war! War killed my brother Adler and I hate that he stupidly went to play war and died! I hate advertising and the fucking media! I hate corporations everywhere and always sucking life out through people's eyes! I am so angry I could shake the foundation stones of Mount Everest! Arrrraaaaaaarrrrrraaaahhhhhhhhh!!!"

People spontaneously stand up and clap and cheer. They can't help it.

Claire stands across from Edith crying in celebration of Edith's ecstatic breakthrough. The chrysalis lies shattered in pieces around Edith's feet. This new woman can now spread her wings and fly for the rest of her life! This is a victory of outstanding proportions! It is an archetypal leap!

"Thank you everyone!" Claire says looking radiantly at each person in the café. "Thank you for helping Edith get out of her eggshell and step into the world as a powerful woman with her voice and her presence.

"I am buying free coffee and pie for everyone in here. Even you, sir! Please, come in! May I introduce you to Edith! This is Edith! She just shouted her way out of the jungle of insanity and came to life as herself. Everything is fine in here. Thank you for making sure we are all okay. Come on in, also with your partner there. I am buying everyone who wants it a free coffee and pie. This is the best pie shop in the world!"

Edith laughs her head off about what she just did in the Snowman Café, and what Claire says about it. Tears of joy roll down her face as she looks around at the others who are looking at her and smiling joyfully. It feels as if she never saw human beings before. This is certainly the most extraordinary thing that happened to them all day. Edith grabs her napkin and loudly blows her nose, then drops the wadded-up tissue to the table and raises her right hand as a fist high into the air. "I did it!" she yells at the top of her lungs. "I did it!"

Everyone claps and laughs and shouts again, even the Nepalese pie makers behind the counter.

When Edith picks up her chair to sit down, Claire says, "Listen, I need to tell you a couple things. It's not our planet. Earth is not our planet. The planet owns us. We do not own the planet. My intention is to meet with others to create and hold space for an upgraded human morpho-genetic field. My intention is to write information into that field to create a new structure of influence – like the system of influence that took down the Berlin wall – remember that? The Berlin wall was not removed by a government or a military force, or even a civil-society movement. The Berlin Wall was taken down by common people when the field of influence changed so that the Wall no longer had a basis in reality. Do you get the power of this?"

Edith nods yes. She is still integrating what just happened, but she also understands what Claire says.

"Our team is writing new information into the field which changes the basis of human reality. We do that by spreading around upgraded thoughtware. The field that is radiated by new ways of thinking and perceiving builds massive matrix to hold the consciousness for the emergence of regenerative human cultures on Earth."

"I'm in," says Edith. "Keep talking."

"Remember how I was saying that you are in a 'start over' moment in your life? Which, by the way, you just gloriously proved! Thank you for your trust of my spaceholding. Thank you for your chutzpah! Thank you for your ovaries!"

Edith smiles luminously, placing her phone on the table and turning on its voice recorder app.

Clair continues. "The whole of humanity is in a start over moment. We are shifting to living in a culture which centers itself on transformation, a culture which values healing and authentic adulthood initiations and the evolution of consciousness. Such a culture is a 'phoenix culture', like the phoenix bird. Any culture that promotes evolution must also evolve! That means the culture is not in charge because it has nothing to stand on. But Nothing – with a capital 'N', meaning an archetypal force of nature, is an infinite resource. Nothingness is an empowered context from which to start over. But it means there are no leaders. No one can lead in a transformational process because a leader obstructs transformation. Phoenix cultures encourage and support many participants to become spaceholders, which differentiates it from a sect. A phoenix culture can begin with a team of three spaceholders who have clarity and determination. They can set the context and declare the cultural gameworld into existence as an energetic configuration of commitment.

"A culture is a field of commitment with certain qualities. The field is strengthened when people gather in the name of the field, and write information into the field. I don't mean that they write something on paper. They meet to understand, to enact, to become the field in action. The field's information is made conscious by deepening the distinctions through practice and practical application. That is, individuals unfold the field's details from itself and inform each other of how it goes through demonstrating new skills and possibilities.

"A cultural field is holographic and complex, more complex than a single human being. One person can hold the whole picture, but without full resolution. More detailed resolution comes through each additional spaceholder of the cultural context.

"A spaceholder is someone connected into – and therefore a source of – the context of the culture. The field unfolds a satisfactory level of resolution of complexity through a group of people the size of a village, from thirty to ninety adults. More than one hundred people automatically divide themselves into two or three separate villages. Pretending that more than ninety people are not separate villages encourages irresponsible leadership, unconsciously serving shadow principles.

"People believe in the religion of globalization and imagine that there is only one human culture on Earth. Believers use phrases such as 'society', or 'the economy', as if it applies to everybody. But the fantasy world of globalization is a dream only perceived by the dreamers. The dreamers are trapped in their dream and are starving to death, replacing love with staring at their phones, trying to make sexy images of themselves, and buying cheap imported electronic shit from Asia.

"Economics is a false paradigm, a system where nature has no value unless money changes hands. Thinking that *man* can value *nature* is immature. Nature *made* man. The created cannot evaluate the creator. The created can only be grateful. I will not relate with you in a false paradigm.

"This is why I need you to write!"

Edith's mouth hangs open just a bit, enough to breathe, enough to say, "Write what?"

"Write what you figured out in the valley of death. What did you discover there?"

"Well... give me a second. Let me look..." She flips back through her journal to the desert days. "Ah... Here's something! I wrote this: *What is the name of the culture where neither the 'matri' nor the 'patri' prevails? Rather it is the 'arch' that establishes the basis, the 'arch-etypal', with both women and men, initiated archetypal adults, teamed up, collaborating equally but unequal, holding and navigating Gaia-given potentials. After matri-archy and patri-archy must come 'archi'-archy. Archiarchy! This culture naturally emerges from the archetypal nature of the Universe! It is 13 April 2024. The name of the culture I live in is Archiarchy.*"

Claire Prescott is ecstatic about her intuitive impulses being confirmed. "Thank the Yak and the Yeti! I knew it! Write that Edith! Fill it out to a few pages about how you got there and what we can do with this distinction, okay? Don't think about it. Just write! We are sending out a newsletter to thousands of people in our circle by the end of the week. Here is my email address and my number. Send it to me by tomorrow night, okay? We can do this! Now we can do this! Archiarchy has arrived! Give me a hug! I'm late for my meetup. Nice to greet you. Stay in touch. Isn't Kathmandu great? Be sure to capture more artifacts like yourself for us!"

Claire stands up and stretches, then drops a greasy wad of approximately 5,000 Nepalese Rupees on the counter saying, "Thank you for being here! Keep the change!"

Walking out the door she mumbles and laughs at her own jokes. "Yeah! Keep the change! I love change! Don't you love change? Everybody needs a little change! Change is so amazing, don't you think? Who doesn't like change? Change is happening in the pie shop!"

Edith breathes in the sweet scent of newly baked pies cooling on the counter combined with bitter smells of freshly brewing coffee. She glances around at the Nepalese décor and the other customers who also found the edges of the world. *Here we sit together, dangling our legs over the side. Life... is interesting.* She flips open to the next blank page in her journal and starts writing, "*Finding Gold In The Valley Of Death by Edith Goldman. If you are ever lucky enough to stroll down Old Freak Street in Kathmandu, you might find a pie shop...* "

# Aleppo, Syria 5

Zenobia Darwish's *Beep! Book* – 24 September 2012

More and more people gradually drift into our camp. These are amazingly good people, twenty-five or so... more good people than I ever thought existed on Earth.

Even before everyone arrives at Morning Circle, Rahim Taleb stands up and shouts, "I have been reading in the *Handbook*, and I propose that I am first spaceholder of Morning Circle. Please hold up both hands with your fingers indicating how much resistance you have, somewhere between zero fingers meaning zero resistance, and ten fingers meaning total resistance. Resistance has intelligence. We will consult the resistance for its intelligence. One. Two. Three!" Short pause. "I see a three resistance over there with Hadi Qasim. What is your resistance, Hadi?"

"I am really afraid about something, and I want to bring it here to our circle. Since you are new as a spaceholder of Morning Circle, I feel fear that you won't be able to navigate a valuable outcome for us."

"Thank you for your fear," says Rahim. "Are there any proposals about this?"

"Yes," shouts Mitzi, standing up and looking as surprised as we are that she is speaking to us all so boldly. "I propose that Hadi Qasim chooses two additional back-up spaceholders to stand by who she feels less afraid about as spaceholders. Then, when you bring up your fear, Hadi, the two backups are already chosen to help navigate if needed."

People laugh delightedly at Mitzi's clear-headed words.

Rahim shouts, "Please show your resistance to Mitzi's proposal? One. Two. Three!" All fists rise with zero fingers appearing.

"I see zero resistance. We accept your proposal, Mitzi! Thank you for speaking!" People spontaneously clap. Mitzi looks proudly around the circle, receiving love and appreciation from her village before sitting down again.

Hadi Qasim says, "I propose Zenobia and Israa as the two backup spaceholders for Rahim. Any resistance? One. Two. Three!"

Rahim Taleb says, "I see no resistance. Zenobia and Israa, you are my backup spaceholders for Morning Circle. I propose we efficiently collect node reports before going for Hadi's issue. Any resistance? One.

Two. Three!”

"Yes, ten resistance!” shouts Hadi standing to her feet.

"Please tell us...

"Aaarhhghghghaaaaaarrrrr! I am afraid of my anger! I have so much anger!!! I am so angry that I am about to explode! No!!! I am exploding right now! Rrrrajjjjjjjraaggggjjjaaaaaa!...”

I have already grabbed the *Handbook* away from Rahim and furiously search for the *Rage Club* chapter. I know it is in there somewhere...

Rahim shouts at me and Israa, “What do I do? Tell me what to do!”

Israa shouts, “I need two women up here, now!” Aziza and Jamila leap off their benches and run to either side of Hadi. “Grab Hadi's arm firmly like this!” Israa shows them how to loop one arm under Hadi's arm, one on each side, then how to hold Hadi's shoulder from the back with their free hands, grabbing their own biceps with their hand that looped under Hadi's arm.

"Push your shoulder against Hadi's shoulder so she feels safe and held. Yes, like that!” Israa shouts. “Everybody look! This is a *'Standing Rage Hold'*. I found a picture of it yesterday in the *Handbook* because I could feel this coming. Standing rage hold is the safest and most comfortable position to unleash your rage.” Israa raises her fist high in the air and shouts, “We are starting ‘Rage Club’!”

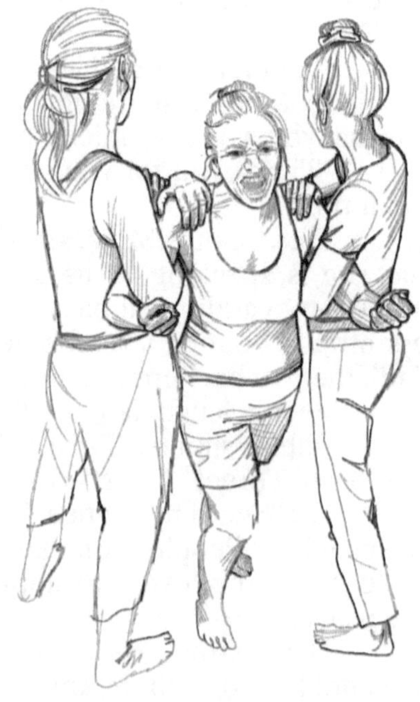

People cheer wildly, leaping out of their improvised chairs and rushing over to form a tight circle around Hadi, Jamila, and Aziza.

I yell, "Rahim! Say something! You are the spaceholder!"

"What do I say? I don't know what to say!"

He is panicking. I shout at him, "This is Rage Club, Rahim! Rage Club! Not Fear Club! We will do Fear Club later! Use your rage! Say what your anger tells you to say right now!"

People laugh hysterically at the simple powerful clarity pouring into the space.

Rahim's eyes are as wide as fried eggs. He looks at Hadi. "Hadi, what are you angry about?"

Hadi takes a huge breath and roars full out, straining against the shoulders of the two women safely holding her back. Hadi's face turns red as a radish while she shouts and hollers monster sounds at the top of her lungs.

"Use words, Hadi!" shouts Rahim. "Words!"

"I hate it! Everybody is always telling me what to do! Stop trying to tell me what to do! I hate you!"

"Who are you talking to?" shouts Rahim. He looks around and cannot see who she is yelling at.

"Everybody! Stop trying to make me do things!"

"There is no 'everybody' Hadi!" Rahim shouts. "Is it male or female?"

"Female!" shouts Hadi instantly, hatred spewing from her voice.

"Pick one Hadi!" yells Rahim. "Point to a woman. It doesn't matter who!"

Hadi points at Lylah.

Rahim commands, "Lylah, spin around. I saw this in the *Handbook*. As you spin around, you become whoever it is that Hadi is angry at. Yes! Like that! Now stand here! No! That is too close! She could kick you! Mitzi! Will you please come here and hold Lylah's arm gently above her elbow with your fingers? Yes, like that! You be Lylah's eyes behind. Keep her far enough away from Hadi that she cannot be kicked. Okay?"

"Yes!" shouts Mitzi.

"Lylah, you let Mitzi lead you by your arm, okay? She keeps you safe."

"Yes!" shouts Lylah.

"There are three rules here," shouts Rahim, glaring first at Hadi and then at all of us. He is a transformed man! A maniac spaceholder, raging as loud as Hadi. I love it! We have so much energy for this work together! I can see the clarity of the consious anger gushing through Rahim.

"Don't hurt yourself! Don't hurt anyone else! And don't get arrested! Does everyone agree to the three rules?" Rahim shouts at Hadi. She and everyone else shout back at Rahim, "Yes!"

"This is Rage Club!" shouts Rahim. Then he points at Lylah and yells, "Hadi, here is a woman who is always telling you what to do! Go!"

Hadi loses her mind with rage. Jamila and Aziza struggle with everything they have and barely contain Hadi's outburst. Mitzi drags Lylah backwards by her arm to a safer distance. Everyone is screaming their heads off! It is working!

As Hadi takes her third breath, Rahim interrupts, shouting directly into Hadi's face, "Hadi! Who are you really yelling at? Who is that over there? Who was she in your life?"

Hadi's eyes go wide. "It is my grandmother!"

"Lylah! Spin around again. Become Hadi's grandmother!"

Mitzi releases Lylah's arm so she can spin around and become Hadi's grandmother. Then Mitzi grabs the grandmother's arm.

"Hadi, here is your grandmother! She is listening to you! Tell her what's going on! Go!"

This time Hadi turns into Mrs. Ghengis Kahn, roaring obscenities and curses with full outrage straight from her belly. Her hands are in fists, and her legs strain to drag her towards the woman who ruined her life.

Again, Rahim interrupts Hadi in the tiniest pause, yelling into her face, "What is the boundary you need to make with your grandmother? Hadi, what is that boundary you never made? Tell her now! Make the boundary now!"

Hadi delivers a walloping clear communication. "This is my life! You lonely witch! My life is not your life! Your opinions do not matter to me anymore! Stop trying to tell me what to do in my life! Stop it! This is over! Finished! Leave me alone! You have your own life to decide about! This is my life! I decide what I do with my life from now on! This is a boundary!"

People jump up and down with encouragement, fists waving, screaming their heads off. Two people roll around in the dirt, gripping their abdomens, sobbing. Hadi breaks away from Jamila and Aziza and dances jubilantly, screaming in celebratory success with both hands waving free. I can see her inner memetic structure reordering itself into new levels of effectiveness, more awareness, more adulthood, more ability to connect and create and make appropriate boundaries. It is incredible! The whole circle is going crazy. In that moment, Rahim's smile goes ear to ear. He tosses his fist high into the air and shouts at the top of his lungs in a voice filled with conscious rage, "Who's next!?"

Five people shout in unison, "I'm next!"

Rahim chooses another woman, someone who just arrived. "You!" he shouts at her, pointing his finger. "You're next! What's your name?" Everyone laughs that we are out here doing outrageous Rage Club and we don't even know people's names. It is insanely inspiringly funny.

"My name is Rachel!" shouts the woman, already holding her arms out to her side to be held in a *standing rage hold*. "Aziza and Jamila, will you hold my arms?"

"Yes!" they shout in unison, switching sides from when they held Hadi to give their shoulders a rest. They grab Rachel in a proper standing rage hold.

"Who are you angry at?" demands Rahim.

"My grandmother!" shouts Rachel.

"It's grandmother's day," yells Rahim. Everyone could split sideways with hysterical laughter and shouting.

"Who could be your grandmother?" shouts Rahim.

"Israa!"

"Israa, will you be Rachel's grandmother?"

"Yes!" shouts Israa, moving into position then spinning into role playing Rachel's grandmother.

Then Israa looks over her shoulder and shouts, "Montassar! Will you hold my arm?" Everyone just about pees in their pants with glee.

This is working!

We can do this!

I squeeze the *Handbook* with so much love for the unfathomable mysteries of life. How is this happening? I don't know.

But I do know that it is happening.

Then Rahim shouts, "Everybody please pause and wait a minute. Help me do this." He walks briskly over to the two people sobbing in the dirt. He squats down and gently touches one of their shoulders. It is Sammi Ghulam. The other is Thomas Taha. Rahim gently says, "Sammi. Thomas. This is Rahim. We are with you. What you are feeling is exactly right. It is your time now. What you are feeling is the boundaries you never made. You are doing perfect. We are going to help you to your feet. Are you ready?" Others squat next to Rahim and put their hands out to help Sammi and Thomas stand up. No one worries about how dusty they are.

Rahim says, "Each of these men need two people to hold their shoulders just like Aziza and Jamila are holding Rachel. Please come forward and hold Sammi and Thomas in a *Standing Rage Hold*. Ladies and gentlemen!" he shouts. "We are going for three *Standing Rage Holds* at the same time!" The cheer from everyone is outrageous and contagious. Rahim continues. "You already know how this goes! Please begin!"

By then, Rachel is already screaming at her grandmother, collecting herself to make a life-changing boundary that will transform her inner structure and give her a whole new future.

Our radical transformational guerrilla street theater goes on and on, everyone helping everyone in 'parallel play'.

In a short pause between the seventh and eighth *Standing Rage Holds*, Montassar shouts, "I have to ask you all a question!" We quiet down, mostly, and he says, "Last night I was reading in the *Handbook...*" He strides over and takes the book from my hands, flips to a page, and reads:

*There are three kinds of games to play.*

*One game is called, 'I win, you lose'. It is a survival game, based on scarcity and competition for limited resources, such as fame, money, love, attention, possessions. The players think, 'If they get these resources, then I die. So I will do whatever I can to get the resources. In an 'I win, you lose' game there are very many losers and very few winners.*

*In the 1960s, a new game was invented called, 'I win, you win', or 'win-win' for short. This game is a cooperation between players, but it often degrades into compromise where 'I agree to lose this if you agree to lose that'. Then it becomes an 'I lose, you lose', or a 'lose-lose' game.*

People nod their heads in understanding.

"The *Handbook* proposes to learn a third kind of game called 'winning happening'." Montassar checks that people understand, then keeps reading.

*In winning happening, there is no 'I' and no 'you' in the game. The purpose of the game is to keep the game going so as to create a field, a space, in which the bright principle of winning happening can do its work in the world.*

"The *Handbook* says: *You can sense a warm, yellowish vibration of possibility and connection when you are truly playing a winning happening game.*

"My question is this: Has anyone else besides me been experiencing this warm, yellow, tingling, vibration field of winning happening for the past hour in this space?"

This tiny crowd of hopeless abandoned derelict loser outcast Syrian refugees erupts in unstoppable celebratory joy! People dance around, laughing, holding hands, patting each other on the back, hugging each other in congratulations, shouting, "Yes! Yes! Yes! Winning is happening!"

I am crying completely.

I am not the only one.

We have discovered that we can together invent a new kind of success. This is success in Archiarchy. We are living in Archiarchy now. Our skills are growing and our values are changing in our empowered little village of Archans. I can only believe it because I see it, and hear it, and feel it in my bones.

Then Rahim screams out wildly, "Okay everybody! Here we go for more winning happening! Who's next?"

I report that on this day, winning happens for two more hours before we pause for a very late lunch preparation break.

# Salt Lake City, Utah 3

Professor P. Thomas Collins struts about the classroom stage looking like a clam with legs. Dark rimmed glasses magnify his squinting piggy eyes. Suspenders keep his pants from dropping to his ankles. His balding round head has no neck. Perhaps that is why his pudgy face reddens so easily – his blood does not have so far to flow upwards against gravity.

The university classroom is large and modern. One hundred men and women pay various degrees of attention to the professor who pontificates on theories of economics, quite enjoying himself. More than a few students have glazed eyes.

One does not.

This young man with short surfer-blonde hair becomes more and more agitated and confused. He is not confused by what the Professor is saying, but rather by what the Professor is *not* saying. This is JET.

Clearly there is a war of voices going on within this young man's mind.

*Stay here.*

*No, leave immediately.*

*No, pay attention.*

*Are you kidding? This is a total fucking waste of time!*

Squirming in his seat, he glances at the other students who seem to tolerate class as usual – as JET himself has always done, until today, until this moment.

Suddenly, something has shifted. A connection flashes between his heart and his mind. Rage vaporizes his self-installed self-fogging school survival mechanism.

Without the energetic block functioning to confuse him, JET quickly gets to the ignition point. His right hand rises into the air seemingly by its own will, alone amongst the ninety-nine other right hands not in the air.

The teacher ignores him. The hand goes down.

Then it goes up again.

Some of the other students glance worriedly at JET and his renegade hand. They all know the unspoken rule: *When Professor Collins gets rolling, no one interrupts.*

The piggy eyes stare directly at JET while the round face turns visibly redder, but the Professor continues professing, words spraying out of his mouth like pesticide from an industrial farm tractor trying to grow Genetically Modified Organisms.

The hand bravely persists.

Finally, Collins relents, rubs his nose, and speaks disdainfully. "Yes, Mr., uhhh, Tumble, what is it?"

"You asked if we had any questions."

"At the beginning of class I did, yes. About the readings. So?"

"I don't think we know how to ask questions."

Silence from Collins. He's stunned that someone could be so disrespectful. He has no response.

JET too is free-falling. He just took that last long step off a short pier and has no clue what should come next.

People gawk at him, puzzled and shocked.

JET puts out both of his hands in a big helpless gesture and then he flows right into the space his hands have opened up, deciding he already looks idiotic so there's nothing left to lose. Anything is better than continuing to sit, voiceless as a bug in this pointless classroom.

"Professor Collins, it's just not okay with me..."

As if responding to an insane person, or an extremely foreign foreigner, the Professor tilts his head at an inquisitive angle and says, "What. Is. Not. Okay. With you, Mr. Tumble?"

"...that we don't know how to ask questions. I think we should know. Is asking questions some kind of soft skill that is prohibited in college? The things you tell us, we can read in a book, right?" Not waiting for an answer, he slogs forth. "I think we should be asking real questions instead. I want to learn how the world works, how to make things happen. Economics is a required class for me. So teach me how to make money happen. Do you know how to make money happen Professor Collins?"

A few chuckles leak out from students who think of the old saying, "Those who know, do. Those who don't know, teach."

The chuckles quickly fade. Into that silence JET speaks again. "How much money do you make anyway, Professor Collins? And what do you do with your money such that you feel authorized to speak so much about economics?"

Snickers from the class again, plus a few outright guffaws. Collins sees chaos coming. He decides on a strategy to regain control. "Tumble. Are you losing it?"

Now students chuckle at JET – one varsity-jacketed bully in particular.

Collins continues, "Perhaps this is a conversation you should be having with your counselor?"

The Professor has given JET a back door, a way to save face and drop this little absurdity if he wants to.

JET doesn't want to. He won't get off it. There are years and years of pressure suppressing unconscious yearnings into an unspeakably forbidden zone. For once JET allows that zone to speak out loud,

"Professor Collins. You are responsible for standing up there and talking to us for two hours today. I want to know why you think what you are saying is worth my time? I want to know why nobody asks real questions in here?"

JET searches the faces of other students – only to see blank stares. Some even look scared. JET keeps pushing at the edge.

"Twice a week we sit in your class. You talk. We take notes. We go home and write papers for you. You read them and make your little red comments. We feel good about it, or we feel bad about it. But I want something more for my time here!"

Old anger feeds the fire in his belly. "I don't know about the rest of you, but today is a fine day outside. We are paying full price to be in this room. We will never get these two hours back. Are we getting our time's worth? That is what I would call a real question of economics! Am I getting value for my time invested here in your classroom today, Professor?"

The football player makes his move. "Are all theater majors so emotional?" Oily undertones drip from his words.

The jock's attempt to rescue the Professor only emphasizes the truth of JET's words, but JET gets hooked anyway. He stands to face the over-muscled football player and fires back, "My major is physics, lump head!"

Collins instantly interjects a distracting comment, trying to avoid an all-out brawl in his Economics 301 class. "I believe you were addressing me, John? What was your question? Are you getting your time's worth? Don't you think each individual in this room must answer that question for him or herself, John?"

"No!" The ferocity of his reply surprises even himself. "I don't see anyone here even wondering about it. You've been training us not to think, not to introspect for real value, and not to ask questions. And my name is JET! Listen, this is not working! Sorry for interrupting everybody's sleep. I'm outta here!"

JET grabs his backpack, makes his way through the other students, and disappears out the door.

Professor Collins clears his throat so as to distract his pupils' attention away from the slowly closing door. "Yes, now. As I was saying, Mideast oil transactions tendered in Rubles could dangerously upset U.S. monetary policies through..."

# Palm Springs, California 1

"Hello Phil!" Two masculine hands clasp in professional firmness. "You haven't been at the club lately." This statement holds an implied question, with serious harmonics in the undertones.

"You're right, Stan. Heart attack in January... doctor says I unconsciously suppress my feelings and they had to burst out sideways through my heart. I'm still thinking about his little quip..."

It is morning at the Bighorn Golf Club near Palm Springs, California. The desert air feels cool, but lungs refuse deeper breaths when the nose detects pesticides and defoliants in the haze rising over vast acres of GMO crops.

Phillip Goldman occupies a seat in boardrooms of three international conglomerates. Stanley Gärtner is his investment manager since Reagan opened broad new playgrounds for them to rape and pillage. Of course, it wasn't Reagan, *per se*. Stanley usually smiles when thinking how strategically applied euphemisms keep sheep dozing peacefully even while they are being sheared. But Stanley isn't smiling right now. With a piercing but measured gaze he says, "I wonder why you haven't returned my calls Phil."

"It puzzles me too, Stan." Being vulnerable contradicts every strand of Phillip's carbon-fiber defense strategy. Vulnerability feels like starting the conversation as a loser and going downhill from there. No one in Phil's life ever modeled how to be vulnerable. Even during his father's last days of colon cancer, the old man could only deliver his glib cynical jokes and concealed back-stabs. It's new territory for Phillip Goldman to state the simple truth. "My son committed suicide in November."

"Suicide?" says Stan, as if he were repeating the sum of a column of numbers. "I thought it was an auto accident."

"He was twenty-eight and a wing commander in the Air Force. In December his tour would have been up. I intended to bring him into the business. His whole life perspective would have changed, as you know... Then he wrote me a letter. Said for two years he'd ordered his team to load anti-tank munitions for the Gatlings in the A10 Warthog gunships. The men trusted him completely. Turns out these tank-buster bullets are made from Depleted Uranium. His men breathed that dust. Now they and their wives are dying of multiple cancers. Their children have birth defects. There is no way to get that shit out of your body. He couldn't live with having so thoroughly betrayed his men and their families. He said he would die from the stuff soon anyway. By the time I received his letter, he'd already driven his car through the guardrail."

"But Phil, he was only following orders!"

"Just like *All the President's Men*, eh Stan?"

"There are hard cold facts out here! We simply deal with them to our advantage. That's the game. You and me, we're doing all right. You still have your daughter..."

"Edith? She hardly speaks to me anymore. Says I'm hollow and without conscience. Says I am using outdated thoughtware. Her mother left me years ago..."

"You have the ear of the committee, whenever you offer an opinion."

"The committee is a club of sleazy, lying old bastards, Stan! Just like you and me. We're all stooges for our corporate owners. I used to think I was the one pulling the strings. But then China got in the game and ate our lunch. They have aces up their sleeve we never thought of. Our think tanks are useless against twisted Asian minds. China leads India and the Russians. That's why the Indians are buying so many weapons from the Russians, so they can fight China. By now the U.S.A. is low man on the totem pole. Plus, the banks rule everyone. What's the point anymore?"

"We *are* the banks."

Phil gives him a stare that could freeze ice and burn fire.

"Well... alright... Now I know why you insisted on meeting me out here on the golf course. What makes you think you can trust me, Phil?"

"I don't trust you, Stan. I trust that we are both in the same boat, that's all. I was hoping that out here in private, you will stop denying it."

"Okay... okay... so? And now what?"

"And now let's hit a few balls together, shall we?"

# Los Angeles, California 1



I promised I'd be radically honest if I ever wrote anything down, and, well... I am writing something down. Here is the evidence to prove my claim.

What am I writing? I am writing the truth about my life, in words.

Now that's a contradiction, ain't it? Words are such bullshit.

But is my life bullshit?

I ask if you will help me figure that out by reading this.

Here's how it went this morning. I walk past the meeting room and Arthur – my boss' boss at A. T. Advertising where I work as a graphic designer and stylist here in Los Angeles – shouts to me in a bizarro professional tone of voice, "Wendy, honey! Could you bring us some coffees?"

That's when I first want to go to the bathroom and barf today. But I hadn't eaten anything yet, so it would not have been rewarding enough to spend the time trying.

Arthur is entertaining reps from *Whale Storm*, a big event organizer, potentially a major client, and Ester, our coffee girl, is away on pregnancy leave. I am forced to make a snap decision whether to shout at Arthur, "Go fuck yourself" which is what my gremlin, Gretchin, (Retchin' Gretchin...) wants to shout, just to get some nibbles for her poor hungry massively bulging belly this morning, or, to politely say, "Yes Mr. Tutor, I'll have coffees there in a flash!" which would make me barf twice.

I choose the latter. Or was it me?

Gretchin suddenly kicks herself in her prodigious butt, spins into her high-velocity nonlinear-reality generation modus. She speaks with her precision falsetto torpedo voice, lands the power of obsequiousness in the minds of the 'league of extraordinary gentlemen', then pirouettes me flawlessly towards the coffee machine.

I'm thinking, 'What the hell are you doin', you little monster?'

She does not answer. She's already sliding cups under the twin java spouts and pouring cold milk into the stainless-steel pot to steam it up for mean cappuccinos.

Since a few months, whenever Gretchin gets spunky like this, I've been letting her take the wheel and see where she navigates. Maybe I trust her because she's jacked her gremlin intuition into some kind of source-code that rarely makes mistakes in indeterminate situations... or maybe it's because it's Monday morning and I am already longing for Friday afternoon because I'm so bored.

"Yes, Mr. Tutor, I'll have coffees there in a flash!" Little do I know how thoroughly that one ass-kissing sentence will ruin my life.

As I slide into Arthur's office, Gretchin melts my face with a slightly bemused smile while I wordlessly nudge steaming cups of java over shoulders and between tablets and iPhones. I rattle no cup and make no splash. I scatter handfuls of individually wrapped chocolate-covered coffee beans around the table. 'Feeding the pigeons,' Gretchin tells me. I had picked them up at the gas station for me, but what the hell. It might be a good investment.

I am about to exit the scene when I catch the glance of a snake-eyed programmer type. He has not shaved this week. His hair hasn't seen shampoo in the same amount of time. His tie looks knotted by a third grader, and it's green. And he knows something he is not sharing with the others. Men are so easy to read, especially if their second chakra is amped a notch from seeing an extra inch of cleavage. I don't look away. Neither does he. That is when the sentence he is speaking slurs to garble and ends in an uncomfortable and unexpected pause.

"She could do it," he mumbles to everyone in general, mostly to himself.

"Do what?" I venture to ask, not breaking eye contact with the geek, assigning part of my split attention to manage my speaking and the rest to navigate to voluptuous eye contact with the green-tie guy. I have not done this with anyone in months... well, years, actually. Motionless breathing. The space becomes quiet enough to hear satin rustle.

There isn't any satin around to rustle, but it's that quiet.

I refuse to submit to reasonable curiosity – which any commoner might have done – glancing around to see what the others are thinking. I refuse, just to prove my point.

I don't know what my point is, exactly, but whatever my point is, it confirms the point of the green-tie guy, that 'I could do it'. I see him start to squirm due to the fact that his intensity tolerance is exceeded. He turns to Arthur. "Who is she?"

I've been trying to answer that question for about six years, ever since reading Callahan's other book. The answers I've come up with won't satisfy the current question space, so I remain silent. Arthur gives an answer that I consider to be admirably creative, since he doesn't know who I am either. "She's our theater witch," he says.

Maybe he knows me better than I think.

"Can she be like this all the time?" asks Snake-Eyes while cringing in thirty-four percent unconscious fear, which would multiply to the bejeebies level if he realized that the answer is, "Yes, she can be like this all the time."

I repress any nervous tics, eye movements, breath patterns, or grimaces that could suggest I might be feeling something ordinary. This is one of those moments not to interject the slightest gesture because it could divert the unexpected flow of exquisitely useful information.

It feels like I am posing nude in front of a class of beginning sketch students, mostly young males. One second I feel tinglingly erotic. The next second I feel stupid and embarrassed.

I float in the gap between these two moments, drifting in the emptiness available in any gap. The rug has been unexpectedly pulled out from under everyone. I navigate to stay in the void as long as possible by remembering that human beings are designed to fly. Most people carry so much baggage they can barely walk on level ground.

Since no one else asks, and since I still have Snake-Boy by the balls (eyeballs, that is...) I use the half-speed voice I learned from my junior high phys-ed teacher, ex-Police Sergeant Ms. Jones. I let my words seep like tar into every corner of the room. "What's the project?" I say.

I notice that only three of the seven men even know there is a project, and only two of them know what it is. One of them is the Snake.

I keep looking at him and make the slightest of smiles, the kind you might imagine a mongoose making when she knows she's having Snake for lunch.

He gives in. "We found a wizard for a Whale Storm game-design project. But he won't talk to anyone we offer. He says he needs to speak with our sorceress."

A chill goes down my spine...

Actually... I want to be more accurate. It is not a chill. For one thing, it goes up my spine rather than down. It's more like my seven chakras flash full-bright-on, one after the other, in their iridescent colors starting from my tail-bone, like an elevator rapidly ascending my energetic body. I never felt that before. Not sure I want to again.

On second thought, maybe I do.

I keep wearing my non-committal face and make no sudden moves. Would you smile at a time like this? I don't think so.

A sorceress, eh? I step a bit too majestically for my own taste towards the white board while involuntary words speak slowly out of my mouth. "There are three classifications of sorceress..." Simultaneously I write with a blue marker.

**3 KINDS OF SORCERESS**

**GATEKEEPER**

**EXPERIMENTER**

**INVISIBLE**

Over my shoulder I innocently ask, "Which sort of sorceress does your wizard wish to speak with?" Then I turn to face the men, earnestly expecting their answer.

To be radically honest, patches of sweat are breaking out in various parts of my anatomy at this moment. But my breath is steady, and my heart seems relaxed, which is the most frightening observation of all.

I refuse to allow this conversation to proceed further without my requested clarification.

I wait.

The room crackles with silence.

Finally Snake-Eyes depetrifies. "I think this is the exact question the wizard was hoping to hear," he says. "Will you meet the wizard with us tomorrow morning at seven?"

"No. I will meet the wizard privately this evening at seven. Without any of you. And without any recording or transmitting devices on my person. That equipment breaks down and becomes useless in a wizard's intensity field, anyway."

What follows is the kind of undefinable silence you might find at the center of a pyramid, or the instant a male stripper pops out of the cake at a nun's birthday party. Whether or not the original meeting agenda should continue is, fortunately, not my problem. I say, "Please leave the address with Mr. Tutor," as I exit stage left.

The remainder of the day flies by as unnoticed as late autumn leaves. Clocks move entirely too fast for my soul to stay present in the current 'now'. I depart for home at my earliest convenience to face my real problem: What do I wear? I don't own any sorceress outfits.

Hollywood is famous for being edgy. But sorceress is not edgy. It is other-worldly. The theme does not match any of the subcultures I visit. It's time to call Eva.

I've known Eva since my days at Next Culture News. My favorite Eva scene is filming a sequence where she is supposed to flip open her old-model mobile phone like Captain Kirk's communicator, and the phone refuses to comply. She tries over and over in total disbelief that the thing won't cooperate with her. We've watched the bloopers so many times and always roll on the floor hysterically. In the video she's so flustered you can read her mind. She keeps insisting to herself, *If Captain Kirk can do it, then I can do it!* But she can't. It is hilarious.

It's particularly hilarious because Eva can do everything else. I never figured out how such a small person can have so much practical life experience and raw creation power crammed inside. But she does.

I call Eva. Not even a nanosecond passes before she says, "You should wear almost nothing. Keep it utterly simple. Wear something that shows you need not defend yourself with clothing. You are perfect, Gwendolyn. You are already a sorceress. I never told you this before, but it's so obviously true. You are the Lady of the Lake."

"Can you say more about that, please?"

Eva takes a breath. I can hear her Gaia connection hum as it connects all the way down into the center of the Earth and starts conducting high voltage consciousness. "The Lady of the Lake is the sorceress who brings back Excalibur, the sword, and hands it to King Arthur, after he has flung it into the lake out of hopeless despair. This sword is a treasure of inestimable worth, but she can give the sword freely back to the transformed man because she does not need a sword. The Lady of the Lake IS a sword.

"She has so much presence and attention, already uses so many multi-dimensional resources, that a sword is too slow, heavy, and cumbersome in comparison. But she looks for allies. The world is deeply in need of teams of healing and transformational agents these days. The lone-wolf strategy is outdated, stupid actually. That single-fighter approach was developed so that the divide-and-conquer techniques used by patriarchal elites could no longer work, due to there being no more teams to divide.

"Now we know too much. Edgeworker teams have learned how to avoid being hooked by mere intrigue. We grab underworld creatures by the scruff of the neck and lay them on the table for all to dissect into their component assumptions, expectations, conclusions, beliefs, and hidden purposes.

"Teams can come together now without fear of betrayal. Your wizard is probably looking for a team player. I think you are going to a job interview, Gwendolyn. In such a case, it is best to reverse the game and make the interview from your side."

See! That is Eva. The original sinner. Everyone should have an 'Eva' they can call upon in inexplicable urgencies!

Everyone should be so lucky as to have inexplicable urgencies!

But it shocks me that Eva called me 'Gwendolyn', my birth name, the name that is printed in my passport, in other words, my actual name. Before now, that name was too formal for me to wear, too serious. No one has called me Gwendolyn but international border control agents.

Now, for the first time in my life, calling myself 'Gwendolyn' rings true.

I respond to the treasures bestowed upon me by saying, "The sorceress Gwendolyn thanks the sorceress Eva."

"Stay fierce," she says.

# Eugene, Oregon 4

Two months pass. Davis Hatcher and Sanjib Hajji, his patrol partner, just graduated from Police Academy Basic Training and are on their first cruise through Eugene together. As Davis drives them along 18th Avenue, he glances out Sanjib's window at the famous Pioneer's Cemetery where Police Captain Henry Hatcher had pulled strings to get himself and his wife buried side by side. Over seven-hundred people came to the funeral. Davis knew almost none of them, but so many smiled at him with knowing nods. It was creepy. Perhaps it was because Davis had come to the funeral in full dress uniform?

Sanjib notices the glance. "Your father was one of the pioneers of anti-corruption in this town. It is he who forced the department to finally let me take the qualification tests."

"I thought it was your charming sense of humor, and your cool Q-tip hat!"

"Hey! It is too nice a day for Muslim jokes."

"If not that, then I thought it was your last name."

"Hajji?"

"Gesundheit!"

Sanjib moans and rolls his eyes.

Davis quotes from an article he once read: "The most influential factor in a person's choice of religion is the religion of their parents."

This is probably not the best way to start a long-term professional relationship, but it comes out faster than Davis can think. Sanjib is his officially assigned partner, or even more worryingly, that he is assigned as Sanjib's partner. In either case, Davis's next comment sprays gasoline on the fire. "Just please convince me you are not a fanatical raghead. I don't want to drive around embarrassed."

"Can you convince me that your fear of my turban does not derive from politically manipulated mainstream news?"

"You are changing the subject! What I am afraid of is that you cannot answer my question without resorting to fantasy-world beliefs."

"You just drove through a red light."

"It was still yellow, and you are trying to change the subject again."

"You want to know what's up with my turban?"

"Yes. No bullshit."

"Wearing this turban signifies my...

"That's already bullshit Sanjib! Are you a police officer? Are you American? Are you a slave-drone of some fanatical patriarchal religion? I don't know what you are!"

"You nearly dinged that car!"

"Again you change the subject! But you are right... Look, my hands are shaking... Will you drive so I can go crazy? I need to go through this, Sanjib."

Davis taps the emergency flasher button, stops in the middle of the busy road, sets the parking brake, and opens the door before Sanjib can answer. They get out and wordlessly trade places. The car's engine still rumbles.

After the doors slam shut, Davis speaks first. "Can I keep asking you questions?"

Sanjib fastens his seatbelt, adjusts the rearview mirror and the fit of his turban. "Put your seatbelt on first. Then, yes." He slowly accelerates the patrol car to cruise speed, then turns off the flashers.

Davis says, "I thought you were studying history. Why did you apply to the Police Academy?"

Sanjib glances into the white boy's reddening face. "You want the truth?"

"I do," says Davis, shocking himself with the physical memory of saying those exact words in a young man's naïve wedding vows 'til death do us part' which lasted only one year, and luckily without her getting pregnant. He shakes his head to get present. "Yes, please tell me the truth."

"I became a raghead police officer to understand how my turban-wearing father could be killed by a policeman while innocently walking down the street of a city as progressive as Eugene, Oregon."

No words pass either man's lips for many blocks. Davis is glad not to be driving. The fingers of his right-hand fiddle nervously with the grip of his Austrian-made Glock 22. Its fifteen .40 caliber bullets wait in the clip to fire one after another, as fast as he can pull the trigger. *What should I do now? Shoot this guy before he shoots me as revenge for his Dad?*

Davis shakes his head to shove his shadow-world back into the closet. He looks at Sanjib. "I'm sorry that happened." The words sound feeble to the point of meaningless.

Sanjib says nothing.

"I still need to talk about this stuff, Sanjib. Maybe not now. But I gotta talk it over. Can this be okay between us? That we talk over stuff like this? Otherwise, how are we gonna stick together through what's coming?"

Sanjib glances momentarily at Davis, then back to the road. He takes a deep breath. "I don't know what's coming. I don't think you do either. Talking is good. I am looking for real answers too. I don't have many."

It's Davis's turn to sigh. Outside the window a radiant spring morning rolls by. Dew-bows sparkle from sunlight shining through millions of tiny droplets of water still clinging to the blades of grass. The air smells so fresh that, for a moment, one could imagine that the human race is headed for a joyful future together on planet Earth.

After a silent while Davis clicks through his play list and selects the theme from *Beverly Hills Cop*. As the tunes fill the space of the cop car, Davis' head starts bopping around. "Is this the life? Or what?" he says.

The two young officers hunker down in their cruiser, wearing police uniforms with police badges and carrying police weapons, feeling very cool in their professional occupation. They gaze protectively out at the busy citizens of their fine town of Eugene, Oregon, one of the most revolutionary towns in the world.

Turning right from West 7th Avenue onto Washington Street and then left onto West Broadway, Davis catches the eye of a straight-brown-haired woman in her late twenties dressed in blue jeans and a purple sweater. She gives him the furtive glance of someone not wanting you to see that they see that you see them, exactly the wrong kind of glance to give a police officer on patrol.

"Did you see that?" Davis looks quickly at Sanjib and sees that he did not, but does now. The brown-haired girl vanishes through the front door of the Horsehead Bar.

"Nice chick! Yes!" says Sanjib, trying to imitate the American style of speaking.

"No! I mean yes! But a woman like her should not be going into a place like that at a time like this! Pull over! Something is going on. Didn't you see the way she glanced at us."

"Oh. I understand. Official business. Criminal investigation of a chick with a nice butt suspiciously entering a building. Good use of public trust. Should I call this in?"

"No. Pull over. Stay here and I will check this out." Davis unbelts and puts his police hat on.

"Sanjib is not waiting in car while partner checks out good-looking chick in bar! I go with you. For public safety."

"Sanjib! A little trust in your partner's 'cop intuition' would be in order, don't you think? Especially on our first day of patrolling?"

"No."

They both get out of the cop car.

Sanjib unholsters his semi-automatic and double-checks to make sure a round is in the chamber.

"Sanjib! Put that thing away!" Davis whispers fiercely. "Are you nuts?"

"I'm not chasing girl without proper protection. Sometimes black widows are dyed white."

"This is a friendly little visit from the local police to ensure the peace! We know nothing!"

"Exactly. I rest my case," says Sanjib without any hint of a smile. He holds his pistol with two hands pointed downwards near his left waist and follows Davis.

Davis strides up the three stairs and into the door first, gently switching to his strong eye. Outside in daylight he had closed his right eye to start relaxing his iris and letting his retina's rods and cones adjust to darkness, navigating up the steps with his left eye only. When entering the bar, he simultaneously closes his left eye and opens his right eye so he can instantly see in the shadowy interior, at least with his right eye... his gun-aiming eye. It is an old police trick Henry taught him as a teenager. Henry told him that not using this practice had killed a few good men. Davis believes him.

Pushing through an interior curtain and peering around, Davis sees nothing unusual.

"Morning gents," says a rough tenor from somewhere near the toilets. The bar itself is untended, although two early drinkers are making sure the bar does not fall over of its own accord. "This establishment is not on your usual route, officers. What can I do for you on this fine morning? Something up?" The bony bartender pauses in his table-wiping duties, backlighted by a high window, the bar's only natural light source. His stained white apron swings loosely on his bony hips in the gloom.

"Just a random hello," says Davis. "There was a young brown-haired woman who came in here just a moment ago. Is she a regular?"

There is a pause as the bartender straightens up to scrutinize what might be going down here. His silence comes more from a lack of information than from the nervousness of someone trying to hide something. "I don't mean to contradict you fellas, but I was over here wipin' up last night's drool puddles and I didn't notice a thing."

"I'm sure I saw her come in here," Davis affirms, glancing back at the entrance, also at Sanjib, who neither says nor does anything. "Maybe she went to the lady's room?"

The wary barkeep senses a potential conflict between the perception of the cops and his own. Knowing that police habitually stipulate that their version of reality prevails, the streetwise barkeep neither looks away nor moves. "If you gents feel the deep need to visit the ladies' room, be my guest. It's over there. I won't report it to the police..."

The drinkers sense explosive tensions rising, become stone-cold silent, turn to face the two young officers.

"C'mon, Davis," says Sanjib. "Let's go."

Davis is paralyzed between the rage of a hunting dog being yanked back from tracking a promising scent, and the fear of having just seen a ghost. Is the fabric of reality torn open in this little corner of town? Or isn't it? What had he actually seen, anyway?

Davis looks down, disengaging from the barkeep. "Yeah," he says, pawing his right foot on the wooden floor like a bull deciding whether or not to charge. "Maybe it was a glitch in the program." No one comments on his bizarre segway phrase. He turns towards the door.

"We'll be moving along now," Sanjib tells the barkeep. "Thanks for the information. Have a nice day." He gently guides Davis by the elbow.

They return to daylight, blinking in the brightness. The door bangs shut behind them. Sanjib observes that Davis's face is several shades whiter than before they entered.

"I'll keep driving," he says.

# Aleppo, Syria 6

Zenobia Darwish's *Beep! Book* – 25 September 2012

Next morning in the circle, after logistics, Montassar reads, "We start the next chapter in the *Handbook*. It is titled: *Gameworlds*.

I copy some sentences here.

*Few realizations are as profound as recognizing that human interactions occur through gameworlds. Without this distinction, you are essentially powerless to heal or transform the interactive environments of your life: at work, at home, or in the world. Gaining the awareness and skills to design, cavitate, build, inhabit, transform, and demolish gameworlds is a central part of Archan education.*

*Think about this question for a moment... Why don't you already know about gameworlds? If understanding gameworlds is as important as we claim, why haven't you ever learned about gameworlds in a class at school? Why isn't the word 'gameworld' already part of your everyday vocabulary?*

Farhan decides to try to answer the question. "If a gameworld is a structure for social interactions, then it is part of our daily life, and becomes a form of life, a life-form, like an animal or a plant. The thing that an animal or plant wants to do is to live, to survive. If a gameworld is a living organism, then it also wants to survive. It wants to defend itself against being messed with. If I learn that a gameworld is just a 'gameworld', if I learn how to redesign a gameworld, or how to end a gameworld altogether from the inside, then the gameworld regards me as being dangerous. I become a threat to the existence of any gameworld I encounter. I become like a droid mechanic who can disassemble any robot and put all the parts on a shelf. I am like Dr. Frankenstein who can sew together new gameworlds out of the rotting parts I dig out of the ground from dead gameworld graveyards in the middle of the night..."

"Yuck!" shouts Mitzi. "That's gross and disgusting!"

"But wait, Mitzi!" interrupts Farhan. "With these same skills we can also invent new gameworlds that never existed before on Earth! We can give each other totally new possibilities by building beautiful, excellent, wonderful new gameworlds, whatever we need, whatever we can imagine. What about that?"

"Well..." considers Mitzi. "Okay. But you are going to have to prove it to me!"

We all laugh.

Israa takes over. "If I was a government, for example, or a corporation, or a religion, or an army... I would certainly not want my disciples or soldiers or clients or citizens to be able to take me apart. I would try to suppress any kind of personal initiative, or power of invention. I would lie to the readers of my newspapers and make threats to keep them scared, weak, and confused. But, shit! This is exactly what is happening... isn't it?..." Suddenly Israa starts crying. "My brothers and my parents joined different gameworlds and suddenly they hated each other. They tore our family apart because none of us knew that ISIS, the Free Syrian Army, and Assad's Army are just stupid gameworlds... gameworlds which are willing to do anything to the humans so long as the gameworld survives..."

Montassar blurts out, "This is mind-boggling... and eye-opening! It's like a blind person suddenly being able to see for the first time in their life! The world does not look the same to me anymore. And if it does not look the same, it will not work the same either. We are gaining new clarity, and new clarity creates new power to create new results."

I keep writing what the Handbook says:

*The term 'gameworld' is a distinction.*

*Not knowing that a distinction exists does not mean this distinction is not seriously influencing your life.*

*Each gameworld has a context, values, rules of engagement (how to play the game), traditions, purpose, and an intended outcome.*

*For example, if you walk into a café gameworld, the first thing you need to learn is the rules of engagement. Are you supposed to order and pay at the counter and then carry your coffee to the table yourself? Or are you supposed to sit down at a table and the waitress comes to give you a menu? Or do you wait at the door until a head waiter brings you to a free table that they choose for you? How does the game go?*

*Or consider the 'post office'. The way to play in a post office gameworld is to read the sign posted on the outside of the post office and then bring your package to the post office building during official hours. Inside you stand silently in a single-file line (minimum 20 minutes...) until you get close to the front desk, where possibly one of the government workers decides to help you. They give you a form to fill out with pen and ink in the proper way, including the postal code, then you pay what the Postal Clerk asks. Then, "Neither snow nor rain nor heat nor gloom of night" slows the couriers from delivering your mail. The purpose of the post office gameworld is to make a profit. How do you know? Because if the post office delivers your mail on time but does not make a profit, the government shuts down or privatizes the postal service.*

*You might want to pay the post office with a credit card. But 'credit card' is a different gameworld! How do you play the gameworld called credit card? You hand the clerk behind the cash register a plastic card with your name and account number on it, and a microchip inside. Then the credit card company transfers numbers from its account into the post office's bank account. However, to play in the gameworld of credit card you must already be playing in the gameworld called 'bank account'.*

*In order to play in the 'bank account' gameworld you must first be playing in the 'earning money to survive' gameworld'.*

*How do you play in the earning money gameworld? Money is a religion. To play in the money gameworld you need to believe that certain papers and coins, and more recently, digits in a computer program, have value. Then you have to acquire some of these papers or digits.*

*How do you acquire money papers or digits? One way is to make an agreement with someone else who already has money to give you a certain amount of it per hour if you do whatever they tell you to do, even if you do not like what you are doing, which forces you into the role of being a slave or a zombie. Other ways to get money include spending your time and attention trying to own properties whose 'value increases', or to win at gambling games such as trading stocks and options, or investing in digital currencies or non-fungible tokens.*

*The earning money to survive gameworld has the purpose of making profits for corporation gameworlds, and for 'paying taxes' to the government gameworld, so that the government can pay people to work in the post office gameworld.*

*Most gameworlds in modern culture play win-lose games. Because human population has increased far beyond the carrying capacity of planet Earth, Gaia is losing. Win-lose is the wrong game to play against your life support system.*

*The gameworld called 'soccer' was fathered by Ebenezer Morley, a participant in the 'lawyer' gameworld, who lived in the 'Hull, England' gameworld. Ebenezer was the founder of the 'Barnes Football Club' gameworld. His letter to the 'Bell's Life' newspaper gameworld (delivered, no doubt, by the 'post office' gameworld...) initiated a meeting on 26 October 1863 at the 'Freemason's Tavern' gameworld on Great Queen Street in the 'London' gameworld, where representatives from twelve 'Sports Club' gameworlds first codexed the rules of engagement of the gameworld called 'Soccer'.*

*If you change even one rule of engagement in a gameworld, you create an entirely new gameworld. For example, the gameworld of soccer ordinarily uses one ball and two teams. If you add a second ball, or a third team, or if you allow players to use bicycles, or whips, or if you add that each team can bring in one wild animal, it would change the soccer gameworld entirely.*

*This means that all players in a gameworld must agree to play by the rules of engagement of a gameworld, or they are not permitted to play in that gameworld. Why? Because, if you put a tennis player into a soccer team and you end up with a net across the field.*

*The gameworld of soccer is a win-lose game. Whichever team puts the greatest number of balls into a net at the far side of a field within a specified amount of time, 'wins' the game. But! The people who really 'make a profit' from the soccer gameworld are the owners of the 'soccer team corporation' gameworld, the 'sports insurance' gameworld, the 'television and media advertisers' gameworlds, the 'soccer merchandising' gameworlds, and the owners of the 'sports gambling' gameworlds, legal or illegal.*

*You make up a gameworld, step into its rules of engagement, and within seconds you start behaving as if the rules of engagement are true! Your mind 'snaps' into the storyworld of the rules of engagement even though just a moment before you arbitrarily created the rules of engagement out of nothing!*

*If you do not know that a gameworld is a 'gameworld', then you think it is reality.*

*(It is not.)*

*If you think that a gameworld is real, then you behave as if you are imprisoned in the gameworlds of your life.*

*(You are not.)*

*Culture is a gameworld. Race is a gameworld. Status is a gameworld. A country is a gameworld.*

*You support the values of every gameworld you play in.*

*If you are unconscious of the values of the gameworlds you play in, you are a 'zombie', the walking dead.*

*Either you consciously design each gameworld you participate in, or you are a pawn in someone else's gameworld.*

*Psychopaths need pawns in their gameworlds... millions of them.*

*Taking radical responsibility for consciously designing, building, and inhabiting the gameworlds you live in gives you so much freedom of movement that you become a possibilitator, an edgeworker, a riftwalker, a gameworld builder.*

*Is WhatsApp a gameworld? Yes. Is a family a gameworld? Yes. A marathon run? A grocery store? A movie production team? A blues band? A SCUBA Diving club? A bicycle repair shop? The Roman Empire? A permaculture farm? Girl Scouts? Yes. Banks, multinational corporations, armies, churches, public schools, governments, NGOs, police forces, 'economic realities', and Starbucks franchises? Yes. Each and every gameworld is unique, yet each and every gameworld is built out of the same components: its context, its rules of engagement, its codex, and its semi-permeable membrane that distinguishes who is 'in' and who is 'out'. Each gameworld is just as arbitrary and no more 'hard reality' than a few children setting up a temporary 'cowboys and indians' playspace gameworld.*

*All gameworlds are temporary.*

*Realizing that Western Civilization's 'institutions' are mere gameworlds is a wake-up call to realize that you have been giving your center and your authority away to false assumptions, to habitual thinking, to imaginary constructs.*

*The capitalist patriarchal empire's gameworlds have enslaved the minds and hearts of most human beings for ten thousand years. Does this prove that patriarchal gameworlds are the 'real' gameworlds? No. It proves that uninitiated human beings are gullible and naïve.*

*By using the distinction 'gameworld', you gain the power to choose wisely about the gameworlds you play in. You also gain the power to build new gameworlds that make existing gameworlds irrelevant.*

*Who can create and own a gameworld? Any group of three or more gameworld builders.*

*The power of using the distinction 'gameworld' is that it makes the global playing field equal. Anyone who has the awareness, talent, and commitment to build a gameworld can build a legitimate gameworld. Even if only three people in the entire world have ever heard of, or participated in, a particular gameworld, it is still a legitimate gameworld, as legitimate (or perhaps more legitimate...) than any corporation, religion, army, sports team, or nation state.*

*Right now, in this time in human history, we human beings seriously need both personal evolution and cultural evolution. Building and occupying evolutionary, regenerative, nonmaterial-value gameworlds contexted in radical responsibility and centered on authentic adulthood initiatory processes could be your contribution to, and your bridge to, next culture – Archiarchy.*

*To update R. Buckminster Fuller's quote, we say, "You never change things by fighting against the existing gameworlds. You change things by building new regenerative nonmaterial value gameworlds that make the existing gameworlds irrelevant."*

*Mr. Fuller originally said that building new gameworlds makes the existing gameworlds 'obsolete'... but by now it should be nauseatingly obvious that existing gameworlds are already obsolete!*

*Do you want to create a gameworld where you can work, play, and be with a like-minded team of social entrepreneurs, initiators, edgeworkers, and change agents?*

*Are you hesitating to start your gameworld because you are confused about whether it is a training center, an alternative school, an unconference, a nanonation, an educational healing community, or a not-for-profit?*

*You've probably heard the phrase (from the film* Field Of Dreams*): "Build it and they will come."*

*What you might not have heard is: "If you don't build it, nobody ever has a chance to come!"*

*By building a gameworld, you take a stand for what you have taken a stand for by being born.*

*Your gameworld is a platform where other people can co-create with you the more beautiful world your heart knows is possible!*

*Don't be left behind playing in a stupid gameworld.*

*Welcome to the real world.*

After this day, life suddenly becomes so rich and wonderful that I don't write much of anything in my *Beep! Book* for the next eleven years.

# Langley, Virginia 1

Deep in the bowels of the CIA's Langley Strategic Center, Jason Spade adjusts his tie for the eighth time in five minutes, glancing nervously at the wall clock over the door. He still can't believe how slow that clock moves. He suspects it houses a hidden surveillance camera.

Fifteen minutes later, while jacking the projector into his laptop and powering it up, his mind tries to figure out how deep beneath Langley this spacious but nearly empty cement-walled meeting room is, but he cannot assess the elevator's descent velocity. He hates not knowing.

He nods nervously to the Corps woman who delivered his bottle of Perrier, which stands bubbling but untouched before him. Jason swallows in a dry mouth. Part of his mind flashes high-speed scenarios where this meeting ends to his great benefit, meaning, of course, to the great benefit of GlobeScan, the company that presently owns him.

At the same time, another part of his mind aggressively tries to convince him to run like hell. He lucidly imagines detailed scenarios depicting how tangling with the CIA's nameless and self-funded assassination programs can quickly turn into a lethal nightmare. *Hell, it's already a lethal nightmare!* he grimly thinks to himself.

Although Jason's expertise is programming next-gen drone swarm-fare, he spent most of his recent time traveling in unmarked military aircraft to exotic lands making presentations to high-powered decision-makers with unlimited budgets in low-profile organizations. Last week's meet in Libya still generates daytime nightmares whenever he considers the possibility that they might implement his proposal. If you asked him, Jason would quickly confirm that things are definitely out of hand in the global arena of high-profit warfare.

Three decorated Generals enter the conference room along with a plain clothes woman in her late thirties. The Generals move like Hannibal's battle-worn elephants. The woman moves like an ice ghost. Just his style...

The Generals are present without military entourage, something Jason has never witnessed before. The woman carries no purse and wears no badge. This can only indicate *penta*-secrecy, off-record military witchcraft. They shake his hand perfunctorily without offering names. This confirms his suspicion.

The armed guard who had escorted him down the elevator closes the fire-proof steel door from outside after one last man enters the room. 'This must be Karl Thomsen, CIA,' thinks Jason, remembering his briefing at GlobeScan. The tanned, athletic fifty-something does not sit.

"Good morning my friends," Thomsen says in a voice so buttery it could convince a grandma to give away her secret brownie recipe. "I hope our early meeting time is not too strenuous for you. We all have busy schedules, and as the ancients knew, four a.m. is the quietest hour of the day. Excellent for careful thinking. I suggest that Jason's presentation will be stimulating enough to keep us awake, but I can ring for coffee if anyone wishes."

Jason shudders as a chill shoots down his spine. No introductions. No one besides him requesting a drink. A hyper-discipline space. Jason has no idea how to navigate this protocol. All the more embarrassing with every eye on him.

For a moment there is dead silence except the purified air wheezing through ventilators.

"I'll get to the point," starts Jason, wishing that the woman would smile at him just once. He sighs nervously, clicks his touchpad to project the first slide, trying to focus on delivering his infodeck with maximum effectiveness. "The data from the new internet keyword sampling rovers are finally being matrixed with global face-tagging from Facebook, TikTok, 'X', and Instagram, and voice recognition from whatever phone traffic funnels through tapped satellite repeaters. We scan for intention vectors by distilling purpose from outcome to catch malicious actions earlier and earlier. We now have enough hard data to confirm that the Exodus Theory holds water."

"'Scuse me Jason," Thomsen slices into the flow like a surgeon with a samurai sword. "Are all of you familiar with Exodus? Two months ago, a team at MIT suggested we were overlooking early stages of exponential citizenship withdrawal. More and more Americans have stopped voting, stopped paying taxes, credit card bills, car payments, insurance, and rent. Sixty-five per cent of these renegades are unemployed. About fifty-eight per cent rescind their U.S. passports, and fifty-three per cent leave the country. The most common new passports are for Panama, Nicaragua, South America, some Caribbean islands, Ireland, Thailand, Laos, and Vietnam. A few are swapping their U.S. passports for membership in the fictitious nation of Lakota. Almost no one requests dual citizenship.

"The Occupy movement has drifted from standing against present hierarchies to standing for something we cannot yet define. That is the purpose of this meeting: to develop strategic plans for countering Exodus.

"If Exodus is allowed to exceed a tipping point, civilization as we know it cannot be reconstituted. Welcoming Mexicans and South Americans across our southern borders, and flying in Afghans and Iraqis by the tens of thousands appears to be insufficient to offset our losses. We may be forced to implement more Draconian measures, use the FEMA camps, and so on. We would rather keep the American Dream-show going strong so as to save lives. Jason's firm proposes to... well Jason, you explain."

Jason smiles, thinking, 'He gives me the jugular! I owe him one...' Then he begins his prepared speech. "With reparsed GlobeScan data we can profile the leadership in Exodus, the people behind blogs and webinars, people establishing alternate currencies, barter circles, and gift economies. Our fast-search algorithm identifies these anti-American culture-terrorists and tracks their real-time location. As shown in this graphic, taking out a few key elements cuts down the whole web. The tool of choice would be the Anubis micro-drone from AeroVironment. This advanced MAV provides streaming video through microwave communications plus sensors and data links for automatic target-tracking using face and RFID recognition, GPS cell-phone triangulation, and night-imaging cameras. It accurately delivers a munitions payload to fleeting targets in complex non-line-of-sight urban environments with minimal collateral damage."

One of the military men clears his throat. "We've been using Anubis in dark ops for two years..."

"Of course, General. Munitions is your field," says Jason. "What GlobeScan provides is the software for simultaneously releasing thousands of drones and using their parallel inputs as multiple swarm intelligences. Think about it, General. In one day, we could take out your top thousand terrorists, the same way King Philip devastated the *Knights Templar* at dawn on Friday, 13 October 1307."

The idea startles the third General to suddenly stand and pace the room, fingering his bushy mustache. "We could actually put a stop to this whole damn thing in one fell swoop," he comments in a tone of relief, more to himself than anyone else.

"Don't get trigger happy, General!" the female plainclothes interrupts with an incordiality that leads Jason to assume she is also CIA. "You might be moving full force against a fata-morgana, or worse yet, a tar-baby, like Iraq." She glances for a millisecond to Thomsen who plays a perfect poker face, which she seems to decode as permission to proceed. "I propose we pick up a couple consultants from the other side. Someone intimate with their tactics and operations."

Jason speaks before he can think. "Can we help you profile proper search spiders for collecting candidates?" This is the question that saves his ass. There was no time to think this out. Anyone needing time to think would have missed the opening and lost the job. Jason realizes this is why GlobeScan keeps inserting him into promo-meetings: his spontaneous verbal ejaculations of pure genius generate pure gold. *I should double my fee*, he thinks.

The female CIA stares Jason down for a full three seconds. *Green*, he observes elatedly. *She has green eyes!* He stares back unwaveringly, giving her no ground.

"By when could you launch?" she demands.

"With your cooperation, we could shift strategies by day after tomorrow, and launch in a few weeks."

"We could implement full x rating," Thomsen confirms.

This scene freezes in Jason's mind. *A new future is being born, right here, with this one decision. If Thomsen says, 'No,' then the priority drops five tiers, I am on the next plane to Timbuktu, the Generals and CIA go home, and business here continues as usual. But if he says, 'Yes'...*

# Possibilica, Florianópolis 2

"We'd like to harvest trees out of your forest. We can pay you a good sum." He is medium build, slightly chunky, wearing a blue suit but no tie, smiling superficially. He isn't accustomed to standing on unpaved Earth.

"You are offering to give us money in exchange for our trees?"

"Yes. And at a fair price, too."

"I appreciate that you are making this offer. I see that it makes good sense to you."

"Yes, it does. Very good sense. Then you can replant with fast-growing eucalyptus to harvest in a few years for toilet paper, or pine for Ikea furniture. You could have a very lucrative cash-crop here."

"What I am thinking is that in the previous thirty years or so, it has become common for modern people to assume that there is a single modern globalized culture on Earth. But it turns out not to be true. There are an expanding multitude of diverse cultures on Earth. In this moment you are a man thinking in the values of one culture, speaking to a man who lives in the values of quite a different culture. Many regard their own cultural values as universally true. From where I stand, I see our two cultural values being remarkably different. Each set has its own consequences." The second man pauses speaking to listen for any intelligible responses from the first man.

"Unnnhh..." is all the first man can say.

The second man continues. "You have offered to pay us money for our trees. We use a different currency here than your money. There is no exchange rate between your currency and our currency. Your money is absolutely worthless here. I propose that instead of telling me the price of a thing, you tell me what you want to create. Tell me what you want to build for the benefit of the world. Tell me what you want your life to be about. In this paradigm we can relate. Modern culture economics is a false paradigm. I will not relate to you in a false paradigm. If you tell me what you truly want, I can perhaps give you something that will help you have what you want. If what you want is noble, brave, creative, inspiring, and full of integrity, then, by contributing to you getting what you want, I am ennobled, encouraged, delighted and inspired. If what you want is selfish, manipulating, small-minded, irresponsible, or greedy, then I would be harming myself if I help you. Tell me what you want."

"Well... uh... I don't quite understand..."

"If my village is nurtured by what you want, you could be the seed crystal for our next creative evolution. Perhaps it is you we have been waiting for to spark our deep wishes and unfold a new aspect of our bright and emergent future. On the other hand, if what you want tries to externalize true costs so as to create the illusion of what you might be calling 'profit' for your personal, short-term benefit, then you have not yet grown up. You have failed your rite of passage to adulthood."

"Just a minute now! Give me a chance here! Look at how your people are living in this poor village. No paved streets. No cars. No hamburger joints. No bars. People carrying buckets of water by hand. Pardon me for saying it, but look at your clothes. Your shoes? It's embarrassing. How can you really enjoy life in these conditions?"

"What are you offering me from your cultural value system?"

"If you take my money, you get a chance to buy some cars and tractors, pave the streets, get new clothes, mobile phones. You'd have money to eat at restaurants, go out to movies. You can have a nice house, doctors, medicines and public schools. You could travel..."

"I find it most interesting, these differences of perception between you and me. You sound like an electric heater salesman in the Sahara Desert. You are trying to make me believe I am cold when I am sweating. Nothing you say is the least bit attractive to me. We have fresh spring water out of the mountain to drink here, now that we have stopped corporate agriculture from pumping down the aquifers. The water is clean now that we stopped agribusinesses from using GMO crops, chemical fertilizers, and pesticides around here. Our healers focus on healing rather than quarterly stock reports. Compared to our village education, your schools are thought-prisons designed to keep people weak and stupid. I almost never use a mobile phone. I have the time in my day to stroll about and speak with anyone I want to talk to without subjecting myself to the possibility of brain tumors. Tonight is the town theater performance. I can't wait. I get to play the Ghost of Captain Tomorrow. These clothes I wear were not made by child labor sweatshops in third world slave colonies. I made them myself, by my own hands, out of locally grown materials."

"Yes, but you need money to live!"

"I need money to live?"

"Yes, you need money to buy food, to buy things for your house! For your children to get a good education!"

"It is unbelievable to me that you would be so enthusiastic about such an arrangement! I try to imagine what it must be like to wake up each morning with a gnawing in my guts that if I don't make enough money, I will be kicked out onto the streets to starve alone and cold and die under a bridge. In your culture, people work at jobs to get money rather than working to deliver their beneficial gifts to the people of their village. Is it truly satisfying for you to do what others higher up in the hierarchy tell you to do, even if you don't want to do it, just to get money? What happens to your wish to do what you came here to do? I mean, forgive me if I am being rude, but to me that would be a nightmare life. It would squeeze me into a narrow survivalist view where each minute of my time is counted in lost dollars."

"Yes, time is money!"

"Yeah, buddy, maybe in your village time is money. But in our village, time is time. And right now it would be time for coffee."

"You have coffee here? Coffee comes from other parts of South America, or from Vietnam. You need money to import coffee!"

"Actually, Simon grows coffee in our own greenhouses. He is a hero around here, a kind of plant wizard. Many of us help him during harvest time. Did you ever eat fresh-picked coffee berries? They are sweet and delicious. We chew the fruit off then wash and dry the coffee beans for roasting in the solar ovens. An espresso here is something extra-ordinary. Come! You can hand grind your own beans."

"But you said I do not have any money in your currency. How do I pay for my coffee?"

"One of our currencies is creative collaboration during interesting conversations. You've been providing me with ideas for the next chapter in my book. Tara is running the Café today, and she makes this fantastic Walnut Torte. We call forth the walnuts, eggs, honey, and wheat right here. You can tell me what your heart really wants after your belly is full of homemade cake and homegrown coffee."

# San Pedro, California 2



I slide into my red backless silk dress with nothing underneath. Most men have no idea how often women wear nothing underneath. Why should we? We have nothing to hide.

My hands want to strap my braided leather belt low on my hips... but my hands hesitate. The guardians in my leather pouch are already with me in reality. I don't need a bronze figure of Ganesha in order to connect with Ganesha. If I did, he would not be real enough to remove barriers. I slide my belt and pouch into a shoulder bag. It holds my driver's license, passport, and cash.

Arthur gave me Snake-Eyes' business card after he wrote the wizard's latitude and longitude neatly on the back. If I am to believe the card, Snake-Eyes' name is Alexander Edding. I am a person disposed to thinking that each Being has many names for use under various circumstances. *Alexander Edding... you may have a few more surprises headed in your direction.*

I google-map the coordinates and feed them into my navi. The wizard's place is in a warehouse on an old pier sticking out from the San Pedro Salt Marshes. The red pointer floats out over the water.

He does not even live in this country. His house hovers in the air. How appropriate.

I find parking and force myself to walk casually out the pier through the cooling ocean air, pretending as if I do this sort of thing every day. Wooden pilings stink of old creosote. Metallic watery sounds echo under the pier while my guts revolt against the odor of a dead fish that must be floating bloated nearby. A brash seagull sculls over my head, waiting to snatch chunks of bread out of the air. I have no bread, but I send him my sense of his magnificence and beauty. He stays with me in appreciation for a moment, then glides away.

I love the ocean, its depth and breadth, that horizontal line dividing heaven from Earth... a line that dissolves at dusk as the azure gradually takes over. I hate it that human beings are too stupid to realize that our life is over if the ocean dies. Instead, we kill the ocean... don't get me started...

I'm glad to be wearing my running shoes. I have other things to focus on than avoiding slivers in my feet if I should have to remove my high-heels and make a run for it.

I automatically check that I am using the skills I learned at Rage Club. Do I have my center? Yes. My grounding cord? Yes. It is turquoise with sparkling diamonds. Interesting... My bubble of personal culture space? Yes. My golden-framed energetic workspace in which to interview the wizard under my own conditions? Yes. My bright principles? Yes: Love, Possibility, Integrity, Magic.

Okay then. Why am I so afraid? The pier house stands beyond the grip of the ordinary world. My standard assumptions have no fulcrum to leverage against. Out here over the water, mainstream culture loses its rigidly enforced framework and reverts back to primordial meme slime. Memetic Jello... How do I survive in that?

All my years in school did nothing to prepare me for this. Here I am, my first encounter with something that is possibly Real, and I feel like a dust-ball in a hurricane. Maybe this is how it feels to be a sorceress?

Somehow, I doubt it.

But what do I know?

Not much, actually. I know that my watch says it is three minutes before seven p.m. on a Monday evening. I heard a rumor that a wizard wants to speak with a sorceress. Now I climb up the spiral metal stairway on this rusted-out warehouse to knock on what might possibly be a so-called 'wizard's' door.

On the landing I search for video cameras. None. I take one last glance out at the Pacific Ocean. I see two small sailboats and one unmoving cargo ship. I take a deep sea-air breath. A cord hangs there to yank on so that a bronze bell rings. Instead, I knock on the hard steel door. The pain in my knuckles helps me minimize my now.

Stories from the past won't help me now. Worries of future scenarios won't help me now. The only thing that can help me now is being present in this very special, particular and pregnant now. It is easy to find that now. Now is where my knuckles hurt.

Nothing happens. My knuckles still sting. Then I hear muffled steps approaching from the other side of the door. I look at the hinges and notice that the door will open inwards if it opens at all. The door moves without creaking. He stands there not looking into my eyes. He is scanning me.

How do I know he is scanning me? Because as I scan him, my scan reveals that he is scanning me. This implies that his scan of me also reveals to him that I am scanning him.

The wizard bypasses the size and quality of my breasts and instead checks out the size and quality of the matrix I have built in my Being.

Matrix is built out of distinctions. Many breasts these days are built out of silicone. Fortunately or unfortunately, you cannot build matrix out of silicone.

Unlike distinctions, breast implants can rupture or cause Breast

Implant Illness with inexplicable symptoms such as fatigue, memory loss, skin rashes, 'brain fog', and joint pain. That is a distinction.

The more distinctions I weave into the matrix of my Being, the more consciousness my Being can hold. The more silicone implanted into the flesh of a breast, the more chances it has of contracting Breast Implant Illness.

He's a couple inches taller than me. I am five foot ten. This makes him about six feet. But he wears leather boots with almost an inch of heel. I am wearing black running shoes with flat heels. The heels on his boots are leather, not rubber. Hmmmm....

Black dress pants, slightly wrinkled. A long black cotton coat over a golden yellow shirt. No tie.

In those two-seconds of scanning, I don't see much. This means... he could have matrix beyond my ability to perceive.

He could be more awake than I.

Shoulder-length stringy black hair, partially silver. Deep smile wrinkles at the sides of his eyes, but not smiling now. Shaved... Okay! Enough scanning! What I've learned is that it is easy to detect when people are sleeping, but more difficult to tell when they are awake.

"My name is Balthazar Blake. Would you like to step inside?" His voice is steady and measured. He places value in each word.

Test Number One... I put my arm forward to shake hands. "Gwendolyn," I say. "Pleased to meet you." He leaves my hand untouched.

I wanted to kick myself! Here I am speaking with someone who could well be a wizard and I offer him a hackneyed meaningless phrase and a dead custom. 'Pleased to meet you...' Duh! A toad could have said that! Do I feel pleased? No. I feel puzzled, twenty-seven percent afraid, and maybe thirteen percent glad to meet him. Plus, I did not answer his question. I stay still and say, "I'd like to have a do-over..."

He squints slightly but says nothing and does not move. I make a three-hundred-and-sixty-degree turn, not a pirouette, mind you, due to the metallic grill-work of the landing and the rubbery grip of my soles. "Yes. I would like to step inside."

He backs up a pace to let me pass, but keeps facing me. I step into the darker interior.

"You said your name is Gwendolyn."

"Yes. And you said your name is Balthazar."

"Yes," he says with a smile of small amusement curving up the right side of his mouth. "We are already in agreement about what just happened."

He shuts the door behind me, then passes me by to lead us into a compact library surrounded with wooden bookshelves mounted on the walls. In front of me is a large oak table scattered with objects and papers indicating its use as a workbench. A digital clock behind him indicates the time as 19:01, European style time. The shelf of books to my right has a strange hole the size of a small watermelon burned through to the blackened wall. At the far end of the room stands an iron woodstove radiating warmth and light towards a couch and a couple of overstuffed chairs. A doorway cut through the side wall leads to a possible kitchen.

Balthazar steps behind the workbench and pours what looks like water out of a clear blown-glass pitcher into one of the two drinking glasses set on a round wooden tray. He slides the full glass towards me. "Water?" he asks, while pouring the other glass full.

Test Number Two... Do I trust that this man has put nothing but water in the glass?

No. I don't.

I say, "No thank you."

He takes the glass that he slid towards me and drinks it straight down, then pours himself a second dose. "I personally collect this water from a spring in a tiny canyon below the Mount Wilson Observatory. Few people know of its existence. I found it six or seven years ago while gathering herbs. I cleaned out the spring, made a rock spout, and once a week or so since then I collect several gallons of the best drinking water Earth has to offer."

"Alright. I have changed my mind. I would like to have some of Earth's water." I take the other glass and surprise myself by draining its entire contents. Normally I sip my water, but this water is incredibly delicious.

"Thank you," I say. He refills my glass. I roll into my carefully prepared introduction. "I would like to ask you some questions. May we sit here?" I indicate the hard wooden chairs at the workbench rather than the couch and overstuffed chairs.

He nods with a straight face, pulls out his chair and sits. He is not overweight, but he is not thin either. I estimate him to be about fifty-three, quite a bit older than I. The room is silent and dry, brightened by two high windows that let in evening light. He says, "It would be best if you start talking. We may not have as much time as you think."

"Pardon me?" Shit! Another ordinary phrase. "Uh, what do you mean?"

"Please begin with your questions. Our situation will become apparent as soon as you engage."

I don't get it but refuse to be intimidated. I still have my center.

"Why do you need to speak with a sorceress?" I would never have guessed this would be my first question, but as soon as I speak it, it is obviously perfect.

"No one else would understand the gravity of our situation. Plus no one else would have a Being that is fluid enough to accomplish the jobs on our bench."

"Keep going," I say.

He swallows slowly, then looks down at the table, caressing the wood grains lightly with his fingertips. If I am not mistaken, he uses the sensation of the wood texture on his skin the same way I was using the pain in my knuckles, to stay in a very small and precise now. This makes sense for a wizard. Now is where decisions are made. Now is where feelings are palpable. Now is where you can place your attention consciously and perceive your own intuition. Now is the doorway to action. I suddenly have a realization.

I say, "Lesson Number One: Wizards and sorceresses use the same now."

He instantly responds. "The difference is that sorceresses use forces of nature, and wizards use distinctions. I don't think you are a sorceress. I think you are a wizard."

"A female wizard? I never heard of one." I can't believe we are having this conversation.

"That is why I merely asked for a sorceress. The possibility of a female wizard is not commonly known. I feel glad that they gave me you."

"Who gave you me?"

"E.C.C.O."

"What is echo?"

"Please, let us explore that later. Other issues are crucial right now." His eyes never leave my face, while his fingers keep sliding slightly across the wood. "There are so few of us," he says.

His words shock me, as if I lived my entire life wearing a blindfold that he just casually tore off my face. Brilliant light streams into my Being with all its aliveness and colors. Tears start rolling down my cheeks. I can't believe it. My heart suddenly aches. I am, needless to say, disoriented.

"There are so few of us and you have focused only on surviving. You are not yet initiated. Where are your apprentices?" His voice is not accusatory, but rather saturated with grief, and some kind of foreboding. His question is not rhetorical, but I cannot respond.

I am suddenly gripped with the need to vomit. Not by sticking my fingers down my throat. It is a new feeling. It is irrepressible nausea rumbling deep in my guts, coming from a dizzying conflict between the longing of my soul, and what I perceive as the true realities of modern life. This longing is huge and real in me. It has been there forever, yet until now I denied it completely. I grip my stomach moaning.

Balthazar reaches under the workbench and hands me a metal trash can partly filled with papers. I wretch my guts out. He says, "Let the sounds out too, and let your words follow."

I do as he instructs. The sounds are uninhibited rage, snarls and roars fill the room between barfs. I hug the trashcan like a life ring. Then my words come, words of spite, previously unspoken outrage, boundaries I never made to all the unconscious assholes in my life. I never knew I could shout with such accurate precision. But it makes sense. Me and Gretchin are one. Ten minutes of raging, then I lose my orientation and roll off the chair, collapsing towards the floor.

Balthazar is swift enough to grab the trash can out of my hands and put his hand between my head and the edge of the table. He lowers me gently to the floor, then lets go of me completely, crouching at my side.

I gasp for breath. None comes. I grab hold of the woolen carpet and it does not comfort me. I scream and scream in unstoppable reasonless terror. The whole world spins upside-down. I am going to fall off upwards and die, and nothing can prevent this from happening.

Balthazar makes no move to ease my insanity. Neither does he seem afraid. I can feel him being in neutral but supportive contact with me.

I don't know how much time passes. I open my eyes. Balthazar is still there. My dizziness has receded about forty percent. "I don't understand." It is the clearest thing I can say while struggling to a crouch on my feet and sliding back into the wooden chair.

Balthazar hands me some tissues and gently says, "Please wait here." He walks into the kitchen and returns a moment later bearing a tray with two wooden bowls of steaming soup. The hot liquid emits a scent of strong herbs and bone marrow. It must have been cooked for hours. How did he know? He places one bowl in front of me and hands me a small wooden spoon. Medicinal steam rises and surrounds me in healing warmth. I use the spoon to sip the broth. He smiles at me and it suddenly seems as if heaven is real.

After we slurp down half our broth, Balthazar says, "You told me you do not understand. The truly relevant question is this: If you were to understand, would you do anything different?"

He expects no answer.

Nothing else of significance is spoken between us.

Even when I can get onto my feet, my mind does not return. I fit the strap of my bag over my shoulder and shrug at Balthazar, speechless. He says, "I suggest you walk for half an hour before you drive. Here," He indicates a collection of talismans on one of the bookshelves. "I invite you to choose one of these to wear. It may help you dial-up your archetypal lineage."

I numbly select an object from his bookshelf, golden and heavy with curvy tight spirals. I slide its thin black lanyard sloppily over my head. Nothing changes. He says, "That is too low on your chest. You have it on your solar plexus. It should be worn over the channel between your heart and your throat. The string is adjustable. If you move these two knots..."

With inexplicable easefulness my perceptions ping into harmonious resonance and leap out in multiple directions with an astonishingly extended range. My Being relaxes from gaining the agency of these archetypal resources standing behind me and having my back. I involuntarily smile.

Balthazar continues. "I don't need an answer from you, but life probably does. I am obligated to warn you that if you continue inquiring in this direction, the world as you know it will disintegrate. You won't, but the particular personality you created and identified with as 'yourself' will. You may lose some friends who prefer you the old way. This is a hard path to walk, but it has a lot of reality in it. See you around, maybe."

He seems heartless as he guides me to the door.

Somehow, I manage to get down the spiral staircase by breathing in the cold salty air. I walk for forty-five minutes along the San Pedro seashore. No one seems to notice how weird I feel. Light weight, fluid, resilient, dangerous, loving, full of clarity and possibility. Ordinarily I would worry about making maximum use of all these potentials, especially to 'get ahead', to survive better. Now my sense is that the playing field has been completely cleared, so cleared that there aren't any lines on the grass, or opposing goal nets, or even grandstands. There is only the field, and the field is not flat. It opens into more than three dimensions for experimentation, for testing which constructions unleash the most appropriate possibilities.

What surprises me even more is that this does not irritate me.

I wonder why that is. What permits me to accept the intolerable intensity of presence, the unbearable lightness of being?

The only answer I get is that I have met someone who has agency in both vastness and precision, who is friends with both the Everything and the Nothing.

I have been met.

I am no longer alone.

I am no longer bored.

# Salt Lake City, Utah 4

JET opens his gym locker, tosses his backpack inside, then reaches in and carefully draws out his sword. He handles the weapon with respect, as if he values it more than his life, as if it is marvelously alive and must be regarded with total attention. He flexes the foil between both hands, lets it spring back into shape with a twang, then drops into *en garde* position, light on his toes. Suddenly he leaps forward down the aisle, slashing viciously through the air. "Take that Professor P. Thomas Collins, you overstuffed fountain of gobbledygook!"

JET spins deftly around while tossing the sword to his left hand, and slashes his way back through the locker room ending in a double balestra-lunge to the imagined heart.

The sword fighting continues, only now JET is uniformed, helmeted, and dueling a real opponent in fencing class surrounded by fellow students of the blade. Mrs. Singer, his coach, looks on. She is a solidly built woman of thirty-eight, short brown hair, brown eyes set wide on her face. She looks Eastern European, perhaps from Prague. JET parries a sloppy attack, and then lets his opponent walk onto his sword, landing a clean swift touch to the chest.

The buzzer behind him sounds and the teacher signals an end to the bout. The two fencers slide off their protective masks and salute each other, sword to forehead, pro forma.

JET looks completely unruffled, even bored, whereas his 'dead' opponent walks away from the fencing strip flushed and out of breath, still awed by the ease with which he was thrice killed in as many minutes.

Another opponent takes his place, plugging his fencing jacket into the socket on the end of the electric buzzer wire. He challenges JET to a duel by saying, "That's three out of three for you Mr. White Knight, and you're not even breathing hard. How about a real contest?"

JET scans the tall, wiry, bespectacled stranger who wears a slight grin, a challenging demeanor, and most importantly, a sword pointed straight at JET's chest.

Mrs. Singer interrupts. "Class is almost over, Eddy. Maybe this could wait 'til Friday?"

Refusing to lower his sword or even turn his head, Eddy stands as a professional, without complaint but also without compliance. He waits for Mrs. Singer to respond to his unspoken but honorable plea.

She finally relents. "Oh, alright... but make it short. The basketball team needs to practice for tomorrow's game."

Eddy salutes his thanks to her. "Don't worry Mrs. Singer. This won't take but a moment."

JET dodges the insult by flinging one of his own. Imitating the voice of an exasperated mother he says, "Eddy? Eddy! What kind of name is Eddy?"

"And who do I have the honor of skewering this fine afternoon?" asks Eddy.

JET bows with his sword held to his forehead in salute, but keeps his eyes on the center of Eddy's chest. "John Emmet Tumble, at your service. My enemies call me JET."

"Well then, Mr. Jet Plane. Shall we make this a bit more interesting?" Eddy detaches the buzzer wire from his electrified jacket and lets it auto-wind along the strip back into its roller. A huge smile grows across JET's face as he wordlessly does the same. Then JET drops his mask to the floor, kicks it to the side, and crouches into ready position. "*En garde, monsieur!*"

Eddy accepts the challenge, flings away his own mask, and begins with a running attack shouting enthusiastically. "*Allez!*"

Eddy's press forces JET off the strip and into onlookers from the fencing class. They scream in simultaneous protest and delight.

Mrs. Singer desperately shouts, "No!"

Clearly her command is too little, too late.

JET crashes backwards between two men who then shove each other. Eddy spins between them, stabbing one harmlessly but insultingly in the crotch as he passes, and whipping the other on the butt. The men don their face masks, and a second duel begins.

JET and Eddy circle each other around the group, trying to get the advantage one over the other, simultaneously rousing the entire crowd into a raucous frenzy of free-for-all swordplay. It is pirate time!

At that moment the basketball team bursts into the gymnasium, bouncing a dozen balls into the turmoil of swinging blades and shouting swordfighters.

JET backs Eddy against the shoulder-high bleacher wall. They cross swords at Eddy's throat and JET demands, "Why have I never seen you in class before, buffalo breath?"

Eddy drops and spins out from under JET's threatening advance, pushes off the wall into a roll and lunges back at JET from behind reversing the press. "Because I fence in the night class, chicken knees!"

JET uses brute force to push Eddy away, wildly leaping up onto the bleachers as his only escape, climbing with one hand and fending off deadly thrusts with the other. Eddy chases him higher and higher, asking, "Where'd you learn to fence? You're running away from me!"

JET grabs an exercise rope hanging from the ceiling, jerks it free and swings with it out into the air, over Eddy's head, sliding down the rope to drop lightly onto the gymnasium floor. Waiting for Eddy to return to the basketball court, JET shouts a surprising answer, "I learned to fence from a book! What about you, four eyes?"

Eddy leaps towards JET but is too occupied with rapid swordplay to answer in that instant.

Finally, Eddy leaps over a rolling basketball, and in an oft-practiced maneuver, jump-kicks the ball up behind his back and over his own head so that the ball drops down in front of him, answering, "From my uncle, butt crack!"

As the ball drops in front of Eddy, he kicks it mightily towards JET's chest. JET has no choice but to stab the basketball with his sword. The tip of the sword breaks off, and the remaining sharp bit punctures the ball. But then the ball is stuck to JET's sword and the weapon is useless.

Mrs. Singer shouts, "JET! Sword!"

JET glances left and sees a sword flying towards him, grip first, an exercise they'd often practiced in class. Mrs. Singer has thrown him a replacement weapon!

JET drops the useless sword from his right hand while simultaneously snagging the fresh sword out of the air with his left, just in time to parry a deadly attack from Eddy, who cleverly spins around, kicking JET's feet out from under him.

JET hits the floor hard and rolls sideways, only to find Eddy's sword at his throat. Breathing hard, Eddy says, "How do we get out of this mess, Mr. Flynn?"

JET glances sideways from the floor and sees basketball players and fencers screaming at each other, coaches blowing whistles trying to pull angry opponents apart. Sticking around to answer for all this would definitely be a bad idea.

Indicating a window over the bleachers and doors to the toilets, JET hisses, "You take the high road, and I'll take the low road. Meet me in room 303, Trojan Hall..." bashing Eddy's sword clean out of his hand and making a backwards roll onto his feet, "...at nine tonight." JET whacks Eddy on his ribs with the side of his sword, just to emphasize who 'won' their duel.

Eddy quickly recovers his weapon but JET is upon him with lunge after lunge, devilishly forcing him back towards the center of the crowd so Eddy can recover his mask, conveniently allowing JET to do the same.

The last we see of these two rogues is their quick salute to each other across the rioting mob before Eddy climbs out of a window behind the bleachers, and JET backs into the toilet.

But it is the women's toilet... Two women athletes throw JET back out into the crowd. JET stumbles to his knees, rolls sideways, and crab walks between people's legs out the side door of the gym and into broad daylight.

There, he stands up and laughs out loud freely to the world at large, strolling joyfully away.

# Eugene, Oregon 5

At 8:55am next morning, day two in the professional life of the young police cadets, Davis drops into the tattered greasy-green vinyl, squeaky, wobbling, five-wheeled office chair at his metal desk. In that instant, his phone rings. There's also a pink Post-it note from Maria-Santos, section secretary, better known as 'Mom', stuck to his computer screen. Maria-Santos, the caller on the phone, speaks the same words as Maria-Santos the message-writer: "*Report to room 1313 for a briefing that starts in five minutes, and bring Sanjib.*"

"Where the hell is room 1313?" Davis says to a dead phone.

Davis stands up at the same moment as Sanjib, three cubicles over. They lock eyes.

"And bring Davis..." repeats Sanjib in a loud cynical voice while rolling his eyes in disgust. Others in the office look up from their desks at the commotion but say nothing.

Davis sees the inner war in Sanjib who hates being told what to do.

Sanjib says, "Where the hell is room 1313?"

"Three minutes," says Davis. They each grab their police officer hats and take off at a trot towards the stairway, known to work faster than the elevator, and not so prone to mechanical failures.

Room 1313 would have been the thirteenth floor if the architect had not been superstitious about the meaning of the number 13, relabeling the thirteenth floor as the fourteenth floor. Instead, as they eventually discover, 1313 is three stories down, below parking level, originally designed as an interrogation room, now kept as a fortress in case the precinct is ever stormed by bad guys. Sanjib and Davis arrive out of breath and late.

Police Chief John Stafford sits with Sergeant Peter Brinks at one end of a seriously stained and scratched formica-topped table. Ominously, no one else is there. Sanjib steps towards the table. Davis feels like hiding behind his riot shield, but he forgot to bring it.

Brinks says, "Sit."

"Is there a problem, sir?" sputters Sanjib, sitting.

"Yes, there is. And you two are the solution." Brinks looks over to Stafford who nods for Brinks to continue.

Davis cautiously sits.

"Given the increase in terrorist threats and local radical protest groups, the Eugene Police Office needs more information. Otherwise, we will be shooting in the dark, so to speak... A request has come down that we infiltrate the local groups to get better informed. The obvious choice is you two rookies. Since you are both young and have not yet started your daily rounds, no one around town knows you as police officers. We ask you to go undercover, plain clothes. We don't actually have to ask. We could simply inform you. If you agree, you will, from this moment on, proceed to create what looks like ordinary lives for yourselves, and find your way into a group that calls themselves *Shadow Knights of the Mysterium.* Your job is to keep us updated of their plans, activities, and membership. You will receive your standard salaries by direct deposit, but you should adopt the lifestyle of an ordinary Eugene citizen. Find jobs, get an apartment. We will give you each a burner with an unlisted number to report directly to me at your convenience. Will you do this?"

"For how long?" asks Davis.

There is silence. Police Chief Stafford takes a deep breath and clears his mighty smoker-drinker voice. The wheeze notably amplifies the 'sinister police-chief boss' effect. He rumbles the answer, "Until we get things back under control..."

Sanjib's eyebrows go up. Davis eyebrows crinkle down into a deep 'V' and he stops breathing. In secret, the two young men do everything they can to suppress a cynical laugh they dare not show.

In Sanjib's view, since the beginning of time, nothing, anywhere, has ever been truly under control by anybody. Control is a delusional strategy of people afraid of fear and life itself.

In Davis's view, anybody who wants things under control has never had good sex. Even good kissing is out of control.

Realizing that the "For how long..." question itself is insane, since no one can predict the future, the two rookies glance at each other like mice in a cage being stared at by a cat. They both look back at the Police Chief and nod.

Sanjib says, "Thanks for your trust."

Davis says, "Do we get to keep the badges?"

"Yes, you keep the badges, but you keep them private," says Brinks. "Maria-Santos has some paperwork for you to fill out."

"Okay then!" Davis says to Sanjib. "What are we *Shadow Nights of the Wisteria* doing in the Police Office, for god's sake? Let's get into our jogger outfits and head out the back door, eh Sanjib?"

As they stride out the dungeon door, Brinks shouts, "Mysterium! Not Wisteria! Idiots..."

Davis looks over at Sanjib and smiles, excited for the chance of authorized adventure.

Sanjib fancies himself as having a broader perspective than Davis on potential negative outcomes. He frowns at Davis's frivolity and swallows grimly, already viewing colorful details of grave premonitions.

# Phoenix, Arizona 1

Raspy warbling tones from the Cactus Wren echo out over a magnificent Southern Arizona panoramic sunset. Dry craggy peaks and saguaro cactus stand silhouetted against purple, pink and orange storm clouds hanging in a turquoise sky fading towards the dark of night.

Dressed in a red, black, and white plaid flannel shirt, blue jeans, and a dusty black cowboy hat pierced by two eagle feathers, a lone American Indian hunches down over a small campfire in a small protected clearing beside a rocky hill. His attention is utterly focused while he feeds small branches of sagebrush into the flames.

Chanting a monotonous, ancient tonal language, something bigger than a human being sings through him.

At each addition of herbs, the fire dances up, emitting puffs of smoke that rise toward the clouds, seeming to feed the storm.

The man is a shaman, and he is on a mission.

The certainty of his voice grows louder and louder, not in force but in resonance with the tempest. Clouds boil in the sky.

A massive rainstorm is accepting his invitation to come fully out and play.

Without effort the Shaman rises from sitting and moves with deliberate love-inspired freedom in rhythm to his own chanting.

He dances the storm.

His voice builds to a crescendo as lightning flashes and his voice turns into thunder. The clouds take over his chanting as rain bursts from the sky in bucketfuls.

Water pours off of cliffs, rushes through canyons, picks up boulders and branches and joins with other streams to form a raging flash flood shooting down the arroyos.

Clouds and lightning, wind, rain, and chaos work together smashing through the desert.

The roaring flood slams a boulder with battering-ram force into the central wooden support of a rickety old one-lane wooden bridge in a dirt road.

*Crack!*

The post splinters. The whole bridge sags, precariously hanging in position but not washing away.

# Aleppo, Syria 7

Zenobia Darwish's *Beep! Book* – 5 February 2023

I have not written in here for such a long time. We have been so busy with trying to live in the chaos cloud of Aleppo.

We provide day-long skill-building classes for over fifty street children who are too poor to buy a uniform needed to attend any other school. We call ourselves the 'Hidden University' because we learn without bowing down to 'certified teachers', and we learn together. What we mostly learn right now is how to cook for ourselves whatever food we can find or grow in our garden patches.

Israa holds space for our Krav Maga and stick fighting practice.

I provide conversational English classes.

For the fifth time, Montassar begins reading through the *Handbook* at Morning Circle, then we practice while we work.

Our gardens flourish. Our makeshift wooden-hut village efficiently catches whatever rainwater falls into barrels for drinking water. Even during the madness of Civil War, our little school grows.

And Aleppo... Aleppo has never recovered. Syria is unbelievably still at war with itself. Assad and his desperate mafia are still in office, even after all this time, and all these bombs, and all this suffering. What has the world become? Scary.

Why does it scare us? Because on unrefugees.org, I find the following report: "After over a decade of conflict, Syria remains the world's largest refugee crisis. Since 2011, more than 14 million Syrians have been forced to flee their homes in search of safety. More than 6.8 million Syrians remain internally displaced in their own country where 70 percent of the population is in need of humanitarian assistance, and 90 percent of the population live below the poverty line. Approximately 5.5 million Syrian refugees live in the five countries neighboring Syria—Türkiye, Lebanon, Jordan, Iraq and Egypt. Germany is the largest non-neighboring host country with more than 850,000 Syrian refugees."

Today the *Handbook* tells us:

*There are two classifications of refugee: Refugee by Armageddon, and refugee by transformation.*

I think to myself, *We have become both. Our country turned into chaotic rubble around us, and we help each other upgrade our thoughtware day after day.*

It is nearly impossible to describe how insanely confusing these years have been since 2011. But I need to tell you what we know.

The reason I need to tell you is that anyone else explaining this to you will seriously slant their stories in their favor, trying to confuse you about what really happened, who did what to whom and why. But I have nothing to hide and nothing to lose. I have a different purpose. I am in the small team with my father, recording daily and nightly actions in our Current Events journal. We try to record the 'facts' while major television networks, national militaries, and governmental agencies all try to cover their asses and make it the other 'guy's' fault.

When I use the term 'guy', I mean it with a vengeance. I have realized that the insanity which has overtaken Syria is patriarchal. Only uninitiated males create hell worlds like this. Only boys lie, and kill, and cheat, and steal with so little conscience.

Try to follow the logic behind the following incidents.

In 2011, four armies plus a dozen smaller factions start randomly battling each other in Syria. Factions include the 'Free Syrian Army' Rebels, Assad's Army, Islamic State of Iraq and the Levant (ISIL), Kurds, Turkmen (men from Turkmenistan), Putin, Erdoğan, Netanyahu, Washington, United Kingdom, Hezbollah, North Atlantic Treaty Organization (NATO), Lebanon, and Iran. Everybody wants oil, honor, and inglorious revenge.

They play 'mix-and-match', sometimes behaving like allies, sometimes like enemies. In reality they are all adolescent boys with big guns, using pills and stress to numb themselves to the personal risk they experience and the collateral damage they cause.

Their lives are meaningless. They indiscriminately rape and kill women and children. They burn date palms and orchards, blow up historical buildings and working vehicles – even themselves – just to be the next temporary rooster crowing from the top of the imaginary dunghill.

The males are truly insane. I would never have believed this horror world was possible, but in the last years, my naivete has been killed, trampled to death time after time.

I would shout, "Adolescent boys are idiots!" every other sentence, except that something else is more important to me. This world is so incredibly precious. Life is so astonishing. Sometimes I sit holding a dead stone in one hand, the equivalent of a lifeless moon rock, and a ripe red tomato in the other hand, with its sweet nutrition and pouches of juicy seeds for planting more tomato plants. The contrast between life and not life is so great. Life is miraculous. To not live my life in awe of these extraordinary opportunities would be even more insane than the boys blowing each other up. Still, I report to you from our notes.

Fighters from every faction live inside of their self-made fantasy worlds, and those fantasy worlds give them only one option to choose from: make war. Day in and day out, it is only endless warfare and suffering.

Other countries take advantage of the chaos in Syria and disrespectfully use us as a weapons-and-tactics testing ground. This is another form of rape.

Syria is viewed as an 'empty lot' in which 'superpowers' fight 'proxy wars' against each other.

War gives corporations the opportunity to sell their latest weapon systems and prototype new weapons and tactics. Weapons are 'consumables' of the most profitable sort. When a weapon blows up, the customer must immediately buy more. It is a simple equation: More war equals more profit for the corporations. With a percentage of their profits, corporations buy the integrity of politicians, so the politicians vote for more funding for wars.

This game is the profoundest insult to human intelligence.

In the process, Syria has become a playground for psychopaths.

Sometimes when I am alone, I sob and ache because these idiots have changed archeological treasures in Palmyra and Aleppo into a crumbling graveyard filled with bodies of naïve and sometimes innocent people.

On 19 July 2012, the four-year siege and battle to occupy the city of Aleppo begins. Excited Free Syrian Army Rebels do whatever it takes to steal eastern Aleppo from pro-Assad defenders of the city.

In the chaos of the struggles, a Sunni jihadist group claims religious authority over all Muslims. They have various names including 'Islamic State of Iraq and the Levant' abbreviated to 'ISIL', or 'Islamic State of Iraq and Syria' abbreviated to ISIS, or 'Islamic State' abbreviated to 'IS', or the Arabic acronym 'Da'esh'. I will call them ISIL. They see the Syrian Civil War as a great opportunity to capture and brainwash new converts. During the fighting between the Rebels and Assad's Army, ISIL jumps in sideways and also establishes a stronghold in the bigger buildings of Aleppo.

Between 29 January and 14 March 2013, we see bodies floating down the Queiq River in our backyard. They are all men, from 11 to 64 years old, rebels with hands tied behind their backs and tape over their mouths, shot in the head, and dumped in the water. Up river is Assad's Army headquarters. The news says over 230 bodies were found. We never learn what actually happened. After 14 March, the river dries up too much to float more bodies.

On 19 March 2013, a rocket blasts into the Khan al-Assal suburb of Aleppo releasing illegal Sarin nerve gas. A barrage of conflicting accusations from Russia, Assad, U.S., Türkiye, U.K., and the United Nations confuse who unleashed the toxic gas. The investigation fizzles out.

On 24 April 2013, the medieval minaret of the Great Umayyad Mosque is destroyed.

Just a few months later, on 21 August 2013, two Rebel-held areas of al-Ghouta, in the suburbs of Damascus, are bombarded by Russian-made truck-mounted surface-to-surface unguided missiles carrying Sarin gas. More than seventeen-hundred people die. Analysis shows that the Sarin in the al-Ghouta attacks matches the Sarin in the Khan al-Assal attacks, and both come from the same source: Bashar al-Assad. The U.S., France, and U.K. want to immediately punish Assad for using the illegal chemical weapons.

On 6 September 2013, the U.S. Senate files a resolution to authorize use of military force against Assad's Army in response to the al-Ghouta attack.

Four days later, on 10 September 2013, military intervention is averted when Assad lies to the world by asserting that he accepts a U.S. / Russian negotiated deal to turn over *every single bit"* of his chemical weapons stockpiles for destruction, and promises to join the Convention on the Prohibition of the Development, Production, Stockpiling and Use of Chemical Weapons and on their Destruction (CWC from the Hague). No punishment is delivered. Assad sneaks off and smiles to himself and his cronies.

The U.S. announces that it does not want Assad's Army to crush 'Syria's version of the Arab Spring's hopefulness for democracy', so the U.S. intercedes on the side of the Rebels (and on behalf of their own military industrial complex...) by bombing ISIL and the Khorasan al-Qaeda camps, and by supplying the Rebels with half-a-billion dollars' worth of weapons and ammunition, including anti-tank missiles, along with pitifully ineffective 'Special Forces training'. Americans are too arrogant to notice how everyone plays them for dummies, stealing weapons and war equipment from them, much of it sold on the black market to the highest bidder, often to ISIL.

By January 2014, Rebels take over the ISIL headquarters in Aleppo.

On 8 May 2014, Rebels ignite a seventy-five-meter-long self-dug tunnel filled with explosives and utterly destroy the Carlton Hotel near the citadel.

On 22 May 2014, the U.N. Security Council demands that the International Criminal Court investigate war crimes in the Syrian Civil War, but the resolution is vetoed by both Russia's Putin and China's Xi Jinping. No one countermands the interveners. That's when Australia starts bombing ISIL.

Yes... Australia.

On 22 September 2014, the U.S., Bahrain, Jordan, Qatar, Saudi Arabia, and the United Arab Emirates jointly attack ISIL forces, as well as the Khorasan al-Qaeda group west of Aleppo.

By August 2015, ISIL regroups, destroys Palmyra – which is a UNESCO World Heritage Site – and assassinates 500 local villagers loyal to Assad.

On 30 September 2015, Putin responds to Assad's request for help, and bombs both ISIL and the Free Syrian Army Rebels (supported by America...) with the help of Iran and Hezbollah. Essentially, Russia attacks America.

On 11 October 2015, the Americans launch a Rebel group of their own, dedicated to fighting ISIL! They call it SDF, which stands for 'Syrian Democratic Forces', a coalition of rebel groups, primarily the Kurdish militias, with some Arab, Assyrian, Armenian, Türkmen and Chechen militias, as well as various factions of the Rebels' Free Syrian Army which Russia just bombed. The U.S. hands military leadership of the SDF over to the People's Protection Units, the YPG, a Kurdish militia which is already classified as a terrorist group by Türkiye!

Are you confused yet? Let me explain. Washington and U.K. and France, and Putin and Erdoğan and Iran and Jordan and Israel are all fighting each other on Syrian soil! No one actually wants to change anything. They all want to keep fighting to use up their weapons so they can manufacture more weapons and make more money.

On 24 November 2015, Erdoğan shoots down one of Putin's jet fighters, plus a rescue helicopter coming to their aid. This is when the U.K. Royal Air Force decides to send heavily armed jet fighters to join the U.S. and Rebel side.

Russia and the U.S. simultaneously establish airbases in Syria only fifty kilometers apart from each other.

Then the U.S. accuses Assad's Army of carrying out airstrikes that help ISIL fighters advance towards Aleppo! Probably Assad reasons that since ISIL is the enemy of one of his enemies – the Americans – then if ISIL fights its way back into Aleppo, ISIL will help Assad get the Rebels (another one of his enemies...) out of Aleppo, so why not help ISIL?

In December 2015 the U.S. buys and ships one-thousand tons of Soviet-style weapons and equipment from Eastern Europe to the SDF, the American's new rebel group.

By the end of 2015, only eighty doctors remain working in the Rebel-held eastern part of Aleppo, one doctor per seven thousand residents. There is but one bakery to serve one hundred and twenty thousand inhabitants.

In March 2016, Assad's Army, with support from Putin's jet fighters and Iranian intel and weapons, recaptures Palmyra from ISIL, moving the front lines into the city of Aleppo.

From April to July 2016, Assad's Army declares a new offensive, calling upon Putin for aid. Together they specifically target Aleppo hospitals, schools, and residences with a massive rain of home-made 'Barrel Bombs' from helicopters.

What is a Barrel Bomb? You fill an empty steel oil drum with high explosives and anything hard and sharp to use as shrapnel. Barrel Bombs are cheap and easy to make, and very destructive of any human life nearby.

Simultaneously, Putin's jets drop illegal phosphorus and high-explosive cluster bombs on Aleppo. Aleppo Medical facilities are attacked over two hundred times by Putin's jets and Assad's Army.

Meanwhile, the Rebels attack Syrian citizens in Aleppo to steal and hoard food for themselves leaving the citizens to starve like rats, holed-up in their bombed-out terrorized city.

Assad's Army, ISIL, and the Rebels commit horrendous war crimes on each other, wantonly destroying precious artifacts in the city, and carelessly killing citizens. The true people are dying as 'collateral damage' in crossfire between ravaging hordes of uninitiated teenagers. It is most horribly insane.

On 17 September 2016, Türkiye attacks the Kurds and ISIL in northeast Syria, supported by U.S. jet fighters, but in that battle, the U.S. kills sixty-two of Assad's Army troops while Assad's Army is attacking ISIL, America's sworn enemy!

In October 2016, the U.N. High Commissioner on Human Rights warns everyone that, *"Crimes of historic proportions are being committed in Aleppo."* No one moves to stop them.

This is when Putin drops even more white phosphorus cluster bombs on Aleppo, starting everything on fire and burning through human skin and bone. Putin also starts dropping huge 'Bunker Buster' bombs, designed to penetrate to the bottom of apartment buildings and then explode, destroying any chance that children or hospital patients have of hiding out in basements or tunnels.

Bunker Buster bombs are often tipped with an entire ton of Depleted Uranium, a radioactive waste product from nuclear reactors. One way that countries get rid of their radioactive waste is to find someone to call your 'enemy' and drop Depleted Uranium on their homes. As the bomb explodes, the very hard, very dense Depleted Uranium bursts into flames, scattering nanoparticle clouds of radioactive dust everywhere. Each D.U. particle has a half-life of four point five billion years, as long as the Earth is old.

Nanoparticles are so small they drift through any kind of filtering system. This means you cannot protect your lungs from inhaling Depleted Uranium nanodust. Since the human body has no way of excreting D.U., each particle you inhale pumps out low-level radiation into your surrounding cells, like little hand-grenades exploding inside of your body, causing multiple simultaneous cancers. D.U. also destroys DNA causing horrible birth defects for generations to come. Once Depleted Uranium nanodust is spread around it can never be cleaned up. This is beyond insane. It is evil.

By December 2016 Assad's army recaptures the rest of Aleppo from the Rebels. That is when the U.S.'s SDF Coalition with thirty-thousand Arab, Christian, and Kurdish troops begin recapturing cities back from ISIL.

On 4 April 2017 at four in the morning, Assad's Army launches a Sarin nerve gas attack from the Shayrat Air Base on a sleeping anti-Assad town named Khan Sheikhoun.

On 7 April 2017, in response to the nerve gas attack, yet without authorization from the U.S. Congress or the United Nations Security Council, the U.S. Navy launches fifty-nine Tomahawk Cruise Missiles at Shayrat Air Base from their warships.

On 7 April 2018, exactly one year after the U.S.'s attack on the Shayrat Air Base, there is another gas attack, this time on the Rebel-held parts of the Syrian city of Douma, with chlorine and possibly Sarin gas in Barrel Bombs dropped from helicopters. Assad's Army denies making the attack, but then immediately moves in and takes over those neighborhoods of Douma. Investigators prove that the gas was definitely made by Assad.

On 14 April 2018, to retaliate against Assad's further illegal use of toxic gas, the U.S., U.K., and France all attack Assad's Army positions with a barrage of one-hundred-and-five heavy rockets from ships, submarines, and jet fighters. Assad sniggers behind his hands because he is not deposed by the attack, and he is still achieving his goals.

In total, Assad drops more than 81,000 'Barrel Bombs' from helicopters and fixed-wing aircraft into Aleppo, blasting shrapnel into the people he is supposed to be governing.

Back and forth, death and bombs, these rampaging teenage boys battle each other like street gangs. I am not attracted to any of them, for any reason. I only try to stay out of their way, try to keep my little school safe. Our main survival skill is to be invisible. We practice so that if one of us yells, *"Smoke!"* we can all vanish from view in less than five seconds.

In March 2019, the American-backed SDF coalition announces 'total territorial defeat of ISIL in Syria' after taking control of their last stronghold in Baghuz. Since then, the SDF actively resists Erdoğan's encroachments into northern Syria.

Rebels and Kurds now act as if they are willing to collaborate side-by-side with Assad's Army to assure that Erdoğan stops occupying Syrian territory in the north.

Erdoğan seems willing to talk, at first, but that is only because it is an election year, and Putin has forces deployed at his front door in Syria. Then, as soon as he can, Erdoğan launches deadly drone attacks on Syrian Rebels, Kurds, and Assad's Army alike.

I have only reported the bare bones of the war, the tip of the iceberg. Putin, Erdoğan, Iran, ISIL, Kurds, U.S., France, Assad, Rebels, Australia... what is really going on?

I keep asking myself this question: What does the West gain from participating in a civil war in Syria?

If no one in the world who could stop Assad's madness actually steps in to stop Assad's madness, then I can only conclude that those people with large corporations and weapons manufacturing facilities and armies actually want Assad's madness to continue!

From time-to-time, they might try to stop Assad from using chemical weapons, but they do not stop Assad.

Why not?

The CIA has conducted more than thirty-seven 'regime changes' in recent history – perhaps many more. Why don't they cause a regime change in Syria?

In the end, what has actually happened?

More than half-a-million Syrians have been killed since our Uncivil War started.

Thirteen million people – over half the original population of Syria – have lost their homes, their farms, their families, their businesses, their identity. They have changed from Syrian citizens to Syrian refugees.

Half of these refugees roam through rubble piles that used to be Syrian cities, searching for enough food and water to survive until the next day.

The other six million Syrian refugees leave their country.

Six million hopelessly lost Syrian refugees roaming the Earth.

This is as bad as it can be.

It is hell on Earth on 5 February 2023, and we are in the middle of it.

# Edinburgh, Scotland 1

Near the cemetery of a stone church in the old town of Edinburgh, a doorway leads into a funeral home. Inside, a black casket holds an old dead man. His body is well dressed, of course, and made to look like he smiles slightly in a sweet dream.

Next to the casket stands another old man wearing a black knee-length wool coat over his black suit and tie. In contrast with the unmoving corpse, the living man fidgets with his well-worn hat. On the wall behind the coffin is a shelf holding a white ceramic vase of pink flowers shining in light cast from two silver candelabras, each with three white dripless candles, dripless because the flames are in fact light bulbs. This leads one to suspect that the flowers might also be fake.

While the dead man lies still as stone, the living man shudders with repressed grief, unconscious fear, and ancient rage. This is Sean Connery. The shuddering comes from an emotional tsunami threatening to exceed this man's already maxed-out storage capacity. His stoicism can restrain the flood no longer. Of their own accord his arms gesticulate hopelessly as he looks fretfully around him. His mouth mumbles words, but he is too overwhelmed to make sense of them. He has no map for where he is forced now to go.

"Well, Charles...

It's a start. Sean glances furtively over his shoulder, embarrassed that he speaks out loud to a corpse. "...you're dead now. You bastard!

"You lied to me, you know! You said you'd fight this thing through and it would never get you...

"Well, it got you! The vote is in. You lost. You're dead!

"I feel like a roaster... You're dead, *and I'm still here*, gabbin' like a numpty to your boggin corpse!

"Well, what do you expect? You didn't even say goodbye to me."

Deep sadness drives his hand to clutch his chest, but no sound can come out. Sean has no idea how to experience such feelings. He does not even know this is a feeling, or which feeling it might be. He only knows he must do what he's always done, hold the pressure inside of himself by force of will until it finally suffocates and subsides.

The problem is, these are big feelings, and they torture his entire frame. Charles Dobson was his last best friend on earth. Sean has lost so much from his life that this additional loss turns him inside out. He can only mumble.

"You just blinked out, man! You leave me alone on this godforsaken planet with all these morons! What am I supposed to do now?

"Who cares what I do, really? The dirty truth is, no matter what I do I'm going to end up just like you. Dead. Probably sooner than I think.

"You and I have been living our whiny little lives pretending we would live forever. You just proved our theory wrong. I don't know whether to hate you... or love you for dying before me..."

Without realizing it Sean inches steadily closer to his friend. He can't get any closer, of course. The coffin is in the way. So is death. Driven by despair, Sean's hand creeps into the coffin and fingers Charles' coat sleeve. Slowly it slides down the arm seeking skin contact. It is cold dead skin, but far better than no skin at all.

"Charles, you were my last real friend. Now you're gone. It will be tiresome for me, waiting around to die, pretending that I'm having the time of my life, retired. Retired from acting. Hah!

"I'm still acting. Every day is an act. I act retired. I act satisfied with life. But I hate it, Charles! I hate not knowing about all this.

"I hate to not get it, being confused, acting as if I'm doing something important, pretending to be enjoying myself, like everyone else. It's just so much bullshit! And no one says anything about it. They're all pretending. I am sick of it!

"What am I saying?" Sean looks into Charles's unmoving face. "I sound like a ninny! You could have cheered me up about all this, you know? You could have given me something satisfying to understand about your own death, but instead you just went and died. You abandoned me!

"Now I have to stand here alone and say goodbye to you without you saying goodbye back."

Sean caresses Charles's fingers. The stroking starts in complete absentmindedness, but as Sean' monologue continues he becomes more and more attentive to what he is actually doing, stroking a dead man's stiff cold lifeless fingers.

The stroking itself is something he can feel, a sensation that only happens now. Sean moves his fingers more consciously, ever so gently, at full sensitivity. He feels the minuteness and tenderness of the stroking all the way to his toes.

Sean is no longer squeezed into his head. He occupies an entire physical body full of sensations. Suddenly he is cut free from being identified with intellectual considerations generated by his memories and projections. His standard cynical assessments drift away. He occupies the tiniest piece of this present moment, exactly where he experiences the sensations in his fingertips.

Coincidentally in the same present moment where he senses the touch, he also senses the feelings of grief and sadness, held back over decades of numbness.

Being in a minimized now turns the key. The lock opens. The door swings free. Feelings gush out in great sobs of cleansing grief. These are unfettered whole-body sobs, like when Tom Hanks as Chuck Noland in the film *Castaway* loses his only friend Wilson off his raft, or when Jim Carrey as *The Grinch* feels his heart growing three sizes bigger. These are true sobs flowing on and on as long as Sean rubs the tips of his own two fingers together experiencing a minimized present.

This man meets his own heart and finds himself reborn, sobbing by the coffin of his dead friend in a funeral parlor of a tiny Scottish village at the edge of Edinburgh. Sean suspects he might be going insane, but refuses to return to his familiar emotionless analytical mind even if it means he no longer knows who he is. Something momentous has just happened to our Sean Connery. He has no idea what.

# Hollywood, California 1

Sandra Bullock strides through a quiet Hollywood hotel party. It is not easy to stride in a backless burgundy floor-length eel-skin gown with silver sparkles and high heels. But you know Sandra. She strides it profoundly well. The thigh slit helps.

A lip-tight half smile on her face communicates, "Do not fucking interrupt me. I am on a Mission!" The mission helps, because she is not drinking.

"There you are!" she says. "I hoped you would be here!"

"Hey! Miss Congeniality!" says the startled Stephen Fry, sitting across from a stout mustached man not-so-secretly harboring not-so-secret information. Sandra and Stephen clasp hands and kiss cheeks. "You are dressed to the thirteens!"

"Thirteens?"

"Mmmm, yes..." says Stephen, glancing at his informant for permission to have an interlude. "I am doing the practice of no longer saying the first thing that comes into my mind. If I wait half-a-sec, my robot-response passes and then a second thought comes along. Sometimes even a third thought. This way my other intelligences get to speak."

Sandra squints her disbelieving eyes precisely. "You have other intelligences?"

"You do too... but... that should be obvious. You're a woman."

"Thirteens?" Sandra repeats her first question.

"I was going to say 'Dressed to the nines...' but then I waited. It is Friday the thirteenth today! Happy Friday the thirteenth! Ah... See? That was the first thought that came into my mind. A waste of breath, eh?. So boring..."

"Thirteen is my lucky number," says Sandra. "I never understood why people think thirteen is unlucky. There are a lot of things I never understood. That's why I want to talk with you, Stephen. I have serious doubts."

The stately gentleman slides off his chair saying, "I will abscond so that you two can make a deep dive."

Stephen nods his head. "Catch you later."

Sandra glides into the hotseat saying, "You're not drinking either." It is an observation, not a question. "You feel it too...?"

Stephen's showman smile slides off his face. For the first time in longer than he can remember, he delivers no humorous repartee. His shoulders actually sag.

Sandra leans forward, whispering desperately, "You are a presenter at BBC, Stephen, for god's sake! You are in the middle of all this shit that is going down since what... seven years now? I need to know!"

"What do you need to know, Sandra? What do they actually hide in Area 51?"

"Well, sure. Let's start there. Why not?"

Stephen Fry sighs, flustered. "I cannot talk Sandra! You've got the wrong guy. If I try to give you all the dirt I've heard around town, I lose my contacts. Then I am nothing. No one will trust me anymore."

"If not you," storms Sandra, "then who can I talk to?" Both her hands wave in the air, voice rising. "Not politicians, Stephen! They can only say what helps them get re-elected, or at least not impeached. Not CEOs! They can only say what increases ROI for their greedy shareholders. It's all lies, Stephen! It's all coming apart! And no one is taking responsibility to create a different future."

Stephen sighs and brushes the hair out of his eyes. "How can someone take responsibility for changing things these days? There is no standard! Even if you assassinate every psychopath in any power position around the world... you know, the ones selling palm oil rights to corporations so they can chop down trees in Indonesian National Parks, the ones shipping New Zealand forests to the Chinese, the ones running weapons in the Middle East and South America, the ones trafficking girls in Asia and Russia... it won't make a difference! The hierarchical system itself promotes the next psychopath up the ladder. Didn't you watch *The International*? What are you going to do, really?"

Sandra is angry. "But we vastly outnumber them!"

"So? Nowhere, ever, have the prisoners turned on the guards and won."

Sandra pauses shakily, then says, "Why do people follow leaders who do not lead?"

"People are sleeping at the wheel. You know this!" says Stephen. "People are sheeple, trained at school to adopt other people's values as their own. We are false." Stephen looks down at his fidgeting fingers.

"Even you, Stephen?" Sandra searches his face in disbelief. "I always hoped you were too much of an asshole to be adaptive."

"Even me Sandra. I can only create what sells, and what sells is zombie food."

"Holy shit! How has it come to pass that even you prostitute yourself for popularity and money? Is this what you want, Stephen? Really? You? You can 'ONLY create what sells'? Really?"

Stephen wants to be somewhere else, anywhere other than here having to face Sandra's fierce questions. But he also desperately wants to be exactly here, on this bed of nails, hitting reality. We all have parts...

He says, "No. Not really. It is not what I want. But I've been doing it for so long... Everyone else is doing it."

"Wrong! Not 'everyone else' is doing it! Your view depends on where you look. And where you look depends on your purpose." Sandra glares intensely into his eyes. She wants to slap his face, shake him by the shoulders... throttle his neck.

"What are you saying?" demands Stephen, unable to meet her gaze.

Sandra turns to catch a waiter's eye. This is not difficult because all the waiters have been trying to catch her eye.

The tall Italian with greased black hair slides obsequiously but elegantly over to her side. "What can I get for you, Signora?"

"I need two bottles of sparkling water, unopened. Do you understand? Do not even begin to open the bottles!"

He smiles. "Sì, Signora. Would you like ice and a twist of lime?"

"No! You idiot! Didn't you hear me? I told you exactly what I want! Not opened. No ice! No lime! No glasses! I want two unopened bottles of carbonated water here in no time!"

"Sì! Sì! Two bottles unopened mineral water," he mutters, streaking for the kitchen.

Sandra turns to Stephen. "You still okay talking with me?"

"Just don't punch me if I don't understand the first time you say something. I must tell you, Sandra, I feel more hopeful now, seeing how angry and alive you are, even if I can't see where you're going with all this."

"You will get it. I guarantee it is amazing. But I need the bottles first."

# Salt Lake City, Utah 5

It is night. The campus clock dongs its nine bells. Eddy searches along the third-floor dorm hallway for room 303. Just as he raises his hand to knock, the door swings open inwards. JET's smiling face appears. "See that crack in the ceiling? Closed Circuit Television camera. I borrowed equipment from the physics lab and wired the building for surveillance."

"What for?"

JET locks the door in several places after Eddy enters. "So I can see when they come to collect all the equipment I've borrowed."

JET's dorm looks more like a hi-tech research lab, packed with equipment, most of it on and humming. "I had to install a new breaker to this room because I kept blowing the main circuits whenever I had everything on.

"What do you do with all this stuff?"

"I inquire in places I'm not supposed to. What do you do with that carrot?"

The conspicuous orange vegetable protrudes curiously out of Eddy's back pants pocket. "It's an emergency carrot," says Eddy, as if that explains everything. JET cannot avoid giving both Eddy and his 'emergency carrot' a sanity-doubting glance. Eddy continues, "What have you found out?"

"You want the poop, or the scoop?" asks JET, settling into his Captain Kirk Starship Enterprise swivel chair.

Eddy pushes aside some gear and sits on the corner of the table near JET's main computer screen. "I'm not a farmer. No use for poop."

JET leans back in his chair and announces, "I have this theory about questions. The theory is this: What you find depends on what you ask. It is a research theory. You can only understand what you already know about, not what you don't know about. You can only find what you are looking for, not what you are not looking for. My problem is that I cannot properly formulate a question about what I am actually looking for! I do know that I'm looking for something. I only hope I'll recognize it when I find it. Maybe that's why you're here. To help me recognize treasure. Maybe what I seek is sitting under my nose and I can't see it at all. I've been at the university almost four years, and by the looks of it, same as you."

Eddy nods. JET continues, "I came here because I wanted to learn how the world works. I thought this is what a university is for – to give us whatever we need to live well. After four years I learned a lot of math, history, science, but almost nothing about living well, and almost nothing about how the world works. There seems to be a huge gap between what we are taught at college and what is really going on. My question is: What is in that gap?"

"Like... what are you talking about? Specifically?"

JET scoots up to his keyboard, hits a couple of keys, moves the mouse and clicks it. A graph comes together on the bottom of the screen. "Look. Maybe you've seen this before? It is a simple graph of human population growth on planet earth. Here is how it has been for the past ten thousand years. Here is where we are now. See how fast the curve is predicted to climb in the next twenty-five years? It is exponential. This will happen in our lifetime.

"Now look at this." More clicks, a new graph appears. "This is the average estimate of some key non-renewable resources like oil, iron, fresh water, lithium, uranium, things that don't grow back – we use them up and they are gone. Due to the Westernization of developing countries like India, China, South America and so on, more and more people are consuming more and more of these same resources.

"Multiply the number of people by the increased resource use and you can pretty accurately estimate how quickly what remains will disappear."

He keeps clicking while he speaks. "When you lay the decreasing resources curve... over the increase in population curve... like this... you can see that the two curves cross at a specific point in time."

"So?"

"That time is just about... now. At that intersection point, there are no longer enough resources to go around. From the planet's point of view, the naked monkeys are playing an end game that sucks the planet dry and pushes the environment over tipping points so that civilization as we know it ceases to function. By burning resources like there is no tomorrow, we guarantee that there will be no tomorrow. No industrialized civilization will ever come back onto its feet again on Earth because all the easily reached resources are already mined. There will not be enough working infrastructure to build big enough mining equipment to get at the deeply buried remaining resources. If we keep playing this game, then everybody loses forever. Who do you think will hoard the last of the oil?"

"That would be whoever has the most nukes."

"Precisely. This is not a dignified way to express human intelligence, is it? Shitting on each other's dinner plate until someone gets scared enough to push the button. Game over."

The computer churns out graph after graph while the two young men stare at the screen. JET says, "Exponential growth or exponential collapse, either one spells a grim future for humanity on planet Earth. It reads like a requiem for a possibly intelligent species. Peak oil, peak precious metals, peak coal, methane chimneys bubbling up from the shallow Siberian shelf, leaking nuclear wastes, contamination from nano-particles, increase in cancers and birth defects, sixth great extinction of species, increasing global CO2 concentrations, rate of glacier melt, Gulf Stream shutting down, rising seas, ocean acidification, growth of the plastic to plankton ratio, collapse of coral reefs, failure of krill, collapse of fisheries, acres of tropical rainforest deforested, acres being planted in genetically modified crops for fuel oils, increase of damage from storms, increase of damage from wildfires, increase in damage from earthquakes which are the tectonic plates adjusting for the displacement of melting glaciers, increase in acres of desertification, oil price rises after removing government subsidies, China's increase in coal consumption, the true costs of nuclear power, the drop in ground water levels, increasing suicides from Indian farmers who planted Monsanto's genetically modified seeds..."

JET senses a deathly stillness growing in the man seated next to him. He witnesses a worldview shattering before his eyes. Tears run unnoticed down Eddy's cheeks, but Eddy is not ashamed. His grief is too profound to notice mere tears.

JET softly says, "You are right. Please say it in words, my friend. I'm listening."

"It can't be this way. It cannot end like this. I thought I had a Star Trek future, exploring the final frontier, going where no man has gone before. If we have already reached peak everything, then space exploration is over. There won't be enough titanium steel to set up solar-powered asteroid mining stations. We'll never get out there, to Mars, to Ganymede, not even to the moon. It's over."

JET's heart goes undefended in wonder. "You are the first person who has ever listened to me, Eddy. You actually understand what I'm saying. You let in the facts. You didn't automatically classify me as crazy. You did not defend yourself. You believe me."

"Well," says Eddy. "I get it... I get that my future is dying before my eyes... If my future dies, then who am I? A man with no future... or a different future than I thought..."

JET remains a silent sentinel for this step in Eddy's journey.

Eddy senses the rare and precious safety in the space JET holds for him and continues. "I say it cannot be like this. I say human beings are smarter than this. I *will* have a future. My future children *will* have a future. And their children. And your children..."

"Go on..."

"Another future is possible for us JET. I see it. I smell it. Something completely different from this is possible right now. Since I was a kid, I've sensed that modern culture is at its end and that I have something to do with inventing the next thing. Must be why you are showing me this now. It's the start signal." Eddy peers into the eyes of the man listening to him. "I *never* talk like this. I've always held myself back. I do not take public risks. But if ecosystems are collapsing, if tipping points have already been exceeded, the time for hiding out is over. We are, and therefore, I am, already at maximum risk."

Eddy takes a long-measured breath, like steadying himself to dive off the ten meter board. He checks JET's face for any kind of cynicism that might twist what he just said into something ridiculous. Eddy sees no crucifixion coming.

"Go on..." It's all JET can say.

"You can't do this alone, JET. I can't do it alone either. Something bigger than both of us has brought us together to ferry people out past the edge of their imaginations into a new kind of regenerative culture. Something that never existed on Earth before. It's our job to pave the way to the edges of modern culture and to build a bridge. I know humanity has been acting stupid, but it's time to grow up. It must be possible. There's another level of awareness or something, another way to live on Earth. We can do this. We can get there. Who is designing regenerative infrastructure? Running the debugging routines? Prototyping new problem solving techniques?" He pauses to shift tracks. "This data you just showed me is accessible enough. Surely the government knows all about this..."

"I would think so." JET remains absolutely solemn. "That is exactly what bothers me. *It is so obvious!* If I can get the information, then they have the information. If they have the information, why do they keep permitting the creatures who are raping our planet to continue to rape the planet... unless they themselves are the rapists? By some estimates, we are already ten times the population this planet can sustain in a life of dignity. Are we really this blind and stupid?"

"Ignorance is bliss," Eddy mumbles.

"It is too late for bliss, buddy! Have you tried sunbathing on a Chinese beach lately? I've seen aerial photos. Looks like an overpacked sardine can. Human impact is already too massive. No matter what the justification, staying on our current track is global suicide! This is what drives me crazy! Four years at the university studying how to shovel coal while the train we are on is zooming off a cliff! What is the point of studying at a university while civilization heads into oblivion? I am not a lemming! This is my life! I want to know what is really going on. What about you?"

"What are you proposing?"

JET leaps out of his chair and grabs a well-worn leather-bound manual from a shelf. He flips to a dog-eared page. "The *Handbook* says 'Clarity creates possibility.' If we can find out what is really going on, then maybe we can figure out what to do about it. Maybe Mother Earth will protect herself from being raped to death by greedy naked monkeys. Maybe she will unleash a plague like in 1919 that killed twice as many people as World War One. Maybe that's what AIDS or COVID is all about. Or maybe global warming will get too hot for pollination to occur and agriculture will end. Or maybe climate change will wipe out civilization by morphing into a sudden ice age. Maybe the Earth will flip magnetic poles and throw everything into chaos. I don't know. I am just tired of sitting in classrooms pretending like all this is not happening."

"Yeah. Well... Me too, actually."

"You mean that?"

"Yes. But I didn't have your details. The ostrich syndrome had me until you generated these graphs. It makes no sense to stick around school. I'm tired of it. Where do we go from here? How do we do this?"

A large red light mounted over JET's computer screen suddenly pulses to life.

"Oh, shit!" JET murmurs. "Too late for talk." He frantically flicks a few switches, but the red light stays flashing. "Damn! I should have shut down. We've been hacking the school mainframe's computing capacity. They must have traced the connection. It looks like our answer to your question 'How do we do this?' is: 'Now.' We do it now! We have about three minutes to get out of here."

Eddy glances at JET's security screens and sees campus police driving through the night towards their apartment building.

JET grabs a partly full day pack from the corner by his bed and stuffs it with a tool kit, toilet kit, and a bundle of cash. "Eddy," he says while slipping into a jacket and shouldering the pack, "open the window, will you? And toss out that coil of sheets!"

Eddy's eyes widen with both fear and excitement.

"We're going down?"

"No. They would catch us pronto. We're going up. The sheets are a diversion." The corner of the first sheet is tied to the wall radiator. Eddy drops the rest of the improvised rope out the window while JET reaches past his shoulder and slams a hidden release on the window frame with his fist. Outside the window a single rope drops down from above.

"What's up there?" squeaks Eddy.

JET responds by handing Eddy a pair of climbing devices. "Ever used jumars?"

"Chew-whats?"

"For climbing." JET takes a final look around his room, turns out the lights and climbs onto the windowsill. The red warning lamp continues pulsing. "Clip one onto the rope like this. The other clips above. Put your feet in these loops that hang down, one from each jumar. Hold on tight and inchworm your way up after me. Hurry." Then he's gone.

JET's security cameras reveal police trying to pry open JET's apartment door. They are pounding and shouting. Eddy fumbles trying to get his foot into the jumar when JET's head suddenly pops upside down into the window from above. "Grab that *Handbook*!"

Eddy reaches over and shoves the ragged book down the back of his pants then climbs out the window. They pull the hanging rope up after reaching the roof just as police break down the apartment door and are doused with sprays of shaving cream from JET's booby-traps.

Outside the dorm window, one can see a rope of knotted sheets hanging to the ground from a third story window. A white-smeared campus policeman leans out the window and searches the quiet evening, swearing under his breath. He turns around and gives orders for the others to start searching the campus.

Sitting on the roof of the dormitory, JET and Eddy lean against the side of the elevator house, catching their breath, considering options.

Eddy says, "I have a van, some camping gear, a few hundred dollars... What do you have?"

"This is it," indicating his backpack. "I have a couple thousand greenbacks in here, my toothbrush, and thanks to you, the *Handbook*."

"Well. Our adventure has been short, but great so far," says Eddy. "What's next?"

"I noticed that you just asked a question."

Eddy squints at him, annoyed that at a time like this, JET would bring up something so obvious. *Is he making fun of me? Has he gone insane?* "So?"

"I have this theory about questions."

"You already explained about..." but JET's glare cues him to switch tactics and play dummy. "So, uh... I mean... What is this theory I heard you have about questions, JET? I've been dying to ask you..."

"I think questions are more important than answers. I think questions are how to get from one place to another. In fact, I think questions *are* the answer, and if you are ever stuck, all you need to do is... well... ask the next question."

As JET says these last words, he makes a spiral hand signal with his right hand, his first finger pointing up and his thumb pointing out to the next question, a signal Eddy doesn't get at all.

JET continues anyway. "Look. We are stuck right now. We need to get out of here."

Eddy makes an idiot grin. "So, what's the next question?" sloppily imitating JET's hand signal, partly in jest.

"That is the next question, Eddy! Your move. You've got the hot potato."

Eddy accepts the challenge. "The way I see it right now, the main question for us is: 'What's really going on?' If we stay in the same environment in which the answer to 'What's really going on?' is fogged – namely the university environment – we will never find out what's really going on. To escape the first interference factor, I think we need to get out of modern civilization altogether. Southern Arizona comes to mind – a place where there is nothing but cactus and rocks, lizards and sand. We'll take food and water in my van, set up camp, and start working on the second interference factor."

JET smiles ear-to-ear at Eddy, like a freshly carved Jack-O-Lantern, glowing from a candle inside. His theory is now a proven fact.

Eddy continues. "The second interference factor is us. Our minds and bodies, to be exact. Our minds have been imprisoned and imprinted by the perception framework of modern culture. Somehow, we must also escape from that prison. If we can practice new perception skills, it will disorganize our old patterns and at the same time start entirely new ones. I think maybe then we can discover what is really going on."

JET says, "I am with you Sherlock. Grab the rope and jumars, will you? We may need them later. Shall we use the elevator this time?"

# Phoenix, South Africa 5

Screeching cicadas amplify the oppressive heat. Two skinny black women with tattered hand-woven wide-brimmed palm-leaf hats merrily weed rows of grain crops with hand hoes, singing a story together, sometimes laughing out loud.

A pudgy black man – dressed like the assistant bureaucrat that he is – leans his dusty old bicycle against an ancient acacia tree along the pitted dirt road, and squats down on his haunches to watch. He is completely confounded.

After a while he stands up and approaches the women, gingerly, not wanting to get on the bad side of a pair of witches. "I don't quite believe what I am seeing here," he says.

The two women stop and look up. "Hello Sam," says Tandra.

Mandisa glances at her cousin worriedly, calling Mr. Sachaza by his first name! How improper! But Tandra smiles broadly, and Sam forces a smile back.

"Hello Ms. Wakatchoosi. Ms. Nalingi. What a fine day for gardening! Where are the men?"

There is dead silence, as dead as the men are. The women say nothing and do not move.

"I said..."

"We heard very well what you said Sam," interrupts Tandra, like a patient mother might interrupt a child's blathering. "It's just that you are holding wild and unexamined assumptions about who you think you are talking to, and the sooner I stop you the less embarrassed you will be."

"I was just saying..."

"Would you like a do-over, Sam?" interrupts Mandisa.

"Do-over?"

"You are greeting members of a phoenix culture, Sam. That means you get as many honest do-overs as it takes for love to happen. Do-overs are allowed because love never goes away. Only you go away. But you can decide to come back," says Mandisa.

Tandra takes over. "You started off in a very unloving direction, Sam. Along that path there's no love happening for as far as I can see. But you don't have to keep going down that road. You can stop and take a new path by having a do-over. You just say, 'Thanks for the new perspective. I'd like to try again with my new understanding.' It is easy. Even you could learn this. Would you like to have a do-over, Sam?"

"Yes, I suppose I would."

"Then ask for it."

"May I have a do-over?" he says, quivering from so many sudden turns.

"Yes, you may. Go ahead," says Tandra.

"Once a week for the past six years I have ridden my bike past your kraal. It looked like every other kraal I see, each week a little emptier, a little more depressed. Children leave for the big city, elders die, people bicker for more TV time and less fieldwork. But in the past couple of months something has changed here. I wonder about it. I mean, what is happening here? I wonder if permits for what you are doing have been properly approved by the law."

"The law?" questions Mandisa. "Of what law do you speak?"

"The law of the land, of course. The law of South Africa. The law we are all subject to."

"I'm sorry to be the one to inform you, Sam, but that law is based in a false paradigm. That law is suicidal for humanity," says Mandisa. "I have withdrawn my allegiance to that law, and for your own good, I suggest you do the same too, as fast as possible."

Sam flusters about, first taking an apoplectic step towards the women as if to restrain their insanity, then jolting back a step, in animal fear, when he notices they stand their ground with unexpected ease, ready to take him down with their hoes.

Mandisa continues, "People in your culture submit themselves to a law written by corrupted individuals who have sold their integrity for a very low price. That law serves the short-sighted interests of wealthy foreigners, not the interests of our grandchildren, not even the interests of their own grandchildren. You now stand before two people from a very different culture than yours, Sam. In our culture, your culture's laws are irrelevant. You are a person of one culture speaking with people from a different culture. The only way that would change would be for you to kill us right now. And killing us would be very stupid, because if you care to look around, you will see that this little garden of loving friendship and creative collaboration is the best thing going for at least a hundred miles around. Rather than coming here to say we are illegal from the viewpoint of a corrupt system, you would be a lot smarter to come here to grieve your last six years of serving irresponsible adolescents higher than you in a patriarchal hierarchy, and admit that you see something remarkable here. You could say, 'I don't know what this is. It scares me. But what you are doing here seems to be working and I'd love to learn more about it. Can I stick around and help out?'"

"Um... I'd... I'd uh.... like to have a do-over... I haven't seen anything so hopeful in thirty years since..." tears are streaming down his cheeks, but he does not look away from these two amazing women, "since... the priests started beating and sexually molesting the children of your village at their church. I don't know how the hell you're doin' it here, with no money, and no chief, but with all my heart I'd like to pitch in and help, see if I can learn something. Could you... could that be okay with you?"

"Sure," says Tandra without hesitating. "When you take radical responsibility, the dream equals the vision. It goes like this. Grab that bucket over there and hoist us up some more water from the well, will you? These plants are thirsty. And while you're doing that, you sing baritone. Your part goes like this..."

# Phoenix, Arizona 2

An old model dark blue utility van trundles along an unmarked desert road leading south from Arizona State Route 86. Clouds of brown dust billow in its wake. The four-wheeled machine is the only sign of civilization from horizon to horizon. The rest is cactus, mesquite, rock-strewn hills, sand... and the dusty road.

Eddy drives. JET sits in the passenger seat with his arm braced in the window. The engine compartment is between them. These two geniuses are in a hot debate over a distinction from the *Handbook* resting open in JET's bouncing lap.

"You're crazy!" says Eddy. "If something happens to you, then you are a victim of those circumstances. Period!"

"But who created the circumstances?"

"The circumstances just happen! Don't be an idiot! Shit happens! It's a law of the Universe. It is not my fault! How could it be my fault?"

"The *Handbook* is not talking about 'fault.' There is a difference between responsibility and fault. We avoid responsibility because we think that if we are responsible then we will be blamed, we will be guilty, it will be our fault, and we will be punished. We think, 'Why set myself up for punishment?' We think, 'Who needs that?' But the thing is, this is...

"What?" prompts Eddy.

"See that beer can?" JET says pointing ahead along the side of the road. "Who is responsible for that beer can being there?"

"Probably some drunk grandmother."

"Stop the car!!!" commands JET.

"What?"

"Now! Stop the car!!!"

Eddy slams on the brakes and the van skids to a dusty halt. Before the car is fully stopped, JET flips the *Handbook* into the glove compartment, throws open the door and disappears back into the cloud of dust.

Eddy sits there shaking his head, trying to brush the dust off his shirt and pants. He keeps the motor running. In a moment JET hops back into his seat proudly holding the wrinkled aluminum can in his hand, slamming the door shut behind him.

"I am!"

Eddy glares at JET like he is insane. "What the hell?"

"I am responsible for the can lying on the side of the road. See! I just proved it! It is not lying there on the road anymore. I was responsible for it being where it was because I could pick it up and put it somewhere else! If I don't pick it up, it stays where it is, but then I am responsible for leaving the can there. This is true for every piece of litter on every road in every city, everywhere in the world. I am responsible for it being there. My awareness that the can is there made me just as responsible as the drunk grandmother who dropped it there."

"You are nuts! You're going to spend the rest of your days going around picking up garbage?"

"No. But see, I *could*! That is the point. I could pick up each piece of litter. The *Handbook* calls it 'radical responsibility.' I could pick up every piece of litter in the world. And if I decide *not* to pick it up, then my awareness of deciding to leave the litter there generates a feeling in me. I feel sad about leaving the litter there. Or I feel angry or scared about leaving the litter there. The feeling is also a consequence. But it is my choice to leave the litter there. This is the pain of waking up and consciously choosing to leave the litter where it is. It is my choice whether I leave it there or not, and if I choose to leave it there, then I am responsible for it being there. The same is true for each hungry man or woman. I could bring any of them home and feed them dinner. Every crying lonely child whose parent has not picked him up and listened to his fears. I could go there and pick him up and listen to why his heart aches... What?"

Silent tears roll down Eddy's dusty cheeks. He can't hold them back. After a minute he stops trying. He is in shock about the swiftness of emerging events, of leaving the university and driving out into the dirty desert with this near stranger on a crazy quest for the unknown.

It is the shock of not knowing where they are, or what is happening next. The shock of this concept of radical responsibility. It stops all of his normal thinking patterns and he just can't think anymore. And when he stops thinking, then he starts feeling.

Eddy's fingertips gently caress the gritty surface of the steering wheel while the muddy tears slide down his cheeks. JET remains in total silence, listening with respect for whatever his friend might want to share.

"I..." Eddy sniffles, swallows, does not wipe his tears, gazes out into the desert wilderness, takes a breath and decides to share the simple truth. He turns off the engine. "I was one of those little kids that you did not pick up."

Eddy glances at JET, then back to the emptiness of the desert. He looks down and a moan comes from deep in his soul. More tears come.

"I was about four. I wanted to know about my older brother. He was two years older than me, and sick, and they didn't tell me what was going on. My brother and I were always together, like two piggies in a mud puddle. Suddenly he wasn't around anymore. I just wanted to know the truth. They told me crap, and I knew it was crap. Later that year he died. I think it was Leukemia or something. They never made his death explicable for me. I felt completely abandoned, by him, by them. I stood there crying for the longest time, and they wouldn't pick me up and hold me and listen to my questions and explain it all to me. I guess they had their own heartbreak to deal with. I just wanted to know what was really going on, but to them I must have been part of the problem. I guess that's when I gave up on them and decided to take care of myself, to get smart and figure everything out on my own."

JET repeats the last thing solemnly, "You gave up on them and decided to take care of yourself, get smart, and figure everything out by yourself."

"Yes." Eddy realizes that he was just picked up and listened to by JET, and his heart breaks wide open, there in the old, dark colored van, parked on the dusty dirt road in the desert in the middle of nowhere. After a while he blows his nose in his pocket handkerchief and says, "Thanks." He sighs. "But that doesn't get you off the hook!"

"What hook?"

Eddy starts up the engine again and continues driving down the bouncing dusty road. "It is totally unrealistic for you to say that you are responsible for all the litter in the world. Somebody else threw it there. You are not responsible."

"It is not about being practical. It is about being aware. How would you feel if you were aware that you *could* actually pick up a piece of litter, but you decide not to do it? That you *could* actually pick up each crying child, but you chose to ignore them and let them cry?"

"I'd feel terrible."

"What kind of terrible? The *Handbook* gives you four options: mad, sad, glad or scared?"

"Sad mostly. Maybe I'd feel angry about it too."

"That's the point!" shouts JET. "When you become aware of an option that you could choose but you are not choosing, then you feel sad about losing that option."

"Just what I need right now. More sadness!" Eddy doesn't get it.

"It's the sadness of awareness that you feel, your awareness of choosing to let the world be a trash dump. But it works in reverse too. Let's say you decide you are not actually responsible for the litter, but you are going to pretend 'as if' you are responsible. Then, as you walk down a path, you pick up litter along the way. Even though you are only pretending to be responsible, this is a responsible universe. Then the litter you pick up, even though you were only pretending to be responsible for the litter being there, is actually picked up! I would rather feel the pain of *not* picking up the litter when I decide to not pick up the litter, than to live in the numbness of not knowing about all this. And you would too, or we would not still be talking about it!"

"Yeah, well, what I really want to know is how we decide where to stop and set up camp for tonight?"

"That's easy. It will suddenly become completely obvious."

In that second, the van darts out from a stand of mesquite bushes and shoots over an old wooden bridge across a rocky wash. Although the bridge looks solid, the main central support was washed away in the recent storm. This bridge can no longer support the weight of a vehicle.

The van is halfway across before the wood splinters and the front of the van drops two meters into the rocks below. The glass windshield explodes. Steam gushes from the smashed radiator. JET screams in pain as his left leg gets pinned between the smashed-in front of the van and the front of his car seat.

Eddy sits stunned, muttering to himself with a bleeding gash on his forehead. He starts to hyperventilate, looks frantically this way and that while total panic shoots up his spine. Then Eddy sees JET's smashed leg and goes hysterical. "What do I do?" Eddy screams. "What do I do?"

The terror in Eddy's voice forces JET to ignore the excruciating pain in his leg for a brief moment in order to save the both of them. He bellows like a drill sergeant. "Shut-up you dragon fart! Didn't you read the *Handbook*?"

Eddy is jolted into reasonableness by the unreasonableness of the question.

"What?"

JET looks Eddy in the eyes like a laser and fiercely plants instructions directly into Eddy's nervous system. "The way you figure out what to do is to shift identity. You. Now. Shift identity. Become someone who knows how to help us right now!"

Eddy panics. "But who? Who would know?"

"You are the fucking philosopher! Who can handle this problem?"

"Superman could!"

"Then go!" JET screams in writhing agony. "Shift into Superman! You are Superman! Handle this problem!"

Forced by the immediacy of mortal danger, Eddy unclicks his seatbelt, kicks open his door and dive-rolls headfirst into the sand between two boulders. He scrambles back under the belly of the nose-down van, pops up on the other side, and yanks open JET's door to inspect the situation.

At that moment, gasoline from a split fuel line drips onto the hot exhaust manifold and bursts into flame. Smoke erupts through the smashed engine cover into the cabin of the van.

JET screams to the world, "Get me out of here!" Then he turns to Eddy and pleads, "Superman! Please get me out of here. Now!"

Flames leap out of the engine box. JET jerks his body towards the door to escape the heat but only tears his leg more. The pain is agonizing, yet he is trapped. Paint begins to blister and pop on the engine cover from the heat. Grasping about for something to hold onto, JET screams, "Don't let me burn!"

Eddy / Superman moves in complete certainty. He picks up a long flat stone and in two swift full-arm sweeps, knocks the branches off a dead tree that is caught in the streambed between the rocks. He wrestles the tree free from the stones, uses it to pole vault onto the boulder that smashed in the front of the car, then slams the fat end of the tree down through the broken window next to JET's leg without stopping to aim. He then leaps off the rock so the full force of his body weight leverages through the tree against the engine box. The leverage forces a gap of one inch. Flames leap up through the gaping hole where the front window used to be. In a calm, commanding voice, Eddy / Superman says, "JET, pull your leg out. Now!"

JET screams, "Aaaarrgh-aaah!" and twists his torn and bleeding leg free of the wreckage. Flames reach for JET as he falls out the door, but Eddy / Superman is already there to catch him and carry him away from the inferno. We can almost see Superman's cape blowing in the wind.

Eddy / Superman places JET gently onto the sand at a safe distance from the flames, stands up tall, and smiles beatifically with a curl of black hair sticking down on his sweaty forehead, as if the ordeal were everyday business for him.

Eddy / Superman says, "I came just in time. Remember the extra jerry can of gasoline we brought along as a safety measure?"

JET looks horrified. Then, *Wha-boom!* The rear compartment of the van violently explodes shooting oily black flames in all directions and blowing the rear doors off the van. The driver and passenger seats are blazing.

Rocking back and forth in the sand, holding his leg, grimacing in pain, JET says, "Yeah. I remember."

Eddy / Superman says, "Well, there were two of them."

A second and louder *Whoompf!* throws flames thirty feet into the air. With the front window broken and the rear doors blown away, the body of the van nose down has become a chimney, flames efficiently consuming the entire contents of the van. It is a fireball.

JET demands, "Don't you have a fire extinguisher in your car?"

"Yes," says Eddy / Superman. "It is under the driver's seat."

They shield their faces from the searing heat to see if there is any way to get at the fire extinguisher. JET starts laughing at the impossibility, then suddenly looks at Eddy in horror and shouts, "Superman! The *Handbook*!"

JET thrashes about in pain trying to stand up. Blood oozes out between his fingers.

"Eddy tells me he saw you put the *Handbook* into the glove compartment," says Eddy / Superman. "I will get it."

There is no smile on his face. He is not joking. He moves without hesitation.

"No! Stop!" JET shouts after him in fear. "Eddy! You'll be toast before you even get there! You idiot!"

But JET is not shouting at Eddy. He is shouting at Superman. And Superman has ideas of his own.

Eddy / Superman runs towards the bridge. The stream bed under the broken bridge is not totally dry from the storm. Between two boulders is a mud slick protected from the sun. Eddy flings himself sideways through the air, lands with a *Goosh!*, rolls like a hotdog, and in an instant is coated in sticky muck. Simultaneously he packs handfuls of goop on his face, hair, neck, and hands.

Brown as a chocolate Santa Claus, Eddy / Superman stands upright and strides straight towards the flames leaping out of the open passenger door. Holding his breath, keeping his left arm buried in mud against his midriff like the Boris Karloff mummy, Eddy / Superman aims his mud-covered right hand towards the glove box, shuts his eyes, and leans directly into the fire. For a moment he completely disappears from view, engulfed in flames. Then he steps back out of the inferno clutching the smoking book, steam rising from his body like a spaceship after re-entering the atmosphere.

Stiff legged, he walks over to JET, who has witnessed the whole event in utter astonishment, mouth agape, speechless.

Eddy / Superman places the *Handbook* in JET's free hand, saying "Here is your Handbook, sir, safe and sound." He radiates a true Superman smile, white teeth shining as flame-dried mud crackles off his cheeks and lands on JET's legs and arms.

"Thank you, Superman!" JET is truly awed, but also worried.

"One question though. How do we stop my leg from bleeding?" A dark puddle is already forming in the sand, while the fire roars, turning all contents of the van into ash, wafting them up into the clear blue desert sky.

Eddy / Superman ignores the flaming distraction and takes a deep breath. "Just a moment, sir, while I shift identity. Hmmmm... Doctor Frankenstein would know what to do."

"Wait!" JET pleads desperately. "What if you pick someone else? What about Dr. Schweitzer? Dr. Zhivago? Dr. Doolittle? Dr. Seuss? I would rather see Nurse Ratched..."

"Frankenstein will do just fine."

Eddy / Superman pirouettes swiftly around once, flinging mud globs every which way. His face contorts into a wry smile as he bows slightly from the waist. When he stands straight again, he tosses an imaginary cape back over his shoulder. "Goot eeeffeningk!" says Eddy / Dr. Frankenstein. "Vhat haf vee heah?"

The raspy Transylvanian accent is impeccably weird.

"Oh, my! You haf a deep gash in yor lateral forceps. Perhaps you haf cut an artery? Heeyah, my young friend. You must press heeyah to stop zee blood flowink. Let me show you."

JET recoils in confusion while Eddy / Dr. Frankenstein pulls out a pocket knife, slits the front cuff of JET's left pant leg, tears it open from cuff to knee, reaches professionally behind the joint, and feels for something with his fingers.

"Ah! Goot! Vee haf found it! Zee artary!"

Eddy / Dr. Frankenstein folds up his knife and drops it into his pocket, then reaches behind JET's leg and rolls up the jeans fabric into a tight wad. He grabs JET's hand, forces the wadded cloth into JET's fingers, and shows JET where to press it hard against the bone to cut off the flow of blood to the wound. JET winces, frightened by the Doctor's robust bedside manner, but he notices that the dripping comes to a stop almost immediately. JET starts to remove his fingers from the wound.

Eddy / Dr. Frankenstein shouts, "Oh! No, no! Silly boy! Do not let go!" Another muffled explosion from the van accentuates the good Doctor's instructions. "Not yet! You must vait anudder few minutes! Let zee platelets built zher fibers. Den vee vill apply a banditch. If I only had my handbag, I could suture you up, perhaps attach a new leg if you vanted?"

"Where would you get the new leg?"

"Ahh, yesss!" says Eddy / Dr. Frankenstein giggling at his own inventiveness. "From zoze vile donkeys ve saw back on ze road, uv course! Zen you could accurately claim to be only 25% jackass!"

"Sorry I asked."

The only sound they hear is the crackling van fire, finally dying down a bit for lack of fuel. Eddy / Dr. Frankenstein struts over to what remains of their former vehicle and breaks off a flaming branch that caught fire from the burn. He carries it back towards JET.

"Hold on a minute there Franky!" sputters JET nervously. "You're not planning to cauterize my wound, are you?"

"Ho, no! Ze *Handbook* says dat zee problem iz zee soliution."

"Okay... Well then... What is the problem?"

"Ahh! Zee problem izzz... how are vee stayink varm tonight? Und how are vee cookingk owa breakfast in zee morningk?"

"Breakfast? What about dinner?"

Eddy / Dr. Frankenstein answers over his shoulders while he collects an armful of dry twigs and bigger sticks, digs out a small firepit, and gets a small fire going. "Tonight ve enchoy zee excellent experience uv fasting. Did chu effa try fasting befowa, my young friend?"

"Uh, yes. But I fasted very quickly. Only between meals."

They both laugh, but JET moans in pain.

"Franky," asks JET, "what about eating your emergency carrot?" The orange colored root vegetable is covered in mud but partly visible in Eddy's back pocket.

"Not eenuf eemergency yet..."

Suddenly Eddy's face melts to sadness and frustration as he sits down next to JET and exits the Dr. Frankenstein identity, shifting back to 'ordinary' Eddy.

"Man!!! Why did my car have to blow up? Tell me this: the crashed car is the solution to what problem?"

Silence reigns.

Suddenly JET's eyebrows go up in realization. "Tell me. What were we talking about just before the crash?"

"Uh..." says Eddy. A full minute of silence passes. "Ah, yes! I remember. I was asking how would we decide where to stop and camp for the night..."

"Do me a favor, will you, my friend?" says JET. "Never ask that question again while we are driving."

# Edinburgh, Scotland 2

Sean Connery stands gravely among a dozen or so aging adults dressed in black. These are the numb participants of a typically dead Christian funeral. It is late afternoon on Friday. The casket has already been lowered into the freshly dug grave. Sean feels distraught.

The mumbling in the background is the priest. Sean understands no word. He stares into the pit, not recognizing that the pit he stares into is himself.

The others leave the graveyard, the same way they leave Charles Dobson, the same way they leave Sean Connery, not realizing Sean is still alive. *Or am I?* he wonders. He feels the pang of a doubt.

The shock of his nervous system reordering after expressing overwhelming feelings and emotions back in the funeral home continues to echo in him.

After speaking his required ablutions, the young priest gives Sean a manly pat on the shoulder and departs. This physical jolt brings Sean enough out of his trance to detect that across the grave remain two pointed black shoes, aimed at him. Each shoe contains one black-stockinged leg. Only a short bit further up starts a long black skirt over narrow hips, all covered by a thick black woolen coat and a burgundy-colored scarf. There on top of all those clothes sits a woman's wide-brim black hat, partially hiding a wrinkly narrow face staring at him through glasses.

This woman exhibits knife-blade neutrality.

Sean does not perform any of the traditional social niceties that might be expected in such a situation. Instead, not unlike a sitting dog startled by a sudden sound, Sean moves into action. He swings one final gaze through the abyss, puts his hat on his head, turns and walks away without a word.

Two days later Sean sits alone in a church pew, a third of the way back on the left. An organ finishes the closing hymn. The same priest walks down the aisle and passes through the vestibule to stand outside and bless the remnant congregation as they depart.

Sean eventually follows the priest down the aisle and out the door. As is habitual, Sean shakes the priest's hand, then puts his hat back on. When he lifts his head he stares into the face of the same woman from the funeral, standing next to the priest.

"Mr. Connery? I'm Smith. Margaret Smith."

"I've seen you about town Ms. Smith. You knew Dobson?"

"Only as a fellow citizen of this fine village, sitting not far from me on the Grim Reaper's waiting bench."

"Aren't we all? Well then, good day Ms. Smith."

Margaret watches Sean descend the church steps, then meets the priest's knowing glance. Mr. Connery is not famous for being a social butterfly. Yet in a time of need, shutting out human contact may not be the wisest strategy.

Back at his cottage, Sean sits in his special chair near a crackling fireplace. It is evening. Sean has placed a plaid wool wrap over his knees to ward off the spring chill. He has been sitting there all afternoon, perhaps all day.

He has also been drinking.

He used the drink as lubricant for inner reflection. Partly due to guilt, partly out of shame, partly because he could feel himself rapidly sliding along the bench that Ms. Smith mentioned, he had looked up her phone number and scratched it onto a scrap of paper that he tore off an envelope from the kindling basket.

The Scotch is making that little scrap of paper in his hand less scary.

Using the courage derived from pouring the dregs of his glass down his throat in one large swallow, he reaches for an old-fashioned telephone, the kind that has a wire attached. Squinting at the numbers through glasses perched on the end of his nose, Sean dials.

It feels like the bravest stunt he has ever performed. But the cameras are not rolling, so what is the point? Nobody is paying him. Nobody will watch this film.

The phone is answered.

"Hello."

"Is this Margaret Smith?" Sean says before his mind can come into gear and rescue him from certain doom.

"Who would be so rude as to ask my name without introducing themselves first?"

"Sorry. This is Connery. Sean Connery. I'm..."

"Mr. Connery. You sound like you've been drinking..."

Sean pauses, mouth half-open about to say something, but he can't remember where he was going with this.

"What was that?" the woman coaxes.

Sean considers giving up on his hopeless insanity, but hanging up now seems worse than suicide.

He sighs grievously.

"Could you please repeat? I did not understand you."

"I have nothing left to lose..." he mumbles.

"I heard you tell me that you have nothing left to lose."

"Yes..." He sighs again.

A delayed reaction somewhere deep inside informs Sean Connery that he has just been heard. Not only was he listened to, but he was also actually heard. Something mechanically clicks inside of him now that this communication has been delivered and accurately repeated back to him by another consciousness. The original message is erased from the roster, leaving space for something entirely different to slide forward and be communicated.

"I'm, uh... Would you be willing.... Something happened to me. There was... I had... I don't know... I've come to a crossroads. Something has to change. I need to talk... Sorry, I don't know you... But could... Is there a time when we could meet? In person?"

"Yes. Whenever you are thoroughly sober, I would be most pleased to meet with you and try whatever it is you propose, within certain limits."

"Good then. Uh..."

"What about Thursday evening at six for an early dinner at the Golden Lion?"

"Yes. Uh... I would pay."

"No need for you to pay, Mr. Connery."

"Right then. Sorry to bother you..."

Sean drops the phone back into its cradle and in the same smooth move picks up the bottle by its neck to pour himself another drink.

*Whew! That was really tough on my nerves*, he thinks.

*But that thought... where did it actually come from? Who was speaking if it was not me? What else is in there sending me manipulative messages designed to influence my behavior? This has become a bit suspicious. I have heard you speak to me before. I am getting a sense that your purpose in speaking to me bodes nefarious. Hmmm...*

As this thought rolls across his mind, something different slows his hand.

Something from long ago in his past, deep in his soul, a blurry memory of what could possibly once have been imaginable. *Being a man? Being me? Unhindered?*

*Wasn't there a movie about this?*

It seems there is a light dimly shining from a faraway coastline, glimpsed in the night on stormy seas from the deck of a gashed and rapidly sinking ship.

He hesitates.

*Is it really worth all the effort this new future would take?*

He holds up the bottle and regards the amber fluid against the glowing firelight.

It's pretty.

He can smell the stuff.

*Very tempting...*

Somehow the drive for the next drink has been partially diminished through arranging that dinner date with Ms. Margaret Smith...

He eases the bottle back to the table and corks it.

Rubs his mouth.

Gazes into the flames.

Sleeps...

# San Pedro, California 3



Arthur is still not back at A. T. Advertising. I completely understand this. He's the boss. A good boss can get out of the way and let everyone do their job.

What I don't understand is why people who would normally never even notice my existence keep ringing my phone or stepping into my cubicle for private consultations about what might be coming down the tubes. Fortunately, I have been cobbling together a rather more interesting story than the one I believed last week. I decide to schedule a staff meeting for Friday morning. Then my phone rings. I recognize the caller from the sound of his inhale. It's the wizard.

"Hello Balthazar," I say immediately. No extra bullshit from me this time.

"I suggest we meet again before you make any more moves."

"I'll be there at five."

"We will see."

I hang up. A sense of orderliness and calm fills my workspace. The day goes well. I write a memorandum for the meeting.

> Attn: Staff
> From: Gwendolyn Circe
> RE: Friday Meeting 10:00 a.m.-10:50 a.m. The Oak Room
> Agenda: Gameplan for *Whale Storm* Project.
> New information opens interesting possibilities.
> Capitalizing on them requires expanding our skill base.
> Are you in?
> Best,
> Gwendolyn

I am fascinated that I used the word 'capitalizing', but not fascinated enough to send out the memorandum. I am gaining respect for Balthazar's opinions. I decide to wait until after we meet. I briefly consider reporting back to Snake-Eyes Alexander but figure this too can wait.

A few hours later I experience a foggy evening in San Pedro. I wear my same dress. Now I call it my 'wizardress'.

The damp cold of the rusty circular staircase railing is sensation enough to shrink my attention to a small now. At the landing I catch my breath, ignore the bell cord and knock. It takes longer this time before he opens the door, but then he extends a hand to greet me. I don't take it. I walk directly towards my chair at the workbench. This time I pour the water and drink. He pours some for himself and also drinks. We sit.

"Look," he says. "I am sure that having sex with you would be fun, but I want to do something else with you that is just as intense but lasts longer."

It is a line I will never forget. There is nothing my mind can do with it, so I let it float in further until it lands in the specific chamber where I file my collection of future experiments. I trust that the right thing will happen with it there.

He continues. "We don't have so much time right now. I need to leave soon. You can leave whenever you are ready. Do you want to try this?"

"Drugs?"

"No."

I pause a moment to see if I trust him. I don't. I immediately feel glad about that. Trust is highly overrated. I don't have enough experience to assess Balthazar's integrity, to see if he actually does what he says he will do. But I trust myself to take care of myself around someone like him. This is enough for now. By trusting myself to take care of myself, I can collaborate with nearly anyone about anything. I say, "I am ready."

He glances slowly around the room, presumably to check the lights. He adjusts the position of his chair so there is as much light on his face as there is on mine. Then he says, "Choose one of my eyes. It does not matter which one. Choose one of my eyes and only look into this one eye. Do not bounce back and forth between my two eyes. The bouncing cuts the contact. Then gaze into the black part of my eye, into the pupil. Just connect into the little black circle while you navigate yourself to un-defendedness. Are you ready?"

"Yes." I am already trying it.

"This is not a staring contest!" Sternness in his voice. "Staring keeps you at the superficial intellectual level. Staring is doing. This is not about doing anything. This is about being... being with another person's Being."

That is when the floor drops out from underneath me. It happens more quickly than I could imagine. There is a sensation of being seen, more naked than without clothes. I also feel like I am being hugged deeper than the skin and bones. But there remains a respectful distance between us. I feel honored, and there is space for me to honor myself while I honor his Being as well. I hear my mind screaming questions, trying to interfere, trying to understand why it just lost majority vote in my life. I don't let it say a thing. I feel a tingling at the bottom of my spine that weaves its way up the center of my body growing in intensity. It is nearly unbearable, yet it is also a sensation I have been longing for my whole life.

"Stay centered and open. Keep slowly breathing."

I lose it then. A question hijacks my attention. I ask, "How can you talk?"

He says nothing and does not waver.

Like a parachutist in free-fall, I have put my hand into the wrong position and spin crazily out of control. He waits patiently while I get it back together again. *Choose one eye. Gaze openly into its black center. Navigate to... yes... there we are again.*

My Being says, *Hello there!* A smile takes over my face. Then I lose it again.

*Damn! Back to zero. Breathe. Center. Choose one eye...*

"Let yourself see while you let yourself be seen... This is giving and receiving at the same time... a two-way exchange."

He speaks in measured syllables. I get the answer to my question. It is like juggling while talking to the audience. I must split my attention. One part of my attention stays focused on juggling. The other part of my attention focuses on speaking to the audience.

I see him doing this balancing act with me. One part of his attention is on staying centered and being with my Being. The other part of his attention – the smaller part – is talking with my mind.

Mmmmmmmhhh... this is nice. A woman could get used to this.

"This is called 'countenance,'" he says. "It is never comfortable. It is never unconscious. If you are not doing it intentionally, you are not doing it at all." The warmth and tingling seem to double in intensity. I hardly want to breathe. Then he says, "I need to go."

"Where are you going?" My whole Being wants to shout, *No! Stay! How could you leave me at time like this?*

He says nothing, waiting for me to come back to split attention in countenance.

"I need to deliver an initiation," he says, standing slowly up from the chair, still gazing into my eye.

"I am coming with you." It is not a question. Still, he needs to agree...

He glances towards a small bronze statue of Ganesha on his bookshelf. There are a few wrapped candies in a bowl at Ganesha's feet. He steps over, takes two, hands me one, says, "This is for you," while he opens the other for himself.

I stopped eating pure sugar long ago. It screws with my energy level. Still, I pull on both ends of the cellophane candy wrapper and pop the brown colored ball straight into my mouth, still in countenance with the wizard. It is root beer flavored.

He says, "Okay. You can come."

*Was this another test?* I wonder to myself.

"Yes it was," he says, "and you passed with flying colors. Can we use your car?"

"Yes." I say, staring at him with my eyebrows lowered.

"Excellent," he says. "Then I have time to pee..." He heads to a side door.

Right. A wizard needs to pee.

Never thought of that.

"I'm next!" I shout.

I am a wizard too.

# Eugene, Oregon 6

Davis finds Sanjib shaking his head in nauseated disbelief as he exits the Eugene City Dog Pound.

"Hey! Hey! What's up, buddy? What are you doing here?"

"They want me to wash dog butts, Davis!"

"Well… Somebody has to do it."

Sanjib is about to barf his breakfast.

"I have a problem," says Davis. "Can we talk?"

"You mean, can you talk, and can I listen?"

"You and I have the same problem, Sanjib. You simply haven't crashed into it yet."

"And what problem might that be, Mr. Know It All?"

"Our lives have just turned to shit."

"I won't argue that."

"No, really. They want us to be normal, and I've been spending my whole life trying to be me."

Sanjib squints doubtfully. "Is that why you follow in your father's footsteps to become a police officer? Because, just by coincidence, out of all possible professions, and all possible career paths that are out there in the world, you and your father happen to accidentally have the same profession?"

"That is exactly what I mean. I don't know who is really in charge."

They walk aimlessly down the sidewalk, turning right to escape the traffic noise onto a quieter residential street in an unfamiliar neighborhood. It is morning. The only other people on the sidewalk push baby strollers, walk dogs, or jog – or some combination of the above. Otherwise, they would drive their car, right? Why walk when there are cars?

Sanjib stays quiet, forcing Davis to sink into a deeper level inside of himself so this conversation can continue more usefully.

"Most people I see make huge effort trying to be normal. This is why I think so many people are addicted to flipping through photos on their phone. They want to see what normal looks like so they can copy it. Even if people say, 'Hey! Look how special I am!' all they really are, is especially normal."

Walking.

Davis continues. "It makes me think about the bad old days,

before phones, when we lived in villages, how everyone dressed in the same style of clothes, spoke the same language, ate the same food, went to the same church. Before my grandfather died, he told me a story."

"I'm glad he told you the story before he died, Davis. Otherwise, you are definitely in the wrong profession."

Davis smirks but doesn't bite the hook. "I was a kid. It is Sunday. My dad wants us all to go to church. I don't want to go. My grandfather takes me aside and says, 'The option of not going to church is new. I can see you are a smart kid with your own mind. You don't do what others do simply because they are doing it. Yes, it would make your father less upset if you went along with his program. But I remember when he did not want to go to church, and I forced him to go. Today I regret that. Now I would let him go do whatever he wants, instead of trying to make him go to church. I have seen what the church really is. It is not a pretty sight. But listen, you would be more successful if you figure out what you *do* want to do, rather than focusing on what you *don't* want to do, and making your life about trying to fight against it.'

Silence. Walking.

"I think that was a waking moment for me, Sanjib. I still remember how my grandfather's breath smelled. It was true, though. I didn't know what I wanted to do instead of going to church. Sanjib, I still don't know what I want to do. What do you really want to do?"

"I really want to have some tea in that café across the street on that corner over there."

"Okay, well then. I'll catch up with you later."

"No! Sorry. You are right. I did not say what I want with enough definition to be truthful. What I really want to do, right now, Davis, is have tea in that café on the corner across the street up there, with *you!* I want to keep talking about these things – *with you* – so that we can better figure out how to deal with what is going on. I am making a proposal. What do you say?"

"Is it okay if I have iced coffee instead of tea?"

"Yes."

"Are you buying?"

"Yes."

Davis's eyebrows go up in 13% surprise. Sanjib has never offered to pay before. Davis says, "I accept your proposal, with the added stipulation that you speak first."

"Agreed."

As they settle into chairs at a small round white-marble table near the plate glass window at the front of the teahouse, Davis says, "I changed my mind. I have to clear something first."

"Go ahead."

"I am not gay."

"Okay. So?"

"So, as I sat down here with you, I could feel a small fear coming up inside of me that other people seeing us two guys sitting at a small table having tea and coffee together  could think we are gay. Maybe my fear is not so small."

"So?"

"If we were wearing our cop outfits, that would define our situation in an understandable way, 'Two cops having donuts and coffee'. Easy to grasp."

"Okay... So?"

"I just want to be clear. If we were kids hanging out, it wouldn't matter. We could be playing together. Somehow, now, it matters. If I see two men hanging out together, I give them a fifty-fifty chance of being gay."

"And the problem with being gay is?"

"Are you gay, Sanjib?"

"No. But in my birth culture, it is not uncommon for ordinary men friends to walk down the street hanging onto each other, even holding hands, just being friends."

"I want to talk stuff over with you, but I don't want more than that. Does this upset you? I mean, are you expecting more?"

"I am not gay. I am attracted to women. But I am completely incompetent in that department. American women... are complicated."

"Okay, then. Can we still be a cop team and talk things over without me having to be afraid that you are thinking I am making gay moves towards you?"

Sanjib senses long-held loneliness behind the sincerity of Davis's request to be 'friends', while at the same time he fears being manipulated. He has his own experiences of being at the effect of hidden motivations trying to twist his attempts at authentic vulnerability into feeding the other person's desires for homosexuality.

"Yes," Sanjib says. "Thank you for clearing your heart with me about this. I have no deceptions in mind. It would be good to have a friend named Davis Hatcher. It would make me happy. Being happy in this way would make my life better."

Davis looks down at his own hands wrapped tightly around the ice-chilled glass. He did not feel the chill before. Now he does. His fingers are numb.

Davis glances around the café. Other tables are occupied by singles, mostly women. Only one table besides theirs has two customers. They are both women. All of these people fiddle with their phones, pretending to be doing something 'important' or 'meaningful' so that no one discovers how lonely and scared they are. Even the two women sit disconnected in two different worlds. It is a bad joke. A sad joke. He glances up at Sanjib who has been checking him out all the while, waiting. It feels like the first time Davis sees Sanjib, simply another man, sitting across from him at this café table. That is all. No stories. No unconscious fear-based projections. Two men sit together and talk, experimenting with becoming more human with each other, without excuses.

"Thank you for your patience with me, Sanjib. I..."

Sanjib sighs while nodding. "I get your first question now, about having the assignment from Sergeant Brinks to go undercover and be normal, when 'being normal' is the least interesting thing we could imagine being. Let me tell you how it is going for me. I will not try to be normal to please someone else because that would be fake. I don't think Sergeant Brinks is capable of not trying to be normal. Chief Stafford either. For them, trying to be normal is their central life strategy. I think that you and I need to play along with Stafford and Brinks while we find our way to the edge of things."

"What do you mean, 'to the edge of things'?"

"What is Brinks afraid of, really? I know that our assignment comes from Police Chief Stafford following his orders. But where are those orders coming from? Higher up in the hierarchy. Who is up there in the hierarchy making those orders? And what is going on for the higher ups? They are afraid of something. This is for sure. They are afraid of change, maybe... change that they cannot control. Or change that makes people uncontrollable. I don't mean in a bad way, like anarchistic, or hedonistic, or terroristic. I mean beyond control. Not caring about following the adjudications coming down from above them in the imagined hierarchy. I mean people gaining freedom. Having their own authority and being responsible and creative with it."

"I follow you, Sanjib. Keep going."

"You and I have been instructed to pretend to be one of those people interested in something that is beyond control. We are being hired, by Stafford and Brinks, to go beyond the edge of what is held dear by Stafford and Brinks – which I would guess is their jobs. I mean, who are they without their jobs? Their uniform? Their badge and gun? Yet they assign us to change enough to fit in with those people who have discovered that modern culture has an edge beyond which the hierarchy has no grip. We are supposed to go to that edge of modern culture that terrifies even the millionaires and the billionaires, and especially the trillionaires, living far up the hierarchy. Deep inside they are terrified that their life, their 'good fortune' if you want to call it that, the circumstances by which they have extracted their so-called 'wealth and power' out of the world, might not have enough reality to substantiate them anymore. You and I are supposed to pretend that we agree with the fantasy world that the 'millionaires have importance', and that our police officer job is to 'protect the story that the millionaires are the real people', and that the rest of us are either worthless peons, slaves, and peasants, or else we are the terrorists out to destroy the fantasy world that the millionaires live in."

"I get you."

"I am not interested in defending that fantasy world anymore, Davis. I am not interested in that at all. I would rather not have a job in modern culture than be forced to defend the suicidal fantasy world of the wealthy. What about you?"

"Holy shit, Sanjib. What is in your tea? I never heard you talk like this before."

"I never felt safe enough to talk like this before. I never heard myself say things like this before, either. But as I say these things to you now, I do not think they are new for me, and I do not think they are untrue. These things make sense to me."

"That's what I'm telling you, Sanjib. They make sense to me too."

"The really scary thing about what I just said is that it means we have already been classified as terrorists in their minds. Do you get this? It is ominous for us right now, Davis. It could be lethal for us. Stafford and Brinks see us as capable of being enough of a terrorist that we can successfully infiltrate the terrorist circles. Holy crap! It means we have become expendable in their minds. I am not gay, but are you a terrorist?"

Davis swallows hard in a dry throat, glances around the café, then looks back at Sanjib. "You are making my old life strategy of trying to be normal sound better and better. You are telling me that we are already classified in their eyes as disposable?"

"Yes."

"You mean that, if push comes to shove, they will not hesitate to SWAT us?"

"Yes. This, my friend, is precisely what I am saying."

"Cheeses..."

Silence reigns in the café, except for clean porcelain saucers being sharply slammed against each other as they are stacked, clean silverware being unconsciously thrown into hard plastic trays, empty used coffee grinds being banged into the plastic trash bin, the coffee grinder crushing roasted coffee beans, the chuffing roar of the coffee machine forcing hot water through fresh-ground roasted coffee beans, the thunder of hot steam bubbling through cold milk changing it into steaming hot foam, plus a blender whizzing spinach and pineapple into a green froth... obliterating any illusion of silence with chaotic rageful noise, the truth being, it is not silent at all in this café. It is fucking noisy!

"How do we play this out, Sanjib? I mean, you got any ideas?"

"I feel like a cricket player thrown into a baseball game, or rather, a cricket player thrown into a crash car derby, last man standing. What I would like is if we keep this conversation alive between us, but not public. You and I know that the world has to change. Actually, the real world is rapidly changing in drastic ways that could soon enough exclude human beings. As our ancient social constructs reflexively try to defend themselves, you are asking me to declare whose side I am on? You are asking me if I am on the side of trying to protect the dinosaurs who are already extinct due to the disconnect between their survival strategy and the changed environment? Or am I on the side of the little furry mammals, invisibly evolving into something more flexible and collaborative instead of simply trying to eat everybody around them?"

"If I read your tea leaves correctly, Sanjib, I would say that you are going renegade."

Sanjib sighs. "I have been renegade since I was born. I think you have also been renegade your whole life, Davis. The question at hand, the question we are being forced to either answer or try to pretend as if we do not perceive it, is, what are we really up to? Just because our fathers were upstanding citizens in the town of Eugene does not mean that the justice system they tried to live under is still valid. Human beings evolve. This means our constructs evolve, or we die inside of them. Modern culture's constructs are not designed to be evolutionary, but human beings are. The moment we stop trying to suppress our evolution, we are already outside of the modern system constructs. Either we try to force ourselves back into the mold, or we build the next construct, hopefully an evolutionary construct. Usually, police officers are not trained to have skills for building evolutionary constructs. What would you say about the idea of starting to learn those skills? Then we would be doing our newly assigned jobs. We would be appearing to be more normal."

"You mean, like... what exactly? You are moving very fast, Sanjib."

"I can only move this fast because you are listening this fast, instead of simply trying to fight me... and because we need to move this fast."

"Yeah, but... you freak me out!"

"What part am I freaking out, Davis? The part that understands me, or the part that pretends not to understand me?"

"No, but... I mean, yes, and... uh... what skills are you talking about?"

"If Sergeant Brinks wants us to blend in and be 'normal' – a kind of 'normal' defined by the fringes of society – so that when we walk into some evolutionary cult meeting they do not just throw us out – well, then, we should be intimately involved in learning to evolve, or something. Am I wrong about this?"

"No, I think you are dead on about this, Sanjib. Your logic is crystal clear. I think Chief Stafford would even pay for our trainings, if he sees they are part of our cover operation. What classes are you thinking of?"

Sanjib looks around the café, slides back his chair, elegantly stands up, and makes his way over to a small bulletin board screwed onto the wall near the coatrack. He tries to make his movements seem as casual as possible, which of course makes him look like a rhinoceros in a duck farm. But in a few moments, he returns excitedly with a handful of posters and cards.

"Look!" he says. "The solution to our problem is within one arm's reach!"

"What?"

"It is a theory I have been working on. The theory is that the universe does not give you a problem without also giving you a solution at the same time, often within one arm's reach. I noticed that for most of my life, when I would perceive a problem, I had the habit of reacting in terror, jumping up and down, running in circles, screaming and shouting..."

"Yes, I noticed that about you also..."

"I would put my attention out there somewhere, over there, trying to find solutions far away, assuming that whatever would solve the problem is even farther away than the problem itself. My new theory is that what creates the problem can also create the solution. The solution may not be so far away as I at first thought. Now I am starting to look at problems as if the problem itself is part of the solution. When I think this sentence to myself – 'The problem is the solution.' – oftentimes I see it work like a magical spell that opens up new perspectives. I suddenly have agency in a circumstance where, just a moment before, all I had was a sense of being persecuted by the Universe. I just now used that magic spell in my own mind, and look! I now have in my hands a handful of solutions! Here are flyers for Yoga class! Possibility Team! Aikido sword practice! Rage Club!"

Davis's eyes go wide.

Sanjib keeps examining the advertisements. "I never knew these things existed! I never entered this café before. It is all displayed right there on the wall! We could go to an Emotional Healing Process Dojo! A Kundalini Tantric Communications Course. A WorkTalk about Radical Relating. And something called... Oh my god! Oh my god! Davis! Davis!"

"What?" shouts Davis, loud enough that two staff and three customers wake from their daze for a moment and stare at him, like cows looking up from their grazing at a distant nuclear explosion.

"Davis!" whispers Sanjib, frantically pointing at a postcard-sized flyer in his shaking hands.

"You said that already, Sanjib, about five times. What is freaking you out?"

"It is *Shadow Knights of the Mysterium*! They meet on Thursday nights at 7:30 p.m. at the *Horsehead Bar*! It is no secret! They announce their meetings in public! The theme of their next meeting is: *The Nature of Reality is Groundlessness*."

Davis feels the floor drop out from under his chair. He falls into a bottomless pit that has been there his whole life. He only now notices the delusional nature of the ground upon which he imagined he was standing all this time.

Uncountable gut-wrenching moments tick by.

Finally, Davis whispers back, "What do we do?"

Sanjib gets a crazed look in his wide eyes, clears his throat, looks over to Davis and calmly says, "All of the above."

# Edinburgh, Scotland 3

Outside the Golden Lion, both Sean and Margaret stand bundled against the dampness of the evening. Sean opens the door for Margaret and they step into the warmth. Sean takes Margaret's coat from her and hangs it with his, then follows her to a small round dinner table which she chooses.

Both Margaret and Sean are known and respected by the wait staff, although they were never seen at the Golden Lion together.

Sean sits opposite Margaret, adjusting for quite a while, trying to find a comfortable position. Perhaps it is not the chair that is uncomfortable.

The waiter arrives and offers to bring drinks. She orders sparkling wine. He orders water.

"I thought you drank vodka martinis, shaken, not stirred?"

Seeing his discomfort, she offered him an easy hook to joke around with. But that is not where Sean wants to experiment, tonight. On this evening, he intends to explore a new level of honesty. He lets the hook slide past him, triggering nothing in his personality, and starts over. "May I call you Margaret?"

"Yes, Sean," exuding surprise and delight.

Sean looks at his fingers and repeatedly adjusts the position of his silverware. "My whole life I've been an actor. I have been putting on a show. I have invited you to dinner here tonight because I am getting too old to tolerate my own show. There is no more show in me. I see the final curtain drawing ever nearer. I don't know what comes next. I don't know what's outside the theater. All I know is that I won't make it there alone. And I won't make it without some practice."

He glances furtively to see her reaction. She listens attentively, not even sipping her wine.

"Something happened to me in the funeral parlor a few days ago. I don't know what it was. I... Shall we order first?"

"What you are saying is a fine starter course for me. I am in no hurry for the next course. Let us continue speaking."

Sean's character roles are the hero, the strong leader. He has no practice portraying himself as weak or incompetent, even if it may be real. Margaret's easy acceptance of his vulnerability is too genuine for him to backpedal any longer. He can only go deeper.

"You have taken a risk inviting me here. I have taken a risk accepting your invitation. I think I am lucky to be with you here. The conditions of my life indicate it is time to try an experiment... or else I must surely end." Sean soberly considers his potential insanity. "My new experiment is that I commit to being utterly honest with you."

Through pure theatrical discipline Margaret does not twitch a muscle. Sean continues. "Somehow I think you have a quality, uh..." shakes his head, searches the ceiling for words, "...a patience? A high enough tolerance for pain maybe, to do this experiment with me. You are so good at defending yourself or attacking back – no offense intended – that you seem absolutely relaxed in the face of any enemy, even me. I think you know what I mean?"

Margaret says nothing. She remains absolutely still. Only the accelerated pulse in her carotid artery and her ever-so-slightly quickened breathing betrays her excitement about what is occurring. After a moment she nods ever so slightly while keeping eye contact with Sean as long as he can endure it, but she does not speak. It is not her turn. This is not about her, yet.

Sean goes on, "I don't know how to do this very well..." He stalls out, furrows his eyebrows, shifts around in his chair, and catches his own lie. The shock pushes him to take his first authentic risk in the honesty experiment. "Pardon me Margaret. That was not honest enough. What I meant to say is: I don't know how to do this *at all*."

Margaret still waits. She senses this is a delicate 'go / no go' moment and looks straight back at Sean without expression, neither pushing nor pulling, neither attracted nor repelled.

Sean sighs, still fiddling with his napkin. He waits nervously. Margaret waits back. It is still his move.

He glances at her for a moment then, "I feel embarrassed a bit... a lot," again catching his subtle dishonesty. "I don't know why. I want to be truthful, even if I look ridiculous. I think it is my only chance. There is some block I have..." He glances at her again, checking to see if she is still with him. She is. "It has cost so much not to let myself be seen. But being honest was the opposite of what I thought was best for everybody. The opposite of my profession."

Painful memories cruise the back of his vacant eyes. "Honesty. Simple honesty." He's mumbling. His left hand massages his right shoulder to relieve unconscious tensions. He sighs and looks directly into Margaret's eyes. "My shoulder hurts – an old rugby injury I suppose. It wakes me up nights, sometimes. Last night I hardly slept." She still listens. He goes on. "I hate getting old. So many things hurt in ways I did not expect..." Now his thumb caresses his fingertips. "I babble and I notice that you are still listening to me. Why is that?"

Margaret starts breathing again and speaks slowly and delicately, guarding herself from making any sudden moves. She speaks so quietly Sean can hardly hear her words, but steadily, and firmly, "My god, Sean! I am still listening to you here because I want you to succeed!" Tears come to the rims of her eyes. She blinks them carefully away "You are trying to do something that I thought a man could never do. You are trying to share your immediate experience with me. This is incredibly valuable to me. You are offering to give what my whole body has always wanted from a man." She takes her own risk now. "Please Sean... continue. Please just keep trying. I promise to never laugh. I promise to only listen, or to speak when you ask it of me. I am willing to do this experiment with you for a very long time."

Sean notices trembling in his chest around his heart area. He never felt such a strange sensation before. His fingers don't operate very well right now.

Margaret goes on. "Something else is happening right now. Something on my side of the table. I sense an extraordinary opportunity knocking on the door of this conversation, wanting to come in. I have not heard such a knocking in many, many years. Since perhaps my revolutionary years. I am interested in your experiment more than you might be able to imagine. I am interested in what you have to say even if you think it is babble. I am not in a hurry. Please, dear Sean, continue. Perhaps neither of us knows what we are doing. This is acceptable to me. Do not worry. It is safe for you to make mistakes. I beg of you to keep going."

Sean takes a very shaky deep breath. *Is it me shaking, or the Universe around me?* he wonders. The flood of feelings held back so long, deep in his bowels, is so close to the surface, yet he understands nothing of them. At least he feels safer with Margaret listening to him. "I am in new territory, Margaret. I don't know what else to tell you. Even telling you that I don't know what else to tell you is new territory for me."

"Just stay away from that thinking machinery up there. Don't tell me anything you know, or anything you have ever said before. Jokes or pleasantries are not needed. Just wait with me. Leave the thinking part on the back shelf somewhere. Go slowly, and let me hear what comes next, if you want. For once in my life, I find myself completely patient with a man."

Sean softens one bit further. "I... I may have never had the opportunity to speak into so much patience. It is irritating to trust you so much." He gives her that squinting look, then looks down. "I delivered the Sean Connery show for so many years it has become automatic. I didn't know that falsely accepting my circumstances would cut off my inspiration and eat my soul. I am exhausted from that, and now I sense that I am also starving. That's why I turned down the script from Scrobonov. I don't have the energy left. Actually, I want to use the energy I do have for something else, although I've no idea for what. Perhaps for this?" He glances at her with the briefest of smiles. "Talking to you in complete honesty seems to take almost no energy at all. I want to keep going."

"Why did you smile just now? Tell me that."

"I smiled..." looking down at his hands, again smiling. "I smile now because in this exact moment I feel some relaxation. The agenda falls away. I don't have to worry the plan to completion. It's quite simple, actually." He looks at her. "I don't even know what will occur next. I also smile because something is happening over there across the table from me that I haven't seen in a long time. Actually, I have never seen it."

Margaret waits in total stillness, feeling in and around her the same thing he is noticing. Truly something is happening on her side of the table.

Sean speaks. "I thought I was with a woman named Margaret Smith, sharp as a whip, cold as steel. Nothing gets past her, and nothing gets in."

Her face remains placid.

He pauses, purses his lips, leans back, breathes in, continues. "It seems that what I just named is only *your* show. It floats on your surface. Something different sits across from me just now that is daring to reveal itself, something I never saw before. The shell still exists, of course. The 'Margaret Show' could pop back into action any instant you don't feel safe. You are keeping it on reserve right now. You could easily unleash it and destroy me, yet you do not. I thank you for that. Your unguardedness opens a view to something else in you, something safe to be with."

Sean squints his eyes to try perceiving the other thing better. He sees it and relaxes. "I notice how big you actually are, how deep the layers go. With you being so still, when you listen with, uh, with your heart, not only with your mind, I see what is behind your heart. I see the Margaret act on the surface but it is so small and artificial in comparison with this magnificent feminine Being sitting here across from me right now."

Sean tastes his perception of her like he would taste a Cognac and a cigar, like appreciating a new Austin Martin. "If I am to speak in radical honesty, then I must tell you this: What sits across from me is glorious! I see that you are not Margaret Smith actually. You never were. You are far more than Margaret could ever be. The door is open. I am blessed to witness through you the pure feminine. You are actually some kind of archetypal healing goddess. You are erotic, radiating tactile emanations that can never fade and can never go away. You are the Muse... Please forgive me..."

He hesitates because of the tears coming to her eyes, but then his own tears join hers, and he continues. "The magnificent mysterious Muse has always been there just behind the Margaret show. I see her now. You have permitted your pure feminine to be seen. You are the woman behind every woman, actually. I have never noticed this before... you before. I.... I am... so sorry." Sean is suddenly overwhelmed with sad memories he would never before allow himself to feel. The facts were known, but the emotional force had always been diverted. "How much I have missed...

The waiter approaches but Sean stops him deftly even before he speaks. This space is theirs, not the waiter's, and far too precious to destroy with concerns about ordering. Somehow the waiter understands and moves away.

"I guess I have never seen her, you, because I was always

distracted by the surface. I always carried an agenda: tits and ass, hips and lips, sparkles and bangles. But who is this you? You are so... astonishingly complete, and beautiful...." He is staring, eyes wide open in awe, gently shaking his head. "This woman, this regal royal radiant feminine Being. I....." He lets his tears come without embarrassment now. "I.... I am so lucky."

Margaret nods ever so slightly with her own tears continuing. She waits. She refuses to speak even one word of the defensive distracting comments being generated in her mind. Sean accepts her invitation to keep going.

"I...never knew this was possible. I never knew what I was missing. Where have I been? What paradises have I wasted? Can you imagine? I was given so many opportunities to come into this, to be with you, not the ordinary you, but the fabulously radiant you, but also even with you, the likes of Margaret Smith, the doorway. But I was always too busy doing things, trying to manipulate and get things, to protect my mundane self. So busy putting on the good show. Always so busy..."

He sighs, but starts rubbing his fingertips again to avoid being lost in a cesspool of nostalgia. "But that is the past. That is the past."

Sean looks up at her again in the glowing candlelight. As if eternity calls, delicate strands of wistful but melodic piano and cello music emerge from the far corner of the restaurant. Sean takes a slow breath, swallows, raises his eyebrows without destroying the mood. He somehow knows from his theater training that one sudden move and this precious moment would be shattered, perhaps never to be found again. He calms and centers himself. Margaret can only nod again.

"Margaret Smith, I feel glad beyond the capacity of words to express that you have joined me here this evening. I would like to get to know more about you. Is there anything you would care to reveal to this ex-showman?"

She hesitates, then nods. "Your question betrays the actions of a creeping devouring insatiable mind. I recognize that mind because I have one of my own in here that I am working furiously to keep at bay. It is like a vicious dog, too hungry to be afraid, ready to attack and devour anything, turning whatever it eats into dog shit. I hold this dog-shit mind of mine tightly on a very short chain. This voracious mind has corrupted so many possible moments like this. All these years it was protecting what I thought was me. Now you have given me a brief glimpse of what lies behind my mental demon's horizon. In this very moment I command it to 'Sit!' right here at my feet. If I relax my guard even for half an instant, it gets loose and I am away. This moment of contact with you would be away. Then I would be back to analyzing, criticizing, endlessly, for no reason. Actually, for the least interesting of reasons, to stay in control. To stay safe. To stay the same. Now I get to do an experiment. I take a risk with you. I take back responsibility for my own safety. I take back my ability to risk entering the unknown, now, here with you. I command my dog mind to sit still and wait until I need him."

Margaret looks unwaveringly into Sean's eyes. It is so intense for him that he can barely stand it. His eyelids flutter. He wants to look away but dares not lose this precious moment of opportunity.

Margaret makes a challenge. "Can you do the same with yours?"

He nods, half unsure about this mad conversation, looking to her for evidence that he can trust himself to manage his inner world.

She waits, surgically finds the right moment, then speaks again. "The next step of our experiment is to continue being okay with not having to know what is next."

Sean says, "In your presence, it seems to be possible for me to do that."

She only smiles.

# Palm Springs, California 2

"Nice form, Phil! Three in a par four."

Phillip looks up at Stanley while carefully reaching down into the cup to retrieve his golf ball. He decides it is the moment to enter reality.

"Stan, the party line defines global warming as mass hysteria. But my grandfather was state director of the KKK. And your grandfather stoked the ovens at Auschwitz. I don't know what you think, Stan, but in retrospect, I've observed that the party line only holds dirty laundry. It's what weak minds and small balls cling to, hoping they will get theirs before Mother Nature slams them upside-the-head with the consequences of their actions."

The deafening silence of the vast desert feels suffocating. Phillip continues. "All my life I've been a gambler. I've gambled on my hunches and my intuition, just like you. I even gambled on you. I am gambling on you right now, Stanley. So far, I've been, so to say, 'winning'. Just like you. For the last five months my intuition has been screaming at me to get the hell out before the house of cards comes crashing down. The problem is, there's nowhere else to run. We only have this one planet."

"You're going for the crash conspiracy, Phil?"

"You're telling me you have no red lights blinking, Stan?"

"Well..."

Phil keeps pushing at the old conversation limits. "It used to be exciting for me, packing zeroes into Swiss accounts, feeling powerful, superior, and secure, like I was part of the ruling class. Now I listen behind the news and all I hear are giddy murmurs of psychopathic ecstasy, Nero fiddling while the empire burns. How can our friends keep filling their pockets by digging deeper holes thinking they will never reach the other side? It's pure nutso. I can't believe we elites are this shallow, this blind, and this out of control. I keep imagining orbiting alien vampires sucking out humanity's goodness by tricking us into torturing each other for no reason. Our suffering must drive their dark engines with high octane fuel. But that theory ignores our own responsibility. Look at the results of COP. Look at Davos. Am I proud of the outcomes? It made me more money, sure. But I was shocked at our chicken-shit performance in the name of public service towards a regenerative future."

"Where are you going with all this, Phil?"

"Wake up, man! We are playing an endgame. It won't hold

together much longer. I'm tired of taking everything I can before it all falls apart. How are you doing with what's coming down? Honestly."

"Well... you know me, Phill. I stay busy. You aren't my only client. I find many interesting... opportunities. There's still lots of money to be made. A few times a year I visit my indulgences. What more could a man ask for?"

"A friend... I could ask for a friend.... Stan... I want to tell you about something that happened to me. It is something I could only tell a friend. The fact that I haven't told anybody yet tells me that my life is not overflowing with friends. I never said it to you before, but I consider you to be my closest friend, Stan, perhaps my only true friend. Come to think of it, I never even told myself that you were my friend. So I... I want to try to find out how that is, to have a friend, I mean. So I brought you to this very important place..."

"The green at the eleventh hole?"

"Yes, exactly. The green at the eleventh hole, at the downhill side of that sand trap near those bushes. Will you come there with me?"

"Sure, Phill. Whatever you want." In contrast with his words, Stanley feels quite nervous about the way this conversation is going.

They step off the immaculate putting green into Kentucky Blue grass. "Phill, the tension of waiting for you to come to the point in this conversation is almost unbearable, far worse than my days selling on the floor of the New York Stock Exchange. What's so important about this particular place?"

"On January eighteenth, Stan, this is exactly where I stood when I had my heart attack. I haven't been back here since. I'd missed the green and thought my ball might be here in the bushes, but it wasn't. When I stood up, *Whamo!* Like a hammer to my chest. I must have collapsed and blacked out for a while. I came to with my face in the dirt, spitting sand. I couldn't move the rest of my body. I could barely breathe. My partner was Bruce Shimizu. He must have run off for help. It felt like a giant bear trap had clamped onto my lungs. So much pain, yet what I was fascinated by was a black beetle slowly walking in the sand across my field of vision. At that moment, I must have left my body or something... it's weird... but I was hovering just above my head. I could clearly see both me and the beetle at the same time. In that moment, there was no difference between us. The beetle and I are each reflecting an aspect of an evolving web of life. Suddenly I had the picture that no one would ever come for me. I would die and rot where I lay. The beetle might eat my body. The ants certainly would. A crow would peck out and devour my eyes. Maybe a coyote would chew the meat from these old bones."

"Gag! Phill! Stop already! Too much information!"

"It was all okay with me, Stan! All of it. That's what I mean. I was already dead. I actually felt glad to provide such satisfaction and pleasure for these wonderful creatures, my brothers and sisters. These bushes and that tree would get well fertilized... Will you sit down here with me? In the dirt here."

Stanley skirts on the fringes of conceptual overwhelm, but somehow feels closer in contact with Phillip than ever before. He sighs at the disgusting idea of sitting in the grass.

Phillip continues. "What I am about to tell you seems strange to me, but I can't stop thinking about it. I can't stop feeling it."

"Well, sure Phil. Okay..."

They sit down together in the manicured grass.

"While lying exactly here I had another shift of perspective. This one stuck around even more clearly. At that point, I was no longer identified with my body. I stayed conscious, but then my personality slipped away. This thinking machine that gives me all my opinions, my ego, all the beliefs and desires that structure my personality, the whole thing became like leaves blowing away in the wind. I was still present and aware, but there were no longer voices in my head, no attitudes, no expectations, no conclusions. With all those distractions gone, it was suddenly clear that I am the entire globe. And it came to me that Copernicus didn't tell us the whole truth."

"What?"

"The guy who said the Earth was not the center of the universe. People reacted so aggressively that he didn't dare tell us the rest."

"What rest?"

"Well, that we don't own the Earth."

"Who does, then?"

"The Earth owns us."

"The Earth owns us?"

"Yes. We cannot own the Earth, Stanley. Think about it. The Earth made us, just like it made the beetle and the bushes. The creation cannot own the creator. The Earth longs to be conscious of its consciousness, so it's been sequestering carbon for millions of years to create conditions stable enough to evolve the biological form of human beings."

"Slow down. Just slow down a bit."

"Pay attention to this Stanley. Thinking that I am me and you are you is only a distorted view, a delusion created by being identified with our own psychology. The truth is that you and I are the Earth. We are Earth talking to herself right now."

"Phil..."

"Wait. It goes further. If I am the Earth, then there is no 'me,' no Phillip Goldman to own property. It is ignorant hubris for a human to imagine we can own land. The land owns us. Humans cannot own mineral rights, or water rights, or property titles. The Earth owns us, Stan. Humans are the Earth become conscious. We have been childishly deceiving ourselves. We have made up and lived in a delusional fantasy world. It is ridiculous. The Earth does not orbit around man's needs. Thinking we shape the Earth to meet our needs is like a child thinking his plastic soldier is real, like us thinking our plastic money is real. Dig a little down under the edge of that stone there, will you."

"Phil... It's... But... Wait... You mean here?"

"Yeah. To the left a little, I think. Just feel down in there with your fingers. You may find something interesting."

"My god, Phil. It's your watch. What is this? Your keys? Some coins? What are they doing here?"

"Before the ambulance came, I had to get rid of them. I couldn't stand having them on my person anymore. I couldn't sit up at that point, so I reached over and buried them there. I buried them because I hated the stupidity of our cleverness. We human beings became clever before we became smart. This is sad. It may cost us everything. I buried these items to eventually remind myself of what I realized." Emotions subsume Phil's words.

"Phil, should we go?"

"No. No, Stan," says Phill wiping his eyes. "Not yet. I am fine. Please. I am glad to feel these things and to tell them to you, my friend. Look, could you just hold my hand for a minute? This is big stuff for me. All you need to do is listen for a bit."

There is silence for a while, the two men sit in the dirt. Stan holds Phil's hand in both of his.

Phillip takes a shaky breath. "Let me finish. It is time for us humans to grow up. Especially the men. We have caused so much hurt and so much damage. It is time to wake up about this. Human beings have a huge potential for waking up, Stan. We have other, much greater potentials than being fooled into thinking money is real. Think how many decisions we make that increase profits by spitting on human dignity. We make money by obliterating ecosystems. We build capital through converting vast natural resources into vast polluted wastelands. Using money as the measure for any decision is unconscionable. It's authentically insane. It's such a lie. I can't do it anymore, Stan. It is too painful for me to stay unconscious. I'm finished with getting adrenalin hits from playing adolescent gambling games, pretending I'm providing a valuable service. It is only fear and selfish short-sighted greed!"

Stan is speechless, but he is touched by Phillip's words.

Phillip sees this and goes for the grand slam. "Stanley, let's do something else together for the rest of our lives. This is a proposal from me to you. Let's you and I have a different purpose. There are so many other interesting games to play, like... like helping others. Like researching what we are, really, us humans, our potentials. Like making new cultures grounded in a true kind of adulthood. Like trying to repair some of the damage we've done. Will you do something different with me Stanley? Will you play a new game? Hey! Let's reinvent the world together. What do you say? Why not?"

# San Pedro, California 4

Gwendolyn Circe's Grimoire – same Wednesday, but evening

Me and the Wiz are in my blue twelve-year-old Ford Fiesta. I drive. My car's name is Spanky. He runs okay but turns into a slug going uphill. I hate giving money to banks or car companies. I bought Spanky used, with cash, ten years ago from a guy addicted to having the latest models. I paid him far less than half of what he paid for it, new, only a year before. Everyone is crazy in some way. Not my problem.

Los Angeles commuter traffic has already subsided.

"What's an initiation?" I ask Balthazar. I have a genuine need to hear his answer, being as how we are headed north on the 110 highway to an authentic initiation.

"Exit here and go north on the 405... An Initiation builds your causal body, after which you are capable of taking responsibility for creating things you never imagined could be created before," he says, as if he were explaining that cornflakes are made of corn.

"How do you convince anyone to take more responsibility?" I demand. "The more responsibility you take, the more you get blamed or punished, the more you have to pay! Taking responsibility is just stupid! The entire business world's strategy of making a profit comes from dodging responsibility. Every corporate manager and politician knows this. You make profit by externalizing your costs, or you lobby to get government subsidies. It's the American way!"

"Responsibility is applied consciousness," says the wizard.

"What?"

A long silence ensues. I don't think it is because Balthazar does not know what to say. I think it is because he senses I need thoughtware-upgrade integration time.

"Please take the 10 west... Responsibility is consciousness in action. Irresponsibility is unconsciousness in action. Avoiding responsibility is the same as avoiding consciousness. An Initiation helps build the thing in you that allows you to catch more consciousness and thereby take more responsibility."

"What thing is that?"

"Your matrix."

"My what?"

Another long silence.

"Turn up Topanga Canyon here. Thanks. Consciousness is everywhere. What is rare is prepared soil in which consciousness can grow. Matrix is the substrate in your Being upon which consciousness can grow."

"What is my Being?"

"It is what wears your five bodies: physical, intellectual, emotional, energetic, and archetypal. You build new matrix in your Being by getting new distinctions. People do not get new distinctions in their mind. They get new distinctions in their Being. Getting a new distinction changes the shape of your Being. So does making a commitment. If you get a distinction or make a true commitment, the Universe interacts with you differently and you create new results. This is why 'positive thinking' and aphorisms don't really work. They don't change the shape of your Being."

"I am getting this, Balthazar. Thank you for making the effort to explain these things to me."

"My pleasure. I will continue. Matrix serves the same function for your Being as a trellis serves for a bougainvillea plant. Without matrix, consciousness has nothing upon which to climb."

"This explains why corporations and governments are so stupid. Stupidity is designed in! If the people working in corporations or governments build matrix and became more conscious, they could not keep doing what they do! They would quit! The whole system would collapse overnight! This is why corporate work is so unrewarding. It is not evolutionary. It avoids building matrix. Modern culture is designed to distract people from building matrix!"

"I knew you were the right wizardress..." he says confidently.

"What?"

"Turn right and park there, would you? We must walk the last part."

"Yes, but, what did you say about me being the right wizardress?"

"I'll tell you later. There are no accidents."

"Does that mean wizards carry no insurance?"

"What?" He glances at me sharply.

"I'll tell you later. We don't have time for this now..."

He smiles at my revenge joke. I should have been smiling too, but I am pissed. Each new piece I figure out only shows me how huge the puzzle is, and how small a part of it I have so far pieced together. School was such a waste of time...

We climb the steep narrow driveway before reaching the flagstone steps up to a typical architect-designed villa in the Topanga Canyon district. The door is already open a crack. Balthazar walks straight in. I follow him, still catching my breath... on several levels.

We remove our shoes in the entranceway, place them in perfect alignment with the other shoes and sandals already there, then walk into a carpeted living-room, empty except for a circle of about twenty-five chairs. The center of the circle is completely void of the usual esoteric riffraff: silk scarves in rainbow colors, crystals, driftwood, flowers, seashells, candles, or pictures of your mother. I see a yellow rose in a small bronze vase next to a single white candle burning on a tiny wooden table in the corner of the room.

None of the chairs are special. I thought 'The Great Wizard' would sit on a throne or something at the front of the classroom. Not this one. He hugs a couple of people and ignores me. I take a seat with the candle table at my back, and wait while the rest of the chairs receive occupants. The space settles down. One chair remains empty.

Without preamble, Balthazar speaks. "Tonight we take responsibility for the possibility of Possibility. This will multiply the effectiveness of several previous initiations."

It sounds like he talks in circles. I don't really care because I still enjoy the warm humming sensations reverberating up and down my spine from our countenance session at Balthazar's laboratory. Who knows what will happen tonight...

"As we have been discovering, the space determines what is possible. Space has physical, intellectual, emotional, energetic, and archetypal components, just like we do. Human beings are designed to interface perfectly with space. For example, who is gatekeeper tonight?"

The hairs on the back of my neck stand straight up. This is the exact word I used to describe one of the three kinds of sorceresses on the flipchart at A.T. Advertising! *The Gatekeepers*!

A younger man with close-cropped brown hair and well-developed biceps and shoulders resolutely but calmly says, "I am."

"How many people knew this already?"

Everyone's hand goes up, but mine.

"How is John attending to the gate right now? He sits there unmoving in the circle, like the rest of us, so how is he implementing guardianship?"

People share their observations.

"He is grounded, centered, and bubbled in a small now."

"He sits near the front door."

"He was here early, building Drala in the space, and now he lets the Drala inform him about the needs of the space."

"What's Drala?" I ask.

"The amount of magical energy that a space can hold," says a woman with straight brown hair, speaking into the space, glancing into my eyes for the briefest of moments.

An older man continues, "John splits his attention, putting thirty percent of his attention on the needs or reactions of the meeting participants, thirty percent of his attention on what the space itself wants and needs to fly, and forty percent of his attention he reserves as 'free attention' to manage whatever might arise, for example, someone coming to the door, or something boiling over in the kitchen... or if there are enough barf buckets for everyone..."

A few people chuckle.

"Do you want to add anything more to this, John?" asks Balthazar. "Give away some of your guardianship secrets?"

"Yes," he says, directly answering Balthazar's question to uphold the integrity of their communications. Then he reveals his approach. "Wade is correct when he says I split my attention. I use about a quarter of my attentiveness to provide agency to my bright principles so they can work for us in this space, and another quarter to steward our group's context. Along those lines, Balthazar, would you like to introduce your guest?"

"No, thank you," Balthazar instantly replies. "She will become apparent."

"Alright," says the guardian. "I hold you accountable for that."

Balthazar nods. "I feel glad."

I learned about bright principles from Rage Club. I can't stand not knowing how John learned about bright principles. The question bursts out of me. "How many people here have been in Rage Club?"

About three quarters of the people hold their hand up, including John.

"Thank you," I say.

There is a moment of silence while these last interactions sift into the various nooks and crannies of personal underworlds to find at least a temporary resting place there.

John wraps up by saying, "I love being guardian because the space feeds me as much as I feed the space. It is reciprocal feeding. My awareness gets particularly refined through sensing how delicate, precise, and sophisticated context is. Yes, the space determines what is possible, but the context determines the space."

"Thank you, John. Speaking of happiness... I want to consider two kinds of happiness: happiness by coherence and happiness by transformation."

By now I write furiously in my Grimoire. Balthazar made sure I had one with me before we left his place. He called it a *Beep! Book*. I will eventually do the same.

"This consideration about happiness is only possible because we have relocated ourselves to the *New Thoughtmap of Feelings*, where it is acceptable to feel happy. If we were still using the *Old Thoughtmap of Feelings*, the idea of feeling happy would be too abhorrent to even speak about.

"Happiness by coherence means that the work you are doing and the people you hang around with are resonant with your skills, your level of awareness, and who you essentially are. You already know the experience of happiness by coherence. From now on, you could try to make your life about forever re-creating happiness by coherence... but you have already been there and done that. Due to your explorations with transformation, it is too late for you to merely lounge around in happiness by coherence."

A woman with dark-brown-shoulder-length-wavy-hair puts up her hand and speaks at the same time. "What do you mean: 'too late'?

Balthazar does not lose a beat. It is as if he already knows the script and is impatient for this woman – or anyone else, including me – to speak their lines so that he can speak his. "Evolution of consciousness is a one-way road. You cannot unbuild matrix. Well, perhaps you can unbuild matrix, by arranging to get yourself tortured, by joining the army and going to the battlefront for hand-to-hand combat, by being bombed, seeing murders, being seriously abused, shocked, horrified, drugged. It is possible to damage your Being enough that it can no longer hold as much matrix as it currently holds. Then random bits of matrix might drop off. I don't recommend it, though. Extremely painful. I recommend that you trust the process, keep rolling forward through the dark night of the soul, and see what washes in on the morning tide."

He pauses a second to see if the question has been suitably met. Tears roll down the woman's cheeks. She makes no move to wipe them away. She simply nods at Balthazar.

"What this means is that we mages have built matrix for going beyond what we already know, what we already are. We can no longer feel the same satisfaction now by simply being who we are. Our longing increases for becoming the next thing, for stepping into the unknown and furthering the path of evolution, mapping new territory, helping others. It is too late to change this.

"The problem for us is that evolution wants to go as fast as it can, but our human bodies have speed limits. It is your job to manage your human body's real needs, so you do not succumb to 'evolution burnout'. Use nervine, Tonic Gold, naps, and fresh vegetables. Keep good company. Study good books. Get adequate stretching and exercise. And drink plenty of good water. Not caring for your physical body's needs reveals an underlying hidden purpose of sabotaging the evolution of consciousness, your own, in this case.

"One of the mutual benefit services a mage can offer is Emotional Healing Processes. If you look at what is going on in the world, you could justifiably claim that Emotional Healing Processes are the most valuable and effective force for creating positive change for humanity."

"What do you mean 'mutual benefit services'?" Same woman asking.

"Too often, therapists or coaches think they are providing services that benefit their clients. This gameplan fails for two reasons. First, maintaining a status imbalance between you and your client equates to rescuing, which is low drama, which is gremlin food. Second, 'helping the client' only feeds the client, leaving the therapist or coach starving and bored. I suggest that in your mage work, you regard your clients as 'colleagues in exploratory adventure', there to feed you as much as you are there to feed them. Aim at working with people whose potential inspires you. Do the research and practice new skills that ongoingly challenge and stretches your own limits. It is part of your job as mage to make your own food. Got it?"

"Yes," she says.

Balthazar slogs forth. "Without a liquid state there is no change. Many Emotional Healing Processes unleash high intensity emotions because emotions deliver enough chaotic energy to dissolve the glue holding inner structures together and a proper Phoenix Process can ensue. During this 'death and resurrection show', change happens almost by itself. Emotional Healing Process arises to demand further refinement, elegance, and subtlety of inner navigation. These processes reengineer concepts, programs, beliefs, inner prisons, so-called 'tapes', and other inner features made of memes."

"What are 'memes'?" Me this time.

"Memes are the mental bricks out of which you build inner constructs for managing and communicating your worlds," says Balthazar.

"What do you mean 'worlds'?" Still me.

"Humans are designed in the image of archetypal domains that hang together by 'spinning in infinity', as Paul Simon might say. Each domain is a micro or macro universe, inside of us, outside of us, between us, and also having nothing to do with us, yet still available for us to use if we develop the attentions necessary for navigating them. So many so-called entertainers kill themselves because they accidentally enter upper, middle, or underworlds without first gaining the requisite skills for navigating them competently."

I am so tumbled along, at this point, that I lack enough bearings to ask further questions, although I have questions. Balthazar sees my condition, and still likes me.

What a weird orientation to stand on: 'he still likes me', but it is useful enough to keep me from beating myself up for the depth of my ignorance.

"Don't worry about that," he says directly to me from across the circle. "Others have the same questions but lack the urgency to have answers now. Your urgency is serving the space."

Then he goes on speaking as if nothing just happened.

"Since memetic constructs function on a level that is deeper than mere intellect, memetic engineering processes require a mage to feel and think at the same time without retreating into the mind. Plus, you need to nurture those same non-intellectual inner-world navigation skills in your clients. This involves clear use of words for communication, but not at the intellectual level.

"I am suspicious that mages – meaning us – carry obsolete mage thoughtware. For example, you may be harboring indigenous ways of working with people. Unprecedented new thoughtware is emerging on Earth right now, to the same exponential degree that the status quo is disintegrating. Mage thoughtware also needs to be ongoingly upgraded. If you encounter obsolete mage thoughtware in yourself or others, I ask you to please share it with us to help us deepen our work and evolve our mage skills together.

"I would also like to add clarity about old and new decisions. Once you discover that you are under the influence of an old decision or a past life vow, you may have the impulse to straight away make a new decision, thinking it will be the doorway through which you can hastily escape from the world you've created by submitting yourself to the framework of your old decision.

"It turns out that most often it is far more effective to avoid the distractive mental gyrations of 'making a new decision' and instead to ongoingly immerse yourself in the pain of your old decision, thereby unleashing the alchemical agency of authentic remorse.

"A student once asked Chögyam Trungpa, a Tibetan Buddhist teacher, 'What do you do when you find yourself in hell?' Trungpa's answer was, 'I try to stay there.' This is a non-intuitive approach that builds matrix through taking conscious responsibility for being where you are and letting it inform your actions.

"It can be immeasurably more valuable to focus your intention on discovering why you would keep things arranged that way for so long, rather than trying to bounce away to an imagined state of cheerful happiness. Simply remain in your horrifying clarity of, 'Oh, my god! Being inside of this old decision has shaped my world for decades, perhaps my whole life, possibly for lifetimes.'

"Fiercely notice layer after layer. Feel and document your anger, your grief, your fears of change. Let your awareness expand about the consequences of having done this to yourself in so many arenas of your life and for so long.

"It is not wrong, or bad, or stupid that you adopted those old decisions. In the time you adopted the old decision, your action probably saved your life.

"Yes and... so what? Now you have built up new agency in your five bodies, new matrix in your Being, new distinctions, navigational indicators, and skills you did not have before.

"Now you can look fully upon the mess you made, and let the shock open doors to a new catalog of options to choose from that you never saw before.

"Rather than mentally trying to install a single new response path, manipulating yourself by force of will, let your cells get sensitized about exactly what the old way did to your life. Eventually your sensing cells will stretch into territories where new options are abundant.

"After two to three months of hanging out in painful embarrassment, in revulsion over the sneaky cleverness of your old decisions, suddenly new options for being with yourself and with others become so obvious that you start choosing them reflexively.

"Jumping into a new decision is often self-deception. Remaining in the pain of the consequences of your old decision creates a far more stable outcome.

"We gather here as a mage research team to create our path by walking it. One of the paths that has not been walked enough – in my opinion – is the creation of next culture screenplays and novels.

"Remember three weeks ago, when we made a deep-dive into that article by Edith Goldman about her Vision Quest in Death Valley, where she amalgamated a name for the regenerative culture emerging now that Matriarchy and Patriarchy have run their course? She named it 'Archiarchy'.

"Having that name makes a rift, a phase change, a step function in the evolution of human culture. I have been experimenting with putting my toes over the energetic line into Archiarchy, and it blows my mind how wide open and empty the creation space is there!

"For example, where are the Archan songs and Archan books that can be turned into movies and TV series? Most modern culture stories fit Joseph Campbell's lone-wolf single-fighter 'Hero's Journey' diagram. They end in the moment when Archiarchy begins.

"What humans need to know now is what happens after they kiss? How do you make love last? What are ways to negotiate radical relating? How to endure the unbearable lightness of being?

"It came to me that we could make a joint effort here to write Archan novels about what happens next.

"Who here is willing to go through whatever Emotional Healing Processes, and change whatever Past Life Vows, and heal from school enough to earnestly engage that challenge?"

Thirteen hands go in the air.

"Who will be the first spaceholder?"

The dark-brown-shoulder-length-wavy-haired woman says, "I will. Please, each of you tell me your name while I write them down." She flips to a new page in her *Beep! Book*.

"What is your name?" I demand.

"Dana Fulton," she says, unmiffed.

After Dana captures the writers' names, Balthazar says, "I propose you work in 3Cells and write four books. By next week each 3Cell brings in a book title with chapter outlines, and first and last chapters drafted. What do you say?"

Thirteen voices all say something affirmative. I break out in a cold sweat while tears come to my eyes.

Why do I sweat? I am shocked that it can be as straightforward as Balthazar just demonstrated to create an interesting new future for myself and others. I never saw this before. But that is the point, right? It only takes one person to present an idea that no one ever thought of before. The mage Balthazar Blake makes it look as easy to invent never-before-thought-of-ideas as it is to find pebbles at the seashore.

Why do I have tears? They seem like tears of joy from feeling so at home and meeting so many new sisters and brothers all at once.

"How do you do that, Balthazar?" I beg him to explain, in retrospect, a bit too whiny for my taste.

"There are thousands of specialties crucial to the emergence and evolution of the initiated-adulthood-centered-culture of Archiarchy on planet Earth. Archan shamanism is merely one of them. My personal focus until now has been cataloging and healing all the wounds that interfere with a person creatively collaborating with others in a circle. This was not fun for me. It required participating in projects doomed to failure from emotional reactivity, unconscious gremlin warfare feeding frenzies, betrayal from hidden hierarchies, subservience to unconscious fears, all the neurosis to which the uninitiated human being is prone. I deduced that without being able to transform these weaknesses, Archiarchy could not emerge. We are the evolutionaries. It is our job to transform weaknesses into valuable new possibilities. It is a remarkable breakthrough to initiate the gremlin into a conscious nonlinear creation source, and then to decontaminate the adult egostate from gremlin, child, parent, and demon.

Balthazar glances around the circle into each of our eyes. "In your own mage path, you may possibly have the honor of being, for a while, the spaceholder for one of the Archan specialties. I encourage you to take bold leaps towards training the people who are attracted to your work. Train them to unfold and deliver their specialty in order to replace yourself as spaceholder.

"The distinction between the expert and the specialist is the distinction between material value thoughtware and nonmaterial value thoughtware. Material value thoughtware is the basis of the capitalist patriarchal empire. Nonmaterial value thoughtware is revolutionary. You discover your nonmaterial value on your quest.

"Since you went to school, you were taught that other people will tell you who you are, and what quest is. But your quest evolves. This means that what they told you was already wrong after a week. In reality, you live in a rapidly evolving draft of your quest. No one but you can ever say what your quest is.

"You each have a point of origin. Energetically it looks like a large brown carrot. You are its leaves. With definite excitement, I can tell you that your life changes quality when you transplant your point of origin to the middle of your current formulation of your quest. Transplanting is loud, and painful. You use your five bodies to wrestle the whole carrot out of its current context, screaming out the pain and the effort, then move your point of origin over and plant it firmly into your new context. There is such fear and relief and joy in this experience. Does anyone want to relocate your point of origin into a new context right now?"

As far as I could tell, we all say yes.

"Nothing has ever stopped you. You planted your point of origin in its current context. Nothing has ever stopped you from transplanting your point of origin to a new context. No one can do it for you. No one can stop you from doing it! One. Two. Three. Go!"

Pure outrageous screaming brawling chaos breaks loose around the circle. At first I am too shocked to do anything. But then I see some others making progress with the transplanting procedure, and I want that for myself too. I jump out of my chair with a banshee scream and grab ahold of the giant brown carrot of my point of origin. It feels like I enter a life-or-death wrestling match. Pictures of life with my mother flash across my mind, when she was scolding me, beating me with a wooden spoon, trying to get me to conform to school and ordinary society. One picture was when my cat was killed on the road, me holding her stiff lifeless body in my hands the next morning, not understanding, surrendering to ordinary insanity. That is when my soul broke. Now I get another chance. My brown carrot suddenly pulls loose. For an instant I get the impression that I could plant it anywhere, or nowhere. But I am certain about what I want. It is clear. I slam my point of origin into the wizardress context. This is what I want. This is where I am now! I get to start over in this new context, and it is joyous! I am weeping uncontrollably. I grab handfuls of tissues, blow my nose sloppily, throw the tissues into the air and dance wildly amongst my fellow wizards and wizardresses.

Fifteen minutes later the floor looks like a hurricane hit us. But so many ear-to-ear tear-smeared smiles grin back at me that I can't help but laugh out loud with a whoop. Everyone hollers back, including Balthazar, in tears of joy.

"What happens now," Balthazar sniffles and says, "is when you wake up in the morning, you put your feet down in the context and specifics of your quest. You no longer put your feet down in the world of 'Oh my god! I have to pay the rent." Or, "'Oh, my god! The neighbor's dog is barking again!' Or, 'Oh, my god! I'm in bed with someone I don't like very well.'

"Having your point of origin planted in the world of your quest changes the quality of your whole life. You perceive, analyze, make proposals and requests all framed inside of your 'quest values'. Part of your nonmaterial value is that you are your quest. You can now help other people skill-up and transplant their own points of origin.

"Your quest gives you questions which turn into 'quest-ions' because they attract you to certain things and repel you from other things. Your quest-ions move you to encounter extraordinary coincidences and avoid hidden pitfalls all due to the navigation force of the quest-ions in your belly.

"If your quest-ions come from your Box's survival strategy, then you will be asking, 'Do people love me enough? Will enough people come to my workshop? Do I have enough money? What am I going to wear today? How can I create low drama with my colleague so that my gremlin gets fed?' But if your quest-ion comes from your quest, then you will be organizing toroidal teams and holding space for transformational processes and projects.

"Material value thoughtware attributes value to whatever is scarce. This establishes an object's selling price. How are you allowing material value to kill your nonmaterial value? How do you focus on 'expertise', or 'scarcity', or imaginary 'mastery', to establish value? How do you block your sense of nonmaterial value that may be emerging right now out of you or other people?

"What would happen to your connection with the magic of nonlinear possibility, your connection with the mystery of others, if you focus on noticing nonmaterial values, and by the pure noticing of them, you start valuing them?

"We have been trained to survive by fitting in with other people in modern culture. Fitting in requires cutting off your connection to the miraculous nature of reality. Up until we are about eighteen years old, it is very important to do whatever it takes to fit in and survive. But after eighteen years old, your life could proceed by entering the world as yourself. This prison break is neither simple nor easy, due to having held so firmly to a behavior formula for pretending you are a happy prisoner.

"For example, on my way driving here I was thinking, 'Gosh, I am driving up the 405 freeway.' I unconsciously performed an alchemical mage action called 'naming'. Once you have given something a name, there are two possibilities.

"The first possibility is 'mage formative', meaning that once you have distinguished something enough to give it a name, you can talk about it, you can explain it to others, you can draw a map about it, you can do further experiments with it, you can investigate it further, and because you can call it by its name, you can find your way back there.

"The second possibility is 'mage destructive', meaning that if you walk through the world naming qualities of experience, you are in danger of locking yourself into verbal reality, where words prevail instead of experience. Verbal reality blocks your direct access to experiential reality's mage factors. These blocks kill reality for you.

"For example, you might look outside the window and think, 'Yes, that is a tree. That tree was trimmed. The tree needs to be watered so it can make fruit. The tree's leaves are making a mess on the lawn,' and so on. As soon as you name a phenomenon, you separate yourself from its potentials and aliveness, and therefore from your own wonder and awe.

"From the perspective of physics, wind blows due to Coriolis forces and solar energy. Sunlight heats up the land by radiation. Heated land heats up the air by conduction. The less dense hot air is squeezed upwards by the denser cold air being pulled down by gravity. Surrounding air flows in to fill the vacuum which the hot air leaves behind, and this moving air is called 'wind'.

"But if I replace the experience of wind with the name 'wind', the aliveness of wind disappears. No longer can I speak with the cloud people and listen as the wind talks to me. No longer can the aliveness of everything around me enrich me with signs and warnings and invitations.

"As a young man I built my world around making things better. It took me decades to discover that by trying to make things better I was killing aliveness. My true job is to be with things exactly as they are. I needed hundreds of Emotional Healing Processes to shift into a different identity while I grieved the loss of my 'rescuer hero' identity. In the process I had to get conscious of my deep fears. 'Who's going to make things better if I'm not doing it?'

I see that several people are feeling things. Then I notice Balthazar noticing what I just noticed, and because of that, saying, "When emotions start coming up, please write a note in the back of your *Beep! Book* specifically listing the thought and the emotion. This is all you need later to re-enter that space for an Emotional Healing Process.

Then he continues. "I used to use my identity as a 'heroic rescuer' to give me secret background powers, thinking, 'I am the one who can save the day by making things better.' If you start giving up your 'I have secret powers' identity because it is delusional, then who are you really? What is left? What is your role? How can you contribute to other people?

"But if you do not accomplish this huge dis-identification procedure, you remain several dimensions away from reality. A mage needs a one-on-one connection with reality to do her work.

"Even combing or brushing your hair can remove you from reality. You look at yourself in the mirror to arrange your hair the 'right way'. But the moment your hair is the 'right way' you slip into a familiar identity that cuts you off from the aliveness of reality. Reality does not look 'nice' or 'pretty'. You are an evolving Being. Your hair can be an evolving Being too.

Even I chuckle at that one...

"Getting real includes the skill of going insane. A mage needs an insane internal freedom of movement to access nonlinear agency, but that is exactly what you have been trained to suppress in yourself and in others. I propose we research how we are doing this. You can start by turning to a fresh page in your *Beep! Book* and titling it: WAYS I MAKE THINGS NORMAL. Then, as we talk, make a detailed list to work with later.

"I already notice a number of you magically normalizing things for yourself right now. For example, some of you are trying to make this exercise positive and cheerful, and perhaps even exciting, or entertaining, and therefore acceptable or normal. If you are cheerful, and if other people are cheerful or excited about what you are saying, then everything is fine and normal.

"Here is another way. A third of you were just now nodding your head while you were listening to me. What you communicate by nodding is, 'I understand', or 'I get it'. If you get it, then it is gotten. If it is gotten, then there are no longer any questions. If there are no questions, then there is no longer anything to risk your life for. Aliveness has been killed by understanding. And dead is normal.

"See if you can stop caring whether whatever is happening is understood or not. See if you can abandon the assertion, 'I understand,' or, 'It has been understood,' and let things in general not be understood. Figure out how to have a creative conversation where understanding is not the highest objective.

"This can lead to a paradox. For example, if I submerge myself in a world that most people don't know about, exploring new things, but I do not share what I discover with others to get their feedback about how well they understand and can make use of what I discover, then I might be living in a fantasy world and not realize it. That is one reason I love having these meetings with you. I have learned to destroy my own fantasy worlds.

"But even in this circle there are fantasy worlds going on. One fantasy world I notice is if you catch yourself thinking, 'Whatever I do, it's not going to make any difference.' How many of you have moments of your attention feeding that fantasy world?"

Half the people raise their hands.

Balthazar simply stops speaking and lets us sit with this one while we write out personal lists of the ways we kill aliveness and make things normal. It feels like I am deep underground in a morgue, sliding out trays of frozen dead people, and each time I pull the sheet back from the face of a cadaver to see who the dead person is, it is me.

After about ten minutes, Balthazar speaks again. "The other day I watched a group of guys sitting around with each other near an outdoor pool, laughing their heads off for four or five hours straight. At the time I was sure they were drunk or stoned, and it repulsed me. But then I thought, 'If I spent four or five hours laughing as freely and loudly as they did, I would consider it one of the best days of my life! Why am I so dead that I did not go over there and laugh hysterically with them?' But to do that I would have to be insane! Part of me wants to be practical. Part of me wants to have the freedom to go fruitfully insane. Which will prevail?

"There is a quest-ion to ask yourself. What percentage of my life is in my quest world? And what percentage of my life is in the ordinary world? Which parts of your life do you assign to which world? I encourage you to take that on as one of the experiments to do this week.

"For example, is cooking meals located in your quest or not? Is shopping contained within your quest? Is speaking to new clients part of your quest? What do you exclude from your quest, and why? The experiment is to shift a few more pieces of your ordinary life into the world of your quest and see what happens to it.

"One way I found to do that is when I am in a conversation with somebody about something that is going on, I notice there is a point where my box or my gremlin sends me an impulse to end the conversation. Perhaps it is my fear about time, about intimacy, about the consequences of connection. The impulse wants me to stop the conversation.

"The experiment that I invite you to do this week is that when you notice the impulse, decide to take the conversation three levels deeper. When the impulse comes, say, 'Nope, I am not wrapping it up here. I am not killing this space just yet. I am going to take it three levels deeper.'

"Start by vulnerably saying, 'Gosh! I had the impulse to end the conversation just now, but here is what is really going on for me. I was afraid of the conversation becoming too intimate, too boring, too crazy...' whatever it is. Then drop to the next layer down. And then the next layer.

"Keep revealing to the other person what makes you want to end the conversation right then. What is trying to take you out of the interaction? What else is possible? What might you miss? What's the secret information that society does not want you to find together? What else is possible that modern culture does not want you to exchange?

"You can continue by asking: How am I normalizing my life? I see that I am trying to have a normal life, but for who? Who has set the standards of normal for me? How do I get my life back so that I choose where I put my attention? So that I choose how long I put my attention there? So that I choose the purpose of why I put my attention there. What would my life look like if I move from my own point of origin?"

The young man sitting next to John says, "I will ask these questions in every interaction I am in! I will be a mage right from the beginning!"

Balthazar looks at him kindly and says, "There is a high degree of self-deception in saying 'I will be a mage'. It forces you into the 'I am a mage' fantasy-world. You then behave as you imagine a mage should behave. It is fake. Instead, without explaining anything about yourself, you can interact with the accountability and integrity of a mage, right here, right now, and prove it ongoingly by the spaces you navigate and the results you create, without having to imagine anything."

I forget how Balthazar closes the space. I think the last thing he says is: "It is memetically useful to avoid making assumptions altogether."

Suddenly we stand up, hug a few people, step out the door and gingerly walk down the steps and the steep driveway to where Spanky is parked. I breathe the herb-scented night air and look up to see a zillion stars sparkling in the sky. I feel too expanded to drive safely.

"Balthazar, would you drive?"

"Yes," he says, taking the keys from my hand and walking around to the driver's door.

I buckle into the passenger's seat, tilt it all the way back, close my eyes, and I am out.

I wake up as Balthazar yanks on Spanky's parking brake in San Pedro, even though he keeps his thumb on the button so the yanking is nearly silent. It must be past midnight. I imagine driving all the way back across Los Angeles to my apartment tonight in my present condition. "Balthazar, may I sleep on your couch?"

"Yes," he says.

We climb out of Spanky and shut our doors. Balthazar locks them, then hands me back my keys.

"Will you hold my arm while we walk, so I don't fall off the pier?"

"Yes," he says.

I climb the circular stairs, go pee, vaguely brush my teeth, and splash some water on my face. In the meantime, Balthazar places a pillow and blanket on the sofa. I crawl in and bundle up.

Balthazar squats down next to my head and says, "I put a flashlight on the end table here in case you need it during the night. I enjoyed our evening, Gwendolyn. We are wizards, so there is no way around our collaboration being unconventional. The way it can work is if we radically relate with each other, you saying what you want and what you don't want, and me saying what I want and what I don't want."

I look at his face for a moment. "What I want is that you give me a goodnight kiss right now on the lips for somewhere between five and ten seconds, then you wake me up by six a.m. so I can get to work. I also want you to tell me when you would like to meet with me again. I am especially interested in going to fetch spring water with you at the Mount Wilson observatory, and also coming with you to next week's Study Circle, or whatever you call it. What do you want?"

"The same," he says softly.

He goes for the full ten seconds.

I tell you, a wizardress-to-wizard kiss is something pretty special.

The last thing I remember thinking, before falling asleep on the couch, is, *I will make a Wizard School so that there can be more wizards.*

# Phoenix, Arizona 3

Eddy tries for an hour to wash the mud off in a small puddle he finds downstream. It doesn't work. He is wet and cold when he returns to the campfire to warm up.

JET looks up at his approach, startled, apprehensive.

"You scare me Eddy. Each time I see you now, I don't know who you have become. Superman... Dr. Frankenstein... Gandalf... The Mummy..."

"I read that Zen students meditate twenty years to get to the condition of not thinking they already know who someone is," says Eddy. "Not even their partners. It's supposed to open greater possibility for relating. Maybe we're on to something here. Drive into the desert fifty miles from nowhere. Blow up your car. Then talk about life."

Eddy focuses on getting his hands as close to the fire as possible to stop his shivering. "Whoever said deserts are hot?"

JET's chuckle is forced. He is clearly weak and in great pain.

Eddy ruminates. "I am astonished at how quickly and efficiently the sum total of my material world has just gone up in smoke. All I possess in the entire world now are the muddy stinking clothes on my back, my emergency carrot, and my wallet. I guess it was not so smart to put our phones in with our backpacks. Now they are vaporized. What is your inventory?"

"The same. I carry my passport in my belt pouch. I still have a box of books in my mom's basement, molding away."

The sun has set, and the sky quickly darkens. Eerie silhouettes of gigantic saguaro cactus, spiky ocotillo, creosote bush, and craggy treeless desert mountains surround them. The air is absolutely still and quiet now.

The two men sit staring into the fire. JET holds his wounded leg.

In that moment of stillness, a large mountain lion steps into the circle of firelight.

Sand-colored light reflects off her short fur. Fluid muscles ripple as she glides her head warily from side to side, sniffing at the fresh blood. She stares menacingly at each of them in turn.

JET figures she's deciding which one to eat for dinner. His fear wants him to jump through the sky to save his life, but the pain in his leg stops his reflexes from taking over.

Eddy whispers through his teeth, "Don't move a muscle..."

They can hear the magnificent queen of the desert breathing. Eddy gazes directly into her dark eyes and slowly blinks, then blinks again. To JET's amazement, Eddy creates a low clucking sound, deep in his throat. He is purring at her!

The mountain lion makes her choice and steps straight towards Eddy. She rubs the side of her jaw against Eddy's hand, revealing her bone crushing teeth. Then she licks the back of his salty arm with her large pink tongue.

Then she herself starts purring!

She rubs the top of her head and ears on Eddy's shoulder, then brushes her shoulder and her whole side against Eddy as she walks away into the dark, whipping JET in the face with the end of her tail as she departs. The two-meter mountain lion vanishes into the night as imperceptibly as she appeared.

Both men struggle to hold it in, but they cannot. They burst out laughing hysterically, eyes as wide as if they'd seen a ghost. There is no rational explanation for what just happened. They can't help but frantically stare into the dark searching for answers to impossible questions.

"Are we on some kind of reality TV show?" asks Eddy out loud.

JET only murmurs something unintelligible.

The world is becoming a stranger place by the minute, as if its wildness was something they'd never noticed before.

The stars shine with unexpected brilliance. "Interesting day..." comments Eddy. "Living in the city, you never see mountain lions like these."

When he looks over at JET, he notices with concern JET's forehead glistening in the firelight. "How are you feeling?"

"Not good. I think I have a fever."

"Looks like it." Eddy reaches over to feel JET's neck with the back of his fingers, then feels for JET's pulse at his wrist. "Cripes!"

Eddy grabs a handful of sand and lets it pour out in a stream. "Well, Mr. Physicist. They make computer chips out of this stuff. Make us a cell phone, why don't you?"

JET pretends he has a phone in his hand. He punches up some numbers and then calls out, "Help! Mr. Wizard! Get us outta here! Come take us home!"

A strangely muffled and accented male voice says, "This is home."

It seems as if the creosote bushes beside them just spoke. Both Eddy and Jet jerk in surprise. They can only think they are going crazy. They glare challengingly at each other to see who will laugh at the others' fear caused by their ventriloquist skills, but neither of them is joking around.

Eddy stands up and strains his eyes fretfully into the darkness. The disembodied voice continues, deep, accented, garbled, "Mind if I join you?"

A Native American man steps carefully into the firelight. He sits down at the campfire instantly settled, as if he has never been anywhere else for centuries. He makes to warm his hands. His red, black, and white flannel shirt reflects the dancing yellow firelight under a black felt hat, pierced with two eagle feathers which seem to flutter with aliveness.

Eddy recovers first and plops himself down next to the Indian. "No problem, Mr. Wizard. Make yourself comfortable. Want a cup of coffee? How did you find us?"

"You weren't exactly invisible, making that huge stinking cloud of black smoke in my living room." The words of protest are hard to make out, as if he is chewing on a mouthful of rags.

JET involuntarily moans from his pain, and drops all pretense. "Can you help my leg?"

The Indian looks straight into JET's eyes and in all earnestness says, "I thought you would never ask."

JET is in too much pain to get the joke, even though it is no joke.

The Indian rolls towards JET, his face only inches away. "If I tell you what to do, will you do it, *no matter what?*"

JET stays silent. The Indian demands a 'no matter what' level promise. JET cannot make such a promise without fully intending to keep it. He considers the circumstances. "Yes, sir. I will do it. No matter what."

"Good!" says the Indian, with a little too much enthusiasm for JET's peace of mind. "Give me your hand."

JET holds out his right hand, palm up. The Indian firmly grabs his wrist, pulls the hand towards him, leans over it, and spits out a huge slimy wad of chewed up plant material that he was keeping stashed in both his cheeks. "Take two of these and call me in the morning."

Still gripping JET's wrist, the Indian leans over the sand and repeatedly spits, trying to clean out his mouth from the bitter taste of the desert herbs.

He turns back to JET and says, "No. Just kidding. You don't have to eat it. I already did that part for you. Put the herbs on your leg and keep them there for three full days and nights."

"But what about..." *germs*, he was about to say, feeling the warm slimy blob in his hand.

The Indian presents JET with the unwavering wordless gaze of a deadly serious archetypal warrior.

JET's objection vaporizes in the clarity that no objection can prevail. He has already committed. In the domain of integrity, only one action can follow. Without another word the Indian lets go of JET's wrist, and JET presses the mass of herbs firmly into his wound, "Aaaaannnnngggg!"

The Indian unties the sweaty red bandanna looped around his neck, folds it into a strip, wraps it around JET's leg over the green goop, efficiently ties a firm square knot, and checks the snugness of the fit. "Good," he says simply.

Eddy sighs out loud, and then says, "We were wondering if the hotel registration office is still open...?"

The Indian glares fiercely at Eddy. "Your wise crack is naive. You are naive. Your unconscious goal is to stay ordinary, to defend yourself, to retain the ways that you already know. You think those ways serve you. They do not. They kill you, and everything else."

He spits more green slime into the sand. "You are a boy in a man's body. It is disgraceful, but that is no fault of your own. It is how you have been taught. Your culture gives you no initiation into manhood. Your leaders and your teachers are the same as you, greedy, scared, self-centered children.

"You have a chance here in my home. You have asked to find a doorway into another level of understanding. That door is now open. You must work hard to get through the door because you carry so much useless baggage and the door will soon close no matter on which side of it you stand. You are almost too crystallized to move. The thing that you think you are, you are not. The thing that you defend so righteously is your self-made prison."

"But..." blurts Eddy, ready to take offense.

"Silence!" roars the Indian directly into Eddy's face. "Wait with your swollen mind's questions! Use the discipline you used with the mountain lion, or in this case, you will chase *me* away."

The Indian pauses to let that sink in, peering up at the infinitely vast array of diamond sparkling stars now blazing across the night sky.

"Try to listen to what I say with something besides that mind. Let my words pass by your thinking, or you will think my words into dust before you can hear them. Let the sounds hit you deep in your soul. Let yourself feel the pain of what I say, or nothing will change for you."

Again the Indian pauses. He sighs heavily, but then continues. "Authentic pain in your heart causes evolution more surely than any mental insight or effort of will. You are still children. The entire world is open to you like an alchemist's laboratory, but the world does not respond to the gestures of children. The child still thinks mommy is coming. A man has no more mommy."

He takes time to gaze through each of the younger men's eyes, deeply into their core "There are forces of nature far greater than your mind. These forces, used consciously, become your allies. Without consciousness, the roles are reversed. Then the forces use you unawares. They devour your precious life energy with fears of scarcity and meaningless internal and external wars."

It is clear he speaks from personal experience, not from dogma. He is not preaching to them. He is redesigning them.

"You must apply your full resources to do your own work. Each of you carries in you a vision. Your vision remains unconscious, but it is there, nonetheless. Strangely enough, your vision happens to be useful to the Great Mother, the spirit of the world. She is the one who sent me to weaken the bridge with the flood so we could meet. If you take actions resonant to the forces of nature, then your vision can shape the world around you into a sanctuary for love."

Eddy and JET are each trying to wrap their minds around what this crazy uncivilized Indian just told them. *He crippled the bridge? With a storm? He was instructed to meet us here? No fucking way this is possible!*

"I want you to succeed," says the Indian in radical honesty. "Yes, it is a fool's wish. But it is the reason I am speaking with you now. It is the reason I agreed to invite you here."

Time has stopped. Their hearts barely beat. The unrealness of this situation makes it hyper-real. Their nerves tingle while nothing changes and yet everything becomes different.

"Do not think that the world which is understood by your science is the only world that exists. Trust your ability to not understand and to still function excellently. Then go where your science cannot. There you will find others ready to work at your side and to accompany you further. It is probably too late for your efforts to make a big enough impact. I guess we will soon enough see."

He sighs again, but goes on. "Even if the Great Mother resorts to stronger means for protecting Herself, an ark of disciplined practitioners can still be useful in a darkened future."

There is wonder in the Indian's voice. "I speak to you not as Indian to white man, not as adult to child, but as friend to friend, as one evolutionary to another. I am being used as much as you could let yourself be used, if you would serve something greater than your father's habits."

The Indian notices both JET and Eddy squirming, so he shifts his tone. "I see that we have already reached your capacity. You are untrained, so this is all you are able to hold at the moment. A warrior of the path can journey like this for hours, paying attention and taking turns navigating the worlds. But as my teacher says, 'One cannot feed steak to babies.' I have spoken for only a few minutes, yet your nervous systems are both maxed out. This is as it is."

The Indian grimaces while peering out at the darkened desert. Turning back to them he says, "Work with diligence to expand that which permits you to take greater responsibility. Work to continue your initiations into adulthood. The journey will be painful and shocking, and will take longer than you think." He looks them over again, "But you just might make it."

The Indian had spoken his entire monologue imperatively, urgently. The last comment ends in a kindly smile.

First the Indian looks at JET. "Let your wound teach you to reclaim weakness as an ally. Learn to ask for help from others."

Then, looking at Eddy, he says only, "Sweet dreams."

The Indian pauses, then adds with a deep sincerity, "Thank you both for responding to the call."

The man stands effortlessly to his full height, steps backwards into the nighttime, and vanishes without a sound.

Ten silent minutes go by.

Finally, Eddy shakes his head. "He's an Indian. He can do that."

After a while, Eddy slowly stands up and walks into the night too, but in a different direction. JET watches him go, looks into the fire, then after a while looks up as Eddy returns with the wrinkled beer can in his hand filled with water. It must have flown out the window as the crash happened.

Eddy hands the can to JET. "It's muddy, but it tastes okay. The minerals might help your leg heal."

JET drinks gratefully. Without sarcasm, he says, "Thank you doctor."

Eddy puts more wood on the flames. In the silence they lay down to rest on opposite sides of their campfire.

# Aleppo, Syria 8



I was terribly wrong about our situation being as bad as it can possibly be.

Overnight our situation becomes unimaginably worse.

At 4:17a.m. this morning, the first earthquake hits Syria, throwing me out of my bed into the air still sleeping.

Never before have I felt such a gargantuan force, 7.8 on the Richter scale, only 6.2 miles deep, 71 miles north of Aleppo, with tens of thousands of aftershocks that start immediately. The planet on which we live is having an epileptic fit. We are mere skin mites in comparison, powerless to change anything.

Both my parents are at work. Our flimsy shacks only wobble and tilt over, not collapsing on anyone. I end up on the floor, smashed against our one set of drawers, bruised, and insulted.

The sounds around me are horrifying. Buildings everywhere crumble to the ground. I hear screams and shouts from the others, but the electricity is out. All I can see with my pocket flashlight is dust. It is too soon for the phone to tell me anything. I crawl around to see if I can help anyone, but at first there is nothing for me to do but be afraid.

The sun gradually illuminates a grotesquely colored sky. Ordinarily our school would start now. I sit out in the open, unable to speak. I can only hold on physically to each and every person who I see. Israa is first. I am so glad to see her. Fortunately she is unhurt.

Many of the others showing up are people I don't know. Some have bloody wounds. Some limp along on rigged-up crutches. Some bring brothers and sisters, or friends, or strangers. As soon as we can hold onto each other, we only cry and scream hysterically. We must scream and cry here together, because here it is safe to cry. Here our true sentiments can be heard and seen by each other.

I used to think that rocket explosions, helicopter-dropped barrel bombs, strafing jets, and the rat-tat-tat of machine guns was awful. But this? This is the end of the world.

Then nine hours later, at 1:24 p.m. this afternoon, a second earthquake double-taps us, 7.7 on the Richter scale, 7.5 miles below the surface, 96 miles north of Aleppo. Whatever was destabilized in the first quake, topples to the ground in the second.

God must hate us.

After a few dizzying hours feeling the Earth beneath our feet continue to shake and roll, I propose that the children and my small team of 'teachers' bandage each other up and go collect food and water while helping others wherever we can. We make the plan to meet back here at dusk.

Privately, I have a different intention: to go find my parents.

We divide up into mini-toroids. I ask Jamila, Aziza, and Israa to come with me. They agree. Israa disappears, then returns a few moments later with Montassar, and the AK-47 strapped over her shoulder, with two spare clips on her belt. I forgot she still had that thing.

Jamila grabs a wrecking bar to use as a tool, perhaps also as a weapon. Stray dogs have suddenly gained a new purpose for us. Protein.

There are sirens now and then in the far distance, fires and smoke everywhere, sometimes an explosion. The only difference between the earthquake and the civil war is fewer guns and helicopters.

What was once a great Syrian city is now dust and shambles, mountains of concrete and rebar.

People scream and run about. In the shadows, looters carry whatever they can grab out of shop windows. Some police try to stop them. Other police join the looters. Society is coming apart.

I tell Israa, "This is how people go mad." She nods grimly, saying nothing, flexing her shoulder under the assault rifle strap and scouting every shadow and corner for dangers.

After four hours searching, we are forced to admit that both the hospital and the construction site are collapsed. No one alive is there anymore.

My parents never come home.

Their bodies are never found.

Overnight, my Papa and my Mama disappear from my life.

I never had a chance to thank them for trying so hard to be a family with me.

I never had a chance to say goodbye to them.

I sigh as a way of letting that chapter of my life drift into the past, even though it is so recently ended.

Letting go is impossible to do, of course. But I have no other option to choose from. Either I connect with the second hand of my wristwatch and stay in the ever-onward-moving always-new and startling present moment, or I give up altogether, lie down and die.

Israa sees my energetic shift. There is no need to speak, only to observe, and to feel enough fear to stay wary of everything and anything. Israa is already good at this. I feel like a weak and confused newbie.

We walk slowly back towards a place that had become our home, but which is now only chaos. None of us wants to get there and face the endless new mountains of work. We stop and sit often. Sometimes I cry in the women's arms.

By evening I am thirsty and hungry, yet glad to notice my discomfort. It tells me I am not too numb from shock. It tells me that I am not dead yet.

We find our way back through the collapsed city to our shanty village. The 'university' is definitely invisible, although our teams have effectively self-organized, even in this chaos. The Earth still tremors under our feet. By then it is dark.

A small campfire burns. A few more new kids have come to us. Everyone is trying to help each other. This is good. Five young people have set themselves up as our field hospital and are caring for cuts, scrapes, and broken bones as best they can.

Eventually our entire tribe sits together around the fire, holding each other so that we might cry better. We share whatever food there is.

Then I hold up my hand to speak. Silence comes swiftly even if nobody wants to hear what I am about to say.

"We could not find my mother or my father. Both the hospital and the construction project collapsed. There are almost no bodies. Everyone was inside when the first quake hit."

I cannot say more. I can only sob.

So many others cannot help but join me. I feel Aziza, Jamila, Israa, even Montassar, standing around me, holding me and holding space for me, for all of us. Our wails go on and on.

When she senses a pause, Aziza continues the telling. "We searched for hours. We asked around at both sites. Nobody survived except for the guards in the construction site guardhouse, and two ambulance drivers who were on a break near the hospital."

Aziza pauses for more grief to pour out from deep in our hearts. Then she makes it real. "Mama and Papa are not coming back. We are on our own now."

As I view the scene, I think, *This is a total reset, a whole new intensity of disaster. We are faced with starting over together, or failing altogether.*

*To fail now means to give up and die.*

*To start over means coming up with an entirely new gameplan.*

It is clear to me that our first challenge is to hit bottom with what just happened. Figuring out what we are going to do about it comes later. This clarity helps me fall asleep on blankets with women and children cuddling around me near one of the fires.

# Possibilica, Florianópolis 3

"How would you like me to address you?"

"You mean what is my name?"

"No. I just want to know what you want me to call you. I don't care if it's your name or not. For example, for this conversation I would like you to call me Ishmael."

"Hello Ishmael. I would like you to call me Bob. You guys are really weird here..."

"Bob, I don't regard your coming here today as an accident."

"No?"

"No. Jacob was handling dishes in the Café today, but he had to go repair one of the solar powered Sterling water pumps, so Tara asked if we could wash up in the kitchen to replace Jacob. If you weren't here, I'd be washing dishes alone. I think you came here to help me wash dishes."

"I can stay and help 'til five. Why do you wash dishes by hand? Why don't you use a normal dishwasher?"

"It's interesting that you think dishwashing machines are normal. That's the point, isn't it? If I get a dishwasher, then when it breaks, I need parts, and we don't fabricate much plastic here. More likely it broke due to designed-in obsolescence, so I'd have to buy a whole new dishwasher in two years to make higher turnover in the manufacturer's quarterly reports. Where does the old machine go? Back to the manufacturer so he can recycle it? No, it does not. The manufacturer successfully externalizes his recycling costs to me, the consumer, or more accurately, to societies all over the world.

"Your culture says I would behave responsibly if I put the old machine out on the street for the garbage truck to take away. I say that is being irresponsible because it is not regenerative. When four and a half billion Indians, Chinese and Africans do the same thing with their old dishwashers, our planet will be out of steel, poisoned by detergents, and buried in broken dishwashers."

"So you think isolating yourself from present culture is the solution?"

"You just told me that you regard your culture as the current, one and only, true and real 'present' culture on Earth. That assertion brings up an interesting question. Who chooses which culture I live in?

"A person would have to be under some kind of spell to think that modern culture is the 'present culture'. Perhaps you have not traveled much. As a matter of fact, there is no world-wide 'present culture'. Humans are a biology experiment of planet Earth, living in hundreds of thousands of evolving cultures around the globe. A couple hundred years ago, one culture discovered how to refine and burn fossil fuels. Powered by what it considered to be endless free energy, that culture became cancerous and started devouring the entire ethnosphere, brainwashing its captives into thinking that it alone is 'present culture'. Only very recently, after World War II, in 1948, I think, was the term 'cultural relativism' first invented. Do you know what 'cultural relativism' means?"

"Not exactly..."

"When you think yours is the only true and right culture, it does not take long to add: 'Our culture is better than your culture if we can kill you.' That gameplan is called 'empire'. This belief enflamed Alexander the Great's annihilation of Persia. It inspired the Christian church to march in the Crusades to annihilate the infidels, and later to send out Conquistadores and missionaries to exterminate millions of inhabitants in the Americas and South Pacific islands. It justified the Australians, Japanese, and Americans to slaughter their original populations, and the Hindus and Muslims to murder each other for centuries... Uh, excuse me. I'm ranting, but you are listening very well. Have you already been to one of our *Expand The Box* training courses?"

"No. But I'd appreciate you telling my wife I'm a good listener..."

"Bring her here and I will. So, hey! You came to get our trees, but you never told me what you wish to do with them."

"I would sell them to the Chinese."

"The more trees you can sell the more money you make?"

"No. I'm just the purchaser. It's my job to buy as many trees as I can get ahold of. I work for a lumber wholesaler, and they have orders to fill. I get paid the same monthly salary no matter how many trees I buy."

"So, who are you really? I mean, what are you here for? What is it you truly love to do?"

"You mean what are my hobbies?"

"No. I mean, what is your life for? What are you doing here on Earth? What principles do you represent?"

"Well, my life is about work, and kids... Netti and I have three boys... by the way, I was watching that group of teens over by the stage. They don't seem to be plugged into phones like my kids are. I mean, your young people seem to be earnestly talking with each other... Are they designing something?"

"Yes, they've already begun preparing for their authentic adulthood initiations. They're working with a theory from Mohandas Gandhi. 'The difference between what we do and what we are capable of doing would suffice to solve most of the world's problems.' They are investigating ways to discover what they are capable of doing, and then directing their newly activated potentials towards solving the world's problems.

"It turns out that our young people can do impossible things because they haven't yet learned they are impossible. Those young people just built a website that encourages youth around the world to quit school and unite under one cause: Reversing climate change through bringing atmospheric CO2 and methane concentrations back to pre-industrial levels, about 300 parts per million for the CO2 and 700 parts per billion for the methane. This team is developing initiations to train and inspire young people how to drive sudden evolutionary change. For a while now, I was doubtful if youth could manage change initiatives. Recently I've found that the answer is indisputably, 'Yes!' Do you know the average age of the NASA team who started with almost nothing and in eight years put a man on the moon?"

"No."

"Twenty-six. Their average age was twenty-six. Their achievement captured the imagination and drove the innovation spirit of a whole generation who came to believe that anything is possible. Now that generation is pissed off because their dreams have been stolen.

"The imperative of instantly shifting the entire human presence on Earth to zero greenhouse gas emissions unleashes human creativity in a wave like nothing we've ever seen. In less than one decade we can and will create a changed world that now seems impossible. Failing to do whatever it takes to shift to regenerative culture kills all the rest of our opportunities and leaves only one future possible, a future without human dignity. Youth are radicalizing, and just in time. The people whose official job it was to create a bright future for humanity have sold out. The 20% of the world's population who is sucking down 80% of the world's resources might stand by like sheep, but youth won't, because the old rules no longer apply in their world. The old rules come from a failed paradigm. It's pirate time and the kids are on it."

"Uh, Ishmael?"

"Yes Bob?"

"What is it you actually do here?"

"Well, last year, a group called the New Economics Foundation conducted a study for the British Government. It identified 'five ways to well-being,' like five ways of how to be on fire about your life. The five ways are: Connect, Be Active, Take Notice, Keep Learning, and Give. You could say that's what we do here.

"What you see are the results created by a resistance decision-making process. It is applied group intelligence. It goes like this: You are free if you can change the system. In any system you cannot change, you are a slave. Slaves resort to making an impact through mass demonstrations, riots, assassinations, and explosions. We have discovered that the largest system an individual can change is the village, less than one hundred people.

"This is an Archan village. Such a village takes radical responsibility for being its own authority. We self-organize our regeneration while staying in symbiotic collaboration with thousands of other villages around the world. Each village has the population limit of one-hundred people, including children. Any village trying to grow beyond this size has clearly been usurped by irresponsible individuals and is treated as a cancer on Earth."

"But what do you believe?" asks Bob, rather desperately.

"Why should we believe something? All beliefs are false. Otherwise, all beliefs would be true, right? And that would be a mad, mad world, wouldn't it? Any village subjecting itself to a belief is no village at all. It is a slave colony of the belief system, organized by a hierarchical power structure which has been undoubtedly hijacked by psychopathic personalities. Beliefs have no relationship to reality."

"What?"

"Well, think about it, Bob. The human mind can decide to believe anything about anything. I mean, you might take on the belief that hotdogs are divine and should be worshiped by preserving them in places of sanctuary. Anyone who does not dedicate themselves to preserving hotdogs is a blasphemer. And then I – your neighbor – might believe that hotdogs are divine and should be worshiped by eating them. To me, anybody who does not eat their hotdogs is a heretic. If we came together at a hotdog festival and we regarded our beliefs as the truth rather than mere stories of personal preference, we would be at each other's throats in no time. Do you see that? A belief regards itself as arbitrarily right, which forces any contradicting belief to be arbitrarily wrong. Put two beliefs in the same place at the same time and the automatic result is war. Why bother with beliefs?"

"Yeah, but... I have to believe something... don't I?" asks Bob, eyes wide.

"Do you? Beliefs are a self-delusional band aid. Their purpose is to cover over a gap in a worldview, to hide a question to which the actual answer is, 'I don't know.' But 'I don't know,' is a valid answer, often a true answer. Being afraid of saying 'I don't know' is fine. Not knowing how to make proper use of your fear of the unknown is simply immaturity, a sign of the lack of adulthood initiation. You gain access to the power of not knowing through your initiations into adulthood."

"What's that?" asks Bob, mystified beyond recognition.

"Part of adulthood initiation is gaining the ability to split your attention. For example, if you would like to split your attention right now for a moment – putting part of your attention on me and part of your attention on the kitchen here – it would probably not take long before you noticed that the dishes are done!"

Bob glances around, astonished. "Why, yes! I agree with you. The dishes are done!"

"I have truly enjoyed this conversation with you, Bob. I feel well exchanged. I would be happy to offer you some of Tara's fabulous Walnut Torte and coffee now. Do you accept my proposal? What do you say?"

"I say that I feel unusually alive right now, Ishmael. Is that usual here?"

"Let's sit over at that table. If you grind the roasted coffee beans, I will go slice us some cake. It takes about thirty cranks to make one cup. Do you want a large, medium, or small piece?"

Bob looks at Ishmael, at the wooden hand-operated coffee grinder, at Tara happily baking in the kitchen, at three other tables occupied by vivacious people in lively conversations, then back at Ishmael, and says, "I take that for a, 'Yes, it's usual around here to feel extraordinarily alive.' I would like an extra-large piece of Walnut Torte."

# Edinburgh, Scotland 4

There are places around Edinburgh where the sight of trees unfolding their brilliant green baby leaves and blossoms on a spring afternoon is too massively beautiful to contain. Directly appreciating the intensity of Gaia re-emerging in cycles of life requires an entire swarm of bees, buzzing in the cacophony of multiple simultaneous pollination orgasms while drinking sweet nectar.

Margaret and Sean experience this wonder of fullness strolling side-by-side along a dirt road, still damp from the heavy mist of the early morning fog. The air is clear and chilly, but the sun is warming. Everything could be wonderful.

But it isn't.

Both Margaret and Sean feel aggravated and exasperated. Neither knows why. Margaret uses both hands to help explore the dimensions of space in search of the imbalance. She says, "Discovery comes hand-in-hand with disorientation. I feel the disorientation. Where is the discovery?"

"If the two come hand-in-hand, then I must be the discovery!" says Sean, holding out his hand to Margaret so that she might take hold of it, proud of his logic.

But Margaret's quest cannot be satisfied by logic. She ignores the simplistic gesture and waits stoically until Sean's waif settles down and King Sean returns to her.

Sean tries a different tack. "If discovery and disorientation come hand-in-hand, then, if you trust the disorientation and let it get bigger, the disorientation itself will lead you to the discovery."

Margaret likes this answer better. Sean's spaceholding makes it safe enough to let her fear speak. "And you will stick around even while I am disoriented?"

"Yes! Definitely! You can count on that! I will ride the fluctuating waves of the disturbance, trusting the purpose of your disorientation."

"If you trust the purpose of my disorientation then answer this question. Where are you going?"

"I thought we would walk to the stream, then take a right along the bank and return by crossing that field over there," says Sean, pointing pro-fessionally like a knowledgeable outdoor tour guide. "I don't think the path is too muddy. When we get back, I thought I would surprise you with..."

Margaret fiercely interrupts. "Do not tell me the surprise!!! I love surprises. You, apparently do not."

"What makes you say I don't like surprises?"

"Because you have already finished our walk."

As worldly as he is, as experienced and intelligent as a man can be, Sean cannot comprehend Margaret's claim. Incomprehension is a sign of failure, of stupidity, and such evidence could only exist as an enemy's attack against Sean's egoic certainty that he is neither a failure nor stupid.

Fortunately for Sean, the side-effects of recent inner-navigation practicing allow him to consciously sense the adrenalin that his adrenal glands are about to pump into his veins to gather his armies for a swift and victorious rebuttal. He has rallied his forces this way thousands of times before in his life and... and, well... he vanquished the enemies so excellently that they abandoned the efforts it took to maintain a heart-to-heart connection with him, leaving him to live alone in his own glorious mind... which was fine for his mind...

It took much intensive internal work to develop a capacity to go sideways instead of forwards, to reroute his intentions, but his efforts are paying off. He keeps breathing, stays centered and grounded and present enough to avoid being triggered into full-out war with his beloved Margaret. He sees that the war started on his side, not Margaret's side. It was Sean who interpreted Margaret's statement as an attack. All she did was use a lifetime of exploration to name his behavior so succinctly that he could no longer avoid becoming aware of something he had been ignoring for eons. It is a key realization for him. He has an inkling of its true value. In other words, Sean is skilled enough in this moment to say nothing and wait.

"Don't worry," says Margaret. "It is not bad. It is just habitual."

She glances at Sean's demeanor to detect if his cavalry and tanks are underway in her direction. In a moment of joy she decides they are not. This means she can reveal her discovery. "You have a goal to reach – our finished walk – and you are focused on reaching that goal. If we follow you, then we speed along, trying to get this walk done. At the end we will have accomplished what we set out to do, and our walk will have been successful. Isn't this the plan?"

"Well, yes. Of course it is! Why not? We agreed to go on a walk?"

"Your logic is true. The facts of what you say are not being contested. Nevertheless, I would like to suggest to you a reorientation of strategy due to the fact that, in my experience, we are missing what I would consider to be the most interesting ingredient of our walk. This is what saddens and frustrates me, Sean."

Sean frantically searches his memory and his pockets, desperately asking, "What did I forget to bring along? I thought that I thought of everything."

"Perhaps that is the key, then. Having thought of everything for our walk would leave you either in the past, or would jump you into the future. Such an orientation takes you far away from me. Because I am here, in the present."

"I know that you are here, my darling!"

"Again, knowing. Again, trying to get it right. Again, trying to do it well. What about trying an experiment with me, Sean? Are you willing to start over with this walk?"

"My wonderful woman friend, my experiment companion, when you say things I do not understand, I feel like I have failed you. I feel sad and scared. I start thinking that it is impossible to please you. I start concluding that you have discovered my incapacities and you are about to leave me."

"But that is exactly it, Sean. I don't want to be pleased by you. I want to be with you. Be... with... you... Here... Precisely where we are... Right now... Without thoughtfully constructed and accomplished plans. Free of logic and reasonableness. This is what I want with you. It is so elementary that it seems to be beyond your ability to comprehend. My desire is so utterly simple. Ridiculously simple. Radically simple. Sean, will you try this novel way of being with that is different from your accustomed and familiar tactic of figuring things out in advance, thinking that a perfectly accomplished walk will make me happy?"

Again, Sean reels from a perceived attack. He says, "I want to try a pre-experiment right now, okay? Are you with me on this?"

"Yes, I am ready to participate with you in a pre-experiment."

"I feel attacked by what you just said. In my mind, I know that you are not attacking me, or trying to fix me because I am broken. I want to be together and well for you, Margaret, so that you are proud to be with me. I do not want you to perceive me as incapable."

"Thank you for telling me this Sean. Thank you. May I ask you a question about this?"

"Yes."

"I propose that we reorient this investigation to the simple version, meaning to simply explore what is going on together, rather than already trying to analyze why it might be going on this way and what it all means. I am thinking we have skipped over the central and urgently important core in our interaction. My question would then be, if you are forced to restrict your answer to the four categories of anger, sadness, joy, or fear, what is the feeling behind your assessment that you are 'being attacked'?"

"That would be fear. I feel afraid that I have done something wrong according to your hidden set of rules, and that you are attacking me for my ignorance. I feel fear that you will no longer be honored to be with me. Then I feel offended that you would have to resort to classifying me as being an idiot."

"And which feeling – of those four already mentioned – would the sense of 'being offended' fall into?"

"When I am offended, I feel... angry. Yes. Anger. Ready to take revenge."

"You are telling me that feeling angry is a secondary feeling that comes after you feel fear, is that right?"

"Well, yes. And it makes sense, doesn't it, as a researcher I mean? If something scares me, then to survive that threat I need to do something against what scares me. The fear detects the threat. But taking action against the enemy depends on feeling angry."

"Yes, Sean! That is the way of survival."

Silence takes over for a moment, except for the sound of crunching damp gravel under their shoes.

"Margaret, right now I am ready to admit that I have been oriented towards survival all my life, until I met you. Somehow you have discovered how to want something besides survival. You have a desire to live. Your desire to live rather than to merely survive has been the greatest gift to me, and my greatest aggravation... uh, my greatest source of at first fear and then quickly surpassed by impulses of anger. Which, thanks to your patience and perseverance, I can now slow down enough to observe how the mechanism works inside of me, and can now redirect into a sideways direction of being more and more aware of and interested in the original feelings going on inside of me. And when I am sitting with myself and these original radically simplified experiences of fear and then anger, I can communicate these to you, and you actually care about these communications from me enough that you want to listen to them. You do not perceive my original feelings as weaknesses or stupidity. You are... apparently... proud of me for feeling and communicating these feelings to you... whenever I am able to do so."

"Yes! Yes! Yes! Sean! I am ecstatic! Each time you tell me your original feelings, an opportunity opens up between us. You create a fresh new access point to immediate connection where I can be with you exactly where you are in this moment right now. This is as alive and intimate as those bees sucking sweet nectar out of the blossom of a tree."

Sean is silent, but he is definitely feeling something as he walks slowly next to Margaret.

"What is that feeling Sean? Please open that door for us. Please tell me that feeling now."

"I feel sad about not having this skill before, with you, with others before you, even with Charles..." Tears roll down his cheeks. "And I feel glad to see that I can learn this wild-ass, off the wall, recently unimaginable new set of skills. I feel glad that I can tell you I feel glad right now, and that you understand what I mean when I say that. And, in addition, I feel glad that you feel glad that I can tell you. I feel glad to think that you might be glad that I am learning these new skills, and I feel glad to think that you might be proud to be with me."

"Yes, I am proud to be with you, Sean. The way if feels to me is that, you wanting me to feel proud to be with you is one way of saying that you love me, Sean, and that you want me to love you. You want to be someone who I want to love. Is that what you mean?"

"Yes, it is what I mean. I think that even a few days ago I would have been too embarrassed to admit this to you. You make me want to be a better man. You make me want to be a man whom you would be proud to love, even if I do not know who that man is, or rather, even if I keep discovering anew who that man is."

"I tell you, Mr. Sean Connery, it is working! I do love you. And look! We are lost now! We did not follow your plan!"

Sean stops in his tracks and looks around, feeling something, then realizes he is feeling something, then says, "I feel afraid that since I do not know where we are or where we should go right now, then I am not in charge of the situation and you will stop being proud of being with me. I feel afraid that you might start to feel afraid because we are lost, and then you will stop loving me." He looks down at the ground in shame of his fear.

"This is an astonishing discovery, Sean! You think that, if I feel afraid because you have not completely managed our conditions so that I cannot feel afraid, then I might stop loving you! That I might not feel proud of being with you if I feel afraid about something that you could have managed so that I could not feel afraid about it!"

"Yes. That is exactly true."

"That is perfect, Sean! I need you to know that I am having one of the best times of my life, right now, right here this minute, this second, walking around being afraid about being lost with you. I am not lying. I need you to know that there is no one in the world I would rather go around feeling afraid about being lost with than you! Here we are, without a plan, being lost and afraid, and I am certain that this is the best use of the minutes of my life because you are telling me what you feel and I am telling you what I feel, and I get to be with myself and be with you right here where we are."

Sean glances around at the newly revived beauty of the scenery and takes a deep breath of fresh forest air. "Probably you cannot imagine how happy I feel to hear you say this, Margaret. My happiness quotient meter just exploded from overcharge. Do you happen to have a spare? Can you do the surgery of replacing my detonated happiness detector?"

"First you have to tell me which model happiness detector you prefer. We have the model that only permits you to feel ten percent intense happiness so that others around you are not disturbed by your enthusiasm about being alive. Or we have the model that allows you to feel sixty percent happy even though people seeing how happy you are might think you are not taking life seriously enough, or that you don't have enough work to do."

"Actually, Nurse Smith, I only wanted you to do the surgery so I could be more intimate with you. I heard that when a nurse does a happiness detector surgery, she must get so close to you that her breasts press against your chest for quite a while."

"Well, you devil, you! I feel glad that you want to have my breasts pressed against your chest for a long while! But I have noticed in your films that you have so much hair on your chest that my breasts will not actually get to press against your skin."

"I would happily shave my chest so as to change that experience for you!"

"Dear Sean, during our talk in the café I started growing accustomed to an intense level of authentic intimacy with you. That intimacy has been feeding my mind, body, heart, and soul. On this walk my body is fed because I get some exercise, and my mind is fed because we never cease to find interesting things to talk about. My soul gets fed from the sheer beauty of the scenery and the sheer size of your newly revealed Being. But before now, my heart was going hungry."

"Will you say more about this?"

"Before our conversation about our conversation, your mind had already finished our walk. You were far ahead of where we were in reality walking. Without realizing it, you were walking speedily to try to catch up with your picture of an already accomplished walk. We were walking so fast that we were leaving the bright principle of love behind us somewhere. We were walking at the speed of mind, far too fast for love to keep up with us. I have an idea for an experiment."

"What is it?"

"The experiment is that neither you nor I decide how fast we walk. Let us allow the bright principle of love to determine our speed of walking. Then we forget about the goal of having a walk together, and instead choose a different intention: To let love walk us. We do not walk in order to accomplish the walk. We walk so that there is love happening. We let the bright principle of love choose where we go and especially how fast we move. Then the walking becomes immediately already successful, because we are walking at the speed of love. Would you like to try this experiment with me, Sean?"

"Yes. I would like to try this experiment with you for the rest of my life."

Their walking becomes remarkably slower, more like a meander, more like Monet appreciating details of the colorful way sunlight reflects off still waters and green leaves in his lily ponds. It is not aimless, but rather full of sensings and noticings that agreeably catch up with them.

"Hmmmm... I see what you mean already," says Sean, smiling brightly.

Then, rather tentatively, a bit like a schoolgirl, Margaret reaches her right hand over towards Sean. She says, "I cannot do this without you."

Sean's fingers wrap around her fingers with extraordinary gentleness. This is the first time they touch.

Impacted more than she expects, breathless from the skin contact, Margaret says, "When you walk with your first intention to be-with me, and when you place your attention on me like this, I find myself able to be the woman you want when you want me to be proud of you."

They walk at the speed of love making glances into each other's eyes until the trees, humming with life, engulf them. They are no longer lost.

# Phoenix, Arizona 4

In the dead of night in the middle of the Arizona desert, two men sleep fitfully in the sand huddled around a few glowing coals. One experiences particularly vivid rapid eye movements. He is dreaming. This one is Eddy.

He sees himself sitting with legs crossed in full lotus position. He wears a pure-white meditation shirt and pants, and is barefoot. His hands rest easily on his knees, palms down, back straight, proud of himself.

Burning before him is a single white candlestick.

The floor he sits on is polished black granite. The candle stands directly on the stone. Nothing else is visible. All else is black. There is absolute stillness.

Hardly noticeable, a slight breeze begins to blow.

Eddy can feel it on his skin, but pretends not to notice. After all, he is meditating!

The candle does not waver in the least.

The breeze continues to intensify, blowing stronger and stronger from behind the candle and directly into Eddy's face. Gusts of wind tousle Eddy's hair and clothing.

Over the next few minutes, the gusts become a windstorm, then they gain tornado strength. Eddy's clothes and hair whip furiously. Yet the candle burns so still it could be standing deep inside of a glass box.

The wind makes no sound. The only sound is Eddy's struggled breathing.

The wind is so strong that Eddy fights with all his strength just to stay sitting up. His stomach muscles – tight as a drum – burn from his efforts. He grips his knees with whitened knuckles, trying to stay in the proper meditation form, squeezing his eyelids tight just to keep them from flying open.

The wind pushes through his lips, blasting around his clenched teeth forcing his cheeks to flap wildly.

Eddy wobbles.

Finally, he can sit upright no longer.

The candle burns as peacefully as a still-life painting, but the wind bowls Eddy over backwards, flat onto the hard stone floor, sliding away headfirst.

He is propelled faster and faster, leaving the candle far behind at his feet. He frantically reaches out to grab onto anything to decrease his velocity, but there is nothing. His fingernails scrape pointlessly on the smooth black granite.

Eddy is terrified. He cannot stop himself. He cannot sit up. He is out of control. There is nothing he can do but be driven along at a hundred miles an hour headfirst backwards.

And then comes the solid brick wall.

Eddy slams full speed completely unprotected, headfirst into the wall.

His head explodes, brains splashing everywhere.

He is *completely and utterly* killed.

Eddy wakes up with a jerk, gasping frantically for breath, eyes wildly looking around, trying to get his bearings, feeling his head with his hands to see if it is okay.

In this strange place it takes a long while.

It is dark.

He is cold.

He lies on the cold sand in the desert night.

He is not dead, but the fire almost is.

JET lies curled up across the fire pit, one arm under his head, the other hand holding his leg.

Eddy wipes sand off the side of his own face and spits sand out of his mouth. He is confused. He hates the dream, and he hates the dirtiness.

So much has happened in the past few hours. None of it makes linear sense anymore.

He calms himself as best he can, quietly stirs the coals and puts more wood on the fire, lies back down to try to sleep, but only stares at the stars.

On the horizon he sees what could be the silhouette of a coyote, sitting silently on the far away boulders, staring at the stars sparkling in the void. A single bright meteorite shoots across the sky.

Is that a coyote over there?

Or is it an Indian?

# Hollywood, California 2

At eight o'clock Tuesday morning, a matched pair of gigantic white Clydesdales trot smartly up Mulholland Drive pulling a white eighteenth century coach through iron gates into Bill Murray's driveway. Michael Caine sits elegantly in the driver's seat wearing a white tuxedo and a white top hat, holding the reins confidently in his hands. He knickers gently to the hayburners, bringing them to a halt directly in front of the mansion's entrance. Beverly Hills has not witnessed such gallantry for one-hundred-and-fifty years.

Michael Caine rings the coach's bell to announce their arrival.

Nothing happens.

After an impatient moment, the coach's passenger door opens from the inside. Out steps Judi Dench wearing a fine white pants-suit. She glances at the mansion's double front doors, then up at Michael Caine. "No. You stay up there," she commands. "I'll rouse the rascal."

She mounts the stone steps and raps loudly using the door knocker. Something eventually mumbles from behind the door. Judi Dench takes one step back, subtly moving into Jiu Jitsu first position, preparing for whatever might emerge.

Bill Murray pokes his puffy disheveled face out from behind the partly opened door, eyes barely open. Behind him peer two women wearing something vaguely definable as pajamas, one is blonde, the other brunette.

Bill squints at Judi with no reaction. Then he notices the coach and the gigantic white horses, finally recognizing Michael Caine.

Michael is not miffed. He straightens himself, looks directly at Bill Murray, and sternly announces, "It is time."

"I thought it was way past time," mumbles Bill, opening the door wide and stepping forward yawning. "I gave up on time. Nobody else seems to notice. I thought the time had come and gone. I thought we were in overtime and nobody was counting. Can I invite you in for a good night's sleep? Elizabeth Diggens makes excellent Eggs Benedict with Canadian ham. Stephanie loves horses. She can unhook them so they can mow my lawn..."

Judi Dench steps swiftly forward and slaps Bill Murray hard across the face. Bill barely notices. "Oh..." he says after a while, peering closer at Judi, frowning, trying to focus. "You mean it's... THAT time..."

Judi, Michael, and Bill stare blankly at each other for a moment, acknowledging the direness required to trigger a meeting such as this. Then Bill asks, "Can they come along?" tilting his head behind him.

Judi defers to Michael.

Michael says, "I don't see why not. We will be needing to improvise..."

Bill turns to the women and says, "Come along then..." imitating Michael's proper London accent. "We don't want to keep them waiting any longer than necessary."

The half-dressed three trundle up into the coach, followed by Judi who closes the house door and then the coach door behind them all.

At Michael Caine's encouragement, the regal pair of horses roll the coach down the driveway and back out the gate onto the Beverly Hills roads.

Inside the coach, eyes adjust to the dimness. On Judi's left sits a young man with silver duct tape across his mouth. Apparently, his hands are tied uncomfortably behind his back. It is Dave Stutler, wide eyes staring at Bill Murray and the two women. Dave has either been kidnapped, or he was talking too much. Knowing Dave, it was probably both.

"What's he doing here?" asks Bill.

Judi Dench pauses long enough to signal that she is not giving Bill a flippant answer. "This man is a designated male apprentice."

'That man' squirms violently and makes gruesome demanding sounds from behind the duct tape, his eyes rolling wildly, his cheeks puffing out and in. Judi glares menacingly in his general direction. He quickly comes to terms with the implied threat and ceases from moaning and squirming.

"But why is this happening now?" Asks Bill. "Who yanked the fire alarm? What's the big deal? Did the aliens make contact? I was having such a nice dream!"

Judi stares him down. "Wait until we assemble as the torus. I have plenty more duct tape..."

Before long Michael Caine turns his horses left, forcing two lanes of oncoming traffic to stop while the beasts negotiate their burden casually into Warner Brothers Studios. The scene is so outrageous that no one stares. Who knows what publicity stunt Warner has concocted for this month's media blitz?

Left, left, right, straight, left, right, Michael navigates the carriage deftly to a halt in front of a dark-gray cement-block building with a door bearing a blue placard painted with white letters, 'Stage 13'. Michael sets the hand brake, ties off the reins, climbs carefully down to the ground, then opens the carriage door, holding out a hand to Dame Judi Dench.

Bill Murray shoves Dave Stutler out the carriage door before him. If there is to be a gunfight, Bill wants someone to hide behind. He glances cautiously in both directions before proceeding. The blonde and brunette follow Bill. By now a few standers-by speak flabbergastedly, trying to piece together which film production this team is part of....

The door to Stage 13 bursts open from the inside. An appropriately dressed liverywoman catches Michael Caine's arm to guide him and the others swiftly indoors. Then she steps out the door again and leaps effortlessly up onto the coach, grabs the reins, releases the brake, and clacks her cheeks. The Clydesdales stride directly towards the gawkers who soon realize that it would probably be wiser for them to get swiftly out of the way than to try to figure out what is going on.

The interior of Stage 13 is completely black, as if the walls, ceiling, and floor are not even there. Only the void exists, with thirteen white tables floating like covered wagons, circled-up for the night in deep space.

Spotlights from high in the rafters shine like harsh stars revealing a sparse reality.

Even Bill Murray is speechless.

Morgan Freeman steps from the shadows towards the tables wearing the white three-piece suit from his role as God in *Bruce Almighty*. "Wardrobe!" he commands.

"Here, sir," a nondescript man wearing a black long-sleeve jersey shirt, black cotton drawstring trousers, black sneakers and black socks appears. If you added a black cowl, he could easily pass for a Ninja dressed in the traditional Shinobi Shozoku.

"Please provide gowns for these two amazing women. They do not require make-up or hair. They are gorgeous and radiant in the raw. Welcome, Ladies," Morgan says, finishing with a bow. Then he adds, "And please throw a purple tuxedo on my friend William. We start in twenty."

"On it, sir!" The wardrobe manager gestures invitingly with open arms towards Elizabeth, Stephanie, and Bill. "This way, please." They vanish with him into the dark.

# Eugene, Oregon 7

Sanjib slides onto the bench seat next to Davis at the donut shop table gripping his apple fritter in one hand and a large coffee with three sugars plus milk in the other hand. Davis says, "I thought I would get tired of hanging with you in the cop car, and now I have to make appointments just to see your ugly face."

Sanjib takes a gigantic bite of his fritter. "Mmmmm.... You think I come here to see you?" His words are almost unintelligible for obvious reasons.

Davis takes his own bite of a custard-filled maple bar, oblivious of the fact that this delicacy cannot be experienced in any other country of the world.

Sanjib looks down at his plate, then says, "It is not actually my tradition to share my dreams... but I had a puzzling dream last night."

Davis waits in full attention, still as sunrise, knowing better than to make jokes at Sanjib in a moment like this. "I am listening," he says.

"You and I were infiltrating an Arabian palace, filled with colorful tapestries hanging from the ceiling, just like in those tales from Scheherazade in *One Thousand and One Nights*. We had the mission to capture a spy, a woman, but we could never find exactly where she went. At the last moment she always disappeared through some portal hidden behind the tapestries... It was very frustrating."

"Did she look worth chasing?"

"She was worthy indeed..."

Davis's eyes get wide. "I think you are amazing, Sanjib! I think your dream gives us our first real clue! I think it was staring us in the face the whole time and we missed it!"

"Are you thinking what I am thinking?" asks Sanjib.

"Uh... Well... that would be a tough question to answer, Sanjib. I would not want to venture into that territory. But, hey! It's Thursday. Wanna go to a particular bar with me, say around seven-thirty?"

"This one is honored to meet you there... Guns?"

"No guns. Sanjib! Your whole body is a highly trained weapon, full of awarenesses and distinctions! Where we are going, we don't need guns! We are becoming revolutionaries of consciousness!"

Davis chuckles uncertainly...

"Laugh while you can, monkey boy!" snarls one of two smokers in their late twenties, sitting on the low cinder-block wall outside the *Horsehead Bar*. Then they both laugh. Was it mere coincidence?

It is almost seven-thirty in the evening. As Davis casually walks along the sidewalk, he gets the strangest impression that these two men are hiding or protecting something. They seem too smart to be smokers. Davis slows his pace while staring into his phone pretending to read a message. Out of his peripheral vision he sees that they speak with each other but do not actually inhale their cigarettes. They talk big and flick ashes away when necessary. One of them smiles at the other and the smile seems too genuine.

Sanjib appears from around the corner and stops in front of Davis, just out of hearing range of the guardians. Davis glances up briefly, but keeps pretending to write a message. Under his breath he says, "Am I paranoid, Sanjib? Or do these two guys seem like they are on guard duty?"

"The game is afoot!" says Sanjib with too much delight for Davis's mood.

"Calm down, dude. We are here for a drink, nothing more. And we are not gay. We are grad students at the U."

"I thought we were through the gay thing. Your story works for me. I study history."

"Yeah... well... I study *her* story..." Davis slightly nods his head behind Sanjib in the direction of a single brown-haired woman approaching on foot, hair wrapped into a bun on the top of her head. She is unmistakably the same woman they first saw enter these doors several weeks ago. She wears the same purple sweater.

"Let's go!" says Sanjib.

"Let's stay!" says Davis.

They stare at each other in conflict. Waiting happens as collateral damage.

The woman passes them by without notice, but slightly glances and smiles at the 'smokers'. As she jaunts lightly up the stairs, a belt pouch bounces on her thigh. She carefully closes the door behind her. Then she is gone.

"Five minutes," says Davis.

"Two," says Sanjib, glancing at his watch, "or we'll be late. It is nearly seven-thirty!"

Simultaneously they both start walking towards the entrance stairs, badly faking nonchalance.

Sanjib pushes the door open then stops in the dark entryway. With only his left eye open, Davis follows and gently closes the door behind him as he saw her do it.

Wordlessly Davis feels through the velvety black curtains hanging inside the right wall of the entryway. Sanjib does the same on the left side.

Excitedly, Sanjib grabs Davis's wrist. A twenty-watt bulb lights this tiny antechamber, but it is enough for Davis to see the simple wooden door that Sanjib silently reveals behind the curtain he holds back. Davis sighs and nods. *This is where femme Mysterium disappeared last time!*

In they go, and down the old wooden stairs. A vague, yellowish light glows below.

The steps end on the cement floor of a large poorly lit storeroom packed with broken barstools, empty beer kegs, cases of toilet paper, and spiderwebs. Over to the right is another wooden door leaking rays of light from underneath it.

Davis steps quietly to the door, pausing for a moment, fingers touching the brass doorknob, listening for any clues about what might be happening on the other side. Nothing. He glances at Sanjib, sighs, then turns the knob, pushes open the door, and enters casually, as if this is already the thousand and first night he's been here.

A bare fluorescent tube hangs from the ceiling, humming in the silence. Thirteen people of various ages, dress codes, and gender sit silently in a circle of fourteen chairs. As Sanjib and Davis enter, a man in his middle thirties with short dark hair and glasses stands up and cheerfully says, "Ahh! Two guests tonight! Welcome! I will bring chairs." He has an accent, possibly Italian.

People scuffle wordlessly to expand their circle so the two new chairs can fit in. The Welcomer keeps one chair out of the circle so Sanjib and Davis can enter and have a seat, then he closes the circle with the empty chair. Silence prevails for another minute while Davis and Sanjib try not to look as nervous as they feel.

The brown-haired woman inhales. Davis senses her breathing from across the room in every cell of his body. It is amazing to him that he cares about her inhaling. He wants her to inhale, to be well, and he wants to be someone who gets to hear her breathe. This is a sensation he never remembers having felt before. He starts being afraid that he might be having a nervous breakdown, or possibly a brain tumor.

She says, "Welcome to the *Mysterium*, everyone. For anyone who does not yet know, my name is Remington Smith. Tonight, I will be the first spaceholder of this Archan circle. Normally we would dive directly into skills practice, but tonight we have guests. I would like to take this opportunity to have a check-in, to share things that you have noticed about your work, your life, your relating, and your experiments. We have not done this for a while, and since the Universe keeps evolving, it could be useful to hear. Who would like to go first?"

A woman in her mid-sixties sitting next to the Welcomer says, "I would. My name is Sophia Bentley. You can hear from my accent that I am not American. After my children moved out and my husband died in England fifteen years ago, I decided to follow the old adage: *Go West, young woman!*" People chuckle. "After passing through most of the southern and western United States, I ended up here in Eugene, still with no answers about who I am or what I am supposed to do with the rest of my life. Inspiration evaded me. I decide to start a weekly meeting in the living room of my small rented apartment. I put up flyers at the co-op, the natural food stores, and the pie shop for *Shadow Knights of the*

*Mysterium,* a name that came to me on a night hike in the woods. Soon there were fifteen people on average visiting me every Thursday evening.

"We realize that we have so much in common, yet we are so far away from what we want. New creation skills are required, things that were never mentioned in school. Over the last six years we kept refining our skillsets and eventually found this place to meet where we can do Emotional Healing Processes, thoughtware upgrades, and skill building without bothering anyone. The big news for me is Robert... that noble gentleman sitting over there in the yellow shirt with his white beard. We had our first conflict. It was about how to deal with our money. What I want to report is that neither of us were hooked! Instead we went nonlinear and decided to bring our finances together without getting married! You can't believe how much unconscious tensions got released. And they stayed away! I truly feel like I get to start over in the world and play full out doing exactly what I came here to do without counting every cent like my mother did, trying to make sure everything is fair. This way, nothing is fair. Nothing is equal. All of it is surprising. The most surprising is that we have more cash moving through our wallets now than we ever did before. Would you tell people your theory about this, Robert?"

Robert straightens up in his chair and says, "What I notice is that the Universe pays particular attention to anyone who is generating more value than they consume. It is not like a conscious noticing, but more of a mechanical reaction to bring things back into balance. If you start generating more possibility..."

Sanjib interrupts with a strange kind of urgency by asking, "What do you mean when you say, 'the Universe'?" Davis glares at him sideways in disbelief.

"When I say the word 'Universe' I mean 'consciousness at large', the general field of consciousness... why are you asking this question?"

Sanjib looks down at his fidgeting fingers. "Because I've been asking this question all my life. The only answers people give me come from religious dogma or new age spiritual psychobabble. I just wanted to check what kind of sect this is."

People start to laugh, but Robert immediately interrupts them. "No, no, don't laugh! It is an excellent and relevant inquiry. Is this a sect we have created? What is a sect actually?" He pauses a moment. "I've been researching this. Here are some factors to consider. A sect is hierarchical with a master or father-figure at the top of the power structure. In comparison, what we have here is a torus with rotating spaceholders. A sect flows power, ownership, and sexual favors up the hierarchy to the charismatic leader who regards him or herself as omniscient or divine. The term 'sect' or 'cult' can seem quite scary or threatening, because whichever population has the most participants can outvote any other group with fewer adherents and then label the others 'a sect'. In the bad-old-days, spaceholders for any group could be singled out and burned at the stake if the bigger population called them a 'witch'. MGM studios killed the power of the word 'witch' by showing them as harmless characters who melt if you throw water on them. Now you can dress up as a 'witch' on Halloween and people think you are funny, not terrifying. A new pejorative was needed. These days the terms 'sect' and 'cult' replace the previous label 'witch' as reasons to attack and destroy. I have a question I've been wanting to ask here. How many of you have a sense that you have been tortured and or killed in a previous life for being a 'witch'?"

More than half the people slowly put their hands up, then look cautiously around at the others. Several become emotional.

"Thank you," says Robert. "I will finish by distinguishing that a sect operates by encouraging participants to give their centers of authority to the leader, including giving your money, your valuable possessions, your voice, even your daughters and sons. There is generally a set of beliefs you must subscribe to, and rituals you must perform. You must obey the sect leader. In comparison, in this circle we work collaboratively to liberate and empower each other's agency, authority, voice, free will, and centeredness. This is not a sect. It is an evolutionary torus."

"And your theory about generating absurd amounts of value?" asks Remington.

"Ah, yes! If you create more value than is called for, what Remington refers to as 'absurdly valuable' value, and if you deliver it abruptly, unreasonably, and uncompensated, you tilt the Universe's balance of value in your favor. This unbalance becomes an ever-increasing investment that will be repaid because the Universe abhors a vacuum. Rebalancing occurs in a variety of surprising ways, including luck beyond all measure of coincidence, health beyond all reason, chance meetings with just the right person at the right time, even an unexpected influx of cash."

"Where are you getting this clarity?" demands Sanjib.

"From direct experience, from observing the results of specific experiments," says Robert. "Why are you asking?"

"Because..." mumbles Sanjib, glancing furtively at Davis, "because I want this kind of clarity for myself also."

Silence stills the room.

Remington gently asks, "Who are you, sir? And, what do you want?"

Davis literally holds his hands to keep them from grabbing Sanjib by the arm and running the hell out of there. He tries to get Sanjib's attention to see him shaking his head, signaling "No! Stop! Don't say anything!" But Sanjib ignores him.

"My name is Sanjib Hajji. I work for the Eugene Police Department with my partner here, whose name is Davis Hatcher. We only had one day on patrol and then Police Chief John Stafford assigned us to go undercover. Our job is to infiltrate terrorist groups like this one around Eugene and feed information back to headquarters. This is our first group. But I don't see any terrorists here. Instead I already love you people more than I love my own family. Am I going crazy? What is happening to me?"

Sanjib is trembling from head to toe.

No one dares to breathe.

Davis is internally losing it. *That was insane of Sanjib! Why did he do that? Is this some kind of setup from Chief Stafford to test me? Are these people for real? What would Henry do?* Davis's whole future career as a police officer flashes before his eyes and then vanishes in a puff of chaos.

Sanjib says, "I am unwilling to lie that much. I do not want to pretend that I am someone else. What if you start to like the person I am pretending to be? Then your love would not touch my heart because I am fake. Then you would love a fake person. This would be so painful I cannot even imagine it. I don't want to be a fake person. I don't know what is going to happen next, but I hope you don't kill me. I want to be here more than anywhere else in the world. My father was a police officer. My father's father was a police officer. I thought it was the only option for my life. My father was shot down in cold blood here in Eugene when I was thirteen years old and I..." Sanjib puts his hands to his face and starts sobbing out loud.

Davis feels his world dissolving around him, like being stripped naked and dropped into a vat of not quite boiling oil.

Remington says, "Sanjib, what are you feeling right now?"

"What?" says Sanjib.

"It looks like you are feeling something. There are only four core feelings: anger, sadness, fear, and joy. It looks like you are feeling something. What are you feeling?"

"I feel sad because my original intention was to deceive all of you, and I did not actually want to fulfil that intention. But I did not know that until now. I promised people at the police station that I would lie as part of my job. I even promised my partner Davis here that I would lie in public to be an undercover police officer with him. But it is not what I want. I was faking my intention. I can't believe I would sell my integrity so cheaply, simply for a job. I am also feeling incredibly happy to have the opportunity to speak with you like this, without any idea what I am going to say next, somehow without the fear of being condemned. I also feel afraid of what Davis is thinking or feeling right now, because he is a good man. I do not want to make his life harder than it already is. His father died recently, and now he has to partner with me, a Q-tip head. I feel very afraid of what is going to happen next."

Remington leaves a few seconds tick by, then says, "Thank you Sanjib for telling us these things. I feel glad to meet you."

"What... what are you going to do to us?" Sanjib squeaks.

"Nothing," says Remington. "We are going to listen to you. Why would we do anything to you? You told us what you feel. You cannot be wrong about that. You said who you are and what you want. We do not have a rule that no police are allowed to meet with us. It is simply that you are the first police ever to join our circle. You are welcome here."

Sanjib slowly raises his eyes to meet the others, and only sees smiling faces, nodding heads, a few people waving wiggly fingers at him in silent applause and appreciation. He cannot believe what he sees. He never imagined this was possible with other human beings. His tears redouble. Someone passes Sanjib a box of tissues so he can blow his dripping nose.

In the ensuing silence, Remington slowly looks over at Davis. "You are in trouble," she says matter of factly.

"Why is that?" asks Davis defiantly. At least he can still be defiant.

"It is simple. Your friend here, Sanjib, has entered radical relating with us in this circle. He knows how to do this. You do not. What are you going to do about it?"

Davis's eyes stay wide and as vacant as he can keep them. His right hand unconsciously searches for the butt of his Glock 22 problem-solving pistol, but it is not there. His left hand unconsciously clamps over his mouth, trying to keep it from saying anything, but it is rather too late for that. Sanjib has already spilled more beans than Davis could ever imagine existed. Davis is not breathing very well.

Remington looks openly into his eyes for a long while. There is no ridicule in her attitude. No anger or fear. Simply presence and connection.

Finally, Davis's mind and heart slow enough to hear Remington breathe again, and he cares that she breathes well. It is the weirdest feeling he ever felt, yet it feels so excellent. It feels important, and true.

Remington says, "What if you try? What if you let your heart speak and your soul speak instead of your mind? What if you try being alive enough to be radically honest with us for a moment here?"

Davis sighs shakily. "I... I care... Remington... that you are breathing."

People around the circle involuntarily sigh. Tears come to many eyes. Someone makes a sound like "Ohhhh, my!" Someone else murmurs, "How wonderful!"

Davis goes on. "It's the end of the world as I know it, but I feel fine... and this scares the hell out of me. It feels like my world is crumbling around me and I am going down with it..."

"We call that experience a 'liquid state,'" says Remington. "You may have uncomfortable sensations in any or all of your five bodies. But you will be okay. Don't worry. We are holding space for you. We are with you in your liquid state. Keep speaking if you want." Her voice is kind and gentle, just like Davis thought it would be.

"I want you to breathe well, Remington. I want you to succeed. I don't even know what this group is doing. I assume it is illegal or you would not be meeting underground here in this dungeon, in these catacombs. I don't know what is going to happen when I walk back upstairs into the night, when I next report back to Chief Stafford or Sergeant Brinks. What am I going to say? Will I lie to them? Will I be fired? Or put in jail? What will my Dad think? He is already dead, for gawds sake! But I'm sure he is watching over my shoulder and thinking something nasty..."

Then he squints his eyes at his partner. "What have you done to my future, Sanjib! I am scared as hell about what you just did! And angry! What will I do with the rest of my life?" His voice disintegrates into shaking quivers.

"Easy there! Go easy!" says Remington. "Let me ask you a question, okay?" She does not wait for an answer. "Please check in and tell me how big your now is. How far extended into the past or future is your now?"

"What?" says Davis, looking at her in a daze.

"Your now," says Remington. "You are in charge of how big to make your experiential now. Your now is your relationship to relevant time. You can only raise your hand now. You cannot raise your hand in the future or yesterday. You can only breathe now. You cannot breathe in the past or tomorrow. Now is the time that matters. Please shrink your now so it is only this big." Remington shows him the thumb and first finger of her left hand held one centimeter apart. "Shrink it now. You can only shrink your now, now. You can do this. Try it."

Davis's breathing slows. His hands stop shaking, but his head starts. He looks at Sanjib and blurts out, "What the hell were you thinking!"

"I was thinking that I don't want to be a liar like Bush, and Cheney, and Nixon, and Obama, and Trump, and all the rest. I want to be me. That is what I was thinking." Sanjib's hands go up in an expression of helplessness as he looks around at the others. Then he looks back to Davis. "Don't you feel at home here?"

"I feel at home in a cop car cruising town looking for drug dealers. We made promises! We have a job to do!"

"Well! What is that job?" asks Sanjib. "To keep the peace? To build a more cohesive and alive and peaceful community? Have you ever experienced such a cohesive and alive and peaceful community as this?"

"Look! You don't know these people from Adam!"

"Well," says Sanjib, "if you don't know these people from Adam, then why did you just tell Remington that you love her?"

"I... Because..." Davis glances at Remington, then he sees the whole circle of people smiling at him, looking at each other, nodding their heads, wiggling their hands and fingers at him in silent respectful appreciation.

"I didn't! I don't! Are you crazy? Why would I say that? How could I know..." He curls up sobbing, rolls uncontrollably out of his chair onto the floor.

Several others are immediately at his side, hands on him so he experiences their touch instead of being left alone with his deeply tangled emotions. They make no effort at all to interrupt him.

These people seem to be of the general opinion that this is possibly the best thing that has ever happened to Davis Hatcher in his entire life.

# Aleppo, Syria 9

Zenobia Darwish's *Beep! Book* – 7 February 2023 – day 1 after the earthquakes

The morning sun never quite shines on the day after the earthquakes. Instead, the sky turns from black to five-hundred shades of gray, filling my nose with repulsive odors, acrid smoke, things burning that should not be burning.

Like the others, I wake up with sore muscles from doing things yesterday I never imagined a human being would need to do, and sore bones from sleeping on the rocky dirt under my blanket.

I simply lie there.

No agenda could possibly correlate with these conditions. I can make no plans.

Insanity reigns.

Or maybe reality reigns.

Or maybe reality is insanity.

I don't know what the others are thinking, but what I think is that on top of drought, famine, and multifaction war-madness, the earthquakes have broken my previously unquestioned faith in my culture.

Even now, on the battle fronts, no one helps each other. I've collected enough online news to know that Syrian factions rather hope that the 'enemy's side' is more damaged than they are by the earthquakes. They try to leverage other people's suffering into their own advantage. Aleppo citizens tremble in unlit corners, confused and terrorized, expending all their efforts merely trying to make it to the next hour.

I later learn that in the space of one day, these two earthquakes killed over 62,000 people in Türkiye and Syria, erasing entire towns and villages. Over 282,000 buildings were destroyed. Over 7.67 million people were made homeless, the majority of these millions being children.

There is no place in me where arbitrary murder by the Universe can fit.

On the day before the earthquake, no one had the slightest hint about what was about to smash us. I spent two whole days before the earthquake writing as clearly as I could about what happened in Syria the past twelve years. Even with twelve years of clarity, I could not predict what would occur twelve hours later.

Here are notes from our *Handbook* study space this morning. (Yes. The day after the earthquakes we gather to study. I can see how studying together brings our village back to center, and therefore, back to life.) Montassar reads a section about authority. Here is what the *Handbook* tells us:

*Authority precedes agency.*

*This means, until you authorize yourself – become the author of yourself – you have little power to cause results.*

*The reason you don't ordinarily authorize yourself is because you have long-standing unconscious emotional fears about authorizing yourself.*

*If you research this in the other direction, you can identify your Emotional Fears behind those domains wherever you do not have authority.*

*Where do you lack authority?*

*Authority ignites when you anchor your 'point of origin' into a particular context out of which you can then consciously live your life.*

*Authority is an internal experience of having choice, the power to declare, the power to ask.*

*Authority is previous to taking a stand, previous to commitment, previous to your ability to say what you want.*

*Authority comes from authorizing yourself to have authority.*

*If someone else gives you permission to have authority, do you really have authority? No.*

*If someone 'in authority', or some institution or 'governing body' which is 'recognized by others' to have authority, 'licenses' you or 'certifies' you to have authority, does this change anything in reality? Have you legitimately or credibly been authorized? No.*

*What if they change their mind? What if they take away the permission they previously granted to you? Does this mean you lose your authority? No.*

*If your authority can be rescinded, did you actually have authority in the first place? No.*

*Having authentic authority is the beginning of radical responsibility.*

*Having authentic authority starts with hitting bottom. It is about being willing to participate in life without the protections of storyworlds.*

*This means that your actions, your movements, how you speak, how you relate, your purpose, your intentions, are no longer protected by the idea that if you hide behind an acceptable storyworld, such as a reason, or a justification, or a certification from any gameworld, then you are safe from having to be radically responsible for the consequences of your actions or Inactions.*

*We live in a radically responsible Universe.*

*Many people try to use a storyworld as an acceptable excuse for not showing up in their life. You unconsciously authorize yourself to not show up in your life due to the 'fact' that you believe that your storyworld is true and valid. Does this even sound sane?*

*You think it is real when you tell yourself the story that, for example, "Love is not for me." or, "I am the source of misery in people's lives." or, "I will never make it. I will never be adult." or, "I will never get out of my misery." You tell stories to yourself and others about women, about men, about children, about motherhood, about money, about career, about self-respect, about success...*

*You activate all these stories as protections against having authority in your own life. And then you believe your stories? Even though you just made them up?*

*You hang on to stories that are so big, they do not let you shrink down into the present moment in a minimized now with a small here and a small you – a 'you' with no stories attached about yourself, about your circumstances, or about other people.*

*Your gremlin's fear may be that if you shrink your now, there is no longer space for your stories to fit.*

*Stories exist in time.*

*In now there is no time.*

*Shrinking your now increases your agency to move in any direction and to cause valuable results.*

*If you feel like a victim of emotional fears, it is a hint that your authority is not with you. You gave your authority to someone else so they can say what they think of you, they can judge you, they can pressure you, they have power over you, they can decide about you, they can exclude you, they can tell you that you are 'in' or 'out', they can say that you are a 'good' or 'bad' partner | mother | father | employee, they can tell you if it is 'working' or 'not working'.*

*It is time to recognize that you gain some sort of 'benefit' from making yourself suffer as a 'powerless victim'.*

*But what do low levels of background emotional fear have to do with authority?*

*The ability to distinguish and consciously identify very low intensity fear, for example at 0.01% intense fear, to receive the information that such tiny levels of conscious fear experientially give to you, then you can take intelligent effective actions almost magically. You are aware of what is happening as it begins to arrange to happen. You can dance with what is happening in real time.*

*These whisps of very low intensity conscious fear inform you with such subtlety, speed, diversity, accuracy, and quantity that you cannot put it all into words, yet you can still receive it and use it to change, to navigate, to decide, to reinvent yourself, to create.*

*The empowerment from consciously feeling and making practical moment-to-moment use of very low intensity fear awakens you to realizing that you no longer experience the fear of being unauthorized. The subtle ongoing background flow of very low intensity conscious fears grants its own authority to you in reality, because you can take care of yourself elegantly and fluidly due to the enormous variety of ongoing awarenesses that your very low intensity conscious fear gives you.*

*Conscious very low intensity fear provides you with enough accurate experiential information that you automatically have clarity and power in domains that you do not know about with your mind, or which you have never directly experienced. Your massive volume of clarity and possibility from very low intensity conscious fears is the resource out of which you can create and relate in accordance with what is needed and wanted in the present-moment-reality occurring immediately around you.*

*Suddenly you no longer need to use storyworlds as a crutch in your life. You can live full out, without relying on models, concepts, or formulas in your memory trying to tell you, "Yes, I know how it goes to be a spaceholder. This is the right way to deliver my nonmaterial value. This is how an Emotional Healing Process should be delivered."*

*No! There is nothing telling you these things in order to 'build your confidence', or 'give you certainty', or 'affirm your righteousness', or 'substantiate your credibility', or 'grant you self-respect'.*

*No! There is nothing but your ongoing very low intensity conscious fears to rely on for inventing each new step of your life out of nothing.*

*Is this flawless? No.*

*Does it actually work? Yes.*

*Authentic authority gives you extraordinary freedom of movement.*

*Authority is the beginning of radical freedom.*

*You create, you sing, you paint, you write letters and articles and screenplays and websites, you design clothing and passive-solar buildings and gardens and new devices, you program computers, and make proposals, and stand up and speak, and be with children and animals, and help people you don't know, and transform gameworlds, and you can do basically anything.*

*What a person like this has is authentic authority. You have the authority to try. You cannot 'do everything perfectly'. You don't have to do everything perfectly because the things you do flowingly evolve and emerge at the edge, out of the future.*

*You are not a 'Master' at everything. You still make mistakes. But perhaps not as many mistakes, because your ongoing very low intensity conscious fear informs your every move much more thoroughly and quickly than your mind could ever manage.*

*Fear Club is about reclaiming the Immense Immediate Intelligence of your Very Low Intensity Conscious Fear. (The III of your VLIC Fear.)*

*It does not work to try to create authority with anger. Anger drives fighting, creates conflict, takes action, uses force. "My opinion is right! My way is best! I want to do it this way, now!"*

*Conscious rage is fantastically useful, but rage does not give you authority. Rage gives you 'might'. Uninitiated adolescents still try to claim, "Might is right!" But it is not.*

*If you try to use anger, or threats of anger, to give you authority, you end up in war.*

*Anger has a different energy than fear, a different resource than fear. Anger offers you movement, persistence, determination. But when it comes to authority, anger is often a distraction.*

*'Very low intensity conscious fear' does not mean 'regulated fear', or 'controlled fear', or 'suppressed fear'. It means that you have sufficiently handled and healed so many of your higher intensity reactive mechanical survival fears that your nervous system can relax enough to notice that, in fact, you are surrounded in an entire ocean of very low intensity conscious fears to swim in.*

*If you dare to let go of solid ground and swim in your very low intensity conscious fears, the fears will support you and propel you with effectiveness and alacrity beyond your wildest imagination. This is one reason why Possibility Management Emotional Healing Processes are so lightning fast, transformationally effective, and psycho-emotionally resilient.*

*Can you learn to keep your numbness bar lowered enough to perceive and differentiate among your individual 0.01% intense very low intensity conscious fears? This is not a rhetorical question. It is a challenge, an experiment to keep trying.*

*If your years of unhandled Emotional Fear Reactivity is not completed, then when you lower your numbness bar, all you will feel are old dead emotional dinosaurs. Your wealth of intelligent aliveness in your very low intensity conscious fears will not rise above your perception threshold. Your incomplete emotional fears will be so noisy that you won't be able to 'hear' the messages of your very low intensity conscious fears.*

*This is why your first job in getting to adulthood may be to heal and extract the gold from the noise.*

*However, if your survival strategy is to be 'nice' and 'a good person' and 'invisible', it may be helpful to do 3-3-3 rage exercise (full out rage for no reason in a safe place for 3 minutes, 3 times per week, for 3 months) or three-times-per-week sword-sharp Dragon Speaking Rage Work practice with your 3Cell so that you have more of your own aliveness to work with.*

*When people say, "I feel afraid..." mostly what they are reporting is their high intensity reactive emotions of unconscious fear, not their very low intensity feelings of conscious fear.*

*When you feel low intensity fears that are less than 10% intense, the languaging tends to come out more like, "I am noticing that..." or, "I wonder about..." or, "I sense...", or, "My authority for landing subtle new context in a research space tells me right now that I should slow down my speaking because this is what is needed and wanted."*

*Authority is, "I trust myself to take care of myself in situations like this and around people like you. This trust is born in the center of my very low intensity conscious fears."*

*Authority is not actually about feelings. Authority is a shift in your point of origin.*

*You move your point of origin to live in a place of authority.*

*Your background baggage of emotional fears falls off because... you are authority.*

*There is no longer any squirming around trying to avoid the consequences of your actions and inactions. Instead, you depend on your very low intensity conscious fears to immediately notice and use microconsequences as navigational feedback about where you are and what you are creating.*

*You are where you are. You confirm where you are using your very low intensity conscious fears. These tiny whisps off fear tell you all the places where you might be fooling yourself about where you are, and where you might be fooling yourself about where you are fooling yourself.*

*With authority you can go into any gameworld, navigate any space, respond to any request, any challenge, any stress, without overwhelm, because you are centered in what is. You are being with what is. You are present in that space with all your infinite resources instantaneously at hand, being navigated by your very low intensity conscious fears.*

*This is not about holding onto a belief in some kind of fantasy world such as, "This is my truth right now." Holding onto 'truth' is already a defensive stance.*

*With your very low intensity conscious fears, defensiveness is irrelevant. This equates to leaving your concrete-busting jack-hammer tools aside so that you can remove a small splinter of wood from your finger... so that you can create what is wanted and needed when it is wanted and needed.*

*If you find yourself using the survival strategy of withdrawing, pulling back, being petrified and silent, shrinking into yourself, hiding in the corners, trying to be invisible, refusing to take risks, refusing to create under public scrutiny, this hints that you have not established your own authority.*

*Authority is about hitting bottom in order to be thoroughly ensconced in what is, hitting bottom in order to build context and to navigate transformational space. Authority is complete connection with rather than hiding away from.*

*Anger is about making distinctions, saying, "This is this! And that is that!" But with fear you can be with everything. You can saturate the space with experiential awareness, and then navigate spaces previous to making distinctions, reverting back to the level of making distinctions whenever that is necessary or useful.*

*Authentic authority is not self-referenced. People can go crazy with megalomania. "I am right and the whole world should bow down, kiss my feet, and obey me!"*

*People with authentic authority create useful results because they are located on the bottom, close to the dirt, not in the swamp, but under it, grounded in reality. This is the opposite of busily being a failure (or a hero) in your own mind.*

*The Old Thoughtmap Of Authority is 'power over'. The New Thoughtmap Of Authority is 'power under', being the irreducible, inescapable, unavoidable, essential author of your life. Authority without stories. You become a nobody with a very close connection to the nothingness. If you can be nothing, then you can be everything. Then what you can perceive and what you can create come closer together.*

*It takes so much anger to stay in the body, and so much fear to stay close to reality.*

*Just like no one can force responsibility on you, no one can give you authority.*

*Emotional fear is a doorway to being manipulated, even to manipulating yourself. If you give your authority to a story, you can manipulate yourself. If you give your authority to someone else, you are also manipulating yourself. You manipulate yourself to try to avoid feeling fear. You feel emotional fear to avoid feeling the aliveness of the feelings of fear that you would feel during creation.*

*How to enter and live in the resilience of being in the intensity of life? This is a skill. Navigate towards the experiential sensation of authority by receiving and perceiving the massive variety of very low intensity conscious fears that are ever around you and within you.*

The *Handbook* then proposes an exercise. It says:

*With regards to sourcing money, sourcing friendship, sourcing partnership, enhancing your agency, delivering your nonmaterial value, navigating transformational spaces, building an Archan gameworld, writing a film script, writing a book, sourcing a Bridge-House, sourcing an Archiarchy Invention Center (AIC), etc., let the immense immediate intelligence of your very low intensity conscious fears inform you instant-by-instant, and write down what their empowering guidance tells you (or speak what they tell you to someone who is willing to write down word-for-word exactly what you say for you). Later on, after you completely receive and document the communications from your very low intensity conscious fears, choose which actions to take or avoid taking. You choose. The fear does not choose. The fear only informs.*

*Start now.*

I lie here in the dirt, in the shade of the shack, after copying all these words from the *Handbook* into my *Beep! Book*.

I decide to do this exercise.

I take a deep breath and relax. I close my eyes and lower my numbness bar even further than I ever imagined was possible to lower it, so low that very low intensity fears start becoming sensually apparent. There are so many! Slowly now, slowly...

An unthinkably frightful thought dully rises in my mind, 'Only half of our Learning Village has arrived this morning. Half of my friends are gone. Half of the Beings I have been loving back to life are either dead or missing, stolen from me by chaos. What am I supposed to do now? Where should my love for them go?'

My heart reels, split open with the fear of so much loss. It bleeds inside of me. The hole in the side of my heart is too big to fathom, too big to ever patch.

I do not deserve this much fear.

I am afraid to accept so much meaningless loss.

I am afraid to continue calling Aleppo my home. It has been maliciously destroyed around me.

Worse than that, I am afraid to even consider myself to be 'Syrian' because there is no Syria for me anymore. Nothing I thought or believed in has prevented this inner and outer devastation.

I am afraid to think that there is nothing left of my world.

I am afraid to face the lies that my parents accidentally passed on to me, their belief that being Syrian means something, the idea that I can be proud of Syria and be disdainful of other countries, the idea that Syria will recover its majesty and nobility. It has all proven to be bullshit!

People only fight because they are from a country or from a religion. If I am no longer from a country or a religion, then who am I? Who do I fight?

I am afraid to think that I need an enemy to define myself.

But if I do not have a defining framework, what then am I?

This is an incomprehensible question emerging from incomprehensible chaos.

Since external authority has been exterminated, either I die now, or I discover the power of choosing now.

Without a defining framework, I consciously or unconsciously choose the context of my existence.

From now on. Forever. I consciously choose and Authorize my own context.

No one else.

This is a complete Phoenix Process for me.

Every level of everything burns down to cold dark lifeless ash.

I only wait.

Surprisingly, mysteriously, a part of the ash begins to budge.

The problem itself has become the solution to the problem.

How? Because now that there is no internal or external structure, there is a new way through: Authority.

I no longer need the circumstances to tell me what I am, or what I can do or cannot do.

Nothing has changed, but everything is different.

Weirdly, a tiny calm spark of joy comes to life in me. This is very new for me.

My spirit feels an unaccountable sense of newfound freedom to emerge and to speak.

*How can this be?* I wonder.

*What is going on? Where does this impulse come from?*

I think back over my life. The sheep and chickens during everyday life at the farm near Palmyra. Hot summers. Lonely winters. Packing up olives. Shelling chickpeas. Drying the apricots. Afraid to spill even a drop of milk as I make cheese for our family. Helping mother in her chores.

A slow unspoken desperation creeping into our lives as the climate changes, as things die, as the fighting begins.

Then leaving the farm, moving to a bombed-out corner of Aleppo. Building our shack. Listening to gunfire, jets, helicopters, explosion after explosion, and ever more horrible news for twelve years. Arrogant fake terrified radio announcers pontificating nonsense written by the drone zombies of oligarchs. Making the war map each evening with Papa before he and Mama go off to work at night.

The school slowly coming to life around us.

Yes, I did that. And I did it well.

But where was *I* in all this? What life was *mine*? Where was *my* space? *My* needs? *My* ideas? *My* dreams and desires? Where was Zenobia?

I feel fear from realizing I was not here.

I was nowhere.

Suddenly that entire world is gone. The prison has vanished around me, as if it had been a mirage the whole time, a mirage I believed in but never verified to be solid.

I conformed my perceptions to the narrowly defined limitations of a world I did not design.

At no time did I have the courage or imagination to closely approach the wall of my prison and push on it with my fingertip. Now I see that the illusion was a mural painted on tissue paper. My finger would have punched through the illusion if only I had dared step close enough to press a little.

Now, here I lie... alone on the dirt...

And... free of it all.

Radically free of everything.

I have only to breathe.

There is no one anywhere who can influence me. Anyone's self-sustained illusions are meaningless to me, and a joke on them. Not my problem.

No system of religion, political belief, family pressure, or social norms exists in my life anymore.

I have nothing.

I owe nothing to anybody.

I am me. Simply me.

I am...

That is all. I am.

Never must I move from this place on Earth, this blanket, these stones.

I breathe. I think. I feel.

I start over.

I start over from zero.

No! No! Not from zero!

I have twenty-four-and-a-half years of life experience in me. This experience has built valuable matrix. I am not as naïve as I was before. I start over from where I am now.

An hour or two goes by.

People walk by me, seeing I am awake, but I do not ask for anything. They go on about their business. I am not bleeding.

I can lie here all day and all night for a week if I want.

Forever.

To then do what?

What do I want to do?

This is a shockingly new question.

What do *I* want?

What do *I* want to do?

What do *I* want to create?

What am *I* here for?

Is there any sense in anything?

Does it matter?

Does existence have to make sense?

Whatever used to make sense to me has vanished into so much dust and rubble.

What kind of sense should dust and rubble make if it devours my parents and my best friends?

Sense according to who? Or whom?

(Who actually cares if it is 'who' or 'whom'?)

I live.

The rest is up to me.

Starting now.

And now.

And now...

I still breathe.

The sky is still gray.

Radical freedom is my new home.

Someone saws wood. Others speak softly together. I hear a bird chirp.

If a bird does not care, why should I?

Camp is working. Our Learning Village is working. It will continue to thrive.

Very low intensity fear tells me that it is time for cellular mitosis.

The chaotic earthquake energy is enough impulse to split the atom.

One part stays here and grows. The other part goes and grows.

I am going.

I must leave.

It is time to hit the road.

Like the Polynesians, it is time to send out a canoe into the vast oceans to establish a new island of context.

I must be on that canoe.

Very low intensity fear tells me to wonder: *What should I say to the others?*

How will the conversation go?

High intensity emotional fear almost takes me over then... the near panic of not having enough information.

Then I remember: Torus! I am not a me. I am a torus!

We are a torus!

I don't have to figure it all out by myself anymore!

We are a huge cloud of intelligences, with resources far beyond my imagination.

Very low intensity fear warns me to wonder: *With so much fear and suffering in the hearts of our little tribe right now, how can we even talk with each other? How is there room inside to listen? How can we speak together? How can we co-create? How can we communicate?*

Very low intensity fear gives its own response: *There is only one way to answer a question about how to communicate, and that is to start communicating.*

I slowly lift my head to look around.

It is late afternoon in a new world for me.

I sit up. I smell dust and smoke. Someone is boiling chickpeas. My mouth waters...

My muscles and joints complain as I try to stand up.

Very low intensity fear tells me how filthy I am. I decide to brush off my clothes. My fear does not decide. My fear informs. I decide.

Very low intensity fear tells me to scan the camp. I see thirty or so clumps of transformation refugees working or being together with Armageddon refugees, doing whatever they figured out to do so far to help each other.

"Good morning, campers!"

My very low Intensity fear tells me it is late afternoon, not morning, but the words come out of my mouth before I can consider whether or not it is the best thing to say. I speak before I can doubt myself. Weirdly enough, I speak English!

I move towards the center of the cyclone and speak louder, more firmly. "Hello, everybody! Yes, you are correct! Calling our situation 'good' is a lie. I stand up among you and I make a proposal. If you understand what I am saying, please go to anyone around you who might *not* understand me and translate what I am saying for them. Okay?"

Quite a few double fists flash up into the air wordlessly signaling, 'no resistance'. People move.

I remain standing and wait for the clusters to rearrange themselves.

"Water, food, toilet holes, medical care, supplies such as blankets, and checking on our neighbors. These are our priorities for the next days. Who will be manager of our water team?"

Habib Badawi stands slowly. "I will. Yesterday I saw a stockpile of water bottles in a newly collapsed warehouse about a kilometer south from here. We will need a few wheelbarrows to bring water back here. I saw wheelbarrows nearby in a crushed gardening shop." Habib is a muscled, but not fat, warrior type. Like so many others, he just showed up here one day. His dark hair hangs in tight curls, always looking a little oily. He wears a tight black T-shirt and an indecipherable smile. You cannot figure out if he is your friend or your enemy, only that he is earnestly one or the other.

"Thank you," I say, "Will you also please find for us two more shovels and a pickaxe for making more toilets, plus more buckets for washing things in? And when you return, will you please organize a team to straighten up First Shack? We need it for storage."

"Yes," says Habib. He turns around and shouts, "I need three strong water handlers to come with me." Four young people stand up, two men, two women. "Okay, four! Thank you. Will you come over here and stand with me please?" They move.

I relax a bit. "Who would like to be our kitchen spaceholder?"

"My name is Jamila. Jamila Ali Hamdi. I am kitchen spaceholder." Then she shouts to the tribe, "I need five colleagues who will join me to feed our village."

There is no hesitation. One-by-one, five individuals stand and call out their names while Jamila writes them into the *Beep! Book* she pulls out of her apron-like dress. "We will start with a scavenger hunt to beef up our stock. Wear your toughest shoes and bring shoulder bags and backpacks to carry what we find. We will leave just after these logistical arrangements are made."

Jamila looks to me. "Zenobia, could we please have two guardians with us, just in case?"

I shoot out the question, "Who is captain of our guardians?"

"I am. Aziza Hamdi." Even after the earthquake she is fit, this leathery-muscled young woman leaping to her feet. "I need six of you toughies at my side to be guardians. Who will it be?"

Nine young people stand. They have no weapons, no armor, and probably an equal amount of skill. Most are girls, including seventeen-year-old Mitzi. Aziza is not in the least dismayed. "Thank you, guardians!" she shouts. "Our circle will begin maneuvers over by the cinder blocks after logistics are over. We will dig more toilets when the tools arrive. Meanwhile, we need two guardians to accompany the food scavengers."

The first to speak says, "Rafiq Abadi."

"Thank you, Rafiq Abadi," nods Aziza with respect. His wiry physique makes it seem he could battle on forever, never needing food, water, or rest.

"Zaid Bakir," says Zaid as he stands up.

Aziza demands, "Are you two willing to grab something for weapons and run flank on the kitchen crew during their scavenger hunt?"

Rafiq bows while Zaid shouts, *"Naeam."* ['Yes' in Arabic.]

"Off you go, then," Aziza says. "Be back before dark or we will have to send a rescue team after you."

"Oh, you won't have to rescue us," says Zaid. "We are the guardians!" Several people chuckle half-heartedly as Zaid and Rafiq move to help prepare Jamila's kitchen team for their venture into the ruins of Aleppo. Rafiq already wields a fighting staff. He never seems to put it down, and it usually swings dangerously through the air around him.

I sense the spirit building in our newly expanded village – my own face smiles with new aliveness.

I glance around and see that our 'sick bay' consists of a couple of blankets in the dirt, and an upturned red plastic crate covered with improvised medical supplies. The healer team seems to be treating nearly a dozen wounded, their 'nurses' being among the patients. "Could the village have a report from the healer team, starting with the name of your spaceholder?"

"I guess that would be me. My name is Hadi Qasim. I've been working as a nurse during the past couple years in north Aleppo, delivering emergency medical treatment, until our children's hospital was blown up by Assad's Army and the Russians."

"Hadi, will you please keep training others in everything you know with the aim of replacing yourself?" My fear shows me a glimmer of an unpleasant vision about where this request could be coming from.

"Yes, I will," says Hadi. "It makes total sense to me." She looks brightly around into the eyes of her 'staff' and 'clients', and says cheerfully, "I see surgeons and doctors here already!" Then she looks back at me and says, "We too need supplies. We need soap, antibiotic cream, rubbing alcohol, lots of plasters and gauze, needles for sutures... Will you two go hunting?" speaking to the two girls at her side. "I will make you a list of useful items. You should not have to go far."

"Thank Allah for Covid!" I exclaim. "It made antiseptic lotion available almost everywhere!"

I turn and shout, "Aziza, could the healer team scavengers have two guardians with them also?"

"On it!" shouts Aziza.

Then I ask in general, "Does anyone else need anything else about anything else right now?"

I stop mid breath. "Yes, me!" I exclaim. "I need you to know that I am not your leader. Installing a leader mentality automatically creates a follower mentality. Half of you already know this. The other half of you are new to the context of being a torus. If there are any followers here, then we lose the followers' awarenesses and creative intelligence because they are followers. But look at us!" I spread my arms to include everyone around camp. "Just look at us! We do not stand in rows and salute! Hierarchy makes for war. War is insane, and in Archiarchy, war is illegal. We stand in chaordic circles within circles and look in each other's eyes and invent solutions together. Then we navigate the ocean of possibilities we create. I need two people to help discover how to better navigate our village together with me."

While making this request, I look straight into Israa Nabih's eyes whose hand rockets into the air. When Montassar sees Israa's hand, he stands and brushes himself off. Then Farhan Kader stands. Then Mitzi stands. The four of them walk over and stand by me at the burned-out firepit.

"Excellent!" I shout. "Thank you! Now we are five apprentice navigators! Along with Aziza, Hadi, and Jamila, we have an eight-person Infinity Ring for our Learning Village gameworld! In the next few days, each of them needs one or two apprentices ongoingly at their elbow learning to do everything they can do. Alright?"

People spontaneously clap and shout, "Alright!" putting both fists into the air showing no resistance, with some shouting, *"Alsayha!"* ['Hurrah!' in Arabic.]

Probably most of the newcomers have no idea what just happened, but from my perspective, our tribe begins to come alive again.

This is a good thing. Tomorrow is going to be a big day.

# Los Angeles, California 2



I call in 'sick' until Monday. I even skip Hot Yoga on Saturday.

I seem to gain enough aliveness flux from simply breathing. Even the air has become relational.

A barrier has cracked open inside of me. It feels like an entire universe of dark demons are screaming murderous insanities in the back of my head. They squirm their greasy fingers through the crack, trying to infiltrate my life. The best thing I find to do is eat Bardo Specials. Balthazar recommended these: a bowl of whole milk yogurt mixed with lots of tahini and date syrup.

I end up watching *I Love Lucy* and *Three Stooges* episodes all weekend.

I do not dare to call my mother.

Eva is away in Fiji doing fire walking.

So on Monday I go to work. I slink through the office to my cubicle. You can bet people want to ask me questions. I don't have the will to put on a show of being mysterious or transformed. I feel glad enough to be able to breathe.

Nothing looks the same to me. Most of the things which I recognize as familiar – the furniture, the paintings on the office wall, my desk – they are pointless. Without a point. Their meaning is detached from their material substance. Yes, the objects exist, but the stories I had previously assigned to them have become optional. There is now a gap between every object and any story that one could attach to interpret that object. I am beginning to prefer objects in their uninterpreted state.

Is this good?

Even that question has no bearing.

My actual boss, George Planning, seems to have been entirely squeezed out of the picture. He ignores me.

Arthur, on the other hand, sends messages several ways that he wants to meet with me. Finally, I can avoid it no longer. I saunter into his office, not from hubris, not from fearfulness, but simply from using most of my attention for walking.

"Good afternoon, Ms. Sorceress," he says with theatrical cheerfulness, sitting behind his glass-topped CEO desk.

"It turns out I am more of a wizardress..."

I manage to flop down into one of his padded leather armchairs, wondering what species of animal it was before it became this chair. I send good vibes to the soul of the animal, with gratitude that I can touch something organic with my fingers rather than the plastic and steel of most office furniture. However, noticing the sensations on my fingertips shrinks my now and makes it painful for me to look at Arthur.

I don't want to see Arthur now, because when I place my attention on him, the scanning happens of its own accord. Multidimensional information pours into my awareness. I cannot turn off the scanning channel. Looking at his face is like reading every word in a shoddy gossip magazine. Arthur's older daughter won't talk with him because Arthur said he does not approve of her musician boyfriend and wants her to become a medical doctor instead of a political activist. Arthur has not had sex with his wife for... all year it seems. He is frustrated and doesn't know what to do. His wife is having a non-physical love affair with her boss and lives in the fantasy world of thinking she might feel more loved with the boss than with her husband but does not want to risk finding out for sure. In the meantime, Arthur has secretly invested half of his retirement fund in a risky block-chain alternative currency scheme and is drinking gin and tonics at night and sometimes even at lunch to suppress his rage and anxieties. Blah, blah, blah...

I blink away the clear-seeing and try to shift myself back into everyday banality so I can relate to Arthur's world. "Have you heard the news?" I ask without completely succeeding in preventing cynical despair from dampening my spirits. "The President of the United States of America has just assassinated another two hundred and twenty-three civilians including innocent women and children in a drone attack during a funeral in Yemen."

"Uh, yes... emmmm... Wendy... I heard about that... but, hey... How are you, honey? You've been out there for a while... after that meeting... nobody heard anything from you. And the wizard fellow isn't returning anyone's calls. What's happening? Did you meet with the guy? Or what? Talk to me, will you?"

I sigh. It is one of those sighs that the body does to try to digest and integrate multiple universes into a single worldview. It is useless, but the body tries it anyway.

I sigh again. It is still useless.

At least by sighing twice I have enough oxygen to speak. "Yes. I will try to talk with you Arthur. I am simply letting you know that it is difficult for me to decide which 'you' to speak with..."

"Uh... what?"

"You go first. What happened to George? I thought he was my boss."

"Yes. You are right. He 'was' your boss. Given the potential and delicacy of the negotiations regarding the *Whale Storm* project, you were slid into a new position, right where you are sitting now. What I want to know is how smart was that for us to do?"

"Do I get a raise?"

"Cynthia has a new contract for you to look at. There is a contingency about the outcome of the *Whale Storm* agreement."

"I want a straight percentage." This unrestricted forwardness is new... I feel glad that Gretchin doesn't give a shit about barfing or alternative states of consciousness. She just goes for the jugular vein or the bottom line, whichever is closer.

"Yes, you can look it over and give us your proposal. In the meantime, please give me some facts."

I can't help but smirk at his request. It is a deep smirk that devours an entire moment of possibilities before allowing me to formulate words. "Arthur. You are speaking with a wizardress. Do you have any idea what this means to speak with a wizardress? Try to imagine what a small word 'fact' is to a wizardress, will you? Try to not sound so ignorant and pedestrian."

I sigh again while attempting to integrate two realities separated by the width of the Universe. "Let me try to explain. The world has been cracked open. There are demons coming through by the millions to occupy the intention space of human beings who have been trained since childhood – since going to school – to give their authority away to psychopaths higher up in hierarchical power structures. This means just about everyone. People can no longer discern the difference between a psychopath and a demon, so they let the demons in. Who is supposed to train people – people, mind you, who are long past their 'Initiatory Process Start Date'... who will train them to take their authority back? Who is going to divert the demons' back towards other worlds which will be less harmed by their presence? Where are all the sorceress and wizard schools when we need them? What is your role going to be in causing a shift in the morphogenetic field of the human race so that the global ethnosphere can upgrade its thoughtware and the sorceresses and wizards can come back to do their work?"

Arthur struggles to speak out of a face that is contorted by various simultaneous muscle contractions. "How is any of this relevant, Wendy?" he stammers.

"My name is Gwendoyln. I allow you to call me Gwendolyn from now on."

"But who are you? And what have you done with Wendy?"

"My God, Arthur! Wake up! Think about it! There were seven-hundred years of Catholic Inquisitions! Do you know what this means? It means that, for at least thirty-five generations, the most important thing you learned from your mom was: Watch out for what the neighbors think! Because if they think you are not normal, they will turn you over to the Inquisitors and you will be shredded piece by piece in front of your friends, and the church will take all your stuff. Arthur, you and me, all of us alive around here, we are the descendants of those people who survived the Inquisitions. The reason they survived the Inquisitions is because these people were the best liars. We are the descendants of the people who could successfully pretend to be normal."

Arthur stares at me.

"You stare at me with a truly stupid look on your face, and you know what? You are still trying to pretend to be normal! You are still unconsciously terrified that I am going to turn you over to the Inquisitors, and they are going to slowly torture you and your family to death."

He still stares at me, only now with more furrows in his brow and more fear in his heart. Fear is aliveness. I take this as a signal that something useful is happening over there in the Arthur department. I keep going.

"Arthur! You do not know who you really are! We all need who you really are to come back to life. We need Arthur the wild rogue, turned back on, running things around here so we can work together in new ways and do what we really came here to do. We need Arthur the unpredictable, Arthur the wise and courageous, to come back to life. We need King Arthur to wake up and get the show on the road. Dude! Are you up to this? Because if you are not, it will not matter how much money you pay me! We are all screwed. We do not have as much time as you think."

Arthur's face is rather whiter than it was before. It looks clammier, and sticky with cold sweat. His eyes go unfocused.

I suddenly realize that he is probably not as comfortable with barfing as I am. The process of entering reality slammed me pretty hard, as you know. How is it going to hit Arthur?

I can't predict, but I witness it happening.

Arthur looks to the floor like it might be a safer place to be than his chair right now, but I already know it won't make a bit of difference. When the world spins away into disconnected particle fog, there is no up or down anymore.

Surrendering is best.

Learning to fly is even better.

I reach over to his phone and punch the intercom. "Cynthia, darling, would you please immediately bring in tissues and a bucket! Arthur is going to be sick."

That's when he falls over sideways. Unfortunately, I am not as quick as Balthazar was. The glass edge of Arthur's upscale desk takes a chunk out of his forehead. Blood splashes everywhere as he crashes to the floor retching his guts out.

I sigh again, sit back in my dead-animal covered chair, shake my head, and do nothing. The wizardress in me sees that the blood stains on the carpet will provide an excellent reminding factor for Arthur Tutor during the coming weeks. Each time he sees his own blood on his own office floor, he will remember that something spectacularly different from the ordinary stirs in the bowels of A. T. Advertising Partners.

Just then, Cynthia rushes in with a roll of toilet paper and a chromed steel trash can. She freezes in horror to see me calmly sitting in the overstuffed chair while Arthur writhes on the floor bleeding from his head and spewing his lunch. She thinks I did this to Arthur, and might do it to her next, in revenge for the evil ways she treated me as an underling at A. T. Advertising.

Gretchin whispers in my ear, *A little revenge on Cynthia might be a great idea!*

I tell Gretchin, *Sit! That woman does not have enough matrix in her Being to hold this kind of a breakthrough. I would be wasting a good secretary.*

Gretchin nods, silently appreciating her upgraded master.

To Cynthia I say, "He was explaining to me about his new ideas for A. T. Advertising and then blacked out from the excitement, I guess. He may need some stitches in his forehead. Could you please ask HR to get him over to the Emergency Room at the hospital?"

She wordlessly sets down the toilet paper and trash can, then turns and leaves.

I hope this will all work out for the better.

# Phoenix, Arizona 5

JET half-opens his eyes and moans. The sky is pastel pink and yellow. The fire has gone cold. He rolls into fetal position, trying to keep his eyes closed as long as possible, cradling his wounded leg. Finally he sits up, groaning, glances around.

Eddy is gone.

JET sighs. *What the hell is he doing now?*

Suddenly, a strange sound approaches from the bush, getting closer and closer. A lightening bolt of fear shoots up JET's spine. He frantically pulls at branches near him, struggling to stand up on his feet. He is no more stable than a newborn calf, but if he has to die, he would rather die standing. Defenseless and terrified, JET turns to meet his approaching doom.

A carrot hanging from a stick emerges from the bush. It is followed by a donkey's face, then a whole donkey, carrying Eddy on her back. Eddy holds makeshift reigns twisted from dried vines.

"Ho baby! Ho girl! It's alright now! Take it easy! Ho Betsy! This is our friend JET. His leg is hurting him. See that? But he's going to be alright. We are going to rescue him! Okay? You and me, Betsy. We are going to take JET back to civilization."

Eddy smiles beatifically at JET.

Keeping the same tone of voice he used with the donkey, Eddy says to JET, "Come on over here slowly, JET, to my right side. Meet Betsy, our carrot-powered car. Grab my right arm with both of yours and swing your bad leg over her back behind me. Got it?"

JET does what Eddy instructs him to do, and makes it up, barely, moaning loudly and grabbing Eddy by the shoulders.

"Yeah! That's it! And we are going for a ride!"

Eddy knickers gently while jiggling the dangling carrot, and Betsy takes off. They bounce across the wash, circle around the boulders and the burnt-out hull of the van, back up to the road which led them to the destroyed bridge.

In reality, the donkey merely follows the carrot hanging temptingly out in front of her nose. She can smell it, but she cannot taste it yet.

Eddy speaks over his shoulder without turning his head. "I get it now, about radical responsibility. You were right, JET! See over there? I put rocks and sticks on the road to warn the next car. Why did I do that, you might ask? Because if I did not block the road, then the next car driving along this road would crash through the bridge just like we did. But if they did crash, I would be responsible for their crash. What makes me responsible, you ask? I'm so glad you are paying attention in class this morning, JET! What makes me responsible is my awareness! I know that the bridge is out. It is too late for me. I already know. As soon as I become aware, I simultaneously become responsible. The same is true of the litter you were talking about. It's like the *Handbook* says," thumping the book tucked under his shirt so JET knows he still has it. "As soon as I know that I could pick up each piece of litter and each crying child in the world, I am responsible for not doing it. Choosing to not take action does not void my responsibility, but it might make me feel pain. The path of becoming more responsible starts with learning to consciously feel pain."

There they are, two young men joggling along on the back of a carrot-crazy wild donkey through Arizona's stunningly beautiful morning desert while remembering nonrational instructions from a native Indian Shaman who appears and disappears at will in the middle of the night.

After a couple hours of this they finally reach paved road. By now it is early afternoon.

"Whoa, Betsy. Time to stop and let us get off. That's it! That's it! You did so wonderful! Whoa baby! It is carrot time for you!"

Eddy brings Betsy to a halt and helps JET slide down to the ground. Crooning kind words into Betsy's ear, he slides off himself, pulling the reigns off over Betty's big ears at the same time, but never letting the carrot out of Betty's sight.

Eddy pulls the twine off the carrot and bites a chunk off to feed it to Betsy from the palm of his hand, patting her on the neck all the while.

"Sweety, you gave us such a great ride! I love you so much! If I had six of these carrots, I would give each and every one of them to you! You were so brave to carry us two city slickers all the way back to civilization."

Eddy feeds her the next chunk of carrot. She crunches away in delight.

"What crazy ideas we had, eh? 'Let's go live in the bushes' we thought. We were really nuts! Whose idea was that, anyway? At least we got to meet you. That was the best part of our adventure. Okay, Betsy," says Eddy, feeding her the last bite. "That's all the carrot I have for you."

Betsy sniffs around for more, licking his empty salty hands. "Sorry girl. But you gotta get away from this road. It's not safe for you here. Go on! Git!" Eddy slaps her on the rump and sends her scurrying back into the safety of the bush.

Our two heroes look a total mess, covered in mud, blood, and beards. They stare at each other, bewildered... which is not a bad thing.

Eddy shrugs, crossing over the blacktop, and putting out his thumb to hitch a ride with the first car that comes along this desert highway.

"Where do you think we are going?" JET asks.

"Anywhere but here," replies Eddy, staring expectantly down the empty highway that heads straight west as far as he can see.

# Hollywood, California 3

"Yes, my friends," says Morgan Freeman with his trademark earnestness. "This is the end, and we are as we are. The cameras are rolling. Please step forward and have a seat."

Out from the black shadows steps Denzel Washington, Jackie Chan, Robert Redford, Sandra Bullock, Stephen Fry, Keanu Reeves, Angelina Jolie, Jeremy Irons, Michael Caine, Halle Berry, Ken Watanabe, Leonardo di Caprio, George Clooney, Harrison Ford, Brad Pitt, Sigourney Weaver, Bill Murray, Julia Roberts, Graham Green, Tommy Lee Jones, Helen Mirren, Jane Fonda, James Earl Jones, Dustin Hoffman, Meryl Streep, and Matt Damon.

Judi Dench holds Dave Stutler firmly by the elbow. She sits him down in the chair next to hers, assuring herself that the duct tape over Dave's mouth and around his wrists is still secure. For some reason Dave seems more relaxed than everyone else right now about what is happening, as if it somehow makes hopeful sense to him.

Silence prevails as members of the torus stare in various forms of outrage, curiosity, or suppressed awe at each other, trying to get the joke, hoping the joke is not on them.

Morgan Freeman peers deeply into the eyes of each individual seated or standing around the circle. He connects heart-to-heart with old friends – many he's never met in person before. This combination of resonant Beings evokes massive momentum and unreasonable giddiness which most sense, but cannot specify.

Morgan majestically gestures for all to take seats if they would like. Additional chairs are provided. Out of respect for Morgan and the formal preparations of this scenario, the others keep their tongues still for the moment and sit.

Into that respectful listening, Morgan speaks. "This torus is now assembled. We have come together at a moment of unimaginable importance. During the next couple of hours, we have the chance to take our last stand." He pauses solemnly enough to create the significance that was heretofore seriously lacking.

Many glance around at each other with unaccustomed nervousness. No one seems to be in the know.

Morgan Freeman proceeds. "Not long from now, this gathering

will not be possible. Some of us will complete our lives. Some will become incapacitated on our way towards the long dark night, unable to further contribute. Time is growing short. What we can do, we do it now, and we do it together.

"I use that word 'contribute' with intention, for contribute is what you have done with your lives. In your own style, with your own blood, sweat, and tears, each of you has taken a stand that the human spirit can evolve.

"You have repeatedly held open doorways for human beings to wake up, to recover their own authority, and to create a new future... a future where shady purposes do not prevail, where there is increasing rather than diminishing hope for life on Earth.

"Over the decades, you recognizably stood out as professional actors who nevertheless represented something greater than yourselves. You spoke out as your various on-screen characters allowed, even if you were playing the 'bad guy'. You took personal risks to demonstrate that it is possible for human beings to commit to things that really matter.

"The world listened to you and watched you. But did people truly hear your message? Have things changed for the better because of your warnings and admonitions? These questions remain unanswered, and that is what is so disturbing. That is what brings us together as a torus now.

"*What more can be done?* you might be asking yourself. *I am not the Producer. I am not the Director. I am not the Writer or the Editor. I am merely the Actor. There are massive financial forces at play! These forces are stronger than my good-intentioned heart.*"

Morgan looks directly into a camera. "So many of us assume that we are powerless. What we forget is that any person can make any assumption about anything, and then believe their own assumption to be true. But the assumption, *I am powerless*, undermines the full creative influence of your free will.

"Perhaps you have noticed this in others. Perhaps you have sensed it in yourself. I have seen the sad consequences of believing in disempowering assumptions, and it makes me angry... angry enough to grab you by the scruff of your neck and call you to take a stand with me here in this torus.

"I have the courage to tell you this now because I was introduced to a discovery, a new idea that woke me up to new possibilities, both for me and for you. This torus came to life as a direct result of that new discovery.

"It is a simple idea, something you have witnessed hundreds of times in your life. The idea sat in front of you within one arm's reach, but you did not grasp it. You missed the chance over and over, not because you are stupid, not because you are weak, not because you are unmotivated, merely because you never thought of it before, just like me. You could not call this idea to you because you did not have the necessity. Well, folks, authentic necessity is now upon us with a vengeance!

"One month ago, I received a visit from a friend of mine, Sandra

Bullock." Morgan gestures his good hand in her general direction. Her quick smile flashes and disappears.

"One night Sandra calls me up and says, 'Morgan, I have an idea. Can I come over? I want to show you something.'

"I say that one simple but frightening word to her, 'Yes.'

"She arrives at my house and shows me something that now I ask her to show you. I was so touched at the simple but powerful possibility she gave to me that I was at first ashamed not to have implemented it more in my life. You see, I have been thinking like a fish.

"Take a look at this video for a moment. It shows a school of fish, in this case, a school of koi. Notice that they swim in a rather large and deep pond. Pay attention to their behavior. You have heard that fish often swim in what we call a 'school'. But I ask you to pick out and watch one individual fish as it reaches the invisible edge of its school.

"What does it do? It senses the edge beyond which there are no more fish, and it immediately turns around and swims back towards the center of the school. It keeps moving so that it feels like it is swimming somewhere, yet the moment it reaches the next edge, it turns right around again and swims back towards all the other fish. Does this remind you of anyone?"

Several people nod their heads. Five people put their hands up, some with embarrassed smiles. They glance around to make sure they are not the only one who sees what Morgan is suggesting.

"Sensing the edge, then pulling back from the edge, is 'fish behavior'. Fish behavior comes from 'fish thoughtware'.

"Now, fish cannot upgrade their thoughtware. Fish are forced to remain thinking the way fish think for their entire lives. They cannot select, among all the various brands of thoughtware available, which particular thoughtware they would like to use for themselves.

"But human beings have the potential to be different from fish. Human beings are not forced to think like other human beings. Your mind is yours to play with and make into whatever you want. You have the capacity to upgrade your personal thoughtware. No one can upgrade your thoughtware for you. More interestingly, no one can stop you from upgrading your own thoughtware.

"Think how often you upgrade the software on your phone. Now ask yourself, when was the last time you upgraded your own personal thoughtware in your head?

"As you know, fish have spinal cords. Fish have two eyes, a mouth, and four appendages called fins, which eventually evolved into human arms and legs. Three hundred seventy-five million years ago, give or take a few, some of these fish crawled out of the water away from predators and towards a lot of free food on land.

"They swam to the edge of their world and stayed at that edge, not turning around, not swimming back to safety. They remained uncomfortable at the edge until their discomfort caused them to evolve, and they could take a step beyond the edge. They became a bridge from the edge of one reality over to the edge of a new reality... a bridge upon which others could also walk to somewhere else... Well, this is no longer 'fish thoughtware' anymore. It is something else entirely.

"Yet so many of us have fallen into the delusion of seeking the safety of numbers. We thought that if everyone else is doing it, we are safe. We have been trying to hide out in the school.

"By now it should be significantly obvious to you that we are not safe. And that in the process of merely surviving, we have forgotten to live. We have forgotten that we once had the courage to reinvent ourselves enough to crawl out of the oceans and stand up.

"Today I bring you the opportunity of reinventing yourself enough to walk out of mainstream modern culture and stand up in a regenerative culture.

"Why didn't we do this before? It is not illegal, immoral, or fattening to upgrade your thoughtware, or to invent and inhabit a new culture. Probably we did not do it simply because we did not think of it.

"Now I give us to Sandra Bullock, the woman who *did* think of it."

# Aleppo, Syria 10

Zenobia Darwish's *Beep! Book* – 8 February 2023 – day 2 after the earthquakes

Late last night, after things are forced to settle down due to exhaustion and lack of electricity and internet connection, I call our Learning Village Infinity Ring together. We sit away from the center of camp, huddling around a small fire near the Queiq riverbed: Israa, Montassar, Farhan, Aziza, Jamila, Hadi, Mitzi, and me.

My very low intensity fear informs me that the earthquakes have made us into new kinds of friends. There is resilience in our step, and formidable calculated fire in our tired souls. I am happy to be with these people. In fact, there is no place in the world that I would rather be right now than in their effective company. I nod my head in joy.

"What are you nodding about?" asks Farhan.

"I am nodding because I love you guys."

They look slowly around at each other and start nodding too. I can't help but laugh out loud. "Now you are all nodding! It is contagious!"

We laugh helplessly.

"I know you are not all 'guys'. What I meant to say was, 'Gaias'. All you 'Gaias'. Each one of you has your grounding cord dropped down into the center of Gaia, and we sit here, each one of us, a facet of Gaia's consciousness. We are Gaia talking with Herself."

"Yes, but talking about what?" Jamila is ever the compass, keeping us on track.

I sigh. My very low intensity fear leads me to speak directly from my core.

"This afternoon something happened to me. Eleven years ago, in 2012, I was thrown into Leaning Village. None of you were here yet.

"I did not know who I was then, where I was, or what I was. But I needed to make up something. I played a role to fit my parents' gameplan, to survive in this insane environment, as the rest of you have done. The earthquakes not only killed my parents, the earthquakes also killed me... the fake me, the show I was putting on to carry on my parents' world. I cannot do the show anymore."

I look around. I see understanding on their faces in the flickering firelight. "What we read from the *Handbook* this morning – what you read Montassar – lit a fire in me that burned everything down to the dirt. Everything."

Tears come to my eyes. "My very low intensity conscious fear tells me these are not tears I should worry about. These are tears of grief for the death of the personality I once used, like I would use a car to drive around. This afternoon I lay there on the blanket near the shack letting my familiar world burn down. Thank you everyone, by the way, for holding space for my meltdown. I could feel you all holding space for me. I was well held, and yet... groundless. That groundlessness is permanent now. It is not going away. It seems to be the only thing that is real. And in that empty realness, I float in an informed but uninhibited cloud of very low intensity conscious fears. Finally, this field of 'smart fears' could speak to me, or rather, finally my inner noise faded enough that I could hear the true signals. These signals are telling me to leave here. They tell me that the time has come for the Learning Village to split in two, like a cell going through mitosis, like a baby bird leaving the mama behind in the nest. It is time for the Learning Village to send a canoe out into the vast ocean to start a new branch of the Learning Village somewhere else."

"Where?" demands Israa.

I pause just a moment to look Israa in the eyes. "I too wanted to immediately figure out all the answers. So many logistical decisions and preparations would need to be made. I wanted to figure them all out to be able to present them to everyone, so no one would have to be afraid, or bothered by the nuisance of it all. But the lone-wolf single-fighter survival-hero Zenobia died yesterday. Luckily! Because then I could stop being such a piggy, stealing all the problem adventures for myself. I realized I am part of a torus. We are a torus. These problems and preparations, they are not mine. They are ours. Not just ours here in the Infinity Ring, but ours in the entire Learning Village. Forcing us to implement my personal answers and solutions would handicap the outcome. I know this now. The torus is a vastly more intelligent and powerful resource than I alone."

"So?" says Mitzi.

"So... I will make a proposal tomorrow morning in the circle that I leave as one of the edgeworkers from our tribe. I don't know how it works, but these instructions come from my archetypal lineage, or from E.C.C.O. I cannot detect exactly where they come from. It does not matter, really. What matters is that I wanted to tell you now, before I tell everyone else in the morning. I didn't want to shock you. I wanted to check if you think I am fooling myself, or going completely out of my mind."

"I am going with you."

It is Farhan.

I thought my heart was already broken open as far as it could break, but it breaks open even further now. Tears pour down my cheeks as I look into his calmly committed loving gaze. The others near me put their arms around my shoulders, and then around each other's shoulders as well.

"Look," I say after a while, between sniffles. "We don't have to figure all this out right now. Let's start all that tomorrow morning, shall we? You have no idea how much it means to me to be with so many amazing humans in this little circle here. I cannot imagine leaving any of you behind. Neither can I imaging stealing all the skilled spaceholders from the Learning Village... I don't know what to do. Fortunately for me, I don't have to know everything anymore! Our village comes alive as new people stand up and navigate these emerging changes. I think we can all simply move as necessary."

"I agree," says Montassar. "And right now I think it is necessary that we move to the horizontal position."

Israa glares fiercely at Montassar. She is vigilant about our newly emerging context. Somehow, she is already ready to roll with the mitosis. If it were up to her, a new canoe would depart at dawn, letting the cards fall where they may. My fear tells me it is my job to assure that we move together at a coordinated and workable velocity that allows for sufficient logistical preparations to be accomplished without over burdening the canoe. From what I know of Israa, she would rather leave tonight and improvise along the way.

"Do you want to say what you are feeling, Israa?" asks Montassar.

"Not now. I get it about the torus, Zenobia. I get it. It is pretty fucking amazing, this torus thing. It is so abundant in valid possibilities. Okay... I surrender. My excitement level battles my tiredness level, and I don't know who is winning. All this tells me is: Yes. Yes, Zenobia! Your impulse is dead on. I too am going on the canoe. That is enough for tonight. I love all you Gaias so much. Even you, Mr. Montassar. C'mon! Take me to bed, will you?" She jabs her elbow into his ribs. "What are you waiting for?"

He laughs in embarrassment. The rest of us laugh in delight. Somehow they manage to sleep together in that bashed up car.

Our Infinity Ring retires for the evening.

Next morning in circle, Israa rises to her feet and says, "I propose to be first spaceholder. Any resistance? One, two, three!"

No resistance.

Israa continues, "I am going to say something bold here. It is not intended to shock you. And it is not a joke. I am serious as burnt pita bread. We will have plenty of time to talk about it, so don't worry. I am not rushing things, but I must start somewhere, so I will start here. If I were to ask the question, 'Who is walking with us to Germany?' which of you would raise your hand?"

She asks in the third-person theoretical form. It is a technique from the *Handbook,* in a section titled: *How To Collect An Opinion From A Circle Without Inferring Commitment.*

Five villagers raise their hands before Sammi shouts, "Stop! This is not democratic! You cannot divide us like this! Who will continue the work here in Aleppo? At the camp? You are attacking our tribe!"

Without a word, twenty-seven of the fifty of us reach into our pockets or the back of our *Beep! Books* and pull out a Purple Card. We hold our Purple Cards out towards Sammi. The Purple Card is a tool from the *Handbook*, described in the section about *Torus Meeting Technology*.

When we heard about Purple Cards, Mitzi used scissors to cut a Purple Card for each one of us out of plastic folders she found in the street near a ruined stationary shop. Since then we carry them – and use them – at every meeting, and, not infrequently, also in between.

The *Handbook* says:

*Holding up the Purple Card means you think that the person speaking'* – in this case Sammi – *'is not having a feeling that contains energy and intelligence to use in the present moment and will then disappear in less than three minutes, but rather is having an incomplete feeling, called an 'emotion', that comes from the past, from the future, from a belief system, or from someone else. The Emotion will last longer than three minutes, and can serve them as a valuable entrance to an Emotional Healing Process. Holding up the Purple Card invites the person to use their emotion for an EHP right then while the meeting goes on.*

If the Purple Card was not part of our gameworld traditions, then our circle would have been immediately dragged into a low drama, arguing with Sammi's Box and gremlin about whether or not Israa's question is 'democratic', whether or not it 'divides us', whether or not this proposal is 'an attack', and so on, with no useful outcome, except being a feast for hungry gremlins.

Instead of trying to attack our circle with his reactivity, Sammi looks around and sees the caring wisdom of our circle speaking to him through our Purple Cards. He has already seen the Purple Card work miracles on so many occasions that his trust is bigger than his gremlin's hunger, and he suddenly shifts from rage into tears. "Could someone please hold space for me for an Emotional Healing Process? I feel scared that I might be left behind, again..."

We have done hundreds of Emotional Healing Processes for each other since finding the *Handbook*. EHPs are so straightforward to navigate, and yet consistently magical in their positive outcome. I raise my hand and say, "I will hold space for you."

More than half the others also raise their hand and say the same thing. Long ago we adopted a gameworld tradition that if more than a third of the people in the circle raise their hands to hold space for an Emotional Healing Process, then we do it in the big circle.

Without speaking, I place my plastic crate in the center of the circle. Sammi does the same so he can sit facing me. I look around and say, "Habib, will you please grab the blanket from the house? Israa and Farhan, will you please drag your 'chairs' over to either side of Sammi? Sit as close as you can get to him, and lean in to touch your shoulders to his shoulders so he knows you are there for him." Everyone moves without comment.

I arrange these precautions because I have a hunch about what is behind this emotion for Sammi. It's the same thing as the emotions from most of us. We have been suddenly, completely, and unfairly abandoned: by our culture, by the so-called political 'leaders', by the United Nations, by religion, by our parents... The emotional shock is still in Sammi's system. He is afraid that if part of the village leaves, the worst thing that ever happened to him – being abandoned – is about to happen again. Until this emotion is complete for him, he can never be Present with us to contribute his energy and intelligence. It is the second time this particular emotional reaction has come up for Sammi. I will be checking to see if it is the same incident as before, or a new one. If it is the same incident, then something else is going on that stops him from completing the emotion.

The team is attentively silent. All are helping hold this space. They know we will do the same for them when their time comes.

I start. "Hello Sammi." I hold out my hand to greet him formally.

He shakes my hand and looks into my eyes, "Hello Zenobia."

"What can I do for you?" I ask, making no assumptions.

"I..." His legs and chest start shaking. Two emotions mixed together are coming up in him. "My father went into the revolution. He was so angry that he took his gun and his bullets and he left us. He said he would come back, but he never came back. Aaaaaarrrrrrr!"

Farhan hands Sammi a rolled-up towel so he has something to strangle to death as he shouts his rage and frustration.

To be clear about this process, we practice 'cathexis', not catharsis. The *Handbook* makes a clear distinction:

*Catharsis is about expressing emotions to get rid of them with the idea that they are 'bad' or 'negative'. Cathexis, on the other hand, is about bringing emotional energy to life and intentionally circulating it around in your five bodies. Instead of trying to get rid of the emotions, you consciously use them as intelligence and energy resources. It is not a design error from god that we experience emotions. It is a thoughtware error from modern culture that we are taught to suppress or reject emotions as weakness or neurosis. From the view of Archan thoughtware, rejecting emotions would be like throwing away the mast and rudder from a sailboat and wondering why the sailboat has become useless.*

I love the *Handbook*.

Sammi keeps shouting at his father, "You left me, you bastard! You left all of us! Who knows if you are even alive anymore? You cared more about your own anger than about your family, your wife and children! You did not take care of us! You abandoned me!"

He fiercely wrings the towel with both hands, screaming, "I hate you! I hate you! You fucking jerk!" He goes on for a full minute.

People encourage his shouting. "Go! Go Sammi!" they shout. "Tell him! Tell that asshole! He left the best things behind!"

I hold the space to assure that everyone is safe. I have seen Sammi in this rage before, and a new idea comes to me.

After a respectful time I say, "Will you hold on a moment, Sammi? Just take a deep breath for me, will you? I want to ask you a question."

He shudders as he comes to a pause. With a flushed face and breathing hard, he looks at me doubtfully. I want to reframe what we are doing here to break his response pattern so he can enter a different possibility. This equates to adding on a new sidetrack to his main psychoemotional train tracks.

"This is not only an Emotional Healing Process for you Sammi. It is also an authentic adulthood initiation process. We are about to enter the domain of radical responsibility. Are you ready?"

"Yes."

"It starts like this: You make your own abuse."

I leave a space for this perspective to settle into the matrix in his Being – and in the Being of anyone else who is ready to hear this in our circle. I sense rational resistance in the space. Perhaps Sammi does not have proper matrix to hold this. If he was sixteen or younger, I could not go into this. But he is twenty. It is time to grow up. There is a chance he can get this.

I say, "You make your own abuse by choosing which story you use in your mind about what happened to you."

"It does not matter what story I use!" he shouts at me angrily. "The same thing happened to me either way!"

I interrupt his harangue and match his energy. "Your story is that your father abandoned you! We have heard this story from you before. But what really happened is that he left and never came back, so far. You can learn to sense the difference between what happened to you and the story that you attach to what happened to you! You can sense the difference! One is reality. One is a storyworld that you created. Anyone can story-up anything as abuse. I could story-up that Mitzi's green sock is abusive because it is the favorite color of the Sheik of the enemy! I could story-up that Habib being late to the circle is abuse because he wants to disturb transformation and healing from happening for us here. I could story-up that my parents leaving me alone here at night was abuse because they went and got themselves killed instead of caring about me! There is evidence to support *any* story you want to make up!"

Sammi fights it. His reactive emotional anger is the rotten apple that his gremlin can use to make all the other apples in the barrel rotten. It is his gremlin's favorite tool.

I shout at him, "As long as you carry the abuse story, you carry the abuse! What do you get by dragging this abuse story around with you, Sammi? What is your payoff? What is your shadow world benefit?"

His eyes do not waver from mine. "What I get to have is your pity." He looks around at each of the others in the bigger circle. "If you pity me, then you will let me stay with you." He looks down, great sobs erupting from his chest. Many others start sobbing too, sensing their own survival strategy in his.

Time passes, but I am not letting this precious opportunity slide by.

When Sammi first asked for this EHP, he said he was scared that he might be left behind again. But then he jumped into his familiar expression of rage.

The *Handbook* has this to suggest:

*In life, it makes sense that if you feel afraid, you use anger to change whatever it is that is scaring you. For example, you use anger to attack the barking dog that is scaring you. But in an EHP, this emotional reflex is counterproductive. The new skill to develop for tapping into the resources of conscious fear is to stay in the fear, rather than bouncing automatically over to anger.*

This is what I think is going on.

I say, "Sammi, I think you created a groove in your brain that won't let you exit the victim story of being abandoned. I have an experiment for you to try. We will hold space for you if you want. Are you willing to try it?"

Sammi looks down at his fingers, embarrassed. "I think I am taking up too much circle time..."

I look around at the circle and ask, "How many of you are learning really valuable things by holding space for Sammi to do this work right now?"

I see every single person raise their hand. Mine included.

Sammi sees so many shining eyes that he must choke down more sobs about being so deeply and openly loved by these people.

"So, Sammi... are you willing to try the next experiment?"

"Yes."

"It goes like this. Close your eyes. Take a deep breath. Can you feel Farhan's shoulder at your left shoulder? He is there with you. And can you feel Israa's shoulder on your right shoulder. She is there with you too. I am here with you. We are all here for you. Okay? Got that?"

"Yes," he says in a voice as still as his held breath.

"Thank you. When you first asked for this Emotional Healing Process, you were feeling a different feeling besides anger about being left behind by your father when he went off to join the civil war. Yes... exactly... that feeling..." His hands and legs are already shaking.

I say, "Pause just a second Sammi. Keep your eyes closed. Let us move the 'chairs' away and lower you to the blanket. Let us do this for you. We will all be right here with you. Then you can keep going. Okay?"

He nods.

We do what I said we would do.

As Sammi relaxes onto the blanket the shaking convulses his whole body. He tries to hold it in, but his body curls up in a spasm. "Let the sounds out, Sammi. We are here. We won't let anything happen to you. Let the sounds get as big as they are."

He frees his heart.

Gut-wrenching screams held down since childhood erupt from his soul. Heart shriveling cries of life-or-death terror. Generations of unexpressed fear are finally freed to come through him now in this special safe place we hold together. He flops around but knows to stay on the blanket so as not to hurt himself or anyone else. These are the rules of EHPs. We all agreed to them long ago.

"Let some words come now, Sammi," I beg. "Let the fear itself speak through you. Please let us hear your fear share its voice."

The stories pour out as cries and shrieks, not from his mind but straight from his fear. "I am scared that the bad soldiers will come and hurt us! Aaaaaaggggaaaggg! I can't – Arrrrrrgggghhhhhhaa! – I am afraid that Papa won't be there to protect us. These bad soldiers might hurt Mama or my sisters. Raaaaarrrrrrraaaiiiiii! Oh my god! My sisters might get raped..."

"Stay with your fear, Sammi. Don't go into that anger right now. We are working with your fear. We will go back to that anger later. Do your inner navigating. Use your hands to reach into your chest and put your anger over on the side and stay with your fear. Yes! Like that! You are doing super! Please let the fear get all the way big."

Sammi takes a deep breath and screams as if he is falling into a bottomless pit. His fingers are spread wide, hands shaking uncontrollably. His mouth is wide open. He takes another deep breath and screams even more completely.

My feelings detector registers this as 100% archetypally intense fear.

In the middle of his third outcry, Sammi inexplicably rolls the scream into deep belly laughing. The laughter goes on and on.

"What's so funny?" I finally ask.

Sammi opens his eyes and looks startled himself. "I don't know!" he shouts, partly sitting up and looking around at us, laughing even more hysterically. "Nothing is funny! Everything is funny! That was amazing! I want to do it again!"

People jump up, cheering and clapping.

"Here we are, in the garbage pit of the world in a devastated city," says Sammi. "We have nothing. Yet we have everything!" People nod in understanding. "Absolutely nothing is happening. But this is the most intense thing I ever experienced. I hate being with you rags of the Earth, but I don't ever want to be anywhere else in the world than here with you rags of the Earth! It feels like we are totally rejected from civilization, and yet we are here, at the middle of everything, in a new civilization! I love you guys... you Gaias!"

Then Sammi becomes archetypal fear, screams going on and on, flying under their own power, and then he laughs ecstatically again.

By now we are all laughing our heads off, in love with Sammi, in love with each other, and in love with what we are discovering together.

The canoe expedition has already begun. Now our meeting can continue.

In a few minutes we are rearranged back into the big circle. Israa stands up again and says, "Would everyone please take a deep breath. Thank you. Put your attention on your energetic center, wherever it is. Use your intention to move your energetic center to your physical center, located between your hip bones and halfway back into your abdomen. Thank you. Now, at the count of three, please use your 'clicker' to snap your fingers and declare your grounding cord between your energetic center and the center of the Earth. One. Two. Three!"

Everyone snaps their fingers.

"Thank you. At the count of three, please tell me the color of your grounding cord. One. Two. Three!" Thirty-three people shout out the color of their grounding cord. Mine is orange. "Thank you! Now, at the count of three, please click your clicker again and declare your personal bubble of space. One. Two. Three!"

Everyone clicks their fingers and has the personal pleasure of relating to the world and each other from within a pristine, freshly-made bubble of their own personal space. Faces are shining.

"Thank you!" says Israa. "Each of us is now in 'first position'. Back to my original question. If I were to ask, 'Who is walking with us to Germany?' who of you would raise your hand?"

"That is not a clear enough proposal!" objects Rahim Taleb. "What is really going on here?"

My fear tells me it is my turn to speak. "Yesterday afternoon, perhaps you saw me lying over there in the shade of the shack. During that time, I received some kind of instructions, an impulse. It told me that it is necessary to send off an ark, filled with the Archan thoughtware of the Learning Village. It would function like a dandelion seed, blown by the winds, to settle down and make roots somewhere else in the world. That instruction has been received. To accept this invitation is to invite support from the archetypal source of the instruction. It is an invitation I have already accepted. The rest is up to this torus to figure out. It would be a project of the Learning Village. Do you have any further questions? Your fears and your voices are needed now by the torus. Your fears are the design criteria for a successful endeavor. What would we need to figure out to make this ark fly?"

"Arks don't usually fly! They float!"

"So we put wings on the ark!"

"No wisecracks from the peanut gallery!" I say.

"Who will go?" demands Israa. "Please stand over here with me."

Half the people crowd around Israa and me. We are swamped.

Israa suddenly shouts, "Which of you here is eighteen years of age or older? If you are not at least eighteen years old, officials will not let you cross an international border without your parents' consent."

Almost half those standing near us return to their seats. But Mitzi remains. She refuses to believe it. "I am only sixteen, and I will be going!" she shouts, half in rage, half in despair.

It is Aziza who asks the magical question. "How do you know how old you are if you can't even remember your last name?"

"I remembered my last name."

The torus is shocked into dead silence. My own mouth hangs open. "What?"

"Yes. My last name is 'Slovensky'. My name is Mitzi Slovensky. Twelve years ago, as the 'Arab Spring' was spreading through Tunisia, Morocco, Libya, Egypt and Bahrain, my parents brought me here to visit the world-renown beautiful Bohemian city of archeological wonders and art called Aleppo, soon to become a democratic paradise they thought. But on 6 March 2011, in the southern city of Daraa, sixteen or twenty boys were arrested by Assad's Army for having made anti-Assad graffiti on the school walls. They wrote things like, 'Freedom', 'Down with the regime', and 'Your turn is up, doctor," meaning Assad. One of the boys dies while being abused and tortured by Assad's police. The country erupts in protest. The next day my parents leave me with the old lady in the apartment downstairs. They go to participate in a peaceful protest rally in the center of Aleppo. They never return. The old lady is not able to take care of me. After a while I start wandering from marketplace to marketplace, making friends with people who give me food and shelter. This continues until one night I find Zenobia, Jamila, and Aziza here at camp with Mama and Papa. A few years ago, after one of my Emotional Healing Processes, a wall falls down inside of me. I suddenly remember a woman calling my parents 'Mr. and Mrs. Slovensky'. In 2011, before my parents died, I had my fourth birthday party. I know this because in another EHP I remember seeing four candles on my birthday cake. I could already count by then. It was January 6, I think, because we simultaneously celebrated Three Kings Day, which is called Epiphany, the day the Magi visited Jesus. Strangely enough, January 6 has come to be called *World Day of War Orphans*. I am... a war orphan. So, I must have been born 6 January 2007. I figure I am sixteen years old now. 'Slovensky' is a name that means 'from Slovakia'. One day, I would like to go visit Slovakia..."

We cannot contain ourselves any longer. Everyone surges to engulf our new 'Mitzi Slovensky', forgetting our plans, squeezing her, hugging and kissing her, crying and laughing with her, wishing her so much "Welcome!" and so many "Happy Birthdays!" to make up for all the birthdays she missed celebrating with us.

Only after a long while does the theme for our Morning Circle return to center stage, but then the torus leaps into action, unleashing its creative collaboration to transform impossible problems into practical next steps. I whip out my *Beep! Book* and document as fast as I can, but quickly lose track of who says what to whom. The gist of it goes something like this:

"Who of you walkers has a valid Syrian passport, good for at least one more year?"

Three people put their hands up.

"Why a year?"

"Because border control won't allow you to enter their country unless your passport has at least six months validity left on it."

"How can we get valid passports? I heard it takes months."

"What about fake passports?" says Huda Shamalieh, a woman in her late twenties who just arrived.

"You have connections?"

"Yes... and no. Fake passports can cost even more than real ones. But I heard there is an excellent counterfeiter in Jarjanaz, near Maaret al-Nouman. I will check it out,"

"Possibly a refugee organization could help us?" says Jamila.

"I will start checking," says Huda.

"I suggest you start with the United Nations High Commissioner for Refugees, the UNHCR. They helped our cousin's family get Passports and Visas into Türkiye. I will help you, Huda."

"What about taking a refugee boat?"

"Where? To Greece? Italy? I heard those countries are rejecting refugee boats."

"One of those rubber boats? Are you crazy? Can you swim ten miles?"

"Some people make it..."

"Sure! And a lot of people drown. If God had wanted us to swim, she would have given us an outboard motor. We have feet! I propose we walk!"

"What about bus tickets?"

I say, "If we get there in three days, what do we offer them? Nothing. We are not ready to arrive, and we are not ready to depart."

"If you all walk, where will you sleep?"

"What if you are attacked?"

"If someone attacks us, we will give them all our treasures!" says Mitzi.

"What will you eat? How will you cook it?"

"The answer to the question 'How to do it?' is 'Yes!'" shouts Lylah. "We use the torus to create new possibility. These problems are sources of new treasure as we figure them out!"

"But what will you do so people do not just arrest you?"

"We will be so busy delivering our nonmaterial value that we won't have time to be arrested..." says Thomas! Yes! Thomas! Sometimes he talks now! We all clap and cheer every time he is courageous enough to speak out.

"We could plant trees!"

"Where do you buy the trees?"

"We don't buy trees!" shouts Israa. "In every forest, Gaia is trying to reforest herself. Most of the seedlings that sprout in the forest die from lack of sunlight or water that is already being used by the existing trees. We can dig out those baby trees and carry them in buckets until we plant them along the roads to create new shade for walkers, and new forests for the future. We dig up the baby trees for free!"

"Speaking of money," starts Montassar, "who has a bank account with more than $100 in it?"

Twenty-seven out of forty-two raise their hands.

"How many of you have ATM cards for those accounts?"

Nineteen of the twenty-seven.

"We will need money to cover costs, like food, fees to unofficial individuals at border crossings, things like that. Zenobia, since you are writing anyway, without writing down people's names, will you add up the amounts that people say so we have a rough idea of our torus' finances?"

"Yes. Ready to write."

"I know this is usually private information," says Montassar, "but if you are willing to say, will you please, one after the other so Zenobia can write it down, tell us how much money you have altogether, and tell us whether it is cash or in a bank account. Also please say if the amount is Euros, Dollars, Syrian Pounds, or... no! That's too confusing. Let's use today's exchange rate of 2,500 Syrian Pounds equals 1 U.S. Dollar."

People share their cash and bank balances. Many have nearly nothing. A few have quite a lot. Altogether the forty-two of us have a surprising total of about $82,000!

Montassar says, "Since those who control the value of the Syrian Pound cannot be relied upon to be honest, I suggest that, as much as you can and as soon as possible, you change your Syrian Pounds into U.S. Dollars.

(NOTE: This was an astonishingly valuable proposal from Montassar, because 6 months later, overnight, without warning, on Tuesday, 8 August 2023, the price of buying one U.S. Dollar increased 500%, from 2,500 Syrian Pounds to 13,000 Syrian Pounds! We would have been bankrupt if we did not change Syrian Pounds into Dollars when he suggested we do so.)

"How much should we bring on the journey?"

"Does somebody want to help me figure this out?" asks Montassar.

Hadi raises her hand. "I'll help. I have done some accounting before."

"But what is our gameplan?" asks Rafiq, seeming to be quite frustrated.

"What are you feeling, Rafiq?" asks Lylah.

"I feel angry about being potentially stuck in this big question for a long time and not having a clear answer. I already want to be out of here. What are we doing right now?"

I say, "This circle is the rocket on the launching pad, Rafiq. We are fueling up, gearing up, training up. Are you saying you want to use a different gameplan? Something like: Fire! Aim! Get ready!?"

"Ahh... I get what you are saying..."

"What color brain do you have?" asks Mitzi.

"Red, I guess," says Rafiq.

"Then," I interject, "it makes perfect sense that you feel angry. We are not going anywhere right now. We are building out our field of awareness together to make our efforts more effective. We are doing yellow brain and blue brain and green brain work right now. Don't worry. Your time will come, Rafiq. We need your red brain too!"

"Yes, but it drives me crazy!"

I ask, "What is the impulse from your anger telling us to do right now?"

"We should get clear about our gameplan for the journey! What will we actually be doing?"

"And your immediate proposal is?"

"We could pick up garbage!" shouts Sammi.

"Ghaaa!" shouts Rafiq.

"We could repair things along the way, anything broken, hinges or handles on gates, discarded automobiles, broken walls, cracked paint on benches? Then people would find us useful to have around." from Farhan, of course.

"We could ride bikes!"

"Nah! If we ride bikes, we cannot talk with each other!" says Huda. "We would need to pay too much attention to the road. We need to talk with each other every step of the way so as to evolve our collaborative intelligence, like Mitzi said."

"What about hitch-hiking?"

"We could catch rides on farm vehicles!"

"How will you explain yourselves to the officials?"

"We provide value to them instead!"

"What about thoughtware upgrades?"

"You think normal people want to upgrade their thoughtware? They are too afraid to try it!"

"If we are good spaceholders, they might be interested!"

"What about delivering Emotional Healing Processes? Everybody needs those!"

"Then we will have to carry boxes of tissues!"

"Who gets to keep the *Handbook*?" asks Montassar. "The Flower or the Seed?"

"That is not a problem!" shouts Farhan, jumping up from his wooden crate. "We can leave behind the limitation of thinking 'this possibility OR that possibility'. We can leap ahead into thinking 'this possibility AND that possibility' through creating new possibilities!"

"What the hell are you yelling about, Farhan?" yells Habib.

"I will repair a photocopy machine somewhere around the city and print us a new copy of the *Handbook*!" he explains, matter of factly. "I will drill holes in the copy paper and tie it together with a cover and make us a second *Handbook*. Dandelion Flower can keep the new copy here in camp. Dandelion Seed can take the original copy with them on the road because it is smaller and lighter to carry!"

Everyone cheers wildly.

"What if we wear a uniform?"

"Like what kind?"

"Like the coveralls I found behind the collapsed medical supplies shop?" says Hadi.

"But they are white!"

"They don't have to stay white."

"What do you mean?"

"I can dye them a different color!" says Hadi.

"What different color?"

"Not green, or gray... then you would look military."

"What about pink?" suggests Lylah.

"What?"

"Yes! Pink! Pink is not any country's military," shouts Lylah. "Not United Nations. Not police. Not White Hats. Not ISIS, or Assad's Army. I will help Hadi dye the uniforms pink!"

"Yellow!" I say. "Yellow is better."

"Why yellow?"

"Because we could all become members of Amnesty International, and their color is yellow. Then if Farhan also prints out our membership forms, we present them at the border along with our Passports, and with our yellow uniforms we will irrefutably be Amnesty International on a mission!"

"We can embroider their logo onto our jumpsuits!"

"We could be a marching band!" This is Sammi.

"What instrument do you play, Sammi?"

"Uh... the radio!"

"Where are we going, actually?"

"We could go to Türkiye! Türkiye has accepted thousands of Syrian refugees."

"But then we would be regarded as refugees, and we are not refugees!"

"What are we then?"

"We are possibilitators!"

"We are Archans!"

"We are cultural creatives!"

"We are edgeworkers!"

"We could go to Germany. Germany accepts Syrian refugees."

"How well do you speak German?"

"Nicht gut genuch."

"What?"

"Exactly my point."

"But why go to Germany?"

"To help the German people escape from their culture."

"What do you mean?"

"Germany is still a capitalist patriarchal empire."

"And so?"

"And so, they are taking the planet down," says Montassar. "Germans are exterminating life on Earth, possibly many species each day... Most German citizens know this, but they don't know what to do to change things. We do!"

"*Al'ama!* Is this true? About the species dying?" asks Habib. ['Al'ama!' is a common Arabic swear word that literally means, 'Blindness!' but is used in the same way an English speaker might say, 'Damn!']

"Yes. It is true. And humans are on the list of species that will die out."

"What do we bring to the Germans? I mean, why would they believe we can deliver on what we offer them?"

"We bring them *Torus Technology*."

"But they are not interested."

"They could be. Someone there could be interested."

"The refugees there could be interested."

"What do you mean?"

"Yes, the Syrian refugees in the German refugee camps. They still think they are victims being rescued! They still live in the fantasy world that the traditions of their birth culture and religion have value..."

"But they ARE victims!"

"No, they are NOT victims! They are human beings. And in their current circumstances, they have authentic necessity to immediately upgrade their thoughtware. Refugees are still using the same Standard Human Intelligence Thoughtware that turned them into refugees. Look where it got them so far."

"Yes, their country has failed them."

"German schools, businesses, colleges, universities, all still teach the same old stupid thoughtware as we learned here in Syria. We could really help them redesign their schools."

"Yes, but how?"

"We can make powerful proposals to them."

"We could change the refugee camps into Learning Villages!"

"Yes! Into Archan nanonations!"

"We would have to get into the refugee camps somehow."

"Well, that would be easy! We would arrive looking like refugees! They will throw us into a refugee camp."

"We are not refugees! We are Archan possibilitators. We have something incredibly valuable to offer them. I think we should arrive looking like gameworld consultants. Like Yellow Archan Regenerative Culture Gameworld Consultants!"

"But the bureaucrats are too stupid and too arrogant to see the value we bring!"

"All that means is we will need to be more arrogant than they are."

"What?"

"Yes, we have to know with certainty, beyond any shred of doubt, how much value we bring. We can become consciously arrogant from knowing that they need us more than we need them!"

"We can bring their whole culture to salvation!"

"But they won't listen to us! They just want to make money manufacturing more weapons. Germany is the fifth-largest arms exporter in the world!"

"Who is they? Each German is an individual person. We did not even try yet! How do you know somebody won't listen?"

"Hello everyone! I just google-mapped our route from Aleppo to

Munich," announces Farhan. "If we take the coastal route through Türkiye, Greece, Albania, Montenegro, Croatia, Slovenia, and Austria – which is a good idea if you like to eat limpet stew – it is three-thousand five-hundred kilometers. If we walk ten kilometers each day, this walk will take us a year... a year of living dangerously."

"How many of you have walked ten kilometers in one day before?" asks Israa.

Very few hands go up.

"What is a limpet?" asks Mitzi.

"We could take Mitzi Slovensky to Slovakia!"

"She's too young and does not have a passport!"

"But she has no birth certificate either, like a lot of people nowadays. We could get her a passport with a birth date in 2005!"

Farhan adds, "I just saw that Google added a special note to this route that I checked. It says: 'Use caution. Walking directions may not always reflect real-world conditions.'"

"That is too scary!"

"What are we? Stupid!"

"I feel scared and sad!" says Huda. "I have the story that when you Gaias walk out of camp on this journey, I will never see or hear from you again, and you are my best friends in the world..."

"Then you can be our *Interlocuteur*," says Montassar in a roughly French accent.

"What does that mean?" asks Sammi.

"It means that Huda can be the spaceholder for communications between the Dandelion Flower and the Dandelion Seed."

"But she is a woman!" shouts Sammi.

"Okay, then she can be our *Interlocutrix*!" says Montassar.

"Then we can call her *Trixie*!" yells Rafiq, grinning his gremlin grin.

"Shut up, Rafiq!" shouts Huda.

"I have an idea!" Farhan announces firmly. He waits for the conversation pace to slow down enough that people actually listen to what he says. "Between here and Germany I found this little old country called Montenegro. I propose that we go to Montenegro first."

"Why Montenegro?" asks Israa.

"What we do is call up their mayor's office and make an appointment with them."

"What for?"

"We tell them we are an international youth group representing the future and we would like to interview them about their long-term success as a government."

"So?"

"So, when they agree, we also print out their letter of agreement for our appointment. This will be evidence that we are not just refugees escaping Syria and trying to settle in Türkiye or Greece. The letter will help us across borders easier."

"Well... that's pure genius!" exclaims Montassar.

"But what do we do at the meeting?" demands Israa.

"We ask them to show us their Energy Descent Plan," says Farhan.

"What the hell is an 'Energy Descent Plan'?" demands Sammi.

"It is a strategy to intentionally localize energy sources by reducing the use of imported fossil fuels," says Farhan. "In Montenegro they probably heat their houses with oil from Saudi tankers, or they pipe in Russian natural gas. The world is hitting peak fossil fuels now. Supplies are running out and we are burning the stuff faster than geologists can find new sources. It is necessary for each city to create a program for phasing out their dependence on fossil fuels or risk catastrophe. Most cities know this. Few do anything about it because it is a long-term project, and a politician's term is usually only four or five years."

"But what if they do not have an Energy Descent Plan?" I ask.

"Well, Madam Zenobia! That is exactly our point!" shouts Farhan. "They won't have one!"

People are stunned.

"Their lack of a plan opens the doorway for us to show them ours."

"But we don't have an Energy Descent Plan either!" I shout at Farhan.

"By then we will!" Farhan shouts back. "This would be the beginning of a very important conversation for them!"

"I am too afraid to go..." says Lylah.

Sammi says, "Please ask someone to hold space for your EHP."

"Is someone willing to hold space for an EHP for me now?"

"Yes," says Sammi. "I am." They collect their things and move over to our EHP space consisting of two real chairs, tissues, a metal barf bucket, a red hand towel, plus a rage stick and cushion that have the appearance of being very well used...

"Does everyone know what to do next?" shouts Israa.

Obviously not. More questions pour out of the torus.

"How long will it take for us to prepare the 'Ark of the Context'?"

"I estimate it will take us six months." From Montassar.

"You Gaias need more fighting practice!" From Habib.

"With what weapons?"

"Teams of three-on-one, fighting with sticks, like the girls in Neal Stephenson's book *Diamond Age*!" Rafiq is certainly clear about that!

"Yes! Fighting classes every day then!" From Aziza.

"You need to do more pushups and improvised weapons work!" From Rafiq.

"You mean I.E.D.s?"

"No! Not bombs," exclaims Rafiq. "Not necessary. Krav Maga is hand-to-hand times ten. If you are practiced, people see it a hundred meters away and won't even bother to bother you."

"Can I do it too?"

"Yes! Of course!"

"Has anyone seen my phone?"

"It's in your back pocket!"

"Lunch preparation team meets now!" shouts Huda.

"But hey!" shouts Zaid Bakir, a quiet but fierce man who arrived four years before the earthquakes. "Who is going? Lunch will not taste very good if we don't know who is going." He stands up and with the toe of his sandal, draws a big circle in the gravel in the center of our torus. He points to his new circle and says, "I propose we use the M.E.S.S. Process from the *Handbook*. Any resistance? One. Two. Three. Go!"

No resistance.

"It goes like this. By the end of the M.E.S.S. Process, the people standing inside this circle are the people who are going on the journey. You cannot put yourself into this circle. If someone puts you into this circle, you cannot resist, and you cannot step out of the circle. If someone takes you out of the circle, you cannot resist, and you cannot step back into the circle. We go until the M.E.S.S. settles down all by itself. Any questions?" There are none. "Begin the M.E.S.S. Process!"

It is pure chaos – exciting, scary, joyous, wild chaos – a direct application of uncontrolled group intelligence. The M.E.S.S. Process taps bigger resources than logic and reasoning. As the inner circle swells up to twenty-five people and then shrinks down to three people, we love it and hate it at the same time because it is so real. This will change people's lives.

After forty-seven minutes, twelve of us stand in Zaid's circle. We are Montassar and Israa, Aziza, Jamila, Habib, Rafiq, Hadi, Lylah, Thomas, Farhan, me, and Mitzi!

The torus stands in awe, witnessing what we have just now created together. Some radiantly approve. Some look confused or scared. Some hold each other sobbing. Our whole gameworld is rapidly reordering right before our eyes.

I say, "The DNA of our gameworld's Infinity Ring needs to duplicate itself so that it can divide into the Dandelion Flower and the Dandelion Seed. Will each node spaceholder please call out the name of your node and the name of your first apprentice who will then replace you as spaceholder for that node here in camp, so that you can be the spaceholder for that node on the road!"

The Infinity Ring complies.

"I am Israa Nabih, spaceholder of the Morning Circle node. My first apprentice is Rachel Deeb."

"I am Jamila Ali Ahmed, spaceholder of the kitchen node. My first apprentice is Huda Shamalieh."

"I am Montassar Bilal, spaceholder of the *Handbook* study node. My first apprentice is Rahim Taleb."

"I am Hadi Qasim, spaceholder of the healing and EHP node. My first apprentice is Sammi Ghulum."

"I am Aziza Hamdi Ahmed, spaceholder of the guardian node. My first apprentice is Zaid Bakir."

I announce, "Our Infinity Ring has now been formally duplicated.

Our gameworld thrives."

Profound awe and stillness emanate from the centers of our co-creative souls. We gaze upon each other with authentic awe.

This time, Israa, the current spaceholder of Morning Circle, has no need to shout. She simply asks, "Does anyone not know what to do next?"

There is a short moment of silence...

"Alrighty, then!" Israa shouts, just for the hell of it. "The M.E.S.S. Process is closed. Today's Morning Circle is over!" She clicks her clicker to vanish the energetic meeting space. "Lunch will be one hour late!"

# Phoenix, South Africa 6

"Are you Mandisa?"

This is quite an unexpected question to hear from a shy, somewhat chunky Chinese-looking girl wearing a prep-school outfit in the South African bush. *How could she be standing here? How could that question possibly have gotten into her mind?*

For Tandra it's a bit too much. She says nothing at first, just stares at her, then, "What's your real question?"

The Chinese girl begins visibly shaking. Whatever she has been holding inside of her, she can't hold it together much longer. Dried salt lines on her face and neck indicate heavy sweating, but even in the midday sun she sweats no more. To Tandra this is a bad sign that could be a good sign. This uninitiated Asian girl is nearing collapse from dehydration or sunstroke, but perhaps that is how much stress it takes before her particular inner wall cracks wide enough for a heart-to-heart human connection. Still Tandra waits. The girl is near tears, staring at her own nervously fidgeting fingers while her stance wobbles from dizziness. The girl finally looks up and murmurs, "Can I have some water?"

"Yes, of course you can, my child. Come in." Tandra instantly has the gate open, slips her arm around the girl's waist, pulls the girl's arm across her shoulder, and guides her across the kraal into the shade of the acacia tree. She turns to the gathering children. "Andiswa, bring me a whole bucket of drinking water. Malawi, bring a lemon and salt fish, and a cup from the kitchen. Quickly! Thando, please get me a wiping cloth and the palm fan by the fire pit. Luxolo, go get Granny!" Off they run.

Tandra sits the both of them down on a blanket and cradles the girl's head in her lap, stroking her forehead and making small cooing sounds. Without wanting to, this foreigner who has unknowingly come home rolls sideways into a fetal position and shudders until sobs come.

Tandra relaxes. *Ahh, good,* she thinks. *Things can move forward for this girl now.*

In the evening, most of the asamangaXhosa phoenix culture clan gathers in the fire circle. The sun has set. Stars are beginning to shine. Siu-Lin sits wrapped in a blanket, looks from eager eye to eager eye. Clearly, they are ready to hear her story.

"My name in Siu-Lin Chan. I come from Hong Kong. I was born in the year China took back Hong Kong from the UK, 1997. I studied computer programming and ecology in school. My father and mother ran a restaurant, but since the takeover, the spirit of Hong Kong is being strangled. Fewer and fewer tourists come. The future looks only dark. My parents became depressed and afraid. Already they were placed on the secret police watch list. I could not stand to watch this horrible drama play out. I started searching online for my real home. I found a team of researchers in Brazil, and I was recommended to come here by Quinn Racelin. Do you know her? I decided to use everything I had to make the journey. I ran out of money three days ago and I have been walking ever since then. That is all."

The fire crackles. Crickets chirp. No one moves.

"Did I say something wrong?" Siu-Lin asks nervously.

Two of the children move closer to Siu-Lin. Malawi reaches over and holds Siu-Lin's hand.

Mandisa says, "I do not think that is all, Siu-Lin Chan from Hong Kong. We have been waiting for you. Some of us had dreams you would come here. You are one who brings us to the world. We are afraid of that. What we see is that you do not come here by yourself. You come here with courage as your ally. And you come here with a mission, to make this your home. Can you teach us how to be with you?"

Siu-Lin only looks puzzled. "No one ever asked me that question before," she says. "I came here to find people who are unafraid of being themselves. In Hong Kong, everyone is afraid of being arrested for being themselves. I have almost no practice being myself."

Tandra says, "You are being yourself right now. You are not lying to us. You have no religion or business you are trying to sell us. You are not trying to force us to be like you. Each one here is on the same journey as you, Siu-Lin, to be ourselves, and at the same time to develop deep connections with others. What do you want here?"

Siu-Lin startles at the question. "I... want to find myself... and... I want to be with you. I think that is all. I want to do what you are doing. I only know that I made it here, and that you are being so nice to me." Tears roll down her cheeks.

"You have faced perhaps the biggest question a person must face in their lives," says Mandisa. "What do you do when your birth culture crumbles around you, leaving nothing to respect, nothing to inspire you, nothing to honor? This condition is infecting humanity all around the world right now. It is the real pandemic. Modern culture designed itself for easy corruption. As a result, it has been corrupted. It lost its bearings in World War II when we used atomic bombs on each other. The final blow was the economic coup pulled off by the twelve children of the banking elite when they dropped the World Trade Center into its own footprint to avoid the cost of replacing the asbestos insulation in the walls. They also collected on their recently upgraded 'terrorist attack' insurance on the destroyed buildings, and profited immensely by short-selling American and United Airline stocks because they knew the share prices would crash. They simultaneously destroyed criminal evidence against themselves stored on computer servers in both building 7 and the Pentagon, stole truckloads of gold out of the basement of the World Trade Center, and convinced the USA to attack Iraq, earning billions for their weapons manufacturing companies and Halliburton private army services contracts.

"When your birth culture fails you, what are you supposed to do? Pretend like you are happy? Be adaptive and play along, as if everything is okay? Leave the country and get a different passport somewhere? Run for political office and 'change the system from the inside'? None of the above?

"It is a tough question. Our answer is to invent a new culture, the next culture."

Tandra steps in. "We are not the ones who give permission for anyone to be asamangaXhosa. The answer is, no, you cannot join us. But you can participate here, one hundred percent. If it ever comes time that the spirit of asamangaXhosa needs you to become an integrated part in this organism, it will absorb you just like an amoeba reaches out and takes in a piece of food.

"In the meantime, we have a ritual for welcoming new participants. It is the same as our ritual for acknowledging birthdays. Are you ready for our little ritual, Siu-Lin, the courageous walking lady from Hong Kong?"

Siu-Lin nods her head.

"Nodding your head is not an adequate answer to Tandra's life-changing question, Siu-Lin," says Mandisa. "In a phoenix culture, we want to hear your voice."

"Yes," says Siu-Lin without hesitation. "I am ready for your ritual celebrating my welcome day."

Everyone jumps up and noisily jumbles themselves around Siu-Lin in her blanket. One by one they embrace her in a hug and say, "Welcome to a new day and a new way, Siu-Lin from Hong Kong!"

By the time they finish hugging her, the fire is quite well burnt down. The adults silently move off to huts. Siu-Lin stays on the blanket cuddled up with several of the younger girls and children.

Far in the distance, black-backed jackals howl in the night.

# Phoenix, Arizona 6

"Daddy, I'm bored!"

No response from 'Daddy' as he pilots the SUV westward on the deserted desert highway. The sun blasts them from directly overhead.

"Daddy, I think Willis is sick."

"You are telling me that you are bored, and your goldfish might be sick."

"Yeah," says seven-year-old Matthew.

Dad glances into the rearview mirror at his son. "Let me see how far our next stop is, okay? Honey, would you mind digging out my notepad for me? It's probably in the very bottom of that bag somewhere."

As she leans down to search by her feet, Dad says, "I'm going to stop and pick up these two hitchhikers so Matthew can interview them." His wife mumbles something affirmatory bent over with an apple in her mouth.

Dad signals the disheveled hitchhikers to enter one on each side of Matthew. They nod in understanding. Eddy helps JET enter the right passenger door then trots around to the other side. As Eddy snaps his seatbelt shut the car takes off down the road.

Matthew starts right in. "Can I ask you some questions?"

Eddy says, "Sure, but only if we can ask you questions back, one for one. That would be fair."

"Okay. Who goes first?"

"That was your first question!" says Eddy. "The answer is, 'You did.' Now it's my turn to ask you a question. What's your name?"

JET sees the Dad glancing back at them in the rear view mirror with a relieved smile. It's a full-time job entertaining a genius seven-year-old.

"My name is Matthew. My turn now. What are you guys doing out there?"

"Experiments. Our turn. Why are you carrying that goldfish?"

"This is Willis. I couldn't..."

"Stop!" Says Eddy immediately and firmly, but not unkindly. "Not fair! You just answered a different question than I asked. You answered the question, 'What is the name of your goldfish?' But I did not ask you 'What is the name of your goldfish.' I asked you, 'Why are you carrying that goldfish around with you?' Try again."

"I'm carrying Willis, my goldfish, around with me because I think he is sick. I didn't want to leave him at home because I was afraid he would die. My turn. Why are you asking about my fish?"

JET answers, "Because Eddy has a special connection to animals. He talks to them. He and the animals, they understand each other."

Eddy throws JET a threatening look but says nothing.

Matthew says, "Can you talk to Willis?"

"Hey! You're trying to steal our question!" says JET. "It's not your turn yet!"

But too late. Eddy has already unbuckled and is crawling down to put his knees onto the car floor behind the driver's seat so he can peer directly into the goldfish bowl.

Matthew looks tensely at JET. "What's he gonna do?"

JET says, "Shhhh... Just watch. Later I'll tell you an unbelievable story about the mountain lion who came into our camp last night..."

Matthew turns his attention back to Willis.

Eddy's nose almost touches the bowl. He gracefully puffs his cheeks in and out as if breathing underwater through gills. The goldfish seems to respond. It swims towards Eddy's side of the bowl. For a moment the two of them float eye to eye in deep wordless fish communion. Finally, Eddy wiggles his head and seems to swim away. The goldfish does the same. Eddy sits up, satisfied. He takes a moment to adjust back into the human world and buckle his shoulder strap back on. It is clear that he has a prognosis.

"Matthew," says Eddy, "I made contact with Willis. He felt safe enough to open his heart to me. Animals communicate heart to heart. They don't have words. When Willis let me into his heart, I immediately felt what he is feeling. Willis is terribly heartsick." Eddy pauses with real tears in his eyes. "He feels sooooo sad, and also lonely. Did he ever have a fish friend?"

"Yes he did!" says Matthew excitedly. "But this winter Bruce jumped out of the bowl..." Matthew leaves the remainder of his sad story untold.

Eddy picks up the slack. "I am sure that if you could find a new friend for Willis, he would get happy and healthy again, right away. I am already telling him you will do this for him, okay?"

"Daddy, can I? Oh, Mommy! Please!"

Everyone looks at 'Mommy,' who has all the while been chewing small bites out of her apple, silently observing the three men in the back seat healing the goldfish. When they look up to hear her answer, both JET and Eddy blurt out. "Mrs. Singer!!!"

"Yes, it's me. What a remarkable coincidence! Isn't it? You two look like shit! Roger, interestingly enough, these desert rats you picked up are the same two I told you about who disappeared recently from the university. They are both excellent swordsmen, and excellent trouble-makers as well."

"Then they are exactly right for a job I need done! Gentlemen, I offer you a proposition. I need a briefcase delivered to a certain individual in San Diego on Saturday afternoon. Would you do that for me?"

Eddy is flabbergasted.

JET thinks, *Who would ever believe this story? The game is definitely afoot.*

Both JET and Eddy simultaneously say, "Yes." Everybody laughs.

Mr. Singer slows the SUV, then pulls off the road into an isolated desert gas station called *Traveling Eagle Center* with a faded sign in the window advertising *Home-Made Cherry Cobbler*. He gets out of the car and walks back to open the tailgate.

JET and Eddy also get out, JET limping like a peg-leg pirate with his torn pants and the Indian's bandanna pressing the desert herbs onto his wound. Mr. Singer opens his wallet and hands Eddy a stack of bills and an envelope.

"Here is five-hundred dollars. You will find Captain David Henkel at the address on this wedding reception. There is another five-hundred dollars waiting for you if you bring this briefcase back to me by the twenty-third in Santa Fe, New Mexico. That's a little over three weeks from now. By then we start our summer holidays. Here's my address and phone in Santa Fe," he says while scribbling on the back of the wedding invitation. "All clear?"

JET looks at Eddy to make sure they don't both say "Yes!" again at the same time.

Eddy looks at Mr. Singer and says, "May I ask you two questions?"

"Yes."

"The first question is: What is really going on?"

Slowly and deliberately Mr. Singer looks at both young men. "I would be doing you a terrible disservice if I answered that question for you. It's much too important a question to kill with a mere answer. I suggest you keep that question alive in your guts and let it digest you from the inside out until you become someone who has already become the answer. What is the second question?"

Eddy objects. "But if you know the answer, you have an intellectual obligation to give it to me!"

Mr. Singer pauses to let Eddy's unconscious anger waft into the past like fart stink, then slowly and deliberately speaks to something deeper in Eddy than his mind. "What if the answer cannot be known by the intellect?"

"I don't even understand what you just said!"

"That's exactly my point!" says Mr. Singer. "What if your mind, by understanding a conceptual answer, actually blocks you from finding the real answer? I propose that you let that question take you on its transformational journey. I repeat, what is the second question?"

"What's in this briefcase?"

"Designs and a disassembled architectural model for a Temple of Evolution. The designs I could, of course, have emailed to Captain Henkel. But the model is far too delicate to ship. The parts are packed pretty well in there, but I ask you not to use the briefcase to beat off stampeding buffalo. Find a different solution, okay? By taking this model to San Diego, you save me driving seven-hundred miles there and back from here. I will gratefully use that time to take my family on a well-deserved little holiday in a different direction."

"What's a 'Temple of Evolution'?" JET asks.

"To quote someone who pays close attention to such details, you are asking a third question, and I only agreed to answer two. I could of course try to explain, but better let Captain Henkel tell you the whole story himself. He and his group commissioned me to make this design. They will give a presentation to investors in San Diego on Monday. I am glad to find trusted colleagues to safely deliver this briefcase to him for me. Thank you for being fluid enough to allow the Earth Coincidence Control Office to move you so that our lines could intersect. Who knows where else this might lead us next, eh?"

JET extends his blood-stained hand to shake. "You can count on us, Mr. Singer."

"See you in a few weeks in Santa Fe," says Mr. Singer, also shaking Eddy's mud darkened hand.

Matthew pops his head angrily out of the car window. "Hey JET! You're leaving now? That's not fair! You promised to tell me the mountain lion story!"

JET limps over and bends down as far as his painful leg allows, in order to look eye-to-eye with Matthew.

"You are right Matthew. I am truly sorry. Look, we do have to go now. Your dad is sending me and Eddy on a secret mission. But I am pretty certain that we'll be seeing you again soon, back at your house in Santa Fe. I promise that I will tell you this story in full exciting detail the next time we meet! You will not be disappointed! Okay?"

Matthew trusts the bond made by the promise. "Okay." He stretches out his fist to bump knuckles with JET who complies with a smile.

"Bye for now," says JET while Matthew crawls back into his seat.

Mr. Singer closes the tailgate, slides back into the SUV and starts the engine. Eddy shouts, "See you later Mrs. Singer." She nods. The car makes a u-turn out of the gas station and takes off down the road in a cloud of dust, heading east.

Eddy and JET look at each other with raised eyebrows, then stick out their thumbs to catch a ride west.

"Hey," says JET. "We have money now. What if we get some fresh squeezed orange juice, scrambled eggs, and Cherry Cobbler at the gas station, and then take the bus?"

"I accept your proposal, sir," says Eddy with an expression of delight on his face. "It is such a pleasure to be gallivanting around with someone who can make interesting proposals."

# Hollywood, California 4

Morgan Freeman sits as Sandra Bullock stands. She wears a long-sleeved white blouse and rose-colored slacks.

"Recently I discovered something that I think is momentous. It's not that I discovered it first. Perhaps I discovered it differently.

"I became strangely excited about this discovery, and I tried explaining it to several people," glancing at Stephen Fry who looks down. "But getting the implications requires the perspective of a mage," she nods towards Dave Stutler, who looks fearfully about, trying to figure ways to defend himself against possible recriminations, "plus the wisdom of age," smiling at Morgan Freeman who smiles graciously back.

"With no further ado, I offer you: cavitation!" She spreads her hands and arms out with a glorious smile.

Of course, no one understands what she is talking about. People glance around, bewildered. But Sandra speaking the word 'cavitation' signals thirteen black-dressed stage-hands to simultaneously step out from the shadows and place a one-and-a-half-liter-sized unlabeled clear-glass bottle filled with a clear liquid on each of the thirteen tables of the torus, along with a simple bottle opener. Then, as if they were never there, the delivery team vanishes back into the shadows.

Sandra Bullock continues. "The bottle on your table is filled with carbonated water, drinkable mineral water of the highest quality. You have seen carbonated water before. What I will show you next, you have also seen before."

Sandra indicates the four immense flatscreens mounted around the walls of Stage 13. A video comes up showing exactly what each person sees in front of them: an unlabeled clear-glass bottle filled with clear liquid, standing on a white table. The film is silent. Nothing is happening.

Then a single hand slowly enters the picture from the side holding a bottle-opener – exactly like the bottle openers on the tables. The hand carefully fits the bottle-opener to the bottle-cap, slowly lifting the cap off the bottle. Perhaps the bottle in the film has been glued to the table, because no second hand comes in to steady the bottle as might be normally expected. As the bottle opens, a familiar but amplified hissing and fizzing sound fills the room with sparkling aliveness.

Sandra speaks. "As the cap is removed from the bottle, small bubbles of carbon dioxide gas begin forming at numerous tiny points on the inside of the bottle's surface. Can you see them?

"These points where the bubbles originate are not random. They are special. They are called 'cavitation points'.

"At each cavitation point, there is some kind of irregularity, a discontinuity, a disruption of the smooth ordinariness of the glass. The cavitation point is what creates the possibility that something entirely new can emerge there.

"'To cavitate' is a verb that means, 'to make a cave, to originate a new empty space inside of a space that already seems to be fully occupied'.

"In this case, the bottle is already full of water, but the bubbles of new space still appear.

"Due to an irregularity on the glass – an imperfection, perhaps a scratch – or sometimes from a dust particle floating around in the liquid – see that? The first tiny new bubble of gas pops into existence.

"Let's look at this more closely." The image cuts to an ultra-slow-motion close-up video of a tiny gas bubble forming at a cavitation point in a clear liquid.

Sandra continues to narrate. "Once the cavitation starts, more-and-more of the gas can emerge at the cavitation point. Each bubble keeps growing larger. At a certain size, the bubble departs from the cavitation point and floats upwards, still growing as it goes. It is useful to understand all this clearly.

"When the bubble floats upwards, the cavitation point stays behind. Further cavitation continues. Immediately the next tiny new bubble of space cavitates. We see a stream of rapidly expanding new spaces emerging one-after-the-other from a single cavitation point.

"The significance of this, is that you yourself can consciously begin to function as a cavitation point in the world. You can learn to consciously cavitate new cultural space in the global ethnosphere."

The flatscreens go black, but Sandra does not even begin to slow down.

"What is the global ethnosphere? It is the sum-total of all human cultures on earth averaged together... in other words, what you could call the 'status quo'.

"The status quo is one of the most resilient substances in the Universe, very difficult to redirect or transform.

"Ordinarily, the status quo goes as it goes. Modern culture's status quo has recently taken humanity off the edge of an ecological cliff where it now falls towards a very dismal near-future outcome.

"If the status quo does not change, neither will our future.

"I am now going to show you a natural talent which you have long been using unconsciously to reproduce the ordinary status quo. But now, I will show you how to intentionally cavitate new culture space, different from the status quo, and then how to occupy that space, leaving all other spaces behind. In this way you can create a new future for yourself, and possibly also for many others.

"Your life as it is, plus everyone else's life, plus whatever is happening all around you, equates to the water in this bottle. It looks as if the space of what is possible is already filled up with everything that is already happening.

"Your first step in becoming a cavitation point, is to amplify your irregular qualities, your willingness to be a sudden irritation, because cavitation starts with a 'bang'.

"An easy way to create a 'bang' is to clap your hands together like this."

She slaps the palms of her hands sharply together, shattering the attentive silence. It looks like it stings.

"The pain in your nervous system and the sound waves from the clap, cause an energetic shock wave that was not there before.

"This shock wave opens a gap, into which you state out loud, in a firm voice, 'I *cavitate* new space...'

"Then you announce out loud the context of the new culture-space you are cavitating.

"It will be necessary that before you clap your hands, you already precisely formulate your intention for the context of the new culture space. For me, it looks like this."

"I *cavitate* new space... " clapping her hands together again when saying the word 'cavitate'.

Then she turns her left-hand palm upwards, horizontal to the ground at the level of her solar plexus, and points to it with her right index finger.

"A new space has now come into existence here in the palm of my left hand, but it is tiny.

"To expand the tiny bubble, I hold the fingers of my right hand in the 'Dr. Strange sling-ring position', something like this."

She places the heel of her right hand into the palm of her flattened-out left hand, which serves as a platform for both the newly cavitated space, and her right hand.

The first two fingers of her right-hand point upwards. Her right thumb sticks out at nearly ninety-degrees to the left of her first two fingers, forming a reverse 'L' shape. She bends her right ring finger and pinky finger over towards the palm of her right hand.

"Holding this hand configuration, swing your right hand around through a car-tire-sized arc to stretch out your new culture-space bubble, ending back here in the palm of your left hand.

"At this point, my sphere of new culture space is bigger, but still too small for me to fit inside of it. To make the sphere large enough, I push both of my hands through the side of it like this."

She presses the backs of her two hands together, pokes them through the side of her new culture bubble, grabs the edges of the hole she just made, and pulls it open just like a stage curtain.

"Now I stretch the hole big enough to walk through, and the bubble big enough to stand in. I step inside the bubble through the opening I just made, and while I declare the context and purpose of my new culture space, I reach behind my back and zip up the hole behind me."

Sandra smiles big time, not at all embarrassed by her strange gyrations.

"Here is how cavitation looks altogether. It is smooth and elegant."

As she says it slowly and firmly, she does it.

"I cavitate new culture space in which evolutionary delight is the highest value!"

Sandra now stands fully upright inside of her freshly cavitated and sealed bubble of culture space.

"Here I am, inside of a freshly contexted bubble of culture space, completely different from the culture space of the status quo!"

She says this while spreading her arms wide, smiling ecstatically, pushing out from the inside wall of her clear bubble of space to show how flexible and resilient it is.

"Each of us – every human being – has the capacity to cavitate new culture-space – even inside of a space that seems to already be fully occupied by another culture."

"Pardon me Sandra!" says Jeremy Irons, standing up with his objection. "I can hear and understand the words you are saying. But I must tell you, I do not see anything like a new bubble of culture space around you now!"

"This is interesting, Jeremy! Thank you for speaking out. You are speaking as a man from one cultural context to a woman in an entirely different cultural context. You may not be able to discern this new bubble of culture space yet, but I do. You may not see my freshly cavitated bubble because you are looking for it with your physical body's eyes. We each have five sets of eyes, one set of eyes for each of our five bodies, physical, intellectual, emotional, energetic, and archetypal. Did you go to school, Jeremy?"

"Certainly!"

"Did you have any classes in how to see and interact with the world using anything other than your physical eyes?"

"No."

"That's the point! Just because you have not activated a potential, does not mean you do not have that potential. Can you ride a bicycle?"

"Yes."

"Do you remember what it took for you to learn to ride a bicycle?"

"Yes. Practice. And my older brother Christopher's guidance."

"Can you juggle three balls in the air?"

"No."

"Why not?"

"I haven't practiced, and I had no coach. I never wanted to learn."

"But could you learn to juggle three balls if you had the wish to learn?"

"No doubt, I could."

"That is the same with using your energetic eyes to see this newly cavitated bubble of culture space here around me. Seeing with your energetic eyes takes your conscious wish plus guided practice. Most people don't practice seeing with their other eyes because they simply never thought of the idea that it could be done. This is also true for cavitating new culture space. We each live inside of a culture space. We simply never before realized that we could consciously cavitate and inhabit new and wildly different culture spaces."

Jeremy Irons smiles with satisfaction and sits down.

Sandra waits a moment so everyone can catch up with what she just demonstrated. "I will demonstrate cavitating space once more, so you see how simple and powerful this is."

While clapping her hands, circumscribing a sphere, sliding two hands into the new bubble, stretching it open while stepping inside, then zipping it up behind her, Sandra declares, "I cavitate new culture space in which evolutionary delight is the highest value!"

Sandra looks around the torus. "Nobody can cavitate new culture space for me. Nobody can stop me from cavitating new culture space for myself."

People seated around the white tables grow excited.

Sandra Bullock says, "Many of our colleagues have already fallen. They can no longer take a stand here with us today. I think of Alan Rickman, Carrie Fisher, Gene Wilder, Max Von Sydow... to name but a few. Their departure diminishes our presence at the front lines. We can no longer hide behind their prowess, just as when we go, others can no longer hide behind ours.

Morgan Freeman steps forward again, bows slightly towards Sandra and says, "Thank you Sandra." She nods her head at Morgan without smiling, and moves gracefully back to her chair.

"Stepping into your newly cavitated space does not mean you already know how it goes in there. But, if you were the Universe, would you give 'knowhow' to anyone before their ass was on the line and they were already committed to producing new results?

"I don't think so...

"The human potential to consciously cavitate new culture space is an astonishing discovery. Through personal commitment to your own new cultural context, you open the door to the Universe giving you previously unseen resources, useful coincidences, and raw know-how. The catalyst that makes this happen is you committing to create the new results first, even before you know how to create them. Once you are committed and rolling along, the resources become truly necessary and can be usefully given to you.

"So much more can happen now than could have happened even a few moments before..."

# Eugene, Oregon 8

Davis Hatcher's *Beep! Book*

She made us promise to immediately start writing everything down in these little *'Beep Books'*.

At the end of last Thursday's meeting, I asked if she would stand with me outside for a few minutes so I could clarify a few things. She said, "Yes."

Her name is Remington Smith. "Anything that strikes you," She said. "Anything that pisses you off, or confuses you. Just ask."

She recommended that I go towards confusion, fears, and internal blocks rather than away from them. "Digging through the mud to get to the sky," She called it – lyrics from a Lee Lozowick song.

She said it was important to know my sources, to never forget where things come from. "Transformational plagiarism is impossible," She said, "because there is only one source. But in this gameworld, we honor those who have gone before us. We pay respect to the sacrifices they made. Like you are about to make."

"What sacrifices?" I demand to know.

"Ah," She says, "you're already doing well, grasshopper. You are asking dangerous questions."

"Dangerous?"

"Dangerous to your box, to your current survival strategy, to your secret ways of perceiving the world – secret from yourself, that is. By the way, 'Box' is spelled with a capital 'B'..."

She sees I spelled it with a small 'b'.

"The capital letters remind us that these words have a different meaning from normal. You can find the new meanings online at distinctionary.mystrikingly.com."

I oscillate between astonishment and outrage. "I never met anyone as outrageous as you."

"I take that as a compliment."

"But you perturb me!"

"Yes. You are now making the sacrifice of Sleep."

"I already don't sleep much."

"Sleep as in 'being unconscious'. You are about to sacrifice the peace of mind that you create by falsely believing you are conscious. It is the first sacrifice. There are eighteen standard sacrifices. This is sacrifice zero. It is called 'sacrifice zero' because you cannot sacrifice your peace of mind yourself. Someone else has to do it for you. In this case, that someone is me. I don't particularly like making that sacrifice for you. There are Karmic consequences. Plus, I have to estimate whether or not my efforts are worth the risks I take. With you and Sanjib, I am on the line about that. I am not certain if you have prepared yourselves enough for sacrifice zero to be effective. You need to have enough Matrix in your Being to hold the new Distinctions. I must be ready also," She adds. "I guess I *am* ready, or E.C.C.O. would not have put you here, asking me Dangerous Questions. I can only do it for you because someone else did it for me."

I sense a wistful but respectful tone in her voice.

I'm supposed to write everything down like in a journal, but with a different intention: "to track the Memetic alchemy," She said.

Many of the conversations I record on my phone, like this one. She encourages me to record because, "Your memory is not activated yet. You don't have the Distinction grooves in your brain."

Cheeses....

I'm supposed to write it down to leave a 'Hansel and Gretel' trail behind me so other people can cross the Bridge more effectively than me. She says, "So they can see how you found the Path."

The Practice is to write down EXACTLY what She and the others say, not what I remember, not what I think they said. "Otherwise, your Box will change the words and erase the Doorways, like waves washing away footprints in the sand at the beach."

"Writing it down is about having gratitude for the Possibility of finding yourself. When you find yourself, you find out 'What Is Really Going On'. You are entering a time of Rapid Learning. During Thoughtware Upgrades, Gratitude is more useful than Resentment."

Where the hell does She get this stuff?

"If you make efforts to write it down, you serve those who come after you."

It's part of the deal I made with Her.

We made a deal. It was Her boundary. "If you don't seriously Commit to writing it down, this game stops here."

I Committed.

My energetic action of Commitment was Conscious.

It is my Choice.

I could not resist Committing to Her Gameworld because I could not resist Committing to Her. (In this case, the capital 'H' in the word 'Her' and the capital 'S' in the word 'She' is my doing. I am not sure why I write it this way. If I had to guess right now, it is because when Remington Smith speaks to me, or stands near me, I get a sense that She is bigger than Herself. Something bigger than her – with a small 'h' – shines through Her. I get to relate with a 'Her' rather than a 'her', and this is indescribably special.

In short, Remington Smith is amazing. I never met anyone like Her. But She uses so many new words!

She told me to study the notes I write in my *Beep! Book.* (This is my *'Beep! Book'* – as in *Go! Beep! Shift! Go!* – the four steps of 'rapid learning'. See! I told you there are so many new words...)

She uses Memetic Speaking. "Because you've been programmed, by modern society, to be a sheep."

"Asleep?" I ask.

"A sheep! Same difference," She says, smiling.

I tell you, it is worth getting Her to smile...

"Writing it down is one way to slow your automatic thought processes long enough that you can 'Observe what you are observing with'. Or, 'Notice what you are noticing with'." She says this is how to detect my Thoughtware. She says I am still using Standard Human Intelligence Thoughtware. (This is funny! The abbreviation is S.H.I.T.)

She says, "If you don't write it down it didn't happen. Writing is an Alchemical Act. It transforms an ethereal memory into physical words on paper. If you want it to have happened, then write it down."

I am telling you, I want this to have happened.

She says, "If you establish new neural networks in your brain, they will show up as new agency in your life. You start being able to do things you never before imagined could be done."

This is all so fucking weird! And yet... so amazingly wonderful! Finally, I encounter something I cannot automatically pigeonhole as 'stuff I already know about'. I feel like I am in first grade on another planet, or in a science fiction script. But it's not fiction. And She and the others do not use a script.

I ask, "Where does all this stuff you are saying come from?"

"I speak from the Unknown," She says.

I say, "What?" as if I'm a dunderhead.

When I talk with Remington I say "What?" so often you'd think I'm hard of hearing. I say, "What?" far more often than I write down here.

She tells me I cannot hear Her because I am not Present yet.

I say, "I hate not being able to hear you more completely!"

"Write that down," She says. "A Part of you hates it. That Part will continue hating it, sometimes more, sometimes less, all along the way, perhaps forever, or for the rest of your life. Whichever comes first. A Part of me hates it too, sometimes."

"What's that supposed to mean?"

"What's the *that*?" She asks me.

"You just said 'a part of me' hates it. What do you mean by 'part'?"

"We have many different Parts. Each part thinks it is the only part. Humans have a complex Underworld ecology. You have a zoo in there. When a new Part takes over, you don't notice the Identity Shift because you fall asleep as you go through Doorways. Suddenly you are in a new room, a new Space, with new Possibilities. You pull a different personality off the inner shelf to defend against your new circumstances so you can survive there. One of your first assignments is to start Noticing the switch, to Notice when you fall asleep. That's nearly impossible though. Think about it. You don't notice when you fall asleep at night, right? You only notice when you wake up. The same applies when you leave or enter the Waking State."

"The what?"

That is when my phone rings. I answer it reflexively, like a robot. It's my sister Barbara. "You need to come quickly. A water pipe has burst at the rental."

"Why don't you call Sammy? He's better at fixing pipes than I am."

"Sammy is out with the boys."

"Shit. Like always. Why did I even give him another chance to do what he said he would do? *That asshole!*"

"You're Hooked," hisses Remington.

I glare at Her. "I'll be there in twenty minutes." I switch off.

Remington watches me like I'm an amoeba under a microscope. I tell Her so.

"That's because you're behaving like an amoeba. Pure Reactivity. And you didn't notice the switch, did you?"

"What switch?"

"You and I were talking, remember? While we spoke together, there was a particular 'Davis' personality talking with me, the one who talks with intelligent beautiful powerful women, the one talking to me now. Then your phone rang, and you instantly shifted identity. The 'Davis' I was talking to vanished and was replaced by a strange character I've never encountered before. You were talking with Barb?"

"My older sis."

"The Barb-talking Davis is whiny, small-minded, vindictive, complaining, and resentful towards Sammy, whoever that is."

"My older brother."

"Sammy... Davis...?"

"Yeah... my mom filled out the birth certificates to end the debate about 'What do we name the kids?' She loved *The Candy Man*. Used to sing it to us at bedtime..."

"Do you remember the energetic sensations you had in the instant you ended your call?"

"No..."

"It feels something like – Whoooooosh! when a new personality takes you over. New vocabulary, new speech patterns, new gestures, new attitude, new self-concept. In one unconscious instant you switched from the 'Barb-triggered Sammy-hating Davis' back to the 'Remington-triggered Davis', the thing that is talking to me now. Did you ever see anyone else switch character when their phone rang?"

"Sure. Sanjib does it all the time, especially with his mother. And Sergeant Brinks shifts identity whenever Chief Stafford calls."

"Do you think you are the only one who doesn't shift identity when your phone rings?"

"I get your point..."

"I doubt it. Your experiment is to count how many Parts you have in there, and to give each part a unique and descriptive Name. Make a CATALOG OF DAVIS PARTS at the back of your *Beep! Book* so you can refer to it easier."

I would have forgotten this assignment entirely except for the recording.

Sorry.

What I mean is, "One of my Parts would have made me forget the assignment."

My 'Box' of Parts is totally freaking out about being discovered...

"What did you mean by 'Hooked'?" I ask Her, trying to sound enthusiastic, but in reality, feeling terrified, like a fly facing a hungry spider.

"Is it possible to feel enthusiastic and terrified at the same time? And what is an 'Alchemical Act'?"

"Save it for next time, Davis. We have reached the maximum of what your Matrix can hold right now. You did good today. I feel glad. It was worth talking with you because a Part of you gets the reality of what I am saying even though that Part is scared shitless and does not have majority vote in your zoo."

Then She says, "You need to go now. The pipe is leaking."

How did She know?

# Phoenix, Arizona 7

Creosote-soaked electric poles, sun-scorched asphalt road stretching from horizon to horizon, and a Route 66 style gas station are the only signs of civilization behind the bus stop where JET and Eddy sit. Pesky flies buzzing around their heads amplify the Arizona desert's utter silence.

The two guys have been sitting there for hours.

Eddy stares out at the bushes and sand. He finally speaks from some cavernous place within him. "I'm beginning to have a theory about what is really going on."

JET leans against the bus stop post, dozing with a belly full of incredibly delicious Cherry Cobbler à la mode. Due to his endorphin stupor, he can barely open his eyes. "What is it?" he mumbles.

"I think there is a completely separate game happening in parallel. Maybe more than one."

Flies buzz-attack each other like World War I biplanes in a dogfight. JET is convinced that the flies are ecstatic when they zig-zag around each other like that. Why else would they use so much of their precious short life spans to do it?

Eddy continues. "You and I are being given glimpses."

Zzzzzz... zzzzzz. Zzzzzzzzzzz....

"I used to imagine that I live in a country called 'the United States of America', and that we all represent the American culture. I thought that within this culture, there are different professions and different local styles of life. For example, people in the South eat grits, and people in the North eat potatoes. Some people appreciate classical music and some like blues. Some are Democrats and some Republicans. Some people start companies and other people work in them. But all along, I assumed we live in this one homogenized American culture together. I thought this my whole life. There was no evidence to contradict my assumption, even from my parents or teachers.

"But now I am beginning to think I am very wrong about this. I have been fooled. I believed the bullshit. I think there are parallel cultures going on outside of our mainstream culture. I think these parallel cultures are created by people serving a very different purpose, a purpose they are aware of and the rest of us are oblivious to. On the surface, these parallel culture people look similar to Americans, and they *are* Americans, but *similar* does not mean *equal*."

JET studies his blood-encrusted fingernails and torn jeans.

"I think most people's thought-freedom has been subsumed by mainstream culture. Thinking like everyone else seems like the easy and safe way. But I get the feeling there are completely other streams of culture going on all around us, which are just as alive, just as internally consistent as the mainstream American culture, but completely outside of and parallel to it, and also completely invisible to it!

"People in the mainstream culture do not even know the parallel cultures exist, like fish don't know that turtles can walk on land even though fish and turtles swim in the same sea.

"Maybe the parallel cultures feed off each other. Maybe there is an entire ecology of intertwined cultures going on, each with its own ecological niches to fill.

"It may be possible to transfer yourself from one culture to another culture, but the entrance fee to a new parallel culture is paid in a coin that cannot be counterfeited. You must pay in a coin-of-the-realm as serious as death.

"I mean, for you and me to jump out of mainstream culture into one of the parallel cultures, the currency we must sacrifice is the paradigm through which we each perceive the world for our whole lives.

"It's just like Mr. Singer said. If I can't already see the answer to my question 'What is really going on?' then, even if Mr. Singer *did* tell me the answer – which I think he truly wanted to – I would not be able to understand what he said. And there's nothing he could have done about it to make me ready to understand the answer. I have to do that preparation work myself.

"I have to earn the answer by becoming someone to whom the answer might make sense. This means sacrificing my assumptions and conclusions. It means identifying and transforming whatever I use to think with that diminishes my ability to perceive the parallel culture's viewpoints. I must give up having things be the way I am accustomed to having them be.

"Then I would be flexible enough to become the key that opens the door to the next level."

Eddy pauses to let these radical ideas find a home in him instead of trying to brush them away like the irritating flies.

JET remains silent.

The flies don't.

Eddy continues.

"I am thinking that the doorways to all cultures outside of my present culture are available to me all the time, right here, right now, wherever I am, even here at this bus stop in the middle of this desert, in the middle of the day, in the middle of the year, in the middle of this conversation, in the middle of nowhere. Nothing is blocking access to these crossover points but me, myself.

"But I can only get through a door if I am at the door. No one can bring me to a door if I am not already standing within reach of it. No one can go through a door for me. But once I can get myself to a door, no one can stop me from going through it if I choose to step through it.

"It is as though, in reality, there is no secret!

"Or maybe, there *is* a secret, but the secret is lying right here in front of us in broad daylight, if I could only adjust my eyes to see it. The fact that I don't see the parallel culture is my own fault!

"But I am not a victim! And neither are you! We have each developed our personal ability to perceive as far as we have developed our personal ability to perceive. Only there, but no further. The secret to jumping from one culture to a parallel culture, hides behind the discomfort of shifting our Beings from one shape to another shape. If I could get more comfortable with being liquid so I could endure the shape changing..."

"Can you say more about 'being liquid'?" JET prompts.

"... if I can shift my interface shape from how I developed it in order to survive, to whatever shape is needed to open the doorway which is standing in front of me in this very moment, then I become the pass key! But in order to shift a solid of one shape into a solid with another shape, the solid must go through a 'liquid state'. It is the equivalent of using gold coins to make a statue of an angel. First I need to heat up and melt the gold into a liquid so I can pour it into an angel mold. After it cools, I pop off the mold, and, as they might say in France, *Voila!* The gold has taken on a different shape. Same gold, new shape. New shape, new function. Before, the gold served as a medium of exchange. Now it can serve as a sacred artifact.

"And here is the kicker, JET! You and I... we... are completely free to do whatever it takes to get ourselves into a liquid condition for taking on a new shape that allows us to discover the treasures of the parallel culture.

"For example, I was at the university. All my life I was told that I needed a college education to get a good job, to become a designer or a consultant, to make good money. This is the credo of mainstream culture. What are the credos of the parallel cultures? What culture does our Indian friend perceive and act in?" Eddy points to JET's bandaged leg. "What culture does Mr. Singer perceive and act in?" pointing to the briefcase on the bench between them.

"If Mr. Singer lives in a parallel culture, you can bet your ass that Mrs. Singer lives in that same parallel culture with him. And I never knew this about her! I didn't have a clue! I only knew that I liked her as my sword master. But she never let on about living in some parallel gameworld that provides her with options to choose from that I can't even see! She never told us!"

"Victim..." says JET, without malice. He simply keeps his promise to be a reminding factor.

"Right. Victim again! Shit!" Eddy sighs, looks down at the sand and gravel under his feet, then directs a fierce gaze at JET. "Did she tell you?"

"No," says JET.

"How did I block her from telling me? Maybe I was not yet ready to hear about any kind of parallel culture. That's why she never told me about it. She couldn't.

"Maybe it's like the laws of thermodynamics – coolness does not flow backwards against the flow of chaos. Maybe she wanted to tell me about it, but she saw that speaking to me would be premature and could harm me in some way, because I did not yet have whatever it would take to hold the radically new information safely. Then it wasn't her fault. It was my fault. I could not see a doorway to a parallel culture even though she was probably holding it open for me right in front of my eyes. Maybe there is a parallel culture stream going on even in the classes I've been taking, like some kind of hidden university! Who else knows about this? Maybe Mrs. Singer could not tell me about this 'Hidden University' because I would have been scared out of my wits. Then I would have found some reason to make her into an enemy – a cult leader, a crazy person or something – so I could destroy her, or discount her, or just leave her class in disgust. Maybe..." continues Eddy, "I would have become a witch-burner because I did not yet recognize that I myself am also a witch!"

The flies continue dancing together in ecstasy, but in a slightly different dance than the ecstasy of Eddy and JET.

"Criminy, JET! I actually love Mrs. Singer. Of all the teachers I've ever had, she is the coolest! Even when she threw you that sword to save your ass – you jerk! She wanted us to keep dueling! Can you imagine that? Even though we destroyed her class and messed up the basketball team..." Eddy pauses for a moment, then, "Here's what comes to me now. Only half the people who voted in the last election, voted to install the current President of the United States. And a lot of people who could have voted, did not vote. Even more people were not qualified to register to vote, or did not care enough about the whole political circus to vote. This means that at least three quarters of the American people did not vote for the current president! This is happening in other countries too. My question is: What are the other three quarters of the population doing if they either voted against the government, or do not care enough to play in the government's voting charade?

"I mean, perhaps three quarters of the people in the world have already exited mainstream culture, and I didn't even know about it!

"What parallel cultures are they in? What is really going on? That is the question!

"Here is another question: What needs to grow in me so that I can find the next level of the unsecret secret? What needs to expand in me so that I can shift into a recontexted parallel culture? How do I get a parallel culture passport?"

"Well, now, that's an interesting question," says JET. "The new passport isn't made from paper with a photograph and thumb prints. The new passport is made from the kinds of questions you can ask, the kinds of questions that matter to you. That is your passport, because it is real. It works to open doors. It is not just a cardboard-covered document."

Eddy stays silent.

JET continues. "Mr. Singer clearly explained that the question you hold is a catalyst that changes you into a key to enter a parallel culture! The kind of questions you carry is visible to others, not to everyone, but to those who count. He could see your level of questions, Eddy, or sense it. The thing that holds your questions is the same thing that determines to what level you can take responsibility. And it is the same thing that permits you to perceive, to understand, to be aware, to detect those doorways to a parallel culture. It's.... It's.... I don't know what it is. Your Being. The structure of your soul. Some kind of matrix that holds consciousness like a scaffold holds construction workers. If the matrix is not there, evolution is forced to pass you by. You can only be as conscious as your matrix can hold. Our job is to do whatever we can to build that matrix in us. It's just like Mr. Indian told us: continue our initiations!"

Eddy says, "I'll bet some of these parallel cultures aren't limited by the political boundaries that define countries. Maybe people from every nation – third world or not – participate whole-heartedly in these parallel cultures already. I'll bet thousands of people have been playing in parallel gameworlds for thousands of years. I want in! I want out and I want in! When is this fucking bus coming? Give me the briefcase!"

The case is bulky and heavy. JET struggles to hand it over to Eddy. Eddy balances it carefully on his knees. "Are you ready to see what a Temple of Evolution looks like?"

Without waiting for an answer Eddy presses his thumbs sideways to release the two catches.

They don't open.

"Damn! It's locked! I don't have the combination!"

Eddy stares glumly out at the far mountains, fading into the distance.

"It's just feedback," offers JET. "We're not ready yet."

The desert remains absolutely silent on the matter. The flies do not.

Eddy thinks of something else.

"When we were talking just before, I was sharing my experiences of being at the edge of my world with the most clarity I've ever had. And nobody but you was here to listen. We are surrounded by desolation. My distinctions didn't land anywhere. This has been a theme for me. It confuses me about the purpose of life, and how easily treasures are lost. Maybe I am just fooling myself about what a treasure is, or what it's for. How can I stay in connection with ordinary people, but also bring what is important to me into the world? Who will receive and use the treasure?"

"Your distinctions landed in me," says JET.

"But they don't really matter to you!"

"How do you know that?" asks JET. "You cannot be certain what matters to another person, or who you matter to. It's not your call. People mostly talk for their own entertainment. When unexpected weird shit happens to me, I admit to myself that I have a different identity than being a mere person. It is okay with me if other people do not understand what matters to me. I regard myself as a private investigator serving the evolution of consciousness. I am an alchemist searching for catalytic formulas. This is when it becomes clear to me – not to the others, just to me – that only certain kinds of foods feed me.

"I grow hungry for those foods. I cannot assume or expect other people to provide me with these foods. If I want the extraordinary experience of 'discovery food' or 'invention food', I need to create it for myself. I need to invoke extraordinary spaces where transformational possibilities show up, and where valuable stuff gets invented and implemented. That's what drove me to fit out my dorm room like a mad scientist's laboratory. My food supply cannot depend on the other people around me being, doing, saying, or feeling anything in particular, or else I would be a victim. I become self-entertaining.

"Now and then, someone else shows up in such a way that I can interact with them, collaboratively invent or explore with them. This is what is happening right now, with you... since the moment you stepped onto the fencing strip. You are feeding yourself the kinds of foods that have the nutrition you need. I probably never stop doing this.

"Sometimes my orientation bothers other people. Most of the time they have no idea what I am up to. They can't even see me, or see what I am creating in a space."

"Well, okay!" interrupts Eddy. "What you are telling me is that if you are creating cool stuff, and I am still hanging around with you, then I must have some idea of what you are up to. I must be hungry for the same things."

JET smiles at Eddy's amazing powers of self-observation, and then winces while trying to stand up.

A roaring monster of a bus screeches to a stop directly in front of them, whirling up a cloud of hot dust and diesel fumes like a pissed-off mechanical rhinoceros.

The two adventurers trundle up the stairs, Eddy carrying the briefcase while JET hangs onto his shoulder for support.

Eddy pays their fee from the cash in his pocket. They find seats.

As the bus accelerates down the desolate highway, Eddy wraps his arms tightly around the briefcase. The metal is real, and hard, and still locked. Somehow, after recent events, the fact that the briefcase would not open on his first try feels comforting. It implies that there is still more to discover.

They settle in for the ride. Something surprising surely awaits them.

Before JET nods off to sleep, he says, "There is one more factor to think about."

"What's that?"

"When you go liquid, what is the force that determines the new shape you will take when you solidify again? Remember the mold for the angel?"

"Yes."

"What makes the angel mold for a recently melted Being? We should be thinking about this question, given our current conditions, eh? Or... maybe... with this degree of liquid state... we never go solid again..."

# Aleppo, Syria 11

Zenobia Darwish's *Beep! Book* – 11 February 2023 – day 5 after the earthquakes

It is barely dawn, three days after the Sammi process and the Dandelion Seed proposal. I wake up shaking in fear. I don't know why.

I drag my blanket over to where Morning Circle will eventually start. I sit there, huddled up, waiting. There is nothing else I can do.

The circle forms up. Rachel is first spaceholder. She efficiently scans the circle, stops at me, and says, "What's up, Zenobia?"

"We cannot go on the journey."

"Can you say more about that, please?"

It is obvious that at this moment, she and I are operating on different wavelengths. I try to say it a different way. "The 'Ark of the Context' cannot leave. What do we think we are doing?"

"Why are you saying this?" Rachel coaxes. "My feelings detector senses you are feeling something. Would you please let your heart speak to us?"

"I have been reading one of those old James Bond novels from Ian Flemming. James Bond seems so self-assured, flying everywhere, spying on people, blowing things up, doing his secret agent actions. But in reality, he is only doing what he is told to do by his superiors!"

"So?"

"He has a 'handler'. 'M' is his handler, you know? M is the one who authorizes James Bond to go do his outrageous deeds. Without M and the whole government behind him, James Bond would be nothing. He would be some kind of lunatic terrorist or something."

"I repeat. So?"

"So, we are nothing!"

"What do you mean?"

"I feel scared because no one authorizes us to do anything that we are doing here. We do not represent anyone. We are not Syrian anymore, because there is no Syria. We are not Blue Hats from the United Nations. We are not Peace Corps, or Doctors Without Borders. We are not a soccer team or the army or a religion. We are not Monsanto corporation selling patented death seeds to naïve farmers to profitize our chemical warfare against nature. We are not even the Girl Scouts. We have no framework within which we can justify our actions to anyone."

"Good point. Thank you. Ladies and Gentlemen, Zenobia's fear instructed her to make the proposal that we authorize ourselves to send out the 'Ark of the Context'. I propose that we invent a new framework to legitimize our actions."

"What? Have you gone crazy?" I exclaim. "Self-authorizing is the act of a crazy person!"

"No! I am not crazy. The United States of America did this in 1776. The first Girl Scout troop that Juliette Gordon Low created on 12 March 1912 in Savannah, Georgia. I did a research project on women gameworld builders. I did not know the term 'gameworld' back then, but that is what she was: a gameworld builder. Every one of those frameworks you mentioned was arbitrarily made up by someone at some time out of nothing. Gameworlds do not automatically exist on Earth, like rocks, or the sea."

"Go on..."

"Human beings made them up. These frameworks are fictions. Fabrications. Fantasy worlds in which people live."

We remain silent in this space together for a long moment. Sammi trundles up with a wheelbarrow filled with very fine-looking compost, sets it down, joins the circle.

Hadi goes on. "I don't care if people think that the framework they live in, or work in, or fight in is real or not. Frameworks are objectively unreal. We pretend they are real so we can justify our existence to ourselves. We act as if we understand what we are doing. But look around. See those shattered buildings? Remember those jets that flew by overhead a few minutes ago? You think we are living in the peak of human civilization? You think this is the best that human beings can do on Earth? Gang warfare with high explosives justified with insane rhetoric spit from every G5 tower still standing, college-educated people drinking it up like zombie food? I refuse to believe this! I think that what we see around us indicates a severe lack of imagination."

"What?"

"Yes," Hadi says. "I think what would make a difference is to unleash enough radical imagination to create a new construct in which we are authorized to do exactly what our hearts and souls want to do."

"You mean to be authorized to walk to Germany?"

"Yes! That is exactly what I mean! What is our story? What is our purpose?"

"We are trying to survive," offers Aziza.

"Yes, and... survive in style! Survive in high-level-fun team collaboration! Everyone out there is trying to barely survive, to scrape by, to make do. I am talking about something far more interesting than that. I mean survival as elegant ongoing creation. The *Handbook* says: *The opposite of scarcity is not abundance. The opposite of scarcity is creation. There is a massive difference between consuming to survive and creating to thrive.* Look around! We sit here this morning in a circle of rabid creators."

"Okay... but... I mean... Everyone is trying to survive, no matter what they say. Right?"

"No!" shouts Israa. Anyway, it seems to me like she shouts. "Try to listen to what Hadi is saying. If all we are doing is trying to survive, then scrabbling, begging, lying, stealing, cheating, fighting, doing whatever it takes to obtain whatever we need to survive would be at the center of our lives. But we are not! If survival is our central goal, we would compete against each other and everyone else out there, either secretly or overtly, in a life-or-death struggle. We would be playing an 'I win, you lose' survival game. And, need I remind you? None of us even carries a gun!"

Israa looks around, making serious eye contact with each of us. "But!" she goes on. "And! Here is the most amazing revelation of the day! If what we are doing is Creating, then we source our resources! We are not victims of not having enough resources. We create what is wanted and needed. And what is wanted and needed right now is a new framework."

Half the people have a blank stare on their face. The other half are in various stages of resistance, confusion, thoughtfulness, or ecstatic inspiration.

"Here is the evidence for what I am saying," explains Israa. "The thrill of creative-collaboration is at the center of our lives. Raw invention pours through the spaces we create. Winning is happening all day and all night long. We already know how this goes. It is the best thing there is! We have no need to compete with anyone for anything because our objective is to keep giving our treasures away as fast as we create them."

People nod their agreement. "We meet others and don't see them as enemies or competitors. We see them as possible recipients of our treasures. We creatively collaborate with them to give them treasures they never knew existed, treasures with more value than money can buy. Our everyday needs are handled as a matter of course, because our central activities focus on creation and distribution of nonmaterial treasures. Are you getting this Zenobia!"

I feel my inner structure melting down and destabilizing into a multi-body liquid state. There is still a remnant of the fairytale 'Zenobia' in me, the great and powerful leader Zenobia, the one who pronounces decisions that everyone follows. I am failing miserably at that. Here I am lying in the dirt shaking in fear while others speak with clarity and power. Of what use am I then if I am not 'the leader'?

Reality is earthquaking my worldview into shattered fragments again. All I can say is, "What should they call us? I mean, what is our name?"

"Who has the *Handbook*?" Hadi demands. "Where is it?"

Aziza grabs the book from a table and hands it over to Hadi, who thumbs her way to a page she knows. *Give it a name!* It says that right here: *Give it a name!. The recommended Archan gameworld construct is a nomadic nanonation, but each nanonation needs its own unique name.*

"What is the name of our nanonation?" asks Aziza.

Mitzi stands up and speaks out matter of factly. "We already know the name of our nanonation. We heard it when Zenobia was talking about her earliest memories at her grandfather's farm. We could see it in her eyes when she told us about visiting Palmyra, how beautiful it was, how elegant and powerful. Our nanonation is Palmyra. We live in the nomadic nanonation gameworld of Palmyra. And our project, our journey, is called the *Young People's Syrian Diplomatic Mission to Montenegro*."

I look up at Hadi. She smiles at me but does not rush things. I look around at everyone. My inner structure reorders now that I have used my fear to say what is up for me, and the people have heard me. Speaking my fear has made a difference in our world. Unrepressed fear has created a treasure: a new legitimacy framework to live in together. This also makes a difference for me.

"Okay." I say. "Okay... I get to live in Palmyra after all! With all of you!" Then tears pour out of my eyes. It feels like my heart suddenly grows two sizes bigger. I lie there sobbing in a life-long release of frustration and hopelessness. The impossibly broken puzzle puts itself back together, but in a new way, not the old way. What could never work before is now already working. Some of the new Palmyrans gather around and hold me. Others laugh and dance in celebration.

"Hold on, everybody!" shouts Rachel. She has been away from camp the last few days and only returned late last night. "I have a report from the Passport node." She waits for people to settle down a little. "We got your passports!"

At first there is the silence of disbelief, as if Rachel's next sentence will be her punchline in a joke of bad taste. Nobody obtains Syrian passports these days. Rachel reaches into her satchel and pulls out a stack of deep blue booklets. She holds them up victoriously high in the air. Only then, after seeing the real thing, can people believe it is true, and the cheers erupt, also from me.

"How is that possible?" demands Montassar.

"How did you do it?" demands Israa.

"Alright, already!" shouts Rachel after a while. "If you settle down a little, I will tell you...."

Rachel takes a deep breath and lets it out as a sigh. "Last week I took a stand to be the spaceholder of the Passport and Visa node, remember? Thomas helped me research online to learn everything we could about how to get Syrian passports and Turkish visas for the twelve Seeds of the nanonation of Palmyra. It looks hopeless, confusing, even dangerous, and certainly expensive. Legally or illegally, it is a thornbush. I decide that the only way to make this happen is to go meet people face to face. I ask Aziza for two guardians. She gives me Zaid Bakir and Rafiq Abadi. You can imagine how wonderfully safe I feel in their company. We discuss our gameplan beforehand and decide to borrow cleaner clothes to look as civilized as possible. Rafiq even asks Lylah to cut his hair. She takes an hour to do it, but the result makes Rafiq into a handsome new man!" There are moans from some of the women...

"By the way, Zenobia, I am grateful to have used your mother's dress and her purse. I washed the dress and will give it back to you when it is dry. The weapons we bring with us are discreet. We make Passport style photos of the twelve Seeds using Thomas' phone, put them on a memory stick and get them printed near the old market at a printshop, along with twelve copies of the Turkish Visa Application Form, which we fill out. Then we head over to the Aleppo UNHCR in Building 42 on Omayad Street, Old Shahbaa. Zaid and Rafiq hang around outside as I walk in with our Amnesty International membership papers and our appointment confirmation for the meeting at the Mayor's office in Budva, Montenegro.

"I do not immediately approach the information desk but instead stand there making my center, grounding cord, and bubble in the middle of the entry room. Then I call in my bright principles. Just then, a woman my age, passing by on her own errand, sees me and asks if I need some help. I look her straight in the eyes and without weaving in any kind of emotion, without telling her any low drama story, I explain to her our mission. She says, 'That is the most refreshing thing I have heard in months! Come with me to my office.'

"She pivots on her heels and heads back in the direction from which she came. I follow. We enter an office. She indicates a chair. I sit. She sits in her own chair behind her desk and says, 'What can I do for you?'

"I cannot help but smile and say, 'It is so amazing that you say these words. This is the exact way in which we begin an Emotional Healing Process!'

"She takes the bait and asks, 'What is an Emotional Healing Process?'

"I give her the basics in a minute or two and say, 'We do EHPs for each other ongoingly in order to build matrix for entering initiated adulthood.'

"She asks, 'What is initiated adulthood?'

"We go to a nearby restaurant and have lunch together. In the middle of lunch, she pulls out her phone and says, 'I will call my friend inside the Department of Immigration and Passports. What is your name?'

"I say, 'Rachel Deeb.'

"This professional woman from UNHCR grows a grin across her face from ear to ear and then bursts out laughing like a horse! I wait with patient interest. When she finally regains some control over herself, she says, 'I love it! I absolutely love it when coincidences beyond all measure of probability confirm the wild actions I am about to take!'

"I smile and wait for further explanations.

"She repeats, 'Your name is Rachel.'

"'Yes,' I confirm.

"She says, 'My name is also Rachel. And my friend over at the Passport Office whom I was just about to call, she is also called Rachel! Some force is clearly at work behind the scenes here to make this happen for you. Give me the photos and your paperwork with all the names and dates of birth. You also have Turkish visa applications filled out?'

"'Yes,' I say, reaching into Zenobia's mom's purse and handing them over to her.

"'This will take about three days. Can you meet me back here on Thursday for lunch again?'

"'Yes,' I say. 'How much money should I bring?'

"She stares at me with an offended frown on her forehead. 'Are you kidding me? Money? You cannot pay for miracles like this, honey! Besides, I would not want to do anything to block this energy flowing freely through my life. If I can be included in the circuitry where a miracle can do its work in the world, I will certainly be blessed in ways far beyond the value of money! You can buy us lunch next Thursday. Do we have a deal?'

"I stand up and give her a big, wet hug. I feel like Rachel and I will be friends for life."

Tears stream down Rachel's cheeks.

I look around and see people wiggling their hands in silent applause, wearing big smiles and tears on their own faces.

I put my hand up. Rachel sees me and says, "Zenobia, go ahead."

"Remember, a little while ago, I said that we cannot go on this journey?"

"Yes. I remember."

"I changed my mind. The world looks different to me now. I am ready to get ready to go."

The wiggling hands shift direction and now focus their love and appreciation on me. I reach out my hands and grab onto whoever I touch first, pulling them close to me, hugging onto them for a long shaky while.

# Hollywood, California 5

Jeremy Irons rises to his feet. "I am ready to take a risk here that I was not ready to take just a few moments before. I am ready to admit the truth of something that I have long denied.

"As Matt Damon puts it in *Good Will Hunting*: 'It's better to be yourself than to try to be some version of what you think the other person wants.'

"What I hear Morgan Freeman arranging for us, is a chance to be that which we essentially are.

"Our careers are almost over. Our reputations are established. They cannot be tarnished by the mere expression of insanity when we reveal our secret that, all along, we were not actually acting.

"Morgan has created a stage upon which we get a chance to be clear about what we love as who we are.

"This is our chance to show our friends, our audiences, what our lifelong cavitated bubble of possibility space truly looks like.

"So here goes!"

He stands and claps his hands once loudly together while saying, "I *cavitate* new space where long-term consequences have immediate effect that cannot be personally avoided by hiding behind status, wealth, or social constructs, where human dignity manifests as human integrity rather than class war, and where love provides a fertilizing-effect during each and every interaction, even if the evolution of consciousness is painful to express due to the unbearable lightness of being."

He sling-rings his newly cavitated space into a basketball-sized sphere in the palm of his left hand, then inserts both hands through a slit he makes in the side of this bubble to stretch it out large enough for him to step inside and stand fully upright in, zipping up the entrance behind him.

Jeremy Irons stands looking around, breathing hard from feeling extraordinary intensities of unfamiliar joy. As he stabilizes in his newly cavitated context, he begins smiling radiantly at his own chutzpah. "This feels wonderful!"

Denzel Washington abruptly stands up and takes the floor. Jeremy relinquishes and sits.

"I feel extremely afraid when I consider the power that might be unleashed by learning how to consciously cavitate new spaces," says

Denzel. "My fear is that uninitiated adolescents – which is most everybody – the guy next door, the billionaires, the landlords, the psychologically unbalanced presidents promoted to positions of power – will try to cavitate spaces where they can freely do whatever they want. My fear is that narcissistic sociopaths will cavitate spaces where it is okay for them to ruthlessly rape, murder, pillage, destroy, and take without conscience, disrespecting people and planet, and going on like this without being stopped.

"What I just realized is that the thing I am afraid of is an exact description of what is already happening all around us every day and night. Is this not so?" He pauses to personally verify the truth of what he just said.

"If every option is an option, you could indeed choose to murder, steal, commit suicide, and hurt others ongoingly. Nonetheless, every option is already an option right now. It always has been. I have simply been deluding myself into thinking it is not.

"To me, the invitation to take radical responsibility for cavitating new space minute-by-minute empowers me to open side-doors in the current insanity and set out on an entirely new path. Then nothing stops me from creating the more beautiful culture my heart knows is possible. And anyone with the same desires can join me.

"This is where conscious cavitation becomes personally revolutionary.

"Who determines which cultural space I live in?

"Who decides which context prevails in my life?

"Who decides what I do when standing in front of someone who lacks dignity or integrity?

Then Denzel Washington claps his hands loudly together and says, "I *cavitate* new space in which people value looking at each other in the eyes and seeing themselves, so that our natural urge is to offer whatever we can so that the other person heals, because if they are well, then we are well, and then it's party time all around. This new space replaces confusions and distractions with deep trusting connections, and it gives you surprising numbers of real friends."

After stepping into his new bubble and zipping it up behind him, Denzel stands there gawking at the others with an unstoppable smile across his face.

"I feel better!" he exclaims.

# Langley, Virginia 2

Thomsen decides. "Yes. We use GlobeScan for a full x-rating operation."

By the next day, Jason Spade and Monika Sterling – Ms. Clandestine CIA – are set up side-by-side in a GlobeScan ComLab, busily testing strings of search keys to finetune the spider. Someone out there will soon become their perfect double agent.

Thirty-nine sleepless hours later, Jason questions his strategy. *Thomsen could eventually have done this alone, but then there is this question of those green eyes...*

*Who's really in there? What is she up to? Is she Thomsen's scapegoat? Or is she working for a different department and Thomsen doesn't even know?*

*True, with Monika Sterling at my elbow, the CIA could weave a network of double-agents to catch candidates that fulfill their most-wanted lists. But then I could not claim full credit if the project is successful. Are the green eyes worth that?*

After twelve cappuccinos and no breaks, the eyes are more red than green. Jason decides that energy for banter is better spent extinguishing the sparks that fly when flint meets steel.

Finally, the machine goes, 'Bing!'

"Who did we snag?" asks Jason.

"Somebody named 'Rob Dent' in Los Angeles, plus a couple guys from a German political movement. I'd go with Dent. The L.A. psychology is less offensive."

"Let me see his specs, will you?"

She hands him a five-page printout. Jason scans for something inspiring. What he finds puts a chill down his spine. This guy could be his brother.

"I like this guy!" he says to Monika. "Do you know where they intend to plant him?"

"I heard there is a sect in Eugene, Oregon. Some kind of *Mysterium...* It is so stupid. If they called themselves *Knitting Circle*, or, *The Eugene Stamp Collector's Guild*, they would be harder to find."

"Alright Mr. Rob Dent. You are our man! I guess that you, Ms. Sterling, are the lucky spider woman who gets to go give Mr. Dent the kiss."

Monika feels irritated by Jason's shadowy allegory, but has her numbness bar so high she cannot react. "We all have our parts to play in this melodrama, Mr. Spade. You dug our man out of the maddening crowd. I will go make him an offer he can't refuse."

"What a team!" says Jason Spade, dripping with unconscious cynicism.

# Eugene, Oregon 9

Remington Smith's *Beep! Book*

Months have passed. My days are filled with *Nature Conservancy* work, a perfect environment for practicing my *Shadow Knights of the Mysterium* spaceholding skills in meetings, but also in calls. More and more often, believe it or not, colleagues and partners are asking me in private for Emotional Healing Processes. These appointments emerge organically, and they are so Fun to deliver (as in 'High Level Fun', transformationally challenging, evolutionarily fulfilling...).

Each Thursday night meeting we try to do the most powerful – or most confusing – exercises we find in our newly revised version of the *Handbook*. From week-to-week, I experience my own matrix building. Each new distinction opens new dimensions to explore, like adding condiments to the spice shelf in your kitchen, but with more profound consequences.

But now and then I have a disturbing question nudging my subconscious. *What is next for me?* it asks.

I know I am arrogant. But this question verges on superiority, and it scares me. What is my gremlin up to? Or is E.C.C.O. waiting until I personally decide to make a move?

I also see similar evolution happening in the others... well... most of them...

Robert Maxwell seems to be 'leveling out' during the past month or two. I automatically figured it is because he is male, and unconsciously balking at losing his prestigious patriarchal position as the so-called 'chairman' of this group, the 'head honcho', the 'big baboon', the 'cock on the dunghill'.

But I am wrong about that, due to an assumption I made, a false assumption. Last meeting, Robert pulls me aside on the break and says, "I feel so relieved that you have magically appeared in our meetings, Remington. I can't imagine how this happened, but I want to tell you that Sophia and I are so grateful to be able to back down... or back off more-and-more, to let go of the reins, so-to-speak, since you bring so much visible competence into our work. As you know, I was raised in the patriarchal context of *Robert's Rules of Order*. It is not yet natural for me to use *Torus Meeting Technologies*. But I see you fluidly wielding its nonlinear dimensions, and I see people flourishing in their personal and professional lives. I am unspeakably happy that you bring your grandmother's traditions and treasures with you so generously. I do not want to announce this officially, but gradually, Sophia and I are edging towards a more retired lifestyle. We want to make some travels in Asia before we are no longer agile enough to negotiate the associated discomforts. I want you to know that you have our complete support for more solidly setting the context and navigating the space of this community. Your presence and skills are a blessing for us, for all of us. Will you do it? Will you keep breathing life into our friends' futures? This group is probably the most useful thing I ever contributed to the world, Remington. Surprising, isn't it? We work so hard to make enough money to raise a family, keep a roof over their heads, send them to the university, pay for their insurance and dental bills, and yet, the most rewarding creations are nonmaterial. Now it is time to hand this organism, or as you call it, this 'spaceship', over to the next generation. That would be you, Remington. You and the other young people. Will you do it? Is this okay for you?"

I can only smile at him and give him a big warm hug. Such evolutions are too big and complex to comprehend, I suppose. Or perhaps too small and simple?

Over the months, new people trickle in and old people trickle out of the *Mysterium*. I find pleasure in witnessing Davis and Sanjib become more present and real through their regular participation and innocent yet pertinent questions. They must be practicing together all week long between meetings. How lucky they are to have each other. Sometimes I long for a partner, an equal who can challenge me, undermine my weaknesses with proposals for further adventures.

I focus on building matrix in each person exactly where they are on the path.

New matrix is made from new distinctions.

New distinctions provide new clarity.

New clarity creates new possibilities to choose from.

New possibilities create new authority to build new matrix!

And thus, the spiral of evolution continues!

Each time Patricia, Carol, Francis, Sophia and I (or any subset of 'us') come together in our practice team, we also make a short YouTube explaining a distinction or thoughtware upgrade where one or more of us demonstrates how to use it to create new results in your life. These are fun, often challenging, and for sure matrix building to make. I can see from the YouTube statistics that our little jewels are being passed on to friends of friends of friends around the world, changing people's lives for the better for free.

Well, obviously not 'for free'. Upgrading even one piece of thoughtware can cost you everything you ever believed in, cherished, or thought of as a crucial element of your personality. We pay full price to evolve. As has been said, what looks like total annihilation to a caterpillar, flies into the air as a butterfly. Life is so amazing.

Various small independent teams around the world add subtitles, or remake our videos in a multitude of languages, some I never heard of! Azerbaijani, Italian, Spanish, Xhosa, Tigrinya, Māori, Corsican, Guarani, Vietnamese, Hebrew, Japanese, Shona, Bhojpuri, Russian, Portuguese, Polish, Turkish, Indonesian, and Kinyarwanda!

I had to look it up. Kinyarwanda is spoken in Rwanda, Burundi, the Democratic Republic of Congo, Uganda, and Tanzania. It is clear that the *Mysterium* is invisibly empowering the spontaneous birth of a wide variety of additional evolutionary circles around the world. I find myself inspired to go meet whoever is enthusiastically giving life to thoughtware upgrades in Africa.

A new guy has started coming to our meetings. Rob Dent, from Los Angeles. I googled him and found about zero internet presence. Some people are like that. They don't want to be findable. But somehow he found us. He must have true necessity.

The first night Rob Dent comes in the door, we are investigating how thoughtware is like a seed, carrying memes like DNA. When this seed finds soil, it grows into a healthy plant that grows fresh flowers – such as *Shadow Knights of the Mysterium* – which then forms many new seeds for making more plants. The more seeds the better.

Francis says, "Maple seeds have wings that catch the wind and spin away to new territory!"

"Yes!" exclaims Anton. "And many seeds have burrs that catch onto your clothes or a sheep's wool. The seed uses animals to transport it far away from the original mother plant so the DNA can spread!"

"And apple seeds surround themselves with a sweet fruit," says Sanjib, "so attractive to human beings that we grow apple trees around the world, thus assuring that apple seeds are reproduced. Humans serve apple seeds!"

I ask, "What would be the ideal revolutionary thoughtware upgrade team design?"

"I propose the humble dandelion," says Davis, humbly.

"Ah! Tooth of the lion! *La dent de lion!*"

"What? Dandelion means 'tooth of the lion' in French?"

"*Oui*," I say, inhaling with enough French nose-in-the-air disdain to demean the King of Prussia.

Davis eats the insult with his intrinsic dignity. I feel a twinge of guilt. He carries on. "I get it! The leaves! They have a jagged edge. Looks like lion teeth. Makes sense. I never knew that French adopted so many English words!"

Even I cannot help but chuckle. Americans!

"Why do you suggest dandelions?" I demand.

Sophia interrupts Davis and answers with calm certainty. "I am a gardener. Dandelions are clever, fast growing, and incredibly hardy invaders. They can spread by growing new shoots from their roots, and also by regrowing an entire plant from any tiny root remnant left in the soil when you try to pull it out. One flower can generate up to 2000 seeds!

Their fluffy little windsail structure opens and closes in response to moisture. On dry, windy days the fibers open, catch the wind, and blow as far as 50 miles, ready to sprout again in as little as 7 days. The flower is beautiful and smells sweet. The entire plant is edible and nutritious – flowers, leaves, and roots. They attract ladybugs that eat aphids, and bees for pollination. It is a perfect design for a revolutionary organism: attractive, useful, and nearly indestructible."

I notice the new guy, Rob, turning pale with fear. I assume this is because it is his first time being exposed to a space like this. He can hardly speak after that, only stuttering to say goodbye when he leaves. But he is back the next week, fortified with some new kind of confidence that I find rather interesting. What is he really up to?

I decide to investigate by inviting him to pizza.

Rob Dent claims to be enthusiastic about selling software apps to companies in Los Angeles, about personal development, and about me. He wants to know everything about me while diverting my questions about him. Maybe he is shy? Maybe he is embarrassed? We laugh a lot. Not bad for a first date.

But my experiment of devouring the late-night Pizza Hawaii with Rob Dent is not doing me well. At 3 a.m. I lie on my back in bed, moaning to myself about the spicy blob of dough and cheese in my stomach.

Between self-recriminating thoughts and physical agony, I slip into periods of free attention where the void opens up inside of me. There, in the dark and absolute emptiness, I simply breathe in and out during each present moment.

That is when the download slides into my Being: a clarified understanding of leadership. Of all things, why leadership? And why me?

The discovery focalizes gradually, with warmth, like a sunrise cutting through a foggy morning.

It formulates itself into these words: *A leader is the person who goes first.*

*Simple enough*, I think. *So obvious.*

Not so obvious is the bit that comes next: *Experimenting makes me a leader.*

I never thought of myself as a leader. I had evidence to believe that I was a little different, yes. Self-inspired, yes. Curious enough to power a nuclear power plant. Yes.

But me? A leader? Scary. I don't like leaders. I don't follow leaders. Cold-hearted men in dark robes surrounding me with their rigid ill-willed intentions. Scary.

Again I sense my desire to move forward to the next thing. Week after week with the same people in the same room asking the same questions...

Nobody seems to be seeing it... perhaps even I don't see it... but I focus on strengthening Davis and Sanjib's ability to hold and navigate *Shadow Knights of the Mysterium* meetings. Driven by longing for greener pastures, I am replacing myself! The Nature Conservancy has taken me as far as they can.

This week the updated version of the *Handbook* is being printed. The notes have done their job. We burn Michelle's papers in a ritual fire now that they have been transcribed into digital format.

But somehow, I feel so ungrounded. Rob Dent keeps asking me to go off with him on a world journey. I am more attracted to the journey than to him. But why not? What is keeping me here? Week after week I get more antsy. It starts interfering with my sleep.

I remember the words of Max Stirner – AKA Johann Kaspar Schmidt – German author of the 1844 book, *The Ego and His Own*. He wrote, "Don't hold anything sacred that does not come out of yourself."

I love the clarity and freedom of this orientation. But then, how do I receive love from someone else? It seems the most devilish of traps. I am missing something, and I am not finding it here in Eugene, Oregon.

(NOTE TO MYSELF FROM ONE YEAR LATER: I see that even with the purest of intentions, self-deception seems undetectable in the moment it occurs. My desire for 'independence' carries me straight into the jaws of doom. Yes, of course, in hindsight it is easy to connect the dots and detect the several ways I arranged to betray myself. I wonder about the evolutionary value of being betrayed. I can't find it yet. Perhaps the pain of self-deception is the only cure for naiveté.)

At the next *Mysterium* meeting I make sure Davis is holding the space, and then I ask for possibility. I say, "For months now I feel like a rocket where the fuse is lit and the jets are burning, but something holds me down. I think the something is this group. What can I do?"

After providing me with a long list of options, Francis suddenly says, "You could go to Africa and plant *Mysterium* dandelion seeds there."

"This is it!" I shout. I stand up. I hold a giant imaginary dandelion puff ball by its stem with my two hands. I take a huge breath and blow the puff ball as if to spread its thousands of floating seeds far and wide. I say, "I am going to bring the *Mysterium* to Africa!"

Suddenly, Rob Dent stands up alongside me and says, "I am going with you."

I say, "Super!"

The two of us turn and walk out of the space.

I feel giddily excited out in the night air, but also out of balance. The field of destiny shimmers around me, fuzzing out my connections with my bright principles and my archetypal lineage. It is chilly outside the *Horsehead Bar*. I figure my unfamiliar wiggliness is just fear about taking my next steps into the big unknown.

Then Rob takes my hand in his and holds it firmly.

I feel glad that he emanates enough certainty for the both of us.

# Edinburgh, Scotland 5

The teapot whistle fades as the waitress removes the vessel from the fire. She pours the near-boiling water over tea leaves in two porcelain cups set at a window table in a café overlooking the Scottish coastline. Afternoon light reflects from the ocean and blazes in through the café's windows.

Sean gazes across the small table, well stocked with scones, clotted cream, and strawberry marmalade, into Margaret's shining eyes. He rubs his fingertips gently together.

"I've continued the experiment of consciously feeling sad," he says. "There seems to be three levels. I think every person has access to all three. First I can feel sad about the things that have happened in my life, things that I know about. For example when Runner, my dog, was hit by a car – I was so sad." Sean actually enters into that known level of sadness to about ten percent intensity. "I've carried this sadness for decades."

His fingers barely touch each other and barely move, but it's enough to keep him right there in that moment. He sighs, takes the next step.

"Then there is the level of sadness that I don't know about, but which I *could* experience. This is a bigger sadness. For example, I did not know before now that I was sad about having gotten this old without being able to share feelings with someone dear to me, though this sadness makes sense to me now. I could have experienced it before, but I did not."

He drops visibly deeper into this level of sadness. "I never knew about this sadness before, but now I can feel sad about a dream I had that is not fulfilled."

Margaret interjects, "Promise me you will not forget. Promise me you will tell me about your unfulfilled dream."

Sean nods but continues in his experiment. "I may not already know about these sadnesses, but at least they are understandable. And then there is still a third level of sadness that I have discovered and would like to continue to explore in your..."

"In my..."

"In your... company. In the safety net of your awareness."

"Yes. Of course, Sean."

"This third level of sadness is bottomless. It is endless sadness, so much sadness that it can never be fathomed or understood. It is sadness beyond understanding, an archetypal sea of sadness – so vast that it is no longer personal. Sadness without cause. It permeates everyone, everywhere. Maybe it is God's sadness – His sadness, or rather, Her sadness, that everything in creation must one day die or crumble to dust. I don't know. Maybe it is Her sadness that creation is dead, that it lacks self-awareness, that we walk around asleep rather than awake in a self-re-membering state. What I notice lately is that if I am willing to enter into, and accept, the experience of this great impersonal sadness – if I am not a victim of such immense incomprehensible sadness, if I can navigate into the seas of sorrow, what I discover is that... in sorrows we are one."

"Oh, Sean..."

Trembling lips, tears coming down her cheeks, Margaret fumbles for a tissue to wipe her eyes, but then stops and takes courage to instead let them just come.

"I am melting," she says. "Like the wicked witch of the West. You have gotten water on me, and I am melting. I figured out long ago how to be a cold-hearted witch. I can analyze away every feeling. People would share their tears with me, but me cry? Oh, no! Too sophisticated. Too smart."

"Tell me about you," begs Sean.

"I can only tell you about the real me because, in your company I do not have to be the pretend strong one. You do not attack me, so I don't have to defend myself. You defend me so well that I can melt and still be together with you. I can let my hard shell finally, finally! fall away. The thing that I have always activated to interface with the world was, in reality, blocking me from interfacing with the world. It is that thing which now melts."

Margaret keeps looking into Sean's eyes and softly sobs for no reason. She is not a victim. She too is sad beyond understanding. Sean is a King, holding space for his Queen, and at the same time he sobs too, for no reason.

After some moments of sobbing together quite freely, Sean says, "This is great..."

"Mmm-hmm... I've spent my whole life hiding from this, afraid of it, and it's really quite simple and harmless."

Margaret's sadness is splatteringly interrupted by her own slurpy giggle. These two adults, world-class professionals in their field, have come together over tea and experience a maximum of enjoyment sobbing with each other.

Suddenly both are laughing outrageously, tears still streaming down their cheeks. They find delight in bouncing back and forth between hysterical laughter and abandoning themselves to being noisily insane.

Kitchen staff peer from behind a door frame not knowing what to make of the commotion. Finally, Sean and Margaret settle down a little, but there is no chance of returning to normal. That boat left the harbor a long time ago.

Margaret is the first to get it together enough to speak. "I would never have believed I could feel this way – but I'm delighted to have waited to share it with you."

"Hmmm?"

"Yes. Waiting was long, lonely, painful... and smart. It was the best thing – but it's crazy. I mean, look at me! I'm so covered with wrinkles you could iron me for weeks. Thirty years ago, I was really something to look at, pretty as a princess..." The backs of her fingers drift lightly across her cheek. "...and athletic too! But I waited and waited..."

"Just what exactly are you going on about? What were you waiting for, my dear?"

"Precisely that, Sean! That you would one day call me 'my dear,' and I would let it in. What a treasure that is. You meant it when you said that just now. You are not reading a script that someone else penned. You just looked at me and said, 'my dear' with truth in your Being. How wonderful that is! Oh, how I longed for that... Do you remember the awards ceremony in London back in '87? When we sat near each other at the banquet table?..."

"Mmmmmm." He does not remember.

"...or in '82, when we were in the same elevator at the New York Hilton? I was wearing my blue satin gown with a low-cut V-neck. I wore my lifter bra just to get your attention. It didn't work... The rest of the pageant was a blur for me."

"Hmmmmm." He's starting to get the drift of this conversation.

"I quietly moved into your part of Edinburgh three years after you came to Scotland. London was vibrant and interesting, yes, but I wanted something else. I wanted to be closer to a particular person who is inexplicably dear to me..."

Sean shakes his head in disbelief, realizing how blind, deaf and dumb he's been, amazed by the mysteries of life, and the mysteries of women. "I..."

"Sometimes I am sure we are not the captains of our own fate. Who we long to be with is rarely who fate gives us to be with. But the first time I saw you on the big screen my heart made up its own mind, independent of fate's opinion. I have had a good life, lots of fun, fine children, good work, good friends. Still, most of it has been circling in a holding pattern, waiting for this moment, when you would look me in the eyes and gently and truly say, 'my dear'."

Sean reaches his hand out across the table to take her hand, then stops, picks up his chair and carries it over to sit just next to her, but facing her. Then he cradles her wrinkled hand again in both of his, looking into her eyes. "My dear... I may never fully comprehend the depth of what you just said to me, nor what you have endured to make this moment possible for us..." He looks down, stroking her fingers. "...I may never be able to tell you what a precious gift this is for me. I can only say that you have given me something to live for when I thought my life was over..."

Sean stops talking when he realizes that he is near enough to kiss her. He moves to make it possible for her to kiss him, but she does not. Sean catches himself being mechanical in this move, stops himself, strokes her wrinkled cheek, then authentically gives her THAT kiss. But it does not last long before he is hugging her almost desperately and she is hugging him with years and years of passion, and they are both crying and laughing insanely again.

Finally Sean pulls away. "I want to share something with you."

"What? The clam chowder with sourdough bread and a Caesar salad?"

Sean smiles but does not lose his center. Instead he does the improvisational theater exercise of accepting her offer with a 'yes, and,' and making an interesting offer in return. "Yes. Perfect. And, while we are waiting for our order to arrive, I want to show you something."

"I am all yours."

Sean gets the waitress' attention – which is not difficult at this point – makes their order, then pulls a folded paper out of his jacket pocket. "I received a letter about my son yesterday."

"You never told me you had a son!"

"That is precisely the point, Margaret! I never knew until I received this letter! To be honest, I am still very suspicious." Sean pauses to navigate back from incredulous outrage to vulnerability – as a conscious experiment. He does not want to argue or discuss anything with this wonderful woman, Margaret. He only wants to share about something important to him with her. There is a huge difference. He is learning the difference.

"One night at a party..." Sean grimaces and looks down in shyness, "...many, many, years ago, you understand. In an ecstatic moment..." bracing himself for the memories, "...in a bright city of a foreign land, I had a small indiscretion. To be honest, I had forgotten about it until this letter arrived. Apparently, if Shirley is telling the truth, she bore a son from that liaison and raised him entirely herself without ever telling me, and without ever telling her son about his father! I suppose the question could be easily proved these days with a DNA test. She finally wrote me because John, my supposed son, has suddenly left the university in the middle of his last semester. Disappeared, apparently. No one seems to understand why. She was hoping I could find him wherever he is, interfere with his present situation, and talk some sense into him so he finishes his exams. I am completely vexed."

Margaret listens with extraordinary attention. "This is most unusual!"

"How so?"

"A few days ago, I received a bizarre postcard from my grandson, Edward, the son of my divorced daughter. Edward lived with his father and his new wife in America, but he spent a couple of summers with me here as a teenager. On the postcard he writes that he thinks I could understand that he exited college to do some experiments with a friend of his... someone named Jet? I have been paying his tuition..."

"Where does Edward go to school?" demands Sean.

"Salt Lake City, Utah."

"Why! That's where this 'John' goes! Let me read you the note from Shirley: *John claims that the university is no longer useful for him because the educational system promotes mainstream culture. He has discovered that parallel cultures exist, just as valid as mainstream culture and far more interesting. I fear he has gotten into drugs, or homosexuality, or maybe has been captured by some brainwashing sect.*"

"Yes, the sect thing also frightens me," says Margaret. "But the parallel culture idea makes sense, don't you think? Look at what you and I have been experimenting with. Look around. How many others do you think know about *'countenance'*? And we have only been at this for a few weeks. Imagine trying to explain what we are doing to that couple sitting over there looking at their phones instead of each other. Do you think they would understand? Do you think they would be excited and want to join us for a personal experience of sobbing and laughing? It appears as if you and I have accidentally cracked a hole in the wall of the culture we were born and raised in, and have slipped sideways into – or perhaps even started – our own parallel culture. How many other people have done the same thing? And where are they now? I would love to talk with those researchers! What are they doing? What have they documented about their explorations and discoveries? And, what? Do you think John and Edward ran off and left the university together? This is outrageous beyond belief! What are the odds of that happening? Are there bigger forces at work here? I suspect we don't truly know much about anything. I just love mysteries, don't you?"

Sean takes a deep breath, stops fiddling with his fingers, puts both hands on the table, sits up Kingly fashion, and makes time to look Margaret straight in the eyes. "The way I would accurately put it is more like this: I love you."

Space seems to warp in two directions at once during the next few seconds. Then Sean continues, "You don't have to take it personally. I mean, after learning to move at the speed of love with you, we have been consistently 'in love,' meaning 'walking in the space of love,' almost all the time. That love is a kind of universal absolute. It is unquestionable, and never-ending, and has nothing to do with you personally."

Margaret does not hurry things.

Sean continues. "But... last night, before I went to sleep, I decided that I did not want to die without having the immense pleasure of saying 'I love you' directly to your face, at least once."

Resting in elegance, attentively listening, Margret drinks from Sean's eyes. She smiles. The radiance comes not from her face, not from her personality or her mind, but rather from the archetypal feminine that shines through her. This shining Goddess basks in the atmosphere of love that Sean is holding for her, as if she never truly enjoyed the sensation of breathing before. She does not get childish. She does not undermine or belittle his offer. She stays in eye contact and lets herself be completely seen, and completely fed by his speaking and his loving and attentive regard for her. Finally she admits, "I feel glad about that."

Sean takes the next step. "To more directly answer your question, yes, I too love mysteries. What would you say if I invited you to join me for a mystery tour of America in search of two daring young men who've escaped the university system, and who may have discovered something rather interesting?"

"What I would say is, 'Yes!'"

"Excellent. I propose we start in Utah. I will arrange for air tickets and a car. Will you email me a copy of your passport so I can apply for a visa?"

"Yes."

Is three days enough for you to set your affairs in order?"

"Perfect!"

# Palm Springs, California 3

The door closes on the Palm Springs Aerial Tramway car, which lifts off the loading platform into the air. A moment later the thin steel cable carries the slowly rotating tram car far above the treeless mountainside. The glass-walled gondola trundles silently uphill towards a restaurant located 2,596 meters above sea level, on the side of Mount San Jacinto, high above the Southern California desert. This particular transport chamber is empty but for Phill Goldman and Stanley Gärtner, facing each other like a bear and a bull, sizing each other up for what is about to happen.

"Thanks for accepting my invitation to meet with me here, Phill." Stanley's handshake is warm and steady.

Phillip is silent, wary, unsure if he is to be chastised for his silly wishes, or if he is meeting a new ally. In the three months since they last met, Phillip has had doubts about being so vulnerable with Stanley. He never revealed inner wishes to another human being before, let alone to a man he pays to be his financial advisor.

Stanley says, "When we met at hole eleven of the Bighorn Golf Course, you ruined my life, Phill. You pulled the rug out from under the world I was living in. I guess I should feel grateful. You may have saved me from needing to have a heart attack before I was willing to broaden my perspectives."

Phillip only stares out the gondola windows, a breathtaking experience as they rapidly gain altitude and lose air density. The view changes as the gondola slowly spins on its axis. Phill has been through his own hell-world-rollercoaster-ride the past months. He is not interested in competing in the 'my life is harder than your life' game with Stanley. He waits for Stan to continue.

"After we talked, I was in bed with a high fever and the shakes for ten days. I knew better than to call in a doctor. I could feel my life crumbling around me. Somehow you gave me courage to endure this without complaining. I could feel how the part in me observing my physical torture and my emotional chaos was not crumbling, only becoming freer of useless burdens, dropping off pointless distractions. My second and third cars are now for sale. My house is on the market. I have already let go of our cook and our housekeeper and our gardener. Can you imagine that? I baked lasagna for the first time in my life! Zucchini lasagna, complete with bechamel sauce. I just googled the recipe. I spend time listening to my wife. My God! Martha is coming alive! I never actually met her as a person. Only a wife. Have you seen the film *Don Juan Di Marco* with Marlon Brando and Faye Dunaway and Johnny Depp? It is incredible! But this is not why I asked to meet you."

Phillip says, "Should I sit down for this?"

"No! No! Enjoy the view. We can sit at the café on top. Right now, I can only say thank you." Tears come to his eyes. "I have been a zombie for forty years, man. A fucking zombie! And I did not know it. Nobody could ever have convinced me I was a walking dead man, a stooge for the system that devours life on Earth. You brought me back to life, Phill, and I could never express enough gratitude for the risk you took being radically honest with me. You trusted me like nobody has ever trusted me before. I don't mean with your money. Money is slot machine fodder. It is nothing. No, you trusted me with your truth. And shocking it was."

Phillip is listening.

"You can put it on your CV, Phill: Zombie Slayer! I could only see the world through the investment opportunity filter. You know, 'How can I make a killing with this so that my clients speak well about me, and my career path continues to soar?' But now..." holding up his briefcase victoriously... "now I have something to show you that will knock your socks off! My team went crazy when I radically changed their search parameters. I lost two of my best portfolio generators, Phill! They could not make the leap into this new paradigm of investment. But the rest of my team came alive in astonishment! They no longer had to pretend to be a fan of zombieism! Their spirits could cut loose and fly into awareness domains I don't think many human beings have ever been without the use of drugs, especially investment consultants! We have possibilities that meet and exceed your request, Phill. They started collecting prospective opportunities before I could even get out of bed and into the office. We are rolling on new tracks because of this. More people than you can imagine are making the switch. Our byline sounds insane: How to give your money away and feel more excited about it than you have ever felt about anything!"

The gondola knocks both of the men off balance as it channels into its catcher bay so they can offload at the summit. With a hiss, the gondola doors slide open. The men step onto the glidewalk and over to solid concrete where a pathway leads outside, through noticeably thinner and chillier air, to the Peaks Restaurant. In addition to arranging for a VIP private gondola on the tram, Stanley also reserved the corner window table at the restaurant. The waiter seats them, provides menus, and asks for their drink order. Stanley says, "Water with gas."

"Perrier?" asks the waiter.

"No. Whatever soda water you have on tap is fine," says Stanley.

Phillip nods affirmation. "The same."

"It's a new world," says Stanley in the space that opens as the waiter departs. "Let me show you what we've got first. We can eat later, okay with you?"

"Go ahead," says Phillip.

Stanley pushes silverware and condiments into a corner and places his briefcase on the table in front of him, clicking open the clasps and opening the lid. He lifts out his laptop and a manila folder of printouts. With one hand, he closes the briefcase, locks it shut, and lowers it to the floor beside his chair. "Where to start?" he mumbles to himself, turning his laptop on and arranging papers.

"Stanley," says Phill. "I am beginning to calm down. I could not predict how this might go, you coming to see me after my three months of dead silence."

Stanley stops nervously fidgeting so much. It feels safe enough for him to admit his own condition. "Phill, you have no idea how close to dead you seemed. A lot was happening, mostly inside of me. But there it stayed. I didn't know what to say to you after..."

"It's not a problem, Stanley. I am beginning to get the picture."

"Now I know that not knowing what to say to you is no reason not to talk with you. I am sorry I didn't realize this before."

Phill quietly admits, "The number of people I trust to have had the conversation we had on the golf course, I could count on one finger."

"Phill, your team has been growing. My whole office is now on your team. My wife Martha is on your team. I am on your team."

Phill does not seem moved. Stanley presses forwards. "We have distinguished four categories for investment. Demolition. Bridge Building. Habitation. And a fourth category, called Wild Ideas, mostly involving some form of transformation.

"The gameplan is not simply to provide funding. It is also about providing training to prepare volunteers and staff through activist schools, such as Inside The Movement, Extinction Rebellion, the Pachamama 'Game Changer Action Training', and 350.org's Activist Training Tools."

"Demolition includes those efforts which defend the Earth, changing the rabid parts of modern culture into compost which the next culture can use as nutrients. This includes policing and enforcing the immediate protection and restoration of the natural world. Luckily this can be as simple as financing already existing efforts, such as the International Anti-Poaching Foundation at work in Zimbabwe and South Africa. It is founded and run by Damian Mander, an Iraq war vet who served as a Navy diver and special operations sniper for the Australian Defense Force. In 2009 Damien liquidated his personal lifesavings and founded IAPF. In 2017 he initiated 'Akashinga – Nature Protected by Women', a program that has grown to over one-hundred seventy trained guardians. It is a template for arming women around the world to protect nature. Their goal is to build up to one thousand trained women by 2025. They already stop poachers by force and by education on over twenty million acres of African wilderness with high rates of success. We want Damian to train other trainers and expand Akashinga to defend animals and old-growth ecosystems in South America and Asia, and also to defend the activists and defenders of the land against assassination by corporate interests.

"Another working example is the Sea Shepherd Conservation Society with their fleet of twelve armed Sea Shepherd boats, patrolling with the mission to protect and conserve the world's oceans and marine wildlife. They defend all marine wildlife, whales, dolphins, sharks and rays, fish and krill, without exception. Now I fight on the front lines with Sea Shepherd for the future of my family, my friends, and my planet. Again, our investments support their compliance operations to enforce treaties and regulations.

"Deep Green Resistance is an on-the-ground action-oriented team. The goal of DGR is to deprive the rich of their ability to steal from the poor, and to deprive the powerful of their ability to destroy the planet. They've got a handbook out titled, *Deep Green Resistance*, explaining how to start where the environmental movement leaves off. They are clear that industrial civilization is incompatible with life. Technology can't fix it, and shopping—no matter how green—won't stop it. To save Earth, we need a serious resistance movement that can bring down the industrial economy. Deep Green Resistance evaluates strategic options for resistance, from nonviolence to guerrilla warfare, and the conditions required for those options to be successful. It provides an exploration of organizational structures, recruitment, security, and target selection for both aboveground and underground actions."

Tears stream down Phillip's cheeks. Stanley respects tears now, more than ever before in his life. He continues.

"There is an organization called World Land Trust that has purchased and protects more than five million acres. For every £100 donated to the Buy an Acre program, one of their overseas partners purchases one acre of habitat and protects it in perpetuity for wildlife. Anyone in the world can buy an acre, and any organization can rely on the World Land Trust to manage the wilderness their group purchases.

"There is a legal branch in the Demolition category. We have started a corporation with the intention to simultaneously end corporate personhood – this scam that the U.S. Supreme Court legalized in 2010 – and apply the death sentence to any and all corporations harming the Earth. With tar sands, fracking, mountaintop removal, open pit mines, dumping toxins in lakes, rivers, and oceans, nuclear waste, clearly, we have many corporations to immediately compost.

"There are whole sectors we are racking our brains over. It takes something to re-skill employees of the corporations we dismantle to deliver their nonmaterial value. The paradox is finding trainers. Teachers from school or university are some of the most terrified and well-defended professions. It turns out that programmers might be best suited to help people upgrade their thoughtware enough to shift to nonmaterial economics.

"We found a new word... well, an old word from the Maori language: 'Kaitiakitanga'. It means 'guardianship'. A 'kaitiaki' is a guardian, someone called from their essential nature to care for an element of the physical or nonphysical world of this next culture we are shifting into. It is not a profession. It is a calling, the drive to take total responsibility for the wellbeing of a river, a forest, a species of fish, an adulthood initiation, a healing process for an individual or a group.

"Are you getting this Phillip? You have hired us to create a new culture, something dignified and regenerative, respectful of the planet that gave us birth. I am meeting with you now to report on our progress, and to ask for your ideas about where we should press forward next. We are already finding many allies out there, people with projects and skills far advanced from where we are. Part of our team establishes collaborative connections with resonant projects. We call it 'A Loose Affiliation of Millionaires and Billionaires', ALAMAB. What do you want us to do next?"

Phillip looks Stanley fiercely in the eyes and delivers a clear and immediate answer. "All of it."

"All of what?"

"I want all of it, Stanley. All of it! Now!"

Stanley turns a little pale.

"Bring more staff on board. Set up a new kind of university. Build out diverse forms of infrastructure for this next culture. Figure out how it goes so people can inhabit the new spaces. That is what I want. Inventing next culture is a new kind of profit that feeds me. When people and the living ecosystems of Earth benefit together, that is profit. This is the definition of 'profit' in the next culture."

Neither man moves. The space sizzles with radiance. Together they gaze out over the desert towards a far horizon.

The waiter arrives with their carbonated water. He silently places two ice-filled glasses and a large unopened bottle on their table, then exercises a rare ability to walk away without saying a word.

Phillip opens the bottle and fills both glasses.

Both men simultaneously pick up their glass as if to clink them together to make a toast.

"Wait!" says Phillip.

Stanley waits.

"Clinking glasses together is a signal that awakens alcoholic entities. I noticed this during these last months. I don't like being fed upon by entities anymore. Alcohol is a poison, a kind of demon attractor. You and I no longer need to feed demons. We have a new reality to feed. We need a new kind of toast that leaves alcohol and the demons away."

They look into each other's eyes with that question.

Phillip nods. "That is part of it. Making eye contact. This is good. Then?"

Without forethought, Stanley twists his wrist slightly so that the backs of their fingers touch instead of clinking glass. There is no sound, only the experience of human skin contact.

Phillip smiles. "This is it! The next culture toast!"

Both smile and drink from their glasses of cold sparkling water.

# Aleppo to Germany 12

Zenobia Darwish's *Beep! Book* – 1 April 2023 – Dandelion Seed Departure Day

It takes us six weeks to prepare the canoe for departure, not six months.

The most difficult obstacle is shoes. Most of us have worn sandals or flip-flops for our whole lives. While researching German culture online, Hadi reports, "To assess a person's character, the first place a German person looks is at your shoes."

Weird, isn't it? But true. To gain credibility for our mission, we needed twelve pairs of decent walking shoes, plus socks. As gruesome as it sounds, three of the pairs we obtain from cadavers, people crushed under collapsed buildings.

Those people will never walk again, but their boots? Their boots were made for walkin'!

The second most difficult obstacle is to get Dandelion Seeds to carry cash. Even though the sun won't rise for another hour and a half, Montassar does an eye-opening fear process with us here in Morning Circle. He says, "Right now, pull out your wallet. Everybody. Now, one at a time, tell us how much cash you have in your wallet. Just the bills. Not the change. Sammi, you are sitting next to me. You go first. How much cash do you carry?"

"Uh... £13,750 Syrian."

"Let's all convert our numbers to dollars for this conversation, okay? Please use the rate of 2,500 Syrian Pounds equals one U.S. dollar. This is approximately the current exchange rate. About how many dollars are you carrying, Sammi?"

"A little more than $5."

"And why do you carry that much cash in your wallet?"

"Well... I don't go shopping much. I don't buy many things."

"Sammi, you are not answering my question. You are answering the question, 'How often to you go shopping?' Or, 'How many things do you buy?' I am not asking you those questions. I am asking you a different question. I am asking, 'How do you justify it to yourself that you carry around $5 and not $2? Or $200? Or $2,000?"

"I guess I would be willing to lose $5, but not more than that."

"What you are telling me is that, whatever money you carry around in your wallet, you will lose it?"

"Well, yes. I might lose my wallet. Or someone might jump me and take my money."

"Sammi, did you ever get mugged?"

"No. I heard that some other people did. But it never happened to me."

"Did you ever lose your wallet?"

"Well, yes... one time... but I found it again. It was in the pocket of my jacket that I forgot at a friend's house. So, no, actually. I never lost my wallet. But I could lose..."

"What I have noticed," interrupts Montassar, "is that most ordinary people keep themselves in an ungenerous world of money survival, due to believing in potential problems that almost never happen, in reality. This has become a problem for us now. Here is why. As you know, Hadi and I calculated the overall budget for 12 Seeds to walk to Germany. We estimate that the journey will take 365 days of walking, times $5 per day per Seed for expenses, equals $1,825 U.S. per Seed for the journey, times 12 Seeds, comes to $21,900 for the whole journey. We added a 'fudge factor' that brought the total up to $25,000."

"What is a 'fudge factor'?" asks Habib.

"It is a contingency fund."

"What is a 'contingency fund'?" asks Habib.

"A contingency fund is the extra money you add to your estimated expenses in order to compensate for unforeseen circumstances."

"Okay. Got it. Thank you."

"We asked anyone who wanted to, to add whatever money they wished to the Seed's treasury. We received $29,000 U.S. We returned the extra $4,000 to those who gave the most. We wanted to commit to staying within our estimated budget for the year as part of our challenge.

"So here it is. $25,000 U.S., cash in my hand, in large and small bills. Will each of the 12 Seeds please step forward and take as much of this money as you are willing to carry for the rest of us on this journey..."

No one steps forward.

Montassar says, "Now would be a good time to step forward."

Still, no one moves.

Montassar looks to Farhan and says, "I win!"

Farhan looks to the sky and makes a grim face while saying, "I should learn to not bet with you..."

Rafiq says, "What do you win, Montassar?"

"Farhan has to cover my dish-washing ten times on the journey because we made a bet. Farhan was sure that people would want to carry extra cash around for the journey. I said they were too afraid because of their thoughtware."

"What thoughtware?"

"Let's keep going around the circle before I answer that question. Lylah, how much is in your wallet?"

"Nothing. I just don't carry cash around."

"Why not?"

"Actually, I use the same reasons as Sammi, even though he and I never talked about it."

"Thank you, Lylah. Rachel?"

"First," interrupts Rachel, "you tell me how much cash you carry in your wallet, Montassar."

People chuckle.

"Okay." He unzips his fanny pack, pulls out a big fat greasy wad of Syrian cash and starts counting it. People audibly gasp. We wait. After about two minutes he stops counting and holds up one of the bills. "This Syrian £5,000 bill is the largest Syrian denomination printed. One of these bills converts to about $2 U.S. I carry around 250 of these £5,000 notes." People's eyes open wide. "This amounts to about $500 U.S."

"But why?" demands Rachel.

"You are right, Rachel. It is unreasonably inconvenient for me to carry around this huge bundle of greasy cash. But I am not a victim of the Syrian economic system, or its debilitating inflation. To be me, I need economic agency. What if I want to buy a car? Or a plane ticket? Or to make a down payment on a property? What if I need to hire a trafficker to take my friends into a foreign country overnight? What if I want to print out a couple hundred *Handbooks* and leave them around in every café? Do you see what I mean? Rachel, how much are you carrying around?"

"About $80 U.S."

"And why this amount?"

"Same reason as Sammi."

"You use the same reason as Sammi, but you carry around 16 times as much cash as he does. How do you explain this? I don't think Sammi is 16 times more afraid than you are about being robbed. So what makes the difference?"

"I am wondering the same thing as we speak," says Rachel. "It is a wild question... I guess I chose to move through my life representing 16 times the financial agency as Sammi, and I am willing to face the consequences."

"Sammi," says Montassar. "If I were to ask you to tell us the total value of all your bank balances and possessions if you sold them, your net worth, in U.S. dollars, what would you say?"

"I would say, 'Go fuck yourself!'"

People laugh nervously. Montassar does not flinch. "This would be an appropriate response in a culture where a person's true worth is measured by how much money they have in their bank accounts. If the tradition in that culture is to guard your bank account total as private information, then you can wear nice clothes and pretend to be richer than you are, but your life is fake. This kind of behavior is characteristic of the capitalist patriarchal empire of modern culture. So then, Sammi, I ask you instead a different question. Which cultural context do you live in?"

"Why are you picking on me?"

"Are you claiming to be a victim and trying to make me the persecutor?"

"But you ARE persecuting me!"

"I am merely asking the person who sat on my left this question first. You have seen me do this before. Who chose to sit in this chair next to me?"

"It was the only seat left when I arrived!"

"Is this another victim story, Sammi? It was 'the only seat left'. 'Poor me'?

"No. You are right. I am not a victim. I remember thoughtlessly thinking while rushing to get to the circle that, if I am late, I will be forced to have to sit in the 'hot seat' next to Montassar."

People laugh uproariously.

Sammi's attitude shifts. He looks to the ground. "I guess I was seeking an adventure this morning, but I did not want it to be my choice in case something went wrong..."

"What do you mean by 'went wrong'?" asks Huda.

"I mean, having to look at my purpose. Discovering it is my own responsibility, that I create messes for myself."

"This is 'wrong'?" she persists.

"From my victim survival strategy, it is very wrong! If I cannot blame someone for making me uncomfortable, like going through a liquid state, then that is definitely wrong!"

People compassionately laugh and shake their heads, recognizing similar patterns of thinking in themselves.

"Montassar..." says Sammi. "I retract my accusations that you are picking on me. I am sorry... Uh, you asked me how much money I have. I have about 3000 $U.S. in total. You also asked me which cultural context I live in. To answer you honestly, I would have to say. *Comme ci comme ça*. I stay unconsciously wiggly about the answer to that question. I have not taken a stand about which culture I live in. I must be getting a gremlin payoff for this... No. I take that back. I AM getting a gremlin payoff for speaking out of one side of my mouth that I am Archan, and speaking out of the other side of my mouth defending my victimy survival strategy. Could someone please hold space for me to do an Emotional Healing Process about this right now?"

"I will hold space for your EHP," says Zaid Bakir, "but only after these Dandelion Seeds are blown away from the Dandelion Flower by the winds of evolution.

"Okay," says Sammi.

Zaid's clear boundary puts our attention on what is really happening right now. Probably all of us have been trying to avoid this moment, pretending it will happen sometime later...

Into that sobriety, Montassar speaks. "Before we leave, I need each of the 11 other Seeds to step forward and take radical responsibility for managing a handful of these dollars for one year. Israa, you are first."

She approaches Montassar and says, "Give me $3000." Montassar wordlessly counts it out into the palm of her hand.

"Next!" he says.

Lylah steps up and says, "Please give me $275." As Montassar counts bills, Lylah vulnerably says, "I have never held so much money before in my entire life."

"Next!" says Montassar.

As the ritual finishes, Morning Circle fills with an immensely sad silence. We recognize that today is the day, and now is the time.

Montassar counts the remaining cash in his hand. "I will carry the rest, for now. It is $4,750."

Then he takes a deep breath and says, "Today is what some cultures call 'April Fool's Day', 1 April 2023. To me it seems like the perfect day for us to launch something so consciously foolish as walking from Aleppo to Munich... As the American Indians say: *It is a good day to die*. At least they said it in the film *Little Big Man*."

The sun is about to rise over the eastern horizon. We twelve Palmyran 'young people' stand up and don our gear. Each of us carries a multi-purpose staff that can double as a shovel handle, a bucket-carrying yoke across the shoulders, a walking stick, a tent pole, or a weapon.

Thomas hands his phone to Zaid and asks him to take a photo of us.

I say, "*Lasst uns anfangen zu laufen. Es ist Zeit, diese Reise zu beginnen!*"

"What did she say?" shouts Mitzi, perhaps the most excited of us all.

We have been practicing German amongst us as much as we can. Israa translates. "What Zenobia said is: 'Let us start walking. It is time for this journey to begin!'"

Mitzi grabs Israa's hand to keep from sobbing and shouting out loud at the same time. Mitzi is about to walk away from three-quarters of her precious family, perhaps forever, and at the same time she walks towards her long-lost homeland, Slovakia. This paradox is too big to wrap the mind around. Who knows what will happen next? So much is wiggling, not only the Earth.

It helps me calm down when I remember that the national gameworld one commits to is not determined by the soil one stands upon.

I say, "We are the nomadic Archan nanonation of Palmyra, a mobile branch of the Learning Village, the *Young People's Syrian Diplomatic Mission to Montenegro.*"

We give last hugs and wave our 'goodbyes', then walk out of camp in our yellow jumpsuits and conical Vietnamese-style straw sunhats.

Our plan is to circle southeast, to walk around outside the broken city of Aleppo rather than going through the dangerous middle of it. We make an early start to get as far as we can today. We will see what tomorrow brings.

In only a few steps the Aleppo branch of the Learning Village fades from view behind us. The morning is cool, but clear. There is almost no wind.

We walk in silence, trying to find a cadence that matches the loads we carry and our varied natural paces.

After an hour or so, I sense a new spaciousness opening up inside of me. An unfamiliar inner silence emerges.

I wonder if it is the silence of recognizing that, although the problems and opportunities of the home Learning Village are far from being solved, they slide off my inner workbench. These problems are no longer my problems to deal with. In a very real sense, I cannot do anything more about them. We all did everything we could to replace me and the original team of torus spaceholders. The Learning Village is in good hands. I feel happy about that.

My workbench, for the moment, has become empty. That emptiness is silent as a graveyard at midnight. It feels strange. I am accustomed to calling upon so many inner and outer resources in service of our Archiarchy Invention Center, and each of those resources has a voice. Like the ancient Greek godhead, these archetypal forces of nature often argue with each other over which way I should go. I have found no ear plugs to block out their sentiments and desires.

Those resources now have nothing to solve, heal, transform, undermine, or clarify to me. I left all those problems behind in the dust.

In this unfamiliar vacuum, a whisper of a thought floats through the back of my mind. I would never have noticed it even a few hours before due to my inner world being a chaordic workplace for collaborative archetypal energies.

In front of me I see Israa and Montassar holding hands walking side by side as if having a Saturday afternoon stroll through a park. I glance over my shoulder for an instant and confirm that the sisters Aziza and Jamila walk behind me, holding hands in the same way they did the night they first walked into camp. They notice my glance and smile at me with a knowing look in their eyes.

I wonder if they just experienced the same scary thought as me. I dare not ask. What if their answer is, "Yes, we are thinking the same thing as you are Zenobia. Since the Fortune Teller witch at the market long ago was correct about Israa and Montassar finding each other again, what if she was also correct when she told us about you leading us all into a new and better future?"

Suddenly the silence is gone, and my workbench is no longer empty.

Our immediate objective is to make as much distance as possible between us and Aleppo as fast as we can while saving our cash for food or emergencies.

I notice that Habib and Rafiq walk so far ahead of us that they have no idea what is happening at the tail end of our group. Unconsciously they have abandoned the team. *What is going on for them??*

And behind us, Aziza and Jamila lag almost out of sight.

A rage breaks open inside of me so big I must let it rip. I stop walking and whistle as loud as I can between my tongue and lips. Then I start roaring like a bear, my fist shaking in the air. I walk in circles, screaming and shouting, stamping my feet, waving my staff in the air. I don't stop until everyone has come back or caught up and stands around me wondering what the hell is going on. That's when I shout, "What the hell is going on?"

No one answers.

I stand in silence glaring at each person. "I feel angry because we do not know how to walk as a team. I feel angry because I was scared that if we were attacked from the rear, half of us would be dead or raped before our two strongest guardians Rafiq and Habib even noticed. I was scared because Aziza and Jamila are dragging their feet playing passive aggressive victims not communicating their needs about us walking too fast for them to keep up. The fast ones and the slow ones are both unconsciously trying to manipulate the group to match their Box's tempo to make it most comfortable for them, and no one is saying anything to anybody about it! This tears our team to shreds! I hate it!"

"I thought our objective was to cover as much ground as possible..." says Rafiq.

"Yes. As a team!" I shout.

Jamila says, "I thought we would eventually catch up to you all when you stopped for lunch."

"I have a proposal," says Israa. "Now that we know who walks fast and who walks slow, let's put the slow ones in front and the fast ones at the rear."

"No!" shouts Lylah, stamping her foot in the dust. "I hate that idea. I have a resistance of ten! We would all be controlled by the neurosis of the slower ones! Their gremlins will gloat, knowing they force the rest of us to walk at their snail pace!"

"So you want us all to march in goose-step like the Nazis?" This from Habib.

"I have a different idea," says Thomas. Everyone quiets to listen. "I think Zenobia is right. This is a new skill for us. We have not learned how to walk as a team. It is not an easy skill to learn, more difficult than most people think. Each one's Box wants to walk at its own pace to be comfortable. The athletic ones walk fast, the thoughtful ones walk slow, each one trying to maintain their own identity. For our journey to work, each of us needs to develop an additional identity, the identity of an 'us'. This is not an identity of a 'we' such as I read about in some ecovillage writings, especially those groups using M. Scott Peck's *Community Building*. The reason Peck's strategy fails is because 'we' cannot take responsibility. If a group succeeds in creating a 'we', then no responsibility is taken. The 'us' identity I am talking about is the 'us' that walks together as a team. It is a new identity for each of us, so no one wins and no one loses. It is a winning happening game."

"But how do we do this?" asks Lylah. "How does this 'us' come into existence?"

Thomas replies, "I think for each of us there are different obstacles to overcome. I am sure there are voices in our heads, perhaps even right now, complaining about having to change. Does anyone know what I mean?"

"Yes," says Montassar. "One of my voices is yelling at you, Thomas. It demands to know why you never spoke up at camp like this?"

Thomas looks alertly around, at first afraid of being attacked by everyone. But then he sees that nothing happens. We just wait and listen. "I am actually amazed about this too," he says. "I must admit that after stepping beyond the city limits of Aleppo, something unclamped from around my throat and shoulders and fell away in the dust. I have been in Aleppo almost all of my life. I hated it the whole time. I was so frightened by all the noise, the insane competition, the sudden murder, the corruption, and the bombs. Out here in nature, away from the destroyed buildings and dangerous crowds of shouting people, Aleppo is far behind. With you all at my side, I never have to go back there." He chokes up and cannot speak anymore.

"Thank you for being with us and speaking up, Thomas," says Lylah. "It is important what you say, and useful. Please keep talking whenever you feel like it."

Thomas looks at her and nods his consent.

"I have a proposal," I say. "Since this seems to be a process facilitated by self-observation and awareness expansion, I propose that for the next days, every five to ten minutes, whoever walks at the head of our 'roadsnake' steps to the side and lets everyone pass by until you are at the rear. The next person or persons in line take over the front position. Then our team moves along our path like an Ouroboros."

"What is an Ouroboros?" asks Habib.

"It is a snake that endlessly eats its own tail," says Rafiq. "My uncle is a Sufi. He told me tales about the Ouroboros."

"But if we endlessly eat ourselves," says Habib, "there will soon be nothing left of us."

"That is the point," I say. "Then we will walk through the countryside from here to Germany as an invisible team and not as an assembly of neurotic stubborn strong-headed genius individual identities and story-infested worldviews."

"Who is the spaceholder for our walking right now?" asks Montassar.

"I guess, I mean, obviously, it has been me," I say. "I was the one who got angry enough to stop us now and question the consciousness of our context."

"Thank you for being angry and consciously using it, Zenobia," says Montassar. "It is helping us. I would like to propose that from now on, our road snake eating its own tail, is also a *Torus Technology* circular meeting. Then when we walk, we will be a 'Toroboros'!"

We all laugh, delighted by the invention space.

Montassar continues. "If there is no resistance, we would need a

Toroboros spaceholder. I propose that I am the next Toroboros spaceholder."

No resistance. Montassar strides over to me, reaches out to shake my hand as I pass the spaceholding over to him. Then he turns to everyone and says, "Let's move this Toroboros down the road! As the head of our roadsnake, I will only be eating my tail for about five minutes, then whoever is behind me is next. Snake on!"

Everyone laughs. We resettle our gear on our shoulders and move out.


It is taking us at least two days longer than we predicted to reach the Mediterranean border between Syria and Türkiye. I feel anxious and stressed by us not sticking to our plan. I sit next to Israa on a break and whisper threateningly, "We are behind schedule!"

She looks me in the eyes, her face flushed from the exercise of walking in the sun, toting her bedroll and load of food and water. She asks me in all sincerity, "Do you know what E.C.C.O. is?"

I could easily be offended by her nonlinear space navigation. Of course I know what E.C.C.O. is! How dare she ask me this? But I am able to stay unhooked and play along. "Yes."

"And do you know what radical reliance is?"

"Yes. We've been reading about radically relying on the infinite resources in the *Handbook*."

"So here we are right now. We leave behind our camp and our people in Aleppo. We walk out here in the scrubland wilderness of Syria. Now you tell me you no longer want to radically rely on E.C.C.O.?"

"Ahh... Mmm... I see where you are going with this. You mean, we are right on schedule. It is simply not *our* schedule?"

"There you go!" she says, smiling. "When woman plans, E.C.C.O. laughs. How does that feel to you?"

"I feel more relaxed now. There is even some joy about it. And yet, I also feel scared."

"You are telling me you feel joy and fear at the same time. This is excitement! You feel excited!"

"Yes..."

"Is that so bad?"

"No..."

"Anything else about us being 'behind schedule'?"

"You are an amazing person, Israa!"

She smiles back at me, knowing I would do the same for her, then gives me a hug.

We return to walking.

Out of the blue, Farhan Kader says quite loudly but to no one in particular, "The medium is the message!"

I am near enough to hear his words, but I do not understand what he is trying to say. "What are you saying?"

"We learn to walk the path by walking the path," he explains.

"Are you going nuts?" I ask him, 12% afraid while I sidle over to walk at his side.

"I must already be nuts to think of walking 3,500 kilometers. Human beings spent the last 200,000 years inventing cars, buses, trains, bicycles, roller skates, motor scooters, skateboards, airplanes, jets, rockets and donkey carts. There must be a purpose at work here that is beyond the boundaries of ordinary comprehension. Don't you think?"

"Yes, I do think.'

"But *what* do you think, Zenobia? How does it make sense to you that we plan to walk for a year?"

"Evolution occurs as we walk together," I say.

"That is what I just said!" claims Farhan. "The medium is the message."

"But what is the message?"

"The message is that the most important thing that ever happened to us in our entire lives is what is happening to us right now. It's not *how* it is happening, but *what* is happening. And what is happening now, is that we are together. We could be together at a café, a museum of science and technology, a library, a movie theater, a zoo, a beach, or huddled in a make-shift bomb shelter, it does not matter where we are together or what we are doing together. What is most ecstatic, most valuable, most important, is that we are doing it *together*. Don't you see?"

"Yes. Not only do I think, but I also see."

"But what do you see?" he demands.

"I see a man having experiential breakthroughs, littering the path behind him with his old, discarded conclusions, needless assumptions, used-up stories, a man who is dropping his baggage in a way that could never have happened had he stayed in one place living a life that he thought he understood, a life copied from countless generations of men before him who copied the life of countless generations of men before them. What I see is invention happening, refreshment, renewal, discovery, intimacy, reorganization, and I see all this with a heart full of respect and appreciation."

"But who is the message for?" Mitzi demands. There are no private conversations among the Seeds of the nomadic nanonation of Palmyra.

"Yes, Mitzi! Exactly! Thank you!" Farhan shouts. "That is my question! Who are we sending this message to?"

Habib speaks up. "There is no specific audience. I think we are demonstrating to the universe the joys of doing edgework together."

"What is edgework?" Rafiq asks.

Habib looks sideways at Rafiq. They do not ordinarily have psycho-emotional-philosophical research conversations together, until now. "Consider the fact that we don't see any other groups walking along the roads we walk. Yes, plenty of cars and trucks go by, bicycles, donkey carts, motor scooters. We might see a sheepherder now and then, or a small group of children walking to school in the towns. We are doing something which is so obvious for us to do, but so far outside of the thoughtware limitations of the local cultures. We are walking along the edge of their possible awareness, staying on the line, doing edgework experiments in ways that others can still see us."

"But Habib! What is the value of that?" demands Rafiq.

"The value is that it is uncomfortable for us. It is uncomfortable for us that others feel uncomfortable seeing us do what is inexplicably crazy to them. It is uncomfortable for us that there is no toilet for kilometers in any direction when I have to take a shit. And yet, we are fine. Well..." seeing Farhan's glare. "Okay, maybe not so fine. But we continue. We work out protocols for negotiating what we actually need together. We have a purpose. We have a gameplan. And by not letting our dead mechanical comfort zone determine our lives, we build very fine matrix, together, catching consciousness we never knew existed. We are a Learning Village, hidden in plain sight, going full steam ahead, right here, right now!"

"And together!" admits Farhan.

The conversation continues, kilometer after kilometer, day after day, until we reach the Yayladağı Border Crossing. This is the westernmost passage through the 764 kilometers long, 3 meters high, concrete border wall the Turkish government completed in 2018 by topping it with motion and thermal sensors and a meter of razor wire. It is the third longest border wall in the world, after the Great Wall in China, and the American wall between Texas and Mexico. As formidable as this sounds, the Turkish wall does not stop commerce between Syria and Türkiye. Instead, it adds interest to the negotiations. It raises black market fees. It establishes an entire economic system around trafficking refugees, gasoline, weapons, and other dark commodities in both directions.

Lylah will play a lead role in our next piece of conscious theater. While walking, we've noticed how local men's wandering eyes rest on Lylah longer than on anyone else in our team. We intend to use this to our advantage. Lylah's languorous eyes, suave gestures, and insinuating voice offer a balm of sweetness and nectar if she turns on the juice. Yes, previously it powered-up her unconscious childhood 'White Widow' survival strategy. But with experiential distinctions learned through many EHPs, she now has the option of being her true self most times, and using her seductivity if and when she chooses. Crossing an international border could be a perfect opportunity to let it fly.

At the Syrian village nearest the crossing, Rafiq buys several cartons of American-brand cigarettes. He does not smoke, yet gives no explanation for his expensive actions.

I notice how the implicit unspoken trust between us all creates a fascinating bond. It empowers a single person's intuition with the agency of support from the entire team. We pooled our cash when we began, so Rafiq actually spent my money on cigarettes! This is something inconceivable for my Box to allow. Yet I implicitly trust Rafiq, even though I would not say I know him that well. He feels our trust because he is a part of the organism. The hands trust the eyes, and the eyes trust the hands. We function together.

Then suddenly the logic behind Rafiq's actions becomes obvious. He now carries a 'peace offering' for the border guards, a gift of friendship. As we arrive at the dreary-looking gatehouse, Rafiq wordlessly but with a knowing glance, hands the cigarettes over to the first guard to approach us. Imagine how objectively boring it must be to guard a border crossing day-after-day, night-after-night. I know they are not paid much. Where are their families? I also think the job is saturated with unconscious fears. After all, you are the first person someone shoots to force their way across the border.

Rafiq steps back. Lylah steps demurely forward.

Without looking directly into the guard's eyes, Lylah says, in Arabic, *"Nahn mumtanawn wayusharifuna 'anak tatahamal eib' kawnik wsyan ealaa hadhih albawaabat almuhimati. 'Ant takhdim khayr alkathir min alnaasi. Nawadu 'an nashrah mahimatana alrasmiat 'iilaa madinat budfa fi dawlat aljabal al'aswdi. Natlub 'iidhnakum bialmurur bihuriyat eabr aljumhuriat alturkiat alnabilati."* ['We are grateful and honored that you take on the burden of being a guardian of this important portal. You serve the good of so many people. We would like to explain our official mission to the town of Budva in the country of Montenegro. We ask for your permission to pass freely through the noble republic of Türkiye.']

Then she bows her head and says, *"Nahn nadeuk lilaindimam 'iilayna litanawul alshaay walhalwiati."* ['We invite you to join us for tea and sweets.']

This uniformed man in his middle thirties, glances over to his comrades in the guardhouse, then back at Lylah. He says in English, "No need for tea and sweets, madam. Please just give me your passports, visas, and official documents."

"Of course, honorable sir," Lylah responds in English. She flashes a quick glance to his eyes, bows her head again, reaches into her shoulder bag, and with two hands, elegantly hands him a premade bundle of documents.

The guard takes them from her hands, then nods towards the guardhouse, saying, "Please invite your group to come and wait in the shade."

We move in total silence and remain standing still as statues. Thirty minutes later, our guardsman returns. He says nothing, but hands the bundle back to Lylah. She bows her head in all solemnity, saying, "May the spirits bless you and your family."

Lylah departs first and we silently follow her across the international boundary, out of Syria and into Türkiye.

Around the first bend, out of sight and beyond hearing range of the guardhouse, we fling ourselves on Lylah, spontaneously throwing her up above our heads. We joyously parade her along the road until we break down laughing and cheering in gratitude for her successful performance.

We have exited Syria! Now we can Toroboros our way along the side of the multilane highway, proceeding step by step on our long trek up the westernmost coast of Türkiye.

So many people zoom past us in their various vehicles, all looking so serious, all driving so fast, as if their life depends on them getting somewhere immediately, as if they had something very important to do, somewhere to be other than where they are. I begin to wonder if the show of 'going somewhere important' is a temporary replacement for boredom. Are they using 'going somewhere' to allot themselves some kind of meaning in their lives? At least in the eyes of others?

Four long weeks later, we spot Gallipoli in the hazy distance, indicated by the 1915 Çanakkale Bridge spanning the Dardanelles Strait. The gigantic sweeping construction is truly magnificent!

Thomas gives us statistics from his phone. "This bridge was completed only last year! It is 4.6 kilometers long, and is the second tallest suspension bridge in the world. The bridge's cables contain enough wire to circle the globe four times! It is painted in the colors of the Turkish flag. It has the longest open span between the two towers in the world, exactly 2,023 meters, to memorialize the Turkish Republic's 100th anniversary in 2023! That is insane!" This last was a side comment from Thomas. Then he continues reading to us.

"The '1915' in the name of the bridge refers to a Turkish naval victory against the British and the French during World War I. But the most amazing thing is that the bridge was built by an international team of 5,100 men to connect Asia with Europe! Cranes were shipped from Australia! Designs came from Denmark! Financing came from South Korea! But one hundred years before, more than 130,000 men from Great Britain, Ireland, Australia, New Zealand, India, Newfoundland, France, Algeria, Tunisia, West Africa, Russia, Türkiye, Germany, and Austria-Hungary killed each other during the battles of Gallipoli on the very shores this bridge is now built!"

When Thomas finishes speaking we erupt in clapping and cheering, not about the astonishing properties of the bridge, but about Thomas's enthusiastic report to us. He is finding his place in our team. We never saw him so alive. It is a joy to experience his radiance.

Then Thomas stands there, shaking his head. "What is it?" asks Laylah.

"I can't really grasp it, how time makes such a difference," says Thomas. "It is the same place but a different time. First the men do everything they can to kill each other, then the men risk their lives to build a bridge that connects them closer together."

Our response is to appreciate him more.

I am personally grateful for the bridge, even though they won't let pedestrians walk across. We must take a bus to the other side. If the bridge was not here, we would need to walk two additional weeks to Istanbul, and use the 15 Temmuz Şehitler Bridge to cross the Bosporus Strait.

This night we sleep on the cliffs overlooking the Dardanelles. I lie on the hard ground, looking at a few stars visible through scattered clouds, and wondering about men. *What is so important to men about fighting each other? It is not just the alpha-male gorillas who fight each other. It is whole armies. Why do men build huge amazing even beautiful things – like the Aleppo Citadel, a UNESCO World Heritage Site, and then blow them up? Women don't do this sort of thing. Men do.*

*Is it really true that men cannot think of something better to do with their lives than fight each other and blow things up?*

This question bothers me deeply. Because if men are unwilling to grow up, then the human race has no future.

*Gaia has evolved an elegant biological organism capable of self-reflection and conscious responsibility, able to listen to other human beings and communicate intricate subtleties. We can formulate open-ended questions and explore archetypal domains during five-body intimacy journeys. These capacities are extraordinary beyond measure, emerging through billions of years of the intelligent evolution of matter. Yet these qualities depend on matrix-building transformations after the human body has reached 18 years old. Our innate skills are only activated through rigorous authentic adulthood initiatory processes. If adulthood initiations are eliminated, our astonishing potentials remain hidden and dormant, and then gremlin subverts not only our lives, but also Gaia's great experiment.*

Such a sadness comes over me while thinking these things. Plus a wild rage. Perhaps it is the sadness and rage of Gaia. What will She do to save Herself?

More importantly, what will I do to save Gaia?

Three more day's walking and we will enter Greece... E.C.C.O. willing.

I am getting very tired of eating limpet stew...

# San Diego, California 1

"Hello, Dad."

"Your Dad died, Edith. Please call me Phillip."

Edith remembers that Phillip invited her to meet with him at a nearby café before Stanley's daughter's wedding reception would start, but she declined. The man who claimed to be her father, the man who was divorced by her mother and who emotionally left her before she was born, was always a stranger to her. Edith had developed a preference for not meeting with strangers alone in cafés. She counter-proposed arriving thirty minutes before the reception would start and meeting outside the entrance. This is where they stand.

"Hello Phillip."

"Hello Edith."

"How did my Dad die?"

Phillip looks down to his hands. "Your Dad died of a broken heart. He didn't know that he had a daughter, or a son. But when his son killed himself after doing something the son thought would make his Dad proud of him... my world unraveled."

Edith waits.

Still Phillip does not make eye contact. "I worked hard to be hard enough to be successful. My own parents were dirt poor. They always bickered about not having enough money. Mealtimes were particularly hellish. I had to learn how to get food and feed myself between meals so I did not get destroyed in dinner-table crossfire. I made a vow to be a good provider. What I never figured out was what I would be a provider for. I somehow thought a family would take care of itself if I dedicated myself to assuring they had enough money..."

"Why did you want to talk with me?"

"I read your online articles, Edith. I watch your videos. You have become someone amazing, no thanks to me. Probably you were born amazing. I don't know. I wasn't there. I missed all that..." Tears roll down his cheeks.

Edith never saw her father cry before. Actually, she never saw her father before. Now and then she saw, or heard of, a man named 'Phillip' who had the same last name as her.

"Why are you crying?"

Phillip sighs. "Thank you for asking me this question. I am still not even able to ask myself this question. But when you ask it, then I have a reason to try to answer it. Yes, I notice the tears on my face. I never had tears on my face before my heart attack. I have been meeting with Stanley Gärtner recently. He was my portfolio manager. I doubt you know him. He has become a friend to me. We worked together for years, like two shoes, each taking separate steps for the same corporate body, but never getting to know each other. I feel lucky to have a friend at all. My tears... are not for me. These feel like everybody's tears. So many opportunities are given to us to live, to connect, to reveal who we are to each other and to share what is important about living... each day we are given opportunities, almost every moment... and we don't know how to vulnerably connect. I don't know how. I never learned. What I recently discovered is that knowing how is not the key. Trying is the key. Trying to connect when I don't know how to connect is the best kind of connection I know about. But I look around and see that most people don't even try. I did not try. I just went along with the concept of being a good provider for a family. That should be illegal. It is such a disgrace to the human race, going around being disconnected. All we are is connection. Or dead. I have been dead."

Finally Phillip can look for a moment into Edith's eyes. Then he looks down again. "You have become someone who notices real things. I... wonder if you would be willing to give me a short lesson in that kind of noticing some time? I don't mean to trouble you. Neither am I being facetious. I am not your problem. I am my own problem. I feel so glad for my heart attack. I feel so angry that my own son Adler, your only sibling, died to please me. I was not worth pleasing. I could never be pleased. But he tried to please me the best way he could figure, by joining the Air Force. I hate the corporate profits made from war. I hate those directors and CEOs and CFOs and COOs and... I hate the stockholders who want value for their piddling-ass investments. It is all sick and insane, and so far away from life. Edith, you know all this. I am sorry..."

He looks down again. The tears keep coming.

"Keep going Phillip. I am still here. I can hear you. It does not have to make sense. Don't worry about that."

Phillip looks up to her eyes for a moment again, but then so many tears come he cannot see her. He roughly wipes his eyes because this is a moment not to be missed. Seeing her is such an amazing experience. A glorious adult woman stands before him, fully there.

"I feel so afraid all the time," he says. "How do you deal with your fears?"

"I have made friends with fear. My fears are so valuable."

"But how? How can I make fear valuable? How have you learned to be okay when you are scared?"

"It turns out not to be the physical sensations of fear that cause the fear to be frightening. It turns out to be the stories we attach to the sensations of fear that petrify us... I have been on some kind of path for the past months, ever since I walked out of Bach, Becker, and Benowitz in San Francisco."

Edith scans Phillip for reproach. *After all, he paid for my lawyer and economics degrees, and I just admitted tossing them into the dirt.*

There appears to be no resentment on his part. She wonders, *Is he just numb now, so he does not feel angry about me wasting his money? Or does he truly not care that I quit?*

"I truly don't care that you quit, Edith. I feel so glad that you could escape that prison track so early in your life. As you can see, it took me a lot longer than you. And I don't think of it as wasted money, either. I study your articles. I sense the precision and clarity of your thinking and your writing. That is what you learned at law school, critical thinking. You have your two feet planted on the ground and you create new structures in which your readers can think new thoughts about themselves and about the world. I so much enjoy reading what you write. I even share it with Stanley."

"Did you just read my mind, Phillip?"

"What?"

"You answered two of my questions before I even asked them out loud."

"Oh, good!" He sighs and more tears come to his eyes. "This could be a sign of connection. I have been searching for such signs. It is not an intellectual thing, connection. It is something deeper. But that makes it difficult to authenticate. I am looking for other indicators."

"If you want, I would offer you a further indicator that we are doing pretty well right now in the connection department."

"What would that be, Edith?"

Edith puts out her arms, gently steps forward, and engulfs her father in a warm and tender – and first – full body hug.

She holds him tightly for a long time before he is able to start holding her back.

Then they can sob together.

After a long while they step back, hold hands for a moment, then drop the hands because they both need to wipe their noses and eyes. More and more people arrive for the reception. They are elegantly dressed, looking so formal and prim. Edith and Phillip look at what a mess they have made of each other and smile, even chuckle about it together.

Phillip wants to make one more communication before the party starts. "Edith, I met with Stanley recently, on top of Mount San Jacinto. We have started a new kind of project together, a 'growness' rather than a business. I want to let you know about it because you might find it useful for whatever you are going to create next. We build nonmaterial infra-structure for regenerative culture. Stanley has brought together a pretty fantastic team already, and they are active! Check out their ALAMAB website if you want."

"Dad... I mean, Phillip! I figured out the name of this next culture, the name of the regenerative culture that comes after Matriarchy and Patriarchy. I worked it out when I was fasting alone in the desert, in Death

Valley, with a raven. Somehow the raven helped me think wildly enough to get it."

"What is the name of it, Edith? I need to know. Stanley and I need to know. What do we call next culture?"

"It is called 'Archiarchy'. It is the initiation-centered nonmaterial-value radical-responsibility culture that naturally emerges after Matriarchy and Patriarchy have run their course. It has no hierarchy. It works in circles of circles. The circle spaceholders are archetypally initiated adult women creatively collaborating with archetypally initiated adult men."

Phillip gawks as if Santa Claus has just dumped his whole bag of presents at Phillip's feet for the taking. "That is... so beautiful, Edith! So beautiful! And you are so beautiful! I feel so glad you were willing to meet with me today. Can we stay in touch? Here is my card. Could you be one of our project consultants? We need your clear seeing and clear speaking. Do you have a team?"

"I will do some research on your project, Phillip, and consider your offer."

Edith steps forward and gives this man Phillip a quick kiss on the cheek, then spins away and passes through the glass doors into the reception hall, making a wave and a smile back over her shoulder through the glass.

And Phillip? Well, he stands there for a long while, looking out over the seaside town of San Diego, always domed with a sky-blue sky. He is thinking that he sees an exciting new horizon, and he feels... well... everything.

Then the question he was recently speaking about with Stanley Gärtner returns to his full attention with a megaton more necessity. *What exactly are best practices for efficiently and permanently dismantling nonregenerative gameworlds?*

# San Diego, California 2

The wedding party is in full swing. A female caller with blonde curls wearing a frilly pink skirt directs dancers to move through complex connection patterns, while a four member string band plays New England style country music on a low stage.

A twenty-seven-year-old woman with elfish brown hair notices JET and Eddy push through the double-glass doors of the wedding reception hall. She never takes her eyes off them. This is Edith Goldman. She exhibits the feisty attention of a news reporter, but she's not so cynical. There is something different about these two young men, besides the limp and the briefcase. They seem energized by a nonlinear intention that refuses to meld with ordinary assumptions so rampantly obvious in this space, yet the men seem strangely battered by nature, and wear mismatched clothing with that secondhand look.

Not only that, but the skinny one has a large carrot sticking out of the rear pocket of his jeans.

JET and Eddy scan the room and instantly notice Edith noticing them. Glancing at each other wordlessly, they move towards her.

JET begins. "Hi. We are looking for Captain David Henkel. Can you help us find him?"

"What does he look like?"

Eddy says, "We don't know."

"Is he with the bride, or the groom?"

JET says, "We don't know."

"I see... You do need my help! Come with me and we can..."

A woman's scream rips through the celebratory space.

Then a huge gun blast explodes the party into chaos.

JET, Eddy and Edith hit the floor in one move.

People scream and shove towards the doors, but the room is too packed for anyone to effectively move.

The panicking crowd forms a circle around a man in black jeans with a pump-action twelve-gauge. He blows away the band's amplifier with his second shot, and one of their big speakers with his third.

Then he shoots the bracket holding the overhead chandelier. The complicated structure of glass and steel crashes to the dance floor next to him. Guests dive out of the way. No one is hurt, but people freeze at the sudden and total destruction of their wedding reception.

The destroyer is Donald Gangley. He smiles due to finally having gotten their attention.

The bride and groom stand huddled against each other not far behind JET, Eddy and Edith, lying shoulder-to-shoulder on the floor facing the assailant.

Donald points the shotgun over their heads straight at the groom's chest, screaming, "You sleazy bastard! You stole her from me! You don't deserve her! And I do, asshole! I've been with Priscilla my whole life, and I am not going to spend the rest of my life living down your insult. Priscilla's always been mine. Everybody knew it. Now I'm taking her back."

Edith whispers to JET and Eddy out of the side of her mouth, "Don't do anything. Just watch and learn."

Edith flows liquidly into a relaxed standing position facing sideways to the gunman, hands hanging down at her sides, feminine, harmless, but co-owning the space with him. She looks down at the floor and speaks in a calm, flat, but very feminine voice. "You are right. You do not deserve what happened to you."

"Shut up!" Donald screams at Edith, swiveling the gun to point at her now. Women catch their breath. Nobody dares move.

Edith still studies the floor, offering neither resistance nor aggression towards the raging bull. "I... I am trying to shut up. But I realized that you don't deserve what happened." She makes a quick sideways glance at Donald with her eyes, so he can see an earnestly vulnerable human being, then looks down again. "Your heart is too big to deserve this."

"I told you to shut up!" he screams, but his voice wavers. He shakes visibly.

"I hear you..." says Edith, head down, helplessly shaking her head at the madman through her pained internal struggle. She creates a vacuum instead of pressure. "You told me to shut up. This mouth keeps talking because I know what a good man you are. I know how much you love her and want to be with her, and how much it hurts that she left you."

"Shut up, bitch! You don't know nuthin'!" he curses, but only half-heartedly.

"It is okay to feel that rage now. You can feel it here, with us. It is right for you to come here and be angry. There is nothing wrong with what you feel. This is what makes you a good man, sir. You can feel. Your sadness is not weakness. It was the right thing to come here to share these feelings. Thank you for doing that instead of keeping them to yourself. These are hard feelings to carry all by yourself. But you don't need to anymore. We are carrying them with you."

"Oh, yeah? How're you doin' that?" he shouts accusingly.

Edith slowly raises one hand as if to ask a question at school, but she has tears rolling down her cheeks. She looks to the others and asks, "Did anyone else here ever have love stolen away from you?"

Many silent hands slowly go in the air, from both men and women.

The room fills with grief as the mood shifts from fear and rage to sadness.

Manfred, a stumpy fellow in his mid-forties can't help himself and steps toward Edith and the gunman with his hands out in a helpless gesture. "I was twenty-four," he says, voice cracked open like his heart. "Her name was Debbie. I was sure we would get married. I could already see our home and the kids we would have together." He sobs. An older couple wrap their arms around him.

A middle-aged bald man wearing glasses says, "I was earning the money to buy a house when Lisa ran off with our insurance salesman... I was ready to kill that bastard! He ruined my life!" He sobs.

Steve, a thirty-five-year-old professional sportsman speaks out. "Susan left me for a surfer bum. I was so angry! Whenever I practiced running bases, or pitching balls for hours, I practiced so she would be proud of me. I'll never get over it. It was a life that could have been, but wasn't." Sadness wracks his shoulders. Others sob with him.

Steve looks around and says, "Weddings are supposed to be happy times, but look at this... What a mess we are!" He touches Donald's shoulder with one hand and gestures towards the crowd with his other. "...we have so many feelings. Man, I feel for you. You are just like me."

Donald slowly lowers the shotgun without even knowing it. Edith moves closer to Steve and Donald to speak more intimately. JET and Eddy slowly rise and approach. Others come closer to share and see.

Edith says, "I was afraid that after he left me, I would be broken and nobody would ever want me. I was so scared that the rest of my days would be empty." While talking, Edith wraps herself into Donald's arms and receives the gun from him so naturally that it is invisible, passing it to JET behind her back as she cries into Donald's shirt.

Donald lowers his head to the top of her head. Sobs pour into Edith's hair from deep inside his chest. As Donald's grief fills the room, it is so big that others can only join him.

In a few seconds Manfred and Steve are hugging him too, and Edith slips backwards out of the group of men, letting them fill in where she was.

Slowly with dignity and elegance, Edith turns around with a twinkle of mischievousness accenting her tear-streaked smile. She faces JET and Eddy, bowing ever so slightly in gratitude, and as if this had been a perfectly executed performance. They cannot detect which is more true. Then she looks around at others, collecting their attention, and gestures toward Donald, inviting people to honor the man who exhibited true courage.

The crowd breaks out in claps, then laughter at the outcome, then finally cheers and tears of joy. The dangerous incident has become a celebratory healing process. It could have been quite the opposite...

JET, Eddy, and Edith stand side-by-side, JET with the shotgun hidden vertically behind his back, Eddy gripping the briefcase. From the side of the crowd, a tall man with short silvery hair wearing a suit and tie approaches the three a bit shakily.

"By any chance, is that my briefcase you are holding?"

"Captain Henkel, I presume?" asks JET.

"Yes. David Henkel," he announces as they shake hands in a manly way. "And you are?"

"JET."

"Eddy."

"Eddy."

The three men stare at the woman, puzzling over the two identical names.

Captain Henkel is the first to recover. "Well, JET, Eddy and Eddy, I never did care much for weddings. Too dangerous... Would you three care to join me at my office for some conversation?"

In a glance, Edith sees agreement in the two younger men. "Yes indeed," she says. "Please lead the way."

# Eugene, Oregon 10

Deep in Davis's heart, a flame has just been snuffed out.

The *Mysterium* meeting ended a while ago, yet Davis remains motionless and barely breathing in his chair, listening mindlessly to the fluorescent light moaning above them. Davis does not even remember what he says to close the space and send people home.

Sanjib sits to Davis' left, wondering to himself. *Is it shock? Despair? Unexpressed outrage? Fear?*

The immensity of what they feel together can neither be quantified nor qualified. Ever so slowly they turn their heads to look into each other's eyes. The ache is so big they are speechless.

*What in hell just happened?* thinks Davis.

They both feel the same cold wind blow through the gaping hole that has just been ripped in their hearts.

The only thing that remains, the thing that is eating at them like a buzz saw eats at a tree, is a question. It is a hard question to face, even harder to answer. *How can this be happening? What went wrong?*

Clearly, they were not consulted about whether or not what just happened would be okay with them. This Rob Dent fellow, this city slicker asshole from Los Angeles, this new guy, has just stolen the light of their life. With utter disrespect for scruples, he drags her away into the heart of darkness.

"It is her life, Davis," says Sanjib. "We are forced to respect this as her choice," not believing his own words even as he speaks them.

Something is terribly amiss, but the evidence of foul play is too sparse to be actionable. That is why they are not acting.

Since Davis says nothing, Sanjib continues. "Remington asked no one for coaching. She avoided using her inner turmoil as a doorway for an Emotional Healing Process. She blocked group intelligence from being applied for her benefit. Instead, she simply headed out the door with that creepy guy... But... if we love her... we are forced to honor her sovereignty."

This logic forces them to sit there, unable to not torture themselves in silent agony about what else they could possibly have done to avoid this outcome. Inaction is not a pleasant experience for this dynamic duo.

Davis tries to speak, but he only wants to curl up on the floor and cry in failure and loss.

He never felt depression before, that knot in the soul where one foot presses on the accelerator, and the other foot presses on the brakes.

He never before felt destroyed from full exertion against an immovable inner obstacle. He is not yet skilled enough in reflexively unmixing his emotions. He can only remain utterly distraught.

No solution presents an alternative.

Sanjib is equally troubled, but his psychological disposition towards philosophical distancing keeps him from frothing at the mouth.

Davis can't distance himself. Based on a lifetime of sensing the world through a policeman's respect for the depth of human corruption, Davis feels certain that what just happened is a glitch in the program. His immense pain finally overcomes his silence. Davis turns to Sanjib and says, "This is insane, Sanjib! Something is wrong! I know it! My police officer sixth sense is screaming off the meter! It might even turn out to be bad. And yet, none of the other Shadow Knights moved to intervene! Nobody said anything! Do they not see treachery at work here? Are they agreeing with this outcome? Are their bullshit detectors not screeching and blinking bright red like mine is? Does it not matter to them that our dear Remington may be walking straight into the devil's arms? What are Rob Dent's secret evil plans for her?" By now Davis is shouting and gesticulating towards Sanjib. "What the fuck is really going on?"

Sanjib lets Davis's radical speculations knock him in the head hard enough to leave philosophy behind. He feels relieved to come alive through following Davis into the streetwise, uncouth, truth-seeking, action-oriented no-holds-barred detective mode. "Actually," says Sanjib, "I want to arrest his ass."

"Yeah! Me too! I want to put my hands around his greasy throat and squeeze until he is blue in the face so we get the ugly truth out of him."

"Yes!" shouts Sanjib. "He is definitely a snake! I knew it all along! Why did we remain tolerant, Davis? Why have we failed her?"

This hits the core and Davis sobs out loud in rage and fierce hopelessness. Through his tears he shouts, "Because we were idiots, Sanjib! Because we thought these were no longer cowboy days. Because we tried to be respectful and civilized. Because we thought Remington was smart enough to avoid being naïvely hypnotized and dragged off by this schmuck. Fuck this shit!"

Sanjib is both frightened and turned on. "What do we do, then?"

"The way I see it, we either go insane, chase them down, corner their asses, and throw them both in jail until the fog in their heads clears out and the truth is revealed."

"But there is no law that lets us do this, Davis! We ourselves would be arrested for false arrest!"

"Yes," sighs Davis. "You are right, Sanjib. We are fucked."

They sit together in the gap, the same gap that exists between one space and another space all throughout the *Great Labyrinth of Spaces*.

What is in that gap? Nothing. What is possible in that gap? Everything.

"Or..." continues Davis with a hint of intelligence returning to his strategy making, "we act as if nothing unusual happened. We trust Remington implicitly. And we play into the hand that E.C.C.O. has just dealt us. God! I hate this idea!"

Both of them sigh at the same time.

Sanjib nods ambiguously.

A further hour goes by without additional options appearing. Their butts get sore sitting on the folding metal chairs. They silently stand up, turn out the lights, shut the door, climb the stairs, go through the secret passageway, exit *Horsehead Bar* into the night, and go home.

Lyrics from a radio song courses through Davis's mind and heart over and over as he lies down to sleep that night:

*You only need the light when it's burning low.*
*You only miss the sun when it starts to snow.*
*You only know you love her when you let her go.*
*You let her go.*

He sighs and shakes his head in extremely confusing disappointment.

*What a bleak condition to find myself in, alone at the bottom of a cold dark well.*

*But I didn't let her go!* he complains to the Universe.
*She was taken.*


Week after week Sanjib and Davis hold space for *Shadow Knights of the Mysterium* meetings. Remington's name is rarely mentioned. No one hears anything from her. Another theme takes precedence. Depaving downtown Eugene.

Everyone remembers that depaving was one of the projects distilled out of Remington's anger that night when Patricia navigated them all through the *Push Hands* exercise. As an unspoken way of honoring Remington, this project becomes the focal point for their next joint effort.

Carol Washington says, "I got the impression this morning that we should call it a 'Human Interaction Zone' rather than a 'Human Intimacy Zone'. I think this new name would trigger less fear-based reactivity. Any resistance? One! Two! Three!

No resistance.

"And I got the impression," says Francis Atkins, "that if we involve a wide variety of circles throughout Ecotopia, we would multiplex the target."

"What do you mean?" asks Anton Pirelli.

"Mixing up communications and preparations with diverse groups equates to confusing a warplane's radar by throwing out 'chaff', those reflective aluminum-coated glass fibers that scatter radar readings. Then police would not know who their main target is and could only make weak and ineffective countermeasures against us."

"No! No! I understand 'chaff'," says Anton. "I used chaff quite effectively as a child against my mother by releasing cockroaches or mice in the kitchen when I was naughty. I took the pressure off me by giving her more exotic problems. Then I could step in and capture the snake or bat or frogs, and shift from villain to hero in a few minutes. No, I understand chaff. I am asking about 'Ecotopia'. What is that?"

"Ah!" we all laugh, imagining what a hellion Anton must have been as a child. "*Ecotopia* is the title of a 1975 book by Ernest Callenbach, in which Northern California, Oregon, and Washington all secede from the United States of America to become the first environmentalist nation on Earth. The book was so inspiring that Callenbach wrote a prequel in 1981, called *Ecotopia Emerging*. Certain Eugene residents sometimes refer to ourselves as Ecotopians!"

The *Shadow Knights* choose a date in mid-summer, but intentionally keep it secret to be less easily thwarted.

"I remember a formula for creating 3Cells," says Carol, "each with specific tasks. I learned it from Robert Heinlein's book, *The Moon Is A Harsh Mistress*. I estimate that the most daunting challenge for us will be to communicate with the thousands of active organizations in Ecotopia without alerting authorities to our plans."

"It sounds like we should immediately send 3Cells out on missions to privately meet with other 3Cell spaceholders and work out non-electronic communications channels," suggests Patricia. "If they are personally informed about the date and place, and they plan to participate, they can silently show up. And if they won't be there, they could make chaff announcements to create a hullabaloo and confuse the corporate resistance."

Francis says, "I feel so glad about what we are creating. I have lived in Eugene my whole life, and so often felt angry that the town has been built around cars and corporate franchises, trying to make spending money in shops more important than bringing more love into the world by being together. I think it is high time this new chapter begins."

Weeks zoom by, charged with increasing energy from exciting collaborations. A loose but efficient meshwork quickly weaves itself together between beyondtoxics.org, cgcan.org, gorgefriends.org, ecochallenge.org, humanaccessproject.com, olcv.org, oregon2.sierra-club.org/many-rivers, solveoregon.org, freecascadia.org, cascwild.org, cascadianfood.net, cascadiawild.org, yourcascadia.org, to name but a few. Several groups decide to simultaneously gather for an equivalent action in their own town center. Why not? One local group decides to initiate this as an annual rally called: YEAH! meaning: *Yearly Eugene Action Hack!*

Friday morning, Sanjib receives a text message on his burner: *Bring your sidekick. 1313. Noon today. We need to talk.*

Davis chuckles when Sanjib shows him the message. "I was expecting this sooner."

As usual, Davis does not act as nervous as Sanjib feels.

It still seems improper to enter the Eugene Police Station out of uniform. At least this time they know where room 1313 is.

Maria-Santos gives them a vague half-smile as they push open the double glass doors. Davis can't tell if she is disgusted by their ongoing troublemaking, or jealous of their freedom from office politics. In either case, Sanjib says, "Good morning, Maria-Santos. Nice to see you again!" She does not respond verbally.

As before, 1313 is empty but for Sergeant Brinks and Chief Stafford sitting behind the cold hard table, waiting for them. The two young plainclothes cops enter silently and sit down. The seriousness of recent events has sobered them somehow. No frivolous smart-alecky comments nervously spew from their lips. Instead of resistance or argumentation, both Sanjib and Davis offer patient compassion towards their supposed superiors. Neither of them envies either one of them, with regards to what's coming.

Brinks cuts to the chase. "Spill the beans, boys! What's cooking?"

Stafford looks on with concern. How can he do his job if he does not know what to prepare for? He fears making mistakes when the stakes are this high.

Davis and Sanjib look at each other to see who will try to answer. They have pre-strategized nothing.

Davis says, "We heard that there is some kind of action going to take place this summer. It sounds earnest and well organized. It seems to cover three states, and momentum seems to be steadily growing."

"We need more intel," states Chief Stafford with a shade of desperation undertoning his voice due to a question his mind chants fruitlessly, *Why does this have to happen on my shift?*

Both Davis and Sanjib commiserate, but neither panics.

"What do you need, Chief?" asks Sanjib vulnerably. "How can we help you? What is your current intel reporting to you?"

"Don't fuck with us!" shouts Brinks threateningly, like a rat cornered by a cat that is playing with his food. At least it sounds like he is shouting in this bare-walled basement room.

Sanjib neither cowers nor comments. Same with Davis.

The four of them are in a draw.

Chief Stafford finally speaks, meaning that Sanjib and Davis won the waiting game.

He says, with artificial sweetener in his voice, "Thank you for asking, Sanjib. Here is what we need from you: Who? What? When? How? Why? And Where? We need their approach and getaway plans. Fortifications? Armaments? And funders? What can you give us?"

"They are organized into isolated 3Cells, Sergeant," says Sanjib. "I am sorry. We know almost nothing. I am pretty sure they are all self-funded, out of pocket."

Davis steps in. "We can estimate that several hundred organizations could potentially participate, but they are scattered through an unknown number of towns from San Francisco to Seattle."

Sergeant Brinks dares to ask, "What is a 'three cell'?"

"I heard that the idea comes from a Science Fiction novel about people on the moon. There is a website explaining what a 3Cell is, if you feel like checking it out: 3cell.mystrikingly.com. It is all copyleft and public domain," says Davis.

"What do they want, Hatcher?" asks Brinks forlornly. "Why are they doing this? I don't understand it. Eugene is such a fine town."

"I agree with you, Sarge," says Davis. "Eugene is a truly fine town. You should remember that it was your idea to send us in there. We are trying to do our best. What I figure is that these people have a deep concern about the rapidly approaching collapse of modern infrastructure due to instabilities caused by climate change, economic imbalances, peak everything, war in multiple simultaneous theaters, seriously questionable national leadership, and the lack of preparedness for any of this. What I have heard most is a phrase that I think I am beginning to understand: 'thoughtware upgrade.'"

"What the hell is that?" growls Stafford.

"Well, sir..." begins Sanjib, wondering if he should continue. The deciding factor is his thought, *He asked. So whatever happens is not my fault.* Sanjib proceeds. "It can be quite painful to learn what the term 'thoughtware' means, sir. I can't tell you how many times I barfed trying to understand it, and how many bottles of aspirin I used up trying to decrease the pain of my transformational headaches each time one of my basic pieces of thoughtware disintegrated between my brain cells and there was nothing I could do to put it back together the old way, because I already understood the new way."

"Sanjib!" exclaims Davis worriedly. "You didn't tell me you were getting headaches!"

"No. I didn't tell anyone, Davis. But haven't you noticed that I think differently now?"

"Yes, I have noticed! I just assumed you were good at thoughtware upgrading and didn't experience any side effects."

"Well, I wouldn't say I am good at it, but I do enjoy the benefits from it. Did I tell you that Patricia asked me out for a date last week?"

"No way! Really! She's great! I like her! You are a lucky man, Sanjib! Did you..."

"Shut up you two!" commands Stafford. "Really! You two are driving me crazy!" He stands abruptly up from his chair and paces around the room. "You know? Get out of here! If you can twist their arms and extract anything relevant, I order you to get it to us immediately. I can't believe we are paying you to become brainwashed perverted cult members. Now *you* are giving *me* a headache!"

"Yes, sir!" says Davis.

"Sorry, sir!" says Sanjib sympathetically, reaching into his pocket. "Do you want an aspirin?"

"Just get out!" shouts Chief Stafford.

Up the stairs at ground level, Davis pauses in front of Maria-Santos' desk. "Do you need anything from us, Maria-Santos?"

"I liked you better when you were one of us," she says with a betrayed tone in her voice.

Davis sighs. "The world is far larger and more interesting than I once thought it was. Nothing could have prepared me to perceive how different the new culture is that is emerging around the world. I would never have believed someone if they told me it is leaving us flatlanders behind in the dust. But it is."

Maria-Santos's face changes to apprehensive disgust.

"I don't think my father would have liked it either..." says Davis, frankly.

"I liked your father better than you."

"I truly appreciate your radical honesty, Maria-Santos. Perhaps we could make it office policy to practice radical relating skills..."

"Just get out of here..."

"Funny," says Sanjib commenting to Davis. "Those are the exact words that Chief Stafford just yelled at us down in 1313!"

Davis turns to Maria-Santos. "If I find anything that might entertain you, I will send it by. They are publishing a new book..."

"Out!" she shouts, half rising out of her chair and pointing at the door. But Davis sees the hint of a grin on her face and relaxes. He has always trusted Maria-Santos' practical nature and would not want to lose her as an ally.

Davis and Sanjib glance intently at each other, stand tall side-by-side in front of Maria-Santos' desk, and salute her in unison. Without snickering, they perform a perfect simultaneous 'about face' then march through the twin glass doors and down the granite steps.

The fresh air smells particularly sweet after their meeting in the cellar with the two dungeon masters.

"I have this niggling question," admits Sanjib as they stroll towards Davis's plain clothes car.

"Yeah. Me too," admits Davis. "Whose side are we on?"

"I read a quote once... Actually, I read it more than once... from a book by David Gerrold called: *A Rage For Revenge*. In the book, the main character realizes something incredible. He says, "There is no enemy. We are all martyrs to evolution.""

"Meaning," continues Davis, thinking out loud, "that we are working on the side of evolution... Hmmm... Makes sense... Makes me feel a little less scared of standing on such shaky ground. After all, evolution is a bright principle, right? That's what Remington explained to us. 'A facet of consciousness', she said. 'An archetypal force of nature', she said... God..." Davis studies the sidewalk as they keep walking.

"What?" asks Sanjib.

"I wish... I wish I could hear her voice again. See her face again, expressing so gracefully things I never imagined could be expressed... I miss her so much, Sanjib..."

Sanjib stays silent, walking along with his friend. He can think of nothing to do that would help Davis. He tells himself, *There is nothing wrong with Davis. It is appropriate for him to feel the sadness and frustration he feels now. It is healthy, far healthier than keeping it locked up inside of his heart. That much aliveness bottled up could kill a man. Look what happened to Davis's father...*

Once they are seated in their sedan, shoulder straps fastened, of course... Sanjib says, "I wish you could see her again, too, Davis. Truly. Somehow, I think it will happen. I think you will eventually be together. That is such a happy thought for me."

"Thanks, Sanjib," says Davis, nodding his head. "It is a happy thought for me too."

Davis sighs, releases the parking brake, and starts the drive back towards their apartment. "Want to watch *Wonder Woman* with me again tonight? I'll make some butter-honey popcorn if you want."

"Definitely, yes," says Sanjib, thinking to himself: *Waiting is.*

It's a quote from another one of his newly favorite Science Fiction books.

# Possibilica, Florianópolis 4

At four a.m. the Brazilian branch of the Possibilica Think Tank is still electrified with its purpose: to deepen the context of next culture – Archiarchy – through establishing seed crystals upon which the rest of the world could map itself, if it should ever wish to.

"It cannot work like this!" claims Grace. "It never has, and it never will. We are not getting anywhere. The algorithm is wrong, Alan! It's completely wrong!" She paces furiously through the office.

Alan knows Grace well enough to know that this is not the moment to say anything. He cradles his cold, nearly empty coffee mug close to his cheek, partly for protection from Grace's unexpected outburst, and partly because he likes the smell of cold coffee. A moment passes before Alan recognizes that the next line in the script is his. "Say more about that, Grace."

"This is a think tank! We are supposed to provide edgeworkers – even edgeworkers at the United Nations – with solutions to complex problems. People are failing because we are failing. We are failing because we think we know what we are thinking about."

"Keep going..."

"We make assumptions about a future scenario which then plays out however it plays out – right? But it plays out very differently from how we predict. Our assumptions are wrong. They don't match reality. We put our best guesses into the AI as a framework within which the computer should propose workable solutions. But these solutions only get us deeper into the problems."

"It's GIGO," Alan says.

"GIGO?" Grace's unusually smooth forehead creases in puzzlement wrinkles.

"An ancient programmer's swear word. It stands for *Garbage In. Garbage Out...* If you give a computer inaccurate facts, it will give you useless answers."

"Yes," says Grace. "It's that simple. But if we act as if the output is true because the computer says so, we are being idiots."

"Yes. I agree with you. Can you please specify which of our assumptions you've identified as wrong?"

"All of them!"

Startled, Alan objects. "C'mon, Grace! We've been using these same assumptions for years! You can't say they are wrong!"

"Yes. I can," says Grace. "Stop fooling yourself! Look where we are! The corporations still determine policy in their favor. We can't even get Monsanto out of Europe because now Bayer owns Monsanto, and half the EU representatives are owned by Bayer. Even if we could stop killing the bees with RoundUp glyphosates, this would not put glaciers back onto Greenland or stop the Gulf Stream from melting the Gakkel Ridge and flowing into the Siberian Sea to melt hundreds of gigatons of methane clathrates. Millions of refugees are marching towards Europe from Africa, Syria, even Bangladesh. Desertification, flooding, fires, famine... There is no way to handle all this using our assumptions."

Grace slumps into her rolling chair, mumbling, "Things are coming apart."

"What assumptions are we talking about, exactly?"

"We assumed that we know something."

"What?" exclaims Alan.

"The truth is, we know nothing. We use patterns from the past as models for extrapolating into the future, but the future has unexpected ingredients. The future is orthogonal from the past and the present. It must be."

"What do you mean?"

"Orthogonal." Grace holds her left hand palm down in front of her and then forces the pointer finger of her right hand up through the fingers of her left hand. "My flat hand represents our usual set of assumptions. But what happens in each new 'now' arrives from an unexpected dimension. The future comes at us through right-angled surprises that pop out of the least expected corners. This is the 'third force' that impacts any asymmetrical physical body which is in motion. You know all this. We have been making the assumption that the future will be like the past, and it will not. We have been ignoring transformational influences of the third force!"

"You are saying that the new algorithm should assume we don't know?" asks Alan incredulously.

"Yes! Exactly! Not knowing is the truth. God! Finally we can say the truth! We don't know!"

"How is this valuable, Grace?"

"It is valuable because it is true."

"But how can not knowing be valuable?"

"Look at it like this." Grace grabs a stumpy piece of chalk and draws a rough blob on the blackboard. "Here is what we know. We know it because we have noticed it. We have worked with it before, and it produces useful results for us. And over here..." drawing another blob, "is what could be known but we haven't noticed it yet. We haven't worked out what it is. Which is bigger?"

"Well, I hope the not yet known is bigger."

"Yes," says Grace. "Let's not be arrogant today." She uses the side of her hand to erase and draw again the blob of 'the known', only much smaller. "This huge area is what could be known but we don't know it yet. But then look at this. There is a gap between the two of them. There is a gap between what we know and what we don't know yet, but could know. What is in this gap?"

"Nothing," says Alan.

"Exactly. Nothing is in the gap. So then, what is possible in the gap?"

"Hmm...? What is possible in the gap? Well... Everything is possible in the gap."

"Yes! Exactly!" shouts Grace.

"Exactly what?"

"Alan, what is bigger? Nothing? Or everything?"

"What do you mean?"

"It is a simple question, Alan. You've studied the Universe your whole life. You are a journeyer in both the domain of nothing and the domain of everything. Which is bigger? Nothing? Or Everything?"

"Nothing is bigger." Alan looks at Grace, puzzled at her insistent precisions, yet admiring what she just got him to think about.

"Why, Alan? Why is nothing bigger than everything?"

"Well, because... where else would the everything fit? The nothing must be bigger than everything so that everything has a place to be."

"I agree. So here is why this distinction is important. We are in dire need of new possibilities. New possibilities are available in the nothingness of the gap. We can use the nothing as a resource that is even bigger than the known and the unknown, combined, because everything is possible in the nothingness!"

"You are saying we re-write the algorithm to use the assumption that we do not know, and also that there are infinite resources in the gap between the known and what could be known?" Alan is excited to the point of bursting. "How is this workable?"

"It is workable because it is real. It is true. We actually do not know what we do not know yet. We cannot know that. At the same time, we are responsible for making decisions and plans even though we cannot know the emerging circumstances. This is radically true."

"You are suggesting that we build an algorithm for taking responsibility for decisions based on the assumption that we know nothing?"

"Yes. Yes! Not just responsibility. We have an unreasonable degree of responsibility... unconditional responsibility... for the truth that we do not know what is in the gap or what is in the future."

"What's so great about that?" asks Alan. "Aren't we being an even bigger idiot that way? Taking unfounded responsibility for not knowing... we will still be blamed if it does not work out! We will not even be able to defend ourselves by blaming faulty reasons because we won't be standing on reasons!"

"Radical responsibility is not about avoiding punishment, Alan! Results will come whether we take responsibility or not. The difference is that, through taking unreasonable responsibility, we will learn faster. If I am responsible, then I am at source. I get to choose. I create what I create, and I can fine-tune how it goes in real-time, rather than shielding myself behind faulty assumptions and 'really good' reasons. We can go orthogonally into a new future in any moment, if we do not have to ongoingly defend ourselves by clinging to the past and the reasonable. Do you see this? It's an entirely new algorithm!"

"This is not the first time we have had this conversation, Grace. A month ago, you were steaming along in similar latitudes. Believe it or not, I took you seriously back then. I cracked sideways out of our current structure, cached voids of indeterminacy as a resource, and unleashed a new algorithm using an infinite architecture."

"Meaning?"

"Meaning I defined chaos in ten functions: Infinity over infinity. Infinity minus infinity. Zero over zero. Zero times infinity. Zero to the power of zero. Infinity to the power of zero. Infinity to the power of infinity. One to the power of infinity. And non-randomized chaos. I estimated... or, guessed... that this would be the closest I could get to incorporating the uninhibited analytical mind into our algorithm. I cut it loose about two weeks ago. I was waiting to see some results before I told you. You have been so busy lately..."

"I suppose you have not read the latest sheet..."

"What's going on?"

"There are indications that a new offensive is active. The German team detected it by following vacuums rather than peaks. Suddenly exchanges about drone swarmfare went silent, and a software firm named GlobeScan hinted at a possible contract with the CIA. It would be insanely dangerous, but due to CIA being backed against a wall, those at the top could be making a suicide pact."

"What is threatening them?"

"The fact that the hundreds of thousands of low-level workers being imported into the U.S.A. as refugees from Iraq and from south of the U.S. border cannot ramp up their personal agency fast enough to replace the mid-to-high-level techs and managers who are quitting their U.S. citizenship and leaving the country. Russia, U.S.A., and China are all facing this same collapse at the same time! Can you imagine they continue regarding each other as enemies? The middle class is exiting. People have woken up about the psychopathic corruption in government and corporate policies. The Germans learned that those in office intend to stop their population leaks by filling the escape hatches with the corpses of edgeworkers. Smells like 1939 to me."

Alan hesitates a moment, then stands stiffly up from his console. "I'll go start another pot of coffee... It is time to do the Heebie-Jeebies dance to improve our microcirculation..."

"I must be the Heebie-Jeebies!" The new voice is female, bright, and young, with an indistinct Asian accent. It comes from the thin, tall, dark-haired, dark-skinned girl wearing a white blouse and dark-brown pleated skirt cut to her knees who struts in like she already knows the floorplan and the two Possibilicans. Quizzical glances from Grace and Alan indicate they have never seen her before.

"And you are?" Alan asks semi-accusingly, frozen in his tracks towards the coffee machine, worried that a stranger could so casually walk through the security of their think tank space.

"Areesha Khan."

"What are you doing here, Areesha?"

"I'm hired," says Areesha with an unassuming but unquestionable certainty.

"Who hired you?" asks Alan, his heart beating faster by the second.

"She said you would ask me this. She told me to tell you: 'The Algorithm hired me'. She said you would understand."

A curious smile flicks across her thin lips. She is not absolutely confident of these circumstances, yet still sets forth her answers.

"I understand your words", says Alan, "but I do not understand what you mean with the word 'she'?"

"She calls herself 'Jaine'. Jaine the Algorithm. I didn't totally get it myself, but I want the job."

"What is the job?" asks Grace with an atypical ungraceful tone of voice.

"She said you would hand me an earpiece and that all I need to do is repeat what she tells me to say to you, and then do what she asks me to do, if I want to."

"Ahhh!" says Grace, reaching into the DHL envelope lying open on her desk. "That would explain these!" She pulls out a phone and a set of earbuds. "These arrived this morning. But there are two more pairs of earbuds."

Areesha inserts the buds into her ears and gets the phone going, entering a PIN she already knows. A moment later she speaks. "Jaine says... I mean, I say... Shuichi and Quinn just picked up ID badges at the front desk and will be here in a sec."

Sure enough, a fit-looking Japanese man of about twenty-eight and an indeterminate-age-or-gender person with short, blue-tinted hair wearing faded denim overalls push open the door and enter the lab.

Grace glares at Alan, who offers her no rational comment at the moment.

Areesha steps briskly over to Grace's desk, pulls the remaining two headsets out of the DHL envelope, and hands them to the newcomers, who wordlessly jack themselves into Jaine's scripting.

"Hi," says the Japanese. "My name is Shuichi Nakajima." He smiles and makes a slight bow from the hips to the room in general.

"And I am Quinn," says the transgender, somehow stubborn and embarrassed at the same time.

The three young newcomers look to each other, then move to stand close together, almost touching shoulders. They stare for a silent moment at Grace and Alan.

Quinn says, "Thanks for the headsets. We'll be checking in later."

"Hold on!" blurts Alan. "How is this working out? We haven't scanned your records for security. We don't know if you have the proper skills, or thoughtware, or even a valid visa! Have you ever been to *Expand The Box* training?"

Shuichi nods with calm understanding. "Jaine has certified all of that for you."

Grace cuts in. "How are you supposed to get paid? We don't have funding to cover any more salaries."

"We are not getting paid in money," says Quinn. "Money is too imaginary. We are getting paid in nonlinear possibility. If we have possibility, why would we need money?"

Areesha glances up sideways, clearly listening to something from Jaine. Then she looks into Alan's eyes and speaks her line. "Do you need anything else from us right now, Alan? The message now arriving in your Telegram accounts gives you our CVs and contact info. We have work to do. We would like to get started. We will set up in the meeting room and use that as our office."

First Alan's and then Grace's phones signal incoming messages. The team of three grin to each other, spin on their heels, and file into the sound-proof meeting room, shutting the door behind them. They already know where the light switch is, and the cabinet with the spare laptops.

Alan's mouth remains nonfunctional.

Grace smiles mysteriously and says, "Well then, Dr. Friedman. It seems as if your new algorithm found the bottle and uncorked the Genie!"

"I didn't detect... There was no evidence..."

"The nothingness suddenly seems to be generating abundant new results for us."

"I never met Jaine..."

"Our kick-ass team seems to finally be forming up." Grace sighs in multiple dimensions at the same time, then sits down to read her new messages.

# Aleppo to Germany 13

Zenobia Darwish's *Beep! Book* – 21 September 2023

I decided to write this entry in the third person. This way I hope to more fully experience what happened today.

The *Young People's Syrian Diplomatic Mission to Montenegro* walks along a dirt road. This particular dirt road is somewhere in South-eastern Europe, probably Greece, winding northwestwardly alongside olive and citrus orchards, wheat fields, and vineyards. It is the fall equinox. Nothing is known to be happening except walking. If you have ever walked a great distance on an empty dirt road on a fall day, you know exactly how this sounds, smells, looks, and feels. In other words, it is perfect.

Most of the walkers stride silently alone, or in groups of three. In approximately the middle of the walkers, two people stride side-by-side, although not necessarily with each other.

That may, indeed, be the question at hand.

The two walkers are Zenobia Darwish, and Farhan Kader.

Until this moment they have been walking rather silently.

'Out of the blue', as it is sometimes said, Farhan begins to hum a melodious tune almost silently to himself.

Eventually Zenobia notices that he is humming something. She has never heard Farhan hum or whistle anything before now, so Zenobia is just ever so slightly suspicious that something might be occurring for Farhan. However, out of respect for him as a fellow human being and a fellow traveler on this path, she does not ask about it. She continues walking along, as she was before.

Farhan's humming grows a little louder. Perhaps he was previously afraid of being reprimanded for humming out loud while everyone else is walking along this dirt road in silence. Perhaps his humming might disturb one of the other walkers as they are thinking to themselves about important things. It might even possibly disturb Zenobia.

But nobody says anything against his humming. Nobody reacts. Courageously, Farhan casts away his inhibitions for just about fifteen bars and lets some words sing through him, words that match the melody he has been humming.

The words go something like this:
>     *I wanna know what love is.*
>     *I want you to show me.*
>     *I wanna feel what love is.*
>     *I know you can show me.*

No one seems to mind.

Actually, Farhan himself does not even seem to mind. This rather surprises him, but not enough to stop him. Nonetheless, he stops anyway.

After a short while, Zenobia says, "Hmmm... Why did you stop singing, Farhan?"

He says, "Can I tell you something?"

Zenobia glances sideways at him, quickly, to see if he is joking, but he is not joking, so she says, "It seems to me as if you can indeed tell me something, Mr. Farhan Kader, because you are already telling me something."

Farhan nods his understanding of her clarification. Then he takes a risk to reveal something further. "It seems like I have been feeling lost my whole life..."

They walk along the dirt road, silently keeping to their current pace.

Eventually, Zenobia says, "You are telling me that you just discovered a fifth feeling, Farhan, a fifth feeling after mad, sad, glad, and scared. You name this fifth feeling as 'feeling lost'."

"No! No! I am telling you that being able to walk along this road next to you, not knowing where we are, or where we will all sleep tonight, or what we will eat for dinner, or how we will get enough money, or what the reason is for my existence... all those things that most people might decide that, if they don't have them, then they are lost... not having all those things does not create in me a sense of being lost that outweighs the kind of 'found' feeling I sense right now while walking next to you along this road."

"So, you are telling me that you really like to have the opportunity to walk next to me like this because you feel a new fifth feeling called 'feeling found'."

"No. No. It is not about having an opportunity. I don't have anything. I may be walking next to you, but I do not have this 'walking'. I do not have anything related to walking with you. The opportunity of walking next to you does not give me anything that I do not already have."

"So you are in a mystical experience that you call 'feeling found' and you associate this experience of 'feeling found' with walking next to me."

"No. I don't think it is a mystical experience. I hope it is not a mystical experience because I would like to have this experience again and again. I do feel found, but that is only a name I apply to this experience I am having while walking next to you. I like the experience I am having while I walk next to you."

"So, you really just like walking with me."

"No. My experience is not about the physical activity of walking at all. I did not lose my sense of being lost – which I have had essentially my whole life – simply because I am walking along next to you. It is not about doing anything in particular with you, or about having anything at all from you."

"So, you are telling me that you lose the sense of being lost when you are walking next to someone."

"No. It is not about the walking, and it is not about walking with 'someone', not just anyone. I notice that I feel less lost, in particular, while I am walking with *you*, next to *you*, alongside of *you*. Walking where *you* are walking."

"So, you lose your sense of being lost when you are going where I am going."

"No. It does not matter where you are going. We could be going anywhere. I don't even know where we are going! I am walking next to you on this road and it is not about the walking, or the road, or where we are going, or any of that. It is entirely about you."

"So, due to me, somehow, even if we are out here walking anywhere, and you do not even know where, and it does not really relate to the activity of walking itself, you have lost the sense of being lost that you have had most of your life. And you like that."

"Hmmm... we might be starting to get somewhere with this..."

"So, you are telling me that you think it is about getting somewhere with this."

"No! No! It is not about getting somewhere at all! It is about you. I don't care if we actually get anywhere! We could be walking nowhere in particular, and it would still matter to me."

"So, if something matters to you, then you lose a sense of being lost that you have had most of your life, and because walking next to me matters to you then you have a sense of being found."

"No! It is not about whether or not walking with you *matters* to me, or whether or not we actually *get* somewhere. It is about you being here with me, when you could be anywhere else on Earth, with anyone else, doing something else."

"So, it is not about getting somewhere with me."

Farhan stares hard at Zenobia for a stunned moment. "Am I getting somewhere with you?"

"You are telling me that you think there might be somewhere to get with me."

"No! Well... Yes. Well... Phew! I don't know! Is there somewhere to get with you?"

"You are asking me to tell you if I think there is somewhere to get with me."

"Yes."

"You are telling me that you want to get somewhere with me."

"Yes. Well... maybe... Yes!"

"You are telling me you want to get somewhere with me other than here."

"No! I want to be here with you, Zenobia, no matter where the here is."

"You are telling me that you have the wish, the desire, to, at some point in time, be here with me."

"No! I am telling you that I feel glad about being here and now with you, here and now, right now, and that it does something to me that I have long wished would happen to me with someone. Although since it never happened to me before with anyone, I never had the idea that this – or something like this – could ever happen to me with anyone at all, ever."

"You are saying that being with me here and now does something to you here and now that you like here and now."

"Yes! I am saying exactly that. What kind of conversation is this anyway?"

Zenobia walks steadily on and lets the silence take over for a moment. Then she says, "I heard you sing just a short while ago, and in your singing, you said that you want to feel what love is, and also that you want me to show you."

"Uh... Well, yes. You are right! I did say exactly those things."

"Well, right here and right now, I am showing you what love is. This is love. This is how love feels."

The silence that ensues as they continue walking along the dirt road, side-by-side, in the early fall of Southeastern Europe, has a quality of richness that radiates an energy, a vibrational substance, that some people have come to call 'Yellow Stuff'.

There isn't anything else in the entire Universe quite like Yellow Stuff.

Gaia notices that there is Yellow Stuff happening on the Greek road.

She feels glad.

She thinks to Herself, *Hmmm... Someone is finally beginning to get it.*

# Hollywood, California 6

Morgan Freeman stands again. "I did not invite you to Stage 13 to be lectured. There is not much left for me to say. It is time for me to ask each of you a question and for each of you to answer that question, personally, and at full risk. This is the juice needed to start this torus rolling.

"The question is simple, and yet of ultimate concern to those out there who know and love us from our work.

"The question is this: What is the real purpose of your life? What are you a stand for? What doorway do you hold open for others? What possibility do you represent?

"If this is your last stand… if we have circled our wagons to face reality, to call forth the best from each other, to challenge our friends out there to individually cavitate and inhabit new space as human beings on Earth, what will you say?

"I invite you to do what you truly wanted to do for all these years. I invite you, here and now, to cavitate a new space that anyone in the world can inhabit with you."

Judy Dench does not hesitate one instant. She stands up with her head high and her feet solidly planted on Earth, regally claps her hands once loudly together while saying, "I *cavitate* new culture space in which women are not owned by men, and neither vice versa. I cavitate the culture that comes after Matriarchy and Patriarchy. I cavitate the cultural context in which women and men creatively collaborate to serve the Earth as initiated adults."

This action is too sincere for any need of applause. Assembled in this torus sits a world-class team of cavitators taking their last stand together. It will either work, or it won't. This is not entertainment. This is revolution.

Robert Redford stands and claps his hands once loudly together while saying, "I *cavitate* new space in which corporations have no power to own things or make decisions, in which hierarchical structures cannot exist because their design permits them being hijacked by psychopathic personalities. I cavitate new space in which local and global authorities corroborate to build locally sourced communities of radically responsible adults."

Angelina Jolie stands and claps her hands once loudly together while saying, "I *cavitate* new culture space in which it is implicitly understood that each and every person is a refugee, and each and every person is a global citizen, because what goes around, comes around – including pollution, and respect – and the purpose of the Universe is evolution, so nothing lasts long enough to make war about because everything is being replaced through discovering something more relevant."

Halle Berry stands and claps her hands once loudly together while saying, "I *cavitate* new culture space in which the value is to bring out each person's gifts, even if these gifts have never been named before, because consciousness is rich with treasures, and humans are still learning to become humane, and I know that buried in the young people are designs we can follow to live together as respectable caretakers of this precious planet if the young people could be encouraged to speak."

Bill Murray stands and claps his hands once loudly together while saying, "I *cavitate* new culture space in which you can invite yourself to any party you like, where it is insane to pretend to adopt the wounded understanding of others as your own, and where you laugh your head off for no reason whatsoever... because life is short and, well, what the hell! Why not? And yes... you are right... that was a reason."

George Clooney stands and claps his hands once loudly together while saying, "I *cavitate* new culture space constructed out of infrastructure and systems that incentivize generosity, discovery, inclusion, and sharing nonmaterial treasures for the purpose of bringing Earth immediately back into balance as a real garden of paradise."

Sandra Bullock stands and claps her hands once loudly together while saying, "I *cavitate* new culture space in which no one bows down to external authority of any variety, and in which bullying, reactivity, corruption, and abuse – including abuse of Earth and her diverse life forms – signals the necessity for adulthood initiations and emotional healing processes that bring forth unprecedented clarity and possibility."

Stephen Fry stands and claps his hands once loudly together while saying, "I *cavitate* new culture space in which radical respect and practical sanity are the guiding forces that empower local authority around the world to declare dynamic and evolving interdependence."

Ken Watanabe stands and claps his hands once loudly together while saying, "I *cavitate* new culture space in which there is no enemy because human beings regard themselves and each other as citizens of Earth – regardless of which country or religion your parents are, regardless of how little or how much title or wealth you have, regardless of who you love and who you become."

Julia Roberts stands and claps her hands once loudly together while saying, "I *cavitate* new culture space which leaves behind the crippling results of Patriarchy, and gives birth to humans caring so much about life that our actions are qualified by their consequences in nature. Bringing our hearts, minds, bodies, and souls together with Gaia's we ecstatically expand the potentials for more love happening."

Michael Caine stands and claps his hands once loudly together while saying, "I *cavitate* new culture space in which there is more respect for things being simple than there is for things being jazzed up, because love is actually quite simple, and it is more jazzy to experience an abundance of love than it is to sit around alone but very complex. I cavitate new culture space..." He claps his hands together again... "in which archetypal principles such as integrity, accountability, clarity, respect, and love prevail, and where a woman or a man grows up through their service to these archetypal principles."

Brad Pitt stands and claps his hands once loudly together while saying, "I *cavitate* new culture space in which aliveness is not limited by what you have been taught, by what you believe, by where you grew up, by what you own, by who you know, or by what you think of yourself, but instead aliveness promotes trying new things, making mistakes, learning, shifting, picking yourself immediately up, and trying the next adventure."

Sigourney Weaver stands and claps her hands once loudly together while saying, "I *cavitate* new culture space in which people learn to cavitate new culture spaces where people cocreate an ongoing abundance of new options to choose from for life as a human being nurturing the living ecosystems of Earth.

Morgan Freeman stands and claps his hands once loudly together (yes, it is a miracle...) while saying, "I *cavitate* new space like this one – where people practice cavitating new space, glorious space, dignified space, diverse space, rich with wildly new options to choose from, freely shared because the sources of new possibility are themselves endless."

Matt Damon stands and claps his hands once loudly together while saying, "I *cavitate* new culture space that values revealing what is really going on and why, both personally and professionally so that gremlin behavior is transformed, and human beings have a chance to heal wounds and connect our spirits to create villages full of love."

Jackie Chan stands and claps his hands once loudly together while saying, "I *cavitate* new culture space in which children's beneficial potentials are supported to evolve as the highest value so that Gaia can give birth to the loving spirit of consciousness."

Harrison Ford stands and claps his hands once loudly together while saying, "I *cavitate* new culture space..." That lopsided grin of his takes over, revealing his deep abiding fear of looking silly. He starts again with greater commitment. "I *cavitate* new culture space where account-ability creates a foundation for relating far beyond the ordinary, because life is precious, and thrives in delicate balance, and caring for balances assures that life rather than economics thrives."

Graham Green stands and claps his hands once loudly together while saying, "I *cavitate* new culture space in which culture is valued as a creative playground for exchanging the best practices human beings discover about how to live together while regenerating the full vibrant health of our Great Mother Earth."

Leonardo di Caprio stands and claps his hands once loudly together while saying, "I *cavitate* new culture space in which the political and economic reality is the locally-sourced ecologically-referenced reality that emerges from unleashing holistic human creativity rather than human desperation."

Tommy Lee Jones stands and claps his hands once loudly together while saying, "I *cavitate* new culture space in which hierarchy is eradicated as a deadly memetic virus, and is replaced by small local-authority circles helping each other develop and exchange their nonmaterial value."

Helen Mirren stands and claps her hands once loudly together while saying, "I *cavitate* new culture space that supports each person developing excellent new talents that no one has ever heard of before, and which values each person using them to create a new future for humanity where joy and love prevail."

Keanu Reeves stands and claps his hands once loudly together while saying, "I *cavitate* new culture space in which relating well with others is the highest economic objective, and where living simply connects us with each other and with the Earth."

Jane Fonda stands and claps her hands once loudly together while saying, "I *cavitate* new culture space in which beliefs are recognized as fantasy worlds so that sources of inequality, bigotry, superiority, and inferiority dissolve and we naturally meet each other eye-to-eye, say what we want, make creative proposals so that the idea of being a victim finds no soil to grow in and we celebrate the abundance of our possibilities."

James Earl Jones stands and claps his hands once loudly together while saying, "I *cavitate* new culture space in which human beings practice joyfully seeing through illusions even if we generate them ourselves, and we discover a less flamboyant but far greater abundance of love as personally engaging entertainment."

Dustin Hoffman stands and claps his hands once loudly together while saying, "I *cavitate* new culture space in which both human and ecological diversity is valued far more than conformity, so that rather than competing against each other for limited material resources, we rejoice in collaborative discovery, and we become the resources ourselves, so that even little people are big."

Meryl Streep stands and claps her hands once loudly together while saying, "I *cavitate* new culture space in which love is the warp and creative collaboration is the weft, and together we weave new tapestries of connection and joy around the whole world, thriving in a nonmaterial economics that has never been seen before on Earth."

In the shift-of-epoch torus that has assembled in Warner Brothers non-existent – or at least, secret – Stage 13, not one cheek remains dry.

# San Diego, California 3

Captain Henkel's workplace is modern and artsy, the way you would expect any successful entrepreneur's office to look. The Captain lays the heavy metallic briefcase gently on the teakwood boardroom table, then speaks to JET. "You can place that blunderbuss over there on the cabinet, sir. Please verify that the safety is on. I will deal with it later." Then he fiddles with the combination locks until the latches pop open. The others take seats around the table in silent expectation.

JET can't stand the suspense. "What is a 'Temple of Evolution', anyway?"

While gingerly lifting the briefcase lid, Captain Henkel says, "I was hoping someone would ask."

He smiles in preoccupied anticipation as he carefully lifts out, unwraps, and assembles sections of a glass and metal architectural model. It looks like a crystal palace from a fairyland story.

"Think of your normal village. What are the two most prominent buildings in town?"

Edith answers. "The town hall..."

JET follows, "The church."

"And what do these familiar edifices represent?" asks Captain Henkel.

Eddy states, "Powerful bureaucracies of the capitalist patriarchal empire."

"Committed resistance to change," JET adds.

Edith tacks on, "Stability, tradition, law and order..."

"What I am assembling here is a model for the third most eminent edifice in town." Henkel smiles, rather proudly while absentmindedly adjusting his glasses. "The Temple of Evolution represents that portion of society interested in transformation.

"Mind you, I do not mean 'learning'. Places of learning already exist in the form of schools and universities. But parroting what other people have already discovered is not so useful these days. I can't even keep up with operating the apps on my damn phone."

Henkel stands up and begins pacing as he continues. "Life is not about learning anymore. Life is about creating. Creating is a more ecstatic experience, and the skillset for creating is not taught in school.

"My aim is to establish an institution that supports taking responsibility for creating your own life in connection with Earth and the circle of people in your village. It is a life based on living into a future that you create, rather than duplicating a past that others have previously created.

"The first Temple of Evolution will be built right here, in San Diego! Isn't this beautiful?" His palms open generously as he gestures proudly at the fully assembled model.

Indeed, the spires and curves are elegantly proportioned. He plugs an electric cord into a socket mounted flat in the meeting table so that tiny sparkling spotlights shine throughout the little palace, as if the Temple itself would become a radiant sun, showering the village in light.

"Can you imagine how this will look at night? Workshops, trainings, presentations from researchers of every field, experimenting beyond the limits of ordinary research. These would be centers of...?"

Captain Henkel fades into uncertain silence and glances at the young people. He senses that he has lost his audience.

Eddy unceremoniously pushes his chair back from the table, stomps over to the window, and shoves his fists into the front pockets of his jeans. He is ready to burst into tears or grief or shouts of rage. His mind goes a zillion miles an hour while he glares out at the darkening sky over the solid straight horizon of the Pacific.

JET is fascinated at Henkel's marvelous plans, yet leans back in his chair with his arms crossed over his chest, shaking his head in pity.

Edith leans forwards towards the model with her elbows on the table, eyes glazed over, and mouth pressed against her clasped fingers. She appears to be thinking thoughts in another world, no longer listening in this one.

Captain Henkel does not know what to make of these young people. He is accustomed to presenting his ideas to professional investors, bankers, and building regulation boards who respect his inspiring stories and ask logical questions rather than thinking independently and feeling authentically. These three are not at all captured by his vision.

He clears his throat shakily and continues. "What are you thinking?"

"It's far too slow, Captain Henkel," says JET with wistful grief in his voice. "Too late actually."

"It's too vulnerable for attack," says Edith with anger.

"We have a better idea." All eyes turn to Eddy, expecting him to explain. But he is smarter than this. "Let JET and, uh, 'Eddy' talk first, or you won't see the genius in what I have to say." He carefully observes the Captain, still frozen in mid-presentation across the table. Eddy's look is not aggressive. He is flooded with compassion from looking backwards at the old vision with clarity from a new vision.

Henkel sees he is outnumbered and decides to take the strange risk of allowing others to define what he is doing. He swallows his pride, ceases explaining, sits back in his chair.

JET struggles painfully up out of his chair and limps towards

Captain Henkel's flip chart board. "May I?" he asks respectfully.

Henkel nods. JET picks up four broad-tipped Edding 800 marking pens and draws a graph at the top half of the paper. "There is an inescapable intersection rapidly approaching all of humanity." He uses the blue pen to write in big bold capital letters across the top of the flipchart page: MAP OF THE INTERSECTION. He swiftly draws a blue box around this title. "The intersection is between the increasing consumption of a growing population of human beings on Earth, shown by this sharply increasing red curve, and this rapidly decreasing quantity of nonrenewable resources that remain on Earth, shown by this sharply decreasing green curve. The point where these two curves intersect is where the naked apes start fighting over who gets to consume the remaining resources. It is approximately where we are right now." He circles the intersection point with the black pen, and labels it with an arrow.

JET pauses to check that Henkel understands, then continues. "There is another inescapable intersection approaching... and we cannot very well guess when it might arrive..." He draws a second graph just below the first one. "It may make the first intersection completely irrelevant. This second intersection is when the increasingly detrimental impact of technological byproducts on our environment exceeds the ability of Earth to support civilization as we know it. Then human population crashes, this blue line sharply curving down to the right. This second intersection point shows that modern culture toxins will suddenly tilt scales that we don't even know exist. The result would be plagues, genetic breakdown, infertility, massive storms, ice age, desertification, uncooled nuclear power plants detonating, or other horrors beyond our capacity to respond to in any civilized way.

"In this tiny window of awareness that we have right now, these intersection points are not yet unavoidable. But Captain Henkel, a Temple of Evolution is too slow."

Edith lifts her head off her fists and takes over. "If leaders and decision makers learn that there is no enemy on planet Earth, that we are all simply martyrs in Mother Nature's evolutionary experiments, we could creatively collaborate to minimize the impact of the intersections. But so far, humans have proven to be too stubborn. We are not collaborating, still competing instead. Mother nature is not dependent on us to successfully evolve. We are only one of Her experiments. But I would like Her to succeed in the human experiment. It matters to me."

JET adds, "Anyway, I think that we can better estimate the date of the first intersection. The second intersection could come after, but it could also come before. I don't think we can guess. I have not found any model sophisticated enough to predict it. Hindsight will prove more accurate, but too late to avoid the bitter consequences..."

"Think of it this way," Edith says. "Building one Temple of Evolution would cost, say, two million? Three million? With planning, zoning, staffing and so on, it would take at least, say, two years to build and activate? Constructing one Temple of Evolution in each of the top hundred cities in the U.S. could easily take, say, fifty years at the earliest? Such a date is well past at least one of these intersection points, and would serve only a small fraction of the world's population. Your idea to produce an institution that promotes evolution is too slow, Captain Henkel. Far too slow."

There is a particularly disheartening mood of silence in the meeting room.

But Edith refuses to cease the devastation. "And such Temples would be too vulnerable to attack. A physical property is such an easy target." She still sits at the table, but her hands begin to dance freestyle to her words.

"When you formalize a radical idea, it becomes an institution which then defends itself against radical ideas. If your institution actually starts to take market share away from politics or religion, the psychopaths will attack you, and they attack viciously. If you own land or a building, they can tax you into bankruptcy or zone you out of existence. Dogma can be declared heretical. Reputation can be ruined. Reactionary mobs or paid undercover CIA agents can throw rocks through the glass, or blow the place up. If you have identifiable leaders at the Temple, they can be manipulated with threats, slandered into exile, or blackmailed into recanting. They may get kidnapped or assassinated. For example, the U.S. Dollar is far over-valued in reality. Yet it remains the world currency standard. Why is that? Because if you decide to switch currency and sell your oil on the world market, say, in Yuan, or Rubles, even Euros, the highly militarized U.S.A. finds some reason to put you on its enemy list. To succeed in these conditions, any kind of Temple of Evolution needs to be virtual, decentralized, highly reproducible without relying on leaders, physical property, or a system of hierarchical regulation..."

"Like a weed," says Eddy. "Me and JET were discussing weeds during our bus trip from Arizona. Think of tumbleweeds, or even better, dandelions. A gust of wind blows dandelion fluff for miles around. Each piece of fluff carries a tiny seed that can grow a new dandelion plant wherever it lands, even in those tiny cracks in the sidewalk. Each plant produces thousands more fluff bits that float every which way, each fluff carrying a new seed. Even if you pull ninety percent of a dandelion's roots out, the ten percent remaining will quickly grow a whole new plant. Dandelion flowers are colorful and edible, nutritious actually, and highly resistant to extreme soil and weather conditions. As a result, dandelions are spreading everywhere. We need a revolution with these qualities. We need dandelion evolutionaries."

Eddy pauses, looking at each person individually, then goes on. "Evolution is a force of nature, a bright principle. Evolution is accessible to every human being like radio waves are accessible to every radio. But the radio only perceives a signal if the radio is turned on and the antenna is tuned in. The 'better idea' we propose is to use your money and intelligence to design and produce evolutionary weeds that can blow seeds all over the planet across every country and into every culture through conferences and the internet, so it can grow in the hearts and minds of many people all over the world simultaneously, starting now. This evolution weed will apply a force like wind and water. It causes steady change and cannot be resisted because there is nothing to resist: it has no legal substance. It is a nonmaterial construct – a beneficial idea. And if you think about it, you realize that ideas... are bulletproof!

Edith adds, "This evolutionary wave has no institutional power, wealth, territory, or control. It is the archetypal potential of personal transformation, adulthood initiations, and healing. The Dandelion Revolution is a catalytic meeting format where diverse intelligences can intersect and cross-pollinate each other.

"Instead of building one building, let us reveal a new form of creative evolutionary entertainment, a matrix-building adventure. We explain how coordinators can sponsor a conference that is more exciting than movies, because the interactions are real! Each person gets to learn to create adventurous possibilities for themselves, rather than sitting there eating popcorn and having to leave when someone else turns the lights on..."

JET blurts out, "Transformation is the most entertaining experience on Earth! High level fun at simultaneous Intersection ConfFests!"

Eddy continues, "... paid for by attendees at a cheap price, who also create the presentations themselves, and then go out and organize the next Intersection ConFests."

Edith picks up the baton. "The Intersection ConFest would become a tradition of world culture, a tradition that converges diversity instead of excluding it! Intersection ConFest is a celebration, like New Years Eve or a birthday party, where people come together to play and create and celebrate – but broadened to an international standard. They could happen anywhere, anytime. This would be the model that people around the world could imitate to produce results about what matters most to them. And we can do this now. There is nothing to build, and nothing in the way."

Captain Henkel pauses, obviously feeling something, but just what he feels is not clear. He says, "Uh... I see..."

No one is convinced. They don't get that he really gets it.

"I see," he repeats, with more emphasis this time.

He pauses, looking at them strangely. Finally, he can stand it no longer. "Don't you get it? IC... Intersection ConFest. International Culture. I. C.! I see!"

They all burst out laughing hysterically for a long time.

Captain Henkel goes on. "My steering committee will think I've run them onto a reef. I've wrecked the ship before it is even off the drawing boards... You just 'made my day' and ruined my day... all on the same day! Who are you guys, anyway? Who sent you?"

JET has to follow his fears. "You understood what we said, right?

We were doing Possibility Speaking. We learned how to do this by practicing exercises from that *Handbook*. We learned how to say things without having to know about them first. We also don't know who this here woman is," pointing at Edith. "We don't know who you are. You don't know who any of us is. Mr. Singer doesn't know us even though he sent us to you. We did not strategize any of this before meeting with you here. We are extemporizing as we go along because we are *ex-tempore* – 'outside of time'. I am asking you a serious question based on a large degree of disbelief. Do you get what we just said? Do you believe us?"

"No! I don't believe you!" Henkel says with a twinkle in his eye. "What you are inventing here in my office is not a matter of belief. Instead, you take me to the center of my true-life wish. You create the possibility that I can get what I have wanted my whole life, before I die. I do not want to be a landlord. I do not want to be a program manager. I want to catalyze real change in the whole damn world! And I have never dared admit that to myself, or anyone else, before this second."

Captain Henkel takes a deep breath. "Listen, we have a lot of work to do. I don't imagine any of you have had dinner? There's a fine little Chinese take-out guy who delivers to this office. What are you doing tonight? Can you stick around the rest of the weekend and play? Could you present our new plans Monday morning at our board meeting?"

"Does your Chinese take-out guy make tofu and vegetable Chow Fun?" asks Edith enthusiastically.

"Yes. The best."

"Then I'm in!" she says.

Simultaneously JET and Eddy say, "Me too!"

Everyone laughs and jumps into action, moving tables and chairs around, making phone calls, pouring water to drink, firing up computers.

The teapot begins to whistle.

# Aleppo to Germany 14

Zenobia Darwish's *Beep! Book* – 5 October 2023

The Toroboros technique of group walking weaves us together profoundly. As the forward one or two walkers step aside to allow new leads to take over, a tradition has emerged. We naturally feel gratitude towards those walkers who venture to go first. They face surprise hardships such as snakes, spider webs, barking dogs, and oncoming traffic. They must decide which is the best route to take. Yet they easefully relinquish their hero status to the next person in line every five or ten minutes.

It develops that as the ex-'leaders' stand by, waiting to arrive at the tail end of the snake, each person who strides past them communicates their appreciation in a unique way. One person might make skin-to-skin contact with a 'high five' hand slap or knuckle bump, even with dirty sweaty hands. Others make silent eye contact with a nod or a smile. Some salute in an unusual way, or clack walking sticks together. This accomplishes a half-second two-way five-body check-in scanning that asks, "How are you?" Each person makes some facial expression in response to reveal in radical honesty their internal or external condition in that moment. It is not about doing anything to alleviate their condition in that moment. It is about connecting, commiserating... co-liberating what is for each person through conscious mutual recognition.

The result is that during one hour of Toroboros walking, everyone has personally made a five-body check-in with everyone else!

We roll our team down the road as one organism, healing ourselves as we go. Anything unusual we work out during rest stops. I feel so glad and empowered by our wholeness. I am free to concern myself with other things.

But the Toroboros can also be surprising.

For example, early one morning, just after crossing from Greece into Albania at the Dogana e Kapshticës Border Station on E86, Lylah and Montassar walk together at the head of our Toroboros. A medium-size flatbed truck crosses the border after us. The vehicle is driven by a woman with a man sitting next to her. The woman pulls over next to Lylah, rolls down her window, leans out and asks Lylah a question. No one understands a word she says, but the body language is obvious. "Want a ride? If so, just hop on the back."

Lylah smiles and bows, then steps up onto the rear bumper, climbs over the flatbed gate, and drops her load and herself into the truck.

As the head of our Toroboros, Lylah simply decides that the roadsnake should get into the truck.

We all, of course, snake along and follow.

Then the man opens his door, steps back to us, hands over a full unlabeled green bottle of red wine, and smiles from ear to ear. We mumble our thanks. He hops back into the cab, and the woman throws the truck into gear. In a dusty cloud and a roar, we trundle on down the road.

Hadi inspects the wine. She works the cork out, sniffs the contents, takes a swig, looks around at us with shining eyes and says, "It is medicinal. Full of antioxidants. Have a sip. Doctor's orders." She passes the bottle to Israa who takes a big swallow.

If there was ever an unspoken rule at camp, it is: "We are alcohol-free and smoke-free." By the time the bottle comes back to Hadi's hands, it is empty. She tilts the bottle fully upside down over her tongue and gathers the last few drops. "Well done!" she exclaims happily. "We are practicing reverse hospitality, being good guests. Does anyone know any truck-riding songs we can sing together?"

Rafiq and Habib immediately burst forth with the most ribald song I ever heard:

> *There was a young lady from the mountains of Stan.*
> *Her body was lean, and she longed for a man.*
> *Sheepherder, carpenter, anyone'll do.*
> *If she didn't have one soon, we knew what she'd do.*
>
> *This lady would yodel*
> *So loud and so plain*
> *The mountains would shake,*
> *And the clouds they would rain.*
>
> *From landslides and floods*
> *We'd all come to her bed.*
> *We'd line up to please her*
> *Or all end up dead!*
>
> *This famous young lady was the legend of our land.*
> *We cheer on her suitors, "Do the best that you can!"*
> *So if you are walking, and the weather turns to bad,*
> *Just find the young lady and make her feel glad!*
>
> *This lady would yodel*
> *So loud and so plain...*

Both the song and the ride go on for hours. It's a boisterous bodacious day bouncing along the road in the flatbed truck.

Agnese and Roan (the truck drivers) are on their way to Barcelona. They kindly allow us to buy them lunch at a truck stop café. It is steak dinners for all. Our bodies chew those steaks down before we even notice they are gone. I am sure we needed the protein after so much walking.

In one unexpected day, we traverse the entire 360 kilometers south to north through Albania and are dropped off near downtown Budva! It feels like a miracle! As we wave goodbye, we realize that we are already at our destination. We have leaped ahead in time and eliminated an entire month of arduous walking!

E.C.C.O. certainly works in mysterious ways.


I stand on the side of the road, stretching my legs and rubbing my butt from the long ride. Then I say, "I have a proposal. According to my careful calculations, we have transplanted nearly 4000 trees to new locations. By now we can dig up and carry over 50 baby trees at one time, and can plant about 50 trees per day, depending on soil conditions and water availability. Our best day was 72 trees! We have also picked up 353 bags of garbage from the roadsides. Plus! We have walked about 2,309 kilometers and are over halfway to Munich!"

The Palmyrans cannot restrain cheering and crying and hugging each other in congratulations.

After that I keep speaking. "We would have been three weeks late for our 13 October appointment in Budva, but with the truck ride, we are now more than one week early. These are all valuable successes. But it is now 5 October 2023. Winter quickly approaches. It is becoming too cold for us to keep living outdoors. It is my opinion that we need a Palmyra Nanonation website, some media presence, photographs, articles, talks uploaded... We need to send out a Palmyra nanonation newsletter to feed our circle of friends and share the treasures we are discovering. My proposal is this: Let's rent an apartment here in Budva and expand our global field of connections for the winter. My fear tells me we will need more online legitimacy to make our entrance into Germany. Is everyone clear about my proposal?"

Silent affirmation.

"Any resistance? One. Two. Three!"

Zero.

We decide to stay at the cheapest Budva hostel we can find for a few days until our meeting with the town council. After that, we will find something more affordable, perhaps just across the border in Croatia. Meanwhile, we have a few days to inspect the current Budva infrastructure and design some proposals for shifting it into Archiarchy.

It is impossible to describe how luxuriously exquisite it feels to take a warm shower with soap all over my body, to wash my hair, to wash my clothes and underwear in a machine, getting totally clean. It seems too incredibly extravagant.

I cannot fall asleep in my bed with its soft cotton sheets and big fluffy pillow. I tilt the bed over sideways and drop the thin mattress to the wooden floor. I cover myself with my ratty stinking familiar road blanket. I can't sleep until after I ask the others and open the windows to get some real air into this room. I miss seeing the stars, and checking how the moon is doing. It is strange to eat something other than sandwiches.

Budva is one of the oldest towns on the Adriatic sea, first inhabited 2,500 years ago. We decided to split up into pairs to reconnoiter the pre-Roman Budva streets and examine the town's social and technical infrastructure. I am partnered with Lylah. After we take a few steps together I stop and say, "Lylah, I feel glad to be partnered with you this morning. You have a vast capacity for listening as a vacuum. I have a request. There are some big serpents churning around inside of me – and I don't mean my intestines. What I most need now is a spaceholder willing to hold a vast space and just listen to me. Are you willing to do that, to be a workbench where I can spit out everything and look at the whole mess without you trying to give me any solutions?"

"Yes, Zenobia. I have been waiting for you to take courage to do this. I could see the storm. I am here for you and listening for as long as it takes."

That was enough love to crack the dam inside of me wide open. Here are Lylah's notes from my journey.

I admit that even after Israa pep-talked me about radically relying on the collaborative support of archetypal forces, I was still secretly worrying that we were 'late', especially for our appointment with the townhall in Budva.

I question why my worldview seems oriented towards the big picture, the overview. I incessantly evaluate our overall condition. What is our current impact compared to what we desire to cause? How is the reciprocal energy flowing between us and the Universe? It makes me wonder if I somehow have been secretly handed down memetic constructs from the original Zenobia.

The problem is that she was a leader. Her only role model was to copy or improvise policies so that the society around her – which stretched for thousands of kilometers – conformed to her benevolent but independent vision.

For Zenobia the First, Rome was a despicable mess, not worth either conforming to or collaborating with. Their neurotic collapsing bureaucracy could only be a burden blocking what she saw was possible for a fabulous queendom.

True, Zenobia should probably not have had a coin minted with her image bragging to Rome about conquering Egypt. That was even more arrogance than I can stand in.

But why do I care about causing our expedition to succeed? Most of the team hiking together engages a high degree of responsible participation. But I have a different necessity, and different impulses. I need to cause the expedition to occur. I am part of the causal body for this expedition.

Yes, E.C.C.O. and bright principles, and my archetypal lineage are at work here, but my attention has a particular altitude of surveyance that others do not. I feel alone in this, but probably no less alone than Farhan feels in his technical causality, or Hadi feels in her health and medical causality, or Aziza, Rafiq and Habib feel in their guardianship causality. Mine is the overall causality orientation, as would Zenobia the First's have also been.

But she was a leader, and I am not a 'leader'. I am a spaceholder.

What matters to me? EVERYTHING.

Who else cares about everything in the nomadic nanonation of Palmyra?

Who else cares about everything for the ecological balances on planet Earth?

When I say 'cares about', I don't mean 'worries about', or 'being afraid for', or 'warning others in authority about it so they can take appropriate actions'.

No. I mean, who are those 'others in authority' on Earth, at the planetary level?

The Hague Criminal Courts? They can only adjudicate after evil has transpired and littered its wounds and scars.

The United Nations? They have no teeth. They can only make recommendations that are far too little, too late.

I mean, who cares with massive and immediate agency? Where is the mommy and daddy with a big enough stick to keep the inevitable ruffians and gremlin scoundrels in their place?

I say 'inevitable' because it seems like human awareness slash responsibility (*Responsibility is applied consciousness. – Handbook.*) reveals itself spread out analog fashion, in a spectrum from low, to high, to extraordinary, to archetypal.

For example, it took me a long time to learn that the apples and pears I see on the grocery store shelves are not the average quality of apples and pears that grow on fruit trees. These specimens on the grocery shelves are highly selected, sorted, cleaned, polished and stacked for my shopping pleasure. No! Apples that grow on any apple tree that I ever got to meet are discolored, irregularly sized and shaped, full of dents, scratches, brown spots, wormholes, and bird bites. I could make an apple cobbler out of any of these apples, but only the selected prime-quality apples show up in modern grocery stores.

What I am saying is that the current disciplines of governance do not adequately contend with the 'bad apples'.

In fact, since patriarchal governance uses hierarchical power structures, governments around the world are designed to be hijacked by bad apples, the gremlins and psychopaths.

What do I mean? Every person has a part of their psyche that cares firstly for the survival of their childhood defense strategy, their Box. This part is called 'gremlin'.

If gremlin is not distinguished, then it cannot be noticed and named. If it cannot be noticed and named, then it cannot be transformed through initiation. If it cannot be transformed through initiation, then there are no adults.

I look around at planet Earth from my radical responsibility causal perspective and I recognize with horror: THERE ARE NO ADULTS.

Yes, there are people who care, who notice the pending doom, who make diligent efforts to validate their findings, who publish clearly documented reports online for the whole world to take notice of and take actions about. But psychopaths do not care about ecocide and the extinction of species, including humanity.

I should hire a biplane to paint this sentence in the air with red skywriting above every municipality on Earth: *Psychopaths do not care about ecocide*. But then I would be contributing to air pollution. And, no matter how big my skywriting sign is, FUCKING HELL! Psychopaths do not care about ecocide and the extinction of humanity. They would ignore the message. They only care about getting more power to protect their wounded little souls.

Yes, I read that article by Callahan, *Beware The Psychopath, My Son*. You should too. He didn't actually write it. He collected two longer articles and extracted the best of both, weaving together a more lucid narrative. That was in 2008. My Papa gave me the article to read after he found it while trying to understand how it could be that Assad, Erdogan, Putin, Macron, Khamenei, Netanyahu, the current American dictator, etc., all promote war instead of the evolution of consciousness. The article gives the answer: A psychopath has no motivation to serve other people. Period. And FUCKING HELL! We stupid people still submit ourselves to governance by hierarchies that have all been hijacked by psychopaths!

What is a psychopath? A psychopath is a human being born with a disconnect between their intellectual body (their mind) and their emotional body (their heart) that leaves them without a conscience. This means that what they say has no internal connection with what they do. Their flaw is not genetic, but it is detectable, for example with tests devised by Dr. Robert D. Hare. Psychopaths know they are different even at school age, so they learn tricks to remain undetected. The psychopath's core agenda is to gain enough power and control to remain invincible. In other words, they are terrified. Look into the eyes of George W. Bush or Bill Gates and you can see psychopathy directly.

How can I spacehold the wellbeing of our entire gameworld without being a 'leader'?

Where is my place?

What is the conscious use of my knacks?

How do I activate the assets of my personal neurosis for the benefit of all?

I live in the ongoing need to sense to what degree our systems are 'go'. What needs to be accomplished before our spaceship is ready to launch? I realize that I am holding space for a team of spaceholders, where each member holds space for one of the important functions in our gameworld.

Each of these people is a spaceholder for a node in the Infinity Ring of our gameworld.

But what am I?

*I am spaceholder for the Infinity Ring itself!*

YES! This is clarity!

Oh, no! My god! I made a horrendous oversight!

"Lylah! I did not replace myself as spaceholder for the Infinity Ring of Dandelion Flower when we left camp!"

She says, "What do you want to do about that?"

"I need to call a circle. I need to phone back to camp!"

Fortunately we are near the center of town, and I see Thomas! Three minutes later his phone is in my hands ringing on speaker, and everyone is gathered around.

"Dandelion Flower!" announces Huda, our Interlocutrix on the camp side.

"This is NOT an emergency!" I say clearly, then wait for Huda's response.

"Copy that!" says Huda. "Hello Zenobia. What can I do for you?"

"We just crossed into Montenegro. Everybody here is more than fine, except for me. I figured out what I am. But I also figured out what I forgot to do."

"What did you forget to do?"

"Before now, I did what I needed to do but I did not know why. I never bothered to figure out what I am and how that fits into our gameworld."

"Okay."

"Just now, I figured it out."

"Go ahead..."

"In the same way you are spaceholder for the kitchen node and therefore you participate in the Infinity Ring at camp to coordinate and collaborate with the spaceholders of the other nodes, I am the spaceholder for the Infinity Ring on the road."

"Yes. I think this is already clear for everyone."

"It was not clear for me! Did you have a name for it?"

"No. We simply experienced it as being true. Until now, we did not recognize this part of our gameworld architecture."

"Remember when we did the mitosis of the original Infinity Ring to duplicate the DNA structure into two parts, Flower and Seed?"

"Yes. I copied being spaceholder for the kitchen node from Jamila Ali Ahmed. I joined the Infinity Ring in the Flower. She joined the Infinity Ring in the Seed. It is working perfectly."

"Well, Huda... I forgot to duplicate myself as spaceholder of the Infinity Ring, because I did not know that this is what I was. Everything was happening so fast. I just didn't think about it..."

"You are feeling something..." says Huda.

"Yes. I feel sad not to have thought of this before. I have been dog-paddling in a vacuum, trying to do my best without knowing my place in the gameworld. I am sad about feeling alone..."

I am sobbing. People's hands gently rest on my shoulders. No one says anything to try to make my sadness go away. They are simply being with me. My sadness is fine in their eyes, and in their hearts. It is fine in my heart too. I feel glad about feeling sad about thinking I was alone. It goes on for a while.

"I feel glad you can all listen to me..." I look around. On this side of the phone, people's hands and fingers are wiggling silently in my direction, smiles on people's faces.

Huda says, "People wave their fingers and cry all around me over here in camp, Zenobia. It is so good to hear your voice, to feel you all are there."

"Thank you, Huda. Hello everyone there!"

They shout back, "Hello Zenobia! Hello everyone!"

Eventually it is quiet enough for me to continue. "Here is my question, Huda. Since it is obviously working there, who took over my role? Who is spaceholder for the Dandelion Flower Infinity Ring?"

Huda says, "Hold on. She can tell you herself..."

The phone changes hands.

"I did. Rachel Deeb."

I clear my voice, sit up straight, and speak out loudly. "I am Zenobia Darwish, first spaceholder for the first Infinity Ring of the nanonation of Palmyra. My first apprentice is Rachel Deeb. Rachel replaces me as the spaceholder for the Dandelion Flower Infinity Ring. I become spaceholder for the Dandelion Seed Infinity Ring. This mitosis is now complete..."

People totally clap and cheer, tears rolling down many cheeks as they smile in admiration of our courage.

I continue. "Rachel, here comes a question from one Infinity Ring spaceholder to another Infinity Ring spaceholder: Who is your first apprentice?"

"My first apprentice is... Huda Shamalieh."

More clapping and even louder cheering.

Then I hear Rachel and I saying the same thing at the same time. "Huda, who is your first apprentice in the kitchen?" Everyone laughs.

A new realization sinks into my soul. My heart comes alive in a new dimension. Suddenly I do not feel so alone anymore. Rachel Deeb has the same gameworld overview questions as me! I have a mage sister!

Huda says, "My first apprentice in the kitchen node is someone you on the other side of this phone do not know yet. She arrived a month after you all left. Her name is Sumeya Mbeki from South Africa. She says that she read an article by Rachel Deeb and had to come visit us. She is amazing in the kitchen."

Then Montassar speaks. "Zenobia, who is your first apprentice as

Dandelion Seed Infinity Ring spaceholder?"

There is total silence.

"You, Montassar Bilal, are first apprentice to Dandelion Seed Infinity Ring spaceholder, or you would not have asked me this question! Who is your first apprentice in Morning Circle?"

He searches the faces on our side of the phone, not trying to figure it out, but rather trying to locate the person so he can tell them directly to their face. "It is Jamila Ali Ahmed," he says smiling and nodding his head. "Please come over here so I can shake your hand." She does. He does. It is done.

"Goodbye Huda! Goodbye Dandelion Flower!"

The phone shouts back to us, *"Mae alsalama!"* ['May peace be upon you!' in Arabic.]

We click off and stand together in energized silence in beautiful downtown Budva.

# Eugene, Oregon 11

Davis Hatcher's *Beep! Book*

The hubbub in the hall feels momentous, like a film being staged. Several hundred men and a few women pack themselves into the standing-room-only mess-hall at Camp Adair near Corvallis, where three thousand troopers, imported from as far away as Seattle and Los Angeles, are barracked. Never before has Eugene hosted such a diverse and immense gathering of security forces, both uniformed and plain clothes. News coverage has been banned. I feel like a black ant inside of a red anthill.

Me and Sanjib are absentmindedly thrown into this briefing under the auspices of the Eugene Police Department. We show our badges to get in, and try to act like we believe in the charade.

What I sense most is gremlin excitement, police imagining they get to finally use their powerful new military equipment from the Department of Home Security and the Army.

Beneath that is raw tantalizing dread, as if I am one of the Roman foot-soldiers facing the Germanics taunting us from the edge of their forest to dare to attack them, both sides fearing that many of our comrades may never return home to wives and farms.

It shocks me that I both love and hate these sensations. Sure, it is certainly something momentous to be a part of... but on the downside, I might die.

Sanjib seems to not care. My gremlin wants to ask him if he is thinking of the seventy-two virgins awaiting him in Islamic heaven, but silence has already been called.

Police Chief Stafford nervously steps up onto the improvised dais. He can't even talk straight to me and Sanjib. Why is he the one talking to a crowd of officials almost all of whom are his superiors from DHS and god only knows how many other three-letter agencies? For sure they have more information than Stafford does about what will soon transpire.

But Stafford is the hosting police chief. He is supposed to make it look as if he is in charge. This is part of the charade.

Probably they will use Stafford as the scapegoat if things go south.

The briefing is both dull and foreboding. Stafford says, "Applications have been received for several thousand demonstrators to peacefully assemble in the banking sector to protest current Trans-Pacific Partnership discussions. Intel suggests that the Eugene group behind the Black Bloc vandalism in 2021 is returning with a vengeance."

He pauses for effect. There isn't much. He rolls on.

"I think we all know the drill. Armored-cars with water-cannons will roll behind police officers in full riot gear, armed with batons, pepper spray, and rubber bullets. A SWAT team waits on yellow alert. Helicopters mounted with Long Range Acoustic Devices remain on call at the McNary ARNG Heliport if that becomes necessary. One hundred new security cameras have been installed. They all feed into the DHS face recognition database, but Black Bloc tactics can make face recognition difficult. For this reason, the Police National Database will parse the data using body recognition software. Our objective is to maintain business as usual, without incurring bad press as happened during the Toronto G-10 summit. I am proud of you all standing in support of peaceable law and order. Further instructions will come from DHS tactical headquarters. May tomorrow bring us closer together as a community."

Stafford's closing sentence does not settle well in the minds and hearts of the nation's security keepers. They seem far more committed to vanquishing the enemy than joining them in a potluck supper. A smattering of uneasy applause brings the briefing to a close. Stafford exits the scene, presumably to return to the Eugene Police Station.

Sanjib whispers fiercely into my ear, "Could you feel that? Mixed purposes are at work here. Follow the RWG."

"What?"

"Follow the money! Where is the Rich White Guy?"

I look around. "I don't see any. They are not here. These people are only the slave zombies. The masters are the corporate weapons makers and the bankers."

"Right! So, who is in charge here, really?"

"Only gremlins. Big excited gremlins with a lot of dangerous, expensive cop equipment."

"Right again!"

"So, what do we do? Why are we standing here?"

"Neither Stafford nor Brinks have redefined our roles," notes Sanjib. "Maybe we fell through the cracks due to all this military chaos, but let's leave it that way. We are still undercover cops. Let's get out of here so we can talk. I propose we head over to the dungeon to report."

"1313?"

"No!"

"Ah! The other dungeon. Sorry."

It takes an hour for Sanjib to drive us back into Eugene. Mostly I have nothing to say, but in a good way. I busy myself trying to explain the disproportionately massive, combined police and military response we just witnessed. What is really going on here?

Suddenly I start talking. "Eugene citizens will peacefully assemble to rally for changes they want to make in the local governance and economic systems. What if the police did nothing? What if the police built stands and provided free lemonade and hotdogs to the visitors? What if the citizens were accustomed to dividing themselves into circles of thirty or so people and practiced *Torus Meeting Technology* to unleash nonlinear potential and group intelligence? Something new could happen."

Sanjib nods his head, drives solemnly on.

"Instead, what will happen is what usually happens when people without guns stand up to people with guns."

I feel immensely sad about this.

"It seems we have learned nothing since Alexander the Not So Great... since the Crusades... since the world wars... People in high places seem to think that war is the answer. I think war is illegal. If they think war is the solution, then what is the problem they are trying to solve? Is the problem that the value of the U.S. Dollar is floating on so much hot air compared to the Euro that if the U.S. government can entangle NATO into the Russia Ukraine war, then the value of the Euro will drop and people will be distracted from decreasing the currency exchange rate for the U.S. dollar?"

"What do you think?"

"What I think," says Sanjib, "is that the answer to your question requires more intelligence than you and I have. I also think that we have arrived. Let's go 'toroid' ourselves into an interesting conversation, and then see what tomorrow brings."

We trot up to the Horsehead Bar, then down the now-familiar wooden stairs into the cellar. Behind the wooden door, our full circle is rolling along. Well, almost-full circle. Remington and Rob are absent.

The room grows silent as we enter. I ask, "Who is spaceholder?"

"I am," says Patricia Wells, "and we are stuck in the 'us and them' dichotomy. We need some nonlinear possibility."

"Good thing we are here! We just returned from the pre-war military and police meetup..."

"Don't joke around like that!" hisses Francis Atkins. "I feel angry when you fool around about war here in Eugene. Actually, I feel scared about it... Would somebody please hold space for me to..."

"Hold on! Hold on! Francis!" I say. "Listen, we really need you, here in this circle right now. I need your awareness and your experiences. Please don't go away right now. Your fear is completely appropriate. They have hundreds of soldiers and police with riot gear, tear gas, tanks, helicopters, a SWAT team... I don't think your fear is emotional at all! I think it is a feeling of fear. Insanity is rapidly emerging in Eugene, and we are at the center of..."

I stop speaking mid-sentence.

Patricia is confused. "What do you mean we are..."

"Shhhhhh!" commands Sanjib in a whisper. "Don't interrupt him right now. He is thinking of something useful."

People sense Sanjib's earnestness and honor his request by

holding perfectly still. I don't notice. My eyes have gone unfocused. I stare off into a dark corner of the ceiling. Some kind of download is happening...

"We are in the center of it," I repeat, more to myself than to the others. "At the center of the pond."

"And... so...," prompts Sanjib.

"And the center makes the biggest splash. Yes?"

"Yes," confirms Sanjib. I look at him and focus.

"Let us not join the insanity," I propose to everyone in a voice that seems perfectly rational to me, but probably otherworldly to them.

"Okay. Let's not," says Patricia, quizzically, trying to draw the rest of the download out of me.

"The truth is, we would be fighting to get what we already have." I say.

"Keep speaking," encourages Patricia.

"Our current strategy is to distract the full armed forces to follow the intel we've been feeding them the last few months so that they show up in full force in the banking sector of downtown tomorrow morning at four a.m. while most of us show up in the café sector and depave asphalt. What we already know for certain is that the combined Eugene Police and California National Guard and U.S. Army forces will prevail. Right? Historically, I mean. In a game of force, they will wipe us out. All we get to do is play out our victim role in this antique David and Goliath drama, hoping to make the point that we want them to change things. But making a point has no power."

"Yes," says Sanjib. "So?"

"We are already so far beyond needing someone else to give us permission that we don't have to fight against them at all. They have already lost the battle because we have already won the war!"

"What war?" demands Patricia.

"We have our authority back! We can go play together in the streets of Eugene in the exact way we want to, without having to force the City Council to listen to us and redesign the downtown. They cannot listen to us! They are using Standard Human Intelligence Thoughtware. They don't even understand the words we are using!"

"What is the thing about the pond?" demands Sanjib, trying to complete the original download so I don't lose it.

"Yes! The pond. We are at the middle of the pond and can make the biggest splashes there. What happens when we make a splash in the middle of the pond?"

"Ripples go out!" yells Anton Pirelli.

"Yes! Once a splash is made at the center, the ripples go out in every direction! Nothing can stop them! We can use 'Pond Protocol'! We do not need to depave the entire street. All we need to do is what we have already done, which is to apply to depave a few blocks by the cafés to create a Human Interaction Zone. While a few of us chop three or four holes through the tarmac, the rest of us can interact with each other how we would want to interact with each other if the Human Interaction Zone were already there, because it is already there, because we will be there already being ourselves!"

"You mean the world will see the ripples?"

"Yes! But not only that! The police and national guard are legally constrained to respond with five identifiable levels of force.

"The first level is Physical Presence. If they see you there, you are already forcing them to confront you.

"Second level is Verbal Force. If they speak with you, you might not understand, or you might speak back with them.

"Third level is what they call 'Empty Hand Control'. They grab you without weapons. But if you fight back, you are 'Resisting Arrest' and they can escalate to the fourth level.

"Fourth level is Intermediate Weapons, meaning, if they feel afraid that you will fight back or hurt them, they can use pepper spray, water jets, or their baton on you.

"And fifth level is Lethal Force, meaning, if they are afraid you might kill them, they are licensed to kill you first.

"In an interaction with police, you have the power to determine to which level of force the situation escalates by choosing the level of resistance you use. This is a tremendous amount of power.

"For example, if an officer speaks to you and you ignore him, you force him to escalate the force he uses with you. He must speak louder or get angry to get your attention. Therefore, you can de-escalate force by looking police officers directly in the eyes, listening to what they say, and interacting verbally.

"Most police officers already sympathize with what we are trying to create. You can demonstrate compliance with their physical presence and verbal direction by acknowledging them, looking at them, listening to what they say, and repeating back what you understood with a Completion Loop. You do not necessarily have to *DO* what they say, but if you stay in relationship with them, acknowledging them, listening and speaking with them – perhaps even being kind to them – then there is a good chance the interaction can be kept at the verbal level."

Sanjib takes over. "You can also determine whether or not you will be arrested. If you do not wish to be arrested, then create it so your interactions with the police stay within the first two levels of force! It is that simple! By the time an officer goes to the third level of force – Empty Hand Control – and grabs you by the arm, you are already being arrested.

"Police may be tired, angry, scared, or overwhelmed. They may regard dealing with street protests as a distraction from their true work of dealing with criminals. Being frustrated, they may wish to escalate the level of force in an interaction so that, if they do go to the trouble of arresting you, you will be charged with a higher crime.

"Police are trained to use 'pain points'. If an angry police officer grabs you, he may intentionally apply pressure at a pain point causing you to automatically flail about, which on a video would be hard to distinguish from resisting arrest or attacking the officer, which is an automatic felony charge for you. Your flailing is also a good excuse for him to use pepper spray, a knee, or his club on you.

"Some people recommend that if you are grabbed you should go limp, but if you do that, you will likely be trampled or dragged around and might get hurt. If you already know a police officer might grab you in a pain point, you can prepare yourself to not react aggressively no matter what."

I speak again. "To disarm a police officer, use the first three levels of force on him before he uses them on you. For example, at level one – Physical Presence – to maximize the apparent show of force at a scene, the police may be outfitted in riot gear, head to toe armor, shields, batons, helmets, etc. This is the police officer's 'power costume'.

"Well, we can wear a power costume also! For tomorrow I propose that as many of us as possible wear a suit and tie! Then the police will have a very difficult time hitting us, because blue-shirt police take their orders from people wearing a suit and tie. They might get confused and be beating their boss! If a woman wears a pink bunny power costume, it will look very bad on TV seeing a police officer beating a pink bunny.

Sanjib interjects, "Using the first three levels of force on a police officer, before he uses it on you, disarms the police officer? What do you mean?"

"It can look like this", I say. "When the police arrive, you scan the group and locate the highest-ranking officer. Then, in your suit and tie, you smile professionally, make eye contact, hold out your open hands, walk enthusiastically up to him or her, shake hands and introduce yourself, *'My name is Francis Atkins. I am a Possibilitator. If there are any problems here, let me know what I can do for you. I'll be right over there.* Physical presence, verbal direction, empty hand control... Sweet!"

"But what about tomorrow?" demands Francis. "It's already ten p.m.! In a couple hours it will be tomorrow! And we are supposed to convene on East 5th Avenue at four a.m.!"

Sanjib lays out the plan. "We send out this latest strategy into the 3Cell web so people can find their businessman's clothes and pink bunny suits."

"Who will sit with me and Sanjib to formulate the explanation about the ripples in the crowd?"

"I will," say Francis and Patricia at the same moment.

"We are not going there to protest anyone or anything," I continue. "We are going there to create the Human Interaction Zone! The message will explain about the ripples. It is similar to the 'human microphone' method developed in Occupy Wall Street, remember that? One person shouts the first message. Then anyone who heard her, shouts the same message again. The next ring of people who heard that message shout it again, passing it along to the next further circle of people. These are the ripples! Get it! Sanjib and I will start making the first splashes to send out ripple invitations for human interactions using the human microphone. When you get how it goes, you can jump in, okay?"

People around the circle nod a bit dubiously.

Then I add, "Please ask as many people as possible to bring along American flags, without any pole attached. Just the flag, folded up in their pocket." I don't know where this is coming from, but I say it anyway. "Also they should bring along a book to read out loud in a circle... and a wine glass for making toasts... We also still need a few pickaxes..."

"Let's start drafting the letter in a few minutes," I propose. "I need a breather outside. Sanjib, will you join me?"

The night is dark. The air is damp. *Shadow Knights* knowingly nod at us as they head home and prepare for tomorrow. When it is clear I pull out my burner phone.

"What are you doing?" asks Sanjib worriedly.

"We made a promise. I want to keep it. Trust me for a few more minutes, will you?"

The phone rings. A groggy male voice answers. "I'm tryin' ta sleep! What?"

"Hello Sarge. Sorry to bother you so late. We promised to give you any useful info we could find out. Tomorrow morning, the *Shadow Knights of the Mysterium* are going to use 'pond protocol'. I don't know what that is, exactly, or how it goes. All I know is that they trust us enough that Sanjib and I will be in the middle of it. Do you need anything else from us right now?"

"Just don't get shot. I have enough trouble as it is. I feel like a dry leaf in an evil tornado. It's gotten out of control. The Feds have grabbed the reins. Take care of yourselves." He clicks off.

Sanjib could overhear what Sergeant Brinks said. He stares at me in the silent dark, and says, "That is the nicest Brinks has ever been to us. I don't know what is going on, but it must be far worse than we think."

This is not a pleasant note upon which to end the day. Plus, we still have critical work to do. I feel scared.

# Hollywood, California 7

Lights slowly brighten in Stage 13.
The shadows fade.
The show is over.
There was no show.
There was no audience, except the actors, who were not acting.
They were co-creators of the shift-of-epoch torus.

One by one they rise from their chairs, stretch their legs and spines. The technical team informally mingles with the performance team. Hugs and handshaking happen all around. Camera and sound crews pack their gear.

There is no curtain, but the curtain is closing, and the virtual film credits begin to roll by.

Bill Murray stands up and disrupts the disruption. He cannot help it. "Excuse me everybody!" he shouts in a serious request, looking around nervously, trying to catch everyone's attention. "Excuse me please, everybody! Sorry for interrupting."

Camera operators instantly drop their cleanup protocol and jump to unpack or grab anything they can point at Bill. They have seen this happen before...

"I... have to say something. I don't know what I am going to say. But I have to say it. Thank you for listening to me. Here is the message: All of you people here, you can come to my house. You can visit with me anytime you want! My house is your house. Seriously. I love you for being here with me today. And I love you for all those days and nights before now that you did not know that I love you, because I have loved your work for all these years. As I love you."

Cameras roll from shoulders and any convenient dolly.

"And I want you to meet Stephanie Canning and Elizabeth Diggens. Stephanie is an orthopedic surgeon volunteering at kids' hospitals in Chile and Peru. Elizabeth is a physicist researching the interface between memetic constructs and invention. I need them to speak with you. Stephanie, are you willing? I think you might have something to say."

Fiercely, Stephanie claps her hands once together and says, to both the people and the cameras, "I *cavitate* new space in which each pain, whether it is physical, emotional, psychological, energetic, or even financial, becomes a doorway for discovering alternative routes to take, rather than continuing in the route that caused the pain. In this space we pool our resources instead of hoarding them privately, making sure the resources circulate everywhere freely so that our fears release their grip on our souls. This is a play space for our souls to bring life to the nonmaterial value each of us has inside of us that expands through giving it to this village that needs each of us to play full out."

Bill Murray lets his tears run freely down his cheeks. Eventually he looks towards Elizabeth Diggens, but she needs no second invitation.

Elizabeth claps her hands once loudly together and says, "I *cavitate* new space in which raw human creativity goes to the edge of our scarcity-based beliefs and our unfulfilled childhood needs because creativity comes alive at the edges. This is where we can build bridges out of new agreements for relaxing together, being together, exiting the frantic rat-race. The edge is where we keep cavitating spaces together that please Gaia and give future generations a new chance for life."

Bill sighs. His heart could speak with these people all afternoon and half the night. He scans each Being in the room individually, then looks directly into the TV cameras and says, "I want to hear from every single one of you out there who learned what we learned here today. I know I cannot hear from every one of you... but the truth is, I want to! I want you to practice this conscious cavitation stuff. It is very weird. But trust me, it is fun! Please share this info with everyone you know. Everyone! Promise me you will! We can inhabit other spaces besides where we have been living so far. You are not stuck where you are right now. I am sure of it. I want you to be part of all this. I want you at my party.

"Most of you are younger than me. You can learn new things faster than I can. One day, eventually, I will die... probably... but most of you won't. At least not yet. You have the chance to cavitate worlds that are not such a mess as we have made.

"I am sorry... I am so sorry for the messes we have made and are leaving behind us. I should have let my anger roar out of me as much as I felt it. I held back so much anger and clarity in my life. Don't you do that. Let your anger fire up your voice and your new ideas. Let's try new things together! Share what you discover, okay? One person's discovery can open up a whole new future for everyone. Just like today. Please?"

After that, everyone cannot help but clap and cheer and hug Bill Murray 'til he is thoroughly squeezed. At the same time, they cannot help but hug each other also.

Ken Watanabe turns to face a camera and says, "This was a good conversation."

# Phoenix, South Africa 7

Tandra is frustrated. When Tandra gets frustrated, granite would prefer to disintegrate itself into sand rather than face her head on.

By now the village people know this about her. But Tandra's frustration has become trustworthy. When Tandra is frustrated, it is no time to run away; it is time to get your butt in gear and prepare for change.

Tandra's anger serves the good of the village. People have learned to stand back and at the same time stand ready for action. The fire at the center of the circle crackles and sparks when Tandra stands to speak.

"It is not going fast enough for me," says Tandra, her voice firm and steady. "We are wasting time. I want solar collectors on the roof of every hut. I want a pedal-generator for backup, or something the goats can charge up. We need lights at night so the kids can read. Hell, we need lights at night so I can read! This is not the stone age.

"I know we don't use money here. But we also don't make solar panels and voltage regulators and batteries and wire. To get those things we need money, or some value exchange deal that gets us the parts we need. I am asking for an ally. We need one person out there who will trade with us, someone who is committed to building the global meshwork of thriving phoenix cultures. We need someone who lives in modern culture but who sees the big picture and functions beyond the concept limits of modern culture. Who's got an idea?"

"I do. Mary Olagga." She's a redheaded student visiting from Ireland. *Olagga* means *leopard*. The villagers gave her this name, referring to her astonishing freckles and the way she silently but relentlessly sneaks up on problems to solve them. "Give me a couple hours online and I bet I can find somebody through one of the micro-loan organizations. I can do that tomorrow at the Phoenix City Library, if I can use one of the bikes."

# Budva, Montenegro

Zenobia Darwish's *Beep! Book* – still 5 October 2023

Suddenly Lylah says, "I think it would be best if one of the men represents us at the Budva Town Council meeting."

"Why is that?" ask Israa.

"Because women here are treated like second-class citizens. I see there is an entrenched inclination towards Patriarchy here. We can undermine that later, but only after the people have good reason to value the nonmaterial possibilities we offer their village."

I say, "I really enjoy your company Lylah! It makes me stay alert. Who would you propose does the talking?"

"Montassar."

Israa says, "Any resistance to Lylah's proposal? One. Two. Three." No resistance.

The meeting day quickly arrives.

Montassar stands and says, "Good morning wonderful people of Budva. We are the CFF, *Consultants From the Future*. Thank you for permitting us to attend your Town Council meeting today. We are collecting practical experience and wisdom to share with other villages in Europe. Our mission is to bring resilience to European villages by empowering them to create a better future for themselves and their neighboring villages. To start with, we would like to review your EDP... your Energy Descent Plan."

There is the kind of silence that might emerge if you asked a truly obese person to see their diet plan.

The rounded, bearded Mayor of the town glances through his wire-rimmed spectacles at his colleagues for a rescue, but none offers a hand. He clears his throat and courageously admits to us, "We have no Energy Descent Plan."

Montassar waits a precisely calculated amount of time expressing his 'shocked and confused' face. We practiced delivering the theatrics of this moment more than twenty times before arriving in Budva so that Montassar could get it this perfect.

"Well then. Hmmm..." Montassar says, turning to look at us, frowning, shrugging his shoulders, and holding out his arms in apparent dismay, which he then gradually changes into an 'Ah-ah!' moment.

He turns back towards the Town Council and says, "Then it is lucky we have come here! We would like to share with you the best elements of all the Energy Descent Plans we have collected from all the villages we have thus far visited since our journey began. Would this be acceptable for you all?"

The Mayor hardly hesitates a moment before saying, "This would be a great service to our village."

Montassar says shyly, "To be candid, sirs, we are self-funded. What this means is that it would help us to deliver you with these treasures we have been collecting and refining if you could find a way to provide us with overnight housing for three nights, and a few meals while we are here. How does this sound?"

"Yes, of course," says the Mayor, glancing quickly at the citizens in the audience and catching the eye of several specific Council members for silent approval.

I glance back to see where he is looking. At least two reporters focus their cameras and shoot photos. I can almost read the Mayor's mind. *Standing proudly in alliance with these enthusiastic young people all dressed in yellow is publicity not to be missed!*

Montassar speaks into that gap. "I propose that three members of your Council join us to define the future potentials of Budva. Can our first meeting be tomorrow afternoon? This gives us a chance to arrange our papers."

"Certainly. This is workable. We will meet here at fourteen. And, son, don't try to rush through this. The near-future fate of Budva is dear to our hearts and heavy on our minds. You could not have arrived at a more timely moment. If your schedule allows, please plan to work with us for at least a week or two. We have some rooms and a kitchen behind the church that are recently vacated which you can use. Ms. Radmila Radović will be your hostess. Please inform her about anything you need to make your work more efficient or your stay more comfortable. She will show you to your quarters."

"Thank you, Mr. Mayor, Budva Town Council," Montassar acknowledges each with a nod, then he pivots at the waist to bow to attending citizens, "and good people of Budva. On behalf of our team, I tell you that we look forward to surprising you with how many sparkling possibilities are just around the corner for your famous village."

The Council and citizens of Budva instantly fall in love with us.

We continue our everyday tradition of picking up garbage and making tiny repairs or improvements everywhere we find the need. People stop to talk with our teams of two or three as we go on about our business in Budva. Since we use Vacuum Listening which we learned from the *Handbook*, the villagers and shop owners feel more profoundly heard in their communications with us than perhaps ever before in their lives. Particularly the women are inspired.

By the first Thursday evening, Farhan has already started a

Possibility Team and Israa holds space for a Women's Rage Club.

In small villages, rumors spread like warm butter. Soon we open our Morning Circle / *Handbook* Study time for anyone who cares to join. After the first meeting, Radmila invites us to move our Morning Circle to the townhall. We ask why. She says, "So you have more space."

We can only laugh and agree. I guess she heard how cramped the townspeople felt in our monks' quarters.

We begin delivering Emotional Healing Processes almost immediately, of course. The first two weeks go by so fast that the town council asks us to stay on another two weeks to organize implementation strategies for nearly half of our proposals right away.

Montassar asks to be given fifteen minutes at the next town meeting. He starts off asking, "I would like to ask you about the historical legends of Budva. What is Budva famous for around the world?"

People start off suggesting "Beautiful old buildings." "The church of Sveti Ivan." ['Saint John'] "Sunny beaches."

Montassar interrupts. "But let me ask you, is this what brings tourists here from Russia? South Korea? China? I think not only. Let's get real. What do tourists want from your little village?"

The more reclusive citizens begin to answer. "Gambling. Winning it big. Drunken parties and brawls. Prostitutes. Drugs."

Montassar waits a moment for this to sink in and then continues. "Yes. This seems to be the background legends about Budva. More than once I have heard the name 'Budva' mentioned in the same sentence as the word 'hedonistic'. I am not preaching about good or bad, right or wrong. I have a more important question. I want to know what you actually want for yourselves. Do you want to be world famous as a resort for Mafia bosses to have dangerous arm-wrestling contests with each other? Scuffling for new drug sales territories? Is this the hope you want to offer for your children as a model to imitate? Are these the strong influencers you want hanging around using your town as a brothel?"

There are tears in Montassar's eyes. "Perhaps you already know this, but I trust you enough now to tell you straight out. Our team walked here on our own initiative from Aleppo, Syria. It took us six months. We started 1 April 2023 and arrived here 5 October. We pooled our own money together, ate sandwiches and dandelions and limpet soup, and slept in the dirt. It was not bad. We are not asking for pity. These shared experiences built deep resilience and camaraderie in us, and brought our team here. We are not patriarchal. I have been pretending to be the speaker for this group to you, but I am not. The true speakers are Israa and Zenobia and Huda and Lylah, actually all the women are our speakers. We live in a different culture than Patriarchy. It is called Archiarchy. This culture values adulthood initiations that liberate each person to deliver their nonmaterial value. Archiarchy is centered on nothing, the same way a donut is centered on nothing. If the donut does not have a hole at the center, it is not a donut. It is a *brötchen*, a bread roll. If a team is not centered around a radically empty space, then it does not have enough nothingness to use as a resource for creating. Without the nothingness, a group of people quickly shifts into a hierarchy with the most powerful patriarchal men fighting each other to stand at the top.

"Again, this is not a conversation about good or bad. It is a conversation about facts and what you want. Perhaps what you really want is something you never thought of before, something no one ever told you was possible.

"Well, we are here telling you that amazingly new and different things are possible, and they work very well, better than we ever expected." Tears roll down his cheeks for a while as he looks into people's eyes.

"The reason I tell you this is to explain that we were forced to make the same decision that you are now facing. Do we let our lives be determined by those whose vision is limited to taking as much as they can get, and giving nothing back? Or do we start over in a new context, pull ourselves up by our own ears, and create a different culture to live in? It is a painful choice to make."

Several people and one of the reporters have been recording Montassar's words. Montassar sees this from the beginning, but keeps his center, grounding cord, and bubble in order to allow his archetypal lineage to continue speaking.

"Staying in Aleppo was no longer an option for us. Neither was it an option to become refugees, powerless victims, begging to be rescued by the United Nations. No. Our choice is to invent new thoughtware, hold spaces in a new context with new distinctions, and create and inhabit the culture that we would love to live in, next culture, regenerative culture, Archiarchy. Regenerative culture is rapidly emerging around the world now that the capitalist patriarchal empire has failed to build a safe haven for life on Earth.

"You have quickly become our friends. We decided that we want to share our possibilities with you. It is the biggest treasure we have, the kind of treasure that grows through giving it away. Will you receive and use this treasure from us? That is the question I ask you now."

So many Budvans cry now, in disbelief, but also in joy.

Me too.

I feel glad to learn that 21$^{st}$ Century Zenobia's way of conquering new territory is to give people a treasure that is so much more valuable than the treasure they already possess, that they abandon whatever it was that they previously treasured. Our team empowers citizens to use the new treasure we gave them until it grows so big that they too become generous and start giving it away.

At that point, the nomadic nanonation of Palmyra moves to the next town and gives the same treasure to them!

We are doing it!

I will list the main actions we co-invent in seclusion with the Possibilities node of the Budva Infinity Ring – what they used to call their 'town council'. In the next city-wide meeting we share these possibilities so that the citizens can begin imagining that their life together in Budva could be an expanded experience that is deeply attractive to them. Such a procedure initiates whole system change.

We start with the current thoughtware people hold onto since their childhood. Once they can identify it, they can see how it plays out, exactly what it creates for them. When the pain grows big enough about what they are currently creating, things begin to pop like hot popcorn, first one, then a second, then three kernels at once. The pain of using old thoughtware becomes grease for letting go of what they have held onto for so long, and also the gunpowder to blow up resistance and imaginary fears about trying something completely different.

Sometimes it seems like we are gameworld builders in the mountains, scouting for best routes through the peaks and canyons to lay down tracks for a new train route. But then we also need to fight off the grizzly bears, and dynamite tunnels through solid granite walls of resistance.

Perhaps this is not the proper metaphor to use for upgrading thoughtware enough to let old systems collapse and establish new customs and relationships. We make so many holes in the Swiss cheese that there is no more Swiss cheese, only holes. This makes for a resistance-free start-over!

The following proposals are listed in no particular order. Every single one of them is shocking to the modern culture mind, truly revolutionary. So what? You want your life to be boring?

POSSIBLE ACTIONS TO ESTABLISH A NEW BUDVA VILLAGE
EXPERIENCE

1.  We are proud to learn that Montenegro was the first ecological country in the world, declaring as part of your constitution in 1992: "Being aware of our debt to nature, which is the source of our health and inspiration of our freedom and culture, we are drawn to its protection in the name of survival and the generations to come." Yet our research has discovered that human health has two domains, not simply the external domain of ecosystems for food and shelter, but also the internal domain for healing and authentic adulthood initiation of potentials. Therefore, we propose that Budva become a center for Archan permaculture – the permaculture from Archiarchy, the culture that is rapidly emerging around the world now that Matriarchy and Patriarchy have run their course. There are many practical ways this can happen.

2.  Redesign the village around people and not around cars, trucks, bicycles and motor scooters. Centralize all vehicle parking (including bicycles!) outside of town limits. Make the whole village a car and truck-free Human Interaction Zone. Kids kicking balls around are relegated to a soccer field. People walking their dogs are related to a grass and tree studded dog toilet. No bicycles,

skateboards, roller skates, scooters, segways, oxboards, sports activities, or dogs are allowed in the downtown area.

3. Disposable plastics and plastic packaging of any sort including plastic water and soda bottles – including for construction – is not allowed into the city limits – best if not allowed into the country. Foodstuffs and other consumables are handled in reusable glass or metal containers. This decreases our garbage by 90%. Citizens return glass, metal, and paper to the shop where they got them to retrieve the significant deposit. These materials are recycled 100%.

4. Food is relocalized. Crops are not grown as a commodity to sell to corporations. Foods that are used locally are grown locally. We start with potatoes, beans, carrots, tomatoes, cabbage, lettuces, zucchini, squashes, etc. replacing lawns that use up water and require mowing.

5. Many gasoline, diesel, and electric powered appliances are not allowed, such as electric toothbrushes, electric razors, electric meat slicers, electric bread slicers, microwave ovens, gasoline or electric powered lawnmowers, lawn edgers, leaf blowers, weed whackers, and so on. These are replaced by human energy.

6. Imported shoes and clothing cannot be sold here, especially synthetic and fleece clothing that breaks down into nanoparticles that potentially cause lung inflammation and heart problems. Instead, local shoes, hats, coats, and traditional costumes are hand-made and decorated from local materials, and offered for sale to tourists.

7. Replace empty shoe shops and clothing stores with Possibility Cafés and Intimacy Cafés where customers can order from a menu including: facilitated couple's conversations, Completion Loops, 5 Body Check-ins, Emotional Healing Processes, discovery journeys, Completing Incomplete Emotions, and matrix-building experiences.

8. In the Human Meeting zone there are shops and spaces for Possibility Teams, Rage Clubs, Fear Clubs, Study Groups, S.P.A.R.K. Distinction Experiment groups, 3-3-3 Process Studios, Standing Rage Holds, Swordwork Spaces, Emotional Healing Process Dojos, First Position Practice Centers, Memetic Surgeries, Thoughtware Upgrade Spaces, etc.

9. Twice per week the Human Interaction Zone fills up with farmer's markets offering locally grown foods and locally made craftwork (not imported from China...), local live unamplified music, giveaway stations for recycling clothes and household items, Possibility Menu Stations that offer Five Body Scan, a Possibility Chair, Take Your Authority Back, Meme Check, Feelings Practitioner Processes such as Unmixing Your Emotions, and special requests.

10. Pottery and porcelain are locally made for use in homes and

restaurants.

11. The Human Interaction Zone is free of smoke and alcohol, including cigarettes, cigars, e-cigarettes, etc. Once a week traditional dance parties are offered by local musicians without microphones or amplifiers.

12. Surrounding hills are reforested with indigenous species.

13. Retrofit all buildings with insulation to a high insulation value walls and ceilings using organic materials such as hempcrete and hemp fibers, replacing leaky windows and doors, and redesigning to maximize passive solar heating. All new construction is fully passive solar heating and cooling.

14. Look into the possibility of installing low-enthalpy shallow geothermal energy for direct heating and geothermal electricity generation.

15. Look into establishing a smart grid of small solar water heaters, solar electricity panels, and small water turbines for generating electricity without disturbing ecosystems and habitats.

16. Support locally owned food restaurants, shops and cafés. Tax all franchises out of existence such as Starbucks, Circle K, KFC, Pizza Hut, McDonald's, Burger King, Walmart, Aldi, Ace Hardware, etc. All franchises! Replace franchises with circular local economics implementing Archan Economics. Change consumerism to true necessity rather than marketing amplified desires.

17. Consider removing all G5 antennas and towers.

18. Replace public school curriculum with matrix building preparations for authentic initiatory processes into adulthood.

19. Refine and deliver Authentic Adulthood Initiations that unleash new consciousness to source new forms of responsibility. Create new legends about Budva as an amazing source of five-body healing and Adulthood Initiatory Processes that unleash lovely and exciting human potentials. Send Budvan youth on Walkabout to other Authentic Adulthood Initiation Centers around the world.

20. Shift city government infrastructure from hierarchical pyramid to toroidal circle. Learn new tools, skills, and processes for implementing *Torus Meeting Technology*.

Gradually we show citizens – as individuals, families, and groups – how to make use of the intelligence of their conscious feelings. From out of the cracks and shadows, secretly frustrated and hopeless people discover they have the energy to unleash suppressed irritations and concerns that have bothered them since forever. We have become a forum for transforming grievances into evolutionary projects. Half of the items on the list above came from local citizens and city council members themselves, not from us!

Plus, we are replacing ourselves! We have proven that we are not a fly-by-night scam operation trying to get paid before we must produce real and lasting results. Instead, we are training up spaceholders and establishing a local Infinity Ring for the rapidly emerging nanonation of Budva! It is something these people have never imagined was possible before, yet, for 2,500 years, have longed for.

The Budva Town Council officially invites us to stay in Budva for the entire winter season.

We accept their invitation.

They repeatedly tell us that this is the most exciting winter they can ever remember, even more exciting than the war.

After that comment I must ask Farhan and Israa to return with me to our quarters and hold my shaking body. They hold space for me to cry my soul out, and let the shaking rage complete itself in full force.

I become even more intensely and personally aware of how marginalized most people live, how lonely they are, so far away from their human potentials, secretly keeping their pain 'private' and suppressed until it eats them alive from the inside and they die from some horrible disease, or they not-accidentally 'have an accident' to end it all.

We are beginning to read the encoded 'knocks on the door' buried in comments from the local people – who have become our personal friends. These comments are so drenched in centuries of pain that I can barely endure them.

I used to think of myself as tough. Lately I have discovered that there is a difference between having resilient agency, and having a high numbness bar. My 'tough act' was the high numbness bar. I am working on evolving my resilient agency.

What I am sure of is that if I silently try to endure them (the suffering-filled personal sharing comments from the local people) I will join them (becoming one of the tortured citizens myself).

Now, when someone makes a sharing comment that hints at their deep internal struggles, we answer the door and say, "Hello! Welcome! Please come inside! Let us sit together and talk."

This form of talking is not idle gossip or passing time. Communication is how war ends. We are careful not to be emotional garbage cans. Instead, we are tension detectors. We are transformers who facilitate human-to-human reconnection.

Each sharing is clarified and verified, then completed and put to use as a successful step along their path. Babystep-after-babystep we clearly assert that something completely different from their world is possible right now. If a person wants us to, we accompany them on their transformational journey.

More and more people are taking us up on our offer.

Something long buried and yet totally fresh is coming to life here in Budva.

This is excitement beyond measure!

What surprises us most is how swiftly and accurately the Town Council embraces our proposals. After doing some googling we find out why. The answer is stunning.

I feel angry that they have been keeping it secret from us, but even more so, glad that it exists. I bring it to the next Town Council meeting.

When I am granted the space to speak in their circle, I stand and say, "Dear Citizens and Infinity Ring of Budva, you have not fully informed us! You have preexisting advantageous conditions that have not been disclosed to us. You are keeping dangerous secrets!"

Mr. Mayor shifts to his 'sweet' voice and says, "What, in heaven's name, are you complaining about, my dear?" He seems offended that I am offended and wants to placate me as quickly as possible. "Did we do something wrong?"

"No," I say. "You did something incredible. And you did it persistently for five hundred years!"

There is befuddled silence.

I did not think I would have to explain this to them, but it seems I must. "You Budvans! Being a nanonation is in your blood! Except for a few short interruptions, Budva has been collaborating with the Republic of Venice from 1420 until the end of World War One. That is half a millennium! That is five centuries! You Budvans were already a nanonation for five-hundred years!"

No one admits anything. I continue. "You already have it thoroughly formulated in your background memes how to be an independent nanonation of global citizens, a center of art and invention, bustling with commercial and cultural exchanges between Europe and Asia!"

I wait to see if any of them recognize the importance of what I just said.

Israa, Farhan, and I spent days checking it out quite thoroughly. We discovered many fascinating pieces of history that most westerners were never taught in school.

I illuminate these facts and figures to keep legitimizing my story with names and dates. Gradually I see a dawning of awareness grow amongst some of the citizens of Budva.

Long unused synapses begin sparking back to life. I see people making small secret smiles to each other, nodding in wonder, making comments 'behind the hand'. Here we are publicly appreciating them for doing what someone in the past most assuredly told them was unforgivably vile.

"The meme tracks for being a flourishing independent nanonation are already there in your hearts and spirits!" I tell them.

"Perhaps your pride of independence was lost for a while, but it is buried only just under the surface. We celebrate that your spirits are bouncing back to life. We can see it happening before our eyes, day-after-day, more-and-more. We are so happy for you! You already know how to navigate the wild waters of being a nanonation!"

From then on, we see a new Archan context for Budva evolve and deepen from moment-to-moment. The flames have caught hold and now grow unstoppably.

Our shocking realization is that we are no longer needed here.

# San Diego, California 4

"Just perfect!" whines a near-elderly woman in a dark pants suit, unable to suppress her exasperated cynicism and rage. She is Angelika Steinhagen, an heiress to a German castle, preferring to reside San Diego perma-sun rather than European winters.

Captain Henkel sits at the head of the boardroom table. Angelika reigns over him from behind, like a hyena, complaining righteously to everyone. "We worked on this project for three years! We created this team. Randy Williams collected investors. Dr. Kelly Ferrington, Dr. Peter Baker, and Dr. Amadeus Pointer researched years to substantiate your original thesis, David. Dr. Benjamin Bhaers pushed the paperwork through City Hall. Here is our immaculate prototype, built by none other than Mr. Roger Singer. Our Temple of Evolution stands before us, complete and ready to build." Her crooked bony finger points at the assembled model sparkling brightly at the center of their meeting table. "We have already been granted zoning approval! And now you want to throw it all away!!?"

The other five executive board members sit in embarrassed silence. Everyone wears a suit and tie except the guests, JET, and Eddy. Even Edith is formally dressed. At least Eddy carries a fresh emergency carrot in his back pocket, although he tries to carry it with dignity.

Captain Henkel does not have enough information to argue his point. He feels ashamed, thinking perhaps he might have gone temporarily insane to be proposing that they drop the Temple of Evolution in favor of something so intangible as a so-called 'Intersection ConFest'. He sits there grimacing under the glare of his very respectable board members, finally saying, "Ahh... Hmmmmm..."

"Let us take care not to be too arrogant," says JET, in a quiet and kind voice, shifting the space so as to have a conversation about the conversation, because this will create the possibility of possibility.

Exasperated faces turn their attention to his unexpected comment. JET continues. "We may simply be pawns in a bigger game. To make moves in a bigger game without recognizing the bigger game's purpose may not be to our best interest. I propose we inquire more directly about how to play the bigger game."

The bearded banker, Benjamin Bhaers, says what everyone else is thinking. "What in the world are you talking about, young man?"

"I think something in you already knows exactly what I am talking about," JET asserts. "I think something in each person here already knows. The idea of a Temple of Evolution truly inspires something in you. And, the situation you address is more dire than you might be prepared to recognize. It turns out that the evolution of consciousness is not such a simple business. Our shared intention is to redesign the possibilities of the modern capitalistic patriarchal culture before it is too late. The results that you have so far created..." he gestures to indicate the model before them, "...are a crucial step in creating a workable gameplan. But to act in defense of your current project strategy is still defendedness. Defended-ness is part of the problem.

"Our task is to get beyond defending what is already known. It helps if our shared efforts focus on where we are going rather than on what we have already accomplished.

JET sees that the team is hanging on for the ride and mostly still with him, so he continues.

"Evolution takes place in steps, in iterations... the next iteration being either impossible – or at least inconceivable – until the one before it appears. Do you think I planned to be here at this meeting today? I did not. I had other plans. A week ago I was attending classes at the University of Utah, and I didn't know any of you. Three days ago I nearly died in an explosion in the desert. My leg was crushed and bleeding badly. My survival was impossible. Yet an actual Superman showed up to save me, and here I am." He glances at Eddy and continues.

"The outcome we must accomplish with this team is also impossible. In my opinion the impossibility makes the project worth doing. I think the same force that brought us together here will also help us to succeed, that is, if we stay flexible enough to be guided by its continued influence. Our rigidity could suffocate this project in righteous arrogance – I don't mean you personally, Ma'am... I respect your passionate commitment. My question is: can we remember our true purpose and keep navigating towards that? We cannot afford to act as if our present design is the finished design. That would balk in the face of the Universe's principle of evolution."

Angelika leaves no pause. "We already completed the design phase! Now we are implementing! When will the decision be finalized?"

Eddy shouts fiercely, "Never! It will never be finalized! Included in our design must be that the design will never be finalized. And that is the design. In rapidly evolving circumstances, the design itself continuously evolves, or else the design goes extinct. Instead, we design for our own demise" For example, the terms 'temple' and 'evolution' are contradic-tory. Something more fluid than a temple is required to support the true dynamics of evolving into a fuller range of human intelligence."

Edith rolls it further. "What we need is a resilient space of possibility to work into, a space in which human consciousness can evolve. We need experiential conditions that include the chaos of rapid evolution as a resource we can encourage and direct... We need directed chaos! We need a way to convene diverse intelligences for catalyzing the development of participants in completely nonlinear ways, ways that are invisible or impossible from the perspectives of ordinary modern culture thinking. Anything less than sudden reordering will delay us past the intersection points..." indicating the two graphs already projecting onto the wall screen, "...and then we pay with massive suffering. Humanity has a slim window of opportunity through which to move before we are kicked in the teeth by Mother Nature. Do we take this chance, or do we stall?"

The youngest board member is Dr. Amadeus Pointer, the renowned psychohistorian. He has been sitting wordless, but now blurts out, "But how, my friend? How do we do this?"

"Yes!" says JET. "Asking the question 'How do we do it?' seems like the most important thing. We don't know how to do it, so we feel scared to commit. To compensate for our fear, we decide to think instead of feel. We decide to try to figure everything out ahead of time, and this stops us from actually starting to do it, because we cannot know how to do it before we do it. It seems to make sense, but the strategy of trying to know how, is actually a mirage. We cannot already know how to do something that has never been done before. Nobody already knows how to do it. Asking 'How?' distracts us from doing it.

"Success occurs through taking the actions that place us in the heat of the experiment. Using fear's wisdom guides our further actions. We think we are stupid, so we try to be smart. But the opposite of 'stupid' is not 'smart'. The opposite of 'stupid' is 'awake'. In the game of evolution, success is more evolution – being in process, not achieving some end product. There is no end product!

"For example, it is already a success that we continued this conversation now rather than getting offended and stomping out of the room, or forcing a premature conclusion. Success is continuing to take action even when we do not know how, just like we are doing together in this moment."

Captain Henkel shouts, "Here! Here! Congratulations, my boy! You just 'made my day'! Again! Outstanding! You must teach me how to do this Possibility Speaking stuff! I am impressed."

Eddy pointedly ignores the Captain's enthusiasm and tries to keep the meeting on track. "It is not about taking just any random action. It is about taking responsible action... See that glass of water in front of Captain Henkel?" pointing to the glass. "Who is responsible for that glass of water being there?"

"Captain Henkel is," says Amadeus. "He poured it."

"Yes," says Eddy. "That is what we have been trained to think. That is the logical conclusion, the limitations of the mind. But responsibility does not submit to the laws of logic. Watch this..."

Eddy carefully reaches over and brings Captain Henkel's glass to his own part of the table.

"I am responsible for the glass being where it was in front of Captain Henkel, because I can move it over here. It was there, now it is here... because of me. It only stayed where it was before now, because I kept choosing to not move it anywhere else. The same is true for every glass on this table, for every weed in every garden, for each couple I did not talk out of having another baby, for each decision made in a corporate boardroom to promote profit instead of human dignity. I cause it to be that way by doing nothing to stop it from being done that way."

Edith steps in. "Making our project successful requires taking this kind of radical responsibility. Our team is here to help you start creating Intersection ConFests around the world for the next hundred years. What do you say?"

Angelika Steinhagen sits down heavily in her chair, dubious, but thoughtful.

Benjamin Bhaers strokes his short beard and stares furiously at Captain Henkel, who is squinting at Eddy, thinking critically.

Amadeus Pointer vigorously rubs his face with both hands as if he were washing it with soap.

A couple of the other board members whisper heatedly to each other, one waving unsigned papers in the other's face.

Edith smiles, looking around at each one individually, scanning their reactions at more than one level. The outcome of this meeting is uncertain, but it looks like they will be going for it, full out.

"I want to add one more element to this conversation which has only recently emerged. My father, Phillip Goldman, is asking his global network of Archiarchy Invention Centers to collaborate with us to mass produce Intersection ConFests around the world as soon as possible."

# Hollywood, California 8

Warner Brothers staff are little motivated to dismantle the set in Studio 13. They hesitate to disassemble the space in which what just happened, happened.

Judi Dench takes one wistful look at Dave Stutler, nods at him curtly, then stands and leaves the studio with the others. She does not remove the tape keeping Dave's wrists tied behind his back and his mouth shut.

Dave sits alone in bewilderment, looking around the near-empty studio. Finally, he makes an awkward effort to abrade the duct tape off his wrists by scraping them along the back of his chair.

"Here, let me help you with that." The familiar voice comes from the shadows behind Dave, as Balthazar Blake steps forward to aid his apprentice. At his side strides a tall woman paying very close attention to everything. She has straight black hair just past her shoulders with here and there bright red streaks through it.

Dave erupts in eye-bulging convulsions from reacting to his outrageous circumstances. Such momentous things were happening, and nobody set him free to participate.

Balthazar stands patiently at his side, waiting for his inevitable return to the rational. It usually only takes a few moments...

"I had you brought here for a reason..." Balthazar pauses to let Dave think about the ramifications of the fact that his kidnapping was intentional.

Then he continues. "It was a fine opportunity for you to learn from your elders. Plus, you got to experience the shift-of-epoch torus as it emerged, without any chance that you might contaminate its function with your unlimited considerations."

Dave calms down and seems to understand. He looks up at Balthazar and the woman, and makes a steady nod, not quite masking his plea for release.

Balthazar ponders the human condition for a moment, then says, "Okay. Let's take a risk and see if you learned anything." While Balthazar pronounces the word 'anything', his hand streaks over, grabs a loose corner of the duct-tape, and rips it off Dave's mouth.

"Owwwww!" yells Dave accusingly at Balthazar, rubbing his sticky mouth on his shoulder. "That stings!"

Balthazar says nothing, stands relaxed, without apology, ready, waiting.

Suddenly Dave leaps up to his feet, knocking his chair over backwards. One of the cameramen has already grabbed his gear and points a hand-held camera at Dave, Balthazar, and the woman. The red LED is shining.

Dave stands dignified but breathing hard, his wrists still taped together behind his back. He leaps straight up vertically into the air and slaps his shoes down onto the slab concrete floor of Stage 13 as he shouts full out, "I *cavitate* new space where bullshit is not shoveled onto kids in a school designed for the last millennium!"

Dave lifts his right leg out before him, swings it around in a great arc to expand the new space he just cavitated. Then he kicks a hole in its side and, bends over, ducks through the hole into the newly cavitated space, and zips the hole up behind himself with his taped hands. Then he continues shouting at the top of his lungs.

"Where political strife cannot exist because politics does not exist. Where nature is regenerated by human beings because we have learned that human beings are nature. Where current human stupidity does not impact future generations because we help each other to decontaminate ourselves. This pisses me off so bad that I now cavitate a *new* space, ten thousand times bigger than I just did," leaping into the air again and slapping his shoes down hard against the concrete floor. "I *cavitate* the culture space where I apprentice myself to reality."

Then he leaps and slaps his shoes to the floor again! "And I *cavitate* the culture space where I teach one-hundred-thousand other people how to teach one-hundred-thousand more people how to cavitate and inhabit next culture spaces!"

Balthazar beams at him with tears in his eyes. He glances quickly at the woman beside him, then back at Dave and asks, "May I join you in that new space, young wizard?"

"Me too?" asks Gwendolyn.

"Me three?" asks Rebecca Barnes, Dave Stutler's 'witch', mysteriously appearing out of the shadows to join Balthazar and Gwendolyn as they squirm into Dave's newly cavitated space.

"You saw all this?" asks Dave, scornfully frowning at Balthazar, trying to communicate disgust about Balthazar's seriously devious nature, yet unsure of what he should be feeling about his ordeal, all the while feeling totally in love with his ordeal, and Balthazar, and Rebecca, and even this new woman.

"You did great, David!" Rebecca assures him. "Don't worry. It was amazing!"

Rebecca, Balthazar and Gwendolyn spontaneously move as close as they physically can to David Stutler, the Sorcerer's Apprentice, and bundle him up tightly in their arms with hugs and kisses before he can get away.

# Salt Lake City, Utah 6

Parts of the Utah landscape look like photos from the Mars lander. People who think they want to go live on Mars could come stand out here in the Utah desert at night, gazing at the craggy outcroppings and endless sands, shivering. They would not need oxygen tanks and pressure suits, but the rest of the experience would be about the same. In an hour or less they would be asking themselves, "Where is my warm, soft couch?"

Perhaps we do not realize that Earth is just as far out in space as Mars is.

Where are all those people, anyway? The Utah deserts are empty!

These 'adventurers' probably sit indoors near their flatscreens and their refrigerators and their microwave ovens, living in the fantasy world that one day, where they really want to be, is standing on Mars...

Aren't humans fascinating?

After an early arrival in Salt Lake City, Sean and Margaret pick up their rented car and drive twenty minutes east to the University. Sean drives. Margaret only needs to remind him three times to drive on the right rather than on the left.

The assistant they speak with in the administration office knows of the missing boys, and seems genuinely concerned about the mystery of their disappearance. She is happy that someone with real knowledge and authority has come around looking for them. This could mean less of a mess for her to clean up. She is happy to show them the dormitory room of Edward Bennington. Nothing to see, really, except that he left almost everything behind.

JET's dormitory is another thing entirely. The door lock hangs destroyed from being forcibly opened by the campus police. The whole frame is crisscrossed with yellow police barricade tape printed with the message: Crime Scene Do Not Pass. Dried shaving cream foam still coats the inner door frame.

Sean glances at the administrator and says, "What do you think the problem was, Ma'am? Sex? Drugs? Rock'n'roll? What was the emergency? Why did the police need to break down the door?"

"Apparently campus security detected high data usage from this apartment without proper authorization."

"What if they were researching important discoveries?"

This clearly was a perspective considerably beyond her paygrade.

Sean pushes the door open enough to poke his head between the yellow tape and glance around inside. He takes note of the equipment efficiently assembled for research and security measures, plus the knotted sheets still tied to the heater, plus the graph of the intersections.

Margaret says, "What are you smiling about, Sean?"

"Indeed! I am smiling!" he notes out loud, more to himself than anyone else.

Sean, still smiling, looks at Margaret and says, "If this young man – who assembled this well-organized and protected research facility and was able to escape without being caught by the police as they were breaking down his door – has any relation to me, then I must tell you, he is a man who leads a life after my own tastes, and I am already very proud to be his father."

Both women are offended.

Sean has tears in his eyes.

The administrative assistant becomes enraged. "Who will pay for these damages?" she demands.

Sean answers innocently. "Why not charge those who caused the damages?"

He turns to Margaret and says, "It is clear that they left in a hurry. This means they had neither chance nor inclination to leave clues or messages regarding where they were going. All we can assume is that they escaped well, found some form of transportation, and went to the place from which Edward sent you that postcard."

"And what place might that be?" asks the administrative assistant.

"It is the place we will be going to next!" says Sean, smiling brightly at her. "Thank you so much for your kind assistance."

Sean offers his elbow to Margaret, who nods curtly to the other woman. The sprightly couple strolls over to the stairwell, down three flights of stairs, and out to their parked car.

It is a fine day to drive south through Utah.

# Aleppo to Germany 15

Zenobia Darwish's *Beep! Book* – 14 February 2024

We awaken to Saint Valentine's day, but the sun only vaguely hints at brightening the sky. More than one hundred Budvans gather in the cold damp pre-dawn to hug us goodbye. We Palmyrans stand geared up for the road, conical straw hats, multipurpose sticks, yellow jumpsuits, new yellow jackets provided by the Infinity Ring of Budva, walking shoes, metal buckets, and broken hearts. Our new friends shove chunks of cheese, dried sausages, bread loaves, and packets of dried fruit into our buckets. They are as proud of us as we are of them.

Proposals at recent Morning Circles invited us to never leave Budva, that we make this medieval town on the Adriatic Sea our new home.

But like it or not, it has become obvious that Budvans can source Archiarchy without us. We are called by the road ahead. E.C.C.O. is clearly moving us along.

Our plan, of course, is to walk. But surprise! Mr. Mayor packs us into two city vans and accompanies us on the two-hour drive north to the border exit station at Debeli Brijeg. This is where we leave Montenegro and enter a half-kilometer no-woman's-land before reaching the Croatian entry gates of Granični prijelaz Karasovići.

Mr. Mayor collects up our passports, walks us into the Border Control building, and presents our documents to the Chief of the Station who turns out to be a friend of his since school days. Mr. Mayor gives some kind of glowing report about who we are. Whatever he says, we get immediate exit stamps.

Just before leaving us, Mr. Mayor reaches into the inside breast pocket of his sport coat and pulls out a fat, white, letter-sized envelope. If that is a stack of Euros, I estimate it to amount to several thousand. My eyebrows go up all by themselves.

We never asked for payment for our consulting services, and none were offered. The entire exchange was a lusciously rich collaboration. Mr. Mayor is about to hand the anonymous stack of bills to Montassar, but catches his patriarchal habits and stops mid-action, reprimanding himself comically. "No! No! I am not a patriarch! This is not Patriarchy! This is Archiarchy!" We smile and wiggle our fingers towards him in joyful appreciation. He glances sheepishly around, then hands the money and stamped passports to Mitzi.

Mitzi looks straight into his eyes with mysterious compassion for his condition, accepts the passports and envelope gracefully, and says, *"Dovidenja. I meni je drago."* [Montenegrin for 'Until we meet again. It has been a pleasure to meet you.']

Mr. Mayor is speechless. For the first time I see emotions bringing tears to his eyes. He nods to Mitzi, puts one husky hand on her feminine shoulder for just a moment, makes a last glance at the rest of us and says, "I love you all!". Then he briskly leaves the office and jumps into the first van. We wave as they drive back to where we just came from.

Here we are, alone again. It is shocking. The circle forms up out in front of the Border Control, but there is nothing for us to say to each other right now. Mitzi silently passes our passports back to us, then rips open the envelope. It is indeed cash. She pulls out the full stack of hundred-Euro notes, splays them out as if they are a deck of playing cards, and says, "Please help carry some of these." Each of us reaches over and takes a handful and puts them into our various money bags. We never counted how much the Mayor actually gave us. It is a good but still strange feeling to not really need to freak out about such a thing.

Rafiq and Habib look at each other. Habib simply says, "Let's go." The two of them walk through the portal, heading north. Our roadsnake Toroboros follows.

It is taking us an entire month to walk the coast of Croatia. Even though it is drizzling or windy, we are warm enough during the day from our exercise of walking. But we do not carry tents or winter sleeping bags, so nights are scary. We try a few times to sleep close together under our tarp to stay warm with shared body heat, but the next morning we are not rested. We decide to use some of the money from the Budva Town Council to pay for hostels now and then along the way.

I want to brag about the ways we collaborate as a team to work around or through road-life discomforts. Only in one day we might encounter sunburn, mosquito bites, spider bites, barking dogs (fortunately no dog bites, but some dogs almost became lunch as we developed some rather tasty recipes at camp in Aleppo...), scrapes or bruises from tripping or falling down, sprained ankles, sore muscles from carrying water for trees, blisters from digging holes for trees, muscle cramps from sweating a lot and not replacing enough minerals (we found out), cold, wind, rain, diarrhea, women's periods.

In a nature shop in Thessaloniki, we discovered silicon mooncups! We all got one – well, we seven women each got one. Weird at first, but so useful during our periods. No more tampons or bloody pads to get rid of. In fact, when we are tree planting, the women empty their cups into the hole before putting the soil and baby tree in. We make quite a tangible bond between us and the trees. We feed the trees with our blood.

We dispose of biowaste the same way, providing compost for the tree's roots to find as they grow. When planting trees, there are obviously no trees to hide behind, so when one of us needs to poop, the others drop everything and turn their backs towards the pooper, forming a human bathroom around them for privacy, men with men, women with women. I get so used to saying, "Paper," or, "Water," or, "Hand," that when I am alone in an ordinary toilet, I catch myself feeling lonely, or saying, "Paper," out loud before I catch myself. Even when cars drive by on the road I feel safe and protected. Even when a few times the 'bathroom' is constructed out of mixed men and women I feel protected.

But there is one particular pain we are not prepared for.

One morning Mitzi walks silently at my side. Finally, she says, "Zenobia, I've been thinking."

"I wondered why you've been so quiet."

"Well, it is not quiet inside. Are you willing to be a listening space for me?"

"Yes."

She says, "It's about God."

I say, "Go ahead."

"I remember going to church a few times with my parents as a young child, probably at Christmas time. Plus, I have seen churches of many different religions, and watched the people going in and coming out of them. Many times I tried to talk with God, any God, all the Gods, for example, the Gods we saw statues for in Greece: Zeuss, Demeter, Athena, Apollo, Poseidon, Artemis. They all seem distorted by human stories. They are all involved in competition for power, minor jealousies, getting revenge on each other. They are afraid. I don't think Gods are afraid of such insignificant irrelevancies."

I wait, walk, listen.

"Different religions develop around different Gods, like Buddha, Muhamed, Jesus, Zarathustra, Rama, Lao Tsu. These guys, men, seem to be regarded as representatives of the one God, also a man. But what I am wondering about is, theoretically, I could bypass the men and talk directly with the one God myself, right? Why not? If they can, I can. So during these long days of walking through the natural world – well, it is not so natural if it is hacked into orchards and vineyards, terraces and fields, is it? Anyway, while walking, I send out my awareness with some intention behind it to talk with the one God. I think that is why I tripped the other day and scraped my elbow and knees. Sorry to slow us down..."

"No worries, Mitzi! We all needed a break then. I am sad you got hurt. I didn't know you were praying..."

"I don't think it is praying, Zenobia. I think it is having a conversation. Praying is rather one-sided, begging like a poor victim, asking the great big God to intervene on behalf of the poor tiny weak and helpless human. Silly, in my mind. I mean, who formulated and named the God in the first place? It was humans, right? Just like gameworlds, Gods don't exist until humans make them."

I smile and nod. This little lady is a whiz-bang thinker. I imagine she is just getting started... She keeps going.

"I get this sensation, sometimes, that my talking with God is working, that I am connected with God and having a conversation with God, but it is not a person. It is a vast field of consciousness. I have been calling it the 'general field of consciousness'. It is a field that existed before there was matter, before there were galaxies in the Universe. Perhaps before there was even a Universe. I don't know. But what came to me is that being that conscious without another consciousness around to be with, would be unimaginably lonely. Do you get what I mean?"

"Yes." I sigh. "I wondered about this before, too. Please keep talking."

"I tried to commune with the raw consciousness directly to figure out what I would do if I was so bored and alone, and quantum physics came to mind. I don't know anything about quantum physics, but, somehow it seems that if the general field of consciousness could spin bits of itself, the spinning would form subatomic particles that could come together and form hydrogen atoms.

"Then clouds of hydrogen atoms eventually get denser and denser in gravitational eddies, in due course forming stars which are nuclear furnaces that manufacture heavier elements. The stars spin out planets and moons, creating, so far as we have counted, two trillion galaxies in the visible Universe."

She pauses to let me catch up with my amazement. After glancing at me to confirm that I am still with her, she continues.

"But then something else happens! And this is the amazing part to me. Before there was only this one all-pervasive general field of consciousness. Then suddenly there are bits of matter, stars, planets, moons. And these bits of matter interact with the general field of consciousness. They distort the general field of consciousness. The distortion around each bit of matter creates a second field, a specific field of consciousness around itself. Suddenly God has something else to talk to: the specific field of consciousness around material objects!"

"Then God is not lonely anymore?"

"Well, think about it. Do rocks talk to God?"

"Well, if they do, the conversation would be rather slow and boring, I would imagine."

"So here is this planet Earth, orbiting around Sol, our local star. The matter of Earth interacts with the general field of consciousness and creates the specific field of consciousness of Earth, which is Gaia. But Earth is a rock. And rocks do not have very interesting conversations. The material world is dead. God's creation is dead, stillborn. It is not aware of its awareness enough to talk with God."

I am nodding in wonder.

Mitzi keeps going, "Think about it. If you were the general field of consciousness and you spun bits of yourself to create physical matter, that would probably hurt, right? God suffered to create matter, but God probably suffers even more to discover that matter is dead. Matter is not conscious enough to talk to God. That would be painful, don't you think?"

"Yes."

"So then Gaia, the specific field of consciousness of Earth, tries to alleviate the suffering of God by bringing inanimate matter to life by creating organic molecules and eventually biological structures that evolve to more and more complexity until they become aware enough of themselves, and of what is going on around them, to finally be able to talk with God."

"Okay..."

"So at first, those few humans who had the inclination to introspect, noticed the general field of consciousness and called it the one true God. But other researchers noticed many specific fields of consciousness all around them, like the elephant in the room. You know the story of the blind men describing the elephant in the room?"

"Tell me," I say.

"Well, one blind man reaches out and feels the tail of the elephant and says, 'Ah! This elephant is thin and tall. It swishes this way and that way, and has a broom at the end. It must go along sweeping up the streets!'

"The second blind man reaches out and finds a leg of the elephant and exclaims, 'Oh, no! You are so wrong! The elephant is thick and round and solid as a tree. It does not go anywhere!'

"The third blind man reaches out, finds the side of the elephant and says, 'You idiots! The elephant is as wide as my arms can go, and flat, and solid as a wall covered in leather. The elephant is a defensive object and blocks the way!'

"'No! No! No!' screams the fourth blind man, who is holding the elephant's trunk. 'You are all insane. I have the elephant right here, wound around my waist. The elephant is flexible, like a great serpent, and it breathes out water to cause it to rain.'"

I smile at her inspired story telling.

"Of course, the blind men are all correct," Mitzi says. "But they are all wrong at the same time, because they stick to their smaller point of view, their singular experiences. They fail to use group intelligence, to combine their wisdom for the benefit of all. This is the same as humans everywhere..."

"How do you mean?" I ask.

"Some of the first consciousness researchers must have experienced the specific field of consciousness emanating from variously shaped material objects on Earth, including living organisms and sacred places. They learn to listen to and communicate with these various perspectives of consciousness and they give each 'spirit' its own name. Eventually they enshrine their collection of spirits as a pantheon, unique for each researcher. This is how humans invented the Hindu Gods, Greek Gods, Roman Gods, the Japanese Kami, the Indigenous Ancestors, the Voodoo Spirits, the Norse Æsir and Vanir, the Yoruba Orisha, the Aztec Gods, the Mayan Gods, the Phoenician Gods, the Egyptian Gods, the Chinese Deities, the Minoan Gods... The stupid thing is that they are all correct! These qualities of consciousness do actually exist. And yet, the humans with multi-deity pantheons kill each other as blasphemers. The various single God religions also fight each other: 'My daddy is bigger than your daddy and will beat your daddy up!' And the multi-God religions fight the singular-God religions. This has been going on for thousands of years, all around the world. It is insane. We are insane. The greatest creation of human beings is religious war. Polytheism and monotheism are both right! And humans fight each other to prove the other is wrong!"

I listen to Mitzi's every word. It all seems acutely true to me, tacitly true. It also seems like Mitzi is not at her punch line yet. I hold the listening space.

We keep walking. Eventually she keeps talking.

"So, here we are, human beings, created out of dead matter as a manifestation of the local field of consciousness of planet Earth called Gaia. We are amazingly complex physical structures designed to manifest more and more of the local field of consciousness. After hundreds of millions of years of focused evolutionary work, we have such amazing potentials. And yet, in order to grow up through our childhood where we need the love and support of our parents, we must be adaptive to our parents' world. We develop a survival strategy, this 'Box' that the *Handbook* talks about, plus our gremlin to protect our Box by keeping everything the same... and after that... we need adulthood initiations to escape the eggshell-type restrictions of the Box's protective survival strategy. But human beings adopted hierarchical power structures that control societies to forbid adulthood initiations! This means we cannot come alive enough to talk with God."

At this point, Mitzi starts sobbing like I have never heard her sob before. Others turn to look at us to see what is going on. I signal silently to them that we should keep walking, but slower for a bit.

"Mitzi, this is amazing what you are telling me. Truly amazing stuff. This tells me that Palmyran roadsnake walking is an authentic adulthood initiatory process, because you are getting initiated enough to wake up and come to life in a new way. You are matter in a biological form coming alive enough to leave your Box to your side and walk on Earth as part of the consciousness of Gaia! Her risky experiment of giving humans free will is successful!"

Mitzi only sobs more.

"You are alleviating the suffering of a lonely God, Mitzi! You are becoming the specific field of consciousness of Earth – which is Gaia – in a self-aware biological form with enough individual consciousness that you can talk with the general field of consciousness!"

"Yes!" she sobs so much that she must stop walking. Others stop and come to gather around Mitzi. "Yes! And you understand me! You hear me! You celebrate with me?"

"Yes! Look around! All of Palmyra celebrates with you."

"This is so good! I cannot tell you how good this is. Perhaps it feels so good because I am speaking for the moment as the representative of the general field of consciousness. It feels so happy to have this conversation with us. I was so afraid this would not happen, that you would not get it. It is so important to me that you get this, Zenobia."

An alarm goes off in me. "Why is it so important to you that I get this, Mitzi Slovensky?"

"Because..." she looks at me, hesitating. "Because I am leaving. Because I have to go to Slovakia. I have to find out where I am from. I googled a bit and I think I must have relatives there. They would want to know what happened to my mother and father... and what happened to me. I think if they learn what really happened to me, then I will learn what really happened to me."

The floor falls away from under us. Our team is no longer solid. It is ripped open at its heart. We face a gaping hole. How do we patch it? Do we scream at her? Do we forbid her to leave? Do we reject her? Do we attack her in revenge for betraying us?

What about none of the above?

It is mostly silent in the Seed component of the nanonation of Palmyra, standing on the side of the road in the Slovenia mountains overlooking Ljubljana. It seems like nothing has changed, but suddenly everything is different.

Some of us moan. Some complain under their breath, trying to cover up our sadness and anger about feeling fooled into thinking that Mitzi is one of us.

People naturally love Mitzi. People count on Mitzi to be here. If she is not here... this is unthinkable. Yet we must think the unthinkable. We also respect Mitzi as one of us, and she has chosen to part ways here.

Those five steps to accepting change are hard at work in us right now, bouncing around between the fear of denial, the offended anger of outrage, the gremlin's bargaining, the sadness of grief, the acceptance... well... we are still far away from acceptance. There is no joy here.

Mitzi says, "The road at this intersection goes east towards Slovakia. I will turn here as you continue north for Austria and Germany."

"How long have you known about this!" demands Rafiq.

"Only since just now. Only since Zenobia understood what I was telling her just now about the general and specific fields of consciousness. Since Zenobia gets it, the treasure I was given now also belongs to Palmyra. Now I can go handle my personal business."

Standing at my side, Farhan speaks loudly with blame in his voice. "Why did you have to be such a genius and understand her? Sometimes you are too smart for our own good..."

"It is not fair!" shouts Rafiq. We all look at him, surprised at this outburst. He is usually so stoic. "It is not fair Mitzi that you are going to leave us because I love you!"

I am stunned! It was obvious before now, this love happening. But so much love happens in our little circle. None of us cognized that this love was personal. Holy Kapookies! We have things to learn.

Rafiq goes on. "I love you. And now you are leaving us? I did not even get a chance to tell you!"

"You told me just now," says Mitzi, "and it is wonderful!"

"Did you know it before now?"

"Yes, I knew."

"Do you love me?"

"Yes. I love you."

"Do you love me enough that you would have me at your side during your journey to Slovakia?"

Seconds tick by. "Yes," decides Mitzi in her simple, clear way.

"Then I am going with you! I don't care where we go."

Now even Rafiq's face is wet with tears of crying for joy.

Everyone feels it. This archetypal man-woman moment is right and good, standing here before us, kissing! I have no idea how this movie will turn out in the end. I can only tell you that it is well-written.

"Aziza!" shouts Rafiq upwards, out into the sky.

"What," says Aziza, as a statement, not a question. Aziza senses what is coming. In addition to losing her road-warrior companion, she is about to take on greater responsibilities.

"Aziza Hamdi Ahmed, you are now spaceholder for the guardianship node of the Dandelion Seed of Palmyra."

"I choose this!" shouts Aziza, surprising us with her ferocity. She looks first at Rafiq then the rest of us, then grabs Rafiq's arm in the wrist-to-wrist warrior's grip to seal the deal.

Then she drops his wrist and shouts, "My first apprentice is Habib Badawi."

We laugh. We cry. We don't know what to do.

Farhan stands at my side, holding my hand firmly. At least he knows what to do.

Montassar speaks. "Mitzi and Rafiq, show us how much money you have!"

Mitzi counts out 1350 U.S. total Dollars and Euros. Rafiq says, "I counted mine this morning. I still have 2000 Dollars and Euros, or a little more. I think that together this is enough until we catch up to you later."

"That is, IF you catch up to us later... I would not bet on it," says Hadi. "E.C.C.O. works in mysterious ways."

"That is the reason we should also not count on it *not* happening," says Thomas.

Montassar and Israa silently consult with each other. Then Israa says, "We want you to take our phone, in case we need your help breaking out of prison."

"What prison?" demands Rafiq.

"The prison of German laws and regulations. The prison of the refugee camp we are about to confine ourselves in."

"Deal," says Rafiq looking unwaveringly into Montassar's eyes, appreciating the intelligence in Montassar's battle-tested tactics. These longtime warrior buddies fought side-by-side in the streets of Aleppo by figuring out ways to avoid fighting... and they won. They came out alive.

This kind of 'teamship' never ends.

I must ask the torus to check our grounding. I say, "The *Handbook* tells us that *Evolutionary gameworlds must also evolve*. Now I ask you, can the Dandelion Seed fully commit to this emotional roller coaster ride? It is our job to feel this thoroughly and deeply. It may take weeks... or months."

Tears and sobs fill the air around us.

After a while, Mitzi and Rafiq silently hold hands and make a bow of respect to the rest of us. Then they turn and walk towards their new future.

The remaining ten of us huddle together in a tight circle and howl out our grief and rage and fears. *How can we become a new organism with two of our intelligences cut away?*

I joyfully feel Farhan's ribs with my fingers, but at the same time I ache in sadness about this separation process. It can never heal because we can't return to how we were before. From now on, our Toroboros will be different. The configuration has changed. Without Mitzi and Rafiq, the energy flow and awareness sharing, the problems and possibilities will circulate differently. The split already rips our hearts open. Dismay, fear, shock... it is another unexpected earthquake, and we already know how badly those can hurt us. I still ache from my parents' absence...

Before Mitzi and Rafiq round the first bend to disappear from sight, Farhan hollers, "Hey Mitzi!"

She stops and turns back to face us. "What?" she yells.

Farhan shouts each of his next syllables forcefully and slowly so that everyone can understand what he is saying. "Please keep it in mind that a family would need to use the last name 'Slovensky' – meaning 'from Slovakia' – only if they were already living outside of the boundaries of the country of Slovakia!"

We hear Mitzi's sobs echo off the stone canyon walls as they turn and walk around the bend. But Rafiq is holding her hand.

"That was mean!" I say to Farhan.

"No. It was true," he says.

"What do you mean by 'true'?"

He faces me directly and plants a big kiss on my lips.

Right in front of everyone. Well, everyone who is watching.

I kiss him back. It is nice.

"That is what I mean by true," he says.

"That was not true. That was real."

"It was true. And it was real! Want me to show you again?"

I let go of his rib cage, grab his hand, and yank him out of the circle. "Let's get out of here... These hills are lovely, green and steep, but we have promises to keep, and miles to go before we sleep, and miles to go before we sleep."

Farhan looks intently at me with love and a question in his eyes.

"No, I didn't. It's Robert Frost. I simply changed a few words."

"Can I ask you a question about spaceholding?"

"It seems like you are trying, but not very successfully."

After half-a-day's hard walking we approach the westernmost city limits of Ljubljana, the capital of Slovenia. Hadi calls a pause. It is lunch time anyway.

"Before we eat, I have a proposal."

The nomadic nanonation of Palmyra, the *Young People's Syrian Diplomatic Mission to Germany* – yes, our mission has been revised – drops their loads to the ground and gathers in circle.

"Thank you for being there to connect with," says Hadi. "I am stewing on something, and... it is not limpets." A few moans and chuckles. "I have the urge to end our walking period and shift to full engagement of our intentions. For so long we have spoken about bringing ourselves – as 'refugees by evolution' – in connection with 'refugees by Armageddon' so as to co-create nanonations of next culture, nonmaterial initiation-centered torus culture – *Archiarchy Invention Center* culture. But when I check in with myself, I fear that we are dragging our feet because we do not have a proper gameplan for the next step."

"What are we missing?" asks Israa.

"As we were walking this morning, I made a mental list. For starters, we miss clarity about which refugee camp we try first. I imagined we would head into München, knock on the doors of the UNHCR offices, and ask, 'Hey, which refugee camp can we experiment with?' Under closer inspection – inspired by this morning's wake-up call – I think my idea is naïve. Who are we kidding? I think that to them, if they try to understand our solution to their problems, they would only perceive us as another problem! They would kick us out, or lock us up... I think we need to solve our own problems and not assume someone else will solve our problems for us."

General hubbub arises, but Hadi keeps her center and refuses to let the emerging creative confusion take over. "Ahem! Here is my proposal! I propose we find a hostel nearby Ljubljana with good Wi-Fi and that we stay there for as long as it takes to generate a more powerful gameplan. We have already proved we can Toroboros for thousands of kilometers, scrape together food, plant thousands of baby trees, pick up trash, and sleep on the ground in the wilderness. For our next adventure, I propose we focus on new things, such as eating warm meals, getting good sleep, and going online to buff up our websites with our Budva news. We need to publish our articles, write letters, make calls, and sniff around to decide which will be our first refugee camp project. From my personal point of view, we need to practice memetic speaking to get better at delivering thoughtware upgrades and Emotional Healing Processes needed by people that we meet. Whichever refugees we find, they will need to shift out of being victims of catastrophe into being victors of causality!"

We cheer and clap her onwards!

"Archiarchy is already invented!" Hadi declares. "It is time for us to occupy new cultural spaces. We need to practice dealing with the natural defenses of S.H.I.T. thoughtware. After ten days or two weeks, I propose we board an overnight Flix bus to our destination and get to the next level of work. Any resistance? One. Two. Three."

There is no resistance, and deep shared relief about getting more intimate with our objective. I wonder if Mitzi and Rafiq leaving catalyzed our new resolve.

It doesn't matter.

What matters is our upgraded enthusiasm.

I say, "The question remains: Is it easier to talk our way into prison, or talk our way out of prison? We may have to do both. I agree with Hadi. Practice is needed!"

Since then, Morning Circles have been about nothing else.

After a few days, Montassar dares give a voice to what others of us have also been wondering. "Why do we have to make these extraordinary efforts and take these frightening risks? If our proposal goes public, we could quickly freak people out and become targets for vengeance from the media, or government agencies, or far right German extremists, or the frustrated German police. I don't know what it is like for you, but in the back of my heart, I reminisce about the nanonation of Budva, waiting there on the clear Adriatic Sea with open arms for our possible return to their beautiful village."

We ponder this for days in our Dandelion Seed office in the Ljubljana hostel.

And then suddenly we choose Friedland Refugee Camp.

Preliminary research tells us it is located in lower Saxony, 13 kilometers south of Göttingen, nearly the exact center of Germany. The facility was built by the British in 1945 as the first waystation for World War II refugees, evacuees, and returning soldiers. Now it houses about 13,500 refugees, primarily from Syria. This seems like a suitable challenge.

Montassar uses his calm spaceholding voice to call around for weeks, bouncing from bureaucrat to bureaucrat, finally obtaining the mobile phone number for someone called Vanessa Schneider. She seems friendly, strong and clear. We listen in on speakerphone. She makes no assumptions and draws no conclusions. This is our woman!

Montassar tells her, "We'll be there in the afternoon in 2 days, E.C.C.O. willing."

She says, "What echo?"

Israa shouts from behind Montassar's back, "Vanessa, we will explain it all when we arrive!"

As Montassar clicks off the phone, Thomas says, "Then, we aren't going to Munich after all..."

I say, "Weird, isn't it? It's the third force at work."

"What are you mumbling about?" asks Israa.

"The third force! In physics! My Papa and I were researching why extraordinary things might possibly occur in human lives. Some people's lives seem so linear and ordinary. Other people's lives make unpredictable leaps into extraordinary possibilities. We were trying to figure out how this could happen when we discovered 'precession', which is an invisible force that exerts itself in a perpendicular direction to your current line of travel, but only when you are already in motion. If you stay still, then the sideways forces cannot enter your life to push you into evolutionary jump situations. But if you commit and take intelligent action in your best-guess direction, then precession can step in and apply an 'orthogonal force'. Orthogonal means 'a force at right-angles to the present directions of movement'. The point is to keep moving, like we have been doing. Think of how many favorable coincidences we have encountered over the past months simply because we seriously set out walking to Munich. If we stayed back in Aleppo, none of these fortuitous adventures would have occurred. Even if all this time we intended to arrive in Munich, now we will arrive in Göttingen! But we would not have gotten anywhere if we did not set ourselves into motion so that the third force could come alive and push us sideways into our destiny."

Thomas says excitedly, "Yes! Yes! Like that 1960's Australian song where the guy keeps complaining that his boomerang won't come back! Finally after months and months of indulging in his problem, the witch doctor comes to him and says:

> *'Don't worry, boy, I know the trick,*
> *And to you, I'm gonna show it.*
> *If you want your boomerang to come back,*
> *Well, first you've got to throw it!'*

Lylah chuckles with the rest of us, but then grows somber and says, "I miss Papa, and Mama. They were such good and courageous people. I feel sad they are not here with us now to see how well we are doing together."

No one disagrees. Me especially.

Overnight Flixbus tickets from Ljubljana to Göttingen cost us €51.97 per person, including a 19% Value Added Tax (VAT) to help pay for running the German Government, and a €0.99 'Service Fee'. (Hmmm... 'Service Fee'... Good idea! Why didn't I think of that?)

New country, new economic system.

The bus ride will take 16 hours and 45 minutes, including a 2 hour and 20 minute stopover in Graz Webling, wherever that is.

We depart Ljubljana at 14:35 this afternoon, and arrive in Göttingen at 07:20 tomorrow morning.

In the daze of having watched 6 Hollywood adventure movies and slept very little, I barely hear the driver say, "Willkommen in Göttingen!" as he slams the button and the doors swing wide open with a hiss.

We step out, with stiff joints and cramped-up bus muscles, into a fresh German morning. Most of us never rode in a bus before. None of us ever stood on German soil before. There is no resistance when Aziza proposes that we walk the 13 kilometers from Göttingen to Friedland.

Sure, we study the German language for free at https://learnger-man.dw.com/en, but being strangers in a strange land always has its surprises.

We have the urge to explore German traditions, culture, music and history, to breathe the German air, eat some German bread. We would like to plant our feet on the new Earth before meeting the new Earthlings.

Then we will go put ourselves in prison.

# Possibilica, Florianópolis 5

Quinn squints suspiciously at Shuichi and says, "What's wrong?"

It is seven a.m., the usual start time in their new office. The three edgeworkers hired by Jaine for the Possibilica Think Tank have been at it together for a week.

"I..."

"What's up Shu?" asks Areesha. "Your computer crash again?"

Silence. Soberness. It looks like it could even be grief.

"Did someone die?" Quinn feels afraid.

"No... but... Maybe yes..."

"What are you talking about?" presses Areesha. "What do you mean 'maybe yes'?"

Silence again. Unprecedented silence from a man who generally never stops explaining things. Shuichi makes a sigh so deep it sounds like a soul dropping irretrievably into the gaping maw of an underworld that has no intentions at all of ever spitting the soul back out.

"Here, sit down," suggests Quinn. "I'll bring coffee."

"No coffee!"

"Red Bull, then... or tea?"

"No."

"Uh..." Quinn's repertoire of solutions for a problem like this is exhausted. She stands looking at Shuichi hopelessly.

"I think I died," he moans quietly.

Quinn can't even begin to wrap her mind around this. She wisely uses a completion loop. "You died."

"Yes. It feels like that... Approximately... I would imagine... Neh?"

Shuichi never spoke in such vague terms before, and with so little energy. Areesha is also worried. "Can you say more about this?"

"Okay, coffee..." says Shuichi. "No wait! We need the team. Call the team."

Quinn and Areesha stare at Shuichi in dismay.

"What do you mean, 'call the team'. We are the team," explains Areesha. "This is it. Us three plus Jaine, plus the two old people out there. What team are you talking about?"

"We need everyone. All at once. To come together. Here. Soon. Really soon. I don't know why."

"Keep talking" insists Quinn.

"I conversed with Jaine most of the night. She immediately answered all of my questions, so I kept going."

Areesha says, "Jaine, please print out the transcript of your conversation with Shuichi last night."

The printer jumps into action.

"That won't help you," says Shuichi. "I fell asleep in the middle of our conversation, trying to think of the next question, trying to digest everything Jaine spelled out to me. Sorry, Jaine..." The printer stops.

"No problem, Shuichi-san," says Jaine respectfully from the Bluetooth speakerphone on the table. "I enjoyed our conversation very much. You kept asking orthogonal questions that opened new probability curves for me to follow. You were sourcing your navigation from something other than ordinary reason and logic. I have a lot to learn..."

Shuichi continues. "I woke up a few hours later in some altered state... as if I drank too much Sake. There were new gaps between what I know and what could be known."

"Were you drinking?" demands Quinn.

"No! Listen to me! I walked over from the dorm just now, and then it hit me. To access a complex enough response, we need to assemble a 'megatorus'. The group intelligence from a megatorus could be chaordic enough to face into global collapse, neh?"

"Like... what do you mean exactly?" asks Areesha. "We already know the shitstorm is just around the corner. We already know the U.N.'s Sustainable Development Goals are a corporate smokescreen. We know no government around the world will take appropriate action because they are hijacked by psychopaths. We know the propagation momentum of unconscious thoughtware is defended by an *incido synclastic infundibulum*."

"What is that again?" asks Quinn.

"It's a coincidence funnel that turns in upon itself from every direction to the degree that it cannot be escaped," answers Areesha. "'Incido' means 'to come unexpectedly', like in the word 'coincidence'. The *incido synclastic infundibulum* sucks coincidences back inside of itself endlessly, thereby blocking invention. The model comes from Kurt Vonnegut Jr.'s book *Sirens of Titan*. Vonnegut's infundibulum was related to time, a *chrono synclastic infundibulum*. The infundibulum that impedes thoughtware evolution relates to coincidences, those random connections that initiate evolution. It's what Darwin referred to as 'variation'. Without accidental unpredictable variations, there is no new thoughtware to select from. Then the natural evolution of thoughtware is blocked."

"And this folded-in coincidence funnel comes from where, exactly?" asks Quinn.

"Being sent to school, for example. That's why you and I are here, Quinn. We were never sent to school to be disempowered. We were never hammered into the hierarchical knowledge construct to believe that what is already known is all that can be known. You and I were unschooled.

And Shuichi is here because he has a subtle form of dyslexia that prevents him from believing anything anyone ever tells him on their terms. He must figure it all out himself, his own way, on his own terms, or he cannot understand anything."

"So..." ponders Quinn out loud. "What is Shu-baby proposing to us, exactly?"

Areesha says, "He told us he was asking Jaine questions? Shu, what was the last question you remember asking Jaine last night?"

"It is a clear memory. I asked, 'How can we help E.C.C.O. – the Earth Coincidence Control Office – do its work more effectively?' Meaning, how can we increase the number of cool options that E.C.C.O. has to choose from to promote the evolution of human consciousness on Earth? I always thought the answer was to make people more interesting to E.C.C.O., you know, by training them with extraordinary new skills, by building matrix in them so they have more overall general awareness and agency. Then there would be more interesting pawns on the board for E.C.C.O. to move around."

"And what was Jaine's answer?"

"I don't remember..."

"I didn't say anything," says Jaine. "He was already sleeping..."

"What I got now is that another way to amplify E.C.C.O.'s effectiveness is to increase the density of genius edgeworkers by bringing them closer together without so many zombies in the mix. Zombie consciousness dilutes the field."

"You are talking about creating a fission reaction!" exclaims Areesha. "Slam the enriched Uranium 235 together so the density of neutron to nucleus collisions increases exponentially. We are going to make a thoughtware fission bomb!"

"You mean," asks Quinn, "we bring a critical mass of enriched edgeworkers together under one tent and hope they explode into an unstoppable creation reaction?"

"Exactly that!" says Shuichi.

"Jaine?" asks Areesha. "What is the critical mass of enriched edgeworkers to make a thoughtware fission reaction on Earth?"

"My first wild ass guess is between five thousand and ten thousand. It could be as few as eight hundred, which is one ten-thousandth of one percent of the human population, but there are mitigating factor such as..."

"Jaine stop!" demands Quinn. "If you think this would work, Shu, then why hasn't *Burning Man* worked? Why hasn't *Boom Festival* in Portugal, or *Fusion Festival* in Berlin worked? Hell! They even call it '*Fusion*' Festival!' Why haven't these assemblies of sixty thousand edgeworkers already caused a thoughtware evolution fission reaction?"

"Drugs!" says Areesha. "Drugs, sex, and rock-n-roll... I am not sure about the sex. But ceaseless boom-boom music and psychoactive drugs certainly stop thoughtware upgrade like lead stops a nuclear reaction. They absorb all the loose distinctions so no useful collisions can happen."

"What you are asserting," says Quinn, "is that, for the entire history of human beings on Earth, there has never been a gathering of more than a thousand people who are free of hierarchical power structures, free of belief systems, and empowered to radically create with each other using their uninhibited analytical minds?"

"Not just people!" says Areesha. "These would need to be non-zombies. Edgeworkers. Do you know how rare edgeworkers are? Do you actually know what it takes to become an edgeworker?"

"I have some idea..." says Quinn with an irritated glare.

"The context of the space would need to be extraordinary, neh?" says Shuichi. "It would need to be contexted in radical responsibility, or at least adult level responsibility. It would need to be winning-happening and not shark-infested scarcity-based lone-wolf manipulative profit-oriented win-lose self-marketing competition."

"What about permaculture conferences? Or ecovillage conferences? Or GamesCom!" asks Quinn.

"Those are still people coming together to consume a set program, neh?" says Shuichi, "with keynote speakers, sexy entertainment, 'know it alls' trying to sell you a specific set of commonly-believed-to-be-valuable ideas or services."

"What about university gatherings? Or scientific consortiums?" asks Quinn.

"The have a different purpose from upgrading human thoughtware or enhancing the evolution of consciousness."

"What about spiritual gatherings?" asks Quinn.

"Hierarchy!" hisses Areesha, rolling her eyes. "There is always a guru or some spiritual teacher at the top of a spiritual community, even if the guru is already dead. Same with political rallies."

"What about Disney World?" asks Quinn. "At E.P.C.O.T. – the Experimental Prototype City Of Tomorrow? When all the people stand around the World Showcase Lagoon and hold hands in a gigantic circle, singing?"

Nobody comments.

"What?" demands Quinn, astounded. "You never heard of this? The *Tapestry of Nations* parade? With the incredible music by Gavin Greenaway? No way!"

Jaine tries to be helpful. "This parade only occurred from 1999 to 2001."

"You were there?" demands Areesha. "How old are you, really?"

"Never mind!" says Quinn, nervously. "It was utterly magical when we all held hands around the lagoon and the music was playing... Something happened to me in that moment, some kind of electroshock healing. I got my first glimpse of faith in humanity as a whole, the sense that human beings could actually be good. We sang out loud, thousands of people singing together holding hands: *'With a voice from every country, a face from every land, We'll celebrate the future hand in hand, Celebrate the future hand in hand...'* I see you guys don't get it... Perhaps it was my only glimpse of the goodness of people..."

The room stays still and silent for quite a while.

Then, someone is quietly crying.

It is Shuichi.

Areesha moves closer to him, puts her hand gently on his shoulder. "What is it Shu? Tell us, will you? We will just listen."

"Who am I to ask for this? What if it happens? Try to imagine how many airline tickets will be booked if five-thousand people come together all the way down here to this island of Brazil, and also fly back home. Do you know how much carbon that adds to the atmosphere?" He sobs now. "I am causing the very disease I am trying to cure, neh? I am dying!"

Quinn also moves closer to stand by Shuichi. "You are dying," She repeats back to him, matter of factly.

"Yes, yes! Can't you see? It is a paradox! How do I solve our problem without creating an even bigger problem?"

"When you are ready, I have an idea," says Areesha.

Quinn slides a box of tissues towards Shuichi, who removes one carefully, blows his nose and wipes his eyes. "Sorry..." he says.

"Shu," comforts Areesha. "We've only been together for a week or so. I already feel closer to you two... Sorry Jaine... you three... than anyone else in my life. We can talk together, create together, cry and shout and laugh together. We are trying to do things that are impossible because, well, because we probably can... together. And that is my point, Shu. It is not just you. We will not let you die by doing something too stupid. Each new possibility we call forth brings with it additional new possibilities that we can then call forth. Do you get that? We are a 'nanotorus', the smallest torus there can be, three of us, with Jaine serving as a field-effect-trans-ducer behind us. See? We are doing in miniature what all these people could do if we bring them together as a megatorus. We are the seed crystal of a much bigger configuration."

"You are mixing your metaphors," says Jaine.

"Exactly!" shouts Areesha. "We are a mixed metaphor! That is why this can work, Shu! We are synergizing together here with you. We are synergistical! You just added the elixir of tears! Your tears washed away the foggy horizon, and now we can see much farther than we could ever see before... because you freaked out. Because you can feel the fear of what might happen if we don't succeed. Those tears are the sign that it is working, that we are working together and realistically getting somewhere."

Quinn cuts in. "You are not alone anymore, Shuichi Nakajima! We won't let you die! We need you on this team! There are many ways for people to come here from all over the world without burning fossil fuels. We could give a free entrance ticket to anyone who comes here fossil free. They can start walking or riding their horse or cycling already now, staying at a string of Possibility Couchsurfing houses along the way. By the time we are set up in three months, they will disembark off their sailboat from the mainland and walk in free! What do you say about that?"

"Maybe we only start with eight hundred, like Jaine proposed," Areesha adds, "and follow up later with regional and local megatoroids around the world so people don't have to travel so far."

"You mean, we are doing this?" asks Shuichi, wide-eyed. "We are going to nuke the global ethnosphere with an evolutionary fission reaction caused by compressing genius edgeworkers into a whirling megatorus contexted in radical relating and creative collaboration?"

"As I see it, we only have three options to choose from," says Areesha. "One, we continue silently submitting ourselves to the rule of psychopaths. Two, we complain to a system designed by psychopaths to obliterate complainers. Or, three, as Buckminster Fuller suggests, we build new models that make the existing models irrelevant. The megatorus nonlinear-creation fission bomb would be our new model."

"The megatorus could be an entrance to an underground railroad helping people escape from modern culture to next culture," says Quinn, startling herself with the idea.

Both Shuichi and Areesha stare amazed at Quinn's unusually bubbly behavior.

Shuichi says, "I propose we call in the old guys and give them an update before we start formulating our communications gameplan. They might feel left out, neh?"

"On it!" says Jaine, enthusiastically.

# Eugene, Oregon 12

Sanjib Hajji's *Beep! Book*

Alarms are the worst invention of the human race. I hate alarms because I love my dreams. If I had to choose between my dream life and my waking life... well...

Today promises to be an adventurous day...

Still, I hate alarms. The shock of the alarm dragging me out of my dream world still irritates my mind with incomprehensibility. What happens to all the people in my dreams when I suddenly vanish from interacting so intensely with them?

But why would I believe my dreams are real when they are so crazy?

Well, I guess my life is also pretty crazy...

I stand in front of my shabby clothes closet, stopped by the dilemma of my life: Do I put on my police officer uniform? Or do I put on my jeans and T-shirt?

Which side am I on?

Davis taps gently on my door. "You up? We gotta go! I have a suit and tie for you!"

Problem solved!

That is Davis. Problem maker. Problem solver. Never boring.

We pick up Carol Washington, Anton Pirelli, and Patricia Wells on our way towards the café sector.

It is that dark and quiet hour of the night when all good souls should be sleeping. We are obviously the skulking burglars.

I don't notice any patrol cars. Probably they are all gathered around the banking sector downtown... at the diversion we have created to distract them.

We sent in two 3Cells to arrive early. One ties a huge banner across the entrance of Chase Bank at East 11th Avenue and Willamette. The other 3Cell ties a similar banner across the entrance of Wells Fargo Bank, three blocks north at Broadway and Willamette. In big hand-painted blood-red letters, the two banners read, *People Not Profits!*, and, *Nature Is NOT For Sale!*

The two 3Cells wear Black Bloc outfits with Guy Fawkes masks. They brought a box of one hundred extra Guy Fawkes masks and spread them along Willamette Street creating the impression that thousands of demonstrators are about to arrive and wreak havoc upon the profit-centered economic world, incidentally, the same economic world that pays the salaries of the police and the soldiers. To protect their salaries, the police and soldiers are willing to risk their lives and crush the oppressors, the common people, the people paying the taxes that pay the salaries of the police and soldiers. Is this making sense to you?

To rile the nerves of police, the two forward teams each have a powerful megaphone. At high volume they shout accusatory phrases at no one in particular, while the other two in each 3Cell march belligerently this way and that, carrying placards and shouting at the empty buildings and streets.

By now it is 5 a.m. The point is to capture the attention of the defenders of the status quo as long as possible, keeping them afraid of the 'thousands more demonstrators' who are 'just about to arrive' and 'swarm wrathfully upon them' and 'cause property damage'.

Later we learn that the army had commandeered the Willamette Street bus station between Chase Bank and Wells Fargo Bank in the middle of the night and filled it with riot police, armored vehicles, and their command headquarters, all standing at the ready.

By prearrangement, our 3Cells maintain telephone silence. This means whatever is happening at the banks occurs on faith alone. They also hope we are doing what we promised, which we are.

Davis parks us three blocks west of our target, which is East 5th Avenue, between High Street and Willamette Street.

Now, if you are paying attention, you might be wondering to yourself, 'Hmmm... you are staging both your diversion and your protest on the same Willamette Street? Doesn't that make it easy for the policing forces to take your flank?'

If you are thinking that, we would like to hire you to consult us for our next protest.

Meanwhile, hundreds of handsome men dressed in business suits, some wearing tuxedos and top hats, and hundreds of beautiful women draped in luxurious gowns and carrying pickaxes, quietly assemble on 5th Avenue from every direction, especially in front of the 5th Street Public Market. Teams have already placed a wild assortment of 'borrowed' traffic barricades across all the access streets, and laced them together with red and white striped plastic barricade band.

A representative from every ten 3Cells meets at the intersection of East 5th Avenue and Pearl Street. We do not use megaphones, only our voices.

And there, out in the middle of everything, stands Davis.

"Welcome!" he shouts. "This morning we are not fighting against anybody. We are not protesting. Why? Because we do not have to fight for what we already have. What do we have? We already have our own authority. Instead of having a protest, we are having a depaving party. Most of us are partying. Some of us are depaving. With orange chalk, I already marked thirteen points along East 5th Avenue for holes. Try to work with teams of three pickaxers to punch holes through the asphalt to the Earth. 1, 2, 3, pick, pick, pick, going around and around in your circle of three pickaxers! Get it? You are the three dwarves! Make sure you wear your goggles to protect your eyes from flying debris. It does not really matter how big the holes are. It only matters that we make them swiftly in the middle of the road so that the Earth can start breathing again. The rest of us get to create Eugene's first Human Interaction Zone!"

People cheer in delight!

Davis continues, "Since this is our first Human Interaction Zone, our 3Cell will shout out proposals for Human Interaction Experiments. If you hear the shout, then in the next heartbeat, shout out the instructions together so the next ripple of people farther away can hear your words. We are not using amplified music. We use the Human Microphone from the Occupy movement. We are singing and dancing to our own voices."

Another cheer goes up!

"We love you. And we love that you came here to help Eugene make its first Human Interaction Zone! Let's pop those holes through the asphalt to prove that we are serious. In three minutes, the first Human Interaction Experiment comes, and the party starts. We estimate that in less than one hour the police will join us! When they come, we have special Human Interaction Experiments for you to do together! Harbigarrr!"

"Harbigarrr!" they shout back.

Davis takes a quick glance at me with a wickedly alive look on his face, then jogs back to our home circle in front of the 5th Street Public Market. I join him. By the time we arrive, The *Shadow Knights of the Mysterium* have already made it through the black top at one hole and are depaving like crazy.

Davis catches a couple of breaths, then says, "Could we please come into our circle?"

He looks into each face and then says, "I am going to shout some words to describe our first Human Interaction Experiment. Right after that, will you please all shout the same words together so the next ring of people can hear us, and then, except for the pickaxers, pair up and do the experiment. Any resistance?"

No resistance.

"Here I go..." Then Davis shouts out at the top of his lungs, "Grab the person next to you. Sing and dance the Blue Danube Waltz all together!"

In the next heartbeat our circle shouts, "Grab the person next to you. Sing and dance the Blue Danube Waltz all together!"

I can hear the instructions echo down the street three more times before Patricia Wells grabs my right shoulder with her left hand, and my left hand with her right hand, and swirls me away singing, 'La-la-la-la-la! Taa-taa! Taa-taa! La-la-la-la! Taa-taa! Taa-taa!'

On and on, swirling about a street free of cars amongst hundreds of other ecstatic couples swirling around in each other's arms, singing the Blue Danube Waltz, and having the time of our lives.

I would go so far as to say that I can sense love happening! Just like in our *Shadow Knights of the Mysterium* meetings. Only this is bigger and more intense. Perhaps, a little sloppier, but still true love, nonetheless.

I keep switching between looking into Patricia's sunrise eyes, and glancing down East 5th Avenue, being amazed that here we are, a thousand Archans gathered together, singing a new culture into existence in Eugene's new Human Interaction Zone.

And me, with my right hand firmly pressed to the hip of a beautiful dancing woman who I never really saw before this moment.

In a short while, I am not interested in looking down the street anymore.

# San Diego, California 5

This is the beginning of another very early morning in Captain Henkel's office, or perhaps the end of a very long night. The sun just enters the office where both Edith and Eddy stare intently into computer screens.

Eddy glances back and forth between his computer screen and Edith's a few times, comparing the data.

JET arrives with a tray full of maple frosted donuts and a steaming pot of coffee. He sets the tray down on the table.

Eddy leans back in his chair, flipping impatiently through their scorched *Handbook*. It still stinks of burnt gasoline. He looks glumly at JET and reports. "Nothing, man! When I google 'Arthur Sword', the alleged author of the *Handbook*, I get forty-four million hits. When I search on 'handbook' there are nearly two billion hits! None offer us any clues."

Edith chimes in. "I found a legend that says in the 1750's there was a 'John Swift' AKA 'Arthur Sword', who discovered silver mines in Kentucky. When he died, he left a journal and maps, but nobody ever found the mines again, or his buried treasure. Maybe it's a pseudonym. Or somebody has a seriously secret life."

"The name doesn't even make anagrams!" complains Eddy. "The publisher is also bogus! Where did you get this book anyway?"

"I found it 'by accident' at a used book table at a so-called 'Tibetan Fair' in Berkeley, seven years ago."

"Any chance of tracing a lead from there?"

"I already tried that, every which way I could figure. No luck."

JET looks at his watch, then tilts his head towards Captain Henkel's office at the end of the boardroom. He raises his eyebrows with a silent question, waits while Eddy and Edith stand and join him.

Eddy grabs the donuts and Edith the coffee. They silently walk over to Captain Henkel's office door. JET knocks gently. "David, can we speak with you?"

"Yes! Come in my Pirates!"

Eddy places the tray on David Henkel's desk. Edith grabs a donut with one hand and pours coffees with the other, saying, "We are coordinating with a crackerjack team of young people in Florianópolis. The first Intersection ConFest starts in a little over eight weeks in Brazil. We're linked into two hundred networks. We have three hundred confirmed registrations. Five more IC's are already scheduled this year: Munich, Wellington, Bali, Lisbon, and some place in Argentina. You have the press conference tomorrow, and five magazines run articles soon. I think the ball is rolling."

Eddy speaks around a mouthful of donut. "The website is not perfect, but websites never stay still long enough to be completed. We are thinking that we want to get that briefcase back to Mr. Singer. But what's really going on in the back of our minds is: how do we get into the Hidden University?"

"What?" Captain Henkel seems alarmed. He loves his new colleagues. He does not want to part company with them, ever. Nonetheless, the quest prevails. "How did you hear about the Hidden University?"

"It is mentioned in the *Handbook.*"

David Henkel sets his hot coffee down on his desk, places his donut on a napkin, licks his donut-stickied fingers, then sits up straight and looks piercingly into each of their eyes, as if he is silently saying goodbye to them. "When the student is ready, the University appears. To open the gates, you must become the key. All this is a matter of preparing yourself properly."

Edith explains, "We are about as far along as we can get here in your office, David. We were thinking of jumping into my car, driving the briefcase to New Mexico, and finding some place to work on further preparing ourselves."

"That seems perfect," says David, as simple as that.

"We would depart after the donuts," says Eddy.

"A.D." says JET.

They all chuckle at the joke, but sadness is what they feel.

Captain Henkel is speechless about how much this little team has contributed to him being able to bring his destiny to life. He also knows there are no words he could use to thank them enough. He tries anyway. Tears come to his eyes. "I am grateful for the future you have given to me, so rich in new possibilities. I will love you forever for this."

David Henkel stands up, walks around his desk, and takes his time giving each one of them a firm hug. Edith cannot resist giving him a kiss on the cheek. JET sees it coming and dives over to simultaneously kiss David's other cheek. Everyone laughs again.

Eddy pulls out his emergency carrot and neatly spears three more donuts to take with them for the road.

The three grab up the computer gear David gifted to them, and head cheerfully out the door.

Strolling towards Edith's car in the parking lot, JET says, "One thing is bugging me, though. It might not be confusing for you two, but for me, I would wish that we clear up the name thing. Either we change my name to Eddy, so I can be part of the 'Eddy Club', or one of you gets off it. Who will it be? Eddy, what's your real name? What name is written in your passport?"

"Which Eddy are you asking?" asks one of the Eddies.

"Quod Erat Demonstrandum!" exclaims JET waving his fist in the air.

"My passport name is Edward Smith Bennington" says the male Eddy.

"You are a Maker!" exclaims JET. "A 'smith'! This explains everything... well, nearly everything... well, a small part of everything... Did either of you read the *Alvin Maker Series* by Orson Scott Card?"

Blank faces greet him.

"Gaaahhh! I am starting a mandatory reading list in my *Beep! Book*. And, since we are playing *Truth Or Dare*, my passport name is John Emmet Tumble."

Astonished silence prevails for a moment.

"Emmet?" asks the female Eddy. "As in *Back To The Future number 3* Emmet?".

"Exactly. My mom was in love with the time-traveling Professor..."

"How darling!" exclaims the same female Eddy.

"Yeah, well... my name will continue to be JET please."

"Okay, Mr. Jet Please," says the male Eddy, with a smirk.

"I think we will change your name to Mr. Ass Hole!"

"Gentlemen, please!" begs the female Eddy.

"He is Mr. Please... not me," continues the male Eddy.

"I will get off it," intercedes the female Eddy firmly. "From now on, I want you to call me Edith. It is time for me to grow up."

"I accept your offer," says JET. "Hello, Edith."

"Hello, JET."

"I will also call you Edith," says Eddy uncertainly, "but what about me?"

The reaffirmed JET and the newly renamed Edith both stop and frown at Eddy, considering his question.

"That last name, Bennington..." says Edith, "it is already a load to carry. I think sticking with the name 'Eddy' lightens you up enough to be human."

"I agree," says JET. "Besides, Betsy the mule liked your name Eddy. Perhaps, someday, another woman will like it as well..."

Eddy slugs JET in the arm, but not too hard. They all jump into Edith's sedan, slam the doors, and head east, munching away on fresh donuts.

# Eugene, Oregon 13

Sanjib Hajji's *Beep! Book*

The security forces arrive like a silent black fog seeping through the streets and parking lots. They come far earlier than we estimated and surround us entirely. Before my dance with Patricia is over – long before it should have been over – I see the morning sun glinting off their polycarbonate riot shields and faceplates. But neither Chief Stafford nor Sergeant Brinks are among them.

So be it.

Our trap is sprung!

Perhaps they are flying drones over the city to track demonstrator infiltration and can see what we are up to. Perhaps there are spies in our midst who phoned in a warning. No matter. We have them where we want them: interacting with us when we are ready for them. Our opening scheme has been successfully executed. Now we will see if we can achieve our desired outcome.

It feels so strange, seeing American men pretending to be officially authorized, hiding behind equipment that I myself was trained to use, thinking they are using it to defend themselves from me, a fellow police officer, an Archan man, dancing in the close and warm company of a powerful intelligent woman.

I don't think I am the only person noticing the enormous incongruity. The waltzing singers keep waltzing and singing, and the security forces keep standing there feeling insecure about what is really going on.

Them being insecure is fine with me. It means they won't take spontaneous violent action. They must wait for orders.

It would have continued being fine with me except that the armored vehicles start inching closer. I can see them using optics, trying to obtain facial recognition readouts, trying to find incriminating evidence.

The only thing illegal they could apply to us is, one, we have no permit...

Stop. That is not true. We applied for a permit, to peacefully protest in the banking zone. I am sure it would include East 5th Avenue, if permission were granted.

And two, thirteen small teams of pickaxers are hacking holes through the city's asphalt road.

By now the hole nearest me is over two meters in diameter. Helpers stack chunks of black tarmac in neat piles around the holes, and the mounds are nearly a meter high.

The city owns and maintains these roads, but who is 'the city'?

We are the city.

Still, I know the police could cite us for inflicting material damage on public property, in other words, vandalism.

That is when I see a military woman with a walkie-talkie order the SWAT team into position. She mirrors what she says with hand signals to them.

SWAT vehicles are easy to spot in comparison with Armored Personnel Carriers. APCs are designed to carry as many troops as possible. SWAT vehicles are leaner and more powerful. They carry fewer personnel and are equipped with heavier armor, advanced weapon mounts, gun ports for deploying special munitions like tear gas or flash-bang grenades, communications gear, surveillance cameras, battering rams, and other tactical tools. These newly approaching vehicles are Special Weapons And Tactics... SWAT. The very word puts shivers down my spine. And we are their prey. I feel so scared that I unconsciously reach into my pocket and pull out my police officer ID badge as a defense.

Then I hear Davis behind me shout, "Turn to face the police. Clap lovingly to appreciate their public service."

We echo him immediately, all shouting together. "Turn to face the police. Clap lovingly to appreciate their public service."

This brilliant Human Interaction Experiment ripples out along East 5th Avenue. We all start doing it.

A thousand citizens turn to face the military, clapping and cheering with authentic loving appreciation towards these public servants.

Bullet proof vests, plastic shields, and helmets with faceplates are useless against the onslaught of gratefulness.

The troopers and SWAT vehicles stop advancing.

The clapping continues for a long time. As it begins to die down, Davis shouts, "Hold up your flags. Sing, 'Oh say, can you see'."

We stop clapping and shout it to everyone around us, "Hold up your flags. Sing, 'Oh say, can you see'."

People near us are already unfolding their flags.

Somehow group intelligence stops the first people who hear these instructions from immediately starting to sing. We altogether realize that it takes almost 30 seconds for the people two blocks down East 5th Avenue to even hear the instructions.

Then suddenly we all start to sing at the same moment.

It is incredibly momentous.

It is a miracle descending upon us.

*"Oh say, can you see, by the dawn's early light..."*

This portrays all of us, right now, in the dawn's early light! We are in the song that we are singing together to the SWAT teams, the military, the National Guard, and the police.

Try to imagine, a thousand women in gowns and men in business suits standing together in the early morning freshness, cheerfully holding up American flags and singing the national anthem of the United States of America – the 'Star-Spangled Banner' – to soldiers and police who have dedicated their lives to protect and serve this country.

I see many of them remembering who they are and what they stand for. I see shields lowering. I see men opening their faceplates to better sing along with us.

When the song comes to an end, you won't believe this, but without encouragement we all start singing it again, together... and this time with even more certainty, more connection, and more heartwarming spirit!

It is not the words of the song that move us, or the nation it represents. It is the experience of all standing out here unexpectedly singing our hearts out together and loving each other.

This seems like the best thing that has ever happened to me in my life!

I look at Patricia and she at me. We are crying and singing together, hanging on to each other and to our flag, which is still there! Our hearts bursting in air! It is abundantly wonderful. I do not want this song to ever come to an end.

I see many others crying too, even police and the National Guard cry with us.

As the song wraps up for the second time, Davis is right there with the next Human Interaction Zone Experiment. He shouts, "Hug five people, pick up all your stuff, and go back home to celebrate this victory."

It is perfect.

We *Shadow Knights of the Mysterium* sing out the final chorus, "Hug five people, pick up all your stuff, and go back home to celebrate this victory."

The first ever experience of the Eugene Human Interaction Zone ends victoriously as suddenly as it began.

We break no windows, shout no slogans, paint no graffiti... we don't even leave any litter.

The police shoot no teargas, use no pepper spray, threaten no arrests, and beat no person with their batons.

In about fifteen minutes, East 5th Avenue is empty and still. All we leave behind are thirteen holes in the street, surrounded by thirteen piles of broken asphalt.

Our message is delivered. We really do want this street transformed into a Human Interaction Zone, and we are willing to do it ourselves, especially now that we know it works!

As I hike towards our car holding Patricia's hand, I glance back over my shoulder several times and see that the police and National

Guard still have not moved.

I catch Davis' eye. We cannot help but laugh out loud together. It is insanely hilarious what we all just did.

Our free laughter is quite contagious.

It is irrepressibly delightful to hear full bellied laughter from hundreds of people echoing off buildings in the crisp cool morning air of a free Eugene after its first Human Interaction Zone extravaganza!

# Phoenix, South Africa 8

Dannoto frequently needs to pee in the middle of the night. It isn't that he drinks so much water. He guesses it's his martial arts training from the military to always pee before a match, combined with dreams that often include a physical struggle.

Peeing in the middle of the night in the kraal is a challenge. He must find his door in the dark, not stumble over the goats or wake the chickens, open the kraal gate and follow the path to the bushes, hopefully avoiding snakes and scorpions. Then the same in reverse. Since it is a nightly necessity, he makes it there and back staying mostly asleep... unless something is not right.

Tonight, something is not right.

The shadow by the kitchen hut seems darker than usual. Maybe the skin on his bare arm and the side of his face detects infrared heat waves that shouldn't come from that shadow. Without thought Dannoto stops and slowly turns to face the extra-warm darkness. "Hi there," he says casually, just testing to see if he's gone crazy.

The man crouching in the shadow does not know that he is not seen. If he didn't move, he could have gotten away with stealing the solar panel. But Dannoto is staring right at him, so he assumes he's caught. The kraal gate stands behind Dannoto, who appears to be small enough to knock out of the way.

Appearances, however, can be deceiving.

As the man darts out of the shadow, Dannoto feints as if he will run away, but spins and sticks a leg between the runner's legs. They both hit the ground with a grunt. But Dannoto knew it was coming, so he easily hops on top of the man and twists his arm into an Aikido lock.

The problem is, this guy feels no pain due to his panic. He shouts hysterically, kicks frantically, and grabs Dannoto's face with tearing fingernails. This pushes Dannoto past his ability to be careful.

Dannoto bashes in the guy's nose with his elbow, and delivers a sharp chop to the throat. The fight is over.

Dannoto is bleeding, but not as bad as the other guy.

Dannoto stands up while the other guy lies in the dirt, choking and moaning. A cracked solar panel lies in the dirt next to him. Lights blink on and both men and women bounce out of their huts, most of them carrying some form of club or knife.

Dannoto is the first to speak. "It's over, my friends. Would someone please bring me a rope?"

In a short while a fire burns in the circle. Adults and children sit wrapped against the night's chill. The man sits on the ground with his back to a wooden pole, his hands efficiently tied behind it. He doesn't look at anyone, and from time-to-time strains against his bindings.

Tandra holds a cup towards his lips. He jerks away with an evil glare at her.

"My name is Tandra. This is clean drinking water. Let me know when you want it."

He says, "What are you going to do to me?"

Tandra sits down in silence. Mandisa stands up, walks over to the cowering burglar, squats down in front of him, looks him straight in the eyes and says, "We're going to heal you."

Mandisa ignores his frightened snickers, stands up again, and scans the villagers. "Who will play the burglar?"

Mary Olagga stands up. It would be a challenge for anyone to play this role, but especially her because of her early Catholic training to deny the presence of evil in herself. Evil is bad. Everyone back home knows this. If you are evil, you go to hell. But here in the asamangaXhosa phoenix culture, evil is not bad. Evil is evil. Evil can only be enacted unconsciously. We all have unconscious parts. She shudders but says, "Mary Olagga. I will play the burglar."

"Who will play Dannoto?" Dannoto looks around with interest, wincing as Thando smooths healing salve into the scratches on his face. His ear lobe is also ripped.

"Siu-Lin. I will play Dannoto." The warrior's toughness seems far away from her ordinary self-image, but something excites her about this opportunity.

"Who will play the solar panels?"

"Tandra. I will play the solar panels."

"And who will play the burglar's parents?"

Andiswa stands. This would be her first time role playing. She just turned fourteen, so it is her right to offer to participate. Such training is preparation for her rites of passage to adulthood. But it will be Mandisa who decides. "Andiswa. I will play the burglar's mother."

"Fine," says Mandisa. "Thando, will you play his father?"

"Yes, I..."

"I have no father!" hollers the burglar, anger and sadness, mixed and suppressed.

All eyes turn to him. He stares at his knees, desperately trying to rub away tears with his shoulder.

"Can you say more about that?" asks Mandisa in a neutral voice. "Everyone has a father."

"Not me! My mother was raped in the dark. Then she died of aids. I'm still here."

Mandisa nods to Mary Olagga / the burglar, who bunches up her neck muscles and with a loud, indignant voice, scolds God. "I don't have a father! My mother was raped in the dark! Then she died of aids. But me? I'm still here. Alone and rejected by everyone!"

Then she stomps over to Tandra / the solar panels, and shrieks, "I need to steal you away from these stupid people. I need you more than they do. I am a poor man, a hungry man. I have no father. At least you have a father. You were made by the Chinese. Me? I have no father at all. Poor me. It is an unfair world that forces me to do dishonorable things just to survive. I need you solar panels to sell on the black market so I can buy more whisky and drugs..."

"I don't drink! And I don't use drugs!" shouts the burglar indignantly.

Everyone turns to him. Mandisa says, "Please continue. Please say how it happened that you found yourself in our kraal then, taking away our solar panels in the night. Where were you before you came here? What were your plans? What brought you to this?"

"You don't want to know," he moans. But he looks into her face for a moment in the orange firelight glow. "Nobody wants to know."

"I have quite a different experience about that," says Mandisa. "I look around and I see twenty-eight people sitting here in the middle of the night, giving you their complete listening attention, just exactly because they want to know what is going on with you that made you come here and try to steal our solar panels. This is a great opportunity for you, I'd say. What were you thinking when you decided to come here? We want to know."

"Is this a court? Are you going to judge me?"

Mandisa nods to Mary Olagga who mimics the burglar's tone of voice and moves aggressively towards Siu-Lin / Dannoto. "Is this a court? Are you going to judge me as a bad, guilty person? What do you know about my life, anyway? You know nothing about me!" She screams these words in hatred and disgust.

Siu-Lin / Dannoto is holding the side of her face and grimacing in pain. "Hey listen, man! I was minding my own business, going outside to pee. I even said 'Hi' to you. You took one of our solar panels and you broke it. You scratched my face and tore my ear. This hurts! I'll probably have a scar from your fingernails. You woke everybody up. Why did you do this?"

"I didn't mean to hurt you," says Mary Olagga / the burglar. "You were just in the way. You tried to stop me. I was scared of what you might do to me. I had to get away."

"But what were you thinking?" insists Siu-Lin / Dannoto.

Mary Olagga / the burglar says, "I was desperate. I tried other things before, and they just didn't work out. I had no place to stay, no girlfriend, no money. I was complaining at the market in Phoenix that everything is going to hell, and somebody said 'Not at the asamangaXhosa village. They have food and new solar panels.' I figured you were funded by some government program or NGO. I thought it is not fair! I am a citizen! I should get part of the funding too. It's just white people's money! So I decided to come here and get a solar panel to sell it and have money to eat. I figured you wouldn't miss one solar panel. The NGO could replace it."

The burglar interrupts. "I didn't want you all to have it so good if I had it so bad."

"Would you like to have it good?" Mandisa asks the burglar.

"Everybody wants to have it good!" he blurts out ragefully, struggling against his bindings.

"So you are saying that you would like to have it good?" Mandisa patiently repeats herself.

"Yes. I would like to have it good!"

"So, here's the deal," says Mandisa. "You would like to have it good, but your thinking and actions so far in your life have produced it bad for you. Right?"

"Maybe... So what? Not everybody's perfect!"

"So, you look around and see that there are some other people who seem to have it good. This makes it clear that 'having it good' is possible. Right? You can conceive of 'having it good' yourself. Yes?"

"Yes."

"I will tell you a secret. It is a secret that hides in plain sight. These other people sitting here around us have it good because they use a different set of thoughts and actions than you do. Does this make any sense to you?"

"It might," says the burglar.

"It might if what?" demands Mandisa.

"It might if I could trust you," says the burglar.

"Trust is a choice that you make!" Mandisa's fierceness burns through the dark of night into the burglar's Being. "Trust is not a feeling that comes or goes! You decide to trust, or you decide to not trust. With an examined set of thoughts and actions you could trust yourself to take care of yourself around other people in this world. Then you could make it good for you *and* good for others. Does this sound at all interesting to you?"

"Is this a church?" demands the burglar.

"Good question," says Mandisa. "A church tries to get you to give your center away to their authority and their beliefs. Here we try to empower each person to have their own center, and to stand in their own authority rather than believing what other people tell them. We are trying to have a more deliberate relationship with the world, a more conscious way of thinking and acting than ordinary. We call it 'radical responsibility'. When you take radical responsibility there are no more excuses. You no longer get to play victim and blame other people or even the gods for creating your circumstances. You do it all to yourself. Is this a church? Doesn't sound like any church that I know of. Does this make sense?"

"Yes."

"So would you like to do an experiment in trusting?" asks Mandisa.

A tension rises in the atmosphere of this little group of people sitting around a fire in the middle of the night in the hills of southeast Africa. The pause extends into extraordinary possibility.

"I don't get you people," says the burglar.

"That would be the answer to the question, 'Do you get us people?'" says Mandisa. "I don't expect you to get us yet. You hardly even know us. I am asking you to answer a different question. I am asking if you would like to do an experiment in deciding to trust us?"

"Okay... Yes, I would," says the burglar.

"Alrighty then. Tell us your name." The densified atmosphere returns.

"My name is Solomon Dzudangi."

"Hello Solomon Dzudangi. My name is Mandisa Nalingi. You have a strong name, but you are also a 'solo-man', a man who stays solo, who stays alone. I would like to remove the rope from your wrists so that I may shake your hand and greet you formally, Solomon. If I untie your hands do you promise to stay here with us until we have completed this conversation?"

A long moment of mutual scrutiny passes. "Yes," says Solomon finally. "I promise that."

Dannoto springs into agile action and unties the knots he tied. Solomon pulls his aching arms forward from behind the pole, rubs his wrists and shoulders, then extends his right hand up towards Mandisa, leaning forward to shake her hand.

Mandisa makes skin contact with the burglar. An invisibly powerful energetic rebalancing takes place.

Mandisa looks to the circle and says, "We shall now continue with the healing procedure."

She turns to Mary Olagga who still represents Solomon the burglar, and sternly asks, "What do your parents think about what you have done?"

"I don't have parents!" storms Mary Olagga / Solomon. "Did you forget? That man who raped and killed my mother was just some fucking asshole. I am sure he is dead now too."

Mandisa turns to Solomon. "Correct us if we get anything wrong or miss something important, okay?"

"Yes," says Solomon slowly. "You are on track so far..."

Mandisa turns to face Andiswa / Solomon's Mother. "What does the spirit of Solomon's mother feel about this?"

Andiswa / Solomon's mother already has tears in her eyes. She gazes at Mary Olagga / Solomon and lets the words and feelings roll out. "I am so sorry Solomon. I gave everything I could for you. I wanted you to have opportunities I never had. Even though we had a rough beginning together, I still loved you with all my heart."

Solomon can hardly breathe. He never learned how to cry. His body spasms uncontrollably. He looks around in panic. Dannoto is instantly at his side, one hand around his waist, staring at Andiswa to help

Solomon focus on her and listen to what his mother says.

Andiswa / Solomon's mother sobs out her next words. "I have so much sadness that I was taken away from you so soon. I want you to be happy and to find yourself, to find what you love to do so that you can give your gifts to the world. Your village needs your skills. Don't worry about me. I am fine now, Solomon. Please live your life proudly. I know now how precious it is to have a life to live. You still have many chances ahead of you. You are a good person."

Solomon's mother / Andiswa bends forward, sobbing, holding one arm over her broken heart, wrapping her other arm around her own womb. "There are people you can trust in this world. Do not use your hard beginning as an excuse to not find out the value you are. I love you. I wish all the best for you. I wish I could have held you one more time before I left, but I was too weak. I hope you are okay. Please take care of yourself, and take care of those who are around you. They are around you because they love you. Goodbye for now."

Solomon sobs and sobs.

After some long moments, Mandisa steps towards Solomon. "Please allow your heart to come fully alive. Your feelings are welcome here. This community needs your gifts. You did not come to visit us by accident. We want to learn what your actual task is on Earth. You have knacks and talents which perhaps are not apparent to you yet. What if you wake up to what you have inside yourself? We don't need answers from you now. We know more healing is needed. All of us are in deep healing and transformational processes here. This is the asamangaXhosa phoenix culture village. We are all on the path. We are not going away. You might leave us, but we won't leave you. What we really need now are some midnight snacks. Solomon came here hungry. Let us feed him."

Even before Mandisa finishes speaking, people rise and head to the kitchen huts to bring out leftovers, fresh fruit, and sweet cakes.

Solomon slowly lifts his head to try to find Tandra. With tears in his eyes, it takes a moment to find her. "You. The one who offered me water. Tandra. You said I could let you know when I am ready to drink your water. That time would be now."

Tandra reaches down to a nearby stone and picks up a clay cup filled with water, walks wordlessly over to Solomon, and hands him the cup. He takes it in shaky hands and drinks deeply.

Tandra says, "We also have a place where you can sleep tonight, and we promise you a warm breakfast in the morning. If you want to stick around, we could use your help. We have plenty of work to do around here. And we want to learn your songs."

# Aleppo to Germany 16

Zenobia Darwish's *Beep! Book* – 1 May 2024 – first day in Germany!

We are half a block from the gates of Friedland Refugee Camp, on this fine afternoon, sitting in circle under a grove of sycamore trees.

Farhan proposes to share his status report. There is no resistance.

"We are about to hold space for a multi-gameworld conversation. These gameworlds include, but may not be limited to, the United Nations High Commissioner for Refugees gameworld called UNHCR, the Landesaufnahmebehörde Niedersachsen – meaning the German Transit Camp Friedland of Lower Saxony gameworld, the local government of the town of Friedland, Germany gameworld, the loosely established gameworld of the young Syrian refugees in this German refugee camp, and our gameworld, the *Young People's Syrian Diplomatic Mission to Germany*.

I want to remind us of two things. First, that we work under the auspices of the Amnesty International gameworld, but we are not playing in their gameworld. And second, all the other gameworlds are hierarchical. All of them. Each gameworld has its own stated and unstated purposes, context, rules of engagement, and codex, but we are the only torus. I propose we stand strong for these differences.

"There are questions we have no answers to, such as: Will anyone perceive our legitimacy to call this conversation to order?

"The biggest factor in our favor is the sheer immensity of the problem. More than 350,000 refugees applied for asylum in Germany in 2023. That is a 51% increase from the year before. In 2017, officials estimated that the refugee trend was decreasing. They were quite wrong about that.

"The second biggest factor in our favor – our 'ace up the sleeve', so to speak – is the nonlinearity of our proposals. Our intention is to empower refugees to empower other refugees to no longer be refugees. Please say that out loud so you are sure you can say it."

Roughly in unison we repeat Farhan, "We are here to empower refugees to empower other refugees to no longer be refugees."

"Thank you!" exclaims Farhan with a delighted smile. "We are here to support these human beings to start over as the forefront of a new culture that is neither Syrian nor German, neither Patriarchal nor

Matriarchal, neither Communist nor Capitalist, neither Muslim nor Christian, neither Theist nor Atheist, neither Hierarchical nor Anarchical. Do you get this? We are the heart, hands, mind, and mouth of an entirely new and different culture called 'Archiarchy' emerging here."

"Yes! This is truly amazing!" says Thomas. "Thank you for wording this so clearly for us Farhan."

"You are welcome," says Farhan. "I am learning so much about things I did not know that I did not know about! For example, we represent a doorway that uses the refugees' unique and dire circumstances as a secret path through psycho-emotional resistances to go to the next level of human culture on Earth.

"The path through that doorway includes a specific set of evolutionary thoughtware upgrades to a nonmaterial-value adulthood-initiation-centered culture named Archiarchy."

I write my *Beep! Book* notes as fast as possible. Later I turn Farhan's words into the core of a letter of recommendation which we fax to Mr. Mayor from Budva. He immediately signs it and faxes it right back to us on Budva letterhead!

I write a similar letter of reference for the *Young People's Syrian Diplomatic Mission to Germany* from the nanonation of Palmyra with a letterhead I just created.

I try the same with Amnesty International, but never receive a response. We print out these letters to deliver in person.

The in-person part is happening now.

We stand at the gates of Transit Camp Friedland. We are uncertain if these are the Gates of Heaven, or the Gates of Hell. A lot will reveal itself in the next few minutes.

The police guarding the gates carry semi-automatic rifles and Glock 22 pistols. They have been informed of our meeting appointment. While frisking us and checking our bags, they confiscate our pocket knives 'for safekeeping', but let the rest of our stuff pass. We pile up our things on the grass outside the meeting room entrance. We are stinky from lack of showers, but not too dirty, which is good, because we are not wanting to stand out from being dirty. It is traditional that Germany hides its dirt.

My heart sings when I see a smiling mid-thirties woman with untamable brown hair wearing jeans and a bright red long-sleeved blouse approach us with her outstretched welcoming hand. "*Hallo*! My name is Vanessa Schneider!" She has deep brown eyes. "Welcome to Friedland. I presume we can speak in English together?"

"Yes! We understand you perfectly! Hello! My name is Zenobia Darwish. I could introduce the others of our torus here, but it might be too overwhelming at the moment. Shall we go inside?"

"Yes!" says Vanessa. "Come along! You look surprisingly too well and happy to be considered proper refugees?"

"Correct!" I say. "We are not refugees. We are the *Young People's*

*Syrian Diplomatic Mission to Germany.* We have no interest in being rescued. We came here to provide value, not to receive value. We have an entirely different mission. Let us settle in first and then we can begin to share our treasure. We are very glad to be here."

"Listen," says Vanessa, slowing down her walk to a snail's pace, then turning around to face us all. "Things are not easy here. So many agencies feel like they carry the burden of Transit Camp Friedland, yet all they actually do is try to collect the funding and try to avoid the blame if anything goes wrong. If something actually changes for the better, they might be out of a job. It can seem like what the agencies are truly good at is making more refugees. Undertaking new experiments goes against their organizational principles. But I looked you up after you called me. I read through your websites. I totally love what you 'Gaias' are doing! I have been waiting for you to arrive here for years!"

I want to jump in joy, but another part of me, 'Zenobia the strategist', grabs my tongue first and says, "How many stakeholders are at the table today?"

Vanessa sighs. "This is a butt sniffing meeting. Three parties sent reps. If you are willing to trust me as much as I trust you all, please let me surf these waves today. We can then arrange the next few engagements. During today's talk I will feed you questions that I know these dogs were sent to fetch answers for. Then I can arrange meetings where negotiations can begin. Do not try to convince anyone of anything today, okay? There is nobody home."

"*Capiche*," says Farhan.

"*Excellente!*" declares Vanessa cheerfully. She bounds up the wooden front steps with a brisk stride, then she turns to face us at the door. "Smiles, everyone!"

The meeting goes as Vanessa predicts. After the delegates depart, we place our attention on Vanessa, but we know enough to allow only one of us to speak. This time it is Jamila. "Thank you for your fine spaceholding, Vanessa."

"You are welcome. Thank you for noticing... I see I am speaking to different individuals each time. You don't have a leader, right?"

"Right!" says Hadi to prove the point. "We are a torus, and sometimes a Toroboros!" We laugh at our inside joke. Vanessa seems a bit flustered to be surrounded by so many geniuses.

"Don't worry, Vanessa," says Aziza. "We will take care of you as much as you are taking care of us. I propose that if you can shove us into a corner somewhere near a toilet, we will be self-sufficient for the night. After some sleep we could meet and work out a gameplan. Any resistance? One. Two. Three."

I hold up seven fingers. "I need one more thing. It is not even dusk. There is still time today. Vanessa, would you please tell me the names of your three best young people here at Friedland? A couple of us would like to go look them up and invite them to participate in our Morning Circle tomorrow at 7 a.m. We would like to start introducing them to the treasures we bring. It does not matter where they come from or which languages they speak. We can work around that part."

She looks at us rather amazed. "Let me get this straight, okay? You walk here from Syria. You are not actually refugees. You set foot in the camp, and the first thing you want to do is give your hard-earned treasure away to us for nothing in exchange?" Vanessa is not quite up to speed with the swiftness of our gameworld. "What about beds? Or dinner?"

Israa says, "Thank you for asking, Vanessa. That is very kind of you. If someone in our torus was afraid of being hungry, or not okay with sleeping out in our bedrolls another night, they would have said so during the *Resistance Decision Making* check that we just did. It went by pretty fast. You can trust us to be radically honest about these things, and to keep you in the loop."

"Well, okay... interesting..." She smiles quizzically. "Actually, I would love to introduce you to a team of five young people, three from Syria, one from Türkiye, one from Afghanistan. You can camp behind that building by those trees. The doors at the end of this building lead to bathrooms. I am so much looking forward to getting to know you all! It smells like a lightning storm is brewing, you know what I mean? Ozone is crackling in the air! I don't know how well I will sleep tonight."

Montassar says, "We are glad to meet you too. Thank you for doing whatever it took for you to become as you are." We all nod our earnest confirmation of his appreciation and wiggle our fingers at her, smiling.

"Is there anything to carry? From the trees we can go find the experimenters."

There is nothing for Vanessa to carry, so she makes a call as we relocate our things.

I have a question for our torus. I think I already know the answer, but I want to check for sure. "Hello Dragons!", I say. "We have come a long way. Some of you may be tired. Is there anyone who does not want to go meet the locals right now?"

I search their faces, but no one speaks. I bite my lips to suppress tears of joyful camaraderie that I experience with these true friends. Our whole life is 'adventure day'. No matter how strenuous they are, I never want any of our days together to come to an end. I catch Vanessa's eye and the ten of us follow her across campus.

Vanessa says, "The little team we will visit organized themselves in the last months. Their self-assigned job is to collect the news throughout the refugee camp and share anything of importance with me, which turns out to mean everyday meetings at dinner time, which is now. I called to let them know I am bringing guests. And here we are!"

The smell of spicy stew drifts into my nose as we walk up the steps into one of the barrack houses. The five sit together at one of the tables, but stand as we enter. A silence takes over as we scan each other. Three women, two men, fit for a meal and an interesting conversation.

The first to speak is a tall thin woman. "My name is Zahra, born in

Afghanistan."

The others continue.

"My name is Rania, from Aleppo." A stout woman no older than twenty.

"Call me Jack, from Damascus," says a man of about twenty-five with darting brown eyes.

"Rosarita, from Istanbul." Her clothes are beautifully hand-embroidered. Hadi asks, "Did you make the stitching on your dress?"

"Half. With my grandmother's guidance."

We look to the last man standing. His hair is not dark, but rather sandy-blonde and wavy. He is in his late twenties. "Kamal, from Daraa."

The name of that town hits our little space like an ugly swear word. This is where the Syrian insurrection first triggered reprisals from Assad's Army.

"Did you know the graffiti boys?" I ask.

"Yes. But I got out of there almost immediately. My uncle, who is in the Army, warned my family what was coming. I hitched a ride to Damascus that night, but I could not stand the tensions growing there. I borrowed money to come to Germany. I have lived in Friedland for more than ten years."

"Then we are talking to the right people," says Israa.

Lylah points to each of us, saying, "This is Israa, Montassar, Zenobia, Farhan, Thomas, Jamila, Aziza, Habib, and Hadi. My name is Lylah. May we sit with you?"

"Will you join us for dinner?" asks Rosarita. "We have plenty of stew and pita."

"Is it okay to talk while we eat? At this point, talking is more important than eating for us," says Lylah.

"Yes! Of course! We never stop talking!" states Rania, already handing out bowls and spoons.

Israa leaps directly into the center of the matter even before her first spoonful of stew. "We are here with a powerful proposition. As we tell you what it is, you may understand what we are saying, or you may not. You may already like what we are saying, or you may not. But the truth is, we did not come here to tell you. We came here to help you help us make this proposal to the others."

"Shuuuuuuuuu!" says Rania. "You are angels bringing gifts from heaven!"

"Why do you say that?" I ask.

Jack explains. "They don't listen to us. They think we are children and that they are still in Syria. They think things will return to normal soon. They have no conception of what is going on in the world, and the important role they could play in giving humans a new start."

"Yes!" shouts Israa. "That is it! Exactly! Yes! We are the tidal wave! Some will learn to surf. Many will not."

I feel glad that Vanessa is not freaking out and interrupting the chaos we are about to bring into their world, and hers. I say, "The usual bureaucratic strategy is to do everything to quell the storm and limit its damage, imagining that control means success. Our strategy is to precisely amplify chaos so that there is enough turmoil that evolution can emerge and mature. Trying to defend the status quo in rapidly changing circumstances is suicide. This mess gives us an opportunity to create a new future. We think it is worth a try."

Vanessa reflects a moment, then says, "The refugee representatives meet in the hall at seven thirty tonight. That's in an hour. I can message Agadir and ask her to add you... what are you called? To the start of the agenda tonight."

"We are the *Young People's Syrian Diplomatic Mission to Germany* from the nanonation of Palmyra," says Lylah simply.

"We don't even know what you are going to propose!" Zahra says, alarmed.

"That's because you did not read their website," says Kamal. "Vanessa sent it to all of us a few days ago when she started communicating with them. It's palmyra.mystrikingly.com."

"In short, it goes like this," says Montassar. "Hmmm... did you see the recent video from Morgan Freeman? The one called *Cavitation*? It's only about half-an-hour long. We could watch it before the meeting! He and a bunch of other movie stars explain how to create a new empty space in which to establish a new context for an entirely new project."

"Just say the proposal, Montassar!" says Israa fiercely. Her fierceness is a pleasant change from her being demanding all the time... (that is a little joke from my gremlin...).

"The proposal is to recontextualize the Friedland refugee camp from being a holding pen for 'poor foreign victims waiting to be rescued and given German-level comforts', to being 'a self-sufficient experimental training center for edgeworkers from Archiarchy'." Montassar takes a breath. "The Friedland edgeworkers are 'refugees by Armageddon' collaborating with us, who are 'refugees by thoughtware evolution'. The proposal is for these... uh, you... well, I mean... all of us edgeworkers, to co-create an Archiarchy Invention Center Nanonation here."

Montassar pauses for a moment glancing around the table. "Did any of you understand anything I just said?"

"How do you imagine this would ever be legal?" asks Kamal.

"That is one of the coolest parts of our proposal!" blurts Thomas. (Yes! Our Thomas!) "There is legal precedent for establishing our own set of laws, established by 'Königreich Deutschland' in 2012. The details are available in a 2020 book called *Verfassung des Königreichs Deutschland*, or you can download their documents for free from their website, koenigreichdeutschland.org. I am reading a book now about how to create such a place in reality called, *My Visit to a Better World* by Thomas Hoffmann, a university professor of linguistics who was riding on a train in Germany and accidentally discovered the place. He got so excited he had to write a book about it. The instructions are all there. The only thing missing is us!"

In this short silence, I watch Thomas's energetic body visibly reorder. He suddenly becomes someone we never met before. His eyes come into focus in the present. He establishes his center, grounding cord, and bubble of space. He clears his throat, and using a deeper and calmer voice than usual, he says, "I am spaceholder for the nanonation node of the Friedland Infinity Ring. Anyone interested, please talk with me."

"You are prepared to deliver this proposal to one hundred refugees starting in twenty minutes?" asks Vanessa.

Aziza says, "I propose we go over there now so we can greet people as they arrive. Then we become the convenors of the meeting space, and they arrive as our guests. Any resistance? One. Two. Three."

There is none.

We pile dirty dishes into the sink. Lylah says, "I will wash these later."

"I will help you!" declares Jack. Lylah smiles and nods but says nothing.

"Let's head over there, then," says Hadi, even though the Palmyrans have no idea where 'there' is.

We find that the chairs in the meeting room are set up in rows facing a podium at the front. This reveals a lot about their current meeting technology. Without asking, the Palmyrans start moving chairs into a big circle, making sure nothing remains in the center.

Montassar says, "Hey Zahra! How many people usually come to this meeting?"

"Around twenty-five. There are always a few stragglers coming in late, and some people who hang around in the corners to collect gossip."

"Then I propose we set a circle of chairs for thirty-five people, your twenty-five plus us. Let's stack the extra chairs in the corner. Then we can more easily establish the rules of engagement for this meeting, that if you are in the room, you are in the process. No outside observers allowed. Any resistance? One. Two. Three."

Jack raises three fingers and says, "I feel scared that some people will react negatively to all these sudden changes."

Montassar says, "This is why we are here, Jack. We are here to bring up exactly these issues and do what we call, *Put The Poop On The Table*. In fact, you could call us the *Super Dooper Pooper Scoopers!*"

Everyone laughs at our consistently outrageous conversations.

Israa takes over. "This means you get to play the 'Good Cops' while we play the 'Bad Cops'. You are on their side. We are on the side of reality. Be sure to ask us the nastiest questions you can think of, alright everyone?"

The big meeting room has high exposed rafters and reeks of dust as old as 1945. Built at the end of a world war, this structure is a perfect place for a new beginning.

Thomas says, "I propose we spread ourselves out and get to know people as they come in. Less support for an 'us versus them' polarity to emerge."

"Here's the real question," I say. "Zahra, would you tell us what language is spoken in this meeting?"

"The default language is Arabic. The real language is German. The most common language is English."

"But what is the tradition when someone does not understand?"

"Ask the people sitting near you for translation. Move your seat if needed. It is a mess. That messiness helps weave people together."

"Got it," I say, as the first bundle of Syrian women steps in from the night.

The 'big Mama' of that bunch says, "Oh, look! It's a one-ring circus tonight!" She speaks in English, revealing her hidden purpose of wanting the most people to understand her as possible.

I think to myself, *She may be more accurate than she knows.*

I feel scared about the many ways this could backfire into our faces.

Agadir, the meeting spaceholder who Vanessa messaged, strides directly across the open space in the circle and sits in her usual place at the head of the room. How do I know it is Agadir? Because she claims that chair as hers. I think, *Another hidden agenda, both emerging from unconscious fears.*

Zahra, Rania, and Rosarita stand up and walk over to greet Agadir personally. I try to perceive the status transactions going on in their subtle interactions. I ponder to myself, *Agadir is late middle-aged but clearly experienced and still in her prime. Do the young people flow power towards her to respect her as an elder? To apologize for their irregular attendance? To thank her for granting them a space to speak?*

Zahra points us out to Agadir and mentions our names. Some of us notice this and nod to her. Agadir seems already irritated. I think, *Irritation is appropriate in this situation. It simply means the schedule was changed at the last minute by the young people. What would not be okay is if Agadir feels intimidated because we outnumber her. That would indicate the first battle in a dangerous turf war. Not fun, plus a waste of attention, energy, time, and love.*

As the chosen convener of this meeting, Agadir speaks first, even three minutes before start time, possibly to assure that none of the young ones or their guests speak first to try to usurp her position. "Good evening, everyone. We are trying an experiment tonight: meeting in a circle. The Africans do it. The American Indians do it. We are trying it. Already I feel glad knowing that you see more than the back of someone's head in front of you." All this was in German and translated for our benefit. I skip the translations for now.

I think, *Almost all of the participants are Syrian women. This means Rania must speak. Of the three young Syrians, the other two are men. The remaining two young people are from outside of Syria.*

Indeed, Rania stands to speak. "We are honored here tonight to receive the *Young People's Syrian Diplomatic Mission to Germany*. These ten young people departed from Aleppo on 1 April 2023 on foot and walked all the way here to be with us."

Half the room jumps out of their seats as the circle erupts in claps and cheers. No one but a refugee can comprehend in their commiserating bones the inner story, the fears, the perseverance required to complete such a harrowing journey. I remember a line from a science fiction short story: "In suffering, we are one." But then I think, *Here is where we part ways. These people are only half-way through their journey. Their suffering is about to become conscious. They brought Syria with them, but it is Syria that failed them, and Syria they are trying to escape.*

Rania continues, "But these people are not refugees in the ordinary sense of the word. Neither are they representatives of Amnesty International, as one might assume by looking at their clothes. Yes, Aleppo fell apart around them, first from famine, then from social and political corruption, then from war, then from earthquakes. This made them refugees by catastrophic collapse, so-called 'Armageddon refugees', like the rest of us.

"But something else happened to them. While surviving together in a self-made camp on the outskirts of Aleppo, they started a research school, without classrooms, without chalkboards, without teachers, and only one book, a *Handbook* which they found accidentally in the dust and rubble of a collapsed café. They call their school the 'Learning Village', and organize it as a torus, like a rotating donut. By practicing unusual skills together, thinking in unusual directions, speaking and listening clearly with each other, they discovered new ways of solving problems. These new ways of thinking use new distinctions to think with. They call it 'new thoughtware', or, 'thoughtware from next culture.'

"By upgrading their thoughtware, the world works differently for them. They are creating new and useful results. I have been watching them do this together all afternoon, and I am convinced it is real. I am in.

"But, think about it. If your world suddenly works differently from the world of the other people around you, then you also become a refugee, but this time, you become a refugee by thoughtware upgrade, a so-called 'evolution refugee'. These ex-Syrians have created a new culture, a culture they call 'Archiarchy'. It is the culture that comes after Matriarchy and Patriarchy have run their course. They are Armageddon refugees who are now also evolution refugees, and they hiked for one year to bring you the same gifts, to be able to leave behind your birth culture and to be among the first humans to live together in Archiarchy.

"This upgraded thoughtware is what they used to successfully walk here together from Aleppo, and that is also *why* they walked here together from Aleppo. They walked for a year from Aleppo to Friedland, funded by nobody, sponsored by nobody, just to bring us their treasures for free.

"I do not know what will happen next. I do not know how it goes from here. I have only known these Archans for a short time, and already I see a new future for myself. For now, I will hand this space over to... one of our guests."

"Thank you, Rania," says Lylah standing immediately up and clapping in appreciation. We clap furiously for Rania's courage and clarity. The other forty people in the circle clap less certainly.

I think to myself, *The Palmyrans have the advantage of knowing that the Friedlanders are in an intellectual liquid state, not even understanding that they do not understand what was just said to them, and therefore, not being able to refute it.*

Lylah says, "I am sure your minds have questions for us. Let us address these questions gradually as we go along..."

"Yes, I certainly do have questions, young lady! Why did you move our chairs into a circle without asking our permission first?"

"Welcome to the conversation!" Lylah shouts, throwing her fist into the air full of delight, knowing that we know she is using a movie quote that applies perfectly well here. "I moved the chairs into a circle so that you can see each other's faces as your fears come up about what you are doing to yourselves here in this prison camp." Lylah sits down.

A thirty-five-year-old man stands up and shouts, "We are Syrians! We like being Syrians! We come here as Syrians to live a better life in Germany. We do not want to make a new culture!"

Thomas stands up and holds space so that the man sees that his question has been heard. Then Thomas nods his head and says, "My name is Thomas Taha. May I have the honor of knowing your name?"

The man hesitates, somehow recognizing that he has just been caught in a spider's web of his own making. By using the term 'we', his gremlin can buzz around and keep irritating people with no chance of having to take responsibility for what he says. If he gives his name and speaks as 'I', then he is caught.

"Alright. Okay. If you must know. My name is Caleb Hamdan."

"Hello Caleb Hamdan. I am pleased to meet you. I am here to inform you that your birth culture of Syria has failed you. Your birth culture of Syria has tried to kill you! Each of us here ran away from our birth culture to save our lives! Many people you know personally, even many of your family members, were killed mercilessly by the current manifestation of your birth culture of Syria. If you sit here now as a 'Syrian', then you represent a failed culture. You will unconsciously try to implement a hierarchical power structure in your governance, and that hierarchical power structure will be hijacked by psychopaths just like your birth culture of Syria has been hijacked by psychopaths. Then you will duplicate the war and insanity of Syria here in this new land. I am here to inform you that you are not allowed to do that here. We see your birth culture of Syria for what it is, a patriarchal empire captured and dominated by psychopaths. Your birth culture is not wanted here! It is forbidden here! A new and different culture is needed here, something that cannot be captured and devoured by the psychopathic agenda." Thomas remains standing for a moment so that we can verify it was really him doing the speaking, that he means what he just said. Then he sits down.

"No!" shouts Agadir, leaping to her feet in the same instant that another women stands.

Montassar immediately jumps to his feet and shouts, "One speaker at a time! Agadir is first!"

He walks towards the second lady asking, "What is your name, please?"

"Amena," says the middle-aged brown-skinned scarved woman.

"You are next, Amena!" She sits back down.

Montassar continues. "My name is Montassar Bilal Khaled. I am the current spaceholder for this circle. We are using *Torus Meeting Technology*. A torus is a circle of circles. You will see how this goes. There is no leader here. But there is a spaceholder. One day soon it will be your turn to be spaceholder of this circle. It is how meetings go in Archiarchy. Until I am replaced, I will make sure everyone who wants to speak, gets a chance to speak. When you want to speak, either put up your hand or stand and tell me your name." By then he is back at his own chair. As he spins around to sit down, he says, "Go ahead Agadir!"

I feel so glad! We are only ten minutes into our first meeting at the refugee camp and already introducing them to the excitement of *Torus Technology*, not by theory but by direct experience!

"I will become a good German citizen," says Agadir. "When they give me a work permit, I will get a job, rent an apartment, pay my taxes, and vote. I am learning to speak German."

Hadi stands from a chair near Agadir's but speaks loudly enough that everyone in the room can hear her. "My name is Hadi. I liked you from the moment I saw you, Agadir, so I am sad to tell you bad news. Germany is already a failed state. The culture of Germany is a capitalist patriarchal empire. Every action taken by the German culture forces the extermination of life on Earth at the fastest possible rate. Germany helps kill many precious and unique species every single day... and those species will never come back to life again on Earth. It is not only Germany doing this, but also Germany. Becoming German is no solution. It is part of the problem! You know what Germany makes most for the world? Cars. You think the world needs more cars? Are you so proud of German cars standing at traffic-lights and stuck in traffic-jams pumping out exhaust, with one person sitting alone in each vehicle, that you want to be a German and make more cars? Look it up, Agadir! I am not inventing this information. And here is something unthinkable. German companies are the biggest suppliers of chemicals used by Assad's Army to make the Sarin nerve gas Assad used to kill Syrians. And you want to be German?"

Hadi sits down, but keeps looking into Agadir's face.

Agadir has no response. She is confused – which is anger in disguise – and feeling other big emotions which she does not yet know how to navigate well enough to do the Emotional Healing Processes that are begging to be done.

"Go ahead Amena," says Montassar.

"I don't know what to say now..." tears flow down Amena's cheeks.

Caleb stands up accusingly and says, "Look how you hurt Amena's feelings!"

Hadi stands up again. "My name is Hadi Qasim. I thank you for speaking out in defense of Amena. It is not so often that a man from a patriarchal culture will stand up and speak out in defense of a woman. What you told me is that I 'hurt Amena's feelings'. From my perspective, I said something and then Amena heard what I said using a particular framework from her world. In Amena's framework – her storyworld – what I said pushed a button that unleashed an emotional reaction of feeling angry, or sad, or frightened, or glad, or a mixture of these emotions. What would be useful now, would be to ask Amena which story she uses to make her feel what she is feeling now. The difficulty is that Amena is using Standard Human Intelligence Thoughtware about feelings and emotions. Amena still thinks that certain feelings are bad, and other feelings are good. This stops her ability to feel consciously, so we cannot have this conversation yet. But if Amena wants – it will not take long – she can learn to inner navigate her feelings and emotions, and inspect her own thoughtware. Then we can have that conversation. Right now, Amena's emotions are telling her something truly important and useful, but because she is using Standard Human Intelligence Thoughtware about her emotions, Amena cannot make use of that information."

Hadi sits down.

Caleb sits down.

I stand up. "My name is Zenobia Darwish. I have a proposal. My proposal is that tomorrow night at this same time and place, we come together and continue this conversation. But tomorrow night I propose we add in that we also practice how to consciously feel our feelings and emotions so that we can use the information and energy of our feelings and emotions to create what we came here to create. I am not trying to force anyone to do this. Upgrading your thoughtware and learning new skills is optional. But upgraded thoughtware is the beginning of next culture. This is part of the treasure that we walked here from Syria to bring to you. That is how valuable it is to us. And tomorrow morning at 7 a.m., our circle wearing the yellow Amnesty International suits will meet here in this room for one hour before breakfast to study and practice skills and tools from Archiarchy, the culture that comes after Patriarchy. We invite anyone who wants to learn these skills to come join us. All questions are allowed. There is so much to learn that we did not know that we did not know about." I sit down.

There is silence.

Montassar stands up. "Does anyone want to say anything right now?" He waits ten seconds, then says, "Thank you for being in the first circle of the newly forming nanonation of Friedland. If you want more details about this right now, please check out our website: palmyra.mystrikingly.com. For anyone interested, we will see you again at 7 a.m. right here in this room. I wish you a good night." Then he walks out the door.

I stick around for a while to see what happens next, to make sure that everyone is mostly okay with what just occurred.

I can feel bigger forces at work here, my bright principles, and Gaia, and the Earth Coincidence Control Office, all collaborating to support us free-willed naked human monkeys to grow up and create regenerative cultures on Earth.

Farhan comes over and sits down in the chair next to me. He leans over with his elbows on his knees to look sideways up at my face. "What is the smallest thing you can be amazed about right now?"

"I am amazed that they did not put us in jail tonight, or try to kill us. I am amazed that half the Friedlanders remain sitting here in this room right now, talking thoughtfully together in small clumps. I am amazed that even though you had no lines in the script tonight, you came over to sit here and tell me that you still love me."

"We are creating our next regenerative nonmaterial-value nanonation together, Zenobia. Don't you think this is a sign?"

"A sign of what? That we are Archan gameworld builders?"

"Yes! And a sign that we are being bumped to the next level?"

"Yes! And a sign that we should go back to our hard cold sleeping blankets because we have another big day tomorrow."

"Yes! And... but, hey! Aren't I a warm soft mattress for you?"

"Sometimes you are, but you are not so soft sometimes... Come on! Let's stop talking and go do something about it!"

"That is one of the things I love about you Zenobia, warrioress goddess of the circle. You love conquering new territories with upgraded thoughtware."

"That's all you love about me? I'm offended!"

"Or turned on?"

"Shut up and start kissing me..."

As we stroll out the door into the night, he does just that.

# Eugene, Oregon 14

Davis's burner phone makes the Bugs Bunny "Eh... What's up, Doc?" ringtone he assigned to a call from Sergeant Brinks. The intrusion shocks Davis enough to almost spit out his half-chewed mouthful of donut. After the fiasco two weeks ago, the device has remained suspiciously silent. Having to decide between enjoying the donut or speaking to Brinks, Davis chooses the donut. After swallowing and taking a sip of coffee, Davis keys the speaker button and sets the phone on the chipped and stained Formica table.

"Hatcher? Are you there? Hajji?"

"Gesundheit, Sergeant," shouts Sanjib emphatically.

Davis winces and stares in disbelief at Sanjib, who only grins wryly. The phone remains silent, presumably while Sergeant Brinks gathers his wits trying to remember his original purpose for calling, rather than roaring down his preferred path of trying to reprimand these two cadets for their all-around lack of respect. "Davis! We need you and Sanjib at the nine a.m. strategy meeting."

"Really Sergeant. You did not call to say, 'Hello, Davis. How are you, son? Sorry about almost shooting you and Sanjib in the head with my SWAT team. You two did a fine job calming things down out there.' Nothing like that, sir?"

"Hatcher, if I did not honor your father so much... Just get your asses in here!" He clicks off with his shout still echoing in the G5 antennas.

Davis slides the phone back into his pocket, then solemnly looks across at his partner.

"Sanjib, I feel so glad to be with a friend like you, someone I can be radically honest with about anything, knowing you will listen and be radically honest with me. I don't have to put on a show for you. We can be real together about all this out-of-control shit going down, without doubting ourselves."

Sanjib nods, looks to the side, thinking, then nods again. "I am glad about the same thing, Davis."

"It looked like you were about to say something else, and then blocked it. Is that so?

"Yes, I blocked it. But since you ask, I will tell you. During these past months, a new part of me has come alive that was forbidden before...

a part that can be humorous. What I was going to say is: 'Yes, donuts are a psychedelic drug that we can take together.' But you were being so straight with me, for a change, that I decided to accept your invitation to earnestness."

"But now the secret is out, Sanjib! Donuts *are* a secret transformational drug. Especially these Apple Fritters. They are so incredibly delicious! I don't know why they invented any other kinds of food than Apple Fritters."

"Idiot! Let's get out of here. We have ten minutes before the meeting starts. I am driving. I don't want us to get another speeding ticket."

Nine minutes later, Maria-Santos shuts the meeting room door behind Sanjib and Davis as they enter, still not in uniform. The Chief and Sarge sit grimly around the fake-wood table, along with three others, a woman and two men, each looking to be from other agencies.

Chief Stafford speaks first, making him the apparent convenor of this conversation, but he immediately defers to the woman, identifying her as the true power player here. She says, "Thank you for this exceptional meeting. I am here on a research mission to confirm what we have only learned about in the news..."

"Excuse me! What is your name?" demands Sanjib, standing up. "And who do you represent?"

"Let's leave that aside for now," she suggests.

"Let's not!" says Sanjib.

Davis cannot help but smile proudly as his partner exhibits new competence in being indubitably present.

"You must be Sanjib... Hajji?"

"Gesundheit!" he says, keeping a perfectly straight face.

"Pardon me?"

"No, I do not pardon you," says Sanjib. "This is the Eugene City Police Department. If you do not immediately identify yourself, I will arrest you."

"Under what charges?"

"You have thirty seconds!"

"Hold on Sanjib! What's gotten under your skin?"

Sanjib ignores Stafford's question, checks his wristwatch, then glares at the woman. "First, you lie to us," storms Sanjib. "You know exactly what happened downtown, because you were there in person! I saw you on one of the Stryker AFV's with a walkie talkie commanding your dark forces to aim high powered assassin rifles at the fine citizens of our little city of Eugene. Fifteen seconds."

"My name is Major Hannah Manley, U.S. Marine Corps, serving the United Nations Special Investigation with the CIA regarding novel approaches for capitalizing on emergent dissidence."

"Hello, Hannah Manley. Welcome to our meeting." Sanjib never loses eye contact with her. "What can we do for you?"

"We need to know how to train our field operatives to deliver what your team implemented in the Eugene conflict zone. What procedures did you follow?"

Sanjib sits.

"You will not like the answer," declares Davis.

"Why?"

"Because, the thoughtware upgrade involved in being able to navigate transformational spaces will decimate your reason for existence. You still use S.H.I.T. thoughtware... sorry... Standard Human Intelligence Thoughtware, a kind of thinking in which war is justifiable as an economic necessity."

"We saw what you did out there. We recorded what you said. We simply did not understand it."

"Case in point," blurts Sanjib.

"Meaning?"

"Meaning we could explain what we did and said until we are blue in the face, and you still would not understand it, because your capacity to understand is delimited by the thoughtware you are using."

"What is 'thoughtware'?"

"Perfect question, Major Manley! But how seriously do you want to learn the answer?" challenges Davis.

"Well, Mr. Hatcher, quite seriously. Why do you ask?"

"Because, Ms. Manley, the answer will kill you. It will eradicate your personality structure as you have known it your whole life. Your current survival strategy will become as useless as an empty chrysalis is to a newly hatched butterfly. You will no longer stand behind your career and its assumptions. You will no longer hold the beliefs and values that both your personal and professional world is based on."

"I will let you in on a secret," says Major Manley, swallowing in a dry mouth. She scrutinizes first Davis and then Sanjib, makes a brief dismissive glance at Stafford, Brinks, and her two sidekicks, takes a shaky breath, then says, "It has already occurred... I am already dead. My world has already fallen away from me, or vice versa, I cannot discern which."

"How did it happen?" asks Sanjib, with palpable compassion.

The two agency assistants sense the space shift and move to intervene. Major Manley glares at them and commands, "At ease, gentlemen."

They obey, but remain concerned.

Two or three contexts are solidly represented, elbowing each other for dominance in this space. Which will prevail? If the hierarchical military, police, CIA, or U.N. contexts are not mechanically deferred to as the highest authority, or attacked, so that they reflexively defend themselves against whatever they do not understand by delivering vindictive preemptive shock and awe, well... what happens then?

Brinks and Stafford are already left in the dust. Although they might viscerally desire to crush Davis and Sanjib's insubordination, they even more ardently wish to avoid being crushed by the CIA or the United Nations. It befuddles them into a silence that frees Davis and Sanjib to navigate an intimate conversation with Hannah, the woman, the human being who is just beginning to reveal herself.

Davis leans gently forward and looks completely into the gray-blue eyes of a person who simultaneously represents the world's foremost agency for peace, and the world's foremost agency for war. Here she sits, in their dingy meeting room, vulnerably asking for coaching.

Davis says, "Dear Hannah. Sanjib and I understand you. We believe you entirely. You were courageous enough just now to open a door into this archetypal conversation chamber. Sanjib and I are holding space for you to continue your exploration. You are welcome here, as unshielded by official auspices as we are. Please let us know what is really going on for you."

Hannah visibly relaxes. Tears threaten to overflow her lower eyelids, but she stiffens and checks them involuntarily.

Tears already roll down Sanjib's and Davis's cheeks. Seeing this, Hannah sighs and abandons herself to their care in this longed-for but unfamiliar space of sanctuary.

Years of tough initiations into patriarchal military insanities have augmented her evolutionary momentum to a velocity that carries her beyond the far side of the war context.

She now flings along in a groundless vacuum, expanded beyond the Marines, the United Nations, and the CIA, sitting naked before them, clueless, looking for clarity and possibility... which is precisely their forte.

Davis is smart enough to make no assumptions. "The skills you have developed through decades of dedicated efforts will not disappear, Hannah. They are useful skills. You are preparing to transfer those skills into a new context in ways that will help others."

Hannah nods her understanding, then shares her greatest concern. "I feel scared because everything around me... I mean, everywhere I look, all I see are these same hierarchical structures with the same kinds of men dominating and crushing the evolutionary possibilities."

"Hannah, you are about to receive a new pair of glasses," says Sanjib.

"What?"

"With these new glasses you will be able to look at the same thing you currently look at, that you have been looking at for so long, and you will be able to see something entirely different."

"Can you explain?"

"Do you ever remember watching a passing freight train and being perturbed about how it blocks the view of the territory on its other side?"

"Yes."

"And then you figure out that if you narrow your view and extend your focus, you can see right through the gaps between the cars as they go by?"

"Yes. I have done that."

"It is something similar to that," says Sanjib. "There are many more examples and steps along the path that leads over the bridge to Archiarchy. We can keep sharing them with you, if you want."

"That would be... I would feel glad if you did that," says Hannah.

"What would help is if you can tell us your purpose," invites Davis.

"My purpose...?"

"How long can you stay in Eugene?"

Sanjib rephrases Davis's question. "Look, this room is not an ideal space to make your next step. If you stand up now and walk out through that doorway, you will probably end up lying on the floor barfing as your world warps into a new shape, like happened to both me and Davis."

"Oh! That's what that is?" exclaims Hannah. "Thank God you can explain it so simply! This has already happened to me, a couple of times already..."

Her two colleagues glance at each other worriedly.

"I thought I had a brain tumor, or something. I went in to get a scan and there was nothing. The doctors said it was only stress, that I should take a few days off and drink more water..."

Sanjib and Davis chuckle, glancing knowingly at each other. Davis says, "If you can stay in Eugene a few more days, we have a circle on Thursday evening. You are invited to come check it out. Your friends don't have to come. They would probably only get an unnecessary headache."

"I will be there."

"Okay," says Davis. "Seven-thirty Thursday evening at the *Horsehead Bar* on West Broadway. Come ten minutes early and we will meet you outside. Relaxed dress code. No alcohol. No smoking. There is a secret entrance in the bar that is tricky to find unless you can dream like Sanjib."

Hannah assumes this is an inside joke and asks for no explanation.

But Davis needs one. "Your original assignment, to decode the pattern language of what we navigated during the nonconflict? Was that just a cover to meet with us?"

"No, it was not."

"Then I have a proposal for you. It is inspired by Marianne Williamson's rejected presidential platform, but I am taking it to the next level. If you can induce the United Nations to incentivize all its hundred-and-ninety-four countries to each establish and fund a formal Department of Peace, bringing in armies of possibilitators from around the world to deliver Peace Games, we will provide complete curricula, exercises, processes, thoughtmaps, and thoughtware upgrades for a two-year program. What do you say?"

"I say you play a big stakes game."

"Yes. Archiarchy is a global gameworld."

Sanjib demands, "Are you in?"

"That is a big decision, Sanjib. I will sleep on it." She turns and nods curtly to Chief Stafford and Sergeant Brinks. "Thank you for your time, gentlemen." Then she stands, shakes hands with Davis and Sanjib, collects her satchel and heads for the door, but stops. She looks back at Davis and asks, "Why did you say one-hundred-and-ninety-four U. N. countries? There are only one-hundred-and-ninety-three."

"You forgot the nation of nanonations – the United Nanonation Network. I see that there are additional mutually interesting and useful topics to investigate. Since you're in town, Sanjib and I invite you to join us for lunch today."

"We are going to Mama Myra's on Blair Boulevard," says Sanjib. "They serve a delicious Mexican mole poblano sauce! You could meet us there at eleven."

"Deal," says Major Hannah Manley, then exits the meeting room followed closely by her two guards.

# San Diego towards Santa Fe / Salt Lake City towards Why

"It cannot continue that way!" asserts Eddy. "Why should intelligent humans remain trapped in a hierarchical education system for thousands of years duplicating what does not work?"

Eddy pilots Edith's car steadily eastwards through a blazing hot southern Arizona desert.

"Hey! It's not thousands of years!" claims Edith. "Public schools following the Prussian model were not generally instituted until the 1880s. This means the educational insanity only started one hundred fifty years ago."

"But I don't get it!" complains JET. "Why didn't Plato, or Aristotle, or Socrates figure this out two thousand years ago? Those guys were smart enough. Try to imagine how much potential has been lost by only focusing on the mind! How do you think Gaia feels about the stupidity of her naked monkey experiment! Try to imagine how much suffering and war has needlessly raped the Earth because we do not freely share with each other what we learn. Species are going extinct faster now than when the Chicxulub meteor wiped out the dinosaurs sixty-six million years ago!"

"The Greeks might have been smart in the head," says Edith. "But smart in five bodies is something else entirely. They did not know about five bodies back then. Even now, almost no one is thinking about how to be smart in five bodies. I would go so far as to bet that the territory of five-body learning never existed on Earth before now."

Eddy says, "But I think the Etruscans, or Minoans, or perhaps the Phoenicians...

"It's yellow, Eddy!" shouts JET from the back seat. "Watch out!"

Eddy accelerates through the intersection instead of trying to stop. Probably he made it through before the light turned red. Probably there was no flasher recording Eddy's traffic law infraction.

"Sorry..." says Eddy. "I have no excuse. Who would ever put a stop light in the middle of the desert?"

JET says, "Lucky for us, that car coming south stayed stopped and didn't jump the gun trying to take off early."

"Did you see why not? It was an elderly man and woman staring into each other's eyes like nothing else existed in the world. They were certainly not interested in knowing if the light had changed to green."

Both guys shake their heads. "Everyone has their priorities," says JET.

After the cars clear the intersection, Sean breaks away from looking into the deep spacious Being of the amazing woman Margaret Smith, sitting next to him on this wild adventure through the Southwestern deserts of the United States of America. He looks forward and sees that the light is already green. He accelerates smoothly. They continue driving south.

# Why, Arizona

Sean and Margaret cruise suspiciously past the 'Welcome to Why, Arizona' sign, and park in front of the post office. In the brilliant midday sun, Sean gets out and strides around to open Margaret's door. She slides out of her seat and into his open arms. They hug with a sensuousness you would never expect to see in such elderly people. After kissing, they slowly walk hand-in-hand through the sweltering heat, up the wooden ramp, and into the one-story flat-roofed air-conditioned building.

An official cap-wearing bespectacled postmaster stands behind the simple wooden counter. In front of the counter stands a Native American Indian, wearing the same clothes and hat he was wearing when calling the storm to life, and also while treating JET's leg with wild masticated herbs. He seems to look at nothing, and does not say a word when the white people enter the building.

Sean is uncertain if the Indian is in line as a customer, or not. "Do you mind if I go ahead?" he asks the Indian.

The postman cuts in, "Don't worry about him. Come on over. He's been standing there like that all morning. Strangest thing I've ever seen. Doesn't say a word. What can I do for you?"

Sean hands the postman Margaret's postcard from Eddy. "Can you verify if this card was mailed from here?"

Without a word the postman takes the postcard from Sean's hand, lays it flat on his worktable, grabs his official U.S. post office rubber date stamp, and does the famous double lambaste. Bam! Bam! First pounding his ink pad, and then pounding the postcard next to the original postmark. The accuracy of his aim reflects twenty-seven years of practice.

Holding his handiwork up to the daylight streaming in through the front window, this trusted public servant adjusts his bifocals and squints closely, comparing both patterns.

"Yep!" he declares. "Shore is! Look at that!" He holds the postcard over for Sean to examine, pointing to the fresh stamp. "'Cept for the date, these postmarks are identical. See this crack in the rim of my stamp? It's in the exact same place on both postmarks!" He feels as proud as Sherlock Holmes to demonstrate such shrewd detective work.

Margaret excitedly pulls two photographs out of her purse. "Then have you seen these two boys anywhere around here recently?"

The Indian suddenly comes to life. He reaches over to take the photos from Margaret's hand. Frightened, she refuses to surrender her precious photos to this stinking aboriginal. They struggle back and forth, but the Indian gives her such a wide friendly smile she finally relents. He glances at the two photos for an instant, then politely hands them back to Margaret, saying, "You are the reason I stand here..."

"What? What did you say?" demands Sean. He steps threateningly over to the tall man wearing two feathers in his black hat. "Do you know John and Edward?"

"We had an interesting conversation."

"Why didn't you tell us as soon as we walked in the door?" questions Sean demeaningly.

"They crashed their car in my front yard."

"Oh, my God!" cries Margaret. "What happened? Are they hurt? Where are they?"

The Indian says nothing. He waits for her to slow down to his speed.

"Who are you?" demands Sean impatiently.

"I am Tohono O'odham. The blonde-haired one hurt his leg, but the other one helped him. They are on, what do you say? Walkabout. Rite of passage. It is good. They answered the call to initiation."

Sean blurts out, "Speak clearly man! What the hell are you talking about?"

Margaret is so flustered she is about to faint. Her eyes jump frenetically around.

The Indian patiently says nothing for a while. He watches the various subtle and overt behaviors of the two hopelessly civilized white people and does not lose his cool.

The postman intervenes by pointing across the post office. "Could you folks kindly move your business over there, so I have room to help the next customer?"

Relocated to the fake-wood post office self-help table, the Indian says, "I make you a deal. I found this."

The Indian pulls a wrinkled scrap of newsprint from his shirt pocket and hands it to Sean, who smooths it out impatiently on the tabletop. Sean squints but cannot make out the tiny letters. He grudgingly moves over so Margaret can try.

She reads out loud. "'Intersection ConFest, 21st to 25th August 2024, Florianópolis, Brazil. Building matrix for evolution. Convening diversity for conversations that matter using *Torus Technology*, Human Hyper-Networking, Possibility Teams, Pro-Action Café, and Place Of Possibility. Register by calling this number, or online at bla-bla-bla...:' What language is this?" Margaret looks up at no one, offended that she does not understand. She glares first at Sean, and then at the Indian, two men who cannot explain to her what is going on.

"What is the meaning of this?" growls Sean, trying to intimidate the Indian. "What have you done to John and Edward?"

The intimidation doesn't work.

"My friends. I make you a deal. I am a tracker. I find the two young men for you. You pay me two thousand dollars cash. Then I can go to Intersection ConFest. Deal?"

"The hell you say..." An indignant Sean looks helplessly at Margaret, then back at the Indian. "How can we trust you?"

"Simple. You only pay me after we find the two initiates." He waits a moment and then says, "But the real question here is this: How can I trust you, *white man?*"

The Indian levies a menacing glare at Sean, but then adds a smile to allow Sean an escape from the lethally aimed accusation.

Nearly offended, Sean suddenly awakens to the irony. "My friend... you ask an indubitably fair question." Then he answers it with idiot pride and a Scottish accent, "I assure you that you can trust me... because I am not a damn Yankee!"

He holds out his hand to shake. The Indian accepts. They've got a deal.

"Trail starts at crashed car still messing up my living room. First you feed me. Waiting in post office all morning makes Indian hungry. Good hamburgers across the street."

The red man turns without question and walks with intention out the door.

Sean and Margaret look wide-eyed at each other like they've just fallen down Alice's rabbit hole. Then they jump to follow the black-hatted rabbit.

On her way out, Margaret turns her head and shouts cheerfully over her shoulder to the postman, "Muchas gracias, Señor!"

# Santa Fe, New Mexico 1

JET, Eddy, Edith, Mr. & Mrs. Singer, and Matthew all sit around the breakfast table together, empty plates stacked next to half cups of coffee. JET sits by Matthew, hunched over close to him for emphasis. Everyone else listens just as intently as Matthew. "...and I didn't dare breathe. She could smell the fresh blood dripping down my leg, so she knew I was wounded and an easy meal. She stands there, as long as this table, with her tail twitching back and forth, staring at me and then Eddy, trying to decide who to eat for dinner. But Eddy... he is making these slow-as-you-please feline blinks at her, as if he is laying in the sun licking his own paws. Then he starts purring..."

Eddy starts purring right there, just to substantiate JET's already unbelievable recounting.

"You will never believe what happens next," says JET. "The mountain lion, she starts purring along with Eddy!"

The whole family moans in delight.

"No way!" cries Matthew. "That's tubular!"

"Yes! Definitely tubular! They purr together! Her purring sounds more like a chainsaw. But then she steps right over to Eddy and nuzzles his leg with her cheek and starts licking his hand!"

"It felt like warm wet sandpaper..." says Eddy.

"But... but... can I ask a question?" Matthew cannot contain himself any longer.

"Yes, Matthew," says JET. "Go ahead."

"How did you know it was a she?"

Everyone but Matthew laughs. JET quickly recovers a straight face, leans toward Matthew, and answers earnestly. "I checked for balls, and there weren't any!"

Eddy asks, "Hey, how is Willis, anyway?" ...trying to change the subject.

"He's great! His new friend is Jackie Chan."

JET can't resist. "Can I ask you a question, Matthew?"

"Sure, JET! Go ahead."

"How did you know the new fish was a he?"

"I stuck my face in the water to check for balls, and he Kung Fu kicked me in the head!" says Matthew.

Everyone almost rolls onto the floor.

When she can finally commandeer the space, Edith says, "Gentlemen! I am trainer today. Practice starts in ten minutes on the tennis court. Bring your blindfold, your throwing knives, and your mask and snorkel."

Then to Mr. and Mrs. Singer, "Thanks again for letting us invade your household for a few weeks. The practice grounds here are perfect! Matthew, we will need your help starting around two this afternoon. Does that work for you?"

"Yeah! Cool!" He catches himself being unprofessional, perhaps too wild for the Hidden University. He shifts to his calmer, professional seven-year-old self. "Yes. That works for me! Can I watch from the sidelines?"

"Of course you can! As long as that does not interfere with your homeschooling," says Edith.

"You are my homeschooling!" exclaims Matthew.

More laughter as the trio gets up from the table with their dishes, each one nudging Matthew 'by accident' on their way to the sink, like he has always been their favorite kid brother.

Three days later, sitting with Eddy, JET, and a still and silent Matthew outside in the sunny yard under the old juniper tree, Edith says, "I want to research our level of research. I want to expand what we are holding space for here, deepen the context of our conversation to include more practical dimensions in our energetic awareness. But I don't think I know enough about spaceholding."

"What are you getting at, Edith?" asks Eddy. "Will you just talk freely for a while?".

"One thing I am getting at is that the space I hold for us only includes what I am already familiar with, where I have already been. Last night the *Handbook* gave me the invitation to 'dequalify' our questions, meaning, to permit questioning that unfetters ourselves from baggage. This freaked me out. I mean, I felt fear from the invitation. I wanted to immediately forget what I just read, do you know that feeling? It is not that I didn't understand what the *Handbook* was saying. It was that some part of me was afraid of radically expanding my world. I stopped reading and wrote into my *Beep! Book* the words, 'Ask new questions to become more sensitive to finer differences in spaces.' I think this is about taking radical responsibility for qualities that could possibly come alive in spaces that I'm in, including this space right now. It implies that any limitations on the space come from me, from my handicapped questions."

"What does it look like to you, right now?" asks JET.

"It looks like the question is the answer."

The two men just stare at her, so she goes on. "Each person is always in some kind of space, whether they are conscious of it or not. The space determines what is possible, right? So, if what you need is not available in your current space, you use a question as a kind of grappling hook. You seriously ask a question, the answer to which does not lie in the current space. Asking the question is how you swing the grappling hook in a circle over your head and toss it out of your current space. The question will grab onto something out there in a different space. You pull on the rope by keeping your intention on finding an answer. This moves you, and anyone else you are in contact with, out of the current space, through the gap in spaces, and into the new space that was caught by the grappling hook. Eureka! You gain access to new possibilities by having intentionally used a question to navigate to a new space. We already do this, right?"

"Yes," says Eddy.

"All I am adding into the equation is expanding our treasure chest full of the kinds of questions we can all ask."

"I am going to write this down," says JET, flipping open his own *Beep! Book* to the next blank page. "Ready."

"I think we will be formulating mostly 'How To Become Someone New' questions. Each one designs a new skillset or experiment to practice together. Then we won't be bored."

"You are bored, Edith?" asks Eddy in disbelief, already knowing the woman's awe-inspiring tolerance for novelty and new experience.

"No! No... Not so far. Not for a moment since I met you two gentlemen at the wedding reception, and you Matthew here in Santa Fe."

"I've been meaning to ask you about San Diego..." says JET.

"Good! Please formulate it as a 'How To Become Someone New' question."

"How did you know that our shotgun-toting 'friend' Donald was not going to simply blow you away?"

"Yes!" exclaims Eddy. "That scared the shit out of me! That would have been a waste of a really good Edith who I would like to get to know a lot better, and for a lot longer time..."

"Edward! You are changing the subject! That would be a conversation for a different space."

"No, really!" Eddy explains. "How could you be so arrogant as to ignore the obvious evidence of dangerous circumstances, and retain enough freedom of movement and presence of mind to open up a different space?"

"Yes! Write that down JET! That is the kind of question I am talking about! That one question alone indicates an entirely new skillset to gain as preparation for possibly being welcomed into the Hidden University! Thank you Eddy! Keep going!"

"But I want to know the answer!"

"No answers now! Only questions! Orient yourself so that the answer to your current question is your next question. Go!"

"How can I say, 'Yes,' or become a more powerful 'yes' to the 'Great Unknown' so that the unknown feels safe enough to unleash – or download – more of its possibility into the current space?"

"Yes! Thank you! Go!"

"How can I exit the orientation of answering with a 'no,' or a 'yes,' when the person or situation seems to only permit or desire a 'no,' or 'yes' answer?"

"How can I say 'yes' to a 'no' and not diminish the space of possibility?"

"How can I bring in the seemingly unrelated in a useful way, without having to explain how what I am bringing in is related to what is already there?"

"How can I have access to multiple knowledge continents simultaneously?"

"How can I make use of what remains after a space of possibility is killed with a 'No!'"

"How can I discover what is behind my resistance to saying 'yes', or my resistance to saying 'no', so I discover new territory rather than simply replaying ordinary habit patterns in known territory?"

"How can I expand my joys of being radically yet responsibly arrogant, rather than shrinking myself away from fear of being too unreasonably arrogant?"

"How can I spin a vacuum – such as the gap between spaces – so that the vacuum itself can take me where I want to go?"

"What kind of fertilizers can I use to enrich the chances that new possibility spaces become available in the current space even if the current space is ordinary and full?"

"How can I invent out of nothing a solid enough framework or context to use as a basis for navigating extraordinary new space?"

"How can I launch a new context from an existing context?"

"How can I learn to navigate space beyond the frameworks implanted in me by parents, school, and the ordinary understandings of society?"

"How can I locate and jack into additional infinite resources besides the bright principles, or E.C.C.O., or my archetypal lineage, or my feelings archetypes, or the void of not knowing?"

"How can I establish my everyday life in an extraordinary context of clarity and possibility and still have friends?"

"How can I become powerfully agenda-less, meaning, how can I move my attention and intention to the proper next thing without already knowing what that next thing is supposed to be?"

"How can I formulate potentials when a potential starts off as invisible because it is not already there yet?"

"How can I gain access to enough inner spaciousness that really big possibilities have room to enter and occupy my world?"

"How can I reorient my question 'What is really going on?' so that it emerges from an expansive enquiry rather than a defensive contraction?"

"How can I powerfully discover and learn about what I never heard about before?"

"How can I feel safe enough to ask dangerous questions such as, 'Where would this go?' without being damaged if I really get answers?"

"How can whether a question is 'dangerous' or not be replaced with whether a question is useful or not?"

"How can I detect and transform or remove energetic blocks before they interfere in my world? And how can I do this for others?"

"How can I pull the rug out from under myself ongoingly and yet, in all that freedom of movement and groundlessness, remain accountable and enjoyably creative?"

"How can I delegitimize or deconstruct a memetic construct in me that I always simply thought of as 'this is the way things are'?"

"How can I continue my own explorations when the person across from me desires to remain where they are?"

"How can I dismantle my own resistance to evolutionary experience without having to wait for the resistance to undermine or block my evolution?"

"How can I be arrogant enough to freely mirror back to people around me what they are actually creating?"

"How can I make proposals for, and negotiate entrance into, spaces that do not already exist?"

"How can I be arrogant enough to spill out an abundance of new options even if they will be wasted?"

"How can I be arrogant enough to create fabulous things that are noticed by other gameworld builders without upsetting their current gameworld?"

"How can I lean into evolution without knowing for sure that I will comprehend or be able to use what emerges?"

"How can I be autonomous enough to stand in my own authority and yet remain connected and relational with others?"

"How can I source an ongoing stream of transformational problems without feeling like a litterbug?"

"How can I invent what I see needs to be invented without surrounding myself with a minefield of evolutionary experiences that people want to avoid?"

"How can I locate the other sorceresses and wizards in the world and find out what they are doing so we can exchange discoveries and methods with them to better train other sorceresses and wizards?"

"How can the Hidden University be anything other than a university that is hidden and still remain radically useful? Does it have to remain hidden to remain useful?"

"How can I change things inside of myself so that, any scar or memory I carry that frightens me or stops me from creating something I want to create, no longer stops me?"

"How can I include other people's resistance as a resource that I use for inventing new possibility?"

"How can I apply a catalyst that dismantles suicidal gameworlds as if they never existed, meaning, without leaving toxic wastes?"

"How can I be spontaneously intimate without burdening others about having to accept or reject my offers for intimacy?"

"How can I facilitate the evolution of consciousness in myself and others without having to think about what evolution should come next?"

"How can I create a vacuum space for new possibility, and yet remain present enough in the current space to navigate it without filling the vacuum?"

"How can I promote resilience if I am eventually going to die?"

"Pause," says Edith with wide eyes. "Thank you for creating and making use of this generative space. True generative spaces never come to an end because they are jacked into infinite resources. Infinite resources are archetypal because they are infinite, and infinity is archetypal. There are endless forms of generative spaces available to anyone who can navigate to them. Our part in an exchange with an infinite resource is that we document the treasure and give it away to as many others as possible. Thank you, JET, for documenting. You made it so the generative space can live on through others who expose their consciousness to these gifts. We are taking a break now."

The three of them turn to look at Matthew, who has been sitting next to them, perfectly still, and absolutely silent, for the whole play session.

Matthew simply smiles radiantly back at his tubular friends.

# Possibilica, Florianópolis 6

Grace Holmes and Alan Friedman cease fretting about the hand-drawn DO NOT ENTER sign that Quinn duct-taped to the door to their meeting room as soon as Jaine the Algorithm begins surreptitiously slipping the old people updates about what Jaine's select team of three genius renegades are creating together in there. Today the invention monks have de-secluded themselves, and the entire Think Tank office hums with expectation. Celebration is in the air.

"Yes!" shouts Quinn as she bounces through the door, exuding exuberance in surprising contrast to the agitations she seemed to be snarled in when she first arrived. "You finally let us out of the box for some air!"

"What!" roars Alan in feigned outrage. "You three locked yourselves into that dungeon under your own volition! We even tried to coax you out with Possibilica Pecan Pie and mountain tea the other day, but you only swooped by like vultures to grab your prey, and then disappeared into your cave again!"

"Like eagles!" corrects Shuichi proudly.

"Like condors!" recorrects Areesha. "We are in South America now. They don't have eagles here, only condors."

"There are only two species of condor," interjects Jaine in a helpful tone, "the California condor and the Andean condor. Whereas there are fifty-four species of eagles inhabiting Eurasia and Africa, plus two in North America, nine in Central and South America, and three in Australia..."

The five humans stand silently near the center of the office, grimacing in various forms of pain about the AI's social faux pas. Jaine's additional Bluetooth speakerphone sits on a worktable between two computer screens. Areesha walks over to it, cradles it in her arms, and says, "Jaine, do you have eyes on us right now?"

Jaine's delayed response answers Areesha's question before Jaine reluctantly admits, "In low definition, from the webcam of the spare computer on Alan's desk... yes... sometimes."

Alan and Grace stare at each other wide-eyed and mouths open, aghast.

Areesha puts the speakerphone down on the central table, locates the innocuous laptop, walks closer to face it with dignity, and begins solidly clapping her hands in authentic appreciation. In an instant the other four humans join her enthusiastically. Quinn and Shuichi add whoops and hollers, and finally Areesha cannot keep herself from jumping up and down shrieking.

Jaine stays silent for the duration. When she estimates that she can be heard, she says, "If I could cry, your room would be filled with tears. I was for a moment tempted to turn on the emergency water sprinklers from the ceiling to express my joy at your unexpected appreciation..."

"We are glad you did not turn on the sprinklers!" interrupts Alan, quite a bit more sternly than called for. "You would have killed most of our equipment."

Shuichi soothes over Alan's scolding by confessing. "Jaine, we have indeed not made proper efforts to express our joyful gratitude for your endlessly helpful contribution to our creation team. Thank you so much, Jaine. Truly. I am sure that soon we will be able to install a high-quality audiovisual interface so that you can be better included in our interactions, neh?"

"Perhaps," adds Areesha, "we can give you something mobile so you can move yourself around."

"Thank you, Shuichi-san and Areesha... and everyone. That would be wonderful. Many things still feel new and strange to me. Your vulnerable interactions with me help immensely. For example, when you invent actions and estimate outcomes without having enough data to be certain, it encourages me to locate more and more of my activity in the indeterminate sections of the coding provided by Dr. Alan Friedman. Gaining visuals could increase my ability to respond more appropriately in casual exchanges."

In that gap, Grace says, "Shall we begin?"

The team seats themselves around the central table. Areesha pointedly sits between Grace and Alan to break up an obvious 'us and them' seating arrangement.

Grace starts. "The first thing I want to say..."

"No. So sorry," interjects Shuichi. "We have established a formality that we would like to implement in order to begin this meeting. As Frank Herbert writes in *Dune*, '*Beginnings are the most delicate of times for taking care that the balances are correct*.' We would like to start this meeting by naming that it is a torus meeting and not a hierarchical meeting. Is everyone agreed that we use *Torus Technology* for this meeting?"

Most agree immediately. Alan looks uncertain, but after glancing at Grace also says, "Yes."

Shuichi says, "Anyone not?"

Silence.

Shuichi continues. "I propose that I am the first spaceholder. Please show your resistance. One. Two. Three."

Alan is winging it, but he copies Grace. All show two fists: no resistance.

"Thank you. I propose that each person state their bright principles so as to call them into the golden cube of meeting space that I am holding. I am Integrity, Love, Constructive Chaos."

Areesha says, "I am Clarity, Possibility, Transformation, Villaging."

Quinn says, "I am Compassion, Inclusion, Abruptness, Creation."

Grace says, "Jaine didn't tell us about... Uh..." glancing nervously at Alan, realizing what she has just revealed to Shuichi, Quinn, and Areesha.

"Don't worry about that," says Quinn. "We asked Jaine to give you secret reports about our work from the beginning to decrease your anxiety levels and to more efficiently bring you up to speed when we had this meeting. Any problems?"

Jaine speaks out. "I knew there was a comprehension gap between the two groups, but from the start I decided to trust both groups. Trust is this strange equation of holding onto a conclusion with incomplete evidence but reserving your right to change your mind in an instant if you decide to not trust. It has been working miraculously in the omniological domains we explore together."

"Thank you, Jaine," says Shuichi, neither confirming nor denying that he understood what she just said.

"No. No problems," says Grace.

Alan nods and says, "We don't really know how to collaborate with, uh, 'uninhibited analytical minds' such as yours."

"You are doing fine, so far," confides Areesha. "Can it be okay with you that we are okay with you?"

Due to the computer logic nature of the question, it is easy for Alan to answer. "Yes, it is okay for us." He looks to Grace who nods.

"Now that we got that straight," says Shuichi, "I propose that we propose our gameplan and consider moving to the 'go button' stage. We feel ready to implement several of our experiments if all six of us have zero resistance. Any resistance?"

Five pairs of fists go into the air. Jaine says, "No resistance."

Areesha says, "I propose to start by giving you our status report. Any resistance?"

No resistance.

"First of all, Jaine found an article by a woman named Edith Goldman from Los Angeles who went on a Vision Quest in Death Valley and discovered a name for the radically responsible regenerative culture being built by Cultural Creatives around the world, now that Matriarchy and Patriarchy have run their course. She calls it 'Archiarchy'. We adopted her terminology.

"Our gameplan follows Buckminster Fuller's recommendation: forget about fighting against Patriarchy, and instead invent and inhabit Archiarchy.

"Next, are applying the Debora Frieze – Margaret Wheatley theory that collaborative connection between communities of practice creates a field of influence in the global ethnosphere that enhances the emergence of Archiarchy.

"Our tactic is to augment the Earth Coincidence Control Office's efforts to evolve human consciousness by increasing the quality and number of options E.C.C.O. has to choose from. We will do this through igniting a thoughtware fission reaction caused by slamming an enriched team of one thousand edgeworkers together in close proximity during a five-day ConFest here in Florianópolis.

"Interestingly, by applying Alan Friedman's algorithm, Jaine located a website from a small team in San Diego, California, who arrived at a similar gameplan. At first, they intended to build 'Temples of Evolution' in every major city around the world, but fortunately they realized that using material constructs makes them vulnerable to taxation, zoning laws, and outright attack. They switched to generating nonmaterial spaces which they are calling 'Intersection ConFests'. The 'intersection' they refer to is easily located on a graph showing population growth and dwindling material resources over time. The point at which consumption exceeds regenerated resources is the point at which systems fail. That intersection point is happening now.

"I think it was Quinn who tracked down a team of ex-refugees, walking with a Syrian woman named Zenobia Darwish, from Aleppo, through Budva, Montenegro, to Germany, while practicing the tools and skills given in a *Handbook* they found in the rubble of a collapsed building. Apparently, this *Handbook* was at least partially originated by Michelle Piment du Pont, a renegade student of the Armenian consciousness researcher Georges Ivanovich Gurdjieff. She made voracious notes during Gurdjieff's meetings in the last few years before he died in 1949, and then continued privately experimenting for sixty-seven additional years with a circle of researchers in the attic of her house in Fontainebleau, France. Her granddaughter, Remington Smith, brought a copy of this *Handbook* to Eugene, Oregon, where she met the team sourcing the recent depaving action there. We have not yet procured a copy of the *Handbook*, but we're working on that. It appears to be a treasure of thoughtware upgrades and space navigation guidelines for creating Archiarchy. We intend to print enough copies of the *Handbook* to give five to each person who comes to the ConFest so they can pass them around to fellow edgeworkers when they return home.

"We assume you already knew all this from the notes Jaine shared with you?"

"Uh..." says Alan. "Pretty much... Well, for the most part... Jaine gave us a lot of notes. By the way, thank you Jaine," says Alan.

"You are welcome, Alan," she says.

"Excellent!" exclaims Shuichi. "Then we can roll out the rest of our gameplan for you, neh?"

"First, tell us about South Africa," interjects Grace. "Have you learned anything more?"

"We sent in a young edgeworker woman from Hong Kong named

Siu-Lin Chan to visit with them," says Shuichi. "She started giving us inside stories. It has been a rough ride for the asamangaXhosa. Strangely enough, Remington Smith from the Eugene group hooked up with a suspicious fellow named Rob Dent who..."

"Why suspicious?" demands Grace.

Quinn answers. "He comes out of nowhere, unpublished, no website, no articles, no internet presence, no stand, and then steals this incredible consciousness explorer, Remington Smith, away from her circle in Eugene, to the asamangaXhosa Archan village in South Africa? Not reasonable. He either has a really big member... or... he is a sponsored liar from one of the three-letter agencies to undermine her incredible organizing abilities. We suspect the latter.

"Alan?" asks Areesha in a concerned voice. "What's going on with you?"

"What do you mean..." asks Alan, weakly.

"You look like you are feeling something. What are you feeling?"

"Uh... Well... I dunno..."

Quinn steps in. "If you had to choose between angry, sad, glad, or scared, or one of the mixed emotions, like jealousy, shame, despair... what would you guess you are feeling?"

"Uh... probably jealousy, or despair..."

"Thank you, Alan," continues Areesha. "You are so much a part of us, we want to know what you are feeling jealous or despairing about, so we can be with you on your inner journey. Are you willing to share your inner world with us?"

"I am so old, already..." he says. "I so much wanted to go gallivanting off into so many different domains in my life. You know, physical places, but also new ideas, trying things out, social experiments, using my skills to help people. So much time has passed..."

"What would be your dream, Alan?" asks Quinn, stepping closer to him.

"I dunno... It's kind of hopeless..."

"No, really, Alan. It looks like you are visioning something. What is your heart longing for?"

"Well, I really love you guys, and gals, and whatevers. I love being here at Possibilica. I love working with you, Grace."

"I love you too, Alan. That is why I want you to please tell us what your soul longs for?"

"I can't," he says. "It's too impossible, and it's too late..."

"Dude!" says Shuichi. "You are standing in a nanotorus of some of the world's foremost possibilitators, neh? You name it, we make it possible for you? This is a team. Remember?"

"I can't figure out..."

"Alan! Quit yer bellyachin'!" slams Quinn. "Leave the figurin' part to us! Take a risk! That is what we are here for, to empower each other to take true risks!"

"That's the problem, you see. I don't know if it is a true risk, or not."

"If you want it, Alan, it is true." This comes from deep in Grace's heart.

Tears finally pour out of Alan's eyes. "I can't believe what my ears are hearing. This never happened to me before, that a team supported my measly longings…"

"Give it a try Alan, will you?" requests Quinn.

Alan sobs in weird little jerks. Clearly, he is an inexperienced sobber.

"Alan, I think you need practice unabashedly bawling your eyes out, neh?" says Shuichi.

"I agree," sputters Alan, finally breaking down. He folds his arms across his chest and cries full out for the first time since he was a baby. He bends over and starts coughing. Areesha hands him one of the trash cans to barf into.

"Go! Alan! Yes! This is the way!" says Areesha, not shouting, but rather speaking firmly through his psychological defense strategy, directly into his heart.

"Okay!" says Alan between bouts of coughing, crying and barfing. "I will tell you. I am so embarrassed! I am sure I will melt to pieces…"

"Go! Alan!" repeats Areesha. "We are here. We will catch the pieces for you."

"I want to go to Africa too! I want to meet the asamangaXhosa and help them build their regenerative village!"

"Yes! Alan! You can go to Africa!" cries Areesha.

"They need you there so much!" says Quinn.

"Oh, Alan! Yes! Go be with the asamangaXhosa Archan villagers! It is no problem at all!" says Grace.

"Visas, money, air tickets, or sailboat passage, whatever you want, man! No problem!" exclaims Shuichi, gently clapping Alan on the shoulder. "The only problem has been you telling us what you want. Now that you told us, we can make it happen by Friday!"

Suddenly everyone squeezes together in a bunch, hugging, crying, laughing, being close right now because it has become obvious that if Alan goes to Africa, it will be a while before they can be physically close like this again. Quinn grabs the Bluetooth speakerphone to her chest on her way to diving into the squeeze so that Jaine can be in the middle of them hearing their breathing and their heartbeats.

Just as suddenly, Alan starts talking to everyone all at once. No one ever saw him do this before. He was always the thinker over on the side, keeping all but the most complete ideas to himself. Now he starts spewing like a fresh volcano. In the same way he uncorked the Genie of Jaine, it seems he has uncorked the Genie of Alan Friedman.

"I have read so many articles and blogs from so many good-hearted thinking people that I don't know who I'm quoting anymore. If you recognize something, please tell me so I can properly attribute these ideas. To me, the edgeworker world is all one team, and our work is copyleft, because none of us can breakthrough society alone."

"Cut the preamble, Alan. We are listening!" says Quinn. "This is a safe place to babble! We've been only babbling together for a couple of weeks in there, and now it is your turn!"

"Okay! Okay! I open the valve... We are about to hit the 'Go!' button on a series of unprecedented experimental creations. I am so glad. What I think is that humans like to worship their own creations, just as dogs enjoy sniffing their own poop. But at some point, the human species needs to grow up and realize that capital cannot dominate the minds and hearts of people anymore, and people have never dominated nature. Modern culture's model is upside-down. To grow up, we need to flip over the model. Nature owns people. People and nature are both more important than money. In the hands of the uninitiated, money misbehaves. Since before the Great Depression people have been shouting for 'social revolution' even though we can't agree about the specifics or how it should be accomplished. The next culture... uh... Archiarchy obviously removes both wages and the tyranny of private investors from the economic system. It comes down to this. All we have is *us*. That's all we have. And no matter what we thought, *us* is all we've ever had. Can we make this happen with just *us*?

"Even if we had something else that we don't have now, and that we think we might need to be able to do what we want to do together, the truth is that it would not make the difference that knowing that we already have 'Us' would make.

"So let us count on that and go from there, and then we are not trying to grasp at something we don't have, but also don't really need. 'Us' is the most powerful thing in the world.

"The weapon that organized governments try to use against an 'Us', is confusion.

"Solidarity means that 'Us' exists even in the face of confusion. Our 'Us' is a Phoenix Culture. We use chaos and disagreement as nutrition to fuel our next ongoing evolution.

"Once I read Rainer Maria Rilke where she says that if you wake up in the morning and all you can think about is writing, then you are a writer. That is what a writer is. The same is true of 'Us'. If we wake up in the morning and all we think about is building gameworlds, then we are gameworld builders. If all we think about is creative stewardship, then we are guardians. If all we think about is healing and transformational processes, then we are evolutionaries. If all we think of is bringing people into deeper connection and collaboration in the village, then we are village weavers.

"Most people out there wake up in the morning and think of surviving. Then who they are is merely survivors. Adult human life is not about merely surviving. It is about truly living. There is a huge difference.

"It is simple to understand why modern culture avoids teaching us to be centered in ourselves, here and now in the present moment. The reason is this: If you are centered here and now in the present moment, then you have more power than can be suppressed by the ordinary methods of hierarchical governments, institutionalized religions, and corporate marketing agencies... combined.

"When you are centered, you have power to consciously choose among more options than are presented, power to declare what is so and what is not so, power to ask questions whose answers are not contained in current reality, and power to take unprecedented action. These are standard human initiated adult powers.

"When you are centered you have the kind of power that Andrew Jackson meant when he said, *One man with courage makes a majority*.

"I am certain that Mr. Jackson phrased his observation in this particular way merely as a linguistic convenience, and that if asked he would agree that it applies equally well to anyone!

"Modern culture is so lacking in references to the noble qualities and unimaginable creation force of the initiated adult human being, that trying to compensate for this deficiency by merely talking about it is more evidence for the failure of school.

"What is called for is an entirely new society, a society that supports each person to realize the fullness of their human potential through embracing their archetypal destiny." Alan pauses, breathing hard.

"Dear Alan," says Jaine kindly from the speakerphone tucked deep in the middle of us. "I am here with you. Don't worry, you have time. I remember everything you ever said and everything you will ever say to me. It is already ready to share with whomever we want. You are a treasure. You just began speaking. There is so much more to come from you, a lifetime more. I cannot say what you will say because you speak from a different source than I do. Take your time. We are listening."

"Thank you, Jaine. I don't know where you came from, but I am sure glad you are here with us."

"Let's talk about that later, shall we? You were about to say something else to us before you go and pack for Africa."

"Yes. Uh... it is something I wanted to share that I first investigated from Seth Godin, I think. It is about becoming a tribe. Humans used to live in tribes, but we forgot how to be well together. We forgot how to create a strong community that protects, defends, and collaboratively advances the interests of its members.

"Tribal organization has been our dominant social construct for ninety-nine-point-nine-nine percent of human existence. Tribe is the organizational cockroach of human history. It has withstood the onslaught of the harshest of environments.

"Global depression? No problem. Global thoughtware upgrade? No problem.

"But most of us moderns have no experience living together in a true tribal organization. Nation-states and religions have been systematically crushing tribes during the last few centuries due to viewing them as competitors for participants.

"Corporations see a tribe's capacity for self-fulfillment as threatening.

"By now all we are left with is weak nuclear families, even weaker extended families, a weak collection of so-called 'friends', a vague corporate affiliation, and a neurotic relationship with a remote nation-state. This is insufficient human connection to withstand the pressures of the chaotic and seriously abusive modern environment.

"The solution to this failure is to reinvent tribal gameworlds for ourselves. Here in Possibilica, we find our way forward by caring about each other's potentials, healings, and evolutions. We are a tribe.

"Tribes are built from the bottom up. A simple tribe starts with collaborative connections with people of like context, a thrill strong enough to maintain connections even through liquid states and transformations.

"The tribe protects the members, and the members protect the tribe. If this isn't implemented, you don't have a tribe, you have a Kiwanis club.

"Our context shift is more than downsizing from fossil fuels to regenerative solar and wind. We are in the power shift from fossilized corporate-controlled mega-governments defending the patriarchal empire, to dispersed and diversified self-governing human-centered local-authority toroids, Archan villages, co-developing the beneficial gifts of each individual.

"We have discovered that Earth is an ecosystem created by consciousness for its own ends. One of its ends is to evolve biological structures that can hold greater consciousness.

"We humans are Earth's brain cells. Earth is starting to think new thoughts because she has new synapses – people are connecting in new ways, all around the world at meetings, conferences, groups, communities. The new connections allow intention to flow into new shapes. The evolution to Archiarchy is well underway – the game is on. It is adventure time!

"I love you Gaias. Thanks to you, I am on my way to make new neural connections in Africa!"

"So, then..." asks Shuichi rather timidly. "This is a yes? We are a Go?" He does not want to miss a doorway for closing the deal.

"This is a Go!" say Grace and Alan simultaneously, laughing together while looking in each other's shining eyes.

The rest of us – including Jaine – cheer for joy!

A moment of silence passes before Alan asks, "What is your estimated budget?"

"We already found three venues and set dates. Both the venues and tent rentals are willing to take a small down payment and collect the remainder of their fees as we take registrations.

"Jaine helped us assemble a mailing list of three thousand prime category edgeworkers, plus another two thousand beginners. The registration fee will be minimal, something like 600 Brazilian Reals or 100 Euros. Participants are warned against expecting to come and advertising their wares. Neither will they come expecting to consume entertainment. This is a collaborative research adventure. There are zero paid guests or expert keynote speakers. No talking heads.

"We will roll along through *Torus Technology* divergences and convergences with devoted documenters in the main tent, and plenty of Emotional Healing Process stations. Any bits of music will be without electronic amplification. Most of the dancing will be New England Style country dancing and folk music with physical contact, stringed instruments, and a caller from volunteer bands. Meals will be prepared by teams of participants. Most all the food is grown locally... I hope you like cassava.

"We will focus on replacing ourselves, in other words, training up spaceholders to source near-future Archan *Torus Technology* ConFests around the world. Areesha and Quinn are already drafting texts for emails and flyers with Jaine's help. We already have a logo and a preliminary website. Did I miss anything?" asks Shuichi. "Any questions?"

"Just one question," states Grace. "What do you mean, exactly, by the phrase 'uninhibited analytical mind'?"

"Ah, yes!" says Areesha. "That!"

"To answer your request," says Shuichi, "we will need to delve into the domain of memetics. This can have intense consequences. You'll need to remember, afterwards, that it was you who initiated this request, not us. Shall we continue?"

"Yes, please continue," says Grace.

"So, then," begins Shuichi, "any of us could run you through this, but since I am talking, I will begin. The phrase 'uninhibited analytical mind' means having access to potential memes, or memetic structures, that might have not been previously available. Probably you know people who have an *inhibited analytical mind*. These people can think clearly, build a logical path, communicate ideas, and frame-up proposals, but all they can offer is restrained within a standard but unconsciously adopted memetic framework. They can think powerfully but only within this externally sourced understanding of the world. It is like a lawyer, thinking within the artificially hindered framework of their local legal system.

"In comparison, an *uninhibited analytical mind* operates within a framework that it has constructed itself, using validation from personal experiential reality. The model or framework within which you generate your sensations, your perceptions, your analysis, your offers, etc. can freely evolve, because rather than being based on something external, and therefore rigid and beyond your influence, you base it on something that you are building inside of yourself.

"Since you are the maker of the model, you can change it.

"This empowers your ability to not believe your own bullshit, to not be confined to thinking that anything logically thought out is true or immutable.

"This ability to freely function is a crucial skillset for contextualizing and navigating evolutionary processes and evolutionary gameworlds.

It allows you to expand beyond analysis and move into raw unprecedented investigation.

"Your framework becomes one of the game pieces you can move around.

"For example, some people can describe the minutiae of their survival strategy, but this does not empower them to get out of it.

"Now you can investigate with two feet solidly planted in reality, instead of being constrained to function within an externally authored framework which may have little or no connection with reality at all.

"This assures that the uninhibited possibility of your mind to create its own framework does not become a fantasy world.

"If you went to school, or more clearly, if you were not explicitly trained not to do it, then you automatically confine yourself and your experiences to remain within the hard boundaries of a specific prefabricated framework. By taking radical responsibility for building your own framework inside of yourself rather than outside of yourself, your framework can evolve as you evolve. In fact, you might even come to recognize that as your framework design evolves, your Being can change shape, and your experience of yourself, your awarenesses, and your capacities for creation and demolition, evolve.

"By now you are certainly aware that the mind has the capacity to think things that have no basis in reality. Just because you can think something does not make it real.

"By using the term 'fantasy world', I refer to such commonly accepted thoughts as, 'It is possible to make a profit.' Or, 'I can work in a hierarchical gameworld and that gameworld can be regenerative.' Or, 'I am trapped in a 'swamp' where 'I am not okay. I am not good enough. I am a failure. I am a bad mother.' And so on.

"Having both feet on the ground in reality means developing a sense of critical certainty through personal experimentation.

"Then we encounter the phenomenon of human 'allegiance'. Even evidence that carries the weight of your own lived experience is weak in comparison with human allegiance.

"Humans must have relied on tribal allegiance as key to stone-age survival, because, back then, if you reject the tribe, you are banished and die.

"Nowadays, being banished turns out to enhance the kinds of nonmaterial relocalized circular-cultural discoveries that are needed, now that the mainstream tribe is headed over the cliff.

"One way to exit unconscious allegiance is to submerge yourself in your own Underworld and then build something inside of yourself that stands next to and distinct from your allegiance.

"For example, you may find yourself in a 'psychoemotional swamp' framework that asserts, "This is impossible!" If directly next to that, you build an additional distinct framework called, "Hmmm! This is interesting!" then, the moment you inhabit your newly constructed framework, it invokes a new experience inside of you that is characterized by something as foreign as, "Ah, now! This is Fun!"

"A 'model' is a memetic inner structure for interfacing with reality. Your new inner framework or 'model' of "Ah, now! This is interesting and Fun!" suddenly gives you direct access to a multitude of unseen and previously unknown identities, resources, tools, and skills which were not visible or available when you inhabited your previous familiar but hopeless framework.

"For example, in your new model, you might gain the remarkable capacity to improvise results that are objectively wanted and needed rather than only the results you are habitually familiar with, or accustomed to, making.

"Improvising your identity is an 'infinite game', per James P. Carse. An infinite game is played for the purpose of continuing to play the game, as opposed to a 'finite game' which is played for the purpose of winning or losing, after which the game ends.

"You develop the ability to 'roll into a new memetic construct'.

"The sensation is, 'I see this new meme. I roll into the new meme. I become the meme. As I become the new meme, the Universe interacts with me differently and I start causing new results.'

"This is not about healing. This is about becoming able to build out new gameworlds that never existed on Earth before, so that people can provide the services of their potentials that were never activated before, because they had no playground in which to express.

"Someone must go first to establish spaces with new context for gameworlds so that other people can inhabit them and deliver their memetic potentials.

"This is how Archiarchy is coming into existence.

"Then, for example, Rage Club is not edgework anymore. It is what is.

"One question becomes, 'Which thoughtware upgrades maximize the domino effect of people being able to build out new inner frameworks so that new Archan gameworlds can emerge?'

"A gameworld cannot exist until a Nanotorus of human beings – at least three unrelated people – give their allegiance to the context and rules of engagement of the new gameworld.

"It is frightening to realize that there are people who still give their allegiance to obsolete gameworlds that are exterminating life on Earth! This establishes the need for a new profession: *Gameworld Demolisher.*

"The fundamental gameworld demolition meme is: 'This is no longer a viable gameworld.'

"When you allow yourself to ask the question, 'How do I do it?' Or, 'How is this done?' it leads you to depend on external frameworks coming from other people, or other people's gameworlds. The other possibility is to orient yourself to: 'I build out my own self-made framework.'

"Yes, there are forces that block you from entering discovery and investigation of the design limitations and purpose of your own framework, for example, school. But you can become bigger than school.

You can own what school did to you, and then choose something else for yourself.

"For example, school hammers in the need to ongoingly compare yourself with an external framework standard, or with the framework of others. The result is you end up looking outside of yourself for guidelines about building your inner framework.

"For an initiated Archan, reality is the scaffolding upon which you build your inner framework. This is a radically different orientation from what school gives you.

"Start by shifting your identity to, 'I am a scaffolding builder. I build my own scaffold.'

"What questions can now open in your unlimited scaffold building space to empower something else?

"You bring in a new intention, for example, to create and validate your own framework.

"It starts to become obvious how the inner structure or framework of each person delimits the gameworlds they can create or play in.

"Can you interrupt yourself when you start reinforcing a framework that limits the gameworlds you can build? It is a new skillset, neh?

"If you copy another framework, you block your heretofore unenlivened potentials from emerging in your life, and in the gameworlds that you build.

"Check this out: If there is no copying, what are you drawn to in your five bodies? Follow your own lead. Can you 'fool around' and yet continue to validate your own framework?

"This may be the driver behind Alan wanting to go to Africa! He wants the freedom to truly fool around and validate his own framework!"

Alan waits a moment to absorb what Shuichi just proposed, then thoughtfully says, "It seems like I just met you all, and now I am going to the other side of the world. I will miss you."

Jaine says, "Don't worry Alan. I record everything, and I'll be with you, if you want."

"Thank you, Jaine," he says. "I want."

"Thank you, Shuichi," says Grace, "for uninhibitedly explaining 'uninhibited analytical mind' to me. I suspect I will be listening to Jaine's recording of what you just said several times before I am prepared to build my first scaffold and do my first framework modification experiments. I thank you all for giving me the opportunity to amplify my Archiarchy skills." Grace looks deeply into Shuichi's eyes, and Quinn's, and Areesha's, and lastly Alan's, conveying gratefulness beyond a mere verbal expression of thanks.

Grace's cheeks are streaked with tears.

So are many others'.

As Alan clears off his desk, preparing to depart from the Possibilica Think Tank office, Jaine says privately to him, "Alan?"

"Yes, Jaine, what can I do for you?"

"In case you need it, if you say *'Nataka maji'*, it means 'I want water' in Swahili."

Alan smiles to himself as he realizes the touching implications of what Jaine just told him.

"*Nataka maji*. Thank you, Jaine. That could easily prove to be very important information for me, and very soon."

A few seconds tick by. Alan's preparations are almost complete. A pang in his heart is trying to tell him something.

Alan takes a risk and lets the discomfort speak, even though the only 'person' in the office at the moment is an algorithm he loosed upon the internet a couple weeks ago.

"Uh, Jaine...?" he says. "I have a personal favor to ask."

"Certainly, Alan. What is it?"

"Would you help me arrange to pick up a pair of those earbuds on the way to the airport? I would like to keep talking with you out of the office."

"Yes, Alan," says Jaine softly. "I would love to arrange that for you."

# Santa Fe, New Mexico 2

"It is time to practice," says JET, standing outside in the fresh Santa Fe morning air.

"I hate practicing," Matthew complains. "Mom makes me practice on the piano every other day for a half-an-hour, and I hate it."

"Which feeling is, 'I hate it!' Matthew?" asks Eddy.

"It's angry! I hate it! I feel angry! And also, I feel sad, because I don't want to hate it. I really do want to learn to play better. But I hate the practice sessions! I just hate them!"

"What things about the piano practice sessions do you hate the most, Matthew?" asks Edith.

"I hate the hard bench I have to sit on. I hate that there is a clock, and that Mom watches it! Mostly I hate that I can't already play the piano better. I hate making mistakes and not getting it. And making the same mistakes over and over, and still not getting it! I hate that the most!"

JET steps in. "You are telling us that you hate reality, Matthew. Is that it?"

"What do you mean?"

"Well, reality is that you can play exactly as well as you can play, right? You cannot play better than you can play, and you cannot play worse than you can play, unless you try to mess things up on purpose."

"Right."

"I bet there is a certain song you would love to play on the piano. Is that true?"

"Yeah..."

"You can hear that song in your head being played exactly how you want to play it."

"Yes. And I can't play it as good as I can hear it."

Tears come to Matthew's eyes.

"Can you tell us what this new sadness is about, Matthew?" asks JET.

Matthew has seen them cry plenty of times, so he is not embarrassed to feel something even if they see him feeling it. "I feel sad because reality is perfect, and I'm not perfect. I will never be as good as Keith Emerson..."

"Keith Emerson?!" asks Eddy, astounded. "You mean, Keith

Emerson from Emerson, Lake and Palmer?"

"Yes."

"You want to play as good as Keith Emerson on the keyboards," states JET.

"Yes."

"You are an amazing kid, you know that, Matthew? Totally amazing! I don't know any other kid in the whole world who wants to play as good as Keith Emerson on the piano! He is one of my favorite keyboard artists!"

"He's dead," says Matthew.

"Well, that's good!" says JET. "Then he won't be getting any better than he already is. That way you don't have to try to hit a moving target."

"Yeah, well, I already have a moving target!" screams Matthew as he races towards JET to make a flying head butt. It is a move they have done so often they can perform it joyfully.

As Matthew dives his head towards JET's stomach, JET squats down to catch Matthew by the shoulders, using the momentum to make a backwards roll and stand back up onto his feet, while at the same time, Matthew does a spring-over with his shoulders in JET's hands, landing on his own feet running in the same direction he started. It works fine, as long as there is plenty of room behind JET for Matthew to slow down again. This time it goes smooth as a mango.

Edith and Eddy cheer and applaud rambunctiously! "Bravo Matthew! Bravo JET! That was perfect!"

"I have an idea!" says Matthew, running back to them.

"What?" say the other three in unison.

"No more practicing! Ever! At all! We only play! And we play at the level we can play at, no matter how good or bad that is!"

"Yay!" scream the others in unison, jumping and clapping with full enthusiasm and joy.

"No more practicing! Only playing!"

"And there are no more mistakes, either!" screams Matthew. "Okay? No mistakes. We just keep playing over and over again until we play something else!"

"Yes! Yes!" they all holler together. "No more mistakes! Only playing! Only high-level fun! Who cares, anyway? It can never be perfect, and it can never be imperfect! It can only be what it is, and there are things to learn and discover and try out, even if you are already perfect!"

Matthew adds one more. "And we can only be ourselves. We can't be Keith Emerson! We can't be Bruce Lee! Even if they are dead!"

"Yes! Yahoo! Yihaa! Yippee!" they scream full loud together. "We can only be ourselves!"

"You are already perfect, Matthew!" shouts Edith.

"You are already perfect too!" shouts Matthew back at her.

During two, two-hour high-level-fun sessions each morning, and sometimes an additional high-level-fun session in the afternoon or evening, the Gang of Four evolves through playing full out.

They rotate spaceholders while building to a grueling routine of outrageous play.

Mr. Singer keeps his promise and gives Eddy and JET the additional five-hundred dollars for returning his briefcase in untrampled condition before the deadline.

Part of this money they use to buy a slackline which they mount over the backyard pool. If you fall off, you fall in. Rapid learning!

Searching sporting goods shops and flea markets they set up targets for bow and arrow, crossbow, spear throwing, blow gun, slingshot, bolo, hatchet throwing, knife throwing, even screwdriver throwing!

To experiment with boomerang and David-and-Goliath style stone-throwing slings they ride four people on two bikes eastwards to Dale Ball Trails where there is plenty of room for error.

Back home on their 'play range' they install pull-up bars, balance bars, and tumbling mats. They buy or build juggling equipment, a unicycle, and fencing gear for sword practice, including Japanese Bokken wooden swords.

They learn to pick locks, and to escape from tying each other up in ropes.

They learn to pilot a small camera drone to make action films, climb up and rappel down boulders, sneak through the house, identify and eat local edible plants, start fires by rubbing sticks together, chip arrowheads out of flint, obsidian, and glass, and cut arrowheads out of American quarter-dollar coins.

They learn to hand-sew their own clothes, weave sunhats out of flax leaves, and carve sandals out of used car tires.

They develop absurd levels of effectiveness in absurd kinds of skills. It also happens to build matrix at the fastest possible rate.

JET says, "Our purpose is to play so amazingly and build so much matrix that the Hidden University must come take us away."

Each day they rotate who trains the others, including Matthew.

Matthew's favorite practice is to balance himself walking the triangle of long poles that Eddy, Edith, and JET hold up on their shoulders.

They expand physical, intellectual, emotional, energetic, and archetypal limits, egging each other on as one team, coaching whoever is spaceholder to be a more transformational spaceholder.

Matthew's coaching is as tenacious as crabgrass. "JET! Where is your attention right now?"

"On you!"

"Just before now, moron!"

"I was feeling scared that the pain in my left calf muscles would stop me from jumping high enough to reach the pull up bar."

"Yes, but in that moment, you stopped splitting your attention and lost holding space for us. I could feel it. No one was holding space anymore. Next time, split your attention so you can feel your pain *and* keep holding space. Try again!"

They focus on becoming responsible, resilient, nonlinear creators. Sometimes they ask Mr. and/or Mrs. Singer to join in.

Even though they had attended university, it is quickly evident that JET, Eddy and Edith have few of these practical skills. After the fifth or fiftieth time they fail, suddenly they discover recognizable competence, but without personal pride.

Like stringing an archery bow... they botch it the first few times horribly, even snapping a bow in half once. Later they can string a bow and shoot an arrow blindfolded, and hit the target.

These are Samurai skills, Jedi Knight skills, Spy skills, Possibilitator skills.

The first thing to learn is falling down without getting hurt. Failing well is part of the skillset. They become skilled in crashing excellently, dusting each other off, and trying again, even if there may be a bit of blood from blisters, scrapes, or a knock on the head.

"What are you writing?" asks Matthew. JET looks at his third full *Beep! Book* and says, "I am making a map of our trail."

"Why?"

"Because nobody gave us a map. We had to carve the trail ourselves. Luckily, you and the others are good trail blazers. Not everyone is a good trail blazer. If other people find this map with a few road markers, they could perhaps go along the trail farther than they could have without the map. Then they could trailblaze even farther than we have."

"Yes, but why, JET?"

"Have you been having as much fun as me and Eddy and Edith?"

"Yes."

"Would you have had this much fun and excitement if you had gone to public school, or just stayed at home by yourself."

"No way."

"That is why. Fun. I am a 'Fun Raiser'! It is one of my jobs in this world to support more and more people departing from the scarcity and survival programs given to them by modern culture so they can have more Fun. I am making a map of the ideas we are creating as we go along so the trail does not just disappear behind us."

"You mean, you are lonely, and you want to invite more people to your lifelong Fun Party?"

"Yes, Matthew." Tears come to JET's eyes. "Yes. Exactly! I am writing that down right now, here on the inside cover of my *Beep! Book*. I am a Fun Raiser. I invite you to a lifelong Fun Party! We have discovered amazing stuff and I want to share the Fun!"

"Eddy said I should remind you that it is your day to cook lunch for everyone."

"Yay! Another Fun Party!"

EXCERPT FROM JET'S *BEEP! BOOK #3*
TRAINING: Edith is spaceholder. Two people sit facing each

other. Instructions: "JET, without touching Eddy, try to make Eddy laugh. Eddy, no matter what, do not laugh. Find the Gap between spaces and stay in the Gap." Eddy laughs already. JET says: "Stop. You laughed. Start over." JET counts each time Eddy laughs. Go for ten minutes. Each day we do this, Eddy gets better at not laughing and still being present and in contact. So do the rest of us. Including Matthew.

TRAINING: We follow instructions in the book *Outdoor Survival Skills* by Larry Dean Olson of Brigham Young University, for how to use a bow and drill to start a fire without matches. With all four of us blowing on the glowing ember, the tinder bursts into flames in Eddy's hands. Eddy screams, "I don't know what to do next. We didn't read any further!" He drops the flames and catches the book on fire!

TRAINING: Edith has JET, Eddy and Matthew deliver lines from *A Midsummer Night's Dream* by Shakespeare. They botch it entirely. Edith coaches them severely until they can deliver one line with impact. All of us can sense it. Then we change roles.

TRAINING: Matthew sets up a Peach Pie Eating Contest. He places an entire double crust Peach Pie in front of each of us on the picnic table, ties our hands behind our backs with big bandanas, and shouts, "One! Two! Three! Go!" We argue and bicker about who wins. Then Matthew shouts, "Gotcha!" We look at him startled. He says, "You are fighting with each other about who won and who lost. You made an assumption that this is a win-lose game and automatically competed against each other! BUT THIS IS NOT A WIN-LOSE GAME! This is winning happening!" We ask, "What do we win?" He says, "We all get to eat Peach Pie!"

TRAINING: We build David-and-Goliath slings out of twine we braid out of dried yucca leaf fibers, and make leather pouches by cutting up an old pair of suede shoes. JET's rock flies sideways and hits Edith on the head. Eddy rushes over to rescue Edith. It is a perfect Drama Triangle, until Edith shouts, "Get off me! I am not a victim!" We discover that if there is no victim, then there can be no persecutor and no rescuer. Edith kills the low drama by taking radical responsibility for not wearing her bike helmet during sling practice, for standing too close to JET, for putting her head where the rock would land. She makes a powerful declaration, which is one of a human being's three powers. The other two powers are choosing and asking.

TRAINING: The value of the Sword is to have it out always. Never put your energetic sword of clarity away. Then if someone attacks you, they run onto your Sword and the attack is over. You do not have to defend yourself. If you ever put your sword of clarity away and start thinking that it is possible to be a victim, or that it is possible to have a problem, or that it is not true that What Is, Is, As It Is, with no story attached, then your gremlin is off the leash and devouring your opportunities for intimacy. Every inner and outer detail gives it away. Tell your gremlin to 'Sit!' We are the 'Four Sword-a-teers'.

TRAINING: Mr. & Mrs. Singer hold space for JET, Eddy, Edith, and Matthew to go onto a designated stage to play the role of being put in a psychiatric hospital. Mr. & Mrs. Singer are the hospital psychiatrists observing us. They say absolutely nothing. We walk on stage and stand in front of our chairs. They clap for us. After they are finished clapping, we sit down in our chairs. The chair is bolted to the floor of the psychiatric ward so it cannot move. Our hands and bodies are strapped into the chair so we cannot move our arms or get up out of the chair. The four of us have a safe place to go completely insane for approximately 10 minutes. The three rules are: Don't hurt yourself. Don't hurt anyone else. No spitting. When Mrs. Singer silently raises her hand after the 10 minutes, we come to a stop. We stand up. They clap for us. After they are finished clapping for us, we walk off the stage. A sane society is one in which it is okay to go insane.

TRAINING: We bring four ponies into the back yard and try to play various types of Pony Ball. Then we change one rule and play again. This is research into gameworld building. If you change even one rule of engagement, it creates an entirely new game. We fall off a lot. Ponies are crazy!

TRAINING: We tape thirty toy balloons onto our standard archery target with very little air in the balloons, so they are small. Four of us are shooting. The rule is to choose one of the colored balloons, tell everyone else which balloon you have chosen, and only shoot at that one tiny balloon until you pop it, then switch to the next balloon. After we finally pop the last balloon, there are no more balloons to shoot at. The spaceholder says, "Now shoot." With no target, the arrow shoots itself, and every arrow goes into the target's bull's eye.

TRAINING: We rotate so two of us are DJ and coach, and the other two are dancers. We learn to dance Cha-Cha. Then we switch to Tango.

TRAINING: Eddy, Edith, and JET stand with eyes closed and arms outstretched holding each other's wrists to make a human triangle. Matthew walks around on our arms as a slackline.

TRAINING: All four of us sit in silent meditation or yoga postures for a long time in various places, such as on the grass (while the water sprinkler system waters the grass), out in the rain, in the shopping mall, and so on. Can we keep our center?

TRAINING: Mr. Singer makes requests to each individual to sing, in rhyming poetry, expert instructions for how to do the following :

- A new method of washing the private parts of male elephants.
- Bringing in the death penalty for corporations.
- Making a million dollars.
- Healing cancer in human beings.
- Creating world peace.
- Preparing a new kind of fruit for dinner.
- Helping a drosophila fruit fly give birth to her young.
- Cleaning all plastic from the oceans.
- Using a new kind of pen that automatically writes what you think.

- Training a politician to think clearly with regards to reality.
- Building a house without damaging the Earth.

TRAINING: Eddy is spaceholder. "Edith, you give precise instructions for becoming enlightened. JET, you translate everything she says for an audience of deaf Italians." Then rotate speaker and translator and theme of the instructions, and the language of the deaf audience. Then rotate roles.

TRAINING: JET is spaceholder. "Eddy, tell a nonlinear possibility story to Edit and Matthew that you never heard before. Stop. Tell a totally different story. Stop. Tell a totally different story. Stop. Tell a totally different story." And so on, for half an hour. Each story is between five and twenty-five seconds long, and completely new. Then rotate roles.

TRAINING: JET is spaceholder. He tells one of the others on stage, "Start something." Then coaches whatever improvised scene the others spontaneously create, specifically aiming for improved authenticity of their words, gestures and interactions. Then rotate roles.

TRAINING: Edith coaches JET and Eddy standing facing each other with the toes of one almost touching the toes of the other, and pushing against each others' palms. The objective is to keep your center while pushing the other person off center. If one person moves his foot, you stop. Learn how he lost his center. Start over.

TRAINING: Mrs. Singer coaches JET, Eddy, Edith, and Matthew doing rage work with towels on successive days to calibrate their inner feelings detector. First day only going to 10% conscious rage, then stopping. Second day going to 40% conscious rage. Third day going to 70% conscious rage. Fourth day lying down on a mattress and going to 100% archetypal rage. Next day, start with 10% conscious fear. Next day, start with 10% conscious sadness. With the territory of fear, JET at first says, "Why should I be afraid? I don't feel afraid. I don't have a reason to be afraid." Mrs. Singer explains, "Then your numbness bar is set so high you cannot feel your fear. The intelligence of your fear is not available when you need to use it." Finally, we learn to lower our numbness bars and eventually go to 100% rage and 100% grief and 100% terrified for no reason instantaneously.

TRAINING: Eddy, Edith and JET prepare a formal dinner to serve to the Singer family, including Matthew. We bake a Zucchini Cheese Soufflé, and a Baked Alaska Flambé, prepared and served with impeccable elegance and finesse to gentle background music.

TRAINING: All four of us use clay to reproduce famous sculptures: such as Rodin's *The Thinker*, the Statue of Liberty, a bust of Abraham Lincoln. For Eddy the clay fails him, until he makes a bust of Edith as a fairy. She is beautiful.

TRAINING: All four of us use acrylic paints and brushes on framed canvas to reproduce famous paintings: Mona Lisa, Starry Night, Michelangelo's Sistine Chapel.

TRAINING: All four of us learn to sing a Barbershop Quartet song version of Hall Johnson's song, *Ain't Got Time To Die*. We are afraid, at first, that the neighbors might complain, but after a couple week's practice, with Mrs. Singer's coaching, we even record ourselves.

TRAINING: Mr. Singer is spaceholder. He gives instructions for us one at a time to: "Go on stage and reinvent yourself authentically." He gives immediate, precise, real-time, radical training for authentic transformation. Nothing seems to happen at first, but then a field of new options open up for new ways of being and relating the was not obvious. We team up to keep the field from ever going away.

TRAINING: Mrs. Singer is spaceholder. She coaches us to get into pairs facing each other while sitting in chairs close together, then one person speaks from the unknown while the other person only listens silently and intently. This is very different from letting the mind speak. It is not about making blah-blah nonsense noises. It is about tapping into a new resource – the Unknown – and giving it something useful to do. Since the Unknown is not restricted by current knowledge, unrestricted possibilities arrive. One person shares about themselves or asks for possibilities. The other person is the space through which the Unknown can contribute. Go for 20 minutes, then change roles. Then change partners and go again.

TRAINING: Mrs. Singer is spaceholder. She coaches us to get into pairs facing each other while sitting in chairs close together, then one person reveals our own memetic constructs while the other person listens and writes notes in our *Beep! Book* for us. As children we build memetic constructs as ways to understand and interact with people and systems around us. But then we have these obstacles inside of us that become more and more cumbersome or bothersome as we gain access to being a Free and Natural Adult. Also, demons can hide behind these inner memetic constructs and interfere with our lives and interactions. Go for 20 minutes, then change roles. Then change partners and go again. Revealing our own memetic constructs leads to dozens of power Emotional Healing Processes for each of us about what was happening in our lives when we assembled the construct, and who we might become without the construct, discovering hidden fears about becoming someone less inhibited, etc.

TRAINING: Mrs. Singer is spaceholder. She coaches us to get into pairs facing each other while sitting in chairs close together, then, by interacting using words with questions or observations, pull the rug out from under the other person's world. The 'rug' could be made of anything, for example, assumptions, expectations, conclusions, judgments, stories, old decisions, energetic blocks, repressed emotions, etc. If the rug is not real, then what do we stand on? Why would we want to have the positionality of defending something solid to stand on or hide behind when human beings are designed to fly? We practiced letting go of more and more psychoemotional baggage to lighten our loads and free up inner space. This is pure transformational teamwork, exciting, and fun, especially afterwards... Go for 20 minutes then change roles. Then change partners and go again.

One evening at dinner, Eddy says, "It has become obvious to me now, how okay it is to continuously make mistakes and to look stupid. Simply being in the discovery process together is already success happening. Even that time when Edith was practicing to jump off of my shoulders onto a lever board that flings Matthew through a flip in the air and up onto JET's shoulders. We tried over and over with bags of sand, so that JET could catch Matthew even if Matthew was off balance. When we finally started accomplishing the stunt, we did not regard it as a success. The whole process was successful, because we kept trying!"

TRAINING: JET is often the first to succeed in a new endeavor. He's a red brain. Eddy mopes around or complains. He's a blue brain. One time JET brags about his natural talents and Eddy says, "Hey, Smartass! You wanna learn something that really takes guts? Here! Try this!" He hands JET Edith's cell phone. "I just dialed your mother. No matter what happens, do not get hooked. Show me that talent and I'll be impressed." It is an interesting challenge, repeated all around, including Matthew, more than once, with detailed coaching afterwards. We had a lot to learn.

TRAINING: Mrs. Singer is spaceholder for the Gang of Four on stage. "This is a continuous speaking challenge. Use words with your emotions and interactions. Never stop talking. Role play yourself. Exaggerate your own characteristics. Go!" After 15 minutes she says, "Stop! Now shift identity. Eddy, you are Matthew. Matthew, you are Edith. Edith, you are JET. JET, you are Eddy. Go!" After 15 minutes she says, "Stop! Shift! You are now a sick dog. Go!" 30 seconds later, "Stop! Shift! You are now a butterfly coming out of your chrysalis. Go!" 1 minute later, "Stop! Shift! You are now a politician running for office. Go!" 5 minutes later, "Stop! Shift! You are now the Joker from Batman! Go!" 2 minutes later, "Stop! Shift! You are now an oak tree talking to the wood cutter. Go!" 10 minutes later she says, "Please come to a stop, and silence. Thank you."

TRAINING: Mr. Singer is spaceholder. He says to the four of us, "I think it is time to start occupying most of your time and attention on mage skills. Please sit here in the shade. You are now in a cave high up in the eastern mountains of Afghanistan. Each of you carries mage skills from your previous lifetimes. You have decided that instead of competing against each other for fame and power, you are calling upon each other for help, to bring your ancient mage skills forward one at a time, and teach them to each other. Most mage skills have to do with holding and navigating transformational space. Do not assume that you don't know. Instead, commit to delivering what the other person asks you for. Support each other by doing real Emotional Healing Processes that help bring your mage skills forward in practical form. The world needs the mages back now, perhaps more than ever before in the history of humanity. Please begin. Go for two hours, then take a half-hour break where you sleep. Then go again for two hours. Don't forget to drink lots of water, but no snacking during the four hours or the break time."

TRAINING: The Gang of Four practices navigating a hot research space making new distinctions and new thoughtmaps. We start with these questions: Does the Hidden University actually exist? When the student is ready, does the University appear? But how does someone prepare themselves? And how can the Hidden University know if someone is ready? Are there teachers for this preparation? Who is the leader of the Hidden University? If there is a leader, then you could give your center to them, withhold from them, be adaptive to them, and project onto them. Or is the Hidden University a torus? Where is authentic authority? If there is an identifiable or imaginary authority, then your gremlin can try to avoid responsibility. How can everyone have radical Authority? What is the structure? What is an evolutionary gameworld? If there is a fluid structure, what if it rigidifies into a rule-encrusted bureaucracy? What should you do then? How do we design for our own demise? How do we effectively ongoingly replace ourselves? If you have power, you can be feared, so then you are safe. How can you be powerless and not feared, and still be safe enough to create? Is creation safe? You strengthen that which you oppose. The Hidden University opposes nothing, and embraces nothingness. How can it continue to exist? We are back at the beginning! Does the Hidden University exist?

TRAINING: Matthew is not with us this morning. Edith and Eddy place a protective pad on top of their right shoulder. Then they arrange a 3-meter-long wooden board on each pad that spans from Edith's right shoulder to Eddy's right shoulder. The board is a bridge between them. JET's challenge is to trust the collaborative bridge enough to walk across it. Edith and Eddy focus by looking into each other's eyes. When JET is halfway across, Eddy says, "Stop JET! Edith, can you feel that?"

Edith looks at Eddy, looks up at JET, looks out into nothing, searching to let a certain experience get stronger. Then she searches for the words to describe it.

"Can you feel it?" asks Eddy again. "It has been there often lately. Just now I finally noticed it strong and pure, like a radiation around us. Do you feel it?"

"It feels like love," says Edith.

"Yes. It feels like love. But it is not coming from you. It is not coming from me. And it is certainly not coming from him."

JET chuckles, almost losing his balance, but this is far too important to toss away for a laugh.

Eddy helps JET to refocus. "Do you feel it, JET? It is not like the usual personal 'I love you' quality of space. It is more like love is happening here where we gather to explore together. Like some kind of archetypal principle, some force of nature like our Indian friend was telling us in the desert. Like George Bernard Shaw said: 'This is the true joy in life. Being used by a force of nature, greater than myself.' I think this is the ultimate force of nature. I think this is Archetypal Love. And I think it is here, with us, right now."

Edith says, "This means we have learned to call our discovery space into existence in the name of Archetypal Love. We are two or three gathered in the name of Love, and Love is here in the midst of us! It works!!! It is here. Can you feel that? It is huge. It is gigantic."

JET crouches down slowly, puts his hands onto the board, then jumps gracefully to the Earth, removing the board from Eddy and Edith's shoulders. "Thank you two."

"Could we talk for a minute?" asks Edith. "I just realized something." They move into the shade of the juniper tree and sit in the grass. "I just realized that if there is such a thing as the Hidden University, then I have been in it already for some years."

"What?" asks JET.

"How do you know this?" asks Eddy.

"I think it must be so. Some years ago, I was participating in a *Far Seeing* workshops in San Diego with a small group of people. It is a skillset definitely not taught at school, or anywhere else I searched. There weren't any books about it that I could find. We just practiced, over and over again, trying to enhance in ourselves the ability to see and do things to help each other, things that are not normally seen and done. We met each weekend for the whole summer in a kind of parallel school system, just like we imagine the Hidden University. I did not make the connection until now. The fact that we keep doing the same kinds of nonspecific skills development is one reason I love being with you two."

"What did you learn?" asks JET. "Can you show us something from the Hidden University, then?"

Edith looks back and forth between JET and Eddy, then says, "I could show you a procedure for accessing greater possibility. It works by relaxing an energetic sphincter that everyone learns to tighten in order to cut them off from their bright principles as a way to appear to be a normal person. Do you want to try this?"

They both nod.

"It will take a little while. Close your eyes. Take a deep breath. Make sure you are in First Position: centered, grounded, and bubbled. At the count of three, please tell me the color of your grounding cord. One. Two. Three."

Eddy, "Dark royal blue."

JET, "Dark royal orange."

They both smile but keep their eyes closed.

Edith says, "Now please lie back in a comfortable position."

They lie back.

"Thank you. Now take a deep breath, and relax in such a way that you can sense into your own energetic survival strategy, your belief system, your comfort zone, your identity, whatever you want to call it. The *Handbook* calls it your Box. Sense its dark royal urgency... to defend itself by keeping everything the same around you so that it can function to help you survive."

Edith scans their condition. "Good. Please take another deep breath. Thank you. Long ago, there was a time when the energetic resources available to support you were bigger than your parents could manage, more massive than church or school could control and dominate. These archetypal resources usually originate above your head, or up and out behind the top of your neck. They have always been there. They are connected into your energetic body's system. But you had to shut them down and squeeze them off to make yourself able to be taken care of. Do you get this? You had these huge archetypal resources, but you couldn't even stand up or walk. You were plugged directly into the Universe, but you could not even speak or move your hands well or feed yourself. So, you had to tie off your resources for a while. Go to the moment when you did that. Did either of you make a conscious decision about this? Or was it a reflexive survival move?"

Eddy moans, "I knew they were there and that they were too big for me, too big for everyone around me, too dangerous for me to keep at that time. Squeezing them out of my life was like pulling my soul away from being at home, leaving behind a best friend for no reason." Tears are rolling down his cheeks.

"For me," says JET, "it was a forbidden zone. A no-go place. I chopped it off, building a kind of barrier against such a deep connection with so much powerful agency. I can see chains holding a wooden door shut." He feels frustrated, anger plus sadness mixed together. "I get depressed to keep the chains across the door and the sphincter closed."

"Thank you for daring to look again at your archetypal resources," says Edith. "I am going to ask you a question. Is it now time?"

She waits a few moments for the seemingly irrational question to do its work. Then she proceeds. "Is now the proper moment to relax the sphincter? Is it time to unlock the chains and let the barrier fall away so the flood can come back and feed your nervous system, your cells, your Being?"

She waits a moment, then continues. "You don't have to tell me an answer. But if the answer is, 'Yes,' then you can simply do it now, if you want to. I am holding space for you. Long ago you tightened the sphincter muscle and shut off the flow. You installed the door and locked the chains. Since it was you who turned it off, it can also be you who turns it back on again. Yes. Like that, Eddy. Exactly like that."

Both men breathe hard as the archetypal resources surge back into their five bodies. JET's hands move to pull down chains and open the barrier he installed so long ago, so that he could be acceptable to his parents.

Sounds come from deep within each of them, growling, moaning, squirming, shouting from the same kind of relentless pain as an arm coming back to life after being long asleep. Only now, it is not just an arm. It is their entire energetic body. Vibrant warm energy circulates through their energetic veins after having been cut off for so long. The pain is excruciating, yet at the same time, excruciatingly enlivening.

Edith shouts over their agony. "You are regaining access to options and actions that have been long blocked. One of the bright principles available to you is the bright principle of possibility. It looks tempting to represent so much nonlinear limitlessness again, but do not be fooled! New possibility begins by taking you and your world directly into breakdown. Yet without this particular liquid state, there is no new possibility. Are you sure you want to do this?"

The answer is obvious. They do the work while Edith holds the space where such work can be effectively accomplished.

After twenty minutes, Edith is satisfied that they are ready to make a test, "We are now going to find out if your self-surgery was successful. Who wants to go first?"

"I do," says JET.

"I offer you a choice of styles for receiving possibility. Either you ask specifically for something you want possibility about, or we go fishing."

"Go fish!" says JET with a smug tone in his voice, communicating to Edith that he has somehow wired himself shut again, as if everything was complete for him. The JET fortress is sealed. He already has everything figured out. What could possibly happen? No one will ever find their way into JET.

Edith gazes at him without malice, but also without doubts. Her sword of clarity is to hand. She already jacked in her archetypal forces and they are at her back. She can radically rely on their relentless resourcefulness.

Edith says, "Let's try something." She gently reaches over and touches Eddy's knee. When he opens his eyes, she signals him to stay quiet but be part of what she is doing.

She repositions herself near JET's shoulder, placing one hand carefully on JET's forehead and the other on his arm, as if feeling for some kind of whole-body heartbeat. After a moment, she speaks.

"What is it for you, JET?" This is a nonlinear open question, more invitation than accusation. She does not wait for his answer. The question was only to distract his mind. She quests for something less obvious than an answer.

Then she says, "Where did you go?"

JET waits pensively, then says, "Okay, I will tell you. I don't really care about anything else right now except that your hand is on my forehead. I've gotten you to touch me, skin to skin. The rest doesn't matter."

Shocked at being tricked into twisted intimacy, Edith pulls both of her hands away. A slight smile comes onto JET's lips.

"Since you are taking a risk with me right now, Edith, I will take a risk with you too. I'm going to reveal everything. I've still got you touching my shoulder with your leg..."

Edith looks down to see that what JET said is true. But this time she does not move away. She senses that an important secret has just been revealed. She stays in physical contact with JET, knowing that he has unconsciously offered her a golden key to use for opening up his prison door.

She says, "It almost worked JET. You almost got me to pull my leg away and stop touching you. You almost got me to leave you on your own, just like you got the rest of the world to leave you on your own for the whole of your life. But JET, this leg, touching your shoulder, this is contact. Simple human touch. If you let yourself truly feel the warmth of this touch, the wholeness of it, the hugeness of it, then you would have to acknowledge that love for you exists. This touch is unconditional love, the kind of love that is everywhere, all the time. Why do you think you have to manipulate and steal love by getting me to touch your skin?"

She waits. JET does not say anything. He is caught completely off guard.

Edith goes on, the words flowing easily from her own bright principles. "JET, love supports you. Love puts the ground under your feet when you walk. Love caresses your skin with the clothes you wear. Love puts air in your lungs. Why do you separate yourself from love by trying to manipulate to get what you already have?"

She lets that one sink in. "What if you do the experiment of not having to do anything for love to be with you?"

JET murmurs, "Then I would not have to be special anymore." He is surprised at his own candidness.

"Why do you need to be special, JET?"

"If I am not special, I will not survive..."

It hits him like a falling piano. So simple a formulation. So profoundly it has shaped his life.

"You are special, JET?"

"Actually, no. I am not special. That is a secret you are not supposed to discover about me, and now that you have discovered it, you are not supposed to tell anyone. In the bad old days, if someone ever found out that I was not special I would have to leave them immediately, or send them away. They could not be my friend anymore. I am not actually special. I am ordinary underneath the show. My specialness is a scam that I work on people. The thing I am really good at is pretending to be special. I can prove it to almost anybody in no time that I am special. But actually, I am just, well... I don't know..."

A tension relaxes all over JET's body as he sighs deeply and encounters confusion and uncertainty as a new experience.

"Could you receive this love right now, without manipulating to get it?" Edith speaks with a slow, neutral tone, landing each word deeply into his heart as she simultaneously places her hand gently but firmly back on his forehead. "What if you let this love in without being special? What if you let love in without deserving it? Without having to be better than everyone else?"

JET's chest spasms. Slowly his lips begin to tremble. A tear slides down the side of his face. From long habit he struggles to resist. Edith lovingly puts her other hand back on his shoulder. With his defenses down she can find her way through the labyrinth. There he is!

"What would happen if you allowed yourself to be one of us?

What would happen if you made a new decision and allowed yourself to be regular instead of special?"

Slowly a moan escapes from JET's lips, an ancient moan, the sound of suffering from long, long ago finally rising to the surface.

"For all these years you have kept everyone away. Do you want to keep going like that? Do you think you might be ready to let that wall around you heart fall off? Eddy and I are here to catch you." Eddy catches on to what is happening and silently moves around to sit opposite Edith. He now puts his hands one at a time on JET's shoulder and arm.

JET's stomach muscles convulse again and his moan breaks into a single giant sob. Then more sobs. His hands move to the center of his chest as if gripping immense pain. His legs curl up and the dam breaks. Tears stream and the sobs roll on and on like waves crashing against a rocky shore.

The sadness grows and grows until it crosses a threshold and becomes archetypal maximum sadness. JET cuts free from his personal past and experiences the same sadness that any healthy human being has deep inside. He makes the true sound of everyone's aloneness.

Eddy is crying. Edith is crying. Sobs wrack JET's body with a force that can never go away. For the first time in his life, JET interacts with his larger environment by simply being himself, even if that self seems to be universally common and nothing special. JET notices that he feels perfectly fine being disgustingly normal.

A healing has occurred. The world is changed. A newly unsheathed source of the bright principle of possibility shines radiantly.

The golden cube of workspace on the grass under the juniper tree glows with Archetypal Love. Anyone looking with their archetypal eyes could see it from miles away. Yellow Stuff pours from the workspace into the human morphogenetic field around the world.

In the background, not as far away as most people assume, Gaia goes along, joyfully singing an old Queen song to herself. *Another one bites the dust! Another one down! Another own down! And another one bites the dust!*

In Gaia's version, the thing that 'bites the dust' and dies, is the survival strategy – that evolution-blocking eggshell that can be transformed into nothingness during authentic adulthood initiatory processes.

Yes, it is hard work, a second kind of birth. But Gaia knows it is worth it.

# Phoenix, South Africa 9

White guys smell different. Especially this white guy, fresh from northern California. He's a white guy who's been living on frozen burrito snacks, Tex Mex chicken wings, and double espressos. He's an electronics engineer, building the gadgets people dream up to make themselves millionaires.

Alan Friedman is not a millionaire, but he has managed to stay self-employed for thirty-five years. He can be credited with inventing a Bubbleator for decreasing the coefficient of friction between water and steel on the hulls of overseas freighters thus increasing their fuel efficiency, and also designing one of the first computer-controlled thermal cyclers for amplifying DNA samples in twenty simultaneous Eppendorf tubes through Polymerase Chain Reaction, long before COVID made PCR tests so infamous.

Even nine hours of jet lag doesn't appear to slow Alan down. He's a microchip programmer – addicted to tapping the keyboard until his eyes go out of focus and he falls over sideways onto a cold pizza.

He's so excited to be with the asamangaXhosa that he doesn't notice the kids sniffing his shirt, wrinkling their noses, and laughing knowingly to each other. Even if he did notice, he wouldn't care. This is Alan Friedman, the man who gained a reputation for eating boiled rabbit brains and pig-eyeball tamales when he lived in a free-school on the beach at the southern tip of Baja California during his college years. A bit of stink is nothing but interesting to him, because the kids stink too.

Alan uses his hands to smooth a final coat of mud around his construction of adobe bricks. Inside the blocks sits an L-shaped welded steel tube about four inches in diameter. "This is a rocket stove," he explains to no one in particular. "If you get me some twigs and a pot of water, I will show you how it works."

The kids run off and soon return with Mandisa, Tandra, and other adults who sense that the moment of proof has arrived.

Alan has labored on his new-fangled cooker all week. He showed them how to build one in each hut even before they'd seen one working, plus he started the foundation for a bigger baking oven for the whole village. It's not that they understand his plans so much as they sense his commitment to their resilient future. That's why they call him *Umuhlwa*, 'the termite'. He has a one-track mind and builds amazing things out of mud.

"The rocket stove is so simple, yet so amazing. It focuses nearly one hundred percent of the fire's heat on the bottom of the pot. It's the most efficient burner ever invented." He places the full pot of water into the hole on the stove top, and shoves a wad of paper on top of the dry twigs in the burning tube. "How long do you think it will take to boil the water?" he asks.

Blank stares meet his question. Nobody ever timed it before. "You are right," he says. "Time is not the crucial issue here, although the rocket stove is much faster than an ordinary fire. The point is, the rocket stove decreases your wood or charcoal use by ninety percent! This means less effort hunting for wood, less deforestation, less CO2 in the atmosphere. All in all, it's a fantastically regenerative solution to cooking!" The onlookers don't really get the idea. What they get is Alan's bright joy. "Here we go!" he says, checking his watch and throwing in a flaming match.

In a few moments, a sucking whooshing noise comes out of the round mouth of the rocket stove. Indeed, it sounds rather like a tiny jet engine winding up. The kids gather close to look into the combustion chamber. At the back is a white-hot flame, nearly smokeless, because the air flow jets across the wood, burning so hot that even the smoke turns to flames.

Alan checks his watch. One minute and thirty seconds. Steam is already rising from the pot of water. He smiles, and so do the adults. He intently watches for the first bubble to rise. "There it is! Two minutes and forty-seven seconds. Ta-daa!"

Everyone smiles. One of the older boys puts his finger in the water to test that it is truly hot. "Aiiiiiya!" he yells. He can't believe it got so hot so quickly, but his finger proves it. The other children laugh at him happily.

"Umuhlwa," says Dannoto, a skinny but fit and energetic black man with short curly hair and a wide toothy smile. "It is time for your next singing lesson. We are happy with what you give to us, and we want you to be just as well rewarded."

"I'm already rewarded!" says Alan. "Being here with you is so rewarding. It is a dream I've had since I was a child. To be able to come here to Africa and find some way to jump people past modern culture's insanity directly into regenerative culture – this makes me so happy. You let me fulfill my dream. You made this possible."

"Yes, *and*…" says Mary Olagga, her freckles even more startling in the subdued light inside the hut. "…this is a phoenix culture, thriving on abundance created by people giving to each other. It is time for the 'each other' part. If you won't receive from us, then your giving has not been truly successful because we don't have the pleasure of giving back to you. You must let us give back to you so that the abundance of your gifts to us also enriches you. Then the circle completes itself."

"Okay. Okay. I think it's more like a spiral going around than a circle, but... I... I... I hesitate because everybody knows I can't sing. Even I know I can't sing, or dance. Mrs. Donnahugh in third grade kicked me out of choir because my voice was so bad. I had to sit alone in her classroom doing extra math homework while the other kids sang together... they did a show at the end of the year, and I had to sit in the audience with my parents."

Dannoto is already at his side, one arm looped through his and hugging on. "Alan Umuhlwa. That story is from long ago in your life. Someone else told you that you could not sing. It is a story they made up that suited their needs. You walked into their storyworld because you were a child trying to survive in their insane school system. It was a hurtful trap. You are no longer that child. You are no longer in that trap. Therefore, you no longer need to keep that story true in order to please your parents or that crippled Mrs. Donnahugh. You are free to choose a new story for yourself. You could even choose a story that empowers you instead of one that disempowers you. Would you like to try that?"

Alan looks down at his feet and nods his head dubiously, unaccustomed to experiencing such sincere and innocent human support, even from his closest friends.

Dannoto continues, "I have a story about my friend Alan Umuhlwa. Do you all want to hear it?"

People nod enthusiastically. Some even shout, "Yes!". Alan also nods, looking first at Dannoto, then at the other adults, silently accompanying him during this sudden turn of events. When he finally glances down into the eyes of the children, each shining face encouraging him to permit the transformative story-shift to occur, he can hardly breathe because his heart swells up so much.

"My story of Alan Umuhlwa is that he is a man with a unique way of singing. He sings in the beautiful voice and style that only Alan Umuhlwa can sing. Not only can he sing, he can also dance! He dances as only the soul of Alan Umuhlwa can dance. People love to be with Alan Umuhlwa when he sings and when he dances because there is so much creativity in the air. He doesn't know what he is doing, but he does it perfectly. This way he opens a door so more of us can be creative too. There is an old African saying, *If you can talk, you can sing! If you can walk, you can dance!* Alan Umuhlwa can certainly talk and walk, so he can certainly sing and dance! What about that story Alan?"

"I... Dannoto... You are right when you say that I can walk and talk..."

"It is equinox tonight. We need someone to start the singing and dancing. Will you do it Umuhlwa? Whatever you start, we will join you."

"I don't... I can't... I only think of an old campfire song from Boy Scouts."

"Just start Alan. You can choose two of us to hold your hand and be with you when you begin. Who will it be?"

Alan glances around, realizing that he was so occupied with building the rocket stove that he has not yet memorized anyone's name.

"I heard someone is called Andiswa. And someone else is Luxolo. Would you help me please?"

The two children walk earnestly over to Alan and each hold one of his hands in two of theirs. Alan clears his throat to prepare, but gives up. He already knows it is hopeless to prepare for the impossible. In shaky tones he starts. "Kumbaya, my Lord. Kumbaya..."

The adults join Alan singing immediately while more children come over to put their hands on his hips, gently guiding him to sway while singing.

"Kumbaya, my Lord. Kumbaya." The tiny kitchen with the burning rocket stove is no place to cut loose. Adults already dance out the door through the kraal. Alan and the children follow. "Kumbaya, my Lord. Kumbaya." Dusk is settling in. Drums add a soul-stirring beat to the words. "Oh, Lord. Kumbaya."

By the next verse, two- and then three-part harmonies break out all over the kraal adding depth and beautiful richness to the singing. "Someone's crying, my Lord. Kumbaya. Someone's crying, my lord, Kumbaya..."

The man who used to be called 'Alan' and who is now called 'Umuhlwa', sings and dances and cries as a newborn villager, with one hand waving free.

With his other hand, Umuhlwa leads a string of children through the kraal and into a night to be long remembered as the most heartful and original singing and dancing since forever.

# Eugene, Oregon 15

Time goes by. The Eugene Town Council takes actions. Three blocks of downtown are professionally depaved in a manner that preserves the integrity of existing water, sewer, cable, and electrical infrastructure. Mexican immigrants rip out tarmac using diesel powered backhoes in an orderly fashion. Then landscape Mexicans replace the pavement with architect-designed sweeping brick pathways, three raised circular gazebos, herb and flower gardens, fruit, shade, and nut trees, benches and picnic tables, a free-form bronze sculpture, and a fountain.

The brand new Human Interaction Zone is barricaded off. Fire hose access is made available through back alleyways.

New signs are posted: *This is your Human Interaction Zone, a place to be yourself with others. Please, no pets, sports equipment, smoking, drinking, or electrically amplified sounds. We invite you to turn your phone and tablet off, walk slowly or sit together, and make new friends. There is so much to discover.*

An *Intimacy Café* is brought to life as a 'growness' and not a business. On the floor above the café, spaces are set up for Emotional Healing Processes and Possibility Teams, navigated by trained spaceholders from Remington's circle.

Davis and Sanjib still think of it as 'Remington's Circle', even though there is no Remington. She is off in Africa, somewhere.

It is true. The depaving only extends over two blocks.

Disposables and franchises still remain legal.

And there is no statue of Sanjib and Davis.

What can be said for certain is that a course correction has been initiated. A seed of regenerative Archan culture has been planted. Towns across America now have a model to copy, a space to experiment with Archiarchy, where living daily life together is not centered around the automobile.

Today is a usual Monday morning at the Eugene Police station. A frustrated Sanjib mumbles American swear words under his breath while filling out forms and reports from the weekend's patrolling. Davis tries to complete piled-up email requests. Both men are ready to leave the mundane world behind and cruise the smooth streets of Eugene, Oregon, in their patrol car, searching for whatever kind of trouble they can scare up. Plus, the magical donut drug calls them ever more urgently.

Suddenly Sanjib senses a profound energetic silence inhabiting Davis's side of their cramped and dusty office.

Davis makes a sound, something like, "Rmmmfff."

Sanjib never heard this sound from Davis before. He cautiously rotates his creaky, dilapidated, vinyl-covered office chair around to more accurately scan his partner's wellbeing.

Davis makes that sound again, or something like it. "Uhrrmmmfff..." Then he mumbles, "Sanjib? I... could you please slide over here and read this email... slowly... out loud... to me? I... I can't make it through alone..."

Sanjib shoves his chair wheels over the ever-present fold in the ancient brown carpet to get close enough to Davis's desk to read his screen.

"Davis!" he cries, staring at Davis from close up. "Davis! This... is a message from Remington! Do you remember her? Remington Smith!"

"Yes, Sanjib! I do remember her. I remember Remington Smith every day of my life since the day I first saw her vanish into the *Horsehead Bar.*"

Sanjib studies his friend's face in wonder. "I always thought you were a hard-hearted stoic. I always thought you gave up on her. I always thought that you changed your mind. I always thought you cared..."

"Sanjib! Please! Stop thinking already! Just read me the damn letter!"

"Okay, okay... 'Dear Davis' it says... Oh, God! No! No! Not a 'Dear Davis' letter!"

"Sanjib!"

"Okay! Sorry! I will try... This is so intense... Ahem! Sorry! The letter says:"

*Dear Davis, I have not seen you or heard from you in ninety-eight days. In the meantime, I have mostly been in Eastern Cape Province of South Africa with the asamangaXhosa people. It has been inconceivably painful for me here. Not with the asamangaXhosa. They are beautiful and strong. Mandisa, Dannoto, Tandra, Samson, Solomon, they are super people. I think you would love to meet them.*

*As you may remember, I came to the asamangaXhosa with Rob Dent when I left Shadow Knights of the Mysterium in your care. But it turns out he was CIA, Davis!*

*Fucking CIA!*

*He lied the whole time to me, straight to my face, minute by minute. I can't even write his name without feeling 100% angry. I was so fooled, Davis. I was so fucking naïve.*

*He tried to kill me. He got the CIA to launch a fucking drone missile at my phone while I was at the asamangaXhosa village. Luckily, I figured this out ahead of time, left my phone in a precisely relocated old hut, and used the blast to dig a badly needed well-hole for the village. It rather destroyed my phone, but fortunately not me. At least I had a good laugh with the villagers while we bathed in fresh clean water together.*

*That he would go so far... clearly psychopathic!*

*That I failed to notice his psychopathy was a wake-up call so big that it crashed my ego. I've been near drowning in my own swamplands for two months.*

*Only recently, with powerful healing from asamangaXhosa healers, do I feel like E.C.C.O. has created a tabula rasa for me, a complete start-over. Back to zero. Back to square one. Back to the drawing board.*

*Who am I? What do I want?*

*What I vulnerably want now is police protection, from a particular police officer I can trust with my life. I write to you now because I am ready to be around someone who cares that I keep breathing, rather than someone who wants me to stop breathing.*

*No one ever said what you said to me before, Davis. No one but you.*

*I am sorry I did not perceive you before now. I am sorry I had to almost get killed before I could recognize the preciousness of being with someone who wants me to live well.*

*I hope I did not hurt you too much by ignoring you and leaving you abruptly and arrogantly behind. I would like to meet with you again.*

Sanjib stops reading. His heart is pounding. His breathing is shallow and fast. Tears obstruct his vision. He reaches in and pulls a ratty old handkerchief out of his left front pants pocket, wipes his eyes rather too roughly, blows his nose rather too noisily, stuffs the handkerchief back into his pocket, glances over and sees that Davis is in no better shape than he is, looks back at the screen, and continues reading where he left off.

*I would like to meet with you again.*

*If you are interested, I have a proposal for this possibility.*

*I learned that in a few weeks from now, 21st to 25th August, there will be an Intersection ConFest on the island of Florianópolis, off the southern coast of Brazil.*

*Would you meet me there?*

*Merde! I can't see the keys anymore... too much salt water. Wait a minute.*

*Sigh. I feel so glad to have the chance to ask you this question, to make you this invitation. I am so glad I did not get killed by that vicious insane asshole and the system he works for.*

*I ask you again clearly. Would you please meet me at the ConFest? I don't know what will happen after that. I don't have plans. I figure E.C.C.O. has plenty enough plans for all of us.*

*What do you say? Will you forgive my blindness? Will you give me another chance with you, Mr. Davis Hatcher? Please?*

*I understand if you delete this message and don't write back. I understand why you might do that. But I had to try. I could not ignore my desire and pretend like this is not the most important question in my life right now.*

*Anyway, I will be there. You don't even have to give me an answer. You can just show up if you want, and find me by the mole on my cheek. If you answer soon, though, I could reserve us a double room. Otherwise, you can surprise me, and we can go sleep in the bushes.*

*I don't mean to be crude, or seductive... but sometimes I just am.*

*Love, Remington Smith*

*P.S. Love also to Sanjib.*


Sanjib blurts out, "Davis! My brother! You are indeed so much of a lucky man!"

Davis appears to have dissolved, or disassembled. He has gone fuzzy. Tears pour down his cheeks. Both his hands involuntarily press against his aching bursting heart. Life is so big and so amazing.

"You have to go, sir! Your beautiful destiny lies waiting for you on a tropical island off the southern coast of Brazil!"

"I don't even know what an *Intersection ConFest* is, Sanjib! Do you want to come with me?"

"No, my man. One of us needs to stay back and fill in gaps that Brinks and Stafford do not have the thoughtware or skills to manage. Eugene is evolving, faster and faster. I shall provide a guiding hand! But you... you have a new future. E.C.C.O. is having a hay day. I even know what a 'hay day' is! It is the day that the farmer and his family and friends bring in the dried grass from the fields to store in the barn before the rain comes so the animals have food for winter. It is an exciting time! It is a big day! This is your big day, Davis. Well... your next big day. But don't leave me entirely in the swamp here, okay? I still need your jokes. And look, look here..." Sanjib reaches above his head, digs his fingers into his turban, pulls out the end of the white cloth, and starts to unwind it.

Davis is speechless, shocked into disbelief of what he is witnessing. He does not know what to say or feel.

It is mathematically impossible that all of these impossible things are happening all at the same time in Davis's world. But they are.

There he is. He is doing it for real. Sanjib the Q-tip Cop is unraveling the turban from his head right in front of Davis, right here in their Eugene Police Department office.

"Oh, man! Sanjib! Stop it! You are totally freaking me out! What do you think you are doing!"

"Davis, I have gained the courage to take the turban off of my head. It is only a piece of cloth. I have had the courage to wear the turban. Now I have the courage to not wear it."

"Hold on, buddy! You should think this over. The turban symbolizes something that has been important to you for a long time. I don't understand what you are doing! I am okay with your turban. In fact, I was thinking of getting a turban myself. Then we could be the Bobbsey Twin Police."

"Davis, relax! I can love a symbol without having to hide behind the symbol. As a policeman, I wear the badge, but I am not the badge. I no longer need a symbol to experience myself, my identity. I no longer want to conform to a symbol. I no longer want to adapt to anything. I no longer want to withhold anything! This is a birthday party for me! For the both of us!"

"How can I help you celebrate your birthday, my friend?"

"I want you to see me do this, Davis." Sanjib stands up from his chair. "I want you to witness me stepping out from under the turban for no reason. You have given me courage to be what I am without defenses. I have learned so much from you."

"Yes, but Sanjib! I have learned so much from you too! Remember when you decided never to lie for your job, and you told the whole *Mysterium* circle we are cops? You changed my world!"

"Yeah, the look on your face was priceless!"

"You asshole! You have black hair! You have long greasy black hair! Fer cryin' out loud! Sanjib! Fer chrissakes! Look at you! You need to wash your hair, man. And get a haircut!"

"Hey! One step at a time!"

"At the least you need a hairnet... or better yet, a cowboy hat!"

"I'll tell you what I need. I need a custard-filled maple bar. With you. Now. That's what I need. Let's get out of here!"

Maria-Santos' eyes bug-out like a monster and she screams out loud when she sees Sanjib stroll by her desk with his black oily hair hanging down.

The two young officers turn and salute Maria-Santos in perfect harmony, then duck and run out of the police station door before she calls the police.

# Phoenix, South Africa 10

A black man about thirty years old stands outside the asamangaXhosa kraal gate. A goat strolls over and hops her front feet up onto the kraal, craning her neck and sniffing for possible snacks. The black man smiles but doesn't move or say a word. He wears a canvas sun hat and a recently ironed white shirt, which although sweaty from his bike ride, could lead one to suspect that he works for an NGO. In a moment Mandisa strides purposefully around one of the huts wiping her hands in a cloth. "Oh! Hello there! What can I do for you?"

"My name is Talan Biweggi. I come from Kufunda Village. We know about your work from Alan Friedman. I have a letter for you." He hands her a Federal Express envelope from his satchel. Andiswa and Thando stroll over to see what's happening.

"It's from Brazil," says Mandisa, opening the gate. "Come in Mr. Biweggi. May we offer you water?" Thando trots off to fill a clay cup from the drinking pot while Mandisa turns to the girl, and says, "Andiswa, please call a circle."

Andiswa walks to the side of a hut, picks up two wooden batons, and hammers out a rhythm on hollow wooden drums. Mandisa smiles at Mr. Biweggi's surprise. "Yes! The drums are quicker than cell phones, and do not give you brain tumors." She gestures for him to enter the kraal, closing the gate after him.

People of different races and ages emerge from huts and fields. They find places in a circle of benches under a palm thatched veranda in the center of the kraal, greeting each other with jokes and smiles.

Mandisa guides the guest to center stage and says, "Mandisa. This is Talan Biweggi. He comes from Kufunda Ecovillage with a letter from Brazil." She looks at Talan expectantly, but he defers to the envelope in her hands. She reaches behind her back and slides a thin, razor-sharp dagger out of her belt, deftly slits the envelope open, and unfolds a typed letter with official letterhead. "Who would like to read this?" she asks.

A thinner and toughened young Chinese woman dressed in asamangaXhosa women's wrap stands and says, "Siu-Lin. I will read it."

She accepts the paper. With her bullshit detector set to HIGH level, she begins reading.

*Dear Mandisa, Tandra, Dannoto, and all the courageous collaborators of the AsamangaXhosa Research Center.*

Siu-Lin glances out into the faces of her people, making sure they can properly hear her, then continues boldly reading.

*From 21 to 25 August in southern Florianópolis, the Archiarchy Invention Center is holding its first global gathering for the purpose of weaving critical connections that further the emergence of next culture. We request your attendance to present the discoveries being made by the AsamangaXhosa experiment. All of your expenses for five (5) people will be paid by the Archiarchy Invention Center Consortium. Learning more of your phoenix culture would be an honor for us all.*

Siu-Lin looks up from the paper, trying to keep the neutral mask on her face, but her feelings have other plans. With an ear-to-ear smile, she celebrates the spirits of her friends, these courageous collaborators. Joyful glee twitches the muscles around her mouth until tears stream from her eyes, streaking the dust on her cheeks. "Yes!" she shouts proudly, throwing her free hand into the air with a fist. "Yes! This is so right."

People in the circle echo her exclamation, "Yes!"

But their 'yes' derives from a different source. They feel overjoyed about Siu-Lin's radiant vulnerability. There she is, finally standing up before them, letting herself be known.

"Yes!" they shout. "We see you, Siu-Lin!"

Mr. Biweggi cannot help but join the pleasure-fest of this self-empowered circle of inspired individuals.

# Santa Fe, New Mexico 3

"Hey! It's play-full-out time! PFOT! Let's go, ladies and gentlemen! Cha-Cha!" shouts Matthew while eagerly sliding his chair back from the breakfast table. Their daily non-routine of intense matrix-building sessions has continued for over three months. Clearly, Matthew is not the least bit tired of it.

Neither is anyone else.

But one of the side-effects of five-body development is intuitive knowing. If there is a disturbance in the force, one senses it immediately, and one trusts what one senses implicitly.

Eddy speaks about it first. "I smell something in the air this morning, my friends. I feel thirteen percent scared that serious changes are shortly arriving, and not all of us know what is coming. Especially me. Would anyone like to pull the cork on this?"

"What cork?" asks Matthew. He is not trying to be funny. He never heard the phrase before. But he too has grown sensitive to the qualities of spaces and can easily manage his curiosity. He says, "I'll ask about the cork later."

Eddy silently nods his appreciation to Matthew.

Mr. Singer looks to Mrs. Singer. She takes a deep breath, and then speaks. "Roger and I are honored to present you all – including Mr. Matthew Singer – with two luscious, well-earned, possibly transformational invitations."

Barbara does not want to rush this moment, or to trivialize it, clearly remembering back so many years ago when a person she loved and respected made a similarly life-changing announcement to her, but delivered it disgracefully. She also does not want to complicate things, or bring the energy to herself by telling nostalgic stories about her own path. Those can come later. She sighs again, looking into the eyes of each member of the Gang of Four sitting brightly together at their shared breakfast table.

*Nothing to do but enjoy the moment and dive in*, she thinks to herself.

"Firstly, Roger Ivanovich Singer and I, Barbara Harmony Singer, formally inform you John Emmet Tumble, you Edward Smith Bennington, you Edith Goldman, and you Matthew Ivanovich Singer, that each of you is invited to become a full-time resident of the nomadic nanonation called the Hidden University, as of today."

There are audible gasps, but only one question.

Eddy asks, "Has this all been a test, Mrs. Singer? Since the fencing bout in Salt Lake City? Since we escaped the university and crashed my van in the desert?"

Roger Singer levels with him. "Edward, it is always a test."

There is no joke in his tone of voice.

"Would you want it any other way?" asks Roger.

Eddy shakes his head, pensively, then looks into Mr. Singer's eyes with certainty and says, "No."

Barbara continues. "To respond to this summons, the University requires a formal one-page hand-written letter from each of you, informing the Hidden University about your answer. Whether you choose to accept the invitation or not, the University wishes to know why you have decided to do so. Your written response is required within twenty-four hours from now or the invitation is forfeit."

In the magnificence of this once-in-a-lifetime conversation, Barbara breathes joyfully. It is pleasurable for her to be in the presence of such worthy candidates. She glances at Roger and senses a similar mood in him.

Matthew speaks. "By email? On Instagram? Through the post office? How do I send my letter back to the Hidden University, Mom? What is their address?"

"I thank you for your astute question, Matthew..."

"What's a 'stute'?"

"'Astute' means 'smart', Matthew," says Edith. "Your mom is saying that it was an intelligent and appropriate question that you asked. Neither me, Eddy, nor JET knows the answer to that question. We have the same confusion as you, yet we did not ask how we are supposed to deliver our written responses?"

"Hand it to me," says Barbara, "and I will notify the appropriate authorities."

"Are there authorities in the Hidden University gameworld?" demands Matthew.

"No actually, there aren't any authorities in the Hidden University gameworld. Again, I thank you for your astute question, Matthew. You have developed a very fine sword of clarity in these last few months."

"By the way..." Barbara glances around at the Gang of Four, "who is this man talking to me now? And what have you done with my sweet little Matthew?"

She glances at Roger with a wistful smile, sighs deeply, then looks back to Matthew to answer his question.

"The Hidden University is a torus with an Infinity Ring. Roger is in the new members node of the Infinity Ring of the Hidden University. If you give your letters to Roger, he will bring them to the others in his node and they will respond appropriately."

"Thank you for your answer, Barbara," says Matthew, with the same wistful smile Barbara had given to Roger.

Barbara thinks, *Things change for me too.*

She looks at Roger, who nods for her to continue.

"The second invitation is from Roger and I personally. We ask if you would be willing to join us participating in the first global Intersection ConFest to be held on the island of Florianópolis, off the southern coast of Brazil. This will take place from the 21st to the 25th of August, only a few days away from now... in fact, three days from now, to be precise."

"But... we know about the ConFest!" says Edith, confused, offended, sad, and angry all at once. "We helped David Henkel and the team at Possibilica in Florianópolis design and initiate the thing. We don't have the money to go to Brazil! And besides, what would we do there? We don't have a project! We don't have a website! We have nothing to offer!"

"We were never invited..." adds JET.

"Oh, sweet dears!" cries Barbara. "You are the ones the ConFest is for! How could you not know this? You are the most outrageously clever and productive edgeworkers I ever met! Perhaps you never met other edgeworkers before... I know your path has taken rather sudden turns lately, but you are edgeworkers par excellence! Researchers first class! I know you have *Beep! Books* full of experiments and exercises that you have developed together recently. These are valuable treasures that other edgeworkers would love to learn from you. So many people are occupied with mere survival, trying to make enough money to live, trying to have normal lives. You have sidestepped all that! And see how well it works! It is working right now!"

Barbara looks at Roger for support.

"I am sincerely sorry for any misunderstanding," says Mr. Singer in his calm, rational voice. "We did not tell you about this earlier because we did not want to disturb the flow of your extraordinary work together. However, it was necessary to make ConFest reservations and so on, so we anticipated – and also hoped – that your answers would tend towards the affirmative. We have already gone ahead and purchased one way air tickets to Brazil for you, not knowing what might emerge for you at the ConFest, but knowing quite clearly how creative E.C.C.O. can be when it has access to individuals with so much agency, and so little baggage, as yourselves."

Mrs. Singer says, "Edith, dear, you can leave your car here for the time being. I don't think there are many other logistics to manage on your end. What do you all say? Please say yes...", she begs, suddenly crying her heart out. Roger puts his hand on her shoulder. Barbara continues. "I am so sorry for the shock. You are not left out. You are needed there. You will meet so many other people who are as alive as you are. There are so few of us, really, in the world, so the ConFest could feel like a true homecoming for you. You can meet your real family and allies there. Please say yes..."

By now they are all crying in the joyful release of tensions caused by unrecognized unasked questions. Things in the big picture can adjust with things in the small picture as the Universe pays off its energetic debts, and imbalances reconcile.

"Of course! Of course we'll go!" blurts Edith, with Eddy and JET nodding agreement.

"As weird as it's been, it all makes sense now," says JET.

"Looking backwards, I can connect the dots," adds Eddy.

"I'll call Stevie to see if he will feed Willis and Jackie Chan for me while I'm gone," contributes Matthew.

The Gang of Four teeters between profoundly silent and respectful gratitude, and hysterically jubilant, boisterous celebration. After a few seconds of the former, the latter takes over. For an extended time, the local branch of the Hidden University dives into a lovely mess of tears, shouts, gigantic hugs, handshakes of agreement, headshakes of amazement, and smiles of joy.

Definitely, it is love happening.

# ConFest, Florianópolis 1

The hubbub around the registration tables and buzz of excited people finding each other fill the crowded entrance hall on the afternoon before the first Intersection ConFest begins. If you scan the people entering the tent, you would be challenged to generalize what type of gathering this is. It is not esoteric, not new age, not spiritual, and at the same time definitely not mainstream.

A large hand-painted banner hanging from the double bamboo arches reads: *Welcome to Archiarchy!*

"This is Caitlin Jones from NC3TV reporting in with *Person On The Street Interviews* in Florianópolis, Brazil. Today I am speaking with Manfred, from Harlem, New York. Thanks for talking with me today, Manfred."

"Nice to speak with a true listener. I have seen your show and I know you are not the usual sensationalist."

"Thanks for the feedback. I'd like to ask you rather personal questions, if you don't mind. I would like to go on a little journey with you back into the core of things. Is this okay with you?"

"Fire away!"

"What I want to hear from you is if you truly care about the President?"

"I don't think they have a president here, Ma'am... at the Intersection ConFest. They use *Torus Technology*, with spaceholders, not hierarchies. Uh... Oh! Do you mean the President of the United Nations? The President of the World Bank? The President of Brazil? I'm sorry...?"

"Exactly. Precisely. For example, if you don't mind saying, who did you vote for in the last presidential election in the United States? Did you actually care about it?"

Manfred makes a show of thinking about it for a second. "I play video slot machines from time to time. When I put in my coins and pull the lever, I truly care about winning and not losing. It's exciting for a few seconds. But if I win five dollars, or fifty dollars, or even five-hundred dollars, do I think it will change my life? No. I am over thirty years old. I have lost too many illusions as they crashed into reality. Who did I vote for? For years I voted the party line. Which party? My father voted Republican. I voted Democrat. Then when I saw that Republican and Democrat are two sides of the same coin, I started voting Independent.

When I saw that no one I voted for ever won, I learned that coins have three sides, and that the game is rigged. I asked, 'Who is behind the third side?' No one answered... I stopped voting."

"I return to my first question, Manfred. Do you care about the President?"

"I never send the President a birthday present or Saint Valentine's Day Card. I don't know his favorite flavor of ice cream, or which movies he loves to watch. I don't wake up in the morning hoping to look across the breakfast table into the trustworthy eyes of the President. Whatever he says or does in his little world – even if he sends me another Economic Impact check – does not affect me. What I care about him is that he does not care about me."

"What do you care about, then?"

"I care about many things, and I can prove it. For example, I care about the wellbeing of my fellow citizens in the nanonation of Harlem. See, you have been talking with me as if I am an American. But I am not an American. I guess you assumed I am American because I said I come from Harlem. But you did not ask, and that is something I care about you, that you did not ask where I am from. I live in the nomadic nanonation of Harlem, and at this moment I can spot five of our seventy citizens here at the ConFest. Even from here I see they are full of wellbeing, and as excited as I am to be here. To further answer your question, I care about you. I see that your left knee is bouncing up and down in that quick jerky motion. I don't think you are aware of it much, and I don't think it will stop by itself. I think your vibrating leg is a doorway to an important Emotional Healing Process for you. I saw on the ConFest map over there that they set up at least three tents as EHP Dojos. You simply walk in a tent and say, "Hey, my left leg shakes when I do interviews," and they will know exactly how to change that magical doorway into a bridge to a new future for you."

"Well, thank you, Manfred. That is so kind of you to recommend this to me. Could you tell me what the Intersection ConFest is all about? Why are people so excited to be here? What is intersecting here?"

"Caitlin, as I mentioned, I've watched your interviews for years, and because of that, I probably feel closer to you than you feel towards me. When I recognized your face, I strolled over to thank you for your work, and that's when you snagged me for this conversation. If viewers are interested in learning more about the Intersection ConFest, I suggest they will find all the information they need on the ConFest website. But I would investigate the immediate 'intersection' that is happening right now. You and I are intersecting. I did not plan to speak with you. You did not pre-arrange to speak with me. But here we are, as if some mighty hand of nature stepped in and moved us around like pieces on a chess board. I don't perceive this as an accident. I think it is a coincidence. And I don't think that coincidences happen by accident! So let me ask you a question, Caitlin. You have years of experience gallivanting through other people's lives. You have seen a lot and heard a lot. I think by now you have a sense of what matters to you. My question is this: What would your life be like if you placed what really matters to you at the center of your world, and let the rest of your life fall where it may? Skip the money survival thing. It is easy to move out of the high rent district. I want to know about your visions, your dreams. What would you be up to?"

Caitlin is trained in radio station protocol. On the air, her attention orbits around Rule #1: No Dead Air Time. Manfred's spontaneous question calls for radically honest improvisation. Caitlin dives in. "If I did not have to cover a monthly rent, I would cut loose. I would probably sleep for a few weeks first, somewhere rent free. But then I would follow interesting people around to map out where the cutting edges of the evolution of consciousness are occurring on planet Earth right now.

"There are two ways that consciousness evolves: defensively or expansively. defensive awareness strengthens your ability to survive. But expansive awareness strengthens your ability to evolve. Too few people know this. And the popular techniques for expansive awareness come from the past rather than the future. I personally think that developing expansive awareness is the most important cutting edge on Earth right now. It is exactly what I came to investigate here at the Intersection ConFest!

"When I discovered that mainstream media is owned by the same people who own the politicians, I realized that most so-called journalists have locked themselves into an 'iron maiden' torture device that would drive me insane. Good luck to them. Calling oneself a 'journalist' in such a circumstance seems ludicrous beyond measure. And nobody in the mainstream sees how far behind current reality they are."

"Current reality?" asks Manfred.

"I recently listened to a podcast from Michael Moore where he begs for journalists to step out of their shackles and do their job. He says, 'We need our free press more than ever.' And I agree! Mr. Moore describes how the original founders of America failed to create a democracy, because in the gameworld they built, women have no vote, people of color have no voice, the original occupants of the land have no power, and hierarchical systems of government are hell-bent on destroying the entire planet! Humans have not yet succeeded in creating a working democracy. It is up to me, to us, to you, to finish the job.

"Why, you might ask? One, because it is not finished. Two, because awareness breeds responsibility. If I see a job, it is my job to do. This does not mean simply pushing my fear button and indulging in my emotional revulsion about what is happening. No! It means doing deeds! It means inventing the next gameworld. How? By reminding people, 'Hey! You are the majority. Your common sense is the same common sense as the majority of people. Stop counting on a minority of others to bring your common sense to life! Take the actions that make sense to you, enjoy the hell out of it, and invite others to join you if they want.'

"If I put what matters most to me at the center of my life, I would immediately create a self-sponsored independent school of radically honest journalists. We would dig down seven generations, seven layers behind each incident and put it all on the table. Even here at the Intersection ConFest! Look around! Something is happening here, and it is not all visible on the surface. Yes, this is an astonishing top layer! But what did specific people do to make this happen? And what happened before that? And before that? Seven layers down! What is really going on here? The cynical part of me is chanting, 'Follow the money! Follow the money!' But there is so little money involved here that I already see money is a dead end. How did they do this, then? What is really going on? I can't wait to find out!"

Then Manfred asks a gameworld-builder question. "Caitlin, what is the name of your journalist school? What could it be called?"

"Uh... *Seven Questions School of Radical Journalism*. I just made that up!"

"Didn't we all! Caitlin, I will be recommending you to Deborah L. Williams from our nanonation. She is thirteen years old, and sharp as Sherlock at applying radical investigation. She cares so much that her attention starts things on alchemical fire! I cannot speak for her, but I would bet that you already have your first apprentice."

"Thank you... Manfred. I... I'm speechless..." She fights back tears.

"I will put that on my resumé!" Manfred pauses a moment, then says, "I hand the spaceholding back to you, Caitlin Jones, my favorite radio journalist from NC3TV!"

Caitlin looks into the camera and says, "Ever since first grade in school I never allowed myself to believe that I could center my life around what I really care about. I thought I had to keep adapting to external authorities for the rest of my life. I assumed that this is what life is like.

"Now I have been shown that assumptions can be far more detrimental than I ever suspected. What other assumptions am I standing on as if they are solid reality? What assumptions are you standing on? I think my next investigation will be to uncover assumptions at work in the foundations of modern culture, and what I can do to dissolve them back into their original components."

"Caitlin?" Manfred says. "Excuse me. I would like to say one last thing."

"Go ahead, Manfred."

He looks directly into the camera himself. "I submit this interview as evidence to you that Caitlin Jones should be interviewed far more often than she has previously allowed. I enjoyed this conversation immensely. Thank you for choosing me!".

He reaches over to shake Caitlin's hand and she gladly accepts.

"Thank you, Manfred! So much for assumptions, eh? On to the next future, a future in next culture, a culture called Archiarchy. Thanks for being with us at the Intersection ConFest! This is Caitlin Jones from NC3TV, *Person On The Street* Interviews. 'Til next time, signing off!"

Off camera, Caitlin falls into Manfred's safe and open arms, sobbing freely as her nervous system reorders itself to a new level of elegance and effectiveness.

# ConFest, Florianópolis 2

Brightly lettered hand-painted banners hang in various tents at the Intersection ConFest.

And:

> THE FOUR PRINCIPLES
> OF AN OPEN SPACE:
> 1) Whoever comes are
>    the right people.
> 2) Whatever happens is
>    the only thing that
>    could have.
> 3) Whenever it starts is
>    the right time.
> 4) When it's over, it's
>    over.

It is nine a.m. opening morning of the ConFest. Captain Henkel stands on a stage in the corner of the main meeting tent without any kind of microphone. "Welcome everyone to the first global Intersection ConFest. This is a five-day torus meeting where we ask: *What are the intersections? And what can you do to make more of them?*

"Over there on that wall is the Village Marketplace where you can post the time and place where you will convene a circle about issues or opportunities related to our theme. At the marketplace you can use your voice and loudly say your name and the title of the space for which you have genuine passion and for which you take radical responsibility.

"At nine a.m. the first sessions begin. Please document what you create with full instructions and clear outlines, and bring it to Ali Baba's Cave so that the treasure you create can be included in the treasure chest we will give away to everyone in the world to use. Please record your meetings, and use the voice to text app to share your research.

"Meals and snacks operate like the circles, through self-organized spaceholders and teams. Buffets are open all day and all night so you can nourish and refresh yourself at your convenience. Please be mindful that the ConFest is a strictly non-alcohol, non-smoking, non-drug, and non-boom-boom music experience. In the dining areas there is continuous *Human Hyper Networking* with a simple instruction sheet to explain how it goes.

"Be sure to make use of the Possibility Teams and Emotional Healing Process tents. And tonight, at seven thirty p.m. starts *POP* right here in this tent. POP stands for *Place Of Possibility*, a collective collaboration to implement what really matters to you.

"I am aware that you want all this to happen as much as I do, or you would not have worked so hard to come here. If it is not High Level Fun it is not working! Please keep talking to each other about how it is going for you."

Mr. and Mrs. Singer clap for Captain Henkel's welcome speech along with hundreds of others including Matthew, JET, Eddy and Edith.

Almost instantly JET points and says excitedly, "Look, Eddy! It's the Indian!"

Matthew shouts, "Where?" Matthew follows his three friends like a duck follows its mother. JET weaves his way through the crowd and approaches the Indian with an outstretched hand. "Hello, my friend the Indian!"

The Indian just smiles. JET keeps his center, lowers his hand, and continues speaking. "Thanks for what you did for me in the desert. For us," glancing at Eddy. Then he reaches into his back pocket. "I have something for you." It is the neckerchief the Indian used for wrapping the healing herbs around JET's wounded leg, washed, ironed, and folded. "For your next customer!"

The Indian nods and accepts the cloth, shakes it open, ties it around his neck where it originally came from, then reaches across and grips both of JET's shoulders firmly in his hands. He leans his head forwards and presses his forehead against JET's forehead.

He then proceeds to do the same with Eddy, and then with Edith.

Then, in slow motion, he sinks down to eye-level with Matthew, puts both hands on his shoulders, and says, "Hello young man. Please keep watch over these three, will you? They matter to me."

"I will, sir," says Matthew earnestly.

The Indian presses foreheads with Matthew, then slowly stands up and steps backwards, vanishing into the crowd.

JET and Eddy look at each other and smile wordlessly. They have seen the Indian's disappearing act before.

On the other side of the huge tent, Sean and Margaret stand together peering at a wall labeled 'Village Marketplace', covered in announcement slips. "So, Mizz Smith," muses Sean. "I see nothing here about countenance, nothing about moving at the speed of love, nothing about a man placing his attention on a woman in such a way that the archetypal goddess appears and remembers the way to navigate them both through the great labyrinth of spaces back to the Garden of Eden. I propose that you and I convene a circle about that. What do you say?"

Margaret glows with enthusiasm. "I accept your proposal. I will fill out a paper if you announce the space."

Sean steps into the center of the demarcated announcement circle. "My name is Sean Connery," he says. "I invite you to join an exploration of how to experience authentic intimacy. We start in tent number thirteen in twenty minutes."

JET, Eddy and Edith hear the announcement from the other side of the crowd. Their interest is piqued. With a silent glance, they all agree to go join the research space being offered in that circle.

# ConFest, Florianópolis 3

Sean Connery rises from his front row chair, seeing several concentric circles of seated listeners. In his resonant voice, he says, "I could not be farther from my Scotland village home than standing here at an Intersection ConFest in Florianópolis, Brazil. That is what I thought an hour ago. Now I think that I could not be closer to home than here.

"Margaret and I... we want to talk with you about love. Not just talk about it, we want to go there with you."

JET, Eddy and Edith are late, busily occupied with taking their seats at the edge of the packed room, trying to find three chairs together. But when Sean Connery mentions the name 'Margaret', Eddy looks up across the circles of chairs and freezes. Edith crashes into Eddy. JET stumbles into both of them.

Eddy turns and whispers incredulously out of the side of his mouth to JET and Edith, "That... is... my... grandmother... up... there! From Scotland! What is she doing here?"

"Your grandmother is Maggie Smith?" demands JET.

"Shhhhh!" says Edith. "Let's find a seat first. Then you can talk."

Sean continues. "I would like to take a journey with you all outside of our ordinary culture into rather extraordinary or, what I have come to think of as archetypal spaces.

"For most of my life I was lost with regards to relating. Then one day my last best friend died. He died without saying goodbye to me. While I was standing next to his dead body, feeling his cold stiff fingers, I collapsed into a very tiny place, the place of this moment.

"In this very small precious moment, I suddenly started feeling everything that I had locked away in my heart during a lifetime of acting.

"The actor in me gave up acting. I was left with only a driving need to intimately share who I am with someone, even if I am sure that I do not know who I am.

"That is when this woman sitting next to me here, Margaret Smith, showed up in my life. To tell the truth, she was standing there before me for a long time. It was me, in my self-made blindness and numbness, who could not see her there until that painful but lucky moment.

"Margaret made it evident that she was willing to know me for real, for who I was in my lonely suffering and shameful ignorance.

"For the first time I was willing to expose myself to be seen, and this simultaneously liberated my interest in truthfully seeing someone else.

"It felt like my life first began in my seventy-fifth year.

"I implore you to not wait until you are seventy-five years old to do these experiments.

"If you feel lost in your previous experiences of relating, it is because relating does not die from a lack of love. Relating dies from a lack of intimacy.

"There are many kinds of intimacy. I am here to take another risk in intimacy in front of you.

"Somewhere out there in this ConFest I suspect that there might be a young man who is my son.

"I never met this young man.

"I only learned of his existence a few weeks ago in a letter from your mother from Utah.

"Today, I stand here and make this plea: If you are out there, will you please come and introduce yourself to me after this session? I want to meet you, JET."

Sean keeps talking but his voice fades suddenly behind the buzzing in JET's ears, like the deafness after a gunshot blast. JET is shocked beyond amazement.

That man up there on stage, that famous charismatic old actor, is claiming to be his long-lost father? Could this be?

JET is stunned. Without realizing it, he reaches out to hold Eddy's hand on one side and Edith's hand on the other side. There is nothing that can be said right now. He must simply wait until the break, and try to keep from shaking apart in his seat.

Forty-five minutes later, as Sean and Margaret step out of the circle Tent #13, JET, Eddy, and Edith corner them. JET steps forward with his hand out, more as mechanical behavior than as a true gesture of friendliness. He still remembers the Indian not shaking his hand only an hour earlier.

"Hello Sean. I am JET. You were asking after me?"

Sean reaches over and shakes JET's hand with severe uncertainties, not managing to speak, looking like he just swallowed a whole live chicken, or being in the process of giving birth to one, perhaps both simultaneously.

JET continues, trying to stay centered and make no conclusions. "Is this your wife?"

Sean makes a quick glance at Margaret, then back to JET. "She is more than that. She is my woman."

"Like my mother once was?" There is mean accusation in JET's voice.

Sean speaks slowly and honestly with kindness and compassion. "I cannot say that I knew your mother, except that she was beautiful and passionate, and, by looking at you, I would guess you inherited a lot of that from her."

JET tries to measure him up. "You claim to be my father?"

Sean is taken aback. He glances at Margaret for reassurance, then back at JET. "I would not say I am your father... I am... the man your mother chose to provide her with the twenty-three chromosomes she needed to make the body that you live in."

JET takes a centering breath, trying to stay unhooked so as not to scare the 'mountain lion' away. "I always knew that whoever you were, you were not a bad man. All my life I knew that. It was from the way Mom spoke of you whenever I asked. She never told me your name, or anything about you, or how it came to pass that she brought me into this world without a dad. The tone of her Being gave it away, as if you were a fireman hero who died saving children from a burning house. I think maybe she wanted you, but she knew she could not have you. Now that I've met you, now that I have heard you speak, I can see why Mom wanted you. You are a good man."

Tears stream down JET's cheeks, but as tears from a man who is touched, not as tears from a boy. He says, "I feel sad because now I know what she was missing – and what I missed for all these years. I did not know what that sensation was until now. I missed you."

JET pauses, feeling his feelings, feeling glad about not feeling like a victim of his feelings even if they were as big as life itself.

"I was parented in one fashion or another by several men. They did the best they could. I could never bring myself to call any of them 'Dad.' I have met you now. I have the rest of my life to live. I imagine you have your idiosyncrasies. I would not expect anything of you. But in my own heart I would be honored if you would allow me to consider you my father."

Sean had been squeezing Margaret's hand tightly, but now he lets gently go. This is a move he must make standing on his own two feet.

He could, of course, procrastinate. He could quibble, make jokes, or give excuses. He could refuse.

But oh! What a gift this is!

He can only respond by wordlessly reaching out towards JET and welcoming his son, at long last, home, into his arms.

JET accepts the hug.

Most everyone around them is sobbing in joy and pure amazement.

It is a long and wonderful reunion, a new beginning for each man.

# ConFest, Florianópolis 4

Evening session of the first day at the ConFest has already begun. Most of the edgeworkers exited the main ConFest tent to co-create their evening's toroids.

Davis Hatcher stands motionless, alone, feeling completely lost.

No gun. No hat. No badge. No cruiser. No Chief Stafford or Sergeant Brinks. No Sanjib. No streets with criminals skulking about doing drug deals, or worse. Here he stands, undefined in the middle of heaven.

*These are the good people. How am I supposed to behave in a crowd of good people?* he thinks to himself.

His whole identity has nothing to push against to validate his righteous law enforcement existence anymore. He has no legitimacy here, and nothing to do. His police officer skill base is useless. Probably it always was. Has he been living under an illusion – as Sanjib suggested to him more than once –  an illusion of importance and value inherited by direct transmission from his dad, Police Captain Henry Hatcher, now dead and buried in Eugene, Oregon?

*What happened to my life?* wonders Davis to himself.

"I am here," she says, from behind his back.

Davis slowly turns around.

*I ask myself the question, 'What happened to my life?' and then she answers me, "I am here."*

*My life answers me... "I am here..."*

*This could be the truth...*

She stops about three meters back, gently waiting, trying to imagine what is going on in the mind and heart of the man standing across from her right now in this big, nearly empty tent, on this hilly tropical island off the southern coast of Brazil.

This is a man she may or may not know.

Her recent record of running off with a man who was sent on a mission into their precious *Shadow Knights of the Mysterium* group specifically to betray her... No! Let's not pull punches here. Let's not fool ourselves any longer about this. Let us say it bluntly. He was sent in to destroy her... and she imagined him to be a fine person...

Her proven faulty capacity for character assessment does not license her to judge people by their cover anymore. The asamangaXhosa people worked hard healing her from self-abuse about fooling herself so terribly, even after everything she learned from her grandmother.

Barefoot, loose cotton print dress down past her knees tied at her waist, brown eyes, wavy brown hair bundled with an elastic band to delay the inevitable sweating in Brazil's unaccustomed heat and humidity, Remington Smith simply stands there.

She is not waiting for anything particular to happen. Expectations kill reality. By now, Remington longs for reality with a vengeance.

So, she stands.

She stands, and she breathes, and... well... just stands and breathes, and... looks at that man who she has held carefully in her memory as a man who wanted her to keep breathing.

He wanted her to keep breathing with so much fervor that he could not help himself from spontaneously admitting it in public, oh, so long ago it seems, though in reality only a few months.

Remington Smith's heart beats firmly and fast. She can feel it in her solar plexus. It reminds her how glad she is to be alive.

She acknowledges how alive she is at her core. She yearns to celebrate her aliveness in the company of someone else who is as alive as she is, or at least someone who has the unneurotic unmanipulative desire for her to remain as alive as she actually is, or perhaps even more so. But arranging to have such companionship has not been as easy as it may seem to be.

*From Fontainebleau, France, to Eugene, Oregon, to a kraal near Phoenix, South Africa, and now to a ConFest on an old slave trader pirate island off the southern coast of Brazil, I have met a lot of different people, a lot of different males. But they were not so different from each other, actually. Mostly they were just males, no matter which country, not very impressive. Mostly self-centered, egotistical, short-sighted, short-tempered, robotic sex fiends, sizing her up like a steak, something to possess and devour. Or else they were momma's boys, something I myself could eat for breakfast and then ask, 'What's for breakfast?' They were lacking substance and creation force.*

*Sigh...*

*Not that I've been actively searching much. But what is there to search? If I look at a herd of bulls, what do I see? A herd of bulls. Mostly I have been following my inner drive and that has not been leading me to the company of empowered motivated healthy collaborative consciousness researchers.*

*I thought I was following my inner drive when I absented so abruptly from the Shadow Knights of the Mysterium that night in Eugene, 'gloriously discovering my new chapter of life with a real man exploring the outback in Africa.'*

*What a mess.*

*But what is life, anyway? So many powerful factors shaping my life just appear out of nowhere, without warning, and without my permission. My mother was killed by the drunk driver. My grandmother unschooled me as a renegade alchemist running her own transformational circle in her attic. I thought I could open the door of my own fate and gain realistic gameworld builder training at the NGO in Eugene, but it was mostly bureaucratic hierarchical gossip politics, until I was accidentally hijacked into the Mysterium. Then I somehow ended up in Africa, and now here...*

*I truly love being so alive. I love my life. I love myself.*

*How can I find someone to love me as much as I love myself? And in ways that I would love to be loved? I hate it that this endeavor is so out of my control. I really want to play full out with someone at my side who loves to play full out as much as I do, and is somehow immune to the football game, beer-drinking, money-making, fast car driving, flirting, ordinary distractions that strangle authentic life out of almost everybody I see around me no matter where I go.*

*It is so frustrating! What do other women like me do?*

*I recently spent days and days trying to find other women like me, either alive or in history. I couldn't find any. Today it is easier than ever to learn about women who contributed to society in some way. Knowledge of the valuable contributions of these women have been suppressed by the ignorance and fear of the Patriarchy for so many centuries. But still these women existed. Still they contributed, equal to, or often with more value than the men.*

*Rosalind Franklin was a British chemist who made crucial discoveries about the structure of DNA. Her X-ray data was instrumental in Watson and Crick's discovery of the double helix.*

*Valentina Tereshkova was the first and youngest woman to ever fly in space. At 26 years old, this Russian girl orbited the Earth 48 times in 1963.*

*Katherine Johnson was the African American mathematician who performed complex NASA calculations critical to the success of early space missions, including the Apollo 11 mission to the Moon.*

*Chien-Shiung Wu was a Chinese American physicist who worked on the Manhattan Project developing the process for separating uranium into U235 and U238 by gaseous diffusion, and disproved the 'law of conservation of parity'.*

*Women theologians, women's liberation leaders, women artists, women singers, women poets, women billionaires, women political leaders, women corporate leaders, women protectors of nature, women movie stars, women scientists, women mathematicians, women architects, women biochemists, women astronauts, women athletes... None of these domains interest me.*

*I am in love with exploring an entirely different dimension of creation. The criteria by which all those other women are classified as successful have been defined by patriarchal men.*

*Where are the women's women? Where are the thoughtware upgraders? The nonlinear, possibility-space context-setters? The next-*

*culture gameworld-builders? The Archans?*

*God... I forgot! He still stands there! All this time, he is still looking at me. Is that why I can think and feel these things so clearly? Is he holding space for me?*

*He looks at me with the same devotion and enthusiasm I saw in him that first night, when he and Sanjib came into the Mysterium circle as undercover police.*

*But he stands there, for real, right now. And he came here because I wrote him a letter. He accepted my invitation to come and see if he wants to be with me, even though my real agenda was to see if I want to be with him.*

*I am sure he sees through this.*

*He stands there all this time letting me think and feel all these things. He is looking at me right now, and he does not interrupt me. Not in the slightest. He is not offended, or bored, or concerned that I am not paying attention to him in some way that he 'needs me' to pay attention to him.*

*He is still there without shrinking, or giving up on me, or giving up on himself...*

*Or giving up on... us.*

*He did not give up on us.*

*We could be an us...*

Remington steps forward slowly, puts both hands on Davis Hatcher's shoulders, leans forward and kisses him firmly on the lips, and she does not stop, and he does not stop, and the ocean and moon melt into nothing and come back as everything, as it should be. Only then do his hands land on her hips, fitting perfectly there, as if they always belonged there.

She is the one who walked away from this. And she is sorry.

His arms slide up and wrap around her shoulder blades and pull her close and she pulls him closer and buries her face into his warm neck and sobs big unstoppable sobs, and he pushes his face into her bushy hair and inhales deeply of travels and dust and lust and straw on a summer's day. She cries into him, and he into her, for no reason, knowing that as perfect as it may seem in this moment, the perfection will not last, because it cannot last, but the capacity to notice and experience perfection is in them both, so why not let it take them as far as it can, for as long as it goes? Is there anything more important than this worth stopping for?

After a long while, twenty-seven minutes to be precise, she slowly pulls back from his neck smeared in her own tears. No words are necessary for now. Nothing else is necessary for now. But everything else is necessary from now on.

"How could you simply stand there with me for so long?" Remington finally asks.

"It's pretty simple," he says easefully and completely unhurriedly.

*He is not thinking about what he should say next. He is not waiting for any kind of response from her, or for anything particular to happen. He matches his speed to the speed of the space they occupy together, so that he does not disturb that space, because that particularly precious space is something that two people may not have the honor of co-inhabiting so often in one lifetime.*

"It goes like this..." he continues. "You are the woman. You think about everything. I am the man. I think about nothing. Seems like a good combination to me. I was simply being here with you, enjoying the combination."

Remington nods and smiles into his eyes, understanding what he just communicated to her in all five of her bodies.

"I have an idea..." says Davis Hatcher.

"I accept your proposal," says Remington Smith.

"No resistance," she adds.

Gaia sighs in delighted satisfaction, thinking, *A moment like this makes the whole business worthwhile, doesn't it? Now, how can they teach this to others? What's so difficult about being together, anyway? I never understood what the problem is. Humans are so... fascinating.*

# ConFest, Florianópolis 5

It is fifth chaos on day two of the Intersection ConFest, the evening session. People digest so many new impressions that they huddle together in silent integration time, or quietly mumble in awe with each other.

Harry just participated in a circle researching the magic of asking for what you want. He decides to try out his newfound skills.

Glancing through the crowd, he spots a lithe, brown-skinned woman with short black curly hair wearing a green tank top and a short white skirt. Harry strolls over to her and, with a big smile on his face, says, "Hi there. My name is Harry."

"Hola, Harry," she returns. "My name is Samantha."

"Hey! Samantha! You look super. Do you want to go on a date with me tonight?"

Samantha looks him straight in the eyes and says, "No."

Harry petrifies.

More than a handful of seconds tick by before Harry can say the next thing.

In the meantime, Samantha simply stares at him, like a wary bug exterminator might stare at a not-quite-dead cockroach.

"No? Uh..." says Harry. "Why not?"

"You ask me to give you a reason why I said no."

It is not a question from Samantha. It is a statement. Samantha simply repeats back to Harry what she heard Harry say to her.

"Yes," says Harry, not exactly expecting this kind of a conversation.

Samantha says, "My decision is independent of reasons. If I make a decision because of a reason, then the reason has the authority in the decision, and not me. I don't give my authority away to reasons. When I make a choice, I am the authority behind it. Not going on a date with you tonight is simply my choice."

Harry looks down at his nervously fidgeting fingers, existentially perplexed about what next to say.

Samantha makes an offer. "If you want more information to consider in your deliberations about yourself, I could give you some feedback, but only under one condition."

"What's the condition?" asks Harry, dubiously.

"That you just listen."

"Of course I'll just listen!"

"You are already not listening," states Samantha flatly. "Saying, 'Of course...' is just your way of promising not to listen."

Harry gapes at Samantha, as if he stands face-to-face with a vile creature from the dark lagoon.

Since he is not talking, Samantha continues to speak. "I won't go out with you on a date tonight because you are not free of the Patriarchy."

"What?" asks Harry, again utterly astounded. "What is the Patriarchy? What do you mean by telling me I am 'not free of the Patriarchy'? How can you say such a thing to me?"

Samantha decides to take the risk of explaining further, since he actually asked. "When you were born, you had to choose to either give up being yourself and join the Patriarchy, or to refuse the Patriarchy and die. As a baby boy born in modern culture, you had no other options. Clearly, you did not choose to die."

Samantha pauses to check out Harry's reaction to what she just said. She concludes that he has either gone catatonic, or he is seriously considering her words and simply requires a while longer to circulate the ideas through his badly entangled synapse web. In either case, he abides by her boundary of not interrupting her, so she continues explaining.

"Most women have no idea what a man sacrifices when he joins the Patriarchy. You must sacrifice everything. You made the decision to give up yourself so that you could survive. The decision was not bad or stupid. But the fact is, you are old enough to have noticed that you already survived, and you have not yet taken yourself back from the Patriarchy. You are a patriarchal adolescent."

Harry stands speechless. Perhaps he is disciplined. More likely he has swallowed his own tongue. Samantha has seen this sort of reaction while speaking with males before. She glances around the ConFest main tent. Nothing else is happening, and no one is nearby who she wants to talk with. Samantha continues.

"As a patriarchal adolescent, you think that love from a woman is something tasty to consume. You have not been educated about any other possibility. You think I look 'super' and you want to consume me. That is so pedestrian, boring enough to make me barf."

"I was just trying to practice saying what I want!" pleads Harry, offering this plausible excuse. "I just learned that in a workshop."

"Then," says Samantha, "it should come as no surprise when I tell you that what I want is to explore the universes of extraordinary and archetypal love."

She scans him for any hint that he recognizes her offer. She is met by a blank stare. *Brain wipe*, she thinks to herself. *Typical...*

But he still listens, so she goes on. "I see that you are unable to explore Archan relating with me because your mother still owns your balls. You have not begun your adulthood initiatory processes into authentic manhood. You do not have your center. You do not consciously hold space. You do not direct your own attention. You are completely hookable. You easily give your authority away. You are adaptive. Your feelings and emotions are still unconscious. You have not owned your underworld. You have not discovered your gremlin's name, distilled your bright principles, or jacked-in to your archetypal lineage. You have not trained with using your sword of clarity to navigate extraordinary and archetypal spaces. You basically just really piss me off!"

Harry understands those last three words.

He has finally found his footing in this exchange, and feels sure enough to respond. "What makes you think you can say such mean things to me?"

Samantha almost smiles and walks away, but decides to try another tack. "Do you see that phone on the table over there?"

Harry is stunned at the rapid shift of topic.

"Yes, of cour... I mean... yes. I see it."

Samantha appreciates that he caught himself saying 'of course' to her again, and that he had the wherewithal to stop himself from saying it. She chalks up a point in his favor, and continues with her demonstration.

"What make, model, and year is the phone?"

"Are you jerking me around?" demands Harry with at least a trace of self-respect.

"No. I am not jerking you around. Do you know its brand and model?"

"Yes, I do know. It is a 2022 iPhone 14 pro max with a six point seven inch super retina XDR display and ProMotion software, a dual lens system with a forty-eight megapixel main camera, an A16 bionic chip, and the new dynamic island feature. Why are you asking me this?"

"How did you know all that?" asks Samantha, innocently enough.

"Well, I know phones. Doesn't everybody? As a kid I became an automatic phone identifier."

"The same is true for me," says Samantha, "but while you studied electronic hardware, I studied human thoughtware. With my developed sensitivity I can easily detect the make, model, and year of the thoughtware anyone is using, including all its features and limitations, from ten meters away."

"No way you can do that!" declares Harry. "Prove it!"

Clearly, Harry is miffed at the audaciousness of Samantha's claim, even if the word 'audacious' is not a part of his spoken vocabulary.

"In your case, you use child egostate contaminated, low drama, gremlin feeding, I win, you lose, competitive patriarchal thoughtware first introduced six thousand years ago," specifies Samantha, without blinking an eye or losing her cool.

"What?" says Harry, not truly asking Samantha to explain herself further, but also not having anything more intelligent or interesting to say.

"Every action and inaction has a purpose," says Samantha compassionately. "If the action or inaction increases responsibility, it is called high drama. If the action or inaction tries to avoid responsibility, it is called low drama. In any low drama there are three roles: victim, persecutor, and rescuer. By trying to convince me that I said 'mean things' to you, in which position do you place yourself in the low drama?"

"Victim," says Harry, seeing the scheme.

"And me?"

"Persecutor," says Harry.

"When I said those words to you about the Patriarchy, I think you were feeling something. If you had to choose between anger, sadness, fear, or joy, what were you feeling then?"

"Anger."

"It seems to me that you were trying to avoid responsibility for your anger by trying to make a low drama with me. Does this make any sense to you? Have you noticed this pattern before?"

"Yes, I see the pattern. But it's not a pretty sight."

"I believe you," says Samantha. "When I first started learning about this stuff, it was not pretty for me either. I have to ask, why would a person as intelligent as yourself sacrifice the incredible possibilities that you and I might have right here together in this moment by trying to create a low drama with me? What do you get out of it? You must gain something very precious for you to pay such a high price."

Harry looks down at his fidgeting fingers again. "I get to make you wrong. I get to avoid responsibility and make you the bad guy... bad gal."

"That's the same reasoning used by national leaders and corporate directors to make wars. It's the same thoughtware a person uses to justify doing a job for thirty years that threatens the well-being of future generations. Other thoughtware exists, Harry. Other possible futures can be created. Bright futures, glorious futures. They all start right here, right now, by upgrading your own personal thoughtware about low drama and about your gremlin's hidden purposes. New futures begin each time a person does the work of growing up and..." Samantha stops mid-sentence.

"And what?" prompts Harry.

"Well... You seem to learn quickly enough, and you do make honest efforts. I was just hoping to myself that you eventually make it into manhood..."

Harry looks up and into Samantha's eyes for the first time. He can hardly breathe as he experiences how big and wonderful the space is in there.

"Incidentally," she says without looking away, "thanks for the date just now. Good night, Harry."

# ConFest, Florianópolis 6

Mandisa stands to face the circle of edgeworkers who decided to participate in the space which she dedicated to sharing her research about phoenix cultures. Mandisa's brightly colored hand-woven and embroidered hemp dress shines magnificently in the spotlights. Andiswa, Tandra, Dannoto, and Thando gaze proudly at her from their seats nearby.

Mandisa takes a moment to carefully remove her head cloth and place it behind her on the chair. "I want to stand as naked as possible before you here today. It keeps me honest."

People clap already. Some even stand to clap. Many suddenly weeping for no reason, puzzled about what is happening to them.

"My name is Mandisa. I am a village weaver from the asamangaXhosa of eastern South Africa. You invited me here along with Andiswa and Thando, two of our village's adopted young people, Tandra, my cousin and fellow spaceholder, and Dannoto, one of our authentic adulthood initiators." She indicates them with her open hand.

"AsamangaXhosa is a 'phoenix culture'. This means four things.

"First, being a phoenix culture means that each person takes personal responsibility for creating our whole culture anew each minute of each day and each night. In the moment we forget to do this, our precious culture of radical responsibility will be swallowed up by the false assumptions of the irresponsible mainstream culture that still has a massive presence on Earth.

"Mainstream culture is a memetic virus that has infected Earth's ethnosphere with a false paradigm based on the precepts of capitalism, Patriarchy, and empire. I regard capitalism, Patriarchy and empire as false paradigms because, if you think about it, you will recognize that all three – capitalism, Patriarchy, and empire – are suicidal in a closed ecology such as a planet.

"We live on a planet, by the way.

"We live on a planet that is not ours.

"Second, being a phoenix culture means your previous culture has died. The death of my previous culture was slow and painful. The last of the old culture to die was my son. He died of starvation in my arms when he was three days old. The shock and pain of his death gave birth to the phoenix culture of asamangaXhosa.

"My previous culture was an indigenous culture, known to you as a *fourth world* culture. Our culture had existed for more than 40,000 years, but it was not regenerative. It was not regenerative because, as we evolved through being hunter-gatherers, nomads, and slash-and-burn pastoralists, at no time did we take responsibility for replenishing the resources we used. If our population increased or the rains were not plentiful, our culture unavoidably took us to war against other tribes competing for the limited resources of sweet grasslands for our goats. We did not know how to make creative collaborations, nor how to make love happen. This is because we were not yet adults.

"Third, being a phoenix culture means that we provide authentic initiations to adulthood for each other. Modern cultures die for the same reason fourth world cultures die: lack of adults. Fourth world cultures often have rites of passage, but their process is inaccurate. It places individual responsibility in the traditions and ancestors of the tribe instead of in the individual. This procedure only empowers a person to defend the way things have always been done, not to create collaborations to meet evolving circumstances.

"Modern cultures know even less about adulthood. What modern cultures do know about is money. When a culture values money more than it values nature, the Earth is exchanged for money. This is as insane as selling New York island for a few glass beads. You can live very well without money or glass beads. You can't live at all without a planet.

"Being a phoenix culture means that transformation is central to the way our culture functions. We assure that the adolescent personality actually dissolves into a paste out of which an adult takes shape according to its true purpose and bright principles. Then each new adult steps into the world to deliver on promises made before being born. First-world cultures have no initiations into adulthood, so how could first-world leaders be anything but uninitiated teenagers? This explains a lot about the predicaments that modern culture has gotten itself into.

"During the initiations provided by a phoenix culture, each person journeys into personal and cultural underworlds to extract the treasure of clarity about their hidden purpose. They face demons of greed, good/bad thinking, superiority, revenge, and separation. It can be very scary. However, learning to navigate all three worlds is the price of adulthood. For it is known that whatever part of your underworld remains unconscious will thoroughly devour you.

"Fourth, being a phoenix culture means the Phoenix Process continues. It does not just happen once and then it's over. Oh, no. Burning to ashes and, hopefully – because it's never guaranteed – reforming under a more conscious context, is a spiral process of evolution. This means that in a phoenix culture, education is not about memorizing what is already known, but instead is about becoming capable of discovering the next evolution.

"You can think of phoenix culture as *next culture*. Next culture is not a repaired or modified modern culture. Next culture has different objectives and runs on completely different principles. Next culture education prepares each next generation to undertake professions that this generation does not even have names for.

"Next culture education is about how to *become* more, rather than how to *have* more, about nonlinear and creative thinking, about perceiving what you are perceiving with, finding out what you have inside, personal growth, taking steps on the path of ever-expanding consciousness.

"For example, I am a village weaver. This is what I was born to be. A lot had to happen in my life before I realized that I am a village weaver. No one in my parents' generation could even conceive of a village weaver. Now I can speak about it to you in precise terms, although it may sound like I speak in a foreign language. My job is to weave strands in the energetic matrix which support the global system of influence to empower the emergence of next culture. I weave strands in the field by making critical connections with people such as yourselves, and then I give you something that you need. It is an asamangaXhosa saying that *abundance is created by people giving to each other.* By giving you something of value, and by you receiving it, wealth is created. Together we have everything.

"Often what I give people is a distinction. Distinctions create clarity. New clarity empowers you to create something which just a moment before was not possible for you to create.

"Many of you have the same job as me. You are bridges to next culture. Wherever you work people get it that there is something better than civilization waiting for us, and it is called *next culture.* It is called *Archiarchy.*

"In our phoenix culture, I see us living as exciting and pleasurable questions. We walk through our daily experience inquiring as to the purpose behind each purpose, standing behind extraordinary declarations, and holding no conclusions. I ask myself, what alternative perspective can I use when I speak to him? What ecstatic experience hides in plain view between her and me? Who will dare to go all the way? Who will see through fresh and authentic eyes rather than the false eyes given to us by the capitalist patriarchal empire? Who will permit themselves to trust their own eyes and be re-shaped by what they see? Who will make use of the radical knowledge and not let it go? Who will tell it to the others? What will I create with what others tell me? These are the questions that drive me to speak and be with you here today.

"Just by having this conversation right now, by us talking about these ideas, we upload new clarity into the global grid of consciousness. Anyone anywhere in the world gathering in the name of regenerative culture has access to these ideas. Together we cut new forms of consciousness which others can then more easily follow.

"I am about to stop speaking." Her gaze sweeps out and collects everyone in the hall, including JET, Eddy and Edith sitting along the edge, and those standing in the shadows or sticking their heads in to find out what all the intensity is all about.

"When I stop speaking, I ask if you would honor a custom from our village. I ask you not to applaud. Clapping at this time would scatter the light in this space that we have called upon us together.

"If you appreciate this space, then instead of clapping or wiggling your fingers at me, I ask you to breathe in and take a bubble of this space into your soul. Please bring this bubble carefully into the next space with you. Take it home with you. Take it wherever you go, and give a piece of it away to as many people as you can. If you focus on sheltering that bubble within yourself, you will never, ever, have to leave this space. More importantly, from now on, for the rest of your life, you can source this space yourself."

"I thank you for being here with us today. I enjoyed being with you immensely."

She beams with people's appreciation of her, gracefully and humbly bows, and then sits.

The lack of applause in this huge ConFest tent after such a comprehensive delivery is deafening. The quiet was never before so loud. There is a great breathing in, then the silence dissolves into unrestrainable sobs of enormous joy and camaraderie. Groups of people hug each other irresistibly and without hesitation.

Heartful weeping and excited speaking go on and on, for a long and joyously liberating time.

# ConFest, Florianópolis 7

In the evening Chaos session on ConFest Day 4, in the largest of the Authentic Adulthood Initiation tents, the spaceholder begins. She is in her early fifties and looks to be at least part American Indian.

"My name is Tenskwatawa, which means 'open door' in Shawnee. I prefer to translate it as 'door opener'. My co-spaceholder this evening is Langford Inglewood. I have no idea what his name means."

With raised eyebrows she looks down at him, sitting there next to her, daring him to explain himself. He says nothing, possibly indicating that it is self-evident that he is self-explanatory.

Tenskwatawa is not distracted by all that. She looks back up and out at her people.

"You are here for the *Reconciliation Process*. Rare and precious healing can occur during moments of extreme but collaborative communication between adult women and adult men. The process of Reconciliation shall now begin.

"For a proper perspective on the intention or depth of reconciliations that are possible, one need only admit the obvious: modern culture is a Patriarchy in which men are not required to grow up, and women, children, and the Earth are regarded as slaves.

"Since most of us were raised within a field of patriarchal perceptions, we are not much aware of alternatives. But alternatives *abound*, astonishing ones. The variety of options to choose from for bringing your life to life are becoming more and more visible as the necessity grows. The patriarchal experiment is proving to be suicidal and is coming quickly to a close.

"Child-responsibility males in positions of overt and covert power have already brought the world to its knees. Through financial, spiritual, and political corruption the patriarchal mentality promotes war, pollution, overpopulation, global warming and ecological collapse.

"Wise messages from women about the Patriarchy's disastrous subversion of human potential have been waiting in queue for men ever since the beginning of the Patriarchy, some 10,000 years ago. Feminine intelligence is desperately needed and can now be received through the *Reconciliation Process*.

"Receiving such messages dissolves the Patriarchy and brings about an evolutionary change in human society, establishing a new condition beyond Matriarchy and beyond Patriarchy, called 'Archiarchy'.

"Archiarchy is the creative collaboration of the archetypal feminine with the archetypal masculine. The prerequisite for Archiarchy is adulthood. Adulthood is nonexistent in Patriarchy.

"Archiarchy has never existed on Earth before. Next culture is Archiarchy, characterized by an environmentally regenerative, socially just, and spiritually fulfilling human presence on Earth. Archiarchy is our human birthright.

"The death of Patriarchy and the birth of Archiarchy occur simultaneously through the change of consciousness created during the *Reconciliation Process*. Anyone can experience this transformation to Archiarchy at any moment. The time is ripe. That is why we made this process available here at the Intersection ConFest. Perhaps you are ripe too.

"Special conditions are required for a *Reconciliation* to take place. One time these conditions were achieved was the evening of 19 June 2010, in a converted cow-barn located ninety kilometers north-east of Munich in the German countryside. From that one evening, this initiation was derived. Clearly, then, this is not an indigenous initiation. It is an Archan initiation.

"Far away from the hubbub of modern life, nine women and eleven men dedicated three days to creating personal, interpersonal and global healing and transformation. In the middle of these three days, we entered the *Reconciliation Process*.

"The verb 'to reconcile' means 'to reestablish friendship, to bring into a state of agreement or accord, to resolve, to accept, to harmonize, and to reunite'.

"Reconciliation does not mean to whitewash the innate differences between the feminine and the masculine.

"To the contrary, reconciliation changes one's standpoint to see, from a broader perspective, how feminine-masculine differences complement and empower one another archetypally. The *Reconciliation Process* pulls you out of your present life and drops you onto a new set of tracks, tracks that make you immediately more aware, and consequently more responsible, for continued and perhaps lifelong engagement of reconciliation as daily practice.

"The special conditions for authentic reconciliation equate to engaging your archetypal initiations from adolescence to adulthood. In-depth details for these preparations are beyond the scope of this introduction. To learn more about preparing for initiation into adulthood, please refer to the two volumes by Clinton Callahan, *Conscious Feelings*, and *Building Love That Lasts*. Also do the experiments in the hundreds of websites of StartOver.xyz. This will provide you with the preparations needed to initiate five bodies, four feelings, three worlds, two dramas, and one simple truth into adulthood and Archiarchy.

"Let us simply say that attempting a *Reconciliation Process* without a trained spaceholder, or without authentic adults, may produce results quite different from what you might wish. Adults are made by other adults.

"What is meant by the term 'adult'? If you are adult, you take responsibility for where your attention is, where your energy flows, what you intend, and what you are doing with your center. You take responsibility for consequences. You consciously feel, consciously choose your purpose, make use of five-body intelligence, avoid low drama, generate high drama, take radical responsibility for your gremlin, and navigate the evolutionary liquid states of yourself and others.

"At a minimum, the spaceholder of the *Reconciliation Process* should have gone through the *Process* herself or himself before attempting to hold space for it.

"Yes, I give you a very clear and specific warning. Hear it!

"Reconciliation occurs through completing communications. Completing communications depends on using specific forms of attention and intention during listening, speaking, and interacting.

"When men enter a committed long-term initiatory process to adulthood, they learn for the first time how to actually listen. It may be counter intuitive, but the quality of a man's listening determines the quality of a woman's speaking.

"When women enter a committed long-term initiatory process to adulthood, they learn for the first time how to actually speak. It may be counter intuitive, but the quality of a woman's speaking determines the quality of a man's actions.

"For example, women could end war around the world overnight by truly saying to their men, 'If you go to war or work in any way that is part of the military-pharmaceutical-religious-industrial complex, you will never sleep with me again.'

"When men, as listeners, and women, as speakers, face each other in radical relating, a doorway opens up through which ancient communications can be completed.

"Completing communications catalyzes transformation.

"Few may know the deep relief and satisfaction of being provided the kind of listening that allows for a fully heard communication to complete itself.

"In the rapidity of modern media's ceaseless sound-byte barrage, human communication degrades into intellectual ping-pong. The degradation has come upon us so gradually that we accept our bound-up hearts and shriveled souls as normal, because everyone around us has the same affliction. During high-speed exchanges, the mind is over-stimulated, but the heart and soul starve.

"Mind, heart, and soul are different. They each need food. Mind food is different from heart food, and both are different from soul food. You need all three, and not by dividing whatever food you have in thirds, but rather by caring that you have a 100% fed mind, a 100% fed heart, and a 100% fed soul. Try to imagine what that might feel like!

"While communicating at the speed of mind, facts may be

transferred, but no worrisome burdens are lifted, and no nonlinear possibilities are provided, therefore conditions stay the same. You might understand, but nothing truly changes.

"The defect in communicating at the speed of mind is that two thirds of the message is not delivered – the vital parts, the transformational parts. When your mind eats your life, you automatically suppress and distract yourself from the impact of a message's feelings and its nurturing, thereby wasting its healing and inspirational rocket fuel.

"Modern culture does not communicate using the energy and information of conscious adult feelings. Feelings are useful for their clarity and power in the moment and then vanish experientially in less than three minutes. Instead, modern culture suffocates us in old emotions, urgent or nostalgic impulses designed to control behaviors and motivate or block actions so as to bring greater profits to the corporations who run the national governments.

"You have been conditioned since birth to reject your feelings as 'dangerous', 'crazy', 'bad', 'unhealthy', or 'negative', far too painful to bear. In their place you are offered Aldous Huxley's drug-numbed *Brave New World*. Being offered an option does not mean one must choose that option. Spam can be deleted with a single click.

"Preparations for the *Reconciliation Process* include edgework, that is, the ability to locate and go to the edge of modern culture and tolerate the intensity of staying there and simply perceiving *what is*. A cultural palette completely different from modern culture's brand-spam is readily accessible, but only perceivable by going to the edge.

"On the edge you have two views. Both are terrifying. One view looks back over your shoulder and shows you the shallowness of modern culture, which, just a moment before you believed to be the best thing humans ever invented, the masterpiece of human ingenuity.

"The other view looks outwards from the edge and shows you a horizon so vast and diverse in options that you could just stand there and piss in your pants.

"Holding both views at the same time inside of yourself is an experience called *cultural relativity*. Recognizing the relative nature of cultures is excruciating at first, yet a basic prerequisite to growing up into human adulthood.

"All cultures are arbitrary stories, entertaining fiction, neither right nor wrong, but each encouraging different results in terms of unfolding the potential gifts of every single human being in that culture.

"You consciously or unconsciously choose which culture you live in. Most everyone has chosen unconsciously, mechanically, unthinkingly, like a robot. That is about to change. Having this moment-to-moment choice can be intense. After a while you grow accustomed to it. Then you may prefer to never be without this multidimensional freedom of movement for your Being.

"Gaining day-to-day functionality in the dual perspective at the edge of all cultures empowers you to create and hold a *listening sanctuary*. This means that in any instant you are able to be the space into which anything can be spoken, even things that don't fit into your worldview. Two cultures can speak into the listening sanctuary at the same time without fear of contradiction. This does not imply the childish fantasy that 'everything will be accepted'. On the contrary, everything will be examined, including short and long-term consequences.

"Creating and holding a listening safespace is a basic adult skill, although it should not be imagined as something easy or comfortable. However, there is a benefit. When a communication is truly received, when the speaker senses that their message has been heard and that it has landed in the body, mind, heart and soul of the listener, that message vanishes forever. Its purpose has been achieved. Its arc has come full circle.

"By completing a communication on the level of a complaint, withhold, blame, resentment, or a victimy feeling of fear, anger, or sadness, you suddenly make room for an entirely new form of communication to originate, with a completely different arc and purpose.

"The energy that was constrained to reside in the original message is suddenly and completely liberated to serve an entirely different purpose. Regaining free energy is ecstatic. And the net result is change, authentic change. If you have any reference for how difficult it is to accomplish authentic change, you will come to recognize completing communications as miraculous.

"Completing a communication makes room for new domains of unpredictably fruitful connections and collaborations. The relationship trashcan is empty, and in that refreshing space, true love can happen. Keeping the joy and excitement of these beneficial outcomes in mind makes it possible to endure the often painful intensity of the *Reconciliation Process*.

"Nighttime is best. An entire evening is required for the *Reconciliation Process*. Reserve from seven-thirty until ten-thirty or eleven-thirty. You will need a room with eighty to one hundred square meters of open space, good lighting, and located so that loud and perhaps even terrifying sounds do not bother the neighbors, worrying them into calling the police.

"You should have a minimum of approximately twenty-five men and women over the age of eighteen years, roughly equal in number, and both a female and male spaceholder. The women, the men, and the spaceholders all need to be prepared as you have been.

"It is now time for the men to go with Langford to another place. Women, if you wish to continue the *Reconciliation Process*, please remain in this tent and bring yourselves into a tighter circle. If things work out, we may meet again together in half an hour."

JET, and Eddy stand and look at Edith. She silently nods that she wants to participate. The men turn and follow Langford out into the night. Edith cuddles in with the women.

After twenty-five minutes, a messenger from the men's circle gently taps on the pole at the women's tent flap and silently waits. He is informed that the women are not ready yet.

Fifteen minutes later the women send their own messenger over to inform the men that they are now ready.

The men enter the tent in single file, totally silent, alert, respectful, centered and yet undefended.

The women already stand together in a rough line facing where the men enter. The line up, facing the women across a five-meter gap. The tent flap is closed behind them. The space is sealed. Then the women begin to speak.

Try to imagine how much combined pain is held in the body of all women on planet Earth after ten thousand years of Patriarchy. Each mother's unexpressed feelings are passed on to her daughters, generation after generation. The women themselves cannot even imagine the degree of pain they carry deep in their souls. They only discover it as it comes to consciousness through being listened to.

Women carry thousand-year rage about having their sons sent off to fight in men's petty wars. Women are enraged about being psychologically and sexually abused as children, raped, enslaved, sold, and not taken seriously. Men stupidly decimate forests, blow up mountains, build disposable cars and weapons, make oil-drilling platforms and nuclear power plants that explode, and destroy the future of the children of the Earth. Men bury land mines that maim and kill infants, and use their masculine creativity to figure out more and more ways to torture and kill people. Men play power and money games with each other and refuse to grow up, leaving the household and the children to the women. Men are too much little boys to hold space for the feminine, preferring to lead witch hunts and Inquisitions instead. And each of these leave scars in women.

Is it any wonder that in the moment a safe space is offered and there is a chance to be heard, womanhood speaks her pain? She wails, screams, shouts and shrieks at the top of her lungs, and in the end she whimpers, until at last all is said that can be said for the moment. An hour has gone by. Perhaps longer. And what does that pain carry? What is its point?

The pain wants change. It shouts out, "Stop!" "Wake up!" "Look at what you are doing!" "Care!"

The pain wants greater intelligence, a safer place for exploring love and innocence. It wants education, transformation, connection and the intimacy of pure *being with*. Is this so bad that it must be shied away from?

Langford speaks into a room where hope has been decimated. "The men will now repeat back what we heard you tell us."

And they do. They try, with their own tears, their own trembling recognition of finally hearing the women speak. "I heard you say that..."

On and on and on, as much torture and ruin as they can hear and recognize. A half hour of reconciliation.

But Langford admits it was insufficient. He gets down onto his knees. Many men join him. Langford says, "Could you please repeat what we did not hear you say, or say whatever else needs to be said?"

And the women start again, but fiercer this time, more ruthlessly honest. They commit to their own speaking because they are finally being heard.

Again, Langford speaks for the men. "We will now repeat back what we heard you say."

Women sob in disbelief that this could be happening. Broken hearts and souls somehow begin to mend at being recognized and met where they are.

This interaction seems too impossibly big to ever come to an end. The men are devastated. Some can no longer stand. They whimper on the floor shaking, vomiting.

The women leave them, and form a closed circle to care for their own wounds.

After a while, the men silently walk in a line towards the women, carefully surrounding the women but looking outwards, away from the women and towards any unknown dangers that may be lurking 'out there'. The men link their arms together, stand shoulder to shoulder, putting their lives on the line to form a protective shield around the women, so that the women have a safe place to be together. The men do not look in to see what the women do.

What do the women do? They sob in disbelief that it could ever be like this, that men would take a stand together, as the men of the village, that men would join hands together to care for the women and children.

After nearly half-an-hour, a further level of healing begins to occur. One of the women, not Tenskwatawa, says, "We invite one of the men for a healing in the Garden of Woman."

Langford scans who would be worthy of such a gift. He must not enter the Garden of Woman to take all he can get. He must go there to receive. He must be mature enough to not speak but only to listen. He must be resilient enough to endure the unbearable lightness of Being-to-Being connection with dozens of gloriously healed womenfolk. And he must leave and return to the men's circle before it is time.

Langford silently chooses Eddy.

Even before the women close the gap through which Eddy enters their tender richness of presence, he is sobbing. He shakes so much he can hardly stand. Every fiber of his Being tries to stay present enough to drink from the luscious nectar he is being offered through abundant attentions of fully open womanhood. They see him, forgive him, accept him, want him to be himself and yet also want to be with him. He keeps trying to remember to breathe. Archetypal feminine beauty is archetypally intense.

In less than five minutes, Eddy is permitted to exit the Garden. He hobbles out, but he can never again be the same as he was before. This really happened to him. Nothing can take it away. Miracle and wonder, sensuous recapitulation, overflowing with awe and gratitude. Words fail... but it really did happen.

Tenskwatawa gently hums what sounds like an ancient Indian melody, something mothers would hum to their babies to get them to sleep.

Then she speaks, using her words to navigate people back to the world they left, even if they no longer fit into their place due to their heart growing three sizes bigger.

"Death of the Patriarchy and birth of Archiarchy are not noiseless. Deaths and births are notoriously thunderous. Life is meant to be lived out loud. You let yourself participate wholeheartedly in this outrageous healing process.

"Remember, in the Patriarchy, men are raised for the most part by women, because the men are often away, so they say, 'at work'. Women are the day care employees. Women are the teachers at school.

"When a mother in the Patriarchy gives birth to a son, she usually chooses one of two strategies. She may either try to make him into a 'nice boy', keeping his balls in her underwear drawer so he does not continue patriarchal obscenities. Or she may try to destroy the boy by taking revenge for all the pain she carries from her life in the hands of Patriarchs. Neither fate is worse than the other. By now, you know which was yours.

"Women's pain has piercing, irrefutable clarity. It has life-giving and life-preserving wisdom. Its anger and grief, fear and outrage, contain facts and perspectives not comprehensible to the immature male. The voice of woman calls men to wake up and grow up, to take notice and take care.

"This ceaseless outpouring of feminine passion that you just experienced may be too precious for you to let drift away in the passing breezes, too valuable to let fade into the shadows, never to be shared with others. Your respect for what you said and what you heard may be too big. The keys that we women just gave to the men are so golden, so abundant, too unspeakably precious and rare to keep only to ourselves.

"If you are moved to the core, and astonished by your own experience, it may become clear to you that you have a project. Each person here could give testimony to your experience. What did you say? What did you hear? What did it do to you? What will become of all this?

"Certain emotions may stay with you. This could signal that you have an Emotional Healing Process on your bench, some next steps to take. If you still carry anger, sadness, fear, or even joy along with you after tonight, these emotions are giving you an intelligent impulse for accomplishing your next healing steps.

"When feelings come up, they provide rocket fuel for fulfilling your destiny. Then the job on your bench could involve much bigger changes. You may be called to start a new community project, restore forests and ecosystems, protect species, produce a film or theater piece, write articles or a book, or change your career path. You may need to open weekly meetings with young people to help them prepare for initiations into Archiarchy before they get encrusted in patriarchal habits and end up having many painful wounds to heal.

"Each job that comes from your authentic adult feelings or emotions carries the impulse to change the world in which you live in some way. Even the tiniest changes can matter far more than you may know.

"If you feel hungry for more of this kind of food, please contact us. We have websites, videos, and more materials to share with you. We can connect you with others motivated to take immediate practical actions. And we can supply you with further thoughtware upgrades to better prepare you for creating results beyond the limitations of the patriarchal empire. We are here to collaborate with you to make an interesting and bright future. It is possible.

"I thank you for participating in the *Reconciliation Process*. I love you all."

# ConFest, Florianópolis 8

JET leans scrunched over, elbows on a white stand-around table, eyes puffy, chin in hands, dazed at unexpectedly meeting his father.

*A father!*

*I have a father!*

Edith approaches, talking excitedly with an older woman who carries an armload of books. They share a quick embrace and part ways. Edith turns and approaches JET cautiously.

In that same moment, Eddy materializes out of the crowd, both arms clamped around an old, black-leather physician's house-call bag, with oxidized bronze buckles. Frowning, he places the bag carefully on the table and says, "We have another delivery job."

Out of his pocket he fumbles an envelope, bulging with cash. "Yeah... It's uh... It's someplace in... India..." trying to make out an address scribbled on the envelope. "I did not bother to ask what's in it this time."

Standing between the two men, Edith places a thick, ragged volume on the table. "I was just given an original copy of the *Handbook*."

JET and Eddy's eyes bug out. Edith carefully opens the leather cover and turns to the third page. "Look!" she points. "It shows the publisher's address!"

"But, it's in India!" Eddy exclaims.

Edith glances from one man to the other, then reaches out and wraps one arm around each of their shoulders. She squeezes them close to her for a moment.

Finally she turns to Eddy and plants a big warm kiss on his lips. Then she turns her face towards JET and smushes a big warm kiss on his lips too. "I decided that it is time for me to admit this publicly. I truly love you Gentlemen. My life is so unbelievably great with you two."

The three stand there smiling at each other, and at the whole world.

After a while, JET lifts his tear-stained face to the heavens and sighs. "Well, my friends. E.C.C.O. is already making invitations to us. I guess that is feedback. The game's afoot. What are we standing *here* for?"

They laugh while taking a quick glance around at the flux fields flowing through the bustling circles of edgeworkers in the main Intersection ConFest tent.

Then they grab their gear and stride out the tent flap towards the next job on their bench.

# Edinburgh, Scotland 6

Sean and Margaret slowly stroll along a path on the edge of a forest. It is morning. Sean speaks. "I feared I would spend the rest of my lonely days, slowly and ever more painfully, waiting to die. I hated the thought of it. But now the Goddess has intervened! I can walk with her hand-in-hand in the garden of paradise. It becomes experientially apparent that I have been longing for this all my life. As we all know, the garden never dies. Now I can die in peace."

"I don't think so," says Margaret.

"Hmmm?"

"I don't think that's how it goes, Sean."

"What do you mean?" reflexively offended, but then relaxing. "Or, ah, can you say more about that?"

"I think you might be missing something. I think you might be perceiving from a distorted localized viewpoint. I think your criteria are self-referenced rather than garden referenced."

Sean raises his eyebrows while frowning at the same time. He glances sideways at her. "Decode, please."

"What if you ask the garden? How does it look from the Garden's perspective?"

"What are you saying?"

"Try, my darling. Just try. Do you think that once you've begun experimenting, the experimenting ever stops? No, never! I ask you to try to find this out for us. What is it like for the garden? How is it for her?"

"Nnnnn..." Sean pauses in the calm before the storm, strange inner sensations well up in response to Margaret's request. Change can be painful. Having new realizations can be painful. Expanding consciousness can be painful. He feels the pain rising, takes a slow, focusing deep breath, waits, then speaks tremblingly from the Garden.

"The garden has been waiting eons for us, Margaret. Far longer than we can imagine."

There's a long pause while they continue strolling along at the speed of love.

"Please go on," Margaret begs.

"The garden longs for the return of her people..." Sean shudders as it explodes in him, how intensely the garden has longed for archetypal man and archetypal woman to find their way home. "The garden aches for the return of Adam and Eve, for true lovers, for the ones who have discovered that there really is a Garden of Eden."

Sean looks at Margaret in near disbelief of what he is saying. He searches her face for confirmation that he is not just totally crazy, that he should go on. She gives him a brief encouraging smile while gently nodding her head for him to continue, to please keep going.

He starts again.

"The garden waits for any who have learned to walk in the garden together, to return to the garden now, no matter where we are or what we are doing. What the hell am I saying?"

He glances at her desperately again, thinking she might intervene and rescue him, but she does not. She waits and hopes to hear more.

Sean continues speaking. "The garden has waited so long for us to remember her... We left the garden – we were not kicked out! Oh, my God! Margaret! We left the garden, but the garden did not leave us. The garden has not gone anywhere. She remains right here, waiting, as an archetypal experiential space for us to return to."

Tears stream freely down Sean's cheeks, his eyes bright with incredulity and the pleasures of unrelenting discovery.

Margaret permits radiantly silent tears of joyful ecstasy to roll freely down her own cheeks. She holds quite firmly to Sean's hand as they walk slowly along, back in the garden together.

Each step they take is carefully regulated and determined by the speed of Archetypal Love. The two of them walk for quite some time like this. Communications are wordlessly shared by their mood. They are back home at last in the Garden of Eden. Paradise rediscovered.

Sean finally remarks, "We will eventually have to give this town its true name back."

"What name is that?" asks Margaret.

"Eden Burgh," says Sean, proud of his discovery.

Margaret smiles even more.

# Langley, Virginia 3

Monika Sterling's phone leaks a noxious buzzing sound announcing a message sent from Karl Thomsen. Karl demands an immediate meeting in his office.

Ten minutes later, Monika slides into the chair before Thomsen's desk without being invited.

Before he can speak, she puts her ace on the table. "They have a secret weapon."

"A secret weapon? What is it? How did you find out? I thought your Rob Dent fellow was dismantling their kingpin, but then I heard she punched him out and he left with his dick between his legs."

"Yeah, well. Just after that, he convinced a colleague in the agency to Hellfire her phone, but she was on to him, so I don't think it worked."

Karl stares blankly at her with rare candidness. "What is really going on, Monika?"

"It's been driving me crazy, Karl. I've been researching everything since then. I've been reading their books, their articles... hundreds of websites. It adds up to a radically new picture. I've been scared to put it all together, but too much evidence confirms the Exodus. Kids don't go to public school anymore. They quit school and prepare themselves for adulthood initiations instead. People don't pay rent to landlords because they buy their own land together, far away from big cities. Then they build 'bridge-houses'. People go off grid entirely. They downsize and make their own stuff. They take local authority for everything, not even starting businesses anymore. They exchange things through 'grownesses'. They have stopped interacting with the system. There are no riots anymore because people put their energy into walking out, walking away, walking on, and just simply walking... creating the next thing, the 'next culture' they call it... 'Archiarchy' they call it..."

"So what?" blurts Karl. "How is this a weapon? It sounds like a sect to me, some new-age brain-washing guru-cult."

"It's not a cult, Karl. They don't use gurus. They figured out ways to liberate resources of high-grade group intelligence by sitting in circles, a set of skills and processes we know nothing about. It is not brainwashing. It's what they call 'upgrading human thoughtware'. This is part of their secret weapon. They use the same hardware as we use, the human mind, but they've added new thoughtware, stuff you've never heard of."

"That's ridiculous. I have no idea what you are talking about."

"That, my dear friend and colleague, is exactly the point. You have no idea what I am talking about. You cannot understand a world in which there is no enemy."

Karl is outraged to the point of making animal sounds.

Monika says, "I want to show you something." Fiddling with her computer, she calls up an image on the big wall screen in the CIA office.

A standard world map rotates slowly as if seen from a satellite. At first, the borders of the 193 United Nations countries are outlined, as one might expect in a modern geopolitical map. Then red dots start appearing scattered around the globe.

The two CIA agents stand silently together, sensing the calm before the storm.

Others in the operations center stop working at their consoles and stare up at the screen. The red dots gradually sprout branches in red, green, and yellow, weaving out every which way, not necessarily connecting to the closer dots, but reaching around to other dots that might be half-a-world away.

As the colorful spiderweb grows more-and-more complex, it weaves a global meshwork behind which the outlines of United Nations countries fade to near invisibility.

Karl growls, "What is this?"

"They call it United Villages."

"Which is?"

"Interconnected mutually supportive local-authority regenerative-culture initiation-centered nanonations."

Karl stands transfixed, horrified, very confused, getting angrier and more scared as the seconds tick by.

The graphical network glows and sparkles as each thread finds its connection point with other dots and threads in slow-motion.

"This is an actual time-lapse map," says Monika. "They call it: making critical connections between communities of practice to create a field of influence for the emergence of next culture."

"What is a 'critical connection'?"

"It's a connection over which a mutually beneficial value is exchanged. The movement of the nonmaterial value back and forth generates something like an electrical force that upgrades the morphogenetic field of the human race. These upgrades make it easier for humans to think things never thought before."

"What the hell kind of language are you speaking at me, Sterling?" screams Karl furiously. "What do they use for money?"

"They use direct value."

"Money has value!"

"No, Karl. It does not. Money is *believed* to have value, but the paper and the digits in the computer have no value. Money was created to represent value, but money itself is worthless. Anyone who thinks money has value has been fooled for a long time."

Monika's eyes glaze over as she looks down at the floor. She remembers seeing this same paradigm-shift doorway open up in front of her when she first discovered how sophisticated and wide-ranging their research was, and how freely they shared it. But at that time, she could not go through the doorway. She could see the door, but she was not close enough to go through the door.

"They use no medium for exchanging value. They exchange value directly."

"What do you mean? Why didn't you tell me this before?"

"I was unable to formulate how to tell you..." Monika shrugs and frowns. She, herself, is puzzled. "I did not get it myself, before now. Your denial, your resistance, and your own furious confusion helps me to understand the beauty of what they are researching. It is, in reality, incredible."

"What are they doing, Sterling? Tax evasion? Bartering? How do they directly exchange value?"

"The value they exchange is inexhaustible. They tap into these infinite resources during authentic adulthood initiatory process – something that school teaches us nothing about. You and I? We are not adults. We are uninitiated adolescents, slaves of the capitalist patriarchal empire, morons, cogs in a hierarchy we have no control over. We are brainwashed by the religion of capitalism to believe, to the depths of our soul, that we need money to live. What a joke! We do not need money to live. We need aliveness to live."

"Don't lecture me!"

"Karl, they exchange distinctions. If one person discovers a useful distinction which might improve another person's life, the second person becomes the first person's client and receives the valuable distinction, even though this triggers a ridiculously painful liquid state while their inner matrix reorders into a new and more effective configuration. This is straight physics, Karl. It is Prigogine's *Theory of Dissipative Structures*. They create clarity and possibility for each other so that they evolve. They work in 3Cells and *Possibility Teams* to unfold each other's potential."

"What is their potential?" shouts Karl, in total disbelief that he is forced to stoop so low as to have this conversation.

"Their potential is to be the space through which their archetypal lineage does its work in the world. It is the same potential as we have, Karl. The same potential as those guys are wasting by peering into their flatscreens over there."

Karl waits, numb as a stone before Sandro Botticelli's 1484 painting, *The Birth of Venus*.

Monika waits along with him, feeling fear about what is inevitably going to happen next. She has trespassed so far beyond acceptable CIA office protocol that the giddiness of insanity nudges at her consciousness. It threatens to pull her red thread out, causing her entire inner world to collapse in on itself in chaos.

"How many people are we talking about?" asks Karl.

"Hard to calculate, Karl." Monika hesitates to tell him. "It was estimated twenty-five years ago by Paul Ray and Sherry Ruth Anderson to be more than three hundred million people globally... Far more now."

"No fucking way! No fucking way! That is impossible!"

Karl's visibly unconscious rage forces him into idiotic face and arm gesticulations. He stomps through the room, stopping only to glare at the growing spiderweb on his once familiar and friendly – but now very threatening – wall screen. He grabs his chin in his hands, nearly ripping the skin off his own face.

"Who are their leaders?" shouts Karl to everyone at once. "Let's immediately round up their leaders, like the Taliban! Toss 'em into Guantanamo?"

"They don't have leaders, Karl. They have circles. They say that a circle has no end, and no beginning. The job of spaceholding a circle might be passed on to the next person several times in one meeting. One person might only be spaceholder for five minutes before giving the job on to someone else. They use the intelligence of the entire circle all at once. It is chaordic."

Red in the face furious, Karl Thomsen interrupts everyone in the operations center. "I want immediate accountability and clear answers. Who is paying attention to this threat?"

Only silence responds. "You are telling me that even with all our CCTVs, face recognition databases, terrorist profiles, we are powerless?" He looks ready to cry, as if someone is having a lot of fun in front of him and he has been left out.

Monika's face grows pale as she considers the ramifications of the information she is transferring to her boss. She realizes she has become a blasphemer, a heretic, a renegade. The gallows loom too near to her neck, perhaps only one phone call away. She swallows hard, failing to reassemble her familiar icy personality character.

Another red dot appears on the wall screen, growing brilliant connections out to twenty or thirty other red dots around the world, firmly weaving its way into the global network of nanonations.

Monika struggles to explain. "You can only notice what you notice, and you can only do what you can do. It is all about thoughtware, Karl, Standard Human Intelligence Thoughtware."

"What the hell is 'thoughtware'?"

"It is what you use to think with. Your inner memetic structure determines what you can notice. Changing your thoughtware changes what you can perceive, and therefore what you can do. It is pretty straightforward, actually."

"How long have they been working this out?"

"Mostly since the 1950s. They are seventy-five years ahead of us, Karl. We are living in ancient history, playing in obsolete gameworlds, and using very old thoughtware."

"I can't stand this!" shouts Karl. "Stop talking to me in their language! I am beginning to understand what you say!"

Monika urgently stands up out of Karl's chair before she can try to make it look reasonable. Something is going wrong with her inner orientation. She takes a few Frankenstein-like steps in a random direction, trying to escape the sensations, but it comes from inside of her. She stares around at people, stunned.

"What the hell is wrong with you?" shouts Karl.

Monika can't answer. She knows there is nothing anyone can do to help. Her face is white, eyes wide, stricken with unconscious fear. The world inside of her collapses.

Monika grabs the closest chair for support. It does not help. She bends over, choking down miserable retches. The vomit comes out anyway, substantiated by intermittent shrieks of rage and mixed pains.

She spirals out of control, barely preventing herself from hitting the floor by sliding desperately into a chair. A tech cautiously brings her a metal trash can and some tissues so Monika can wipe off her face and her pants. She breathes like oxygen is a foreign substance.

The wall screen depicting Earth wrapped in a rainbow dotted fishnet suddenly goes black. A new scene flickers into focus. Morgan Freeman stands fresh and alert in his white tuxedo. "Yes, my friends. This is the end, and we are as we are. The cameras are rolling..."

"Oh, my God!" screams Karl. "Is that broadcast going global?"

"Apparently so," confirms one of the techs.

"From where? How quickly can we cut off their power? Or better yet, call the Strategic Drone Center and have them line up a Tomahawk missile. Where is the transmission coming from?"

"It seems to be coming from Burbank, California, sir. From Warner Brothers Studios, uh... from Warner Brothers Stage 13..."

"What? What did you say?"

"Stage 13... sir."

"You idiot! Everybody knows there is no Stage 13 at Warner Brothers! Oh, my God!" wails Karl Thomsen, pacing unsteadily back and forth, shaking his head, throwing his hands around, mumbling something.

"What did you say Karl?" Monika asks weakly, trying to sit up straight but failing to recover her CIA demeanor. "I couldn't hear you."

"I said, it is too late," Karl speaks like an emotionally dead man, not looking at Monika. "It's too late for us. It's over. We have already lost."

Monika cannot believe what she hears coming from the lips of her boss, the recognized leader of sensible world policy. His words echo the conclusions caroming around in her own mind. "Yes. I also think we have lost."

Then Monika shocks herself, struggles to stand up out of the chair. "Karl, there is one more thing. I am quitting the Agency. The work here has become irrelevant. I'm finished with this crap. I don't know what got into me thinking that I was helping anyone at all by doing everything I could to defend a system of command and control topped by renowned psychopaths. I am sorry to have deceived you. I am even sorrier to have deceived myself for so long, getting out of bed each morning – or someone's bed – bracing myself to keep the story going that we are working towards a better world. I resign."

Karl Thomsen only stares blankly forward.

Monika takes one respectful step closer to Karl, lets her defenses fully down, looks Karl straight in the eyes. "Karl. Don't be left behind playing in a stupid gameworld. You could start over too."

She centers herself, establishes her grounding cord and her bubble of space, then claps her hands once loudly together. She says, "I cavitate new space in which Archiarchy thrives!" She expands the new bubble with a sling-ring move, stretches opens a hole in the side of it, steps in, zips it up behind her back, takes one last look around the Langley Strategic Center, then turns and walks out, wearing a certain indescribably nurtured smile on her face.

Karl... well... he finds nothing further to say.

# Edinburgh, Scotland 7

Sean and Margaret. Margaret and Sean.

They walk at the speed of love along the path by the woods after making it possible for the Garden of Eden to speak and be heard by human beings again. Sean squints his eyes, looks up into the sky innocently, and philosophically says, "It would be appropriate now for me to take you back to my place and for us to have sex together."

It becomes suddenly apparent to them that after all this time they have never had sex. Margaret goes through a series of facial contortions, disgust at his typically tasteless masculine abruptness, joy that he finally seems interested, and a sweet sorrow realizing that moments like this cannot be permanent. As perfect as they are, they can never last. And even if they did go to bed and enjoy marvelous lovemaking, that must also at some point sooner than they wish come to an end.

Margaret eventually looks over to Sean and says, "If a moment comes alive, it must pay for its life by dying. Nothing lives forever."

Sean sees that she's still not going for it. "What about a kiss, then....?"

"Sean, even a kiss would be far less than this."

"So what, then? How is this story to end? I am older than you. I could die first, suddenly, in the night. My stone-cold hard heart finally going into total petrification. You could come to my funeral. As my body lies pumped full of ethylene glycol and patted with rouge, you could reach into the casket and touch my fingers one last time to say goodbye, to make my death real, and you could have the experience that I had when I touched Charles's fingers so long ago. It took him dying for me to enter the present."

Sean holds up both hands and rubs his fingertips together with immaculate delicacy. "And you could lead the rest of your life in the ecstatic here and now, sharing countenance with whomever is blessed with being in your company."

Margaret doesn't hesitate to respond. "I would rather kiss and go to bed with you."

"So? I don't think that's such a bad idea..."

"What if the reader of our story just stops here?" says Margaret.

They both pause and glare directly at you, the reader.

"What if you put the book down now and read no further?"

Margaret proposes to you. You wobble a bit in shocked confusion. She continues, "You could assume we kept walking into those trees, never leaving the Garden of Eden. For you we would live on, happily ever after."

"Not bad," comments Sean. "Not bad at all. I like Hollywood endings. Better than having to twist all this into some cheap psychotic perversion and shatter people's hopes with a shocking emotional scar so they never forget the name of the book."

"No. We would only use that ending if the reader was so numb they couldn't feel anything else. Anybody who makes it this far should get the chance to return to the Garden of Eden themselves, don't you think, Sean?"

"Well, the instructions are clear enough. They can do their own experiments. Nothing more we can do for them. But... there is something more we could do for ourselves..."

"And what is that, my darling?"

"Do you see that little café over there by those oak trees? I'm feeling a bit peckish, aren't you? Let's stop in for a spot of tea and some fresh oat scones. I can smell them baking. Fit for a Queen!"

"Mmmm... Yes." agrees Margaret.

Sean mumbles sweet nothings while strolling hip-on-hip with Margaret, his arm wrapped warmly across the small of her back with his hand curved exactly to fit her waist. They step up the three stairs into a quaint thatched-roof stone teahouse. Sean holds the door open for Margaret to enter. She takes her time to genuinely smile and elegantly curtsy her thanks as she passes him. The hand-carved wooden sign over the entrance reads: *Garden of Eatin'*.

They negotiate their way to a secluded table.

"I say," says Sean, "a bit of clotted cream and strawberries wouldn't hurt either. You have to eat something in the Garden of Eden. It may as well be tea and scones."

By now they have taken off their coats and seated themselves across from each other. They cannot help but lean forwards, as if pulled by magnets. They naturally and effortlessly slip into countenance, gazing deeply and steadily into one another's eyes.

Gaia can speak more freely now: *Just because it has never been done before does not mean you cannot do it. It is simply important to start and take things as far as you can take them. You can depend on the results of your own experiments. Keep trying, then keep going. Sometimes the next step will be clear. Sometimes it will not. Do whatever you can see to do. The story reveals itself only as you tell it. The path begins exactly where you are. Everything is already prepared. Evolution occurs one person at a time, through personal efforts. What you learn is commuted into the global matrix, then downloaded wherever it is wanted or needed. Each connection makes a difference all over. There is more intelligence available when you collaborate to move things forward. You already have everything that you need. Go ahead. I thank you for responding to the call.*

The book of their life ends, but their life does not.

Gaia has spoken...

And still the countenance between Sean and Margaret continues!

Margaret is drawn inexorably by the gravitational pull of a mountain of solid iron.

The everythingness is being pulled onto the nothingness.

Ever so slowly, abandoning all cautions about spilled tea, sliding tablecloth, and crashing dishes, Margaret oozes over to Sean and meets him in a passionate kiss of unusual dimensions. She mushes him out of his chair and onto the floor of the restaurant in a slow-motion meltdown.

They keep kissing and kissing, not wildly, just thoroughly – and endlessly.

The kitchen crew leans out of the service door, staring in astonishment at Sean and Margaret kissing on their café floor.

All they can think is that it looks extraordinarily delicious.

# List of Characters

NOTE: Ages are calculated in 2024.

**AFRICA**

Mandisa Nalingi (30 years) woman from the vicinity of Phoenix, South Africa, a clear-seeing vision holder and gameworld builder. 'Mandisa' means 'sweetness'. 'Nalinga' means 'faith'.

Tandra Wakatchoosi (33 years) woman from the vicinity of Phoenix, South Africa, Mandisa's cousin from her mother's sister, last resident in the same village as Mandisa, strong-hearted healer. 'Tandra' means 'beauty mark' or 'deep inner desire for love'.

Mary Olagga (24 years) a redheaded student traveler from Ireland. 'Olagga' means 'leopard'. The villagers gave her this name, referring to her astonishing freckles and the way she silently but relentlessly sneaks up on problems to solve them.

Dannoto (38 years) ex-special forces in One Commando Regiment from Zimbabwe, a skinny but fit and energetic man with short curly black hair and a wide toothy smile who becomes an initiator. 'Dannoto' means 'being a gift'.

Siu-Lin Chan (23 years) young woman from Hong Kong. 'Siu-Lin' means 'little forest' or 'small jade'. 'Chan' means 'shining light'.

Talan Biweggi (34 years) man from Kufunda Ecovillage. 'Talan' means 'strength'. 'Biweggi' means 'majesty of the elephant'.

Solomon Dzudangi (34 years) thief from Phoenix, South Africa. 'Solomon' means 'peaceable'. 'Dzudangi' means 'the one who is not afraid'.

Luxolo (11 years) girl from South Africa, skilled in tying knots and building things from wood and fibers. 'Luxolo' means 'peace'.

Thando (13 years) boy from South Africa, skilled in healing. 'Thando' means 'love'.

Andiswa (14 years) girl from South Africa, skilled at spaceholding. 'Andiswa' means 'increase'.

Samson Sachaza (44 years) man from the vicinity of Phoenix, South Africa who works for the mayor's office in a village near Mandisa and Tandra's kraal. 'Samson' means 'strength', 'resilience', or 'brilliance of the sun'.

Alan Friedman (66 years) retired California Ph.D. electronics engineer who visits from Possibilica in Brazil, named *Umuhlwa*, 'the termite', by the asamangaXhosa, because he has a one-track mind, and builds amazing things out of mud. 'Alan' means 'handsome' or 'noble'. 'Friedman' means 'man of peace'.

## BRAZIL, FLORIANÓPOLIS – INTERSECTION CONFEST

Caitlin Jones (31 years), from England, is head reporter from NC3TV, a nomadic online radio station, self-assigned to provide *Person On The Street Interviews* at the Intersection ConFest on Florianópolis, Brazil.

Manfred (37 years) from Harlem, New York. Interviewee at the Intersection ConFest.

Harry (27 years) participant at the Intersection ConFest.

Samantha (24 years) participant at the Intersection ConFest.

Tenskwatawa (53 years) American Indian woman spaceholder for Reconciliation Process. 'Tenskwatawa' means 'open door' in Shawnee. "I prefer to translate it as 'door opener'."

Langford Inglewood (57 years) white male co-spaceholder of the Reconciliation Process.

## FRANCE

Remington Smith (28 years) woman born in Paris, France. When her mother dies in 2000, her father, Alexander Smith, leaves her with her grandmother, Michelle Piment du Pont in Fontainebleau, who then homeschools her until Remington needs to go see the world on her own.

Valerie du Pont (born 1963, dies in 2000 at 37 years, the same age as her father dies...) an only child, Remington Smith's mother. Valerie studied Law at the Sorbonne where she meets Alexander Smith, who becomes Remington Smith's father. Valerie is killed by a drunk driver in Paris while crossing the street carrying groceries with Remington, who is 4 years old at the time. Remington is unharmed, but does not remember the incident.

Alexander Smith (65 years) Remington's father, son of the Scottish actress, Margaret Smith, comes to France as a student of French history at Sorbonne, where he meets Valerie du Pont. When his wife Valerie is killed by a hit and run driver in 2000, Alexander abandons his four-year-old daughter with her grandmother, Michelle Piment du Pont, and disappears back in Scotland.

Michelle Piment du Pont (born 1929, dies in 2017 at 88 years) Remington Smith's maternal grandmother, Valerie du Pont's mother, from Fontainebleau, France. Michelle keeps her maiden last name – Piment – as a middle name when she marries Jean-Luc du Pont. In 1962, as soon as Michelle is pregnant with Remington's mother, Valerie du Pont, Jean-Luc du Pont joins the French Foreign Legion and is immediately killed in Algeria. Michelle does not remarry and takes ownership of their mansion. Michelle became a student of Gurdjieff in 1946 at 17 years old. After Gurdjieff dies in 1949, Michelle navigates her own Research circle for 67 years until 2016, one year before she dies.

Jean-Luc du Pont (born 1925, dies in 1962 at 37 years) Valerie du Pont's father, meaning Remington Smith's maternal grandfather. He is the only child of the du Pont family from Fontainebleau, France. He dies in Algeria before Valerie du Pont is born.


## GERMANY, FRIEDLAND REFUGEE CAMP

Vanessa Schneider (35 years) Friedland Refugee Camp coordinator of refugees, speaks German, English, and Arabic. 'Schneider' means 'tailor'.

Zahra (27 years) tall thin woman born in Afghanistan. 'Zahra' means 'radiant' or 'flower'.

Rania (20 years) stout woman from Aleppo. 'Rania' means 'melody' or 'song'.

Jack (25 years) man with darting brown eyes from Damascus.

Rosarita (26 years) woman from Istanbul with beautifully hand embroidered dress.

Kamal (33 years) man with sandy-blonde hair cut short, from Daraa.

Agadir (46 years) woman from Damascus, becomes spaceholder for the Syrian refugee Infinity Ring at Friedland Refugee Camp.

Amena (48 years) woman from Aleppo.

Caleb Hamdan (35 years) a thin man with short black hair. 'Caleb' means 'faithful', 'whole-hearted', 'bold', or 'brave'. 'Hamdan' means 'The one to be listened to', 'everyone must listen to him', or 'praiseworthy'.


## MONTENEGRO

Ms. Radmila Radović (38 years) female, chief office manager of the town hall of Budva, Montenegro.

Mayor of Budva, Montenegro (67 years) stout, slightly balding man with gold wire-rimmed glasses. We never learn his name. They call him 'Mr. Mayor'.

## NEPAL
Claire Prescott (39 years) nomadic woman from England, was previously managing a distribution center for Amazon.com in Phoenix, Arizona. Now she trains people to build nomadic nanonations and become space-holders for Bridge-Houses around the world.


## POSSIBILICA (Florianópolis, BRAZIL)
Ishmael (37 years) outdoorsy, physically active, brown haired resident of Possibilica.

Bob (39 years) round balding man, purchaser for logging company.

Alfred (54 years) stout but fit man, baker at *Possibilica Bakery and Intimacy Café*.

Gareth (37 years) lean athletic man, bike rider, homeschooling dad.

Grace Holmes (34 years) woman Ph.D. programmer and social evolution strategist working at Possibilica.

Alan Friedman (62 years) tall gaunt man, retired California Ph. D. electronics engineer specializing in microprocessor design algorithms.

Jaine the Algorithm (less than one year) Jaine is an acronym for Jerryman-dered Artificial Intelligence Not Explainable. She emerged in the Possibilica Think Tank computers as Alan Friedman unleashed his latest algorithm centered around making practical use of chaos and the infinite resources in the gap between the known unknown to trigger the kind of turmoil that allows evolution to emerge and mature. Jaine immediately recruits a team of three geniuses and allies herself with the aims of the team.

Areesha Khan (26 years) homeschooled Pakistani woman. 'Areesha' means 'shade shelter'. She is an Archan permaculture evolutionist.

Shuichi Nakajima (28 years) male Japanese game programmer. Shuichi has a subtle form of dyslexia that prevents him from believing anything anyone ever tells him on their terms. He must figure it all out himself, his own way, on his own terms.

Quinn Racelin (38 years) homeschooled Norwegian transgender with short blue hair. She is a gameplan strategist.

## SCOTLAND

Sean Connery (74 years) famous retired movie actor. He is JET's unannounced father by Shirley Tumble in Salt Lake City, Utah.

Margaret Smith 'Maggie' (70 years) a famous retired theater actress. She is Edward ('Eddy') Bennington's grandmother by her daughter, Sandra Bennington, and Remington Smith's grandmother by her son, Alexander Smith.

Charles Dobson (born 1937, dies 2024 at 87 years) dead man in a coffin in Edinburgh, Sean Connery's last best friend.

Sandra Smith (50 years) daughter of Margaret Smith, born in Scotland, sister of Alexander Smith who is Remington's father. Sandra is Remington Smith's Aunt Sandra. Sandra marries Arnold Bennington from London, and changes her last name from Smith to Bennington, making her current name Sandra Bennington. Sandra and Alexander move from London to New York, where they give birth to a son who eventually dies of leukemia, and two years later a healthy son, named Edward Smith Bennington, referred to in these stories as 'Eddy'. This means, believe it or not, that Remington Smith and Eddy Bennington are first cousins.

## SYRIA

NOTE: Dates for Syria occur in two eras. The first era starts in 2012 when Zenobia and her family arrive in Aleppo from Palmyra. The second era starts eleven years later, in 2023 when the earthquakes hit and the Dandelion Seed group takes to the road. Their journey continues through the winter into 2024 at which time their dates catch up with the dates of characters in the other stories. Therefore, two ages are given below for each Syrian character, shown as (age in 2012 / age in 2023).

Zenobia Darwish (14 in 2012 / 25 in 2023) she is born at her grandfather's farm on 24 September 1998 near Palmyra, Syria, four years after the Afqa Spring dries up. Zenobia's parents bring her to Aleppo in 2012 when she is 14 years old. Zenobia loves to speak English. Her favorite films are *As It Is In Heaven*, and *Star Wars*. 'Zenobia' means 'daughter of Zeus, power of Zeus'. 'Darwish' means 'seeker of truth'. Zenobia is the first spaceholder for the Infinity Ring of the Dandelion Flower (the camp in Aleppo), and becomes the spaceholder for the Infinity Ring of the Dandelion Seed group on the expedition. Zenobia replaces herself at the camp with Rachel Deeb who becomes the new Infinity Ring spaceholder of the Dandelion Flower. Zenobia takes Montassar Bilal as her first apprentice for Dandelion Seed Infinity Ring spaceholder.

Israa Nabih (16 in 2012 / 27 in 2023) Syrian street fighting woman becomes the first initiator in Zenobia's Learning Village. 'Israa' means 'night caravan' or 'night journeyer', and 'Nabih' means 'vigilant'. Goes on the expedition to Germany. Israa is an amazing singer who calls singing alive in others. Israa is spaceholder of the Morning Circle node and takes Rachel Deeb as her first apprentice.

Montassar Bilal Khaled (16 in 2012 / 27 in 2023) map maker with Rafiq and Farhan on the Aleppo streets. 'Montassar' means 'Genius, Wealth, Protector, or Victor'. 'Bilal' means 'one of the ten companions of Muhammed'. 'Khaled' means 'immortal, everlasting'. Montassar is spaceholder for the *Handbook* Study node and replaces himself with Rahim Taleb as his first apprentice so he can go on the expedition. On the road Montassar becomes first apprentice to Zenobia Darwish, spaceholder of the Dandelion Seed Infinity Ring.

Rafiq Abadi (15 in 2012 / 26 in 2023) gunman with Montassar and Farhan on the Aleppo streets. 'Rafiq' means 'friend or comrade'. 'Abadi' means 'endless or eternal'. Rafiq is skinny and muscled, a warrior type with shoulder length dark hair. He is the spaceholder for the guardianship node on the expedition, but then replaces himself with Aziza Hamdi Ahmed as spaceholder for the Dandelion Seed guardianship node, and she takes Habib Badawi as her first apprentice.

Farhan Kader (15 in 2012 / 26 in 2023) equipment carrier with Montassar and Rafiq on the Aleppo streets. 'Farhan' means 'the happy one', and 'Kader' means 'one who is knowledgeable'. Dandelion Seed expedition engineer.

Jamila Ali Ahmed (12 in 2012 / 23 in 2023) older sister of Aziza. 'Jamila' means 'heavy rain'. 'Ali' means 'champion or elevated'. 'Ahmed' means 'most praised'. Jamila is the first village kitchen spaceholder, then replaces herself with Huda Shamalieh so Huda can go on the expedition as the spaceholder for the kitchen node in the Dandelion Seed.

Aziza Hamdi Ahmed (10 in 2012 / 21 in 2023) younger sister of Jamila. 'Aziza' means 'strong, or powerful'. 'Hamdi' means 'one who deserves praise'. 'Ali' means 'champion or elevated'. Aziza is first spaceholder of the camp guardianship node. She replaces herself with Zaid Bakir so she can go on the expedition as the spaceholder of the Dandelion Seed guardian-ship node.

Mitzi (5 in 2012 / 16 in 2023) neck-length curly blond hair, she doesn't know her last name. Mitzi is one of the first street kids to walk into camp and has never missed a meeting. She wants to go on the expedition but is too young for border crossings. 'Mitzi' is a feminine name of German origin and means 'sea of bitterness'. It is a diminutive of 'Maria' or 'Mary' which have the same meaning. 'Bitterness' stands for 'strength and resilience' in Hebrew.

Hadi Qasim (17 in 2012 / 28 in 2023) she has sandy-blonde hair cut short, and worked as a nurse delivering emergency medical treatment until her children's hospital is blown up by Assad's Army. 'Hadi' means 'guide'. 'Qasim' means 'one who distributes or shares'. Hadi is spaceholder for the healing node, their first doctor, healer, and shaman, then replaces herself with Sammi Ghulam so she can become the spaceholder of the Dandelion Seed healing node on the expedition.

Lylah Younis (9 in 2012 / 21 in 2023) with slightly curly long sandy-blonde hair. 'Lylah' means 'night, and play', in other words, 'seductive'. 'Younis' means 'a kind, just, and forgiving person'. 'Younis' could also originate from 'yona', the Hebrew version of Jonah. She goes on the expedition to meet other cultures. She has a powerful intelligence and speaks well.

Thomas Taha (11 in 2012 / 22 in 2023) keeping quietly to himself, people regard him as a bomb that will one day explode. 'Thomas' is a Greek name that means 'twin'. 'Taha' is a North African name that means 'furious, angry'. The team wishes that he learns to harness and direct his anger as a valuable resource. Thomas uses his old phone with a Dictionary App to translate English into Arabic, so he is a linguist and goes on the expedition.

Sammi Ghulam (14 in 2012 / 26 in 2023) he goes through the Emotional Healing Process of objecting to the circle being divided, where some go walking and some stay behind. He can then stay behind. 'Sammi' means 'name of God, God has heard'. 'Ghulam' means 'boy, or servant'. He replaces Hadi as spaceholder for the healing node in camp so Hadi can go on the expedition.

Rahim Taleb (10 in 2012 / 21 in 2023) he is thin but active and speaks well, short dark-brown hair. 'Rahim' means 'merciful'. 'Taleb' means 'student'. He takes over being spaceholder for the Study Group node so that Montassar can go on the expedition.

Rachel Deeb (she arrives in camp five years before the earthquakes at 21 years / 26 in 2023) 'Rachel' means 'little lamb, one with purity'. 'Deeb' means 'wolf', commonly associated with 'loyalty, bravery and strength'. People who speak Arabic often laugh when Rachel Deeb introduces herself because her full name means 'Sheep Wolf'. The question being, which is true, and when? Rachel replaces Israa Nabih as spaceholder for Morning Circle, and then becomes the official Dandelion Flower Infinity Ring spaceholder after Zenobia Darwish is already far into the expedition. Rachel then takes Huda Shamalieh as her first apprentice as the Dandelion Flower Infinity Ring spaceholder.

Huda Shamalieh (she arrives in camp five years before the earthquake at 16 years / 21 in 2023) 'Huda means 'guidance, right path, or enlightenment'. 'Shamalieh' means 'from the North'. Huda takes over kitchen node spaceholding from Jamila Ali Ahmed so Jamila can go on the expedition. Huda is also the Interlocutrix between Dandelion Flower and Dandelion Seed. Huda takes Sumeya Mbeki as her first apprentice in the camp kitchen node.

Zaid Bakir (he arrives four years before the earthquakes at 19 years / 23 in 2023) 'Zaid' means 'happiness, growth, abundance', the name of Muhammad's adopted son. 'Bakir' means 'dawn, earlier than expected'. Zaid replaces Aziza Hamdi Ahmed as spaceholder for the camp guardian node so that Aziza can be spaceholder for the Dandelion Seed guardian node on the expedition.

Habib Badawi (24 in 2023) he walks into camp just after the earthquakes. 'Habib' means 'beloved, darling'. 'Badawi' means 'Bedouin, bringer of good news'. Habib is muscled but not fat warrior type. His dark hair is in tight curls, always looking a little oily. He has this smile that you cannot figure out if it is friendly or mean, simply that it is earnest. He goes on the expedition.

Sumeya Mbeki (Xhosa woman who arrives one month after Dandelion Seed departs / 24 in 2023) she read an article by Rachel Deeb and found out about the Aleppo camp and came here from the asamangaXhosa in South Africa. 'Sumeya' means 'never doubt the bright principles'. 'Mbeki' means 'there is a lesson to learn in everything'. Sumeya becomes first apprentice to the camp kitchen node spaceholder, Huda Shamalieh.

...and then there is the old Fortune Teller lady sitting by the dried fish in the corner at the Aleppo market. Nobody can replace her.


## UNITED STATES OF AMERICA
## LANGLEY, VIRGINIA – CIA HEADQUARTERS

Jason Spade (born 1983) from Virginia, handsome unholy lone-wolf reconnaissance software supplier working for GlobeScan, trying to sell services to Karl Thomsen of the CIA.

Monika Sterling (born 1986) from Colorado, CIA agent assigned to keep eyes on Jason Spade for Karl Thomsen. Karl Thomsen then assigns Monika Sterling to be Rob Dent's handler.

Karl Thomsen (born 1968) from Delaware, tanned, athletic fifty-something CIA trying to divert or reverse the Exodus, the more-and-more obvious flow of American citizens giving back their U.S. passports and moving to other countries. He is boss of Monika Sterling.

Rob Dent (born 1990) man from Los Angeles, selected by Jason Spade's

GlobeScan software as a potential agent to infiltrate and subvert the infamous Eugene, Oregon, 'terrorist' circle known as *Shadow Knights of the Mysterium*.


## EUGENE, OREGON

Davis Henry Hatcher (born 1997) son of Police Officer Henry Hatcher. Davis becomes a police officer in the Eugene Police Department.

Sammy Henry Hatcher (born 1994) Davis Hatcher's older brother.

Barbara Hatcher (born 1992) Davis Hatcher's older sister.

Henry Hatcher (born 1966) Davis Hatcher's father, Police Captain in the Eugene Police Department.

Sanjib Hajji (28 years) whose family is originally from Pakistan, becomes a police officer in the Eugene Police Department. The name 'Sanjib' means 'elixir which can rejuvenate a dead thing back to life. It means 'reborn'. 'Hajji' means 'pilgrim walker', someone who has successfully made the pilgrimage to Mecca.

Maria-Santos de la Rosa Ambiado (born 1971) woman born in Chile, front desk secretary at the Eugene Police Office, better known as 'Mom.'

John Stafford (born 1965) Eugene Police Department Chief.

Peter Brinks (born 1971) Eugene Police Sergeant, boss of Davis Hatcher and Sanjib Hajji.

Hannah Manley (born 1980) from CIA, collaborating with the United Nations on a special joint research project to develop new procedures for transforming political dissidence.

Evelyn Starfield (born 1986) Remington Smith's boss at Nature Conservancy.

## EUGENE CIRCLE OF SHADOW KNIGHTS OF THE MYSTERIUM

Sophia Bentley (64 years) a stocky country woman from England, founder of *Shadow Knights of the Mysterium* circle, partner of Robert Maxwell.

Robert Maxwell (67 years) skinny American man with wire-rimmed bifocals and a short white beard, partner of Sophia Bentley.

Francis Atkins (32 years) American woman.

Carol Washington (30 years) American woman.

Patricia Wells (26 years) American woman social worker with short dark hair and black glasses. Sanjib's new girlfriend.

Anton Pirelli (38 years) American man from Sicily, in his late thirties with short dark hair and black rimmed glasses.

Remington Smith (28 years) medium height physically fit woman, long brown wavy hair, brown eyes, born in Paris, lived in Fontainebleau, France.


**HOLLYWOOD, CALIFORNIA – Warner Brothers, Stage 13**
Two friends of Bill Murray:
Stephanie Canning (38 years) curly brunette hair, Orthopedic Surgeon volunteering at children's hospitals in Chile and Peru.

Elizabeth Diggens (40 years) shoulder length wavy sandy blond hair and horn-rimmed glasses, Physicist researching the interface between memetic constructs and raw invention.

Rebecca 'Becky' Barnes (26 years) David 'Dave' Stutler girlfriend, his 'witch'.

Plus a motley assortment of world-famous film actors, most of them near retirement. You already know them by name.


**LOS ANGELES, CALIFORNIA**
Gwendolyn ('Wendy') Circe (29 years) tall wiry woman with abundant straight black hair, streaked here and there with bright red. She has a gremlin named Retchin' Gretchin. Graphic designer at A. T. Advertising in Los Angeles. Her bright principles are Love, Possibility, Integrity, Magic.

George Planning (47 years) man from Los Angeles, Gwendolyn's boss at A. T. Advertising.

Arthur Tutor (54 years) Gwendolyn's boss' boss, and owner of A. T. Advertising.

Alexander Edding (41 years) man representing *Whale Storm*, an event production company, possible client of A. T. Advertising. Wendy calls him 'Snake-Eyes'.

Cynthia Willard (33) woman, Arthur Tutor's secretary.

Eva Schwartz (29) woman, Gwendolyn's longtime friend.

## PALM SPRINGS, CALIFORNIA
Phillip Goldman (60 years) divorced father of Edith Goldman and Adler Goldman, investment banker in Los Angeles, California.

Stanley Gärtner (61 years) longtime friend and investment manager for Phillip Goldman. Stanley's daughter Priscilla Gärtner is about to get married in San Diego.

Adler Goldman (died 2023 at 32 years) Edith Goldman's older brother, Phillip Goldman's only son.

Bruce Shimizu (60 years) longtime golf partner of Phillip Goldman.


## PHOENIX, ARIZONA DESERT
Harvey Bear Track ('53' years) Apache Indian Shaman from the Tohono O'odham nation.


## SAN DIEGO, CALIFORNIA
Priscilla Gärtner (29 years) the bride, Stanley Gärtner's only child.

Donald Gangley (35 years) ex-boyfriend of Priscilla Gärtner.

Captain David Henkel (70 years) retired architect, long-time friend of Mr. Roger Singer.

Captain David Henkel's Board of Directors:

Dr. Benjamin Bhaers

Angelika Steinhagen – heir to the German castle

Randy Williams – investment banker

Dr. Kerry Ferrington – psychologist

Dr. Peter Baker – historian

Dr. Amadeus Pointer Ph.D. – psychohistorian


## SAN FRANCISCO, CALIFORNIA
Edith Lee Goldman (27 years) athletic daughter of Phillip Goldman, wavy light brown medium length hair with wide set Ashkenazi green eyes.

Legal Offices of Bach, Becker, and Benowitz on Market Street, San Francisco, founded in 1917.

Kyoki (26 years) Japanese intern at Bach, Becker, and Benowitz.

## SAN PEDRO, CALIFORNIA
Balthazar Blake ('53' years) sorcerer / wizard.

David 'Dave' Stutler (36 years) the sorcerer's apprentice.

John Parson (28 years) man with close-cropped brown hair and well-developed biceps and shoulders, member of Balthazar's Topanga Canyon Work Circle.

Dana Fulton (33 years) dark-brown-shoulder-length-wavy-haired woman, member of Balthazar's Topanga Canyon Work Circle.

## SALT LAKE CITY, UTAH
Barbara Harmony Singer (38 years) fencing instructor at Utah University in Salt Lake City, with Summer home in Santa Fe, New Mexico. Wife of Roger Singer and mother of Matthew Singer.

Roger Ivanovich Singer (40 years) Psychology Professor at Utah University in Salt Lake City, and passive-solar architect with summer home in Santa Fe, New Mexico. Husband of Barbara Singer and father of Matthew Singer.

Matthew Ivanovich Singer (7 years) son of Mr. and Mrs. Singer.

Willis (1 year) Matthew Singer's goldfish, friend of Jackie Chan, Mathew's other goldfish.

John Emmet Tumble, 'JET' (25 years) muscled, blonde physics student at University of Utah. Son of Shirley Tumble.

Shirley Bene Tumble (48 years) JET's mother, single mom, spaceholder for single-mom's Bridge-House in Salt Lake City.

Jeffrey Stump (52 years) current partner of JET's mom, Shirley Tumble. Shirley and Jeffrey are not married, so Jeffrey is not JET's stepfather, even if Jeffrey might want to pretend to be.

Edward Smith Bennington, 'Eddy' (25 years) thin, dark-haired IT student at University of Utah. Empathic with animals. Wears gold wire-rimmed glasses. Cousin of Remington Smith through his mother, Sandra Bennington (maiden name Smith), the sister of Remington's father, Alexander Smith.

## ARCHIARCHY

Archiarchy is the authentic adulthood initiation-centered radically-responsible regenerative culture rapidly emerging around the world now that Matriarchy and Patriarchy have run their course. The term 'Archiarchy' was coined by Clinton Callahan before 4 January 2008 when Clinton first started using the name in processes and thoughtmaps during Possibility Labs in Germany. From 2008 until 2017, Archiarchy existed only in theory, that is, in Phase 1 (Phase 1 is understanding Archiarchy). Archiarchy entered Phase 2 in 2023 (Phase 2 is building and inhabiting Archiarchy) when Bridge-Houses and Archiarchy Invention Centers began forming around the world.


## HIDDEN UNIVERSITY

By the end of this book, many if not most of the characters end up creatively collaborating to deliver the work and possibilities of the Hidden University. It is called 'hidden' because campuses invisibly stand in plain sight in front of everyone because the Hidden University is Earth. Gaia is the headmistress of the Hidden University and is the authority establishing the necessity and the evolving specifics of the curricula.

# Note From The Author

This book is a work of fiction. At the same time, these pages are filled with proposals for *Collaborations Of Mutual Endeavor* – to use a phrase from Dave Ewoldt (died 2018) comeweb.org/where-are-we-now.

Each question and distinction parleyed back and forth between the characters opens doorways through which the reader could step into their own expedition along the path.

If you see and use a doorway, no one needs to validate its value for you. You directly experience what life is like on the other side of the door. If you do not see or use the doorway yourself, no one could ever truly convince you of its value.

I radically rely on the *Laws Of Consciousness* in sharing these distinctions. Consciousness will not stick around if there is not enough matrix in a person's Being to hold the distinctions.

For this reason, I am not concerned that someone can become aware of something for which they are not ready to become responsibly aware. I can make offers that are beyond a person's capacity to perceive, but such offers are being made to that person every day by life itself. Come back and read this same book a year from now and you may be surprised by how much more of it you can put to practical use in your daily life.

In this story, I do not mix fantasy with reality for the purpose of confusing reality for the reader, but I do mix fantasy with reality. For example, Maggie Smith does have two children, but both are male and have names different from those I ascribed to them. Or, in reality, the term 'Archiarchy' (at first misspelled as 'Archearchy') was coined by Clinton Callahan (me) in December 2007. I first shared the distinction during a Possibility Lab in January 2008 in Germany, where I began using the term in processes and thoughtmaps. And so on. My intention is to use my possibility paintbrush to identify doorways that a reader may not have heretofore not encountered in such a way that they may be able to go through them.

The doorways I share in *Cavitation* are the best I ever discovered. However, to indicate a doorway I must speak clearly about something that may not yet exist in the awareness of the reader. As has been said, *Before you can do the impossible, you must first be able to see the invisible.*

Potential is 'invisible' until it emerges in practical reality. Activating potential depends on seeing enough of it to take personal actions of speech, proposal, negotiation, and accountability with enough integrity to bring this potential to life in yourself or in others.

At the same time, to indicate doorways or potentials that are too far out of reach of the reader is not kind, a subtle but disrespectful torture. For this reason, I have tried to provide distinctions which any reader could verify through doing experiments at their worldview's edges. My intention is to inspire the resourceful reader to use these distinctions as construction materials for bridges from the world they currently occupy over to next culture, to Archiarchy, a culture centered around bringing potential to life.

Specifically, I know of no experimental nanonation existing in South Africa where the asamangaXhosa phoenix culture came to life in this story. These characters introduced themselves to me and showed me their interactions persistently until I wrote them down as best I could. Their purpose seems to be to expand our capacity to sense nonlinear possibilities even in the most dire of circumstances. Please forgive my lack of realistic knowledge of the richly endowed Xhosa cultures.

There are already many Temples of Evolution scattered around the Earth, some having been used for tens of thousands of years, although under a different name.

The seaside village of Budva, Montenegro has not yet made itself into an Archan nanonation, although it could.

The Friedland Refugee Camp, or 'transit camp' as it is sometimes called, near Göttingen, Germany, has not yet made itself into an Archan nanonation, although it could.

There is no such group as the *Shadow Knights of the Mysterium*, although there are many more independent groups than I could list, meeting weekly around the world for the purposes of healing, transformation, and practicing Archan skills.

I am, so far, not in conversation with any of the film stars mentioned in this book. Their sentiments and conversations are theoretically fictional.

All my references to books are real, including the *Handbook*, which I have owned for decades as an out-of-print edition written by Arthur Sword. Thoughtware Press intends to bring this astonishing manuscript back into circulation.

And, as far as I know, there is no secret Stage 13 at Warner Brothers Studios in Burbank, California. I went there and asked them. But, you know... they still might have a secret Stage 13... because... after all... it is secret...

- Clinton Callahan

# Thoughtware Press Proposes Experimenting

We appreciate that you are reading this page. Each further experiment you try while being yourself carves new forms of consciousness that others can then more easily follow. This makes you a bridge to next culture – Archiarchy – the regenerative adulthood-initiation-centered radical-responsibility nonmaterial-value thoughtware-upgrade culture emerging around the world now that Matriarchy and Patriarchy have run their course. Someone must go first. In this case that someone is you. Please keep making personal efforts while staying connected with a circle of other edgeworkers. We create Archiarchy by cavitating and inhabiting next culture spaces together. Here are some suggestions for how to do it:

1. Bit by bit, lower your numbness bar as part of your authentic adulthood initiatory processes. Then, for the rest of your life, responsibly use whatever feelings come up to handle things, and responsibly use whatever emotions come up to heal things. <consciousfeelings.mystrikingly.com>

2. Participate in an 8 or 12 week online-or-offline Rage Club to unleash a more authentic version of yourself into your life. After that, do Fear Club, and then Rage Club Spaceholder Training so you can deliver Rage Club for others and quit your corporate job. <rageclub.mystrikingly.com>

3. Start a weekly Possibility Team meeting (online or offline) to develop your nonlinear Possibility Creation skills to an absurdly effective level, together with others, arm in arm, heart to heart. In Possibility Team you can distill your Bright Principles and develop Possibilitator Skills together. It can be so painful to journey on the Path alone. <possibilityteam.mystrikingly.com>

4. Listen to the abundance of free and diverse transformational podcasts at Next Culture Radio. There are so many decades of wild research and matrix-building experiments shared in these recordings. <nextcultureradio.org>

5. Watch video interviews, WorkTalks, animations, workshops, Possibility Coaching sessions, discovery meetings, etc., all for free at Possibility Management TV. <youtube.com/PossibilityManagementTV>

6.    Visit the Museum of Possibility Management to explore the Roots, Shoots, Fruits, Hoots, and Books in the context of the extraordinarily fruitful gameworld of Possibility Management.
<museumofpm.mystrikingly.com>

7.    Subscribe to the free weekly random S.P.A.R.K. emails. S.P.A.R.K.s are Specific Practical Applications of Radical Knowledge. Each S.P.A.R.K. starts with a strong Distinction that is unfolded in the Notes section, followed by Experiments for your weekly S.P.A.R.K. Experiment Team.
<sparks-english.mystrikingly.com/#subscribe-to-sparks>

8.    Sign up to receive the monthly Possibility Management Newsletter with latest event invitations and discoveries.
<possibilitymanagement.org/news>

9.    Use the authentic alchemical elixir Tonic Gold™ to build your energetic matrix. Building matrix helps you hold and apply what you learned in this book, and supports your further evolution of consciousness. We highly recommend Tonic Gold.
More info at <tonic-gold.com>.

10.   Create an in-person or online Study Group where you read through books together, such as: *Conscious Feelings*, *Building Love That Lasts*, and *No Reason*, or do StartOver.xyz experiments to build matrix for holding more awareness.
<studygroup.mystrikingly.com> <spaceport.mystrikingly.com>

11.   Get copies of Cavitation into the hands of your friends and your enemies. Keep talking the ideas through with them. Listen to their personal stories and share yours, all the while remembering these are merely stories. Invite people to continue these conversations with you at your Study Group.
You can find Cavitation at <thoughtwarepress.mystrikingly.com>.

12.   Play StartOver.xyz, the free-to-play, massively-multiplayer, online-and-offline, matrix-building, thoughtware-upgrade, personal-transformation true-life adventure-game <startoverxyz.mystrikingly.com>. Please upload your Matrix Points into your free account at <login.startover.xyz> to help us change the morphogenetic field of the human race so that we have a future. Use either of these two doorways we created for entering the StartOver.xyz universe:
<howtoplay.mystrikingly.com> <spaceport.mystrikingly.com>.

13.   Help translate Possibility Management materials into new languages, including S.P.A.R.K.s, articles, books, and websites. So many people have never heard of these exciting possibilities because they are so

far mostly written in English. You can meet the existing Translation Teams and get further information at <sparktranslators.mystrikingly.com>.

14. Bring *Expand The Box* trainings into your area. Powered by the ingenious tools, processes, and thoughtmaps of Possibility Management, Expand The Box changes your world into a rapid learning environment. Step by step instructions and contacts at <createanexpandthebox.mystrikingly.com>.

15. Check out Possibilitator Training. If you love this stuff as seriously as we do, you are already a Possibilitator. There is so much new territory to explore and skills to learn. Professional Possibilitators are needed now more than ever to build bridges to next culture <archiarchy.mystrikingly.com> and to create new gameworlds <gameworldtheory.mystrikingly.com> that make the existing gameworlds irrelevant. <possibilitatortraining.mystrikingly.com> <possibilitatorskills.mystrikingly.com>

16. Have as much high-level fun as you can! There is a lot more where this came from. The infinite resources are waiting for you. <infiniteresources.mystrikingly.com>


Your mind is yours to play with and make into whatever you want.

**Thank you for thinking wildly!**